BLOODLINES

ROBIN SAXON
AND ALEX KIDWELL

Dreamspinner Press

Published by
Dreamspinner Press
5032 Capital Circle SW
Suite 2, PMB# 279
Tallahassee, FL 32305-7886
USA
http://www.dreamspinnerpress.com/

This is a work of fiction. Names, characters, places, and incidents either are the product of author imagination or are used fictitiously, and any resemblance to actual persons, living or dead, business establishments, events, or locales is entirely coincidental.

ISBN: 978-1-62798-319-8
Digital ISBN: 13978-1-62798-320-4

Printed in the United States of America
First Edition
November 2013

My lovely Robin,

I think we dream, it is said, so we don't have to be apart for nearly so long. I dream of you so we can be together all the time.

Your Alex

A-
To hear your voice is pomegranate wine to me:
I draw life from hearing it.
Could I see you with every glance,
It would be better for me
Than to eat or to drink.
(The Flower Song, 1539-1075 BC)
-R

CHAPTER
1

Jed

PLANNING A vacation, Jed was finding, was a lot fucking harder than planning a job. For one thing, it required far less calculation of the correct amount of C-4 to use and a whole lotta discussion about *gas mileage*. One was math that Jed was good at. The other made him want to set things on fire. Redford had also strictly limited the number of deadly weapons he was allowed to take to ten. Ten! He was practically going to be naked. The thing was, for as long as Jed had been talking about taking his dream fishing experience, he was ill prepared for the *reality* of the whole thing.

A reality that included searching for a cabin that had both private beach access and a king-sized bed, but one that didn't require him to clean up after himself. Seriously, this was a vacation. If he wanted to play maid, he'd buy a feather duster and high heels and stay home. In the three months since they'd gotten off the plane from Cairo, Jed's life had turned from plotting out the best sniper posts to deciding if they wanted to fly, drive, or take a train. Driving had won out, because public transportation seemed to frown on people taking bitchy Siamese cats and shotguns.

Dealing with vampire politics and crazy daddy issues had *nothing* on planning a vacation.

"Babe?" Jed was sitting on the couch, surrounded by piles of clothes, fishing gear with the tags still on, his chosen ten weapons, and two bags filled with road snacks, like a little fortress of things to pack. He'd abandoned shoving everything into duffel bags in order to page through the book Redford had insisted on purchasing. It had pictures and everything. "How do we get the worms?"

Every picture in the fishing guide had happy people with funny hats and worms. Jed had a funny hat—two of them, actually, one for him and one for Redford—but the worms he'd been kind of at a loss about. Flipping through the book, he scowled. Fifteen fucking pages of how to hold the goddamn reel and not one page on worm hunting.

Jed tossed the book aside and figured he'd just wing it. Surely he could dig for them. Worms were in the ground, right?

There was a crash, a loud, churlish yowl, and Knievel stalked out of the bedroom, tail twitching in irritation. Redford trailed after her, a long scratch on his arm, looking positively crestfallen. "She doesn't like the life vest," he explained as Jed vaulted over the back of the couch, immediately fussing over the wound. "I'm sorry. I was just trying to make sure it fit."

"Fido? Shut up." The words were biting, though his tone was anything but, absolute distress radiating from the set of his shoulders, the tenseness of his body as he herded Redford to the couch. With a muffled curse, he threw all of his piles of stuff every which way to make room for Redford to sit down. His weapons were treated with a passing iota of care, his clothes, not so much. Jed grabbed the first aid kit and started to clean off the scratch, calloused fingers gentle as he smoothed a bandage across the reddened skin. Yes, he was aware it was just a scratch. It'd barely be a mark by this time tomorrow. Didn't stop Jed from pressing a kiss to Redford's wrist in apology, huffing a sigh as he took the vivid-pink cat-sized life vest away from him.

"You are going to wear this," he told the cat, who was washing herself vigorously on the opposite chair, ears flattened back. "It's a floatation device. Everyone wears them while we fish."

Turning back to Redford, Jed cupped his cheek, searching his eyes. He could read Redford's face like one of the books the man loved so much, those blue-gray depths that he'd drowned in, the worried little crease between them that seemed to insist Jed lean in to kiss it away. Every line and curve of Redford's face, Jed knew. It was like the light in Redford's eyes was written on the very bones of him, in the breath of his lungs, in the muscle and blood that made him up. "You okay?" Jed rumbled, concerned.

A little sigh was huffed out, Redford's lips twitching upward fondly. "I think I'll live," he intoned solemnly. His hand twisted up to catch Jed's, bringing their joined fingers in to rest over Redford's heart. "It's just a scratch, Jed. We've both had far worse and been just fine."

Inevitably, Jed's eyes went to the scars on Redford's face, the long, jagged tears that marred perfect pale skin, sloping over the bridge of his nose to his cheek. Leaning in, Jed kissed them, like he did every night before bed, a quiet promise to the both of them that he failed at more often than not. So Jed made it again. He wasn't good for much, Jed knew. Fucking and fighting and pretty much nothing in between. But Redford, he was *good*. He was heaven, as much as a man like Jed Walker could hope to touch. He was glory, more than Jed would ever know outside of him. So he kissed those scars, he kissed the scratch their spoiled cat had given him, and he swore to himself, one more time, to never let Redford get either one again.

"Yeah, well," he muttered gruffly, covering his tenderness with a glower. "Doesn't mean the cat's not a bitch."

Knievel seemed to take that as her cue. With a chirping purr she hopped lightly off the chair and wound her way around Redford's legs, apparently in apology, before jumping into Jed's lap. He rolled his eyes, rubbing a hand over her ears, chuckling quietly when Knievel immediately sprawled out for better cuddles. "Goddamn cat," he said, but he was smiling again.

Jed snagged the life vest, holding it up to Knievel. She arched her neck up lazily, sniffing it twice before batting it with a paw. Jed let her fuss with it as she bit the straps, showing it who was boss. In the end, she apparently decided that having a tummy rub was distracting enough, not noticing when Jed and Redford slipped her front paws into the vest. Jed buckled it up, making sure her fur wasn't caught in the straps.

"There you go, Miss Priss," he crooned, setting her down on the couch. Knievel immediately fell onto one side with a mournful look, as if the life vest itself was so heavy her body was unable to hold it up.

Jed rolled his eyes at her. "You are such a drama queen." Redford had found the jar they kept the cat treats in and Jed offered her one. With great difficulty, Knievel reached out to touch her nose to it. The martyr act didn't last long. In a moment she was gnawing happily on the tuna fish flavored snack.

"So that's how you get a cat into a flotation device," Redford mused, voice that low little rumble that sent all kinds of electricity along Jed's skin. "Bribe them."

With a grin, Jed pulled out a matching adult-sized vest in the same eye-searing pink. "Want to see how I get a wolf into one?"

Knievel had picked out the color. Or, rather, she'd head-butted the screen when Jed had clicked onto the pink vests, but Jed figured that was good enough. Now licking her paws, Knievel looked content enough in her life jacket. Redford, however, gave Jed a horrified look, holding up one finger to stop Jed from talking.

"No," he insisted firmly. "Just *no*, Jed."

With a positively wicked smirk, Jed pounced. The life jacket was forgotten in the first flurry of movement, in Jed blanketing Redford and Redford, with a howl, rolling them off the couch onto the floor. They turned again, Jed laughing loudly as Redford got the best of him, pinning his arms in a very dirty move that involved grinding their hips together and then sitting on his chest.

"No fair," Jed protested, but he was grinning. "Who taught you to cheat like that?"

With a smug smile that looked *far* too good on him, Redford leaned over, hands braced on either side of Jed's head, knees still pinning Jed's arms. "You did," he said, lips just barely brushing against Jed's.

That little coil of heat in Jed's gut surged into flames, and he moaned softly, head tipping upward, chasing the kiss Redford was holding back. "Fuck yeah, I did," he muttered and grinned as Redford crashed down onto him, as their mouths found each other in panting bites, in a long, slow kiss where Redford's tongue fucked into his mouth and Jed twisted under him, desperate for more.

Redford pulled back first, ghosting his lips across Jed's, chuffing a laugh at Jed's frustrated growl. "There are two men outside our door," Redford whispered.

"Good for them." Jed narrowed his eyes, and he reluctantly turned his head to stare at the doorway. "Who—"

Redford took a deep breath, smiling suddenly. "It's Victor."

A knock sounded, sharp and brisk, and Jed groaned loudly. "Goddamn it." Heaving himself upward with one last regretful look at Redford, Jed went to answer the door. "You know," he mused conversationally, "I can't decide if you doing that is freaky or sexy."

Jed swung the door open, then leaned against the frame as he took in the sight of one Victor Rathbone, in all his sweater-vest-loving glory. Behind him, standing nervously at attention, was some kid with dark hair curling to the nape of his neck and thick glasses that he awkwardly shoved up onto his nose. "Princess," Jed drawled, dismissing the flunky for now. He did look oddly familiar, but Jed didn't feel like playing a game of Who's Who, Nerd Edition. "I didn't know we had a tea party scheduled." The time since Cairo had turned the professor freaky pale again, all the better to highlight the dark circles under red-rimmed eyes. He had the decided look of a man who'd been in a bed other than his own last night. Probably one he couldn't have found again with a map and a flashlight. So Victor was doing the whole one-night stand thing. Of course Jed recognized the signs. He'd practically *invented* the signs. It was a perfectly valid way of coping after a breakup with a vampire.

"Oh, how I missed your wit," Victor said, eyes narrowed behind his glasses. "Randall, I don't believe you properly met Journey Walker. Jed, Randall Lewis."

"Don't call me Journey, sweetcheeks." Jed's gaze went to Randall, looking him up and down. Recognition sparked. The last time he'd seen Randall, he'd been bloodied up and in a dank vampire cave. People tended to look a bit different in the daylight. "Course I remember the kid. Got his blood on my shirt. Don't often forget shit like that." He held out his hand, which Lewis took, giving him a firmer handshake than Jed would have expected from someone wearing a waistcoat.

"Yes. Thank you for that," Randall started, but Jed waved him off. He hated that part. The thank-yous, the gratitude, the talking about shit like pulling people out of buildings or the details of what they'd been saved from. He just wanted to do his job and be done with it. The aftermath was what he'd always been bad at.

"I'm sure you remember my partner, Redford Reed." Jed moved aside slightly, drawing Redford in. "Best nose in the goddamn business. If it wasn't for him, you'd be vampire chow." Redford shifted his weight, his shoulder bumping up against Jed's. When Randall's hand was offered, Redford took it tentatively—the man had made a lot of progress in becoming more confident, in becoming his own person, but he still shied away from people that he didn't know all that well.

"Then thank you to you both," Randall said quietly, a very real strength under his words. Jed had met a lot of people in his life, had dealt with a lot of men who thought they were strong. Whether it was due to money or position or just how much they fucking loved themselves, there were a lot of people who mistook bullying for power. This kid, though, all soft eyes and hair in his face, reminded Jed of Redford, of the wild, feral *something* that was wrapped in a mild cloak.

Then again, maybe it was a wolf thing. According to Redford and David, this kid was one of the real ones. Jed had no fucking clue what that was supposed to mean and how it was different from werewolves in any way, but with the way Redford was staring at Randall, he thought it might be an important distinction.

"Don't suppose you showed up at our door to sell cookies?" Jed really hoped the answer was yes. "'Cause if it's anything else, we're fresh out of it. We are two hours away from a well-deserved vacation."

Victor, ignoring things like personal space and the lack of an invitation, pushed his way past Jed into the apartment. His gaze fell upon the mess of clothes on the couch, the duffel bags, and the cat staring venomously at them. "Where would *you* go for a vacation? Somewhere you can play with your guns all day long? I'm sure you can do that perfectly well here."

"Fishing," Jed said, arms folded, eyes narrowed. "As in sun, sand, and nothing to do with whatever it is you're here to ask. The answer is no."

Randall blinked at him. "We didn't even ask for anything."

"Yet," Jed pointed out. "Don't think I don't know what it means when people knock on my door all puppy eyed, with the princess over there pretending to be civil. You want something. And the answer is no."

4

Walking over to the couch, Jed started grabbing the rest of his stuff and shoving it into bags, like if he did it fast enough, the inevitable wouldn't happen. People didn't just *show up* at Jed's apartment. In fact, people *never* showed up at his apartment. Not unless they were delivering food, trying to shoot him, or asking for help. And he didn't see Victor carrying a pizza or a gun. "Thanks for stopping by. Really. It was a blast. Now you and Professor Sunshine can just skip your way back to wherever you came from. Redford"—Jed struggled to zip up his duffel—"and I"—he stomped his foot down on one end of the bag, yanking the zipper harder—"are going goddamn *fishing*." There. The bag was stuffed full and zipped up, Knievel was wearing her float vest, and Redford had shoes on. They were leaving.

"I need your help." It was Randall's voice, soft but firm, saying those four goddamn words Jed hated more than anything. Well, almost anything. *I forgot the lube* was still number one.

"Yeah, well"—Jed turned, leveling Randall with a glare—"I'm on vacation, sweetheart. You're outta luck."

There was an awkward beat as Randall glanced between him and Victor. Jed got that sick little jerk in his gut, the one that told him he was missing something. He hated it when he missed shit. Usually that wound up with him hungover in Thailand, surrounded by six passed out sumo wrestlers, without his goddamn pants. And missing his favorite gun.

He still mourned that gun.

"I wish you a good vacation, then," Randall said, choosing his words delicately. "I actually wasn't speaking to you." Before Jed could get a word in edgewise, Randall turned to Redford. "Mr. Reed, I need your help. Please."

Redford took a reactionary step backward in his surprise. "Me?" He stared at Randall, looking like he was waiting for some kind of punch line. "No, if you need help, you should ask Jed. I just help him."

Before Jed could say anything, before he could figure out what the hell had just happened or kick Victor for that fucking smug expression on his stupid English face, Randall had moved toward Redford again, so much *earnest* dripping off of him it was kind of ridiculous. "I'm afraid Mr. Walker's particular skills won't be of any use to me. I appreciate, more than I can ever say, what you all did for me in Cairo. And believe me, I don't want to be even more in your debt." Randall's eyes cut to Victor, just for a moment, color faintly touching the high curve of his cheeks. Why the fuck he was looking at *Victor* was beyond Jed. Unless he felt an obligation to the goddamn *getaway driver*, Jed's recollection of Cairo was very different. In the "Victor doesn't do wet work" kind of way.

"And yet you're here," Jed pointed out bluntly. "And I'm not sure what your point is. So spill."

"I need Mr. Reed to help me because I need a wolf," Randall said with a very slight shrug. "A human—no offense—is not going to be able to talk to the people we'll need to speak with."

Redford had progressed to wringing his hands in worry. Jed didn't like it when Redford got that look, the pinched nervous concern, the expression that said Redford

5

thought he wasn't good for anything. Before he could even form the thought, Jed was there, right at his side, arm around Redford's waist. "I—I'm not *really* a wolf," Redford said in a stutter. "I mean, I was a werewolf. And now I'm not, but I'm not a real wolf like others I've seen."

"I am," Randall said very simply. "I know what you are, Mr. Reed. And you are exactly who I need. You are of Filtiarn. And you are the only one whom the Gray Lady will speak with."

"The whosa-whatsit now?" Jed was scowling at, well, fucking everyone. Goddamn people with their *goddamn* problems. "We aren't going to talk to any of your freaky furry people. We're going fishing. Both of us. Together." There was a meow from the couch, and Jed added, without missing a beat or lightening up his frown one bit, "All three of us." Damn fucking right they were.

Victor gave a low sigh. "Jed, will you at least let Randall talk? He wouldn't be coming to Redford if the matter wasn't serious."

"Office hours are between eight and nine every fourth Wednesday," Jed returned. "And you must have missed the big 'fuck off, gone fishing' sign I put on the door, so why don't you just see yourselves out."

"Jed." Redford's voice was low. "I know we want to go fishing, but we should at least take five minutes to hear them out. The fish won't go away if we're five minutes late."

Jed closed his eyes, taking a deep breath. "Fine," he growled. But he pointed his finger at both Randall and Victor. "Five minutes. Redford is going to get a vacation if I have to *build* an ocean, and I don't care what you have to say about it. Five goddamn minutes."

"You'd do that for me?" Redford looked utterly charmed.

"No, he wouldn't. It's quite impossible," Victor said archly, impatient. "He—"

"If Red said he wanted the moon, I'd ride Buzz fucking Aldrin up there and get it myself," he told Victor in a calm tone, arms folded. "He wants an ocean? I'll flood the streets until he can swim. Impossible's got nothing to do with it. Besides," Jed snorted, "you can too build an ocean. What, you think *Jaws* was real?" Clearly a fake ocean. And a fake shark. And possibly fake boobs.

Victor fell silent with an annoyed little grimace, giving Randall a chance to speak. Randall sighed, sitting, hands folded tightly in his lap. "My brother is dying," he told Redford simply.

And just like that, Jed shut the fuck up.

He'd gotten a lot of jobs in his life. Most of them didn't matter. Powerful men wanting more power, rich men wanting more of whatever made them rich. War, all of it, only this time the enemies weren't clear at all. Jed wasn't a superhero. He wasn't even a good guy. No one had ever come to him like this. Of course, the first time it happened, it was for Redford.

"We're wolves, like you," Randall continued. "It's just me and my two brothers, and Anthony is dying. You're the only one who can help. Will you?" After a beat, he cut a glance over at Jed. "I believe that was less than five minutes."

"How am I the only one that can help?" Redford looked confused. He glanced at Jed quickly, seeking help, before looking back at Randall again. "I'm not a doctor. If he's dying, you should go to the hospital, shouldn't you?"

"Ah." There was a wry twist of Randall's lips. "That, I'm afraid, will take much longer than five minutes to explain."

Jed hesitated before heaving a sigh. He already knew how this was going to end. Some wolf, some bright-eyed kid, comes to Redford claiming he needs help saving a dying brother? Yeah, they weren't going fishing. Maybe he'd known that since they opened the door. All his bitching and moaning, all his talk of leaving, he'd hoped that Victor and Randall would give their polite excuses and be gone.

It never worked out that way.

Jed scooped up Knievel, unbuckled the life vest, and set it aside. "Okay," he said, the cat prancing off his lap over to Randall, sniffing him curiously before sneezing at him and heading back to Redford. "So talk. Apparently we've got all day."

Randall sagged back a bit. Even Jed hadn't noticed how tightly wound the guy was until his shoulders eased and some of that tense worry lining his face relaxed. Randall nodded at him, glancing again at Victor. If it was for reassurance, Jed was pretty sure he was looking in the wrong place. Victor just looked satisfied that they hadn't gotten kicked out.

"In order to understand what's happening, you have to know why my family is rather unique among the wolf world," Randall started, taking off his glasses to clean them. "Most wolves, true wolves, are parts of a pack."

"And you're a true wolf?" Jed asked, frowning. He was standing next to the wall, leaning against it, arms folded, looking almost lazy and half-asleep. His gaze, though, kept cutting between the three other men, trying to figure this out. It hit him then, all at once—he was the only human being in the room. Now that was a goddamn trip. "Which is different from a werewolf... how, exactly?" He knew the basics, but Jed figured more information couldn't hurt.

Randall gave him a slight smile, shrugging. "How is a Homo erectus different from Homo sapiens?"

Jed burst out with a laugh, rubbing a hand across his mouth in a very failed attempt to hide his smirk. "One of them sounds like a very personal problem?" he guessed, grinning. "Or a porn title. I've got a little homo erection going on right here."

Randall just gave him a vaguely bemused look. "I was more referring to the fact one of them shat in caves and drew on walls, and the other created the Louvre."

"The former sounds exactly like Jed," Victor mused idly. "Perhaps we have history standing across the room from us."

Randall laughed at that, low and husky, grin crinkling up the corners of his eyes. Jed had no fucking idea what was so funny, but he glowered at them both anyway. "Okay, homo nerd-us," he shot back. Even Redford had a small smile on his face. "How about you use non-prissy-professor language for ten minutes."

"My apologies," Randall said. He didn't look sorry, though. "My point was that the werewolves are a decidedly less evolved version of a true wolf, or Cano, as named in the old Gaelic. They are the result of the Cano mixing our blood with humans."

"But Fil was trying to fix that," Jed said, eyes going to Redford. "Shooting them up with his blood." Turning werewolves, who were probably *lesser* in the eyes of someone like Fil, constrained by the moon cycles, unable to hold their own minds, into wolves that could turn when they wanted to. And Redford, without the full dose of whatever freaky mojo, was stuck in between. He could shift to furry form when he liked, but not without pain. And his instincts were all haywire. Hell, even a shrink couldn't seem to make that part of it better.

"That is what I gather from what Victor has told me, yes." Randall nodded. He turned back to Redford. "And that is why you can help. My parents left their pack when my mother found out she was pregnant with my eldest brother, Anthony. They never told us exactly why, but my father talked about disagreeing with the direction the pack leaders were going in. The Gray Lady is the mother of us all, the eldest of all the packs, and she was the one in leadership when my mother and father decided to leave."

"You realize that none of that makes sense, right?" Jed was frowning, looking over at Victor for a moment. Maybe this was more smart-people gobbledygook. "Gray Lady?"

Redford was looking intent, leaning forward on the couch. "You mean she's the *actual* mother of all wolves? Was she the first? She must be incredibly old."

A very faint smile touched Randall's lips. "It depends on who you ask. If you study the texts, the old stories of the Cano, it talks of a pair of wolves who were the first. Filtiarn and Liadan. They brought forth the first wolves. They started the first pack. But Liadan and her mate fought, and Filtiarn was cast out, taking his favored pack mates with him."

"And Líadan means *gray lady* in old Gaelic," Victor injected helpfully.

Now, Jed wasn't much good at math. But even he knew that anyone claiming to have started the whole wolf line was getting far more than the senior's discount at Denny's. "That's impossible," he told them both bluntly. "It's a scam, or someone who just really likes the name. But what you're saying is that—"

"What I'm saying," Randall interjected mildly, "is that we are not human. And our lifespans are not yours. It's impossible for you, yes, but I think you'd agree that the world is rather a lot bigger than what you're assuming."

Baby goddamn Jesus. Jed sat then, trying to wrap his brain around everything. So, vampires were real, they didn't die with garlic or silver knives, crazy ass wolves *did* die with silver knives, and both of them apparently could live forever. That was kind of a lot more than he'd been ready to handle today. Or ever.

"You're quiet, babe," he murmured, nudging Redford with his foot. "What's going on in that big brain of yours?"

"Just absorbing new information," Redford said lowly. He nudged Jed's knee with his own, a silent *let Randall keep talking.*

"I apologize," Randall was saying, a frown pinching the corners of his lips. "This is a lot, I know. If I had anywhere else to go, I would."

"The history lesson is fascinating and all, but I'm still missing the part where you need to involve Red," Jed said gruffly, eyes still on Redford.

"Ah. Yes." Randall shifted a bit, leaning forward. "I need to get help for Anthony. I need to get him back to the pack. The problem is, I don't think the Gray Lady will let us in, because our parents left. There are rumors, though, that she is gathering up the remnants of Filtiarn's pack, giving them refuge. While she won't talk to me, I know she will talk to you. And you can be our ticket in to see her."

Redford shifted slightly, and Jed took care not to say anything to interrupt—the guy needed at least two seconds of silence to indicate that it was okay for him to talk. "Earlier, you said you'd explain why you couldn't take Anthony to a hospital," Redford pointed out. "That's where most people go when they're dying, isn't it?"

"Redford," Randall started softly, before fading off into a sigh. "We're not people," he pointed out, deep-brown eyes flicking up to Redford before falling again. "Anthony has signs of Parkinson's disease. The canine version."

Oh. Well, yeah, that probably would be fucking difficult to explain to your average Doogie Howser. Jed snorted softly, but he didn't speak. He just reached out to take Redford's hand, a silent show of support. This was his gig, his play. Jed was going to let him decide what they did.

"So you want a ticket into the Gray Lady's pack," Redford said. "Because they have a hospital there for them? Or because you think they'll know what to do?"

Randall fidgeted a bit, hands fiddling with the side seam of his pants before he deliberately folded them together, trying to maintain his composure. "We weren't raised in that pack," he explained. "Some years after our parents left the pack, they were killed by hunters, when I was young. Anthony took care of us. I don't know how to help him, what to do, if this is curable, anything. I'm only sure that a human hospital would be a death sentence. If I can just speak to the Gray Lady, if I can plead our case, I know I can make her understand and I can get information on how to help Anthony. But I need to be let into the pack in order to do so. That's what I need you for."

Randall fumbled in his pocket and pulled out a white envelope. It looked rather anemic from where Jed was sitting. "This is everything I have. It's not much, but I can figure out how to get more. Please." Randall's gaze was on Redford's face, begging. This wasn't a guy trying to pull one over on them. He genuinely thought he was pleading for his brother's life. "Just tell me how much more you need and I'll find a way. I promise."

Redford had a thoughtful look as he studied the envelope. "Actually," he remarked, "I don't think there'd even be a budget on this one. It's not like we need supplies or ammo or—"

"But the retainer fee," Jed jumped in smoothly, shooting Redford a wide-eyed *what are you doing* look. They did not work for free. Ever. That was practically rule number one. "Half up front. Figure two days' work at five thousand a day."

"Really, Jed?" Victor gave him a withering look. "Randall is not exactly swimming in money."

Randall's cheeks flushed at that, his shoulders bunching up in shame. "I'm fine, Victor," he said shortly, pulling himself up to his full height as he searched his pockets. He was a proud guy, though apparently Victor didn't get that. "I, uh, have half of your required fee there. I can get more. There's some things I can sell. I only require time."

"No, that's ridiculous," Victor said firmly. "You are not selling your possessions. Journey Walker, you give Randall a discount, and you give it to him *right now*."

"Victor," Randall snapped, eyes darkening. "I am not a charity case. This is what it will cost, and I'll pay it. I don't need favors. You've all saved my life once. I'm hardly going to *beg*."

"Um." Redford tried to cut in, his shoulders a little hunched at the raised voices flying around the room. "We can knock off a thousand per day, because we won't be needing things like explosives or a place to stay. If we go, we'll be able to stay with the pack, right?" He looked like the idea terrified him a little, but he stood firm, trying to mediate the argument and make things easier for Randall all at once.

"That's what you think," Jed sighed, staring up at the ceiling, twirling a pen between his fingers. In his experience, there was *always* a need for explosives. But he relented, cutting a glance over at Randall. "Fine. I'll waive my normal rate. Redford can decide how much he wants to charge. It's his job; he's the boss." Jed clambered to his feet, dropping a kiss to the top of Redford's head. "You set the fee, babe, and get half. I'm going to make some coffee."

"I'm the boss?" Redford looked even more terrified at that.

"Damn straight." Jed paused in the doorway to the kitchen to give him a positively wicked leer. "Don't worry. We'll practice tonight in bed. Start thinking of all those orders you want to give me." With one last wink, he moved to start up the coffeepot, leaving Redford to finish the negotiations.

For a while now, Redford had been doing the business side of things—budgets and invoicing and keeping the books. All shit Jed was terrible at. As much as Jed didn't really like this job, it was Redford's. He got to take point. Normally, giving up his control would send Jed into fits, but this was for Redford. It'd be good for him, to plan his own op, to be the one calling the shots. It might just show him what Jed had known for a while: Redford was smart and capable and more than ready to do something on his own.

Also, it was hot as hell. So basically this was a win-win.

"We'll take the job," he heard Redford say. "I'll need a few minutes to figure out the budget, and I'll need information like where we're going and what we're expected to do." Redford paused and added, a little defensively, as if he expected to be denied, "Jed is coming too. I'm not doing a job without him."

A smile crept across Jed's face, and he ducked his head, fussing with the mugs. Maybe that was predictable. Still nice to hear, though.

"That's perfectly fine," Randall was saying, and Jed came back around the corner to find Randall holding out his hand for Redford to shake. "Why don't you come to our house tomorrow night? That will give you and Mr. Walker time to discuss matters, and you can prepare your proposal. We can talk over details then. I'm afraid I don't know the location of the pack offhand, but there are a few different ways you might go about getting that information."

Redford looked surprised. "It's that well hidden? How big is the pack, do you know?"

Shrugging, Randall absently pushed his glasses farther up onto his nose. "I honestly have no idea. Could be dozens. Could be hundreds. Liadan is notoriously secretive, and the pack's location is jealously guarded. There are other, smaller packs, obviously, but if anyone will know how to help Anthony, it will be her."

He *hoped*. That subtext was miles deep. Putting your hopes into some possibly mummified old chick with a dubious background and no real info was, in Jed's mind, just begging to be let down. But rule number three was *don't goddamn argue with the basic premise of the hire*. If someone wanted Jed to stand guard over a pile of *dirt*, for enough cash, he'd do it. Same went here. So what if this was probably a fool's errand. If Redford wanted to take the job, Jed sure as hell wasn't going to point it out.

"Okay." Redford nodded, beginning to look a bit more confident about the prospect of leading a job. "Is Victor coming too?"

"I'm sure Victor has far more important things to do." Kicking back on the couch, giving Victor a shit-eating grin, Jed lifted his mug of coffee in salute. "What was it, princess? Lucky night at the senior home?"

Victor didn't seem to get the joke. "I'll thank you not to pry into my personal life, Jed," he replied. "It's not particularly pertinent right now."

"I mean, I am *assuming* you wore his clothes this morning by mistake. Because even you can't think that a plaid jacket is anything but tragic." Jed smirked widely. "Come on, don't tell me you didn't do a little bump and run last night. I can see it all over you."

"You're not going to let this go, are you?" Victor rolled his eyes heavenward, as if asking for patience. "Fine. Yes, I had sex last night with a man whose name I don't recall. It was satisfactory. Are you done?"

Jed gave Victor a golf clap, wiping away a fake tear of pride. "Our little baby's all grown up," he told Redford, voice teasingly thick. "I just... get the camera. I want to make sure we remember this moment." At Victor's withering look, Jed couldn't stop the laugh, shaking his head. "Okay, fine. Now that I will have to brain-bleach tonight for any hope of a nightmareless sleep, we hauling your ass out to wolf-ville with us or not?"

"I would like to go," Victor said carefully. "If you're okay with that, Randall, of course. I'm well aware that I wouldn't be terribly helpful, but I'd like to go nonetheless."

"No, that sounds perfectly acceptable," Randall assured him, nodding, struggling to look completely uninterested. "If you don't mind making the trip. Our house is about an hour outside of the city, rather out of the way. I can give you directions. If you'd like, you could join us for dinner?" A very slight smile touched the corners of his lips. "Anthony makes a mean rabbit stew."

Victor's eyebrows had lifted in surprise. Jed thought the guy probably didn't get invited to social gatherings very often. Then again, neither did Jed. Of course, one was because Victor was a stuffy, boring stick, and the other was obviously because Jed's good looks and charm scared people off. "That would be lovely," Victor replied. "I've never had rabbit stew."

There was a strange *softness* in Randall's smile. He directed it all toward Victor, as if he'd forgotten anyone else was in the room. "Of course. I know my brothers will be very happy to meet you." Jed cleared his throat, and Randall immediately turned to include him and Redford, flustered. "All of you, of course. Ah, let me just write out the directions and I'll be going. I don't want to take up any more of your time."

Once Randall had completed a map, Redford studied the offered directions closely and handed them over to Jed. It seemed easy enough. Over the river and through the woods and all that shit, but they'd find it just fine. "We'll be there at six," Jed decided, clapping Victor on the shoulder. "The professor is buying the gas. Don't be late, princess. I know how you like to primp."

"Are we carpooling?" Victor looked completely unamused at the prospect. "Do you not trust me to drive myself? Or are you just incapable of bearing the thought that I may be in control of my own car?"

Jed blinked at him. "I just want you to buy the gas. You can strap yourself to the hood for all I care."

"As long as you hold off on the drive shaft jokes," Victor sighed.

"Jed is very good at restraint," Redford assured him. Which immediately killed the five jokes Jed had at the ready.

"Well then, I'll see you all tomorrow." Randall nodded, moving toward the door. "And Mr. Reed—" Randall paused, reaching out to very lightly touch his hand to Redford's arm. "—thank you. For listening to me." He nodded at them all, holding the door open for Victor, who was following him out. Victor gave Jed an indiscernible look as he left, something that might have had gratitude buried deep in the expression.

Randall's hand hovered behind Victor, almost as if he was going to rest his fingertips on the small of the man's back. But he lost his nerve, hand falling away, and the two of them walked down the hallway, separate and removed.

Redford closed the door behind them. He looked utterly pleased with himself at handling the talk of his first job so well, but as he looked at Jed, that beaming smile slowly dimmed into guilt. "I just ruined your fishing trip," Redford realized. "You planned it for so long and you were so excited and I just took a job and I'm horrible."

Looking around them, at the clothes and supplies strewn about, Knievel asleep on top of Redford's pink life vest, Jed shrugged. "It's just a vacation, Fido," he reminded Redford gently. He reached out, taking Redford's hand and tugging the man in close. "It doesn't really matter."

And it didn't. It might have, before. The idea of a fishing trip, of sun and sand and water and zero responsibilities, had been kind of a talisman to Jed for a long time. It was the idealized version of what Jed kept promising himself, of the *good life*, of relaxation and weeks spent away from his normal life. But it seemed kind of empty now, if he didn't have Redford in the picture too. The vacation had become a getaway, the solitude had become time spent with just the two of them, and Jed figured he didn't need a beach right now to have that.

"Besides," he murmured, brushing some of Redford's hair out of his face, grinning slow as he wrapped his arms around Redford's waist, "I get to see you be all commanding and in charge. I think I like that idea."

Redford gave a huff of a laugh. "I'm not sure that's going to happen," he admitted. "I'm not very good at that. But when we're finished with this job, we'll have more money to spend on fishing. We could add another week or two to the plan?"

Jed made a pleased sounding hum, nuzzling his nose against Redford's. "We'll practice the commanding thing," he assured Redford, swaying a bit, like they were dancing together to unheard music. "Lots and lots of practice. We might not be able to leave the bed for days, but that's a sacrifice I'm willing to make." He laughed as he leaned in for a kiss. "It's just a couple of days, and then we get to take off. Easy job, in and out, and then it's nothing but you and me and the water."

CHAPTER
2

Jed

SO, FAMILY dinners. Not exactly Jed's forte. He'd kind of spent a great many years avoiding them, matter of fact, and now here he was, speeding down the highway toward one that would be populated with wolves and a prissy professor. Some days, he really had to take a step back and look hard at how fucking *weird* his life had gotten.

"I really do think we should have brought something," Redford fussed from the passenger seat, beautiful face crumpled into a frown. He pushed his hair back, fidgeting with the sleeve of his shirt, obviously worried, and not just about their lack of a hostess gift. "The etiquette books my grandmother had said you should never show up empty-handed."

Redford was wearing a dress shirt. It had buttons and a collar, and it was officially the most dressed up Jed had seen Redford in months. Frankly, Jed wasn't sure where Redford had *found* the damn thing. Or when he'd found time to iron Jed's jeans. Who ironed jeans? Wolves who were fretting over leading their first job, that's who. He'd agonized over clothes, over how he should stand, and Jed could tell he was just looking to be worth the trust people were placing in him. Jed thought it was kind of silly, really. Like Redford was ever anything other than *worthy*.

"We're not going for social calls, Red," Jed pointed out, taking their exit and heading into the countryside. "Trust me, Miss Manners did not anticipate this particular scenario." He gave Redford a reassuring little smirk, reaching over to find the other man's hand. "Two mercenaries showing up for dinner isn't exactly covered in polite society."

Huffing out a little sigh, Redford allowed, "Maybe." But his hand tightened on Jed's, and that simple gesture was all Jed needed to know that everything was right with the whole damn world. Their fingers threaded together, resting on Jed's knee as he started watching for street signs to find their next turn. "I just want to make a good impression. They're trusting me with a very important job."

"Nobody alive would meet you and think anything but that you're amazing," Jed told him stubbornly, eyes flicking up to the rearview mirror. Victor was seated in the backseat, wearing another one of those ridiculous sweater vests. Seriously, did the guy get them on sale? In bulk? Was his mother the secret heiress to a sweater vest factory? "Ain't that right, princess?"

"Undoubtedly," Victor replied drolly, taking off his glasses to clean them. He continued, more genuinely, "Try not to fret too much, Redford. Unless you do something truly alarming, I'm sure they'll be quite happy with you."

Redford just looked even more worried. His episodes of doing "truly alarming" shit because of his instincts gone wild were less frequent now, but they still happened. The other morning, Jed had been completely unable to leave the bed for two hours after he woke up, because Redford had been feeling a bit too overprotective and growly. Not that Jed minded staying in bed half the day, but the idea that Redford had been so convinced Jed stepping outside would lead to his instant death hadn't exactly been the grounds for the best mood in the world.

Slumping back in his seat, Redford carefully hooked a light grip in Jed's sleeve. "They're wolves," he murmured. "I've never really... you know, *socialized* with wolves."

Turning to look at Redford, cutting glances back at the road to make sure they were still on it and not about to hurtle into a tree, Jed reached up to cup Redford's cheek. "They're wolves," he repeated calmly. "If anyone's going to get Chuckles and Mr. Bitey Pants, it's them, right? Besides"—Jed grinned then, turning back to his driving before Victor had a heart attack—"who the fuck cares? They're clients, Red. Remember? In, out, and then we're on to the beach."

Simple.

Redford gave him a mystified look. "Who are Chuckles and Mr. Bitey Pants?" He twisted in his seat to glance at Victor, as if he might have brought some uninvited guests along.

Jed just waved his hand in dismissal. "You know. Chuckles is when you decide that chasing the mailman is the height of fun, and Mr. Bitey Pants is when you pin me down and—"

"That's quite enough information, Journey, if you please." Jed could practically *feel* the British Beams of Disapproving Prudeness hitting the back of his head from Victor. "As Jed said, Redford, they are indeed like you. Not exactly, of course, but they will understand your, ah, *situation* much better than the average human." A beat and he added mildly, "No offense intended, of course." It took Jed a moment to realize he'd been insulted. Then again, he wasn't exactly sure when *human* had turned into something nobody wanted to be. Victor went on, a bit more upbeat, "They may even be able to help you."

"Really?" Redford sounded surprised, like he hadn't thought of that. "I guess. Jed's been helping me a lot, though, as much as anybody possibly can." He gave Jed a fond look. "And I'm still seeing Dr. Alona. Even if Jed doesn't like my head being shrunk." Another amused look in Jed's direction. Jed just huffed a neutral little noise. He hadn't decided yet if he trusted the shrink. "I think he's human, isn't he?"

"Ah, well, that's up for debate," Victor replied dryly. "I don't know the man personally, so I couldn't say for sure."

Redford appeared to be considering this. He got a little crease between his eyebrows when he was going over something in his mind, and Jed cursed the fact he was stuck being a responsible driver and couldn't lean over to kiss it away. "He pretty much smells human," Redford decided. "I think. Even if he's a bit weird about the name Rufus and has three different animals named that."

Victor tilted his head in interest. "Out of curiosity, what do *I* smell like? I've never been told."

"Kind of like what I imagine a snake smells like." Redford inhaled. "It's all... scaly? I don't know how to describe that very well."

Heh. "Told you your mom was a snake fucker," Jed said with a smirk, ignoring Victor's irritated grumble. "Now do me, Fido. What do my manly, human genes smell like?" This could be a fun party game! Kind of like reading palms, only way more prejudiced against bad BO.

"I've never told you?" Redford lifted his eyebrows in surprise, leaning across to rest his cheek on Jed's shoulder. "You smell like pine forests and gunpowder. I like it."

Lips creasing upward slightly, Jed turned to press a kiss to the top of Redford's hair. "And manliness," he prompted. "Pine, gunpowder, and pure, distilled manliness."

"Yes, that too," Redford added. "Beer, sweat, and gasoline. Pure manliness."

"Damn straight." Jed was smiling, his hand stealing over to find Redford's again. This was so fucking good. Just this, just the two of them. And yeah, okay, so his life was weird. His life also included moments like this, with the two of them in the car—and Victor, apparently, in the backseat, but hence the aforementioned weirdness—and Jed wasn't about to trade it for anything more normal. Normal didn't have Redford in it. Normal could go fuck itself twice.

"I don't suppose *I* smell like manliness," Victor mumbled half to himself, staring out the window. Jed snorted out a laugh, rewarded by the faint smile touching Victor's lips, the soft crinkle that looked like genuine amusement. What did you know. The princess could crack a joke. At his own expense, even!

"Do tea and books count?" Redford teased lightly. "Those, I think, are very masculine things. David seemed to like them."

And just like that, the moment broke. The almost smile faded from Victor, Jed's shoulders tightening, and Redford looked utterly crestfallen at his mistaken mention. They didn't talk about David, he and Redford. Three months since Cairo and Jed hadn't found a good time to do so. Or maybe he just didn't want to think about it too much. A guy he'd almost trusted, a guy who'd gotten as close to Jed as people got, before Redford, and he'd turned out to be... well. Not a regular guy at all.

Yeah. They didn't talk about David. Victor, Jed assumed, didn't talk about him for his own set of issues. The same issues that had him showing up yesterday looking like a poster boy for one-night fuck aftermaths.

"Sorry," Redford said guiltily. "I wasn't thinking."

Victor pinched the bridge of his nose between two fingers, suddenly looking exhausted. "It's fine," he said lowly. "Just because things ended between David and I doesn't mean you can't mention him ever again."

"Don't worry about it," Jed said, wrapping his arm around Redford and hauling him in close. He could drive just fine one-handed. "It's just David. And, for whatever reason, he did get off on tea, books, and nerds. No point in pretending he didn't exist."

15

Not that he wanted to continue that line of conversation, but hell if he was going to let Redford feel bad over it. "Can anyone read these fucking directions?" Jed said, promptly changing the topic, scowling at the slip of paper. "For a giant fucking dweeb, that Randall kid has drunk monkey handwriting."

"Or doctor's handwriting," Victor agreed. "Here, let me look at them." He reached forward to take the directions and turned the paper around. "It may help if you read it the right way up, for starters."

Jed just beamed him a wide, shit-eating grin. "Hey, it's not my fault you're the only one here who can read nerd. Seriously, I think he just threw that paper in a coop and let them go wild."

"It really is just regular handwriting, Jed," Victor corrected, sounding bored. "Right, you're going to want to turn after the upcoming lake. There will be a dirt road to your left, and we'll be on that for...." He paused, trailing off as he studied the rest of the writing. "Goodness. Ten miles? Randall wasn't lying. This is certainly out of the way."

"I think I saw a horror film that started like this," Jed pointed out darkly. "Good shit never happens this far from a bar."

Redford looked like he wasn't sure if he should be wary. Maybe Jed should stop showing him movies—he'd tried to explain to Redford that movie situations and real-life situations differed greatly, but Redford never quite seemed to grasp that. It wasn't lack of common sense, Jed knew, it was just from growing up with no socialization and a hell of a lot of books. Redford, Jed was pretty damn sure, was half expecting fairies to come back to life when he clapped. Or at least he had enough faith to think it was possible. Jed, however, wouldn't believe in Santa if the fat guy built him a chimney, climbed down it, and then gave him a lap dance.

"Don't be ridiculous," Victor dismissed, leaning his head against the glass to peer up at the trees as they turned down the dirt road into the forest. "I think it's quite lovely. Very private. I'm sure that the location helped the Lewises immensely, considering."

"Considering they like to go furry and chomp on cute woodland creatures?" Jed snorted quietly, concentrating on driving slow enough so that they weren't all bounced around like breasts at a rodeo. "Yeah, I'm guessing they don't want to be cramped up in a high-rise."

Redford made an affirmative noise. "With them being the kind of wolves they are, it'd be nice for them to have a lot of forest that they can run around in." He hesitated, frowning a little. "Not that I could do something like that. I'm still not really in control."

"Well, that would be even better for you," Victor pointed out. "If you lost control here, there's not exactly any neighbors you could traumatize."

Jed had never been much of a dog person. His parents had one, back when he was a kid, but he'd never *bonded* with it. Had never seen the point of running around outside chasing a stick or whatever. Jed liked cats. He liked how little they demanded, how Knievel would go from desperate for affection to barely remembering he existed in a swing of her tail. When Jed had felt the need to *run*, it hadn't been through the goddamn woods. It'd been a new life, a bigger city. It'd been forgetting who he was and hiding in the masses.

When Jed thought of freedom, it was in the way he could sleep 'til noon whenever he fucking wanted. How he'd never, not once, had another lima bean since he'd sat all night staring at his plate, refusing to touch his mother's cooking. How he could take the jobs he wanted, leave the ones he didn't. How he had money in the bank and the man he loved next to him and nobody said fuck all about either. Or if they did, Jed didn't have to stay and listen.

It was how he felt good in his own skin most of the time. How his ass fit perfectly in his couch, how he had weapons at his fingertips and he knew full well he could survive just about anything that got thrown at him. Because he had before.

When he was *home*, it was with a roof and windows and buildings in close. He liked the noise of traffic to sing him to sleep. And he'd never, not once, considered the fact that Redford—or, more specifically, Redford's *instincts*—might not feel the same way.

But as they drove, as the dappled sunlight flashed over Redford's face, the trees bending gracefully above them, it was like seeing a glimpse of that *something more* that seemed buried away in Redford. Being out in the woods was exactly what someone like Redford needed. Not a cage, not a basement hidden under lock and key and chain. Not a tiny apartment, four walls, a roof, and no room to run. Redford still hid himself away every full moon when he had no choice about turning, still looked to that cage. To both cages, really, because Jed suddenly couldn't think of so many differences between a bitter old woman's bars and his apartment. None of it was fresh air. None of it was dirt under Redford's feet and a chance to actually *be*.

Fuck.

"Yeah, well, the woods doesn't have a hot dog cart on the corner," he pointed out with a sudden manic grin, gripping the wheel tighter. He wasn't going to look over at Redford, at the way the dappled sunlight through the leaves was lighting up his whole expression. Wolves in cages were just a fucking sad thing to contemplate. Wasn't that what he'd been trying to save Redford from all this goddamn time?

"I do like the hot dog cart," Redford agreed. "Jed brings me a whole pack of hot dogs on full moons," he said to Victor, grinning. "I think I've gained five pounds."

Hot dogs, like that was somehow better than being free, and fuck, Jed needed to stop thinking about this right the hell now. It wasn't doing anyone any good. They were here for a job, to meet the fur balls and get the details of what they needed to do to get paid. Any other random thoughts could be shoved aside until later. That was what insomnia was for.

The drive curved, and all at once they were in a clearing, a low-slung log cabin in between two tall pine trees. Jed parked in front, vaguely surprised to see a sandy-blond-furred wolflike dog curled up on the porch, tail over its nose. When they piled out of the car, the dog raised its head and chuffed at them, trotting over with tail wagging to head-butt all of their legs. It wound up next to Redford, looking up at him with a happy doggy grin, tongue lolling out.

Redford stared back in mute anxiety.

Jed immediately dropped down beside him, grinning, scratching behind its ears. Hell, he might not be a dog person, but that didn't mean he couldn't appreciate a good petting. And he'd gotten way better at this since Redford. Apparently even growly wolves liked cuddles. "Who's a fluffy puppy?" he crooned, rewarded when the dog immediately flopped onto its side, showing its belly as it wiggled ecstatically under Jed's attentions. "Who is a furry, fluffy big boy?"

"That would be Edwin." The dry, faintly exasperated voice came from the doorway, Randall stepping outside with a worn flannel robe in his hand. "Who knows better. Ed, come on, you know the rules."

The dog—no, *wolf*—underneath his hands gave a forlorn sounding yip and nudged Jed's hand with his nose a final time. He shifted, and then instead of fur, there was skin, a blond mop of hair, and a broad grin staring up at Jed.

"Son of a bitch!" Shocked, Jed sat back on his heels while the kid—who wasn't a kid and who was definitely naked—stood, and trotted up to where Randall was standing. Edwin shrugged on the robe and wrinkled his nose at Randall.

"You're such a stick-in-the-mud," he declared.

"Edwin is my younger brother," Randall explained, arching his eyebrow at Edwin and looking completely unaffected by Edwin's assessment of him. "And he apologizes for going wolf on you."

"No, he does not," Edwin replied, arms folded, all sun-kissed skin and long limbs, defiant and proud. "We're wolves, Randall. I'm not going to apologize to a bunch of two-legs about that."

Randall sighed. "Fine. Go see if Anthony needs help, would you, Ed?" As his brother scrambled inside, he called after Edwin, "And put some pants on, please!"

When the door shut behind Edwin, Randall came down the steps, offering his hand to Redford. "I'll apologize then, if Ed won't," he said quietly, gaze touching on each of them before finding Victor's. "Anthony taught us not to shift around people. It's common courtesy that Edwin sometimes chooses to forget."

There were rules for that kind of shit? Jed was just left to stand up again, staring, baffled, cutting little glances over at Redford. Sure, he'd known they were going to a little wolf family. The *reality* of it was slightly different. Redford had always seemed, to Jed, like a guy who just happened to go furry. Randall, though, and Edwin even more so, struck him as wolves who sometimes walked around like people. It was something in their eyes, in how they stood, in the way they carried themselves.

Around Redford, Jed felt like he was the traditionally normal one, the one who was altogether *human*. He'd never seen a full moon as anything other than too much light for wet work before Redford, where Redford lived in fear of the goddamn thing. But now, standing there, Jed realized all at once he was the odd one out. He was the one who didn't fit in.

Seemingly bereft of words, Redford took Randall's hand to shake it. Victor did the same. "You have a lovely house," Victor complimented. "Did you or your parents build it themselves?"

"I did." A man wearing an apron and a cooking glove stepped out of the front door. "Anthony," he introduced himself, giving them a bright grin in greeting. "Let me guess, the one who smells like gunpowder is Jed, the wolf is Redford, and the other guy who looks like Randall's wet dream is Victor."

Jed choked out a laugh, a broad smirk tripping across his face. Randall immediately turned bright red, giving his brother a positively mortified, wide-eyed stare, and Victor turned much the same color. "I like you," Jed declared, holding out his hand for Anthony to shake. "Right on all counts, although I'm not sure the princess could really wet any panties."

Instead of the handshake he'd been expecting, Jed found himself engulfed in a floury hug. Anthony then did the same to Redford, who looked stunned. Jed was still watching Anthony, shocked, hands instinctively going to make sure his wallet and his gun were still in place. The last time he'd gotten an unsolicited hug, his pockets had been picked cleaner than Tom Cruise's straight genes.

"Well, you're all welcome to treat this house as your own," Anthony said. "Randall has told me everything, and trust me when I say that all three of us are damn thankful you want to help."

Victor looked startled when Anthony grabbed him in a hug too. "He told me about Cairo," Anthony continued, looking between them, his expression turning serious. "I can't thank you enough. You three are the reason that he's alive, and for that, I'm more grateful than I can tell you."

"Yeah, well, don't try," Jed said gruffly, shoulders rounded, hands in his pockets. "Seriously. We did a job, we got paid, your brother was just one of the lucky ones. No gratitude necessary."

Redford looked uncertain. "Are you the alpha?" he asked Anthony, obviously trying to put as much confidence in his voice as he could.

"Am I the what?" Anthony's nose wrinkled in confusion. As he took in Redford's shrinking posture, though, he seemed to connect the dots, a faint smile touching his lips. "We don't really use that terminology," he corrected gently, like a parent nudging a toddler on simple manners. "I'm the oldest. I'm sure Randall can explain it to you much more academically if you want an explanation of pack dynamics, but I won't be ripping your throats out for stepping on my territory." He almost looked amused at the thought.

Randall had disappeared inside the house. Jed was betting he was hiding from Victor. Which was just damn funny, really. "Someone promised us food?" he asked, clapping Anthony on the shoulder as they walked toward the house. "And then we can talk details. Redford will be taking point on this job, but I'm here as a consultant. Victor's here because he's tired of eating those little frozen meals alone and crying in front of his TV." Jed looked over his shoulder, giving Victor a wide, innocent grin. "What was that show you liked so much, princess? The Everyone Hug and Dance and Sing and Twirl Fairy Story?"

"Yes, that sounds about right," Victor said wryly. "I do love that show."

"I'm making rabbit stew," Anthony announced. "Don't worry. It's not from the supermarket either."

"So, you guys hunt and all that shit?" Jed was interested, his hand going, like always, to find Redford's. "Like, on all fours? Or do you do it the old-fashioned way?"

"Wolf hunting predates modern humans by a few years at least," Randall pointed out dryly as he emerged from the dining room. "Even if you count the point where your ancestors were running around with blunt sticks, hoping they could find something slow enough for them to catch. So I'd say our way was the *old-fashioned* manner."

The place wasn't huge on the inside, but it was neat. Well, neat by Jed's standards, which meant it wasn't on fire. None of the surfaces had anything growing on them, so in his opinion the Lewises were right up there with Martha Stewart and his mom. It was obviously rustic, the axe marks visible on some of the roughly hewn walls. There was also a television and a record player in one corner, along with shelf after shelf jammed with books. It was lived-in and cozy, and Jed liked it, from the soft rug slung out in front of the fire to the dining table set with sturdy blue plates.

"We make sure that we don't overhunt, of course," Anthony was saying, making his way back into the kitchen. He gave Edwin's hair a fond ruffle as he joined him at the counter. "Does it need anything else, Ed?"

Edwin, dressed now, thank God, took another taste from the stew pot. "Nah, it's perfect," he said, giving his brother a wide-open grin, nudging his shoulder against Anthony's. Edwin didn't have a trace of guile in his expression, nothing hiding or held back. He just *was*, this kid who looked to be all of twenty, broad shouldered and so goddamn alive. He looked like Redford did sometimes, when Jed did something good enough to shake off the years of care and worry and fear for him, when Redford stopped hiding behind the ghost of an old woman and his own scars.

"Good." Anthony nodded. "Make yourselves at home, please, get comfortable. Do you want anything to drink? We've got water, beer, tea, and coffee. I'm sure we have juice in here somewhere."

Redford picked out a seat close to the roaring fire, the tense expression slowly leaving him. "I'd love an orange juice," he ventured.

"Let me get that, Ant," Randall said, immediately going to the stove and putting a coffeepot on. Jed was brought a beer, and he nodded his thanks to Randall as the man went out to hand Redford his juice. "Why don't you sit? I've set the table. Edwin and I can take care of the rest."

Jed watched Anthony carefully. Up until that moment, no one would think the guy was sick. He was bustling about, equal parts wolfish and strong, still wearing that goddamn apron. In a flannel shirt and equally worn jeans, he looked like the grinning love child of Martha Stewart and a lumberjack, messy brown hair and bright-blue eyes, dark stubble lining his jaw. But right there, when he reluctantly handed off the pot of stew to Randall, Jed saw his left hand shake. Anthony frowned, quickly curling the trembling hand into a fist, and stuffed it in his pocket to hide it.

Under the smiles, under the easy warmth, Jed saw the tension. This whole family was holding their breaths, desperate and hopeful and terrified. And they were making them dinner. Instead of pushing for their help right the hell now, instead of demanding, they were setting out plates, Edwin cutting up bread, Randall finding the butter. It was a family here, but more than that, it was one that wasn't afraid to let them in. Maybe that was just because of what they wanted from Redford, but shit, the stew smelled good and he had a cold beer. Jed wasn't going to complain about ulterior motives.

Redford tugged Jed down to sit next to him on the wide couch, nudging his side with an elbow. He looked at Jed, then tilted his head toward Anthony, silently asking if Jed had noticed. Letting out a slow breath, Jed wrapped his arm around Redford and nodded, eyes narrowing slightly as he went back to watching the brothers. "Yeah," he murmured lowly. "Yeah, I know."

"You're a wolf." Edwin had appeared at Redford's side, easy grin as messy across his face as the faint freckles and the wild tangle of blond hair. "I mean, you're a wolf like us. I can smell it." Leaning in, he took a deep breath as if to confirm. "Nice to meet you."

"I—I'm not really like you. Sorry." Redford had leaned backward slightly from being sniffed. "I used to be a werewolf. Now I'm somewhere in between."

Cocking his head, Edwin studied him. It was the longest Jed had seen him be still yet, those pale-blue eyes tracking across Redford's face. Then he shrugged, tapping the side of his nose. "Yeah, well, I can smell you. And you're near enough to a wolf to count. Come on." He held out his hand. "Dinner's ready, and Ant's stew is legendary."

Anthony gave a self-deprecating laugh. "Yeah, a legend in this household."

"It smells amazing," Victor piped up, eagerly migrating toward the table. "Thank you, once again, for all this. I haven't had a home-cooked meal in quite some time."

As much as Jed gave the guy a hard time, he had to kind of feel for Victor. Not a *lot*, but he knew what it was like to think "homemade" meant the instant noodles you'd heated up using the coffeepot because your microwave had something stuck to the inside that smelled like death. Or maybe that was just him. In any case, Jed knew he was damn lucky to have Redford, and Victor.... Well, even with David, he hadn't been lucky like that. Most people weren't.

"You're always welcome here," Randall ventured, though his head was bowed over the bowls as he ladled up the stew. "I mean, we take turns cooking, and there's usually something edible around." His gaze cut over to Victor quickly, before he determinedly looked away again. "After all, I owe you quite a bit more than a simple dinner."

"Oh no, you don't owe me anything," Victor replied, looking startled but pleased at the offer of further dinners. "You have Jed to thank for your rescue in Cairo and Redford for helping here. I'm merely tagging along, though I do hope to be helpful."

"Jed and Redford are more than happy to accept dinner in trade for lifesaving." Jed waved Randall off. "In fact, if you get me another beer, I'll say we're even." He'd rather have a simple meal than a bunch of thanks he didn't know what to do with, any day.

They took their seats. Jed held out Redford's for him and claimed the chair next to him. Edwin easily took the bowl from Anthony, almost seeming as though the gesture meant nothing. He and Randall got Anthony's food ready, filled up his glass, all without missing a beat or appearing like they were even deliberately helping him. It was a choreographed dance between people who didn't want to acknowledge why they were doing what they did.

Anthony took a few moments to encourage everybody to put more on their plates than what was really necessary, making sure they had enough to drink, fussing over bread. Jed noticed that he subtly switched out his bread plate for Edwin's, giving the larger slice to his brother. He did much the same thing with his bowl of stew and Victor's, like it was ingrained in him to make sure everyone else had enough before he let himself relax into his own place.

"Well, before we get started," Victor said, lifting his glass, "may I propose a toast? To working together, and to hopefully finding a solution." His gaze went to Randall, a reassuring smile tugging at the corner of his lips. "With Jed and Redford on your side, I've no doubt they'll find a way."

Jed laid his hand over his heart as he raised his beer. "Was that a vote of confidence? Professor, I'm touched." He mimed wiping away tears, sniffing loudly.

21

"God, and I didn't get you anything. Red, remind me to stop at the pocket protector store on the way home. Victor deserves something pretty."

Victor looked thoroughly unamused. "As an addendum," he continued, as if unaware that Jed had spoken, "I apologize for any explosion, property destruction, or loss of limbs. All three regularly happen in Jed's vicinity."

At that, Jed laughed genuinely, leaning over the table to clink his bottle against Victor's glass. "Now that I'll drink to," he said, giving the man a grin. "And to the professor. If we play our cards right, he might just use that big brain of his for good instead of putting me to sleep."

"Cheers," Randall said with a sideways little smile, raising his glass. Everyone else followed suit, and they settled down to eat.

The rabbit stew was fucking fantastic. Jed had eaten some weird shit in his life—once, while embedded in Cambodia, he'd eaten roaches the size of his fist off of where they were crawling all over him after his rations ran out—but this was less *well, it's eating this or my own foot* and more just plain delicious. "Goddamn, this is great," he enthused, reaching for a second helping, sopping up the last drops in his bowl with the bread. "Seriously, holy shit."

Beside him, Redford gave a low laugh and nudged Jed in the side. Yeah, okay, Jed was well aware that he said the same thing every time Redford cooked. But come on, they'd taken a bunch of nothing, and now it was something way better than frozen chicken patties. That was like a form of magic in Jed's book. Forget water to wine, this shit was the real miracle. Besides, he was more of a beer guy anyway, and no holy son of God had ever made a decent brew.

"I suppose we may as well get down to business," Anthony said, leaning back in his chair as Edwin reached over in front of him for more bread. "The first thing we'll have to do is find the Gray Lady's pack."

"Which might be easier said than done," Randall said, offering Victor more stew with a hopeful little look, which Victor returned by happily handing his bowl over. "We're going to need to find a place where people will be willing to talk about such things."

"And where would that be?" Redford piped up. "Do you know of any places like that, Jed?"

"Oh, yeah, me and the Easter Bunny were hanging out just last weekend." Jed snorted quietly, giving Redford an apologetic wince. "I'm kind of thinking my contacts are going to be about as worthless as tits at a bathhouse."

"You could go to Murry's Bar," Edwin offered, stealing the spoon from Jed to dish himself up yet more stew. "There's always a bunch of naturals hanging around there." Catching Anthony's look, Edwin immediately tried for an innocent expression. "Not that I've ever been there! I just heard. You know, from other people."

"Naturals?" Bewildered, Jed frowned around at the rest of the group. "What the hell does that mean?"

Randall sighed, slipping off his glasses to clean them on a corner of his shirt. "It's a rather crude slang expression that ought not to be used. It means other than human. The supernatural community, if you will, though generally we don't have a universal name for the differing groups of us. Those that use the term *natural* are arguing that we are the normal ones. It's humans that should be considered others."

"Supernatural...." Jed trailed off, eyebrows raised. This was a fucking weird conversation. He was half expecting someone to come out with a herald and a trumpet and hand him the Sword of Destiny or some shit.

"Werewolves, vampires, half bloods," Anthony clarified, giving Edwin another suspicious look. "And who exactly did you hear this from?"

"Oh, you know," Edwin said, carefully not meeting Anthony's eyes. "Just around. Hey, you should totally go!" He changed the topic swiftly, turning to look at Redford. "You'd definitely get in. They just have a couple of wolves at the door that sniff you to make sure you're not a preter or anything."

"Edwin," Randall barked sharply, eyes narrowing. But instead of continuing, he just looked to Anthony, as if awaiting his mediation.

Jed and Redford shared twin looks of utter confusion. "Preter?" Jed asked. "Maybe slow down the crazy talk around the uninitiated. What the hell is that?" It sounded like a slur against penises.

"It's more slang." Anthony smacked Edwin on the shoulder as a rebuke. "Only this time it's pretty rude. Preternatural is what *some* call regular humans. You know, *other than* natural. It's not something any of us should be saying, not in this household. Edwin, seriously, we have a human sitting right here at the table. Can you curb the racial insults?"

"And it's less than polite in mixed company, even if you choose to use it in private," Randall muttered, shaking his head.

Jed shifted, suddenly uncomfortable. "Hey, I'm just.... I mean, come on, I'm not different."

Except yes, he was. He was wildly different. He was part of a whole different *race*, and apparently all the things that went bump in the night got together and voted him out of the clubhouse.

Jed sagged back in his chair. Edwin looked abashed, murmuring, "I'm sorry," but Jed waved it off.

"Hey, don't worry about it, I scratched your ears and saw your ass. In some cultures, we'd be married."

Anthony just shook his head. "In any case, Edwin's suggestion was a good one. If anybody's going to know where the Gray Lady's pack is, we might find them in there. Although I think he and I should have a discussion about the people he hangs out with."

"I'll go," Redford said. "You said that she's looking for the remains of Filtiarn's pack. If anybody has information, they'll know she's looking for people like me." He hesitated, eyes darting over at Jed. "But, um. I guess Jed can't go?"

"Fuck that nun, I'm going," Jed said, arms folded, jaw jutted out stubbornly. "You go, I go, babe. That's how this works. We're partners, remember?" And like hell was Jed letting Redford walk in anywhere he hadn't vetted first. God only knew what kind of shit might go down, and Jed wasn't going to leave him without someone to watch his back. And his front. And all side portions of him.

"I *want* you to be there, but if this is a bar where wolves and vampires and everybody else hang out, it might not be... well, Edwin says they sniff out humans." Redford looked apologetic. "You might not even get past the front door."

"He could go if he's escorted," Edwin said, sighing heavily at the looks his brothers gave him. "I didn't say I *agreed* with that option. I'm just saying, sometimes naturals bring their preter in. They have to be under control and stuff. I even think they use leashes sometimes. The vampires at least." A pause, and then, very unconvincingly, "So I've heard from people who I have no real association with."

"Edwin, *how* do you know this?" Anthony looked appalled. "Please don't tell me you've ever done that."

"Ew, no." Edwin wrinkled his nose. "Collars are gross. I just... have friends who told me." His voice went up at the end, an overly innocent look affected, as if that was going to make Anthony stop pinning him to the chair with an expression that brought to mind a patient bulldog.

"Which friends?" Randall said dryly. "I wasn't aware that your reflection counted."

"Shut up. I have friends." Edwin rolled his eyes at Randall. But, fidgeting guiltily under Anthony's glower, Edwin finally sighed and admitted, "I went last week to hear someone speak at Murry's. It was a lecture. Educational, even!"

"Who would you hear speak at that place?" Anthony folded his arms. "It's a *bar*, Ed."

"A guy called Phoenix." Once again Edwin tried for the guileless uptick of his tone at the end before apparently giving in and simply shrugging. "He's doing all these rallies around lately. I saw a poster for it and went to check it out. He talks a lot about preters... um, humans and their relationships to naturals. Um. Us."

"You and I are going to have a *very* long talk later," Anthony threatened. He looked apologetic as he turned back to Jed and Redford. "Would you be okay going there? It sounds like there might be information to be found."

Jed smirked. "Nah, that sounds like just my kind of scene. Count me in. I'll provide my own leather pants."

"What? No, we're not doing that," Redford yelped, horrified. "I am not putting you on a *leash* or anything. That's degrading."

Reaching out, Jed took his hand, holding it between both of his. "It's a cover, Fido," he reminded Redford. "I'm just there to back you up. A collar's an accessory, is all." He grinned, a flash of amusement crossing his face. "Not the first time I've worn one." Though probably in this instance he wouldn't be calling anyone *Daddy*.

Redford was still clearly not happy with the idea, but not protesting in horror anymore. "I just don't like the thought of you in a stupid collar," he muttered.

Jed's smile faltered.

The cage. The goddamn *basement*. And here Jed was throwing that shit around like Redford wasn't still that scared kid, tied up and thrown away by the one person who was supposed to take care of him.

His whole face crumpling in guilt, Jed wondered if he could beat his head against the wall. Probably would be rude to do that to someone else's walls, and God knew his thick skull would break something. Goddamn, he was so stupid it was a wonder he kept breathing without hurting himself somehow. Immediately, Jed gathered Redford into his arms, kissing his shoulder in penance. "It's not going to be like that," he murmured. "No collar. No leash. Not if you don't want it, not for either of us. I'll just go and let you do the talking." Jed tried for a little smile, not quite making it. "I can be real quiet. Subtle, even. Like a mouse."

That, at least, made Redford smile. "No, you really can't."

"I wasn't aware mice used such copious amounts of explosives," Victor hummed, peering over the tops of his glasses. "How unusual."

"Fuck you all," Jed responded, but more cheerfully, only really caring that he'd pulled a smile from Redford. Turning to the Lewises, he nodded. "We'll get the info and then give you a call." Jed hesitated, glancing over at Redford. "And...." Fuck. Being second in command after all this time alone was not the easiest thing in the world. Popping up out of his chair, Jed bustled about, clearing dishes. "Redford, why don't you talk details or whatever you need. It's your job. I'm just here as a silent and extremely good-looking shadow."

Jed made his way into the kitchen after loading himself up with bowls and cups and spoons. He poked around a little, once he'd filled up the dishwasher. The fridge was decently stocked, as was the pantry. Nothing fancy, lots of meat, most of it looking like the butchered pieces of things they'd caught. Jed wanted to give Redford some space, the chance to do things his own way. The guy was more than capable of handling everything, really. Jed just wanted to give *him* a chance to realize that.

Redford and the Lewises got down to talking, the sounds of the conversation washing over Jed as he looked around the kitchen. A few minutes later, Redford sidled up to him. "Jed," he whispered urgently, "How much is gas right now? I need to know for the budget."

After a moment, Jed huffed out a little laugh, taking Redford by the shoulders and tugging him in, kissing his forehead, the bridge of his nose. "Nervous?" he murmured, ignoring the question for a moment in favor of massaging the tense knots he could feel in Redford's neck.

"Very," Redford admitted. "I don't know how you do this. There's so much to think about, and I can't keep any of it straight in my head."

"Sure you can," Jed responded. He kissed said head again before wrapping his arms around Redford. They fit together so goddamn well. It still amazed Jed sometimes. "Remember the Southfield job two weeks ago? Instead of just charging gas money, you charged mileage. That way it paid for the wear and tear on the vehicles too." Although Jed's version of *wear and tear* was slightly different than other people's. Removing some stains from upholstery was apparently more expensive than just ripping the seats out and starting over. "Just use that amount and charge them per mile."

He pulled back just enough to study Redford's face, fingertips brushing along the man's cheek. "You can do this," he repeated, absolute conviction in his voice. "You're brilliant, and you're damn good at the planning part of things. Just take a deep breath and do what you do best." He smiled at Redford, and he could feel the expression mostly in the corners of his eyes, in the softness of his gaze. "Use that beautiful big brain of yours."

Redford, as suggested, took a deep breath and exhaled slowly. At the end of it, he leaned in to kiss Jed, resting against him for a moment. "You're right," he said, nodding. "I can do this."

"Damn straight." Jed smirked a little, tugging gently on a strand of Redford's hair. "I only have the best for my partner." He softly nudged Redford back toward the dining room. "Now go in there and be amazing."

"You make it sound like you auditioned for a partner," Redford huffed, amused.

"Kinda did." Jed wasn't good at the big, grand declarations. He'd never been one for genuine emotion. But he met Redford's eyes steadily, for once not hiding behind a manic grin or a cocky smirk. He just *was*, he was just Jed, and Redford got to see all of him. The only person who ever really had. "Waited my whole damn life for you, didn't I?"

Instead of replying right away, Redford just tugged Jed into a tight embrace. "Me too," he said. "Now are you going to come back out to the table with me? We're partners, and I want you there."

Their hands slipped together, just like that, and Redford led the way back out to the table. He sat down with a notepad and a pen, going over numbers and paperwork he'd draft up for the Lewises to sign, contingency fees, and even the damn mileage. He handled it all, grasping Jed's hand the whole time, and Jed was sure his heart was just going to balloon up and burst for how much *pride* he felt, how much he adored seeing Redford comfortable in his own skin.

Anthony gave them a plastic container filled with leftover stew. Edwin darted around them, still on two legs but moving every bit like the wolf, seeing them out to their car, making Redford *promise* he'd come back. Randall was more subdued, but he went out to say good-bye as well, hovering behind Victor, opening his car door for him with a slight, shy smile.

"Thank you for coming," Randall said. To all of them, but really just to Victor. "It was…." He breathed out a little laugh. "Interesting."

"It was my pleasure," Victor replied. He took Randall's hand in a brief shake. Jed rolled his eyes when he saw Randall's expression brighten at the contact. How Victor could be *that* oblivious and still keep breathing, he just didn't know. Maybe not being able to look into people's eyes made him miss the most obvious things in the world.

"We'll call you as soon as we have a location," Redford promised. "Hopefully tomorrow."

Jed felt a little like the goddamn Waltons, driving away from the Lewises as the three brothers stood on their porch and watched them go. Any second now, someone was going to say *Good night, John-Boy* and he'd die of some kind of diabetic coma from all the domesticity.

At least they had a job. And as soon as it was done, they could leave the Little Wolves on the Prairie to their knitting or whatever the fuck and get back to real life.

CHAPTER
3

Redford

THE CLUB didn't look like much from the outside. They were parked on a little-used backstreet, the entrance to the club nothing more than a painted wooden door and glaringly red lights above it reading *Murry's Bar*. The cab driver didn't even seem bothered that they were there. There was no indication at all that the occupants of the bar were anything other than human. Redford didn't know what he'd been expecting, but this definitely wasn't it.

Victor had elected to come along for the taxi ride, though he had declined to go in with them. He didn't seem as impressed with the idea of a club of nonhumans as Redford was. Then again, he probably was more used to things like that. "Remember, if you need an exit strategy, I'll be in the diner across the road," Victor said.

"And, what, you'll come in and nag everyone to death?" Jed snorted.

Redford just squinted at the bar sign. "We shouldn't be long," he said to Victor. He touched Jed's shoulder, making sure he was ready. "Show time, I guess." They got out of the taxi, heading in toward the bar. Victor exited as well, in the opposite direction, leaving them very much alone.

The door seemed to open of its own accord when they approached, but a closer look into the shadows revealed a well-dressed bouncer, eyes narrowing as he inhaled. "You're gonna need to put that human on a leash," he rumbled.

Redford summoned up every ounce of courage within himself and met the bouncer's eyes. "I don't need to," he said dismissively.

"Yeah, sweetcheeks," Jed smirked. "I'm just fine right here." Moving forward, dismissing the bouncer, Jed headed in toward the bar. He was stopped by a beefy hand on his chest, though, the large wolf—Redford could smell him, an overwhelming wave of aggression and fur—blocking Jed's path.

"No preters without restraints," the wolf growled, showing his teeth. "Club rules. Either control your little friend here or get the hell out." The whole conversation had obviously been directed toward Redford. Jed didn't even warrant more than a glance from the bouncer, as if he were some errant bug that had wandered in and needed to be shooed away.

The thought of putting Jed on any kind of leash sickened Redford, but it didn't look like the bouncer was going to let them in if Jed was free. "We didn't bring anything," Redford said, losing some of his courage when the growl was turned toward him. Jed was remarkably quiet, though Redford could see his fingers flexing, obviously wanting to go for a weapon. Which would be a disaster of the highest order.

"There's a room right there. Lost and found." The bouncer jerked his chin to a small door to the side of the lobby. "Should be something in there you can use."

He gave Jed a little push. Jed's lips split into a grin, not a nice smile. No, Redford knew that look, and violence usually followed pretty close behind it. "How about you keep your meat hooks to yourself, there, bubba?" Jed took a step forward, getting into the bouncer's face.

"Get a muzzle on this bitch." Far from intimidated, the wolf rolled his eyes at Jed, moving back to his position at the side of the door. "He talks too much."

Redford didn't like that idea either. As the bouncer looked away, Redford traded a glance with Jed. He sighed and opened the door. Inside there lay all sorts of things that Redford didn't want to think about too much, including several absolutely barbaric looking contraptions. He settled on a short length of soft rope, hiding a cringe as he picked it up.

"Sorry, Jed," he murmured under his breath, low enough that even the bouncer wouldn't hear it. "We'll just use this."

As gently as he could, Redford fastened the rope around Jed's throat—Jed had taught him how to tie a range of knots, and the one he used only *looked* solid, but could easily be tugged apart at a moment's notice if need be. Jed gave him a quick thumbs-up to show he could still breathe.

Once the bouncer saw that Jed had been appropriately attired, he waved them through into a dark hallway that stank of disinfectant, malfunctioning lights flickering on and off, the walls painted a sickly shade of green. Brightly colored posters littered both sides of the hall, the sound of thumping music growing louder as they approached the end.

Redford reached out to open the second door and cringed at the wave of *noise* that came rushing out. Music, voices, and above all of that, a cacophony of scents that threatened to send his brain into overdrive in the effort to process them all. The dimly lit club was packed full of people, an area off to the left crammed nearly shoulder to shoulder as the crowd swayed to the music.

He leaned over to Jed, putting his lips close to Jed's ear. "I'm going to take us to the bar," he said, raising his voice to be heard. "Do you want anything?"

Jed bumped his shoulder against Redford's, a reassuring weight, grounding Redford as the room pulsed around them. "No, sir," he said with a mischievous twist of his lips. "Thank you for thinking of me, but I'll be fine."

That was strange. Jed was refusing a chance to drink? Redford pulled back to frown at him faintly, and Jed gave a subtle jerk of his chin, motioning toward the crowd. Of course, many of them would have excellent hearing and would likely be highly suspicious about Redford treating a human nicely.

Redford hated this place already.

But he took another deep breath and squared his shoulders. Though he wasn't typically in the business of appearing totally in control, he fit himself into that persona then, thinking back to the Lewises and their comfort in their own skin, particularly Anthony, with his casual confidence. Redford tilted his chin up slightly, pushed his hair back from his face, setting his expression in vague indifference like he wasn't impressed or startled by any of this, and guided Jed toward the bar.

Jed had given him tips on body language before, so Redford settled his hand on the back of Jed's neck, pushing his head down ever so slightly. He didn't like doing it, but apparently doing so gave off the air of control over a lowly human. Jed, he noticed, seemed tailor-made for the club, fitting in easily with his leather and, again, the kind of confidence that Redford could never call up naturally. The blinking colored lights flashed across Jed's skin, turning it red, blue, yellow, a dizzying quick change.

Redford leaned in again. He wanted to tell Jed he looked amazing. Instead, he lightly bit at Jed's earlobe. He hoped it would convey the same message. He used the closeness as an excuse to breathe in deeply, focusing himself on Jed's scent, grinning at the shiver that went through Jed's shoulders.

The man behind the bar turned toward them, revealing a face that had more piercings than free skin. His eyes glittered yellow in the flashing lights, and he smelled of old blood. Vampire, Redford realized.

"Nice," the vampire smirked, nodding at Jed. "Haven't seen either of you around before. He new?"

It took everything Redford had to bite back the growl that wanted to emerge. Instead, he shrugged, the motion casual. "I'm new in town. I just picked this one up," he replied, raising his voice to be heard. "I don't even know his name."

The vampire laughed, fangs flashing as a bright-red light hit his face. "It's better not to know," he replied, filling a glass from the tap and pushing it toward Redford. "On the house. Everybody gets a free first drink."

Redford took the glass and faked a sip. He didn't particularly enjoy the taste of beer, but even he could tell that this one would be considered a cheap brand. Tightening his grip on the back of Jed's neck, he nodded in thanks at the bartender and took Jed over in the opposite direction of the dance floor. There were tables set up in the far corner, the kind of place where Jed would typically set himself up—his back to the wall, a place where he could keep an eye on the whole room.

He wasn't sure of the protocol, so he motioned Jed toward a chair. With a quick wink, Jed sprawled out into it, legs spread, arms hanging loosely, looking every inch as though he wasn't scanning the room for possible escape routes or for makeshift weapons, or for anywhere that could be used as a trap. The leash tugged tighter when Redford tried to take the seat across the small table. He slid his own chair closer, making sure Jed had enough slack. Once he did so, Jed nudged his shoulder in close to Redford's, giving him a little smile. "You're doing great," he murmured, just barely moving his lips. "Free drinks! That's a good sign."

Redford just summoned up a sickly smile. If the wolves treated humans like this, he suddenly wasn't so sure he wanted to find them.

He cast his gaze over the crowd of people again. Unless he spent a decent amount of time here to get used to the chaos, Redford knew he couldn't rely on his nose. Instead, he looked for body language and eyes that might look yellow. There were more vampires off to the side, gathered in a group, some of them sneering at the rest of the room. When he inhaled, he could smell, well, *everything*: old blood, earthy scents, something that smelled more like fire, another that hit his nose like fireworks. More half bloods than anything else, he assumed.

Jed nudged his arm slightly, surprisingly quiet. His eyes were on a group across the room, a few older men, a woman with gray hair and a kind smile, and then five or six younger people. They were sitting at a large table, drinking and talking quietly, one girl leaning against another, eyes half-shut as she listened to the music. The group held themselves apart a little. A woman with dark hair was giving Redford sidelong glances. Unlike the side of the bar they were in, with men and women in leather and a few humans in ropes and chains sitting adoringly by the vampires, that one group just looked like some friends out for a few drinks.

Redford liked the look of that side of the room better. He touched his hand to Jed's shoulder, giving it a quick squeeze to let Jed know they were moving, and got to his feet, picking his way through the crowd. As he got closer, he breathed in, and the scents he noticed were definitely wolf.

The woman with the dark hair, twisted into a braid, gave him a faint smile. "Redford," she greeted. "I knew I'd see you around again."

Redford froze in place, trying to remember where he'd seen her before. Recognition sparked at the back of his mind, bringing up a picture of her face in a vastly different situation. Filtiarn's pack. She'd been one of them.

"Sophia," he said, stunned. She smelled like the Lewises did, a real wolf, not stuck halfway in between like him. Since Redford assumed Filtiarn's pack had all been dosed with his blood, she must have gotten the full treatment. "I thought—"

Jed had blown up parts of the building and presumably taken down a large portion of the pack with it. Maybe more had escaped than they'd thought. That was just fine with Redford though, considering the majority of them had been victims. He'd had no problems with Jed killing the ones that helped Filtiarn with the kidnapping and the violence, but knowing that the ones like him, the people who had gotten pulled in and used, had gotten out? That was a good thing.

Sophia rose, putting her hand on Redford's arm, a more genuine smile lighting her features. "You look good," she told him. "Here, come sit with us. It's a lot more peaceful over here." She pulled out a chair for him but paused when she caught sight of Jed and the rope leash. A frown settled in at the edge of her lips.

"Howdy," Jed said, sounding rather cheerful for a man who hadn't had a drop of alcohol since they'd gotten there. With a graceful movement, he pulled up a seat next to the chair they'd indicated for Redford.

Redford settled his hand on the back of Jed's neck again as he sat, and he didn't miss the looks that the wolves were giving one another. None of them seemed particularly happy that he had a human on a leash. He put his untouched beer on the table, listening attentively as Sophia went around the group, introducing them to him. She was the only one that had been part of Filtiarn's pack, Redford noticed.

"So, Redford," one of the men—who Redford had been told was named Frank— spoke up. "What brings you here?"

Redford found himself having to internally compose his answer before he spoke it. Luckily, he had Jed to use as a suitable apparent distraction, taking a few moments to make sure the rope was still in place and comfortable, that he hadn't tied the knot too tightly. "I'm looking for information," Redford said honestly. Then not so honestly, "I'm looking for a pack to join. Since Filtiarn, I've... pretty much been on my own."

He hated having to say it. He was well aware that Jed knew he was lying, but it felt like dismissing him, somehow. Redford would make it up to him later.

"There's not many of Fil's pack left wandering around alone," another of the group said. "Which is good for them. A wolf without a pack is just about the saddest sight you'll ever see."

Redford tilted his head, curious. He was getting closer to the topic he wanted to discuss. "I haven't had any luck," he admitted. "Are you all pack?"

Sophia gave him a warm smile, leaning against the side of the man sitting next to her. Even in the chaos, Redford could smell that their scents were mingled. "Oh," he said, surprised, and nodded toward Sophia. "Um, congratulations?"

Her smile brightened into a grin that was verging on a laugh. Redford noticed she looked younger, almost. The lines of stress and wariness she'd worn with Fil were gone, replaced with a lightness in her expression. "You too," she said dryly, indicating Jed. "He's not really your pet, is he?"

"I should fucking hope not," another wolf growled. "That shit is for the bloodsuckers. We don't keep *pets*. We've got enough leeches trying to do the same to us." Redford almost asked him to explain, but he remembered in a flash, the big wolf that Gabriel had kept chained in his office. That wolf had seemed slavishly devoted to Gabriel, to the point of ignoring his own imminent danger in favor of mourning Gabriel's apparent death.

"No, I, uh—" Redford gave a sheepish smile. "I was told that it's the only way to get humans in here."

"And it's true," Sophia replied. "We just don't involve ourselves with humans all that much. We definitely don't keep them around on leashes."

Redford wanted to untie the rope then and there. But just because they were on a different side of the club didn't mean they were invisible. They'd have to keep this up until they left.

"Well, I look fucking fantastic in leather, darlin'," Jed drawled, winking at the table at large. "So trust me, this is not a hardship."

"You definitely do," Redford approved. Not that Jed needed a club to wear it to. He was far too happy to make leather pants or too-tight jeans his everyday wear, and Redford fully supported that choice.

As he sat up straight again, his eye caught the edge of a poster plastered to the wall near the table. In bold, blocky letters it proclaimed *Half blood Revolution*. There was a picture of a man, angular features, lean build, standing behind a podium. At the bottom of the poster, it said that someone named Phoenix was going to be giving speeches there every Thursday for the next few weeks.

It was the man Edwin had spoken of coming here to listen to. And that wasn't the first poster of its kind that Redford had seen, he realized. They were all over the club. Sophia noticed what he was looking at, and she made a derisive noise under her breath, but she didn't comment on it. "What were you looking to find out, Redford? We know of a few other packs. We could point you toward some."

"Actually," Redford started, dragging his gaze away from the poster. There was something oddly hypnotic about it, like the old World War II posters he'd seen pictures of, with propaganda smeared everywhere. "I heard that there was a big pack looking for the remains of Fil's group. The Gray Lady?"

"That she is," Frank confirmed. "Says she's looking to right Fil's wrongs, or something like that. It's the biggest pack we know of."

"I'd like to know where she is," Redford replied. Then, deciding he may as well be honest, he added, "It's not really for me. I have a friend who's sick, and his family thinks that the Gray Lady might be able to help him. It's not really a case where he can go to the hospital."

Sophia's expression softened. "A wolf sickness?" she murmured, trading looks with the other wolves around the table. "Yes, she would be the best person to go to for that. Frank can give you directions. From here, it's about two days drive."

Redford breathed out in relief, giving her a grateful look. "Thank you." He hadn't anticipated it would be that easy. He'd thought he'd have to find someone he didn't know and gradually get the information out of them. Redford watched as Sophia passed Frank a slip of paper and a pen that she'd retrieved from her handbag, then turned his gaze to the directions Frank was writing down.

"It's not exactly just off the highway, so you'll have to keep an eye out for landmarks," Frank cautioned. "Once you get into the forest, you're not far from the compound, though. And if you get lost, you can always use your nose." He gave Redford a quick grin, passing the paper over to him.

Redford tried to figure out how he could properly convey how appreciative he was. He reached across the table to shake Frank's hand. "Thank you," he repeated. "This really means a lot."

"Don't mention it. We're all wolves." Frank smiled easily, leaning back in his chair. "We might separate off into little groups, but we look after our own."

"Promise you'll find us if you need help with anything else," Sophia insisted, and what else could Redford do but agree? It was odd to him, to have more than one person who wanted to look after his well-being.

He said his good-byes, and Jed stood with him. Redford didn't really want to spend any more time in this club than he had to, so he led them toward the door. He noticed Jed giving a longing look toward every dark corner they passed, and a few seconds later, his neck was getting enthusiastically attacked with lips and teeth.

"You're so goddamn hot when you're in charge," Jed breathed, sucking kisses along the slope of Redford's throat. "You've got me at your beck and call. Be a shame to waste that, wouldn't it?"

"Maybe when we're not in the middle of a club," he replied, wrapping his arm around Jed, though his steps kept faltering when Jed found a particularly sensitive spot on his neck. Jed knew him far too well.

"Prude," Jed teased, but he was smiling as he nipped lightly, just under Redford's ear. "I wish I could ride you right here and now. Club be damned."

That made him stumble even more, and Redford had to gather every shred of willpower he had to make it out the door. They got into the dimly lit hallway, the blinking lights none too kind on his eyes, but Redford was pretty sure it was the perfect place to tug Jed into a proper kiss. Pressing Jed back against the wall, Redford bit at Jed's lower lip. "You're terrible for my self-control," he said, attempting to sound stern. "I was trying to be all confident, but you kept distracting me."

"You were confident," Jed corrected, dropping to his knees. Nuzzling his nose against the front of Redford's jeans, Jed flashed him a wicked smile in the dim light. Redford was too startled to make a move to haul Jed back to his feet—and he hadn't been lying, Jed *was* terrible for his self-control. "And sexy." He slid his lips along the outline of Redford's cock, sucking at it through his pants. "And perfect. I barely could watch the crowd, I was so busy looking at you."

"Wait, wait a second," Redford insisted, though he was starting to find it difficult to think. His higher thought functions always started to sink down into the gutter when Jed got going. "Can you—" He broke off, wrapping his hands around Jed's shoulders and tugging him up again. "I'm just going to get the leash off."

He nudged Jed to turn and started plucking at the rope around his neck. "There's a storage room two steps to your left," Jed rumbled, green eyes bright in the flickering light, looking back at Redford. "See if it's unlocked?"

When the last of the rope had fallen away and was tucked into Redford's pocket, Redford took the few steps to his left and checked the door handle. "It's open." He beamed at Jed, reaching out to take his hand, absently sliding his fingers along Jed's neck, making sure there were no marks from the knotted collar.

He swung the door open and happily dragged Jed inside, hauling him in for a kiss as he kicked the door shut behind them. They were cloaked in near-total darkness, the only light coming from under the door. Jed's hands were on Redford's belt, yanking it open with a sharp movement. The only sounds were the faint, low thrum of music from the bar, the harsh panting of their breaths, and the creak of leather as Jed sank back to his knees.

Redford tangled his fingers in Jed's hair, stroking through the short, messy strands, looking down to watch him. "I wish there was a decent light in here," he admitted, running his thumb over Jed's jaw. "I like seeing you."

He felt Jed pause under him, a low huff of air lifting his shoulders. Fingers fumbled a bit on Redford's zipper, and then there was Jed's tongue, running along the underside of his cock. Redford hissed in a sharp breath, just barely stopping his head from colliding with the wall when he tipped it back. "Same to you, babe," Jed murmured. "Best sight in the whole damn world."

Jed apparently wasn't in the mood for any kind of slowness or further lead up, and Redford really did thump his head against the wall when Jed's mouth wrapped around him. His eyes were beginning to adjust to the low light, but not enough to see Jed—instead of staring down at the sight of Jed on his knees, the lips wrapped around him cherry bright, the gleam of a smirk in Jed's gaze, Redford was forced to focus only on the physical. His whole world became nothing but scent and sensation, the incredible feeling of Jed's tongue and the slide of his mouth. Redford clenched his fingers in Jed's hair, struggling not to turn his grip painful.

It wasn't that they hadn't done this before. Jed had shown, time and time again over their months together, that he was quite willing to partake of this specific activity with little to no provocation. But somehow, it was so *intense*. Maybe it was that it was dark, or that Jed had decided that sliding his lips down to the base of Redford's cock in one fell swoop was the right course of action—which Redford could hardly argue with— but Redford found himself biting his lip just to keep from moaning so loud everyone could hear. He'd never exactly done this in a *storage room* before, especially not with an entire bar of strangers less than thirty feet away.

Closing his eyes, he leaned his head back against the wall, summoning every scrap of restraint he had to stop himself from advertising their presence. He wasn't going to last long, not with Jed doing his best to make him come undone as quickly as humanly possible. Not with the strange allure of doing this in a place where they could so easily be discovered—Redford wasn't sure why *that* was hot, but he didn't have the brainpower to figure it out right then. He'd ask Jed later.

When arousal built to its peak, Redford tried to warn Jed, but all that came out was a stuttered version of Jed's name, pleasure sweeping over him and leaving his skin alight. His head was definitely going to hurt, with all the times he'd smacked it against the wall, but the sensation drowned that out.

He sagged back against the wall like it was the only thing holding him up and managed to loosen his grip on Jed's hair, rubbing his fingertips over Jed's scalp in apology. "I don't think I can move," Redford said vaguely. "But I'd like it if you stood so I can kiss you." If he attempted to kneel or pull Jed up, Redford was sure he might actually fall over.

With a very quiet laugh, Jed stood, arms bracing on either side of Redford, body blanketing his, pressing him back into the wall. "You're incredible," Jed murmured, ghosting his lips over Redford's. Nimble fingers were gently getting Redford's pants zipped back up, his shirt straightened again. Redford's sudden movement to wrap his arms around Jed briefly halted Jed's progress, but getting himself neat and tidy was the last thing on Redford's mind.

He nuzzled in against Jed's neck, burying a smile against the skin as he pushed a thigh between Jed's. "We're not done," he pointed out, biting at Jed's lip. Jed's response came a little slower than normal, but then there was the blush of a smile against Redford's lips, Jed leaning in to catch another kiss.

"Yeah?" Jed rumbled, sounding a little surprised. "What, you got another go-round in you? And here I thought Cujo would be tired after that workout."

Even after a Jed-mandated viewing of that movie, Redford still wasn't sure about that nickname. Then again, Jed's names for things rarely made a lot of sense to anyone but Jed. "No, I mean—"

A sharp knock at the door made Redford jump. "If you're quite done" came Victor's dry voice.

Redford gave Jed a guilty look. He knew there wasn't exactly a time frame on this part of the job, though, so he couldn't feel *too* bad about it. Reaching down, he gave Jed's cock a fond pat through the leather pants. "Hold that thought until we get home."

Jed pounded on the door, smirking at Victor's audibly irritated reaction on the other side. "It's not nice to eavesdrop, princess," Jed informed him, swinging open the door and walking out, looking vastly pleased with himself. His hand was laced with Redford's, and he pulled the man into his side happily. "Especially not when I'm busy with a cock down my throat. That was important to the mission." Off of Victor's disbelieving expression, Jed tried out his best innocent look. "What? It was! Crucial job-related activities were happening in there. I'll be billing for our time."

"Incredibly crucial," Redford agreed solemnly. "We might not have gotten the mission done without it."

Victor looked completely unsure of the validity of that. He obviously wasn't used to Redford being able to lie and play along with Jed. His eyes narrowed in suspicion, and he turned to walk back to the hallway. "The meter's running on the taxi. Unless you want this trip to cost more than your entire fee, I suggest you quicken your pace," he called.

Whistling sharply, Jed strolled past Victor, hastening to open the door for him and Redford while he tried to hand Victor what appeared to be some folded paper. "Move your very pert asses," he told them cheerfully. "And, Victor, see what you can find out about that guy."

"Has that been inside your *trousers*?" Victor sounded scandalized, refusing to touch the poster.

Jed blinked, looking down at it and then back up at Victor. "Well, yeah," he drawled, arching one eyebrow. "Not like I have *pockets*."

He ushered the two men into the cab, giving his address and leaning back against the seat. Jed shook the poster out, and they leaned in to look at it. It was the same poster Redford had seen on the wall, the one that called for a half-blood revolution. "This guy. Phoenix. I want to know what his deal is."

Victor gingerly took the poster between thumb and forefinger. "His name is Phoenix Green." Redford gave a snort at the name, which Victor smirked at. "Yes, I know. Odd name. Word is that his parents were hippies. But beyond that, I'm afraid I can't tell you much. Much the same as Edwin was saying the other night. He advocates for half-blood superiority over humans, and that half bloods are equals to wolves and vampires."

"Is he a half blood?" Redford asked curiously.

"I'd assume so." Victor leaned closer to study the fine print at the bottom of the poster. "Nobody has a clue what *kind*, though. He's kept it very secret." When Redford gave him a quick look, Victor simply shrugged. "Apparently he smells of old metal and earth. That's hardly a definite species as far as we know."

"Feel like I've seen him before. Or maybe he's just got one of those faces." Jed shrugged. "Probably not in any of my type of crowds, right?" He smirked a little, humorlessly. "Dirty human and all that shit."

"Perhaps you have seen him around. He's been doing a lot of public appearances in the last few years." Victor folded the poster back up and handed it to Jed.

"You got ears to the ground on this?" Jed asked Victor, gaze sharp despite the lazy sprawl of his body.

Victor gave a one-shouldered shrug, a wry smile touching his lips. "Somewhat. I am part of the half-blood community, after all, even though I don't converse with the fanatics that Phoenix is beginning to cultivate. I'm usually treated with a reasonable amount of respect, due to the dwindling numbers of my bloodline."

"Good." Jed's eyes slipped shut as he thought. "Got a feelin', that's all. Wouldn't be the worst thing in the world if we kept one eye on this hippie."

Redford glanced over at Jed, questioning. "What do you think is going to happen?" It seemed fairly harmless to him; what were one man's words, really? People talked all the time. Redford saw them on television, in the news, even on the street corner, sometimes. Everyone had an opinion and sometimes felt the need to shout them. One man standing up and saying that he thought humans were less wasn't going to suddenly turn into something much more.

"What always happens." Jed shrugged. "People talk, people listen, everyone gets all het up, and then either they get tired and go home or shit goes to hell. Kind of hard to tell what a group of anyone, human or whatever, is going to choose to care about on any particular day. I just want to keep eyeballs on the situation, especially if you're going to be chummy with any of the fanged or furry types."

"I'll keep an ear out for whatever information I can," Victor agreed. "Phoenix is becoming more popular lately, so gossip is easier to come by, at least."

"And maybe when we visit the Gray Lady's pack, the wolves there might be talking about it too," Redford said.

"Doesn't look like much, does he?" Jed was studying the picture on the flyer, head cocked, still frowning as if searching his memory for why the man looked so familiar.

"Well, he has just had his face in your pants," Victor said idly. "Anybody would look terrible after that." Redford wondered if he should be insulted.

Leaning forward, Jed gave Victor a smirk, expression absolutely wicked. "Well, just to let you know. Not a lot of room in these pants, so that poster," the one currently resting on Victor's lap, "got *real* cozy with Winston Churchill, Margaret Thatcher, and Rambo, the True American Hero."

Instead of reacting with horror, Victor's expression turned as confused as Redford's had been. Then, very slowly, recognition dawned on his face, and with a vaguely irritated noise he shoved the poster at Jed. "I'm not sure I want to know *why* those three people."

Laughing, Jed grinned at him, arm slung around Redford's shoulders. "All you need to know, princess, is that in my pants? Churchill wins the war *every time*."

CHAPTER
4

Victor

"JED, IF you're going to pull up outside my classes, you could at least have the decency to not lean on the horn with quite so much enthusiasm." Victor readjusted his grip on his bag, peering into the rental van. Inside were Jed and Redford, three wolves, and a cat. "Good morning," he said dryly. "It's certainly a lovely day to be crammed into Jed's idea of transportation, isn't it?"

"Well fuck you too, princess." Jed was behind the wheel, looking none too happy about his current ride. As far as Victor could remember, the man preferred his vehicles with a few more bullet holes and grunt to them. He was certain it was some of kind of overcompensation. "It's not *my* fault that we're the fucking Brady Bunch on acid in here. I had to get something that would fit us all." The minivan chugged back to life, and Jed grimaced at the automatic transmission. For a moment his hand had flailed out as if to switch gears, which, obviously, wasn't necessary. "Goddamn soccer mom shit."

"I only narrowly stopped him from trying to put a V8 engine in it," Redford piped up from the front seat, twisted around to look at Victor. Jed sighed mournfully, revving the engine. It sounded like a wailing cat, the van shuddering a bit in protest before it evened out again.

Victor frowned at the thought of it. "That would handle terribly," he admonished Jed, climbing into the van. He shoved his bag under a seat, looking around to figure out where he could sit. Edwin was taking up half of one of the seats, a Siamese cat taking up the other half. Anthony was seated near the window, and Randall had gotten himself near the back, head down in a book. His options seemed to be to remove a very possessive-looking cat or to press into the backseat. It was not exactly first class. Victor made a mental note not to entrust Jed with the traveling plans in the future.

The cat lifted its head to study Victor intently, and Victor suddenly felt a bit like a schoolchild who had forgotten his homework. But then she rolled over, dismissing him out of hand, much too busy kneading happily into Edwin's leg to bother with him. Edwin gave Victor a helpless little look, torn between amusement and bafflement. "This is Knievel," he informed Victor, cutting a quick look up at Jed. "Apparently she's coming with us."

"Damn straight," Jed informed them all cheerfully. "My baby is not doing that kennel thing again." Knievel, for her part, didn't appear concerned at all to be surrounded

37

by wolves. In fact, if the way Edwin was putting up with claws digging in and out of his thigh was any indication, she was coming out on top in the whole matter.

Victor felt his nose start to itch. Thank God he'd had the foresight to pack some allergy medication. He'd met Knievel before in the times he'd been to Jed's apartment, but those had always been brief visits, and his allergy to cats had never had time to play up too much. Now he was going to be stuck in a van with one for two days. Wonderful.

Backseat it was, then. As he settled into his seat, Jed kicked the van into gear, and they peeled out of the parking lot far faster than Victor was comfortable with. He dragged his bag closer with a sigh, digging into a front pocket to retrieve the medication. Out of the corner of his eye he caught the title of Randall's book: *Mittelalterliche Liste gefährlicher und unerkennbarer Bestien.*

"You know German?" Victor said, pleasantly surprised.

Looking a bit startled, Randall raised his head, glasses falling half down his nose from where he'd been bent over the book. "Oh. Er, yes, a bit. Well enough written, my spoken is quite terrible." A very faint smile touched his lips. "I have the worst accent. I only really learned it because I was interested in Old English, but that wasn't an option in my high school. So I taught myself, using what I'd learned in German classes."

"How wonderful." Victor beamed. "You're on the right track to getting close to Old English, then. They do have many similarities." He motioned at the book. "Why a medieval index?"

Randall rifled his bag, pulled out a bottle of water, and offered it to Victor almost shyly, eyes darting to the bottle of allergy meds. With a grateful smile, Victor accepted and took a drink to wash the pills down.

Randall's eyes fell, warmth touching his cheeks. He fumbled a bit, pushing his glasses back up, explaining, "It's, uh, research. A list of 'dangerous and unknowable beasts,' which, of course—" He turned the book to face Victor with a slight amused smile. There was a woodcut print of a snarling beast, eyes wild, fangs dripping. It was labeled *Übelster und gefährlichster Wolfsmensch.* Most vile and dangerous wolf man. "—includes our great, great ancestors. Including a mention here of Liadan and Filtiarn. Well, not directly, but it talks about the wolf mother and her mate, and the birth of the curse of the Wolfsmensch."

"Really?" Victor's interest was piqued. "That's fascinating. I'd love to glance over it later, if that's okay with you."

"Oh, yes, absolutely." Randall immediately handed it over, nodding a few times. "I've read it numerous times, so, please. Be my guest. I have other books."

Victor was careful as he handled it, putting it on his lap. The book was obviously well read, the pages slick at the top corners from frequent turning. Overall it was in quite good condition, loved and cared for. Victor did respect people who treated their books well. "You must be quite interested in this line of research," he murmured, turning a page, his gaze skimming over a frightful woodcut of what looked like a demonic infant. "I think you'd like my personal library. Study of the supernatural is something of a passion of mine."

"You're a professor of linguistics, right?" Anthony said from a seat over.

"Indeed." Victor leaned forward to talk to Anthony, so that he could be heard over the rumble of the engine. "I have my masters in linguistics, and I teach a few classes here and there. This is actually my semester off—they like us to write research papers every now and then, but that doesn't take much time, so here I am. I have no formal education in the study of the supernatural, but then again, what they teach in classes is hardly the truth in that area."

Anthony laughed in agreement. "I imagine not." He glanced at Randall and said, "You know, Randall's a fan of yours." His leg jerked back, and he laughed again, rubbing his ankle.

"Are you all right?" Randall asked dryly, head down as he carefully went through one of his bags for another book. "How terrible, you've hurt your ankle. Perhaps you should stop talking and tend to it."

"Yeah, must be one of those mysterious phantom ankle kickers." Anthony smirked. "But seriously, Professor, I had this mental image of you being sixty years old. None of your books have a picture of you."

Randall was bright red, and Victor felt like he might be headed in the same direction. He'd written a few books over the years, but because of the fact that he was significantly younger than most of his peers, he of course had never included photos. Mostly, he was just surprised that someone had actually *read* his books. They'd been accused of being rather dry.

"Well," he said, temporarily at a loss for words. "I hope they didn't put you to sleep, Randall."

"Oh no, he loves them." Now Edwin was in on the conversation, his grin huge underneath shaggy hair as he turned around in his seat. "Reads them over and over. Once he tried to explain to me why they were...." He trailed off, hiding a laugh behind an entirely innocent look. "How was it you put it, Randall?"

"I think I changed my mind," was all Randall said, grimly, gaze very deliberately down, whole body flushing. Where his and Victor's legs touched by accident, his body gave a little twitch, but he didn't move away. "I no longer wish to attempt to save either of my brothers' lives. In fact, if you want to drop them both off here, on the side of the highway, I would be most grateful."

"The most brilliant pieces of literature to come out of academics in the last twenty years," Edwin recited, ignoring Randall completely, smile absolutely wicked. "Was that it, Randall?"

"I hope your tail falls off," Randall replied.

Laughing, Anthony turned away from them, ruffling Edwin's hair. And despite the teasing that had gone on, Victor found himself smiling.

He'd never had siblings, and due to his parents' deaths when he was young, he'd never particularly been part of a family group either. But now he watched the three Lewis brothers interact, the way they knew one another so well, the ease of their words and the gentle teasing. They were close; that much was obvious. Even when they were being embarrassing to one another, they loved one another.

"You're very fortunate," Victor found himself murmuring, looking at Randall.

Despite the glare he'd shot at Edwin, despite the huffed sigh he'd given Anthony, when Randall looked over to meet Victor's gaze, his expression was soft. Randall gave him a very small smile, one corner of his lips curving upward. "I know."

Victor fell silent, ducking his head to study the book Randall had given him. As he lost himself in it, he was dimly aware of Edwin and Anthony talking lowly, of Knievel shifting so she could appropriate Redford's lap instead. At one point, Jed turned the music up to ear-ringing volumes, only to turn it back down at the number of glares sent at him.

He'd read books like this before, as part of his personal studies. It had a slightly different take on the origin of wolves, shaded by the perception and moral values of the author. This one seemed to think that werewolves only turned into their wolf forms when they smelled blood in the air, and Victor suppressed a laugh as he read a passage about using swan fat rubbed into skin to "soothe the wild mind." The next time he looked up, they were a decent distance into the drive, having already reached one of the major towns along the path.

"If you'd like," Randall's quiet voice reached him, and he turned to find the man looking at him in concern, "I could move up to the empty seat. So you're not crowded. Or you could, I suppose. I just...." Randall looked down, to where their legs were pressed together, fumbling a bit on his words. "I don't want you to feel claustrophobic."

Taken aback, Victor took a few seconds before replying. In his experience, when people termed things in the perspective of *you probably want to*, it actually meant that *they* wanted that thing to happen and they were too polite to say so. But Randall didn't seem the type to be passive-aggressive. Idly, he rubbed his hand over his neck, fingers bumping over twin scars, and said, "Oh, no, I'm quite fine here, if you're fine."

"I'm very fine here," Randall said, voice dropping a bit, eyes going to Victor's fingers and then up to his face. "I.... Yes. It's very nice here. With you."

"Distanced from the rabble?" Victor smiled, turning his gaze back to the book. "I agree."

Randall almost said something; Victor could see it in his face. But, in the end, he simply sighed and said quietly, "Yes. That's what I meant."

The road slipped by under their wheels, Jed actually keeping within the speed limit. Victor was shocked, though he did hear Jed muttering something about a death box on wheels, so it was possible the van simply couldn't go much faster. After a while, Anthony was lulled to sleep, his head resting lightly against the window, but his legs shoved against Randall's in a way that made Anthony seem like he took up far much more space than he really should be able to. Randall had shifted a bit closer to Victor, shrugging off his jacket to tuck around his brother with a fond little sigh.

Edwin, a row in front of them, had instigated a car game with Jed and Redford. Redford had expressed confusion over what "I Spy" was, so now Jed was teaching him. From his position in the back, Victor could see a smile curved at the corner of Jed's lips, fondness clear in his eyes as he looked at Redford.

"You try it, Red," Jed was prompting, cutting quick glances over at Redford in between watching the road.

Victor caught the edge of a frown on Redford's face. "I spy... something green," Redford decided, making it sound like a question.

"No." Edwin heaved a long-suffering sigh. "You do it with the first letter. Like, I spy something that starts with *T*."

"Only in Loserville," Jed shot back with a smirk. "Here in man's country, we play with colors."

"Yeah, cause you can't spell." Edwin was laughing, grin lighting up his face.

Jed stuck his tongue out at Edwin in the rearview mirror, because that was obviously the most mature way to win that argument. "Driver's rules, Shaggy. You get your balls to drop, you can take over. Until then, we're playing my way."

"Shouldn't I be Scooby?" Edwin teased, not at all minding Jed's vulgarity. "I think you've got the Shaggy part all taken care of."

"Seeing as how there's *four* Scoobys in the car, I think we can share the title." Redford laughed quietly. "Okay, how about we do both? I spy something that's green and starts with a *G*." He paused, uncertain. "Does that give it away too easily?"

"Nope," Jed said, ignoring Edwin's nod in favor of kissing Redford's knuckles. The motion was so easy, so automatic, that Victor almost looked away, feeling like he was looking in on a private moment. "Is it gophers?"

Edwin and Redford started laughing again, Jed's impish grin belying his innocent look. Gone was the usually guarded expression that sat on Jed's face, discarded in favor of genuine affection. Victor hadn't seen Jed get like that all that often, not when the man was too busy walling himself off. Something about Redford, Victor concluded, made it difficult for Jed to remain distant.

He envied them.

His gaze shifted to Anthony and Randall, watching them out of the corner of his eye. Anthony was still asleep, chin tucked to his chest, looking weary in a way he hadn't looked while he was awake and too determined to not seem ill at all. He looked smaller right then, a contrast to the loudly cheerful, fiercely protective man that Victor had seen at dinner.

Randall had his head down to read another book, his shoulder idly wedged against Anthony's to make sure Anthony stayed upright in his sleep. This time, Victor's gaze didn't immediately go to the book. Instead, he looked at the man, the way dark hair fell over his forehead, the absent motion to push his glasses farther up his nose when they slipped. His hands were gentle, deliberate as they turned the pages, treating them with care.

Victor, in his history of dating, had a type. He didn't *say* that he had a type, but every boyfriend he'd had had been the same. Before David, they'd been safe. A little boring. People like him who had no real ambition beyond sitting in the parlor room at noon and drinking tea. David had been the outlier, a man who had come along at a time when Victor had needed something *different*. Something that wasn't what Victor had grown up with and was surrounded by.

David had been dangerous, darkly handsome, confident, a predator's sway to his movements that had utterly captivated Victor.

But in the end, it hadn't worked. David had been too wrapped up in issues of blood and sex tangling together, and Victor had gotten too addicted to the same. And everything Victor had wanted with David—the danger, the darkness, the chaos—had seemed *too* dangerous. He still recalled perfectly that night in Cairo where David had nearly drained him. Victor remembered laughing, being so high on adrenaline that he wouldn't have cared if he'd lived or died.

And a small part of him still craved that. Though David was gone, and Victor tried to keep telling himself it was for the better, he still couldn't stand the thought of going back to a boring life and boring boyfriends who asked how his day went and wanted nothing more than to come home from work and watch the television for a bit before going to bed. The thought of domesticity, of settling down, was horrifying.

So as he looked at Randall, Victor couldn't help but try to place the man into one of those two categories, dangerous or safe. He found he couldn't. On the surface, Randall was mild mannered and soft-spoken, tentative in the way he approached most things. But there was an undercurrent of strength that Victor found himself fascinated by. A firmness to Randall's words, a dedication to his passions, the protectiveness of his brothers.

Randall was a wolf. There was no way he could fit in the *boring and safe* category. And yet he was sitting there reading a book entitled *Japanese Water Demon Myths*.

Shifting slightly beside him, Randall looked over just in time to catch Victor's gaze.

Victor didn't think anything of it at first, idly noting that Randall had quite nice eyes, a dark hazel that seemed lighter when the sun caught them. He didn't notice the sound fading out around him. Only when his vision started blurring around the edges did he catch on, and fear spiked through him. There was no time to do anything other than shove himself away from Randall as far as he could, trying to brace himself on the opposite edge of the seat, and then—

Safety. Warmth. A small cabin in the woods near a lake. Small, but full of love, of hugs good night, of silly bedtime songs. Hey diddle diddle, the cat and the fiddle. Forks running away with spoons. He was happy. Randall was happy with Anthony, with a mother and a father. With Edwin, barely able to walk, unsteady legs, two and then four.

Running through the woods, following Anthony. Chasing the moon.

Coming home to find Edwin hiding under the bed. Randall didn't know why, knew that something bad had happened. Anthony telling him to stay back. Blood on the kitchen floor when he caught a glimpse over his brother's shoulder, Mom and Dad lying so still.

Living in the woods, knowing that his parents weren't coming back but not understanding why. Anthony hunting to feed them, keeping them alive and warm and safe, the three of them living mostly as wolves in the forest for a few years since none of them were old enough to get jobs. Never quite sleeping, because the men with guns might come for them next. The hunters might take Anthony away if he closed his eyes. In a cave then, curled up together, three wolves huddled against the winter cold.

A larger cabin. Helping Anthony, sneaking books from the library on how to build houses. He walked in the first time, to a sanctuary filled with books and things he could learn about, and he never wanted to leave. Randall found, there, every friend he'd wanted, every life he'd dreamed of, every country and every culture and every possibility given ink and paper. He'd spent hours there, that first day, and went back as often as he could. But his first book had been a guide to building a cabin out of logs, and he'd spent the next month chopping trees. He was all of eight, and he helped his twelve-year-old brother build their home.

Randall going to school, getting there early in the hopes the teacher would impart more lessons before the bell rang. Edwin getting homeschooled because he couldn't sit in a confined classroom for too long. Anthony working, lying about his age to get jobs. Growing up depending on each other for everything, sharing every chore.

Years passing, faster, school and books and college, finally. Acceptance to his chosen university after two years of saving, two years of local courses. Coming home with the letter to find his brother's hands shaking so badly he couldn't open the envelope. Doctors and tests and too many questions. Faking the paperwork so they could leave without giving too much away.

Cairo. He shouldn't have gone, but it was his last chance, his final escape. It was his dream, and the program had taken him out of hundreds of applicants. Fear. Blood. Pain. Good doggy. Chains.

"Victor? He's not responding. Anthony, hand me that water. Victor, can you hear me?"

The face of the man who had saved him. Pale and exhausted, a bandage wrapped around his neck. The bustle of the airport around them. His Beatrice, leading him through heaven.

Then—

Possibilities. Arcing off into the distance like threads vanishing into the mist, only Victor could push that mist back, could see exactly where those threads ended, if they were cut or frayed or burned at the edges. Colors twined around each other, memories and emotions.

Anthony growing sicker. Wasting away. Dying. Randall and Edwin alone at their brother's grave. Randall going off to try to live, guilt eating at him, souring every attempt. Every start became an end, at the same grave. Bitter, alone, grieving.

More death. Hunters. A hole through Randall's chest. His head. Over and over, the threads ended in him falling, young and innocent and simply gone.

One of those had Randall in Victor's arms when the bullet came. Blood spattering Victor's cheek, his glasses, as Randall gasped in pain. As he reached out. Apologies, only half said before the dark end.

Or—

There were other men. Happy, holding hands, tuxes and flowers and cake and family. Some of them stayed, some of them faded, but those threads didn't burn as bright as—

In bed, while flares of red and yellow from the bonfire lit up the room. Randall smiling, eyes reflecting the bursts from outside the window. Victor kissing him, soft, then urgent, fumbling together for the first time, for many times to come. Tuxes and flowers and cake and family. Anthony better. Anthony worse. Anthony gone, Randall clinging to Victor by a gravesite. Older then, with children. With Edwin coming over for dinners. With no one but themselves. Age finding them, white haired and holding hands, sitting on a long pier and looking out over the ocean.

And then—

Something dark in the distance in all the possible futures, but so far off that Victor barely grasped the sensation of it.

Then—

"Victor!" There was water splashed in his face, a hand shaking his shoulder. Jed's voice, sounding like it was very far away and once removed, calling him back. "Come on, princess, wakey-wakey."

There was some kind of material shoved in Victor's mouth, clamped between his teeth as his muscles shook, trembling out a last few painful spasms. He tried to make a noise, tried to tell them he was quite okay, thank you very much. He didn't need to be fussed over.

He scrambled out of the van, fell heavily on the ground beside the road, and threw up.

Wonderful.

Randall was next to him a few moments later, rubbing his back soothingly, handing him a fresh bottle of water. The man didn't say anything at first, more concerned with taking his coat from where it had been in the car, obviously discarded when Anthony had woken, and wrapping it around Victor's shoulders. After a moment, Randall asked, worried, "Are you all right? Do you have something you need, medication or... or something I can do to help?"

Victor fumbled with the water bottle as he tried to open it, but he managed to twist the top off, swishing the water around in his mouth before spitting it into the grass. Christ, he needed to brush his teeth.

At least he seemed to be coherent and cognizant. He hadn't snapped. Yet.

"There's medication in my bag," he managed, lifting the water bottle to press against his forehead. The coolness of it sent waves of relief through the pain throbbing in his temples. "It's in blue packaging. For migraines."

Randall scrambled back to the van. Redford was immediately there to take his place, hovering in front of Victor and helping him move to sit on the running board in the open door of the van. Jed was standing a slight distance away, Edwin and Anthony beside him, watching Victor carefully.

"You really need to stop doing that," Redford said quietly. "You've probably never seen what you look like, but your eyes roll back and you seize. It's terrifying. And sometimes you make these *noises*, like you're scared or angry."

"Yeah, like a pea soup spewing freak show," Jed interjected, arms folded over his chest, squinting at Victor as if he was trying to figure him out. Possibly there was concern there too, but Victor was too busy trying to not have his head explode to look for it. "So, you know. Cut that shit out."

"Here, take this." Randall's soft voice came from over his shoulder. The pills were pressed into Victor's hands, followed by the toothbrush and toothpaste Randall had obviously found in Victor's bag. "Just, uh, I wasn't sure if you wanted those, but I thought you might."

Victor slowly took the pills, trying not to move his head too much. He managed to unscrew the toothpaste cap, which he counted as a personal victory. "No, I think you may be a mind reader," he said, barely whispering. He figured out the mechanics of brushing ones teeth without access to a tap and basin—toothpaste on the brush, a bit of water from the bottle, brush and spit. It was hardly dignified, but it got the horrendous taste out of his mouth.

He could hear Redford and Jed talking lowly, but Victor stayed right where he was, waiting for the pills to start to kick in. So far, none of the Lewises had demanded answers, though Victor had a feeling Edwin was only being contained by the force of Randall's glare. Minutes later, Victor estimated, the pain in his temples *finally* began to die down, and he gave a groan of relief, cradling his head in his hands.

"I'm so terribly sorry," he said, trying to raise his voice to be heard by everyone. Especially Jed, who Victor was sure was likely staring at the clock and being none too happy that they were losing driving time. "It was an accident."

He was normally so careful. Ever since he'd first learned about his ability, he'd had to get used to the idea of never meeting the eyes of another human being. He'd had accidents, a few of them when he was young, but Victor normally kept such rigid control over where he directed his eyes that he hadn't had an accident in years.

And even though he'd go insane from it one day, even though his mind would crack and he'd no longer be *himself,* Victor still remembered the eye contact fondly. A little piece of human connection that most took for granted. A little piece of knowledge that nobody else had. He craved it, a little. That *knowing.* It was like, despite the pain, despite the threat of madness, in that small moment he was fulfilling something he *needed* to become.

"I'll be right in a few minutes," he continued, raising his head to squint at them. "Just as soon as I'm sure that I'm not going to vomit in the van." He was sure Jed would appreciate that.

Out of the corner his eye, he caught sight of Anthony, and the pang that hit his chest surprised even him. For a moment, Victor wasn't sure where the emotion had come from—until he saw, in his mind's eye, the moment that Randall had realized his older brother was sick, and the worry that had come from that. Remembering that tipped his mind in the direction of the future threads he'd seen, and—

Well, one of those was not the sort of thing he'd expected to see.

He'd been *married* to Randall. Not only that, but they'd adopted children, they'd grown old together in the most perfect, normal, picket fence life that Victor could ever imagine.

The thought made him slightly queasy. It was nothing against Randall. It was the thought of two-point-five children and a perfectly idyllic, perfectly *boring* life that didn't sound like all that great of an ideal to Victor. It wasn't what he wanted out of life. He wouldn't have dated David if he'd wanted a little white house and a dog. Or a wolf, as it were.

"Right, I feel like I'm not going to fall over," he announced, bracing against the edge of the van to push himself to his feet. He nearly tripped over Knievel, scowling when the cat hissed at him and darted away. Randall was next to him instantly, leaving off the argument he'd been having with Jed over pulling out his battery-operated hot plate to make a pot of tea, slipping an arm around his waist to help support him. The man blushed, the tips of his ears turning bright red, but he very gently, very carefully, helped Victor into a seat.

The sheer *contentment* that settled inside Victor's chest was alarming. This was the worst part of his visions, the way those memories and possibilities broke off inside his mind and left little shards that remained. Thankfully, as Randall had not lived nearly as long as David had, this time around it wasn't quite as disorienting.

"You shouldn't be moving," Randall chided softly, crouching down next to him, fussing with a washrag that he was pouring cold water over. He even fished out some ice from the cooler and wrapped that inside of it, hushing Victor's protests and easing him to lean forward so he could wrap the wet cloth around the back of his neck. "Just close your eyes. Jed is going to stop at the first place we can find, and I'll get you some tea. Do you need anything else?"

"You sound like you've dealt with migraines before," Victor said, reaching up to press the cold cloth tighter to his skin.

There was a brief fumbled movement, an awkward clearing of Randall's throat, and then his fingers, light and unsure, touched Victor's temples. "I used to get them a lot," he said lowly, voice pitched into a reassuring rumble as he rubbed circles against Victor's skin. The light pressure combined with the cool cloth was absolutely heavenly, and Victor found himself leaning into it. "Before I had my glasses. And Anthony gets them now, from time to time, even though he pretends he's unaffected."

The pills were starting to kick in, combined with the care Randall was giving him. The pain was starting to leech away, and Victor had to bite his tongue to stop himself from letting out a groan of relief. He always forgot how painful these episodes were until he experienced them again—and once he *was* experiencing them, he tended to forget he'd ever been in a state without pain.

"Okay, does somebody want to tell me what just happened there?" Anthony's voice came from the door of the van. He sounded concerned, a little gruff in his worry. Jed and Redford had maps spread across the hood of the van. Victor could see them through the windshield. Apparently they'd decided to let Victor explain himself to the wolves as he saw fit. "Do you have epilepsy, Victor?"

"Not quite." Victor shifted the cloth to press it against his eyes. The movement, the little motion away from Randall, immediately had Randall's touch falling away. "I'm a half blood. Medusa, to be exact."

There was a pause before Randall breathed out a noise, both intrigued and pitying all in one. "My God," Randall said lowly, eyes wide. "You... you had a vision?" Another beat and Randall went pale. "Of me?"

"Yes," Victor admitted reluctantly. "I'm sorry. I truly didn't mean to look." He always felt sorry for the people he accidentally made eye contact with. It was an invasion of privacy of the highest degree. By himself, Randall might have only told him that his parents had been killed by hunters, for example, but Victor had just seen all the gory details. Had shared in a moment that Randall had not *wanted* to share with him.

"I don't get it." Edwin was standing there, looking far more content now that he'd gotten to run around outside. Victor's little episode had apparently saved him from extreme car boredom. "What's a medusa?"

Randall, instead of giving the answer Victor assumed he knew, just looked vaguely like he was going to be sick. "Excuse me," he said, pushing past Anthony and half stumbling out of the van, taking off into the grass by the side of the road, obviously wanting as much distance as possible.

Victor didn't blame him.

"It means that when I look into somebody's eyes, I see everything about them," he answered Edwin. "Their past, their present. Their future. Because my brain is not designed for such an influx of information, I tend to pass out." He didn't go on to talk about the eventual insanity. It seemed too morbid right then, to tell to a carefree young man like Edwin, who was already dealing with his brother's sickness.

Nose wrinkling a little, Edwin looked to where Randall was pacing back and forth, arms folded tightly across his chest. Something dawned in his gaze, and he glanced at Anthony. Then his frank blue eyes went back to Victor. "You saw what happens to Randall in the future," he mused. "I guess you're not going to tell us, huh? That's how it always works in stories. The fairy godmother knows all the answers, but she just gives people dresses and lets them figure out the rest on their own. Otherwise the story would be over in the first chapter."

"No, I'm afraid telling people about it usually gives the game away." Victor turned his gaze back to Randall, frowning slightly in concern.

Anthony shifted his weight from side to side, looking uncertain. "Did you see what happens to me in the future? I—ow! Edwin!" He glared at Edwin, rubbing his arm where the punch had landed. "I'm just asking."

"You're not going to die." Said with all the conviction of the young and the strong, as if by *willing* it, Edwin would order the universe. As if by his own hands he could pull his brother back from the brink of wherever he was falling. "We don't need a medusa to tell us that. You're going to be fine, and we're all going to go home." He gave his brother another punch to the shoulder, though this one was much lighter and really was more of a pull in so he could wrap his arms around Anthony. "I don't care what anyone sees," he murmured, clinging tightly. "You're going to be fine. Okay?"

Anthony huffed out a laugh, ruffling a hand through Edwin's hair. "Of course," he replied. "I've got way too much to do; there's no way I can get *that* sick."

"Besides," Victor felt the need to chip in, "I don't see *the* future. I see many possibilities." He shared a quick look with Anthony, and it seemed to reassure the man that there were potential futures in which he lived just fine.

Anthony looked over at Randall, who was still looking none too happy, and gave a short sigh. "Randall's an extremely private person," he told Victor, a protective rumble in the back of his throat. "I don't think he's going to be too happy with you."

"Princess, you done puking your guts out yet?" Ah, the dulcet tones of an irritated Journey Walker. "As fun as it is to escort you to your fainting couch, Scarlett, if we want to hit the halfway point we need to keep moving."

"Yes, I'm quite done," Victor returned dryly. More genuinely, he added, "Thank you for stopping. I'm fairly certain added motion sickness would not have helped." He wasn't used to seeing Jed be *thoughtful* about anything. Usually the man's method of dealing with things was explosives. And if that didn't work, more explosives.

Then again, watching as Redford came up behind Jed, slipping arms around his waist, kissing his jaw with a smile, maybe there really was a softer side of Jed. Maybe that's what happened when one spent months in domesticity. Jed was smiling slightly, murmuring lowly to Redford, opening the door for him—like he was a normal man in a normal relationship. If Victor didn't know better, he wouldn't have even assumed Jed had five different weapons on him at the moment.

Randall was the last person in the van, head bowed, hair tumbling down to hide his eyes. He very carefully got into his seat, fingers fumbling with the seat belt before he finally got it latched. Embarrassment and, oddly, shame were etched into his expression and every hesitant move. The glimmers of confidence, the spark of intelligence and wit that Victor had seen before were hidden now, under an almost painful shyness.

It made Victor feel like the worst sort of bastard. Even if it had been an accident.

The van rumbled to life, and they got onto the road once more. Victor was left alone to his thoughts, keeping his eyes closed this time. He didn't want to risk another moment of eye contact, not so soon after the last one. Slowly, conversations started up around him once more. Jed and Redford were cheerfully bantering over whether finding a pancake place or a burger joint was more road trip appropriate. Anthony and Edwin had started a game of go fish, and Anthony was trying to get Randall to join in. Knievel kept trying to walk over the van's dashboard. The noises washed around him, soft ripples against the rush of the road under their tires, and Victor sank into that contented feeling of not being alone.

It gave him the much-needed time to sort through what he'd seen. Like they were a pile of papers dropped carelessly onto the floor, Victor picked the memories up and shuffled them until they were in order, making sense of them.

"I'm sorry." It was Randall's voice, several miles down the road, after he'd declined the card game, after they'd both sat in silence for long enough that the sound of him speaking seemed out of place. Randall wasn't looking at him, instead focusing on his own hands, laced tightly together and resting neatly in his lap.

At the sound of his voice, all Victor could see for a few seconds was split-second flashes of memory, other instances that Randall had said those words. "You have no need to apologize," he replied, keeping his voice low. "It was my fault, and I'm sorry for invading your privacy like that. If I could give it back, I would."

A frown touched the corners of Randall's lips. "I know I don't *need* to apologize," he murmured after a moment. "The thoughts in my head are... well, they're supposed to be my own. But I'm sorry you had to see them. That you know—" Cutting himself off, deep red curling around his ears, down his neck, embarrassment plain to see, Randall sighed and ran a hand through his hair. "God. You must think I'm a complete idiot."

For a few seconds, Victor had no idea what Randall was talking about. He first assumed it was something to do with Randall's past, but that couldn't be it. The bits of present that he saw weren't as clear as the past or future, but he saw them well enough.

And he had seen a fragment of memory concerning himself. The day that Randall had sought him out to inquire where Jed and Redford were. There had been a warmth of emotion there, an admiration. Something beyond what one felt for someone they wanted to be friends with.

The realization startled Victor. Randall had *emotions* regarding him. Emotions that were none too platonic.

"Yes, well." Randall had obviously taken his silence for confirmation, a quick flash of misery on his face before he shuttered it all away behind polite blandness. "Again, I apologize, I—"

"No, I'm sorry, I was...." Victor rubbed at his forehead. "I tend to get easily distracted after the visions. Don't mind me." Although he had to admit, some of

Randall's memories were very pleasant. Especially the ones about his family. "I meant to say that there's nothing you should be embarrassed about, Randall. It may sound trite, but if I'm allowed to comment on what I saw, I have to say that I admire your strength."

Cutting a sideways glance over to Victor, Randall hesitated a moment before breathing out a quick, startled laugh. "I don't think anyone's ever mistaken me for strong." His lips twisted upward into a rueful smile. "That would be Anthony's forte. I'm just very fortunate. But, um, thank you. For not judging me too harshly."

"Well, I didn't look into Anthony's eyes," Victor replied. "So I couldn't comment on him." He wasn't sure what there would be to judge, in any case. It was hardly his place.

"Really?" A slight, teasing smirk touched Randall's expression. "He's right there. About six two, brown hair. Penchant for flannel. Comment away."

Though the thought of looking into somebody else's eyes so soon was slightly terrifying, Victor breathed out a quiet laugh. "I'll have to decline the offer, but thank you. I've already broken enough privacy boundaries for one day. No need to have the entire van pissed off at me."

The smile slipped away, and Randall reached out, fingers touching the back of Victor's hand. "I'm not mad," he said very seriously. "I'm just not used to anyone… knowing. There's supposed to be an order to things. A mutual learning. And now you know all the answers, and I'm still making mistakes all the way back at the starting line. It's scary, to have you know that. But I'm not angry at you."

Victor hadn't thought about it that way before, and he could see Randall's point. It must be very strange to talk to somebody that you didn't know very well, when that someone knew everything about you. "How about I promise to be very forthcoming in any questions you ask of me?" It was a weak promise, something that would hardly make up for the accident, but Victor couldn't think of anything else to do. "So that you don't feel quite so unbalanced?"

Ducking his head, Randall hid his smile. "That sounds like a whole lot of trust you're giving me," he said softly. "But thank you."

"Trust is earned through knowledge of another person," Victor replied. "I feel I have enough to trust you rather implicitly."

Quiet for a moment, as if considering that, Randall ventured hesitantly, "Tell me about being a medusa. I've heard of them, read several legends, but—"

He was cut off by the noise of the brakes and the soft jolt of the van coming to a stop. "Everyone out," Jed shouted. Edwin happily climbed over everyone with Knievel at his heels. "Pit stop. Take a piss and then meet at the diner."

Randall sighed quietly at the interruption, then eased himself out of his seat. With a rueful backward glance at Victor, he was engulfed by Edwin and hurried along with the exuberant promises of cheeseburgers. Anthony was on the other side of them, Randall's arm instinctively going out to take his brother's, to support him without even appearing to notice Anthony was unsteady. Victor caught sight of Randall's smile, the tense uncertainty easing as he laughed at Anthony's joke, as Edwin grinned at the both of them, carefree and content.

Knievel wound between all of them before Edwin picked her up and the cat perched on his shoulder. Victor somehow gathered that neither the cat nor Jed or Edwin would care that most restaurants did not welcome pets. Which was amusing, considering that five of their diners were hardly strictly human, and four of them would shed far more than Knievel on her worst day.

The greasy smell of diner food didn't exactly do wonders for Victor's lingering headache, but he fought hard not to visibly wrinkle his nose. He'd already given everybody in the van enough trouble today. For now, he'd just order a coffee and maybe a scone, if this place would even know what those were. Considering he had a lot of trouble finding a decent scone in America, he didn't think his chances would be too good. Perhaps he'd chance a muffin instead.

They settled in a booth in the corner. Edwin and Anthony immediately made a grab for the menus, and Victor would bet they'd order the largest dish available. Redford was seated next to Jed, darting nervous glances at the waitresses, and Randall was sitting opposite Victor, so he supposed now wasn't the time to carry on a conversation about what it was like to be a medusa half blood. He felt grateful that Randall wasn't truly angry at him, because the man had every right to be.

Victor tried a tentative smile for him, an amused expression at Anthony and Edwin's enthusiastic discussion of food, and was rewarded with one in return. He wasn't sure if he liked the warmth that hooked into his chest as a result.

Jed somehow managed to convince a sleepy-looking waitress that Knievel was his seeing-eye cat. As they ordered drinks and food and got their drinks delivered shortly, he noticed that Randall had deliberately placed himself on the outside edge of the booth, seemingly so that he could take Anthony's mug from the waitress and put it down on the table in front of Anthony. Victor took a quick look at Anthony's hands. They were shaking, though he'd clasped them tightly together to try to stop it. He looked ashamed that he needed the help.

"So what's the plan for tonight, expedition leader?" Anthony said to Jed, trying to grin, though it was rather dimmer than his usual cheerful expressions.

"We're about four hours' drive away from the halfway point," Jed said, easily looping his arm around Redford, absently rubbing his thumb along the man's side. It was a calming gesture, Victor noticed, if Redford's reaction was anything to go by. Some of the sharp nervousness melted away, Jed providing a casual buffer between Redford and the rest of the world. "There's a little town that'll do to stop. We'll find a cheap motel and hole up for the night. Red and I are going to take the bathroom, provided the door locks from the inside. The rest of you can divide the room however you want."

Anthony looked startled, then a little suspicious, and finally, somewhat worried. "What exactly are you going to be doing in a locked bathroom when Redford is a wolf?"

Jed glanced around the table, apparently confused. "Being with him during the moon?" Jed finally ventured slowly, like this was incredibly obvious and he was worried Anthony might have some form of brain damage to not understand that. "I don't know what your freaky furry family does during full moons, but Redford's a lot calmer if I'm there. I'm sure as hell not leaving him alone." He paused a beat and grimaced. "Aw, shit. You guys need to be all locked up too, don't you?" With a sigh, he seemed to accept that, though he grumbled during the startled silence of the Lewises, "We're looking for a place with a damn big bathroom."

"You lock yourself in a room?" Anthony's eyes were wide. "Don't get me wrong, I'm glad my earlier suspicions were unfounded, and it's nice that you want to be there, Jed, but...." He trailed off, seemingly horrified by what Jed had suggested.

There were twin expressions on Edwin and Randall's faces. "Fuck no," Edwin declared. He glanced at Anthony and amended, "*Fudge* no."

Shifting a bit in his seat, Randall offered, "I, uh, think what my brothers are trying to say is...." He appeared at a loss for words before adding, with a quick, wry twist of his lips, "Fuck no."

Victor barked out a surprised laugh. He wouldn't have guessed that Randall would openly curse. Randall was now grinning at him, corners of his eyes crinkling, a warmth there that made it clear the whole expression was directed straight at Victor, and despite himself, Victor grinned back. He could definitely appreciate a well-aimed curse.

"But what do you do?" Redford looked just as confused as the rest of them, but for very different reasons. "I grew up locking myself down and muzzling myself in my grandmother's basement. It kept everybody safe. But now I can be in a small room and not go crazy."

While Redford was looking proud of himself for his achievement, the other wolves had gone distinctly pale. Edwin reacted first, lip curling up in a little snarl. "That's disgusting," he said, looking Redford up and down as if quite sure he was making a sick joke. "What kind of fucking—" He darted his gaze toward Anthony and hesitated before plunging onward. "No, it is, Ant, it's a *fucking* gross kind of person who'd tie down a wolf. Even a were."

Randall cleared his throat, nudging his shoulder against Edwin's. "Ed, not everyone was raised the way we were," he offered mildly, though he looked just as disturbed as his brothers. "It's abuse, to a wolf." His voice was kind as he explained, gaze going to Redford. "We all react to the moon in different ways, as individual as the wolf themselves, but at our core, we need our freedom. We get to choose where we run, how we run, when we turn. We're full wolves—*you* are a wolf now. But to tie us down and take away that freedom?"

"It'd make us crazy," Edwin interjected, frowning at Redford, at Jed. "It's some sick preternatural thing, to use cages and muzzles. It's not right. We'd hurt ourselves or each other or, shit, I don't know. Go nuts."

Redford looked like he was beginning to regret ever saying something, and Victor noticed that one of his hands had risen to rub nervously along the edge of a scar, the ones that traveled over his nose to the edge of his jaw. "Jed did say that I seemed calmer when I wasn't tied up," he ventured. "I just assumed that it was what happened. The thought of being free, well, I could hurt someone."

"Not if you've got other wolves with you," Anthony replied. "Not if you're *free*. Why would you want to hurt people when you've got better things to do?"

"It's the function of a pack." Randall smiled at Redford softly. Knievel had been drinking water delicately from Randall's glass. She now pranced across the table to rub her head under Jed's chin and hop down to curl up between Jed and Redford. Jed looked stricken and guilty, hunched in on himself more than a little bit. He looked as small, at that moment, as Victor had ever seen him. "We care for each other. We run together. It's what makes us safe, what makes us wolves. That support."

Redford leaned against Jed's side, wrapping an arm around Jed's. "Jed's my pack," he said confidently. "He's been helping me adjust. He makes me happy."

"Pack wouldn't tie you up," Edwin protested, eyes narrowed. "And pack wouldn't keep you in a cage. He's not very *good* pack, is he, if he doesn't even let you run."

Redford just smiled a little. "I ask for it. It's safer."

With a hoarse little noise, looking pale and sick, Jed stood, disrupting Knievel and pushing his way out of the booth. Hands clenched at his sides, fingernails biting into his palms, he stalked away, slamming out of the doors and into the parking lot, leaving them all staring after him.

They had to pause as the waitress delivered their food, awkwardly silent about stopping a conversation that wouldn't do to be overheard by regular humans. Knievel batted a piece of bacon from Jed's plate down onto the booth seat in front of her, chirping happily. Edwin had ordered a mountain of food, which he eagerly dug into.

"I think I said something wrong." Redford was staring miserably down at his food and then back up to look out the window, trying to keep his eye on Jed.

"I think *he* did." Edwin shrugged, digging into a steak easily as big as his head, bloody rare and dripping from the fork. "Maybe he just realized how much he's hurt you."

"He has *not* hurt me," Redford growled, anger rising suddenly to his eyes. "Jed is the best person I've ever met. He doesn't *want* to tie me up on the moons. He's the only reason that I'm not still caging myself in my basement."

Edwin didn't seem too concerned with Redford's aggression. He just blithely kept eating his steak, wrinkling his nose at the vegetables that had come alongside it. Redford, upon seeing that his anger had no effect, promptly wilted, his shoulders hunching in embarrassment at his outburst. "He might be the best person, but he's still just a *person*. Not a wolf. He doesn't understand," Edwin said.

With a sharp sigh, Randall shook his head. "God, Edwin. Shut up."

"What?" Edwin glanced at Randall's salad, rolling his eyes and promptly shoving half his steak onto Randall's plate. "It's true and you know it."

"What I know is that Redford is not *you*," Randall said. "Which means that he gets to decide what he wants to do on the moons. He's coming from a different childhood than us. Not everyone had a family that tolerated them flashing their furry tails every ten minutes because they couldn't be bothered to learn any form of control." Randall's anger wasn't like Edwin's or even Redford's. It wasn't sharp and sudden and flashing teeth. It was more quiet, more the way he pronounced every word with the hint of a bite. The way his eyes glinted dangerously as he threw himself, verbally, in between Redford and the sharp barbs Edwin was throwing.

"Guys," Anthony cut in, his voice firm. "Enough. Now isn't the place or the time."

With that, Edwin and Randall fell silent. Victor poked at the scone that had been delivered to him. He didn't particularly feel like risking a bite, because he just knew it would be ridiculously dry. He caught sight of Randall tugging Anthony's plate closer to him, cutting up the steak, and though Anthony gave a grimace, he let it happen.

It was the full moon tonight. Victor had never been around wolves on the full moon, but the effect was beginning to be obvious. They were getting jittery; it was the only word for it. Randall, who was normally rather mellow, as far as Victor had observed, had a tense line remaining in his shoulders after he'd snapped at Edwin.

"Just stop pretending you don't want red meat on full moons," Edwin was sighing at Randall, nudging the half a steak he'd given his brother closer.

"Fine," Randall snapped. But then, with just as much bite but with a very faint smile touching his lips, "Thank you."

Edwin's eyes went to Redford's plate, and he carefully sawed off a large chunk of the third steak that was piled high on his platter and deposited it onto the other man's. "You can go running with us." He shrugged, a peace offering of sorts. "See if you like it."

Redford was still watching out the window for Jed, but he turned back around at Edwin's comment. "Maybe," he said reluctantly. "I still can't control myself very well. Not like you guys."

"So half werewolves, half wolves, are more like pups who chase their own tails and trip over their own paws, barking at everything that comes close?" Anthony smirked. "Don't worry. I've raised two of those." He cut amused looks at Randall and Edwin. "One of them is still a bit like that."

Edwin tipped a wide smirk around his mouthful of meat. "Just because I'm totally going to outrace you tonight, old man," he teased.

"Please. You haven't come close to winning a race since Anthony took a nap halfway through your first moon out," Randall snorted. Under the table, his foot gently kicked Victor's, a quiet moment of inclusion.

To be honest, Victor *was* feeling rather out of place with all of this wolf talk, but he was content to sit back and listen. As someone who had long studied the supernatural, it was quite interesting to hear how actual wolves lived and acted. He smiled back at Randall. "Just out of interest, how do you three react to full moons?" he inquired politely. "I've read a lot of conflicting reports."

"Well, probably because they asked conflicting wolves," Randall laughed quietly, and Edwin grinned, nudging Anthony as he easily reached over to refill Anthony's coffee mug from the pot the waitress had left behind. "It's as different as the individual. We all feel the moon, though. Wolves tend to get more aggressive, more…."

"Wolfish," Anthony supplied with a quiet chuckle.

"Yes," Randall agreed. "Though that means differing things to each wolf. The one rule is that we all have to change. It's in our instincts, it's our blood, and we can't deny the pull of the moon. We do get to choose when we do so, however. I, uh, I'm not one for running, really. I tend to change later in the night, run a bit, and then sleep. Edwin and Anthony are much more interested in spending the night chasing rabbits." It was said fondly, though Victor noticed the hunch of Randall's shoulders, the familiar expression of one out of place. Yes, it would be hard, Victor thought, to grow up in a culture that embraced things you yourself weren't so inclined to participate in.

"You can choose how late you change?" Redford had obviously never heard of that before. "I didn't know wolves could do that."

"Yeah," Edwin said with a shrug. He was now looking over the dessert menu, having finished all of his meat and the large portion Randall hadn't eaten. "We're not werewolves."

Seeing that Redford was clearly confused by this, Randall explained gently, "Werewolves are the result of a bad combination of wolf and human blood. The sides aren't joined well. So you were human most of the time, but the wolf instincts won out on the full moons. Now, though, you are much more Cano than not, which means you *are* wolf. All the time. The form you take doesn't change your instincts or how you see the world. Your mind remains the same whether you're two legs or four."

"Yeah, but your nose is better on four," Edwin grunted. "Too bad, cause this place smells great *now*. I bet I'd be able to tell what everyone's eaten for, like, a *year*."

"This is fascinating," Victor enthused. He dearly wished he had his notepad so he could write all of this down. Perhaps he'd ask Randall to repeat everything later.

Redford looked like he wanted to say more, and Victor could guess what it might be about. He'd seen the result of Redford's change, in Cairo, where the man seemed to have little control over what his wolf side did. But Redford obviously changed his mind about speaking about it, giving the Lewises a small smile instead. "Thank you. It's... nice to talk to people who can give me information."

"Okay, look." Jed was back. Victor was somewhat amazed that he'd missed the stomping. His short hair was standing up all at ends, like he'd been running his fingers through it, and he had a slightly green around the gills look. "I didn't know. And I know that's no damn excuse, and I know that I'm shit at this, but I love him, okay? So just tell me what I need to do to make it better."

Edwin blinked at him. "Have some steak?" He glanced down at his plate. "Oh, wait. I ate that. And Knievel ate your bacon. Um. Sorry. Dessert?"

"Jed," Redford started, right back to looking concerned. He reached out to take Jed's hand. "It's okay."

"It's *not* okay, Red." Jed looked genuinely distressed, though he did collapse back into the booth, lowering his voice slightly in deference to all the perfectly normal humans who were trying to have their dinner. "Jesus." A beat and he frowned. "Wait. Who ate my bacon?"

"Knievel," Edwin told him mildly, nudging Randall's half-eaten salad toward Jed. "You can have the rest of Randall's dinner."

"I was eating that," Randall sighed.

"I don't want *salad*," Jed said at the same time, pulling a face.

"I'm going to order pie." Edwin was perfectly happy to have moved on from the argument, studying the menu. "A whole one."

Jed sighed, slumped half down in the booth. "How come this was a big-ass deal ten minutes ago and now we're talking about pie?" he muttered.

"Full moon mood swings," Victor informed him with a slightly amused look. "They get overly aggressive, I'm told."

"Well, this is going to be a treat." Jed snorted quietly. "Four growly furbutts at once." But he wasn't over the earlier conversation. That was obvious from the way he kept glancing at Redford, from the guilty slant to his lips.

"Do *I* get overly aggressive?" Redford frowned in worry. "I didn't even think about it."

Jed took Redford's hand and rested their joined fingers on his stomach. "You get all bitey and possessive." A quick leer crossed his face, missing some of its usual bluster. "I like it. A lot."

"Please do refrain from talking about your sex life at the table," Victor muttered. "I'm debating ordering dessert, and I'd like to keep my appetite." Still, he was glad to see that Jed didn't look quite so upset anymore, and Redford was happily leaning against him.

He did hear Jed whisper "Sorry" to Redford, carding fingers through Redford's hair. Which was more than a little shocking. Victor wasn't aware that word was in Jed's vocabulary.

They ordered dessert and strayed away from the topic of what wolves should and shouldn't do. Instead, the conversation fragmented, with Victor talking to Anthony about his work—an auto mechanic—Edwin too busy with his pie to talk, and Randall getting up to take a walk around the outside of the diner. Victor watched him for a moment, noticing that he seemed to be more jittery than previously. Perhaps, with time until the full moon growing shorter, Randall was feeling its effects more.

The waitresses didn't look all that happy with the mess they had left behind, but Victor made sure to tip generously, which considerably brightened their expressions. Jed was uncharacteristically quiet as they marched back to the van with Knievel bundled up in his arms. Randall joined them, his face smooth and calm even while his fingers played restlessly with the cuffs of his sweater. "We can't stay in a motel tonight," he informed Jed. "Well, the wolves can't. There's no reason at all why you and Victor can't find someplace with a bed. But we'll need to figure out a good place to stop where my brothers and Redford can go running."

"Someplace without a lot of people." Jed nodded, considering. He gave a quick glance at Randall and reached into the van for his maps. "What, you don't run?"

Randall shrugged. "Eventually. What about fields? We're bound to hit some farm country if we keep going. Ant? What are you thinking?"

As Jed opened one of the maps, Anthony stood at Jed's side, looking at it carefully. He pointed to a circle on the paper. "Is this the halfway point?" At Jed's nod, Anthony gave a quiet hum of contemplation and tapped a green area a few miles away. "There. It's a nice big forest and it's got road access. We can drive into the middle of it, and if you and Victor need a bed, you can drive back to the hotel."

"That's up to Victor," Jed said shortly, rolling the maps up. Victor just shrugged at him—he'd decide if he wanted a hotel room when the time came. "I might just be human," Jed continued, fixing Edwin with a challenging look. The wolf had the good grace to squirm a bit, embarrassed. "But I meant what I said. I'm with Redford on the moons. Always."

"Good." Redford beamed at Jed, pulling him close. "We've never been in the forest before. You could come running with me."

Anthony chuckled as he got into the van. "Yeah, Jed. You should try to keep up, might work some of that dessert off of you."

"Hardy-har," Jed grumped, but he flicked a look back at Anthony that wasn't entirely sour. "I'm not the one that ate their body weight in steak and fucking pecan pie."

Edwin grinned, lopsided and unashamed. "I'm young," he said, patting his flat stomach. "And tonight I'm going to run until I can't move. Just you try and keep up, human."

"You're a brat, kid," Jed said, getting the van underway. "So I'm going to beat you with twice the usual amount of gloating."

Victor settled into his seat with a sigh as they started driving again. The almost tangible tension in the air from the wolves was thicker now, shown in the way that Randall needed to have something to do with his hands where before he'd been perfectly content to sit still. It was in the way that Edwin decided to put his head out the window and howl, much to Anthony's despair. Anthony had started being hypervigilant, his gaze flicking to absolutely everything that moved. Knievel, Victor noticed, was glaring at all of them, perched up front like she didn't even want to be near so many canines.

It looked like he was going to be sleeping in the van tonight. If Jed was going to go out with them, then Victor could hardly drive back to the hotel on his own—he'd feel terrible, leaving them out there, even if they could take care of themselves.

Redford, for his part, had shuffled closer to Jed until he was practically draped over the man's side, though thankfully he didn't look to be interfering with Jed's ability to drive. Jed had wrapped his arm around Redford, playing fingers through his hair, eyes focused on the road ahead. They looked relaxed at first glance, but a closer look revealed lines of tension around Redford's eyes, a longing stare out the window. Perhaps the close confines of the van were getting to him.

"You smell really good," Randall said, looking at Victor, immediately looking embarrassed. "God, sorry. I just.... You do, and my mental filter is... lacking right now."

Victor blinked at him. He was suddenly tempted to take a surreptitious sniff of himself, just to see what Randall was talking about. But his nose was as human as it got. "Thank you? I'm pleased that I'm not offensive, at least."

Randall grimaced in apology. "I usually spend the full moons hiding with a book. I just blurt things out. It's rather embarrassing." He paused and then gave Victor another sideways glance. "And you are definitely not offensive. Believe me."

Aside from the jitters, aside from the lack of mental filter, Randall *looked* different too. Victor couldn't quite pin down what it was at first. It was something about the way his eyes seemed darker, his stare more intense and a lot less hesitant than usual. The way his shoulders were straighter, his movements more fluid and graceful. He seemed ill fitting in his sweater and glasses right now, like they were a mask, a very literal sheep's clothing.

It was, Victor realized, rather ridiculously attractive.

"What do I smell like?" Victor couldn't help but ask. He recalled what Redford had said on the subject, tea and scales, and he found himself curious if Randall would have the same answer.

There was a beat where Randall seemed embarrassed, uncertain, color blooming on his cheeks again. But there was a heated look in his eyes, a sharp, hungry gaze as he leaned forward. One hand rested on Victor's shoulder as Randall nudged in under his ear, taking a long, slow breath.

"Parchment," Randall murmured, the warmth of his breath stirring along Victor's neck, his lips just barely brushing against that scar that David had left behind. "And tea.

But under that there's oranges and spice and something like scales, dry in the sun. You smell like the earth under trees after a rain. It's rather addictive, to be honest."

Victor had barely heard what Randall said, too distracted by the feeling of what Randall was doing. For a moment, all he could think about was David. About the first time David had bitten him—reluctant to do so at first but finally giving in, fangs sinking into Victor's throat with a pain that was much more like pleasure. At that very first moment, Victor had gotten addicted.

But now it was nothing but the gentle pressure of Randall's lips touching against a scar left by a person who wasn't in Victor's life anymore. The murmur of Randall's voice was a low rumble, pushing the memories away and replacing them with the present.

"Well, that is certainly a complicated scent," he managed.

"Oh my God, Randall," Anthony said, sounding scandalized. "Keep it behind closed doors."

The wolfish confidence disappeared from Randall's face, and he was pulling back, eyes wide. "Oh, God," he started, running his hands through his hair. "God, I'm *so* sorry. I just...." He winced. "That was unforgivably forward of me. I apologize, Victor. That, um, that won't happen ever again."

Victor found himself absently rubbing over his scars, fingertips searching out both the too-smooth skin and the memory of the sensation of Randall's lips. He almost wanted to tell Randall to not apologize. He certainly hadn't minded.

But with that sensation came the full knowledge of exactly how Randall felt about him. Victor had seen every inch of it, the depth and breadth of a wolf's passion and the conviction of family. The want that wasn't merely physical, wasn't even touching on sexual. It was no casual interest. It was a bone-deep need for connection in everything, in running under a moon, in sleeping, sated and content, in a heap the next morning.

And Victor's feelings were the tortoise at the starting line, thinking of Randall as a nice friend to have. The responsibility of knowing Randall's feelings was confusing, to say the least.

"It's quite all right," he told Randall. "I was just startled by someone touching, er...." Victor trailed off, taking his hand away from his neck. He was surprised at the low, possessive growl Randall gave, seeing the scars again. Then again, it seemed Randall was surprised as well.

The man briefly closed his eyes, shaking his head. "Sorry," he muttered. "Yes, I noticed those. I should have been more careful. In fact, I shouldn't have done that at all. It's a wolf thing. A very intimate wolf thing and I was wrong to take that liberty. Your throat is...." Randall tried valiantly for a smile. He failed. "Not something I should be sniffing, that's for sure."

"Well, I did recently see all of your memories. I think we're past apologizing for things we can't help," Victor murmured. He felt guilty, knowing he didn't respond to Randall's feelings. He felt like he was letting the man down. But he knew that was irrational—Randall's emotions were his own and didn't affect Victor's. The possibility for more was there, which Victor had witnessed with stunning clarity, but there were several paths for Randall that didn't have him in them at all. Knowing the potential did not immediately imbue Victor with feelings or an obligation to return them, regardless of any crushes Randall might have.

That didn't stop the vague guilt from nagging at the back of his mind, though.

"I can help this, though," Randall told him with a slight, sad smile. With a low word to his brother, he switched seats with Edwin, going to sit in the row in front of Anthony. Edwin took his place beside Victor with a grin.

"You really do smell like tea," the wolf informed him.

Victor gave a quiet laugh. "It's *good* tea," he clarified. "Not the weak dirtwater you Americans stock over here." He glanced at Randall. He could guess why the man had moved.

"I don't drink tea." Edwin flopped back on the seat, legs restlessly jittering. "Randall does, though. By the truckload. He drinks more since Egypt. I think he has nightmares, and he's a dork who tries to will them away through books and green tea."

"Yes, I would expect anybody to have nightmares after that ordeal," Victor murmured. "It wasn't pleasant, by any means."

"He won't talk about it." Edwin was watching Randall, who'd curled up against the window to flip through a book. His fingers were a bit too rough on the pages, tension seeped into his shoulders. "Not to anyone. Anthony barely let him out of his sight for a month after, and Randall wore stupid looking turtlenecks for ages."

"You are aware that Anthony can hear you," Anthony said dryly. "Randall can too."

Edwin looked over at his brothers, baffled. "I know," he said, as if speaking to a very slow child. "But Victor doesn't know, so I'm telling him."

Victor didn't feel the need to tell Edwin that he *did* know. He'd seen the nightmares that Randall had, the way he hadn't been able to sleep for a long time afterward.

Randall said, very casually, "Edwin chewed all his pillows to shreds until he was fifteen and still sleeps with a stuffed bear named Sprinkles." At Edwin's indignant howl, Randall looked back, eyebrow rising. "Don't make me tell them about the first time you saw a train."

Anthony barked out a laugh. "Yeah, Edwin, we've got plenty of embarrassing stories about you. Don't get too smart."

Grumbling, Edwin sprawled back down in his seat with righteous indignation. After a while, lulled by the motion of the van, Edwin's agitated fidgeting calmed and he wound up sleeping, pressed up against Victor's side. The first time Edwin had flopped over, Victor had given Anthony a helpless look, but Anthony had just grinned at him. Knievel had paced over and appropriated Edwin's lap as her bed, the both of them happily pressed into the warmth of Victor.

Victor wasn't entirely sure how he felt about all of this, but he didn't want to disturb their rest, so he stayed as still as he could, even when his arm started to get pins and needles. He spent the rest of the drive watching the passing scenery, seeing the light grow dimmer and dimmer. By the time they arrived at the edge of the forest, Victor calculated that they had perhaps half an hour left, at best.

Though Victor was not the one sizing up the woods to see if it was adequate for running, he couldn't help but think of it that way, taking note of how densely the trees were packed, that the ground was mostly made up of dead leaves and pine needles. It wouldn't be pleasant for a human to run through, but he imagined it would be a very different story for a wolf. The sun all but vanished as they wound their way deeper into the forest, and Edwin woke up with a jolt, swaying away from Victor's shoulder. Sleeping at an angle like that, his neck should have been killing him. Instead, Edwin was grinning, his hands going to his shirt.

"Ed, wait until the van's stopped at least," Anthony sighed, though he was sitting rigidly in anticipation too, his eyes glinting yellow in the darkened interior of the van.

Victor wondered if he should be scared, being in a relatively small vehicle with four wolves that were getting antsy. He wasn't, though. He wasn't even wary, which surprised him somewhat.

The moment Jed found a turnoff, Edwin was out of the van, clothes falling into a puddle behind him. Victor caught a glimpse of tanned skin and long legs before fur flashed in between the trees. A long, joyous howl lifted to the sky as Jed switched off the van and the headlights dimmed, halving the light that shone out into the woods.

Anthony was next, bounding out of the van. He grinned at them as he shed his shirt. "Have a good night, guys," he said to Victor and Jed. "We'll find you in the morning." Then he too was stripping the rest of his clothes off, smoothly shifting and sprinting away on all fours, chasing Edwin with gleeful barks.

Jed was carefully helping Redford take off the dog tags, the bracelet he wore. "I'll be right here," Jed murmured, kissing his forehead. Knievel seemed to join her owner's mood, chirping as she rubbed against Redford's arm. "Hell, go blow off some steam, and then I'll race you and the little fur ball, okay?"

"Okay," Redford replied, but he looked nervous. He kept darting glances at Randall, seemingly embarrassed. "I, um. I'm going to go find a tree or something so nobody has to watch." He took Jed's hand, a silent plea for Jed to come with him.

"Well, let's find you a tree, then." Jed smiled softly, kissing him, concern in his expression as they started toward the tree line. Edwin came barreling out of the woods, tackling Jed and licking his face before bounding happily around Redford's legs. Apparently he was ready for that run now.

Victor stepped out of the van, taking a deep breath of the night air. He wished he could block his ears, because he'd heard Redford shift before, and it wasn't pleasant. "You might want to concentrate on your book," he said to Randall. "The sounds you're about to hear are... well, somewhat horrifying."

Randall looked up with a frown. "Because he's not full Cano?" He put the book aside, coming to stand next to Victor, eyes sharp as he looked through the deepening dusk. "I can't imagine going through the shift like that."

Victor had anticipated that there might be a few more minutes to wait, but apparently the wolf in Redford had decided to come out early. It started with the sickening snaps of cracking bone, echoing around the forest, closely followed by the distinct sound of someone trying not to scream. Anthony had come back, a dark shape of fur hovering at the edge of the road. Edwin was curled up next to Redford, little rumbles of encouragement coming from him as he nudged his nose against the other wolf. Jed was on the other side of Redford, arms wrapped around him, the two of them holding Redford close as he changed.

When it was all said and done, Victor was just glad it was over. Redford was flopped on the ground, panting softly, but he happily nosed at Jed's head, recovering quickly. He was more cautious about Edwin, but he looked fairly content to just accept that another wolf was there.

"When do you usually turn?" Victor asked Randall, curious. "I know you said you do it later, but is there a set time?"

Randall watched as Edwin nudged Jed toward the woods, butting against Redford, encouraging them both to take off running. "I don't like to be ruled by a lunar object." He shrugged. "I turn when I want to." There was an implied *or when I can't put it off any longer* that Victor recognized, the steel of control that was tempered by the knowledge that control could only go so far. But unlike David, Randall didn't seem to hate the wolf instincts. It was merely preference. "Am I bothering you?" Randall looked over to him. "I can go elsewhere."

Getting back into his seat, Victor dug out his own book. "Not at all," he said. "Consider me relieved, actually. I'm not entirely sure about spending the night in a van, in dark woods, by myself all night." He gave a wry smile. Not that Randall would be there all night, but it was nice to have some company.

"Oh, you won't be alone," Randall assured him. "Jed won't last twenty minutes with my brothers. I'm actually surprised he isn't back yet, or Edwin isn't here to tell us all about the human that passed out in the woods."

Victor snorted. He was surprised at that too. Though Jed was incredibly fit—he had to be, for his job—keeping up with excited wolves did sound exhausting. "He's doing better than I would," Victor admitted.

"Have you ever gone running?" Randall asked. His eyes weren't yellow, not yet, but there was something intense about them that seemed to cut straight through Victor, even without being able to meet them fully, like Randall was the one who could read souls and futures.

"I'm a professor that reads books all day, and my idea of fun is doing the crossword," Victor said dryly. "The only times I've ever run was when something was chasing me."

Huffing out a laugh, Randall pushed away from where he'd been leaning against the van. He paced a little, movements languid, graceful. "It's like nothing else," he mused. "Not even just the *running*, but the experience of being out there. The ground under your feet, the breeze against your skin, like the whole night is just rushing through you. Like you're captured by it, pulled in and enmeshed in every beat and throb of it."

It *did* sound nice. But it also made Victor think idly about the similarities between wolves and vampires. Both of them had something that meant the world to them, something that they needed, otherwise they'd go crazy. He had to wonder if his own breed of half blood had something like that, and he just hadn't discovered it yet.

"It sounds very freeing," he replied.

Randall stretched, arms up to the sky, before collapsing down on himself and going back to leaning against the side of the van. "That's the point," he agreed. Then, whole body pricking to attention, he murmured, "Here comes Jed."

Sure enough, there was the muffled noise of cursing and someone crashing through the underbrush toward them. Jed came into view, red-faced, and stumbled to a halt, hands on his thighs, puffing out huge, shuddering breaths. "Oh, fuck me," he managed between gasps for air. "I think I have a hernia. Can you die from a running fucking hernia?"

"I'm not sure that you can get hernias from running," Victor pointed out calmly, looking up from his book, shadows cast out onto the grass from the sour yellow glow of the van's overhead light. "I thought you'd last longer. You do always boast about your stamina."

"Blow me" was Jed's eloquent answer as he flopped down onto the grass, spread eagle, looking worn out. "Oh, God, I think I'm dying."

Victor rubbed a hand over his mouth to smother a laugh. He retrieved a water bottle from his bag and stepped out of the van to stand over Jed, holding the water out for him. Redford came running out of the undergrowth, nosing at Jed and pinning him down with ninety-five pounds of contented wolf.

Groaning a little, Jed did manage a smile, genuine behind the fact he was still heaving in air. His fingers tangled in Redford's fur, rubbing behind his ear. "See?" Jed muttered, head falling back onto the ground. "Told you I could keep up."

Edwin was next, racing out of the woods and piling on top of the two of them. His tail was wagging frantically, and he happily licked everyone he could reach before he took off again, howling loudly. There was a howl in the distance in reply, likely from Anthony. At the sound of it, Victor could see Randall starting to look longingly at where Edwin had run off to, his knuckles white as he gripped his book.

"Randall," Victor murmured. "You should go."

Randall glanced between Victor and Jed, hesitating. "I feel bad leaving you. Both of you," he hastened to add. "No offense, but it's dark and you don't have my eyes."

"I also have no doubt that you three will smell any potential danger *long* before it even comes close to us," Victor said. "Go, have fun. We'll be quite fine." It was, surprisingly, almost painful watching Randall deny his urge to change. It seemed wrong to have a wolf hold back like that.

After what seemed like a long few moments, Randall finally nodded. Some of the tension eased from his shoulders as he gave in. "Fine. But I'll be in earshot." He flashed a smile, wolfish and eager. "And I can run faster than you'd think. You'll be fine."

Randall stripped off his sweater, folding it neatly on the seat of the van. His shoes were next, followed by his jeans, until it was just Randall standing naked under the full flush of the moon.

Victor knew he shouldn't stare. It was completely rude of him to stare. He had the feeling that if this were happening at any other time, Randall would be stammering and blushing, embarrassed. But now, with the shift approaching, he was standing straight and tall, confident, his eyes slowly changing to yellow.

And he was *startlingly* well built. Victor hadn't anticipated that a body like that would be hidden under the sweaters and shyness. The muscular definition on the man was something that Victor felt he could quite happily spend a very long time visibly appreciating. He was all lean limbs and smooth skin, and oh God, Victor should really stop staring.

Randall shifted, skin becoming fur, body elongating, until instead of a man there was a wolf. In contrast to Edwin's dark-gold fur, Anthony's deep brown, and Redford's dappled red, Randall was more mottled, cream-colored muzzle fading into tan. Randall circled Victor's legs, lightly nudging him with his muzzle.

Victor had very briefly had contact with Redford in his wolf form, once, back when they'd been taking some of the kidnapped victims to the hospital. But he was still hesitant about reaching down to gently place his hand on Randall's head, his fingertips bumping against his ears. It seemed wrong to just put his hands all over a creature so free.

Randall pushed into Victor's touch, chuffing softly. Apparently he didn't mind getting his ears scratched, so Victor kept it up, careful in his touch. He was well aware that Randall was not like, say, Knievel—Randall wasn't going to bite his hands if he touched him in a way Randall didn't like—and he was still cautious, though Victor was relaxing into it somewhat. Wolf fur was a lot coarser than he'd imagined.

A soft, contented rumble came from Randall, and he rolled over, showing his stomach. There was amusement in Randall's expression. If a wolf could be said to smile, he was now. Victor frowned down at him. "Are you all right?" Why was Randall rolling around on his back?

Randall's tail stopped wagging. With a sigh, he got back onto his feet, shaking off his coat. Redford was making a low huffing noise in the background like he was laughing at Victor, and Jed was laughing too. "What?" Victor gave Jed a questioning look. "I'm missing something incredibly obvious, aren't I?"

"Goddamn, princess," Jed said with a grin. He was sprawled on the ground with Redford, rubbing under his chin happily. Knievel was stalking Redford's gently waving tail through the grass. "You never had a dog, did you?"

Victor shrugged. "I've never particularly had the time to care for one. I can't even keep plants alive. Why?"

"For someone who's supposed to be so smart, you're kind of missing the point," Jed commented. The man looked awfully smug. "You never heard of a pack animal showing their stomach before? He's submitting. Giving you his throat. I think it's kind of a big deal."

Randall had moved away from him and was sitting now, back to Victor, staring out into the woods. He lifted his head, howling, listening for his brothers' response.

Victor promptly felt rather stupid. He took a tentative step closer to Randall, lowering his voice. "Er, my apologies. I'm afraid I'm not well versed in wolf body language."

Randall looked back over his shoulder to regard Victor for a moment. The moon was pouring down onto him, silver light making his eyes shine, making him look like so much *more*. He got up, shaking himself off, and stalked over to Victor. He pressed his head against Victor's stomach, pushing him back toward the van. When Victor's knees hit the edge of the van floor and he sat, Randall put his paws on Victor's legs, half standing so they were nose to nose.

Then he licked Victor across the cheek.

Chuffing out hoarse noises that Victor was beginning to suspect were wolf laughs, Randall then turned and ran into the woods, disappearing with a flash of his tail. Victor pulled a face, wiping his sleeve across his cheek to clean off the wolf slobber. "I bet you don't drool on people, Redford," he said.

In response, Redford opened his muzzle and licked Jed across the cheek, going over his ear for good measure. He looked far too amused about doing so.

"Yeah, that's another wolf thing," Jed informed Victor, wiping off his cheek and sprawling under Redford. Knievel had caught his tail and was now happily wrapping her paws around it, her own tail lashing back and forth. "I think it means he likes you, princess. Either that or he's thinking about eating you in your sleep."

"Emotional communications via saliva," Victor said dryly.

"How is that any different than what you normally do?" Jed pointed out.

Victor threw an empty water bottle at him and retreated back into the van.

Two hours later, Jed made his way into the vehicle. He and Redford had been sprawled out together on the ground, the gentle noise of Jed's voice just barely audible over the cacophony of the night sounds. They'd even run together, back and forth in the tall grass of the clearing, Jed laughing loudly when Redford tackled him to the ground. They seemed to fit together now just as well as they did when Redford wasn't shifted. It was odd to watch, Jed Walker being so *human*. So very vulnerable.

Finally, though, Redford took off into the woods—after much prompting and encouragement from Jed. Heaving himself into his seat, Jed stretched and groaned before toeing off his boots. He pulled a gun from his waistband and left it on the seat next to him while he settled in and made himself comfortable. Victor just gave him a brief glance and went back to reading. The moon had risen high in the sky now, half the night whittled away, and he couldn't even hear any howling anymore.

"I'm somewhat surprised you let him go off on his own," Victor murmured, still more absorbed in his book than the act of talking. "With not even a cell phone or a flare gun or something."

"I keep trying," Jed sighed heavily, head tilted back. He'd shrugged off his jacket and was squirming in the seat, trying to find a good position to sleep in. Knievel had appropriated one of his knees, draped over it like a scarf. "But for some reason he won't wear a fanny pack. Also, no opposable thumbs, so...." Jed shrugged.

Shockingly, Jed didn't seem to feel the need to fill the silence. Time passed, the overhead light seeming so dim compared to the darkness outside, making Victor feel a little like he was stuck in Plato's cave with only a single fire to ward off the night. Victor turned the pages of his book, and Jed's breathing evened out into something quite like sleep.

The idea of chasing sleep was a tempting one, but Victor didn't think he was going to have much luck trying to get comfortable in the minivan.

"Have you heard from him?" Jed's voice was low, but not that of a man who'd been asleep. He didn't indicate who he was talking about. Then again, he didn't really need to.

"No." Victor sighed faintly, looking up from his book to glance out the window. David had loved nights like this: clear and cold, completely still. "Have you?"

Barking out a quick laugh, Jed dragged a hand over his face. In the garish light of the overhead he looked tired, worry pinching the corners of his eyes. "Yeah, I don't think I'm exactly on Davey's Christmas card list at the moment." After a beat he shook his head, lips tight. "I tried. Burned through every contact I could think of that we'd used together, tracked him to Russia, maybe, and then Peru. Trail kept going cold. I gave up a few weeks ago, when I lost wind of him someplace in Argentina. Then again, probably was just chasing ghosts."

"Perhaps," Victor murmured. "If David doesn't want to be found, he won't be. He's a bit more experienced at doing so than the average human contact you have. No offense."

Jed didn't look exactly thrilled to be reminded of David's *otherness*, of the fact that he'd been both something more and something less at once. "I knew him," Jed muttered, staring up at nothing. "Shit, princess, I knew him for *years*. Now I don't really know fuck all, I guess."

Victor hadn't seen much of Jed's reaction to finding out that David wasn't human. He'd seen the first part, when Jed had thought that throwing garlic pizza at a vampire was a hilarious thing to do, but all he knew of after that was that Jed had hidden in his hotel room for some time. He imagined that the knowledge must have been quite a shock, especially to Jed, who didn't really mingle with the supernatural crowd.

"And in those years that you knew him, he was exactly the same person as he was after you found out what he was," Victor pointed out. "Except for the numerous lies he told you, I assume." He frowned, staring out the window. Honestly, he had no idea how David had convinced Jed for so long that he was human. "He wasn't at his best in Cairo, either. If you're going to judge him, don't judge him because of that."

"This ain't some after-school special about giving your mommy and daddy the 'I fuck boys' talk," Jed growled. "He sure as hell *wasn't* the guy I knew. Because instead of being a kind of stick-up-the-ass contact who dated like it was changing socks, he was a guy who *ate* people. And now I gotta live with the fact that, as close as I was, as much as I thought I understood, everything was wrong. So fuck you, Victor, and fuck Cairo. He would have killed you if Redford hadn't smelled it going south. And you wouldn't have been the first."

Victor just stared at Jed for a few seconds, then dipped his gaze back to his book. He really had nothing to say to that. What *could* he say? That if David had killed him, he wouldn't have particularly minded at the time? It was true, but it was also likely to send Jed into a cursing fit, and Victor wasn't in the mood to put up with one.

After a long moment, Jed murmured, so quietly that it almost didn't count as out loud, "Just wish I didn't worry so much about the stupid fucker." Leaning forward, Jed twisted the key, turning off the lights. "Go to sleep, Victor. You're gonna run down the battery."

Victor blinked hard as he tried to adjust to the sudden darkness. At a loss for what to do, he slotted a bookmark between the pages he'd been reading and put the book down on the seat next to him. There was a far-off noise, a long, drawn-out howl that reassured him somewhat. At least one of the wolves must be close.

"As much as David could trust anybody, I think he trusted you," Victor said into the darkness. His sight was beginning to adjust, bringing Jed and the interior of the van into sharp relief, the pale moonlight shading everything white and black. "He'll contact us when he's ready."

There was a sharp snort that summed up what Jed thought of that. But Victor could see him rustling around, and then a blanket hit him in the face. "Sleep, princess," Jed commanded, but there was a softness in his tone, under the weariness. "We've got a long day coming."

Victor heaved a sigh, but he nonetheless dragged the blanket off his face and twisted himself to lie across two of the seats. It was hardly comfortable. "Pity. I was looking forward to braiding your hair and watching romantic comedies together. We were having such a nice talk too." One that he was glad was over.

Jed gave a loud, genuine laugh, and Victor could see the other man peering over the back of the seat at him. "You'd be surprised, professor," Jed said around his grin. "I do a mean french braid."

CHAPTER
5

Redford

REDFORD RAN.

Nothing else existed but him and the forest. The wind through his fur, the ground under his paws, the noises of insects and night birds that guided him. To his sight, the forest was alive with movement, flora and fauna swaying together as a single organism, one that he was instinctively in tune with.

He had never felt so free.

The aggression and the fear that his instincts were usually edged with were nowhere to be found. It was just him and the forest and utter freedom.

Every once in a while, he caught a glimpse of another wolf. His instincts reacted first, wanting to chase and growl, but once his human mind kicked in, he recognized them for who they were. Edwin, a lighter streak amongst the darkness. Anthony, stalking a deer. Randall, curled up next to a stream to watch the play of moonlight over water. Then, later in the night, the three of them gathered together. Redford could smell them and the deer they were eating.

He approached cautiously, loitering on the edge of the clearing they'd dragged their prey to. Though Redford understood that they were wolves and they were just eating, the whole scene looked briefly terrifying to him: three wolves gathered around a carcass, blood shining on their muzzles. But it was just the Lewises, all of whom gave him a happy welcome. Redford sounded a low huff in return and trotted over.

Edwin had saved him the liver. Redford wasn't sure why, but from the expectant body language of Edwin, it was probably his favorite part. They fed, and splashed around in the river to clean, and wound up collapsed in a pile afterward, warm and full. Randall's nose was pressed into Redford's stomach, Edwin was draped across him, and Anthony was warm at his back. The moon bathed them and the river sang to them and they were at peace.

Redford closed his eyes, and the rest of the night drifted past him. His instincts and the wolf in the back of his mind were peaceful and satisfied, for the most part. But Jed wasn't there. That was the only thing that would make it better.

As the sun started to rise over the horizon, Redford lifted his head and opened his eyes, taking a deep breath. He hadn't slept so much as he'd *rested*. Detaching himself from the pile, he sneaked a few short steps away to change back, biting his tongue so he didn't disturb the brothers. They didn't look like they were waking up anytime soon, so Redford left them, unable to help smiling briefly as he started the walk back.

He wished he'd had the foresight to bring along clothes or to change back closer to the van. It felt very strange, strolling the woods in nothing but his skin, but it also felt like an extension of the night and everything it had contained. Freedom. Freedom from worry and boundaries. The freedom to do exactly what he was doing.

It felt *amazing*.

The walk back didn't take him as long as he'd anticipated. Jed was hovering at the tree line, looking anxious and worried. The playful spirit of the night lingered in Redford, and he grinned to himself as he stalked behind the trees, keeping himself hidden until he got close enough to pounce on Jed, tackling him to the ground.

"That was *awesome*," Redford enthused, happily thumping his hands on Jed's chest. "We should do that every full moon."

The tension faded from Jed's face into a slow grin, his fingertips brushing along Redford's cheeks. There was guilt under the smile, but Jed shook it away to laugh lowly. "You look like you had fun, babe," he murmured, kissing Redford's chin.

"It would have been more fun if you'd been there," Redford replied. "But it was good. I ran around, and Anthony killed a deer. And then we rested a bit." Self-conscious, he reached up to swipe a hand over his mouth, making sure there wasn't any blood remaining. Thankfully, there didn't seem to be. "And I liked it earlier too, when it was just you and me."

Jed's hands ran through Redford's hair, down his back, Jed's idle touch exploring his skin. Making sure he was all in one piece. It was a touchstone for Jed, Redford knew. A way to assure himself that Redford really had come back to him. "Nah," he huffed out a rueful breath. "Couldn't have kept up with you. You're much better off with the furry brigade."

Redford rolled off Jed and flopped down to lie in the grass next to him on his back, their arms still pressed together. "Our time together was my favorite bit," he murmured, finding Jed's hand with his own, linking their fingers together.

He hadn't felt quite this *satisfied* in a long time, like every part of him was exhausted in the best kind of way. It was actually similar to how Redford felt after a round of really good sex with Jed, only this time his instincts were happy too.

Jed raised their joined hands to his lips and kissed Redford's knuckles. He almost looked embarrassed by the gesture, but he didn't let go. "It's always mine too, Fido," Jed said gruffly. He wore the same look he always got when he said something sentimental but didn't want to acknowledge it. So Redford rolled over again, sprawling himself on top of Jed to kiss him, reaching his arms past Jed's head to stretch.

"I'm going to need a massive breakfast," Redford announced, nosing his way in against Jed's neck. He smelled the same as always, pine and gunpowder, mixed together with what Redford knew was his own scent. "Did you have a good night?"

"I slept in a van with Victor goddamn Rathbone," Jed muttered, head arching back to give Redford more room, a pleased little murmur as Redford found that one spot on his throat that always made Jed's toes curl. "What do you think?"

"Poor Jed," Redford laughed. "Did you have to put up with lectures?" He didn't know what Victor could possibly think of to lecture Jed about, but he was sure Victor could come up with something.

"It was *terrible*," Jed pouted, a gleam in his eyes as he wiggled a bit under Redford. "I'm traumatized for life."

Redford lifted his face from Jed's throat to briefly sniff the air, glancing up at the sun. If he figured correctly, the Lewises would still be an hour away, considering how deeply they'd been sleeping. Victor too smelled like he was fast asleep. For now, it seemed, they had the entire forest to themselves.

He wanted to say something potentially cheesy about making better memories for Jed after his lecture-based trauma, but instead Redford just kissed him, leisurely and slow, lifting up to grin at him. "I'm sorry. I'll never make you sleep in a van with Victor ever again."

"Good." Jed arched his neck up to catch Redford in another kiss, his legs wrapping around Redford's hips to keep him there. "I missed you."

"I missed you too." Redford ducked down to kiss Jed's throat, biting him lightly. The instinct was there, wanting him to bite harder, to give Jed a mark that would last for the next few days, but that could wait. For now, Redford was content and comfortable, the sun warming his back, and he had Jed underneath him. He wanted to relish this.

He kissed Jed, smiling into it, lazily running a hand down his chest. Redford still wondered if he should feel weird about the fact that he was naked in the middle of a forest clearing, but it felt like the most natural thing in the world, especially with Jed there. "You have *far* more clothes on than I do," he pointed out, getting his hands under Jed's T-shirt.

With a laugh, Jed tumbled out of his shirt, tossing it away and sliding his hands through Redford's hair, down to his shoulders, tugging him in to meet in a sweet clash of lips and tongue. "God forbid," Jed mumbled with a smirk, kicking off his jeans, sprawling out under Redford happily. He looked more than comfortable to be in the same naked state. If a car happened to drive past on the nearby road, Redford had no doubt that Jed would just flip them off and attempt to charge them for viewing rights.

Jed's hand slipped between them, wrapping around Redford's cock, his lips trailing along the slope of Redford's shoulder. "God, you're gorgeous," he murmured, nipping lightly at Redford's neck, burying a smile into his skin. "How do you just keep getting more beautiful?"

"Wolf secret," Redford replied, giving the words a lofty tone, grinning down at Jed. He still felt heat rising to his cheeks, though, just like every time Jed complimented him. There was a laugh buried against his skin as Jed painted a trail down his chest, tongue teasing across his nipple. In retaliation, Redford bit harder at Jed's neck, grinning to himself at the gasp it produced. "You're getting predictable," he teased fondly, doing it again. Every time, Jed would get this glazed look in his eyes like he'd temporarily lost all sense of anything else that was happening.

It was satisfying to know that Redford could have that kind of effect on Jed—a man who normally divided his attention between fifteen different things. Not now, though. Now the hands that would be reaching for weapons, that would be focused on violence or planning, were gentling down his sides. Now the eyes that scanned rooms for exits, that picked people apart, that looked for weaknesses and opportunities, were dark with want. Were only focused on Redford. Every part of Jed was in tune with him, every shudder and sigh was only for Redford. Jed tipped his head back, baring his throat, a slow smile slipping across his lips.

"Yeah, I'm predictable," Jed muttered. "I'm so fucking into you, Red, you have no idea." Redford smiled against Jed's throat at the words, soothing the bites with a kiss.

"Predictable is good," he replied lowly, moving his way down to Jed's collarbone, giving him another bite there. He liked knowing exactly what to do to make Jed lose his mind, and knowing the steps didn't make it any less exciting.

As for himself, he thought he might try to be a little unpredictable this time around. Redford knew he was still a little shy when it came to things like this, something he hadn't quite managed to break out of yet. But on the morning of the full moon, and after a night of running, he was feeling confident. It was a good feeling. So he bit at Jed's throat again, then down lower, nuzzling over his stomach, then licking a long line up his cock, grinning up at Jed. Jed certainly seemed into it, if the moan was anything to go by, so Redford grasped his hips, settling in, contentedly ducking down to wrap his lips around Jed, sucking him gently. He could go hard and fast, and maybe he would later, but for now the sight of Jed, free and happy, sprawled out on the grass, was something Redford wanted to savor a little longer.

Jed's heels dug into the ground as he sucked in a quick breath, as he spread his legs farther for Redford. One of Jed's hands dropped to Redford's hair, fingers tangling in the soft strands. "God, Red," he managed, voice throaty and low. "Fuck, that's so good." As much as Redford could with his mouth full, he grinned again, the expression in his eyes. He was addicted to making Jed come undone.

He let his eyes fall closed, concentrating on the scent of pine and gunpowder, the heavy weight of Jed's cock on his tongue, the gasps and groans Jed was making. Redford knew Jed's favorite moves, and he employed them with enthusiasm, drawing back to tease, licking at the tip and using his hand, watching the almost frustrated little frown that Jed would get. But making Jed lose his mind also had the effect of making Redford very quickly get single-minded too, so he stopped teasing, stopped the light touches, and took Jed as deep as he could—he was *almost* at the point where he could deep-throat Jed, and practice made perfect, as Jed was fond of saying—lifting Jed's hips to encourage him.

Yelping out a surprised little whimper, Jed scrambled his free hand into the dirt. His eyes were closed, that look of blissful concentration on his face as he gave himself over to Redford. There was so much *trust* there. Jed wasn't watching his back, wasn't worried about what happened next. His body rolled up into Redford's mouth, and Jed was moaning loudly, uncensored and uncaring who might hear. All he cared about in that second was Redford. Reaching up, Redford took Jed's hand, twisting their fingers together.

Maybe he'd have to practice deep-throating more often, if *this* was the reaction he got.

His eyes still closed, Redford redoubled his efforts, one hand curled under Jed's hip to lift him up slightly. If Jed's whole world was the pleasure right now, then Redford's was the giving of it, in tune with every little noise Jed made, every faint twitch of his muscles. He smoothed his fingertips over Jed's hip, down to his thigh, smoothing his palm over the trembles he could feel that told him Jed was getting close. He wanted to turn his head and bite at the muscles, but with his mouth busy, Redford used his fingernails instead, scraping over soft skin, laughing to himself when Jed's leg jumped.

That little touch of pain with the ecstasy was what tipped Jed over. Redford could see it happen when he opened his eyes again—the blush that curled across Jed's body, the way his eyes were glazed over with need, the twitches in his muscles, the soft, keening gasps of air. With a hoarse moan of Redford's name, Jed came, body jerking up like it was caught on a string before he sagged back into the grass, panting and spent.

Redford gave in to the urge to bite Jed's thigh then, just lightly enough that it only left a faint red mark, and propped his chin on Jed's hip. Their hands were still joined, and he squeezed Jed's fingers, thumb rubbing over his knuckles. Redford heaved himself up and knelt next to Jed. Though he was still aroused, he was content, more than happy to just watch Jed come down from the high.

"I think that might be my favorite sight in the world," he murmured, carding his fingers through Jed's hair.

"Nah," Jed said, voice still all slurred and happy. "Best thing is you smiling. Then a good steak. Then you smiling with a good steak. I'm, like, number five, tops." But he slowly arched his neck up to kiss Redford, hands painting a path down his back.

Bending down, curled over Jed, Redford hummed a happy noise against his lips. "I said *my* favorite thing," he replied. "I have my own list, and you're at the top of it. Steak is much lower down." And, needless to say, Redford's smile wasn't on his own list. He wasn't a big fan of looking into the mirror.

"What about Knievel?" Jed asked seriously, but his fingers were creeping up Redford's sides, brushing just below that spot Jed *knew* made Redford squirm. Redford gave him a suspicious look. "She's very important. Is she on this list of yours?"

Jed's fingers sneaked higher, and, grinning, Redford attempted to bat his hand away. "Yes, the cat rates on the list," he replied. Jed's oh-so-innocent face wasn't fooling him. "Getting to my ticklish spot is *not* on the list."

"I don't know what you're talking about." With wide eyes, Jed looked up at him, the very picture of innocence. That was, until he attacked, hands sliding just above Redford's ribs, tickling him, with a huge grin. Redford yelped, scrambling away, slapping at Jed's hands to no avail.

"Jed!" Redford protested, laughing, leaping up and taking a few short steps away—and now he felt ridiculous, standing in the middle of the woods, naked, still very turned on.

Jed didn't seem to care. There was a very predatory gleam in his eyes as he stood gracefully and stalked over to Redford. He grasped Redford's hips, pulling him in with a low little growl, which Redford happily responded to, leaning into him. Nipping sharply at Redford's lower lip, Jed murmured, "I'm counting to ten, and then I'm coming to get you, Fido."

Taking a step back, Jed grinned, covering his eyes. "One," he counted, apparently not caring that he was stark naked, fifty feet away from the van where Victor was sleeping. "Two. Three." He peeked through his fingers. Redford hadn't moved, staring at Jed in vague confusion. "Better go, babe. I'm not going to go easy on you." Then, eyes covered again, "Four."

If this was a game that Jed knew, Redford definitely wasn't familiar with it. But he caught on pretty quick, because the rules seemed easy, and Redford could never resist that grin. So as Jed said, "Five," Redford turned and took off, trying not to laugh. For the first few steps, he felt awkward, like he should be running on all fours if he was going to be running at all. But he settled into it, concentrating on the ground under his feet, the wind rushing past him, and it was just as good as last night. Better, even, because he knew Jed wasn't far behind him.

When Jed started running, Redford could hear him. Jed was stealthy when he wanted to be, but at that moment, to a wolf's ears, he sounded like an elephant crashing through the forest. Redford took a sharp left turn, ducking behind a tree, grinning to himself as Jed ran right past him. The sound of Jed's laughter trailed after him, and Jed turned, spinning in a tight circle, looking for him.

"Come out, come out," Jed called, eyes bright in the early morning dimness. "Or I'll huff and puff and suck you right off."

Redford couldn't help it. "That's not how it goes," he replied. Then, realizing he'd given his position away, he darted out from behind the tree, tossing Jed a smirk over his shoulder as he sped in the other direction. Next time he'd just have to refrain from questioning Jed about incorrect references.

He heard the quick noise of Jed's bare feet through dried leaves, the soft puff of breath hanging on the chill morning air, and then Jed tackled him from behind. They rolled together through the underbrush, Jed finally pinning him, both laughing until they couldn't move. "I win," Jed crowed, arms in the air like the prizefighters Jed liked watching so much.

Which, of course, gave Redford the perfect opening to twist them around, sprawling on top of Jed and giving his own little smirk. "Who won?" he asked innocently, a gleam in his eye as Jed sagged back onto the ground.

"Nice moves, Fido," Jed teased. "And who taught you how to do that?"

Jed had, obviously. "Maybe I'm just a natural," Redford replied. "It could all be part of the wolf instincts, you know. How to get out of a hold."

Snorting out a laugh, Jed reached up, hauling Redford in for a kiss. "That must be it," he mumbled against Redford's lips. "You're all natural." As if to demonstrate this, his hand closed around Redford's cock again, stroking it slowly as Redford arched into the touch with a hiss, eyes falling half-closed. Far from making his arousal die down, the chase had magnified it. Jed's thumb rubbed against the head of his cock, and he huffed out a laugh. "Left the lube in the van," Jed grumbled. "I'm just going to have to finger fuck you the old fashioned way." The words had a bolt of heat shooting through Redford's body, and he kissed Jed again, hard and wanting.

Grip strong on Redford's hips, Jed hauled him up to sit over his face, tongue teasing down his cock to press against his hole. The suddenness of the move had Redford's legs jerking, and he slammed his hands against the ground above Jed's head, fingers digging into soft soil and brittle leaves, laughing shakily. "Maybe a little warning next time so I don't fall over and break your nose," he breathed.

Jed's voice was rather muffled. "What's the fun in that?" And then he buried his face under Redford, tongue licking along the curve of his ass, twisting around his hole, long moments of nothing but teasing until Redford was rocking back, desperate for more.

71

Jed's tongue pressed inside of him slowly, fucking in and out with deliberate restraint. Jed knew how much Redford loved this. He took great pleasure in making Redford go crazy with want. It was amazing and frustrating all at the same time, making Redford grab a handful of Jed's hair and tug.

Responding with a low moan, Jed nudged his finger in alongside his tongue. Slowly, carefully, just to the first knuckle at the start, Jed toyed with the pressure and friction until his finger was sliding in and out of Redford, brushing against his prostate with every other thrust. His tongue moved with it in time, hot and wet and perfect.

The threat of accidentally falling over and breaking Jed's nose was becoming more of a possibility by the second. Jed loved this position, Redford knew quite well, but every time he felt like he was just going to collapse and something *very* unsexy would happen. Still, it was difficult to think about any of that, with Jed so intense.

"Jed," Redford tried to warn, tugging at his hair again, muffling a moan around a bitten lip as Jed decided that adding a second finger was an awesome idea. "Seriously, I'm going to—" Oh, God, his knee was beginning to slip, and he didn't care because everything that Jed was doing felt incredible. All he could think about was moving into Jed's fingers and tongue, his gaze focused sightlessly on the woods ahead of them, the scents of pine and arousal and gunpowder overwhelming him.

One moment slipped into the next, the sounds of the forest waking up around them, of Redford's bitten off gasps and moans, surrounding them. It was like everything stopped, everything, and Redford was achingly aware of the wind through the trees sliding over his skin, of Jed's heartbeat a steady throb underneath him, of the way Jed was moving and the growing twist of arousal. Every second turned into a wave, every wave crashed into him, over and over, until Redford couldn't feel anything but this.

For once, everything in him—the wolf instincts and his own mind—were in perfect harmony. And it wasn't that unknown growl that rumbled *Mate-Jed-Journey* in the back of his thoughts, it was his own voice.

Digging his fingers deeper into the soft ground, Redford tipped his head back as Jed eased his fingers still deeper, and the orgasm that crashed through him made his vision blur at the edges, unexpectedly intense, a kind of *freedom* to it that Redford had never felt before. He was dimly aware of grinning, laughing, and then flopping down on Jed to happily nuzzle at his neck, feeling like every inch of his skin was buzzing.

He couldn't believe how good he felt. How, for the first time, every part of him was perfectly content. Blowing out a happy sigh, Redford leaned up on hands and knees to give Jed a light kiss. "You're amazing," he murmured, eyes still half-closed in contentment. "We should do that every full moon."

"Sweetheart, I'd do that every *morning* if you'd let me." Jed's voice was teasing, but he was looking up at him with a strange mix of expressions. Jed kissed his forehead and combed his fingers through Redford's hair, that softness on his face that only seemed to come out in moments like this.

There was that guilt on Jed's face again. It was nearly impossible to notice, and it was mostly covered by Jed's usual look of tired contentment after sex. Redford knew why now, but he didn't think Jed *should* feel guilty. His staying in the cage and the basement was his own choice.

"Come on, we should probably get dressed before everybody else arrives," Redford sighed, reluctantly getting off of Jed. He offered a hand to Jed, helping him up, wrapping an arm around his waist. As much as he kind of wished Jed could go around naked all the time, it sadly wasn't feasible. Even if he was sure Jed would love the idea too.

"Gonna need your nose on that one, Fido," Jed murmured, kissing just in front of Redford's ear, their hands lacing together. "Not even sure where we left them."

Redford raised his chin slightly, closing his eyes as he scented the air. "This way," he decided, leading Jed back through the woods and toward the clearing again. Truth be told, he wouldn't have known the way back either, if not for his nose. He hadn't really been thinking about directions during their chasing game.

Jed had left his clothes scattered in the clearing, and they were now appropriated as Knievel's napping spot. She'd come out of the van apparently for the sole purpose of shedding all over Jed's shirt. They both showered her with attention until she stalked off, and Redford left Jed to get dressed while he cautiously crept up toward the van. His own clothes were packed in a backpack, left resting against the wheel, and since there was no flustered exclamation, he had to assume that Victor was still asleep. He got dressed, tugging boxers, jeans, and a T-shirt on, then socks and his boots. After digging deeper into the backpack, Redford put his necklace on and tucked it under his shirt, and then slipped his bracelet onto his wrist. These days, he didn't go too long without wearing both items—the whistle and Jed's dog tags looped on a chain and the lapis lazuli scarab bracelet Jed had bought him in Cairo. They were good-luck charms, things that he wanted to keep with him at all times, even if Redford knew the idea of "good luck" was just a superstition.

Jed had gotten them for him. And if he was ever apart from Jed, for any reason, Redford could look at the jewelry and know that Jed was coming back. He'd always come back, because he'd promised.

Behind him, Jed was cursing as he accidentally put his shirt on inside out, so Redford opened the van door as quietly as he could. The sound still woke Victor, who blinked owlishly at him and then seemed to remember where he was with a faint groan. He sat up, rubbing the back of his neck. "It's morning already?"

"The others should be getting back soon," Redford replied, reaching for a water bottle. "How did you sleep?"

"Horrendously." Victor smiled dryly. He rolled his shoulders with a wince. "But I'm sure we'll all get a decent night's sleep when we arrive at the compound."

From far off in the forest, Redford could hear the distant noise of the Lewises coming closer—one two-legged beat and two four-legged beats. When they emerged, Edwin was happily running circles around Anthony, who was still a wolf, and Randall, who seemed more comfortable being human. Randall nodded at them both, a faint blush staining his cheeks as he reached for his clothes.

"I didn't think you'd be awake yet," he mumbled in Victor's general direction. For his part, Victor had gone red and seemed determined *not* to stare at Randall and his current state of nudity. The confidence that Randall had worn so easily last night seemed faded a bit in the sunlight. Edwin, however, changed back to his human form with the same rakish grin, climbing into his clothes and sprawling over Randall's back in a hug.

"Wasn't that *great*?" he enthused. "You got up early, Redford. Shoulda said something. I totally would have gone for a swim before we had to come back. Also, you missed breakfast. Ant got us the best rabbits. Randall ate *two*. That's how you know they were good."

Randall flushed deeper. "No one cares, Ed," he said, straightening his sweater, grimacing as he pulled a leaf out of his hair. "Get in the van."

"I'm sad I missed it," Redford said, the end of his sentence trending upward in a tentative tone. He surprised himself by saying the words genuinely, though. It *did* sound nice. He was just still unsure as to whether he really fit with them and their family, and whether or not he was intruding.

Anthony, still a wolf, was circling around the van, nose to the ground as he, presumably, checked to see if anything had happened over the night. When he'd made a full circle, he changed back, grinning as easily as Edwin. "We'd love to have you along, Redford," he said. "As often as you want."

There was a moment where Redford was sure Anthony would hug him—the Lewises seemed so *easy* with their affection, so free about tumbling all over each other in a very wolfish manner—but the man just smiled at him, squeezing his arm and moving over to ruffle Randall's hair. It was kind of a relief. Redford wasn't sure how to *do* things like that, how to hug and roughhouse and be a part of something that messy and big. At the same time, he did like hugs. Jed gave very nice hugs.

Randall had ducked out of his brother's grip, grabbing a bottle of water and a small bag. He walked a few steps away, dug out a toothbrush, and quickly scrubbed his teeth, following it with a gargle of mouthwash. Victor had climbed out of the van, stretching with a groan, and Jed had finally managed to get dressed and was walking back to the van with Knievel under one arm, who was yowling her protests about leaving.

It was all more than a little domestic, Redford realized. Getting ready for a long trip in the early hours of the morning, with Anthony bustling around and making sure everybody was okay. Victor had turned bright red again because Anthony was cheerfully rubbing his shoulders, talking about muscle knots and how bad they were if you left them alone.

Randall came back and handed the bag off to Edwin, urging him to wash up. Digging around in the luggage, Randall produced what appeared to be a battery-operated hot plate, which he immediately set about making tea on. His shoulders slumped a little, and Randall absently rubbed the back of his neck, looking tired. He kept cutting glances over at Anthony and Edwin. Redford realized, all at once, that he was worried. It was easy to forget what was happening, especially after last night. Anthony didn't seem to be letting his illness slow him down, Edwin was relentlessly cheerful, and Redford almost didn't notice how Randall appeared to be gathering all the stress and piling it onto his own back, bit by bit.

"Oh my goodness, Randall, you are a lifesaver," Victor announced. "Tea is exactly what this morning calls for. Tea will solve everything."

"Ah, yes," Randall replied dryly, pulling out several travel mugs. "I heard about the recent Parkinson's cure. Cup of tea and everything will be fine."

74

Anthony's happy chatter was cut short, and Victor rubbed a hand over his face, looking guilty. "My apologies," Victor sighed. "I wasn't thinking, I'm afraid. Unfortunately, I do that a lot."

Looking horrified at himself, Randall closed his eyes, forcing out a breath. "No. No, I'm sorry. That was completely uncalled for. I don't know what I was thinking."

"You're thinking your brother is sick and you're worried." Jed's brisk voice cut in, and he nudged Randall out of the way to rifle through his own bag. "Jesus, kid, if that's the worst thing you say then you probably got something up your ass bigger than a Chinese stripper pole. It sucks, the whole situation sucks, but we're going to fix it. That's the point of this little operation." He found the gun he was looking for and strapped it on. "Now have your tea. We're moving out in ten."

"And we're nearly there," Anthony said, giving Randall a playful shove. "So stop looking so down."

Redford had to admit, he was starting to admire just how *cheerful* Anthony seemed most of the time. If he had a degenerative disease with no known cure, Redford knew he'd be incredibly depressed and probably wouldn't work up the motivation to get out of bed. But Anthony had his brothers to take care of—whatever his own feelings on his illness were, he wasn't indulging them.

Rolling his eyes, Randall bumped his shoulder against his brother's. He poured the tea, which both Edwin and Jed promptly declined. "I'm afraid I only have the horrid powdered creamer." He sighed heavily. "Anthony? Victor? Can I fix you something?" He gave Redford a slight smile. "How about you, Redford? It's my favorite blend, and I think Victor is right, it's exactly what's called for this morning."

Victor took a mug appreciatively, wrapping long fingers around it and taking a grateful sip. Jed brought out his instant coffee, and between himself and Randall they got everyone a hot morning beverage of choice. Redford tried the tea. It was better than coffee, not as bitter, but he still didn't see the appeal.

Redford and Edwin gathered around the hot plate, joining Victor and Randall, while Anthony puttered around in the van, cleaning up, and Jed attempted to shave in the side-view mirror one-handed while never letting go of his coffee. After a brief discussion between Anthony and Jed, Anthony got into the driver's seat, and Jed squeezed himself into one of the backseats, with Redford seated beside him. For a while, he watched Anthony's driving closely, clearly not sure about giving up control. But Anthony handled the van well enough, and eventually Jed's head dropped onto Redford's shoulder and he drifted off, snoring quietly when sleep finally claimed him.

Redford woke Jed up as they pulled into the first diner they saw, and got breakfast to go. No one argued the chance to eat on the road and shorten their trip. They were cramped and exhausted, anxious to reach their destination. Once they were back on the road, Redford entertained himself by stealing pieces of Jed's bacon out of his to-go box. Redford had ordered himself a gigantic breakfast platter, eggs and sausage and ham, and he hardly needed more, but Jed's possessiveness over his bacon was too fun to not antagonize. The drive passed in peace, with Victor flipping through the pages of a book and Randall reading too, while Edwin and Anthony kept switching the radio channels.

The closer they got to their destination, the more nervous Redford was feeling. He liked the Lewises, and he was starting to feel relatively comfortable around them—but where they were heading, there would be a *lot* more wolves. Dozens, possibly hundreds. While Anthony had laughed at the idea of calling wolves by rank, like alpha and beta, Redford wasn't sure if that was unique to their family or not. He'd already had one bad experience with a wolf who thought himself an alpha. What would happen if there were wolves like that at the compound?

As per the directions they had, they turned left at a lake and started heading down a long dirt road, walled in on either side by tall trees. Jed had taken over driving duties and was muttering under his breath every time the van hit a bump in the road. Edwin had stuck his head out the window, taking deep breaths. Randall was holding onto the back of his shirt with a long-suffering expression, nose still buried in his book.

Redford didn't know how far away they were, but with the window opened, he could smell it. Wolves. A lot of them. He couldn't pin down exact numbers, but there had to be at least a hundred. Probably more.

But showing nervousness wasn't going to help, so he gritted his teeth and kept watching out the side window. He just had to trust that these wolves wouldn't be like Filtiarn.

The van jolted to a stop, and Jed muttered, "Fuck." There was a steel and wire gate across the dirt road, overgrowth heavy around it. The whole thing looked like it hadn't been touched in years. There was even a rusty *No Trespassing* sign hanging crookedly from one side.

For a moment they all just sat there, considering it. Jed unbuckled his seat belt. "Stay in the car," he ordered, opening the door and stepping out. There was the quiet *ping, ping, ping* of the van alerting them he'd left the keys in the dash, echoing in the eerie stillness of the woods. Jed's boots were loud against the gravel as he walked closer to the gate. Redford watched as Jed slipped his gun from his holster, the tense set of Jed's shoulders easy to read, even through the dusty windows of the van.

Anthony huffed a sigh. "Humans," he muttered, climbing out of the van and grabbing Jed's shoulder to tug him back from the gate. "You might want to let me do this, Jed," Anthony said, an amused little smile on his lips. "They might not be all too happy about a human just stomping up to their gates."

He tested the gate with a brief push, but it didn't budge. Then Anthony tipped his head back and howled. It was long, wavering only slightly at the end, and Redford could pick up on the meaning of it right away.

I need help, the howl said.

It faded into the stillness of the air, echoing slightly off the trees. Surely, Redford figured, *someone* would hear that. Jed had jumped a little at the howl, just a quick jerk of his shoulders, and growled under his breath. "Fucking freaky loud wolves," he muttered, but he took a step back, just behind Anthony, though his grip hadn't loosened on the gun.

For a long moment, there was simply stillness. Edwin and Randall were tense, leaning into the quiet, as if waiting for something. Knievel's ears pricked forward. The cat was sitting on Edwin's lap, tail lashing in irritation. After seconds ticked by with nothing but the faint rustle of tree limbs, Randall sagged back in his seat, slumping in disappointment. But Edwin grinned, eyes flashing. "They're here."

Five wolves appeared, flashing in between the trunks at the tree line like ghosts half-seen. As they came closer, the drumbeat of their run turned into stalking forward, ears flat back against their heads. They stopped a ways away, teeth bared, a low, menacing growl rippling through the pack. Anthony held up his hands, showing that he wasn't armed and he wasn't going to shift, and put himself between them and Jed. "Jed, it might be a really good time to put away the gun," he muttered. Then, to the wolves, with a pleasant grin, he said, "I'm Anthony Lewis. Our parents used to be part of the Gray Lady's pack."

Redford directed his gaze away from the growling wolves. If his instincts had been perfectly happy this morning, they were clamoring for attention now, rattling in anger at the back of his mind, snarling *protect Mate-Jed-Journey, no other wolves*. He shut it out as best he could, because the last thing that anybody wanted was a fight to break out.

Well. The last thing anyone but *Jed* wanted. Because he still was holding his gun, though he had, surprisingly, lowered it to point at the ground. Which was pretty much as relaxed as he ever got in these situations.

"Inside the van are my brothers, Randall and Edwin," Anthony continued. "The other wolf you can smell is Redford Reed; he's a friend. The two non-Canos are Jed Walker, Redford's mate, and Victor Rathbone, also a friend."

"Whoa, whoa, not a mate. Not... mating." Jed glanced at Anthony, who gave him a baffled look in return. "But we're just here to do a little business with the boss lady. Want to drop the furry act so we can talk?"

One of the wolves sneezed, a sound that almost might have been a laugh. It took a step forward, and then it was a man with red hair past his shoulders, arms folded across his bare chest, completely unconcerned that his altogether was, well. Swinging in the altogether. "We could talk before, two-legs. And that one"—clear blue eyes darted over at Victor—"isn't Canos and definitely isn't human. Though he does smell rather—" The wolf huffed out a laugh. "—scrawny."

Victor gave a muffled squawk of indignation, but seeing as he remained inside the van, he didn't seem set on protesting *that* hard. "He's a medusa half blood," Anthony explained, smirking at the wolf's description. "Just don't accidentally meet his eyes, and you'll be fine."

"My name is Mallory. We patrol these woods." Mallory studied Anthony carefully. "How do I know we can trust you, Lewis?"

Far from the posturing and growling that Redford had expected from two wolves of their status, Anthony and Mallory were merely calmly studying each other—a little defensive, perhaps, but they didn't look close to starting a fight to prove dominance. Anthony lifted one shoulder in a shrug. "I can't really say anything that'll make you trust me," he apologized. "But I need help. That's why we're here, and you know it, because you can smell it. I'm not in any condition to start fights." He sounded pained to say it.

Mallory simply nodded, circling Anthony, ignoring Jed altogether. Anthony stood still under the study, meeting Mallory's eyes when he could. "Why is the rest of your pack hiding in the van?"

"Hardly hiding." Randall climbed out, Edwin following him, Knievel fast on his heels. Apparently she felt as if she had to keep him in line. Both of the remaining Lewises shed their clothes easily and shifted, flanking Anthony even as Mallory's group did him. Edwin glanced over at the van, yipping softly. Victor clambered out to stand beside Randall, and Redford was last, shoulders hunched. If Edwin expected him to turn, he wasn't going to. Not here. Jed was right there, arm pressed against Redford, seemingly unfazed by all the wolves.

Randall stood in front of Victor, keeping his place by Anthony's side. Mallory looked at each of them by turn, gaze lingering on Redford for a long moment, a twitch of a smile appearing when he studied the cat, who was mildly staring them all down, unimpressed. Then he chuckled softly. "You definitely need help," he told Anthony. "This is the sorriest pack I've ever seen." But he smiled, holding out his hand. "Come on. I'll take you to see the Lady."

Laughing at the comment, Anthony reached out to clasp Mallory's hand. "Thank you," he said gratefully. "Jed, Victor, Redford, you guys follow us in the van. We'll go on foot with Mallory."

Relieved—and still a little nervous about why the wolf's gaze had lingered on him for so long—Redford got back into the van. Once Jed had scooped up Knievel and gotten himself behind the wheel, he checked to be sure both Redford and Victor were settled. They watched out the dusty window as Mallory swung the gate open. The wolves started trotting their way down the road, flanking the Lewises on all sides, though Redford didn't know if that was for protection of the Lewises or their own security.

"Well, that went okay," Redford said hopefully as the van slowly crept along behind the wolves, Jed keeping his foot just barely on the gas. "I think. That went okay, right?"

"No one's dead, bleeding, or spewing out either end" was Jed's reply. "I count it as a win."

Redford rubbed his nose as the scent of wolf grew stronger. The dirt road started to falter as the trees grew denser, and Jed began to curse under his breath as the path became harder to find. The wolves obviously didn't have vehicles come in very often, because the only trail looked to be worn by foot. Occasionally, the wolves leading them would look back, a distinctly amused glint in their eyes at Jed's struggles with the van.

It seemed that the camp came into sight very suddenly. One minute the view outside the van had been nothing but trees. Then they emerged into a clearing which Redford hadn't even seen glimpses of through the forest. The scents hit him like a truck—wolves, a nearby river, fire, the smells of an entire community of hundreds living in secret.

Victor leaned forward to peer out the windshield. "Goodness," he remarked, looking fascinated.

"Holy fucking LARPers, batnerd." Jed hung his head out the window, staring around, eyes wide. "What the hell is this place?"

Redford thought that might be a good question. He leaned over alongside Victor as they continued to drive, his gaze darting back and forth, trying to take everything in. The clearing the camp was set in was massive, circled by thick tree cover. As far as Redford could see, there were cabins lining the edge of the circle, rough-hewn, hand built but sturdy looking, some so small they must only be a single room, some that must surely fit a few dozen people.

To the right stood larger buildings that Redford thought might be for community use. He twisted his head to look through the windows of one as they drove past, and stared in stunned silence at the rows of desks covered with books and pencils, young children attentively watching a teacher write on a blackboard.

"Jed, they have a *school*," he said, reluctantly turning away when he could no longer see through the windows. He caught a glimpse of a playground at the back of the school, a clearly hand-built slide and a seesaw, kids in human and wolf form alike playing happily.

There was a painful kind of sadness on Jed's face as he watched them, one fuzzy wolf darting around underneath the slide, apparently on the receiving end of a game of tag. For a long moment, Jed didn't say anything, fingers tightening on the wheel as he followed their escort to park the van alongside a building. "Yeah, Fido," Jed finally answered, quiet, voice thick as he ducked his head, checking his weapons, tightening the straps on his chest holster. "I see it."

Redford moved aside as Victor got out of the van, but didn't follow. "What's wrong?" Redford frowned at Jed. "Did you not like the school you went to?"

Jed seemed to be taking quite a long time to check all his guns. "My school was just fine," he said, words clipped, jaw tight. "Not my school that I'm thinkin' about, here." Before Redford could form the next question, Jed was swinging out of the van, tossing the keys to Anthony with a sharp whistle. "Come on, Red. Time to meet the furries."

Redford, as he hopped out of the van, worriedly hoped that the wolves wouldn't be insulted by Jed calling them *furries*. Knievel seemed content to march alongside their feet, tail thrashing in irritation when Jed attempted to pick her up. Randall was grabbing his clothes out of his bag, having changed back. Edwin didn't seem so inclined. Hopping on one foot as he got his shoes back on, Randall gave him a slight smile as Redford closed the van door behind him and looked out into the camp. They had parked near one of the bigger buildings, though Redford couldn't guess what it was used for—his gaze was more drawn to the bonfire set in what looked to be the direct center of the camp. There were wolves gathered around it, relaxing, reading, some of them curiously looking back at the newcomers. Redford instinctively hunched his shoulders and put himself near Jed's side.

"The Gray Lady is expecting us," Anthony called, absently dodging as Edwin— still a wolf—ran past his legs. "Jed, lose the weapons. This isn't a war meeting."

"Yeah, that's not happening, Lassie." Jed didn't even look at Anthony, his eyes restlessly roaming over the camp, the buildings, his shoulders tense. Jed didn't like to be put in situations where he didn't know the lay of the land ahead of time. Redford could see his gaze darting to the shadows of buildings, the edges of the bonfire, the thick darkness of the trees beyond the camp.

"Jed," Anthony tried again.

"You got fangs, princess fluffy?" Jed snapped. "You got teeth? Well I've got my damn guns. So shut up and keep walking." Redford could hear Anthony give a sigh, but he let the conversation drop. With every step, Jed seemed to get more irritated, fingers tight around the butt of one of his guns. He dropped to the back of the group, suspiciously studying the wolves they passed.

Edwin found this all rather funny, apparently, chuffing at Jed's knees before taking off in a run toward the large cabin they were approaching. "Edwin," Anthony barked, a sharp tone of urgency to his words.

It was echoed in Randall's more desperate, "Edwin!" His ears going back, Edwin skidded to a halt, looking over his shoulder mournfully. Redford glanced between the brothers and saw Victor doing the same out of the corner of his eye, wondering what was happening.

Anthony put a hand on Edwin's nape. "We're in unfamiliar company." Redford could only barely make out Anthony's words. "What's more, we're in the home of the oldest wolf alive. You can stay as you are, but please don't run around like a pup who thinks he owns the place."

Edwin's ears were pointed back, his tail still for the first time Redford could remember. After a moment, Edwin huffed a sigh and rolled over, showing his stomach with a whine. Randall rolled his eyes. "And stop acting like we're beating you, just because we want you to behave."

Wriggling his body, Edwin arched his head up, blowing a huff of air into Randall's face. Randall's stern expression didn't falter, but he, along with Anthony, gave Edwin's stomach a pat. "I know, I know. Lots of stuff to smell," Randall agreed with a sigh. "But later, okay? They might kick us out."

Redford sidled up to Randall as they continued walking. "Didn't Anthony let him off really easily?" Filtiarn—the alpha, the wolf in charge—would have reacted much more violently had any wolf under his command disobeyed him. "I haven't been in a pack in a while, but I remember punishment being, um, harsher."

Randall gave him a baffled look but didn't have time to speak. Anthony said, "We're here."

The wolves that had guided them into the camp had sat themselves nearby, and Mallory nodded toward the entrance of the building. "She doesn't like to be kept waiting."

Nervously, Randall straightened his sweater, pausing to fix Anthony's collar. "It's going to be fine," he murmured to his brothers, stooping down to fuss over Edwin's messy fur. "Just let me talk. It'll be fine."

Anthony gave Randall a look; it seemed to Redford that he wanted to speak, his mouth even opening as if to start. But Randall didn't need to meet his brother's eyes in order to immediately cut him off. "We've talked about this, Anthony," Randall said quietly.

"Doesn't mean I like it." Anthony sighed, pulling back to fidget with his shirt himself, purposely undoing the top button Randall had just finished putting into place. "It's my place."

"But this was my idea." Randall sounded so practical, so matter-of-fact, but Redford could see faint creases of worry lining his face. "Do you want to flip a coin?"

"Yes," Anthony grumbled.

"Too bad." Randall's hand paused halfway toward reaching out to Anthony, a low breath leaving him. "Ant...."

"I know." Anthony didn't sound happy, but he moved to close the distance between them, shoulder butting up against Randall's palm. "It'll be good. We'll all be fine." Randall's eyes met Anthony's, a silent conversation between the two; Redford felt suddenly awkward to be staring. He'd just never seen wolves interact like this before. He was half expecting Anthony to snap, to show dominance. Instead all he did was allow Randall to once again fix his shirt buttons, snapping his fingers once to get Edwin's attention. Edwin had apparently gotten distracted, rooting around under a nearby bush, but at the sound he immediately jerked around and came trotting back up to them, tail wagging happily.

"You're a mess," Randall informed Edwin archly.

Edwin didn't seem to mind. Randall and Anthony, though, immediately set out to try to brush dirt from his fur, much to Edwin's apparent distress.

Knievel was helping, grabbing Edwin's head between her paws and aggressively grooming the fur between his eyes before she stalked off to find Jed again, crying at him until he sighed and stooped, letting her jump up and settle onto his shoulders. Even Victor was running his hands through his hair, trying to look presentable. Redford chanced a look down at himself and grimaced. Perhaps he should have dressed nicer?

Edwin whined softly, nudging his nose into Randall's shoulder. Randall bowed his head, rubbing a hand over his brother's ears, obviously worried. But then he stood, brushing off his slacks. "Right. Okay. We should—"

"Oh, for fuck's sake." Never one to hesitate, Jed brushed past them all and strode into the cabin, rapping on the door as he passed. "We're here, sweetheart. Let's get this over with."

Redford winced as he followed. Normally, Jed's way of doing things didn't faze him, but there was an air of reverence to the cabin and the wolves waiting outside it. He could hear the Lewis brothers behind him, Victor at the very back, as they made their way through a short hallway that opened up into a wide meeting space. It was lushly decorated, brightly colored silk hanging over the windows, plush chairs lining the edges of the room. The only light within was provided by candles and the sunlight that struggled to filter through silk.

The Gray Lady herself was sitting cross-legged at the edge of a lavish rug woven in many different colors. Like the room she surrounded herself in, she was regal in appearance and brightly clad, dress nothing more than soft folds of fabric gracefully draping to the floor, her white hair falling loose around her shoulders. The candlelight seemed to flicker in dark eyes as she opened them, lips parting in a white smile against olive skin. She seemed young and old at the same time, an ancient sadness in her gaze even as she moved elegantly, welcoming them all in. "Come, my children," she said, sharing her smile equally with Redford, Randall, Edwin, and Anthony. "Sit."

Jed started forward, his hand at Redford's elbow, to be stopped by a low growl. The Gray Lady's eyes flashed yellow, her smile never fading even as her expression darkened. "Not you, human. You may stand, if you must be present. But this is a conversation for wolves." Her mood shifted slightly as she nodded to Victor. "Half blood, you are welcome to listen. Keep the human in line."

Redford glanced at Jed, unsure. He didn't want to sit now that Jed had been refused it. The choice was made for him by Anthony's hand at his elbow, tugging him down until his knees buckled and he sat awkwardly. "Sorry, Jed," he murmured, reaching over to curl his fingers around Jed's calf, wanting to keep in contact.

"It's an honor to meet you," Anthony said, his head bowed. He'd placed himself closest to the Gray Lady. "Thank you for agreeing to see us."

"I would ask you how you found me, little wolf," the Gray Lady said, tone kind once more. "But I can smell Filtiarn's foul work from here. I take it you have sought me out, werewolf?" All eyes turned to Redford as the Gray Lady sat, expectantly awaiting his response.

Redford flinched under the weight of her gaze. "Sorry," he said automatically. Did he smell bad to wolves? He really hoped not. He hated to think that riding in a van with him might have been awful for the Lewises. "And no, that's not exactly why we're here. We, um...." He looked at Anthony, waiting for him to jump in and save Redford from himself.

But when it came time to speak, Anthony seemed to hesitate. He'd curled his hands into his lap, the same knotted stiffness that Redford recognized as Anthony attempting to stop the shaking. So it was Randall who stood, bowing before the Gray Lady, all that nervousness and quiet restraint bundled up and forgotten. He spoke softly, yes, but there was a strength to each word. "My lady. I'm afraid we came with Redford because we weren't sure you would see us otherwise."

"And why would I deny you?" she asked, head tipped to the side, watching Randall carefully.

"Because our parents were once part of your pack. We are the Lewises."

There was a long pause before the Gray Lady clucked her tongue with a quiet, "I see."

"We've come back because we need your help, my lady. My brother, Anthony, he's sick. You're the only hope we have for a cure." Randall took a step forward, hand reaching out to the Gray Lady, pleading. "Please. I will do anything. Pay any price. Just... help my brother."

"And what would you have me do?" The Gray Lady turned to Anthony. "What ails you, wolf?"

"If you can't help, I understand," Anthony said hastily. "It may be beyond your ability." He glanced back at Randall and Edwin. "But human doctors can't help me. It's...."

He hesitated again before saying it, like he was embarrassed.

"Canine Parkinson's," Anthony finally said with a sigh. "It's degenerative."

The Gray Lady stood, going to her window, looking out over the camp. The sound of voices filtered in, the noises of a thriving pack, the smells of meat cooking. It was all so calm and peaceful, like something out of one of the books Redford had read in his childhood. It was a home. "Do you know why your parents would not have been welcome here again?" she asked, looking over her shoulder at the Lewises.

"Not exactly, ma'am," Anthony said politely, though his expression had tightened. "But I can hazard a guess."

"There are men who hunt us. There is a world that does not know of our existence, a fact which I work very hard to maintain. A lone wolf is a danger to all of that. One family, one mated pair, it is not a pack. It's a risk that I cannot allow. Letting you come back after your parents chose to leave, what would that say? How would I begin to explain to the rest of the pack why you should not be shunned, as we shun all others who chose to walk away from our protections? As we shun those who put all of us in danger."

Jed shifted beside Redford, lips tight, fingers curling around his gun. He cut a quick glance over at Anthony and stayed silent, though it was clear he desperately wanted to make a point.

Anthony drew in a deep breath. "If you'd like to shun us, ma'am, I'll accept that decision," he said, his tone still polite. A thread of steel crept into his voice as he continued, "But we are not our parents. We did not make the decision to leave. And if your decision to shun us is based solely on how difficult it would be to explain to others, we'd be glad to leave however quickly you'd like us to."

There was a long, tense moment, Jed shifting a step closer, Edwin's hackles rising as he backed up against Anthony's leg. But then the Gray Lady smiled. Tight and powerful, yes, but she smiled and waved her hand. "Go. You wolves may stay the night so I can think on this matter. Your human and half blood may even join us for the evening meal. I will meet with you in the morning to discuss this further." She reached out, taking Anthony's shoulders in her hands, leaning forward to rest her forehead against his. "For now, Lewis pack, leave me, and sleep well."

"Thank you," Anthony whispered to her. He stepped back, and inclined his head, the lines of tension eased out of his expression. "Thank you, ma'am."

He turned and hustled his brothers out of the building. Redford followed at a slower pace, absently finding Jed's hand with his own. Jed's fingers tightened on his immediately, though he kept cutting glances back as they left the cabin and the door was shut firmly behind them.

"So," Jed drawled once they were all huddled around together, blinking in the sunlight once again, "that was a trip. Not exactly big on welcomes here."

"I'm really sorry, Jed. Victor." Anthony shook his head, looking surprised. "I wasn't aware they'd be so xenophobic."

"No apology needed," Victor said. He didn't sound bothered by it at all. "If you think that's bad, you should see some sections of the half-blood community. You'd think it was the apartheid all over again."

"Wait, so, she hates bugs?" Jed was looking between them, confused. "Doesn't everybody?"

Redford, like everybody else, gave Jed a questioning stare. "No, she hates humans," Redford explained. "Not bugs."

"Oh." Nose wrinkling, Jed turned to Redford. "Isn't xeno-whatever a bug? The one with the legs all...." He wiggled his fingers and did a face with all his teeth showing. "Or wait. No. That's the alien from that movie, right? So she hates bug aliens." Knievel, disrupted by his motions, jumped lightly down and wandered away, tail waving, eyes shining in the sunlight. She apparently wanted to explore, though she didn't go far.

Anthony started laughing, a deep, full-throated sound. "No, Jed. Xenophobic means she doesn't like people foreign to her."

"But you have a good point about the xenomorph aliens," Victor said brightly. "The key word is *xeno*, meaning foreign or alien, hence—"

"The point is," Anthony cut in, still smiling, "She doesn't trust anybody that's not a full-blooded wolf. I'm sorry, again, I didn't want you to get treated so...." He glanced back at the cabin, seemingly torn between bluntness and reverence. "Rudely."

"But at least we have a chance to speak with her again," Randall said, stubbornly clinging to the good points. "For now, at least, she hasn't forced us all to leave."

"Just the humans." Mallory had come up behind them, smiling, clapping Anthony on the shoulder. "And then, only after the meal tonight. That's practically a warm welcome."

"Hold on." Jed's eyes narrowed. "What do you mean we're getting kicked out?"

Mallory shrugged. "Just got my orders. You and the half blood are to be escorted out of the camp after evening meal. We don't allow humans on our territory, not while everyone's sleeping."

"What, cause we're going to slit your throats?" Jed bitched.

That scenario didn't seem to be too far-fetched to Mallory, though, who simply said mildly, "Or something like that. Look, friends, I'm sorry. That's just how it is. No one trusts humans, and half bloods are too close to them. Especially with the trouble we've had with hunters. There's a town two hours north. You can find a room there, I'm sure. And it's not as if we're kicking you out immediately. Food gets served a little before sundown. That's plenty of time to visit the gift shop on the way out."

Redford saw Victor give Jed a horrified look. Jed nodded, seemingly accepting this. "Fine. Red, Vickie, and I will go have a spa day and—What now, Pippi Longfur?"

Mallory had been shaking his head, then arched an eyebrow at the nickname. "We can't just let a wolf wander off. Even if it's with you. Aren't you listening? We've got hunters out there, looking for us. A lone wolf is a danger to the whole pack. I'm sorry, but until the Gray Lady says otherwise, the wolves stay inside, the humans stay outside. End of story." He paused, eyes flicking to where Knievel was happily fighting with a flower stem. "Though if you'd like to keep your cat with you, I can't see a problem with that."

Redford hated that idea already. The concession for Knievel was hardly the same. Redford had barely spent a night apart from Jed since Jed had first burst into his grandmother's house pretending to be a repairman. There had been a few nights, times when Jed had been out on a job in the early days when Redford hadn't helped as much— but even then, Redford had stayed at Jed's apartment.

He'd never told Jed this, but staying there surrounded by Jed's scents had reassured him far more than Jed's occasional postcard had. Though Redford did appreciate the postcards!

But Mallory looked like he wouldn't be swayed. There were a lot of wolves around too, ones that would probably back him up if they argued the point.

"Yeah, that's not going to happen." Jed moved a step closer to Redford, arms folded, an almost bored expression on his face. That wasn't a good sign. "Me and Red, we're together. Period. End of story. Finito. Whatever wolf barky thing that means full stop. Where he goes, I go. So either find me a place to bunk or he and I will head to the van."

"Jed," Victor said. He gave a nervous glance over his shoulder, where several wolves were beginning to look distinctly unhappy at Mallory being disagreed with. "Perhaps this isn't worth a fight. We are in *their* culture, on *their* territory."

"Fuck you, princess." Jed's voice rose. Mallory shifted a bit, eyebrow raising, moving a step closer to them. Jed's hand was on his gun, eyes flashing in anger. "You think I'm going to let some teen wolf with a hair gel problem separate me from Fido, you—"

Randall shoved Jed backward, giving them space. Redford instinctively straightened his stance, scowling at Randall—though it looked like the flash of yellow in his eyes went without notice. Randall's hands were on Jed's shoulders, voice low and urgent, a thread of steel and worry running through his words. "Listen to me, human, and listen very carefully. You are not in your world. You are not anywhere you understand. You can use your guns and your explosives and start a fight, but if you do, the very *best* thing that could happen is that we'll be shunned. And I know you don't care. I know right now you think that's a great idea." Randall's eyes slid over to Anthony, and something painful entered his expression. "But if you do that, you are killing my brother. Do you hear me? You will be killing him. All for a night spent with Redford."

Redford could hear the very distinct sound of Jed's teeth grinding, his hand tightening on the butt of his gun. Redford knew that look, he knew the way Jed's shoulders were tightening, how his gaze was flicking between Mallory and the other wolves—he was trying to decide if he could fight his way out, if there was a way beyond the path he really didn't want to take. But, in the end, he let out a slow breath and nodded, a sharp jerk of his head.

"Fine, Cujo," Jed relented, jaw tight. "One night. One. We solve this shit or I am going to get really cranky."

Randall seemed relieved at that, his shoulders slumping slightly as he nodded. His "thank you" was ignored as Jed shoved past him, going to Redford and wrapping an arm around him possessively.

"I was going to get really cranky too," Redford said. "You know, if anybody cares to actually feel threatened by that." He doubted they would. Explosions were a lot scarier than a man who couldn't even really shift properly.

"I'd feel extremely threatened," Anthony said, patting Redford's shoulder consolingly. "I'm going to take Edwin and Randall to unpack, check out the guest cabins." He looked at Jed and Victor, apology crossing his expression once again. "I'll see what I can do to sway their decision to keep you out."

"Or you'll focus on the reason we're here," Randall said under his breath. "Honestly, you people are acting like it's the end of that movie with the boat and the iceberg."

"Nerd," Anthony said fondly. He gave Randall a light shove. "Come on. Mallory's taking us to our cabin."

"*Titanic*. Even I know that." Edwin had shifted back, not bothering to find pants as he curiously walked around, eyes wide while he watched all the other wolves. Redford determinedly kept his eyes above waistline—that was just awkward. "Come on. Let's see if we can figure out where they keep the food. I'm starving!"

Redford's gaze went over Edwin's shoulder to a pack of wolves walking past. His eyes widened. Apparently Edwin's clothing choices—or lack of them—weren't actually all that unusual here.

"Is this part nudist colony?" Victor grumbled. He sounded torn between being scandalized and giving a few of them an interested eye.

A growl rumbled in the back of Randall's throat. He bit the noise down with a quick cough. Victor looked even more startled at the sound than Randall did. "Right. Edwin, pants. Now. We'll put our bags away, and Anthony can rest while we get food. Redford? Do you want to come with us to the cabin?"

Edwin protested, shifting back to wolf form as if to keep away from the dreaded clothing, streaking off after Mallory, who was waiting a short ways away. Edwin yipped loudly back to them, tail wagging eagerly. Knievel gave him chase, speeding off like a demon and then stopping, grooming herself and pretending she wasn't the least bit interested. She, at least, seemed fully comfortable here. Jed was keeping half an eye on her, but the cat seemed perfectly content to explore and stay within sight.

"I'll stay with Jed until dinner," Redford replied. "I'll find you later?"

Randall nodded, hand easily cupping Anthony's elbow like he wasn't doing anything odd. Like he didn't need to help hold his brother upright. "Sounds good. Try and stay out of trouble."

Redford watched them leave. Anthony was walking slower than usual, his shoulders hunched, though Redford wouldn't have noticed anything wrong if he didn't know that Anthony was sick. A glance at his watch informed him they had about an hour until dinner.

"I don't know how I'm going to sleep," Redford admitted. "It's usually... you're usually there."

Rumbling out a sigh, Jed reached up to rub his fingers across Redford's cheek. "I know. But hey, you'll be with all the wolves, right? That's going to be good."

Redford just shrugged. "Still nothing compared to you." As soon as he heard his own words, he sighed mentally at himself. Moping wouldn't help anything. "Maybe I'll stage a jailbreak," he continued, perking up at the thought of it.

Jed drew him in for a kiss. "You stay put," he ordered, nipping lightly at Redford's lip. "Last thing I want is a bunch of flea-bitten mutts getting pissy. Besides, I won't be that far away."

"Venturing outside for a wolf may not be the smartest idea, either," Victor said cautiously. "Twice now we've heard mention of hunters."

"You think that's legit?" Jed, arm still looped around Redford's waist, keeping him close, squinted out into the woods, like he could magically see everything that lay beyond. "Might have to do a little hunting of my own, we stay here much longer. Just to see what everyone's so worried about."

"Just not tonight," Redford insisted. "I don't like the thought of you tracking hunters on your own."

Huffing out a little laugh, Jed drew Redford in, both arms slipping around him, fingers pushing up under Redford's shirt to play along warm skin. "No hunting tonight," he murmured, lips trailing along Redford's jaw. "We're a team. I'll just be sleeping right on the other side of this damn camp, dreaming about you. Deal?"

86

"Deal," Redford replied, smiling against Jed's cheek.

"*Ew.*" An unfamiliar voice broke Redford out of his Jed-induced distraction. Startled, he glanced over Jed's shoulder to see a woman watching them, her nose wrinkled.

"Um, sorry," Redford offered, flustered. "Are public displays of affection not okay here? I'm really sorry, I'll—"

"It's not that." She cocked her head, staring at Jed. "It's just... *him.*" She nodded toward Jed, looking baffled. "How can you even stand to get so close, with that scent?"

Redford growled in response before he could restrain himself. The dark instinct that had made itself at home ever since Fil was curling hot in his gut. Redford dug his nails into his palms to try to force it away. "Jed smells fine," he said, his voice more a snarl than anything else.

There was the light touch of Jed's fingers on his back, Jed's voice interjecting calmly, "I shower and everything. Pardon us, sweetheart. We're just going to keep moving, if you don't mind." Then Jed was leading him away, Victor following worriedly behind. "It's okay, babe," Jed was saying. "Doesn't even matter. We're fine."

Redford made himself close his eyes, take a deep breath, and then another one. The woman was shaking her head in disbelief as she walked away—Redford could hear her murmur something about *humans* under her breath, the tone of it distinctly displeased.

He rubbed his hands over his face, hard, hoping there wasn't any yellow in his eyes. "Sorry," he muttered. "I just don't like it when people insult you. Or *us.*" It had been a problem a few times before. Once, a client had been confused about why Jed would hang around with a hobo. Another time, a complete stranger in a bar had told them they looked completely unsuited for each other. Redford had not quite figured out how to just ignore the comments.

Jed's hands ran through Redford's hair, pulling him in close so that Jed could circle him in a tight embrace. "I just figured," he drawled, voice sounding a little amused, "that as much as I like to stir up fights, maybe you shouldn't. These are kind of your people, right?"

Redford looked over toward the center of the camp. As dinner was getting closer, more and more wolves were gathering around the bonfire. They looked content in one another's company, easily sharing space and cooking duties alike. There were no scuffles for dominance, and nobody looked miserable. He still didn't quite believe Anthony when he said that ranks like alpha weren't actually a thing. But looking at them now, maybe Anthony was right. Maybe these wolves—these Cano that could shift painlessly whenever they liked—had no rankings. That still didn't ensure that Redford would fit in any easier, though. He wasn't a werewolf, and he wasn't a Cano either.

"Not really," Redford finally murmured in reply to Jed. "Should we get ready for dinner? I don't want to be late."

For a moment, it looked like Jed was going to say something else. Long fingers touched the edge of Redford's eye, like Jed could capture the wild yellow that curled up in them sometimes. But then Jed smiled that cocky grin and pulled away. "Sounds like a plan. Vickie has to primp, and you know that takes ages."

The only response that came from Victor was an exasperated sigh. He looked even more awkward than Redford felt. Redford might be caught between the two types of wolves, but Victor was the only half blood in the camp. Jed, however, being the only human, looked nearly perfectly at ease, if a bit wary.

Victor didn't wind up primping, but Redford did. He wanted to look his best if he was going to be judged from all angles. He changed his sweater three times before Jed took the luggage away and insisted he looked perfect. Redford wasn't sure of that, but he supposed Jed knew what he was talking about.

Then again, Jed might say the same thing if Redford wore a potato sack, so perhaps Jed's opinion was not to be trusted.

A loud bell was rung to indicate that dinner had started, and Redford nervously made his way back into the center of camp with Jed at his side, Victor trailing behind them. They'd left Knievel curled up in Redford's cabin with a can of tuna. She seemed perfectly at home. Redford just wished he could be so content. Many more wolves had gathered outside—Redford was willing to bet it was nearly the entire population of the camp. He was hit with a chaotic mix of too many scents, all of them underscored by one thing: *wolf.*

Some stared at them as they got closer to the bonfire. Some, visibly uncomfortable, shifted away. But some seemed not to mind, and those were the wolves that handed Redford, Jed, and Victor plates heaped with meat and bread, pushed glasses of water and home-brewed beer into their hands. Though Jed's gaze was near constantly darting back and forth, his expression brightened as he tasted the beer.

They found a more sparsely populated area a short distance away from the bonfire, sitting on long logs that served as communal seats. While Redford might be feeling a little anxious from being around this many wolves, he had to admit their food was amazing. He'd never been able to cook meat *this* good.

Halfway through dinner, Victor had found himself a wolf that obviously didn't mind the smell of half blood so much and was excitedly asking him questions about wolf culture, having to shout to be heard over the din of conversation. Redford was more than happy to keep to himself and Jed, leaning against Jed's shoulder as the sunlight grew dimmer and the bonfire was stoked higher.

He found himself envying the wolves. They were so comfortable with one another, perhaps something that was brought about by communal living. They were like the Lewises on a much larger scale: completely at peace with what they were.

Redford didn't want dinner to end, because as the food grew scarcer, his time with Jed for the night grew shorter. He rubbed his cheek against Jed's shoulder, feeling Jed's arm tighten around his shoulders in response. But time, like it always did, had a bad habit of continuing to tick onward. The wolves started leaving, and the noise around them grew quieter until there were just a few small groups of people remaining.

Redford caught sight of Mallory across the bonfire. The man was talking with a few friends, but when he saw Redford watching, he nodded in the direction of the gate.

It was time for Jed and Victor to go.

Jed, surprisingly, didn't argue. He stood, fishing the keys to the van out of his pocket. With a whistle, he tossed them to Victor. "Take it into town if you want, princess," Jed said. "I'm going to sleep by the gate."

"Really?" Victor blinked at Jed, perplexed. "Though I'll only admit this under extreme duress, I wouldn't mind having to share a hotel room with you again. I saw one on the way here that wasn't too terribly far away. I'm sure they'll still have some available rooms."

Jed smirked, clapping his hand on Victor's shoulder. "That's the nicest thing you've ever said to me. But I'm not leaving Red. If the closest I can be is the damn gate, then the gate's it."

Victor didn't look inclined to argue the point too much. "All right." He pocketed the keys. "Before I leave, get what you need for the night out of the van."

"Come on." Jed's hand had dropped to clasp Redford's, like he couldn't bear to let go. Redford knew the feeling. "I'll walk you to it, grab my bag."

They walked back to the van, and Redford waited patiently while Victor tutted at Jed and kept reminding him of things Jed might need for the night, such as reading material if he got bored and a pocketknife should he ever need a small screwdriver to unscrew something. Redford hid his smile as Jed grew increasingly more and more exasperated at the suggestions, and finally, he and Jed watched Victor drive the van out of the camp.

Redford winced as Victor nearly hit a tree. He obviously didn't drive much.

"Okay, where to?" he asked Jed.

"By the gate. So you know right where I am if you need me." Jed cupped the back of Redford's neck, lightly pulling him in for a kiss. "And so you know I'll hear you if something happens."

"Okay," Redford agreed. Needless to say, he wasn't particularly happy about it. He deliberately walked as slowly as he could as they made their way toward the gate, staying close. When they got there, Jed carefully closed it behind him, fussing over it like it was very important he get everything just so.

"I'll be right here," he finally said gruffly, unrolling his sleeping bag. "And if you need me...." He paused, looking up at Redford, giving him a very small smile. "Well. Just whistle."

Redford absently clasped his fingers over his necklace. Given to him by Jed in the midst of the chaos with Filtiarn, the necklace had never been taken off unless absolutely necessary. He bumped his fingers over the cold metal of the whistle and the smooth edges of Jed's army dog tags. "I will," he promised. "Are you sure you'll be okay?"

Jed hooked his fingers into Redford's belt, tugging him closer to the gate slung across the dirt road. "I've slept in worse places, Fido," he rumbled, resting their foreheads together. The gate was cold metal, digging into their stomachs, but Jed didn't seem to notice. "Go. Sleep. You need your rest. And keep an eye on our spoiled cat. You know how she fusses if she doesn't have someone adoring her."

Redford couldn't leave without kissing Jed good-bye first. He'd see Jed in the morning, he knew he would, but he still clung to him like he wouldn't see him for days. Maybe he was being a bit overdramatic; he just hadn't slept without Jed in the same bed for a long time now.

He had to make himself pull away. That didn't last long as Redford ducked closer for another kiss, but after that he squeezed Jed's hand, forcing himself to separate from Jed for real this time. "Good night," he said. "I'll see you in the morning."

Jed didn't seem to want to let him go, either. But he forced his hand away, cupping Redford's face briefly. "Night, babe." And then, so much softer, "I love you."

"I love you too."

He wanted to stay. Or to haul Jed back over the line that separated them, the small bit of iron and dust that was keeping them apart. But just as Redford was reaching out again, to insist that he *could* leave, that he could so easily just slip free of the camp, there was a rustle in the woods beyond them. Two yellow eyes blinked out of the shadows of the trees; a wolf was watching them. Watching the human, Redford realized. One of the pack's sentries was making sure that Jed didn't go anywhere.

The walk back to the cabin that had been assigned to him was miserable. Redford kept looking back at Jed every few steps, just to make sure he was still okay and hadn't suddenly vanished in the few seconds he hadn't been looking. And then he turned the corner and Jed was out of sight completely, the bend in the trail hiding the gate from the rest of the camp. Redford trudged to his cabin, head down, already wishing it were morning.

He could hear the Lewises in the next cabin over. His own, Redford had discovered, was perfectly bland. As he went inside, the only colors he could see were brown and white, though it seemed comfortable despite the sparseness. The most comforting part of it was Knievel, already asleep on the bed, just like she would have been at home. After pacing around the small room, Redford realized he had nothing else to do besides get ready for bed.

Half an hour after his head hit the pillow, Knievel graciously sharing the mattress with him, Redford was forced to come to the realization that he was not going to be able to sleep. Frustrated, he turned, and grew even more frustrated when he nearly rolled off the single bed, having gotten used to Jed's ridiculously large one.

This wasn't working.

He knew, logically, that this was only for the night. Tomorrow they would be able to speak to the Gray Lady again, and once she saw that Jed and Victor were trustworthy, she might let them stay. Redford knew he wasn't going to fall apart over one night without Jed. But his instincts were clamoring in the background of his mind, pushing a dull ache into his chest with how much he missed Jed.

Redford growled to himself in exasperation, flopping over to stare at the ceiling. The wolf in him wanted his companion. His thoughts were pacing back and forth uneasily with a steady mantra of *Jed, Jed, Jed.*

He gave up and got out of bed.

The air was cold when Redford stepped outside. The bonfire was smaller now but still glowing in the distance, splashing orange light over the camp in contrast to the moon's white glow. Footsteps crunching on dirt and gravel, Redford rounded the bend of the faint trail, heading toward the gate. His eyes were still adjusting to the dark when he spotted Jed, a fair distance away.

Jed couldn't sleep either, it seemed. Redford could hear the steady pace of his footsteps, could smell his wariness even from here. The scent of the wolf sentinel was just as strong, though Redford couldn't see him any longer. As he drew nearer, Redford expected to be stopped. There was nothing more than a warning snort, though, the almost silent noise that let Redford know they were being watched.

In the chill of the night, wearing only the old sweatpants he slept in, Redford silently padded closer. "Jed," he whispered when he reached the gate. "Why are you still up?"

He heard the huff of noise that was Jed's nearly silent laugh. "I could ask you the same thing," Jed murmured. "What are you doing out here?" Redford could hear a rustle of fabric, and then Jed was leaning over the gate, wrapping his own sweatshirt around Redford's shoulders. "You're cold. You should be inside. Is something wrong?"

"No. I just can't sleep," Redford sighed. Even as he stood, his eyelids felt heavy, and the ground looked awfully comfortable. He just wanted to sleep.

He hugged Jed's sweatshirt closer around his shoulders. In the distance, there was a very faint howl, joined by two others. These wolves, of course, didn't have to wait until the full moons to go running whenever they liked.

Neither did Redford, he supposed. But he didn't want to think that way right then, not when those howls were an invite to come join them. *Come run with us*, they said. *Be free.*

"I think I'm going to sleep here," Redford said decisively. He could definitely sleep on the ground. At least he'd be close to Jed.

"No way" was Jed's instant response. "It's freezing and the ground is hard. You have a cabin, Fido, and a bed. That's where you should be."

"Oh, stop protesting," Redford grumbled. He sat down, bundled Jed's sweatshirt up for a pillow, and then lay down fully, stretching out on the hard ground. "This is fine. You're not the only who has slept in worse places."

There was a long pause, and Redford could almost smell all the arguments Jed was biting back. Finally, with a drawn-out sigh, Jed reached down to grab his sleeping bag. "Stubborn wolf," he muttered, but his tone was fond. He leaned over the gate to spread his sleeping bag out, followed by his pillow and the extra blankets Victor had insisted he bring. "Here. You are not trained in sleeping in shitty conditions. You are going to be warm and slightly comfortable."

Redford gave Jed a *look* and opened the sleeping bag. He laid it out like a mattress, half on his side, half on Jed's side, the gate between them. He did the same to the blankets, then crawled under them, putting his head on the balled-up sweatshirt. Now he almost felt like he could sleep. It was uncomfortable, to be honest, but he'd spent many a night on his grandmother's cold basement floor. Having a thin mattress and a blanket was luxury compared to that.

Jed reached out, took Redford's hand, and held it in the space between them, the line that delineated the wolf's pack and the rest of the world. "You are something else, Fido," he said, bending his head to kiss Redford's knuckles. He lay down on the other side of the sleeping bag.

"Get some sleep," Redford urged. He echoed Jed's previous fond teasing. "Stubborn human."

"Damn straight. I am all human, baby." Jed grinned, a leer in his tone. "You like it like that."

Redford laughed quietly. Only Jed could possibly turn that into innuendo. "I do," he confirmed, squeezing Jed's hand. "And I think you smell great." No matter what the wolves here might say or indicate.

"Well, you're the only one who gets to sniff me," Jed murmured, approaching sleep starting to slur his words slightly. "So that's a good thing. All those other furry asses, they can smell someone else. No smelling for them."

Redford let his eyes fall closed as he smiled. "Good. I wouldn't be happy if they tried." He fell silent as he absently rubbed his thumb over Jed's knuckles, relishing the one point of contact they had. "Night, Jed."

CHAPTER
6

Randall

LONG BEFORE birdsong crept through the morning, long before the mist was scorched away by the rising sun, Randall was out of bed, standing at the window and watching the camp beyond. Some wolves were early risers, creeping out on two legs or four to greet the barely-there morning.

Randall's nose twitched as the faint scents of bacon and coffee drifted from the communal kitchens. He should get some, for Anthony. The morning cold lately seemed to make Anthony stiffer, make walking just a little bit harder. Randall tried to think ahead most days, to simply provide alternatives to the actions that caused Anthony the most issues. So he should go and get breakfast now, before Anthony was awake, or else he'd be pretending everything was fine, that everything was *normal*, and shuffling a painful path across the camp to get it himself.

Sighing softly, shoving his hair out of his face, Randall glanced down at his watch. Given how deeply Anthony was sleeping and how long the past few days had been, he probably had another two hours before his brother would wake up. Enough time, maybe, to do what he needed to. And then he would bring breakfast.

Edwin was passed out in one of the beds, limbs sprawled everywhere, blankets tangled by his feet. Randall paused to cover him, to smooth the blankets around Edwin and gently rub his hand through the messy waterfall of blond hair. Edwin snorted in his sleep, rolling over, ever the exhausted pup, even now. Randall turned to Anthony, who slept in wolf form. Always protecting them, Anthony, always doing what was necessary to keep them safe. So he slept that way to have every advantage possible, should the worst happen. The chill in the air would make it even more difficult for this form to get out of bed. Brow creased in concern, Randall gathered the blankets from his own abandoned mattress and tucked them around Anthony, careful not to wake him as he fussed over the covers.

He grabbed a sweater and slipped into his shoes, then silently crept from the cabin. He left footprints in the mist-dampened grass, a ghost trail over bent green, making his way toward the Gray Lady's home. Two wolves were standing at attention outside her door, but they did no more than flick an ear toward him as Randall passed. The door seemed larger today, more imposing without his brothers at his side, without Anthony to lead them.

But that was why he was here. So, after a moment, Randall straightened his tie, smoothed a hand down his worn gray sweater, and lightly knocked on her door.

There was no answer for a long while. Randall shifted his feet, awkward and cold, but he didn't leave. Both of the guardian wolves ignored him. The faint sounds and scents of the camp seemed far behind him. It was just him, alone on a porch, waiting. Finally, there was the soft noise of movement from within, and the door released, swinging open slowly to admit him.

Randall hesitated. He wanted to move swiftly, with purpose. The way Anthony would. He wanted to march in and demand respect, to earn their way into the pack. But he hesitated. Hand on the doorway, he paused, listening to the measured footsteps from within, the hiss of boiling water, the clink of a spoon on china. And he nearly left. Because who was he to approach the oldest of them all? He was books and research, he was knowledge of things long past. There was no *power* in him.

Not like Anthony.

Not like her.

But his brother was sick. Anthony was dying, was *fading*, bit by bit. So Randall screwed up his courage and stepped inside.

The Gray Lady was seated, pouring a cup of tea, seemingly unconcerned with him. Randall politely stood by the doorway, closing it behind him to keep the damp morning air from her warm cabin. Long seconds turned to minutes, ticking away, but Randall was silent. The Gray Lady seemed to demand that kind of patience.

A low table filled one half of the room, but Randall didn't dare sit. The Gray Lady was at the head, holding court with ghosts, the gentle morning breeze curling around the bright fabrics that covered the windows. Last night the room had seemed so much more welcoming. Then again, last night Randall had his family by his side. Now it was only him.

Finally, she spoke. "You have sought me out, little one." There was a laugh in her voice. Her eyes sought his over the rim of her mug. "I did not realize we had an appointment."

"You said you needed time to think." Randall took a step forward, hands spread in supplication. "I realize that it's only been a day—"

"Less than that." The Lady set her cup down, legs crossed and arms resting loosely on her knees as she leaned forward to study him with that intent, piercing gaze. "Barely a full night passed before you were back at my door."

"I know," Randall admitted, having the grace, at least, to sound sheepish. "I apologize. But the matter at hand is not one that allows for procrastination."

"You think I am dawdling?" Her voice trilled upward, not entirely in amusement, a warning entering her words.

"I think that if you are who I believe you to be, you hardly needed time to think. You knew what you wanted to do the moment we arrived." There was a faint accusation there, Randall raising his jaw slightly. "My brother is a wolf, my lady. He is one of yours. Whatever our parents' sins in your eyes, I do not believe you intend to deny him."

"Oh, really? And tell me, little wolf, how do you know my mind?"

"You are Liadan. The mother of us all. I've read about you all my life. My father kept books, and I read them all. You wouldn't turn away a wolf in need." Randall took another step closer, daring in his desperation. "My brother is ill, my lady. Tell me what you need me to do, what I should say, what the magic words are. Tell me anything and I'll do it. Just tell me you'll help him."

Another silence descended on them, this one unbearable. Randall wanted to scream at her, to rip the silence apart, to force her to speak. But he made himself stand still as she stared at him, eyes calm. She stood, every movement liquid, turning her back to him while she prepared more tea, as if there was nothing else to do that day besides make *tea*. At the fireplace in the corner, she made busy work with the kettle and water, pouring in careful, measured moments. In that moment, Randall hated her. She held Anthony's life in her hands, and she refused to speak.

"He is a leader, your brother," the Gray Lady mused as she added sugar to the cup. "We have need of those. You and your brother are strong, healthy, so he must be fit to lead."

"He's taken care of us our whole lives," Randall said, voice tight, studying the line of her back, the set of her shoulders, trying to read anything at all from her. "He's never gotten to be anything but our brother. Even when he was a kid, all he did was protect us. He's the best man in the world."

The clink of her spoon against the china was like nails grating against his back. He wanted an answer. He'd done the research, he'd read the books, and he knew what it *should* be. But she was refusing to give him the satisfaction of it, the peace of knowing that he'd done what he was supposed to. When she at last returned to her seat, Randall's hands were all but shaking, his nails digging into his palms as he forced himself to remain silent, waiting for her.

"You are very impertinent, speaking to me as you do. You are not your pack's leader."

She didn't sound angry, but Randall instinctively took a step back, his shoulders losing some of their defiant slant. "I know," he agreed quietly. "But—"

"But it's for your brother," she finished, and Randall nodded. The spoon was moved slowly in her tea, silver dragging through tan. She seemed entranced by it, letting the quiet fall once more. Her next words held an edge of warning. "The pack is kept safe only by its cohesion. I will not tolerate any lone wolves. Those who leave will be cutting themselves off from my protection."

Randall nodded. Whatever the price, it would be worth it, if it got Anthony the help he needed. "We are not our parents," he reminded her.

"No," the Gray Lady agreed. "You are not." That seemed to decide her. She put the tea aside, standing and holding out her hand. "You and your brothers may stay. We will give you whatever assistance we have."

It was like a dark, tangled ball of sour fear was suddenly pulled from his throat. Randall took her hand, bowing his head to kiss her knuckles, gratitude babbling out of him, the words all slurred together and meaningless. She smiled at him, and with a graceful gesture she led him to the door. "Geoffry"—she gestured to one of the wolves— "let the healers know that Anthony Lewis is to be put in their care. Give him whatever help he requires."

Randall turned to thank her again, only to find her shaking her head. "I do not know if there is anything we can do," she warned quietly. "His sickness may be beyond the scope of our healers. But if your brother is to die, at least he will do so with his own kind."

And then she was gone. Geoffry had taken off, leaving the remaining guardian to watch Randall climb down the stairs, walk across the grass, in a daze. It felt like he'd been in the Gray Lady's presence for hours, and yet the sun was barely peeking above the horizon. Nothing at all had changed.

He wanted to feel relief. Instead, that knot of fear simply settled back in, clutching at him. They were there. They were accepted.

But it might not make any difference at all.

His feet led him. Randall barely paid attention to where he was walking, his shoes damp in the grass, faint shivers sliding down his arms. Randall wasn't one for wolfish running, for letting go of everything but instincts. At the moment, though, he felt the need to be *wolfish*. He didn't shift, but he wandered around the outside of the camp, near the trees, lost in his own head, in a thousand thoughts and none at all. The wild woods called to him, and he let himself be drawn in, barely aware when he walked past the van that had brought them there, now parked by the path that had led them to the clearing.

"Randall!" Victor's voice sounded decidedly croakier than usual. "Good morning. Did you sleep well?"

At the sound of his name, Randall jumped, startled, turning toward Victor and showing his teeth. His eyes blazed yellow, a growl rumbling out before his thoughts managed to catch up to what was happening. Randall choked back the rest of the warning sound, fumbling his glasses off to clean them on the edge of his sweater, trying to look like he hadn't just acted like an idiot puppy during a thunderstorm.

"Sorry," he mumbled, shoving his glasses back on his nose and giving Victor an embarrassed look. "I was a bit distracted."

"Oh. Er, that's quite all right," Victor said haltingly, peering at him. He was sitting in the driver's seat of the van with the door open, a takeaway cup of what smelled like tea sitting in a drink holder. "I apologize. I didn't mean to startle you."

"No, my fault." Randall hesitantly took a step forward. Victor looked incredible first thing in the morning. Then again, Randall was hard pressed to think of a moment when Victor *wouldn't* look incredible. The problem was, Victor had no interest at all in Randall, he was sure, other than as some amusing idiot who sometimes stumbled into his path. And the *worst* part of it all was that Victor had seen inside Randall's head. All those stupid thoughts Randall pretended weren't there had gotten trotted out and shown off. Really, if the option existed to just hide under a rock for the rest of his life, Randall would have taken it.

Then again, if he did, he'd never get to see Victor first thing in the morning, with his hair just a bit out of place and a little hoarseness to his voice. So maybe rock dwelling wasn't all it was cracked up to be.

"They let you back in," he observed, almost immediately internally kicking himself. Of course they had, otherwise Victor wouldn't be there. Next Randall would be pointing out that the grass was very green that morning and that sometimes people inhaled oxygen.

"Surprisingly, yes." Victor laid the book he was reading down on his lap. "Mallory was at the gate when I arrived. He mentioned the Gray Lady wanted to speak to all of us later, so I have something of a day pass." A small smirk curled the edge of his lips. "I nearly ran over Jed and Redford. Did you see them?"

"No." Randall took another cautious step forward. Victor smelled like tea and shaving cream and a tang of oranges, but Randall wasn't sure if under that there was acceptance for his presence or not. Reading nonwolves was hard sometimes. "Where was Redford? His cabin was next door to ours, but I was busy convincing Edwin not to go for a midnight run with strangers. I didn't see him after he went to bed."

"Oh, he was out at the gate with Jed." Victor waved a hand in the direction of said gate. "Lying on the ground with a sleeping bag underneath the gate. I'd almost call it cute, if it wasn't so amusingly melodramatic."

Randall wrapped his arms around himself, warding off the morning chill. "They acted like it was forever. I don't understand. It was only one night. You would have thought one of them was shipping off to war."

"The perils of being in love." Victor looked torn between being amused and exasperated. He gave Randall a look he couldn't quite identify, something deeper than the idle smirk Victor was still wearing. "I suppose one only understands when one has felt that way about another person."

"Haven't you?" The question was out before he could stop himself. Randall wasn't sure if he wanted to know the answer or not. Dropping his eyes, he shrugged, striving for a casual tone. "I mean, I would have assumed someone like you would have."

The way Victor absently rubbed his fingers over the two scars on his neck made Randall's hackles rise. "I thought so," Victor said contemplatively. "It was love, in a way, and very much *not* love in others. But it was acknowledged—" He paused and gave Randall a rueful smile. "Well, it's probably not something you want to hear me prattle on about. I do apologize." He abruptly changed the topic. "Have you had breakfast yet?"

Actually, Randall did want to hear. He wanted to know what made Victor have *that* expression, who gave him those scars that sent tight, sickening waves of jealousy through Randall every time he saw them. He wanted to know, but at the same time, the mere topic had him wishing he could run away. Not that it mattered. Victor had the person whom he'd loved, he had whoever else he was with, and none of it was any concern of Randall's.

He shuffled a few steps away, forcing a smile. "No, I haven't. I, uh, I had some things to do this morning, I haven't had a chance. I was going to go get some to take to Anthony and Edwin. They're of the 'hearty breakfast' school. If they don't eat first thing, they complain for the rest of the day about starving to death."

"Excellent." Victor sounded revitalized by the prospect of food. He hopped out of the van, tea in one hand, book tucked under the other arm. "I wonder if the pack will have anything other than meat? Not that a bit of ham or sausage isn't excellent at breakfast, but one does wish for variety."

"I certainly hope so," Randall said, falling into step beside Victor, careful not to walk too close. He *wanted* to. He wanted to get close enough to bury his nose in under Victor's ear, to wrap himself up in the scent and warmth of him, and then to go chasing after him to find breakfast. Because he was, at heart, an idiot. Being around this many wolves was apparently making him more and more like Edwin every day. Since when did he like *cuddles*? This was most disturbing. "I prefer a bit of fruit and tea to massive quantities of meat products. We can hope for the best, I suppose."

Victor gave a hum of agreement as he sipped his tea. He glanced at the sky, his eyes narrowing at the brighter light that was starting to spread over the tops of the trees. "If I may ask, what were you doing up so early?" He sounded like he could scarcely imagine that anybody woke up before nine in the morning. "I'm only awake because I barely slept."

Randall hesitated. "I had to get up before Anthony," he admitted. "Otherwise he wouldn't have let me go see her."

He didn't need to explain further—Victor obviously understood what he meant. "And how did that conversation go?"

Randall puffed out a silent sigh, watching as his breath left a faint curl in the air. It would be blazing hot later, once the sun came up fully. One of the things he loved about early autumn, it was like two seasons at once. Then again, he usually enjoyed the cold while curled up in bed. This wasn't so bad, though. "Frustrating. I begged." He glanced over at Victor, looking embarrassed and defiant all at once. "I'd do it again. But in the end, she agreed to let us stay. Not that she knows if it'll make a difference, but it's a step, I suppose."

"I'm glad to hear it." Victor, though his tone was a little distant, did genuinely sound glad. "I doubt I could be of assistance in any way, but if I ever may be helpful, I'd be more than happy to offer."

Just that little tendril of kindness felt like far too much. It felt like Randall had been fighting and pushing, making lists and doing research and creating plans he couldn't ever talk to his brothers about, since the day he'd found out Anthony's diagnosis. And to hear the offer of help, even if Victor probably didn't mean it, was enough to make Randall's eyes burn, all the exhaustion and fear catching up with him at once. Like that polite offer, which meant nearly nothing at all to Victor, made it so Randall could feel all the weight he was carrying.

"I'm sorry," he murmured, taking off his glasses to scrub his hand across his face. "Thank you, I mean. That's, uh, that's extremely kind of you. I know you have better things to do than watch out for a bunch of silly wolves. You've already done too much."

Victor stopped walking to turn to face Randall, lightly putting a hand on his arm to halt him. Where anybody else would be meeting Randall's eyes, Victor's gaze was focused somewhere around Randall's left temple. "Randall," he said firmly. "I came on this trip, didn't I? Believe me when I tell you this is the best, the most worthy thing I could be doing right now. I want to help in any way I can."

Randall took a deep breath to get himself back together. It was embarrassing, the positions Victor had seen him in, the number of times Victor had witnessed him at anything but his best. Randall had his own set of scars, though he hardly touched his with anything resembling fondness, and it had been Victor who had pulled him out of that hell. And now it was Victor again, assisting him out of another one of his nightmares come to life. "Anthony appreciates it," he told Victor, a very faint smile touching his lips. "As do I. You are a good man, Victor."

"Far from it." Victor looked bemused at the compliment. "But I do mean it. You don't have to shoulder this burden alone."

With a perfunctory smile, one that didn't reach his eyes, Randall turned and began walking again toward the kitchen. "Yes. I do."

Victor caught up with him with a few short strides. "Randall, you have *Jed* helping you, and Jed doesn't normally help people like this. You have Redford and I, and Edwin, and now the Gray Lady. You—"

"You don't understand." Randall cut him off, lips tight. "This is our pack. Anthony has been our leader, has taken care of us, since we were kids. All of us were *children*, Victor, and Anthony was figuring out how to feed us and find shelter and…. This is our pack. Only Anthony is sick. He's sick and he's not getting better. So I have to do this, I have to be *him* now. But I don't want to."

God, he'd never said that out loud.

"I don't want to be him," he repeated in a miserable whisper. "I don't want to be in charge or have to be responsible for them. Because I'm a terrible, selfish person."

"Randall, you just disrupted your entire life to find a cure for your brother," Victor said gently. "Are those really the actions of a selfish man? You brought your family here; you got the mother of all wolves to agree to help him. Does that sound like the actions of a man that cannot be a leader?"

"I dropped out of school." Randall sounded horrified. He *was* horrified by it. It still hurt to think about. All that work, all the sacrifice, and he'd never even gotten to step on campus. "I was supposed to go next month. I'd transferred from our community campus to a university I've wanted to go to since I was eleven. But I dropped out. And I'm mad that I had to. I'm *mad* at Anthony, at this stupid disease. I did all this because I *need* him, Victor. I need him to be better. I need him to be who he is again so that I can be who I am. I need my brother. I would move heaven and earth if I had to, to get him well again. Because I love him, yes, but also because I'm *terrified* of being without him."

Of all the reactions he would have expected from Victor, a quiet little *laugh* was not one of them. Randall immediately withdrew, expression shuttering away, shoulders tense. "You hold yourself to incredibly high standards, it seems. It's quite all right that you're not some flawless protagonist in a fiction, Randall."

"You've clearly never met my brother," Randall offered after a moment, hesitant, still not sure if Victor's laugh was something he shouldn't shy away from. "Because he's kind of horribly perfect."

Victor took a breath as if to say something, but he paused. His expression looked distant, like he was thinking of something so clearly that he didn't have time to notice the real world at that moment. Randall wondered, with a sudden horrifying realization, if Victor was mentally replaying what he'd seen of Randall's memories.

"You're a better man than you give yourself credit for," Victor finally said. "I hope, one day, you'll see that."

The instinct, of course, was to brush that off. Compliments were never easy to take, much less from someone who gave Randall as many confusing emotions as Victor. But Victor wasn't saying something nice just because; he wasn't offering empty flattery. He'd seen Randall, all of him, just as clearly as Randall knew himself. His memories were Victor's now. And that was a huge, scary, horrifying idea, yes, but it also meant that he couldn't exactly blow Victor off. When Victor said that, it was with the full weight of knowledge.

"Well," Randall said after a moment, taking a step closer, studying Victor's face, "who am I to argue with my Beatrice?"

There was a moment, he thought. Maybe just in his head, but it felt like a *moment*. Like heat racing through him, like shivery fire. And there were things he could do in that moment—he could be brave, he could sprout wings, he could dare a thousand things that seemed impossible any other time.

"Randy!"

Of course, he could only do those things in the moments where his younger brother was not tackling him.

Edwin shoved himself into an overenthusiastic hug with Randall, grinning at them both. "Hi, Victor! You got back in, awesome. I was hoping you would. Hey, Randall, let's get Ant breakfast, okay? Man, do I smell bacon? I love bacon!" And then Edwin was gone again, charging up the stairs to the kitchen, beaming a smile at everyone he met. He was a force of nature, Edwin. And he'd completely ruined the moment.

Then again, maybe that was for the best.

Anthony followed him at a much slower pace, giving them a greeting and a smile, the corners of his eyes crinkling in amusement before he labored his way up the stairs. Clearly Randall had been right. The cold early morning air had not done his joints any favors. Randall bit back the urge to help him. Edwin was right there, circling around to casually loop an arm with Anthony's, talking about all the meat he could smell and pretending, of course, that nothing at all was wrong.

With a slight smile and a sigh, Randall gestured toward the building. "Shall we?"

Victor was blinking, startled in the wake of Hurricane Edwin. He shook his head, collecting himself. "Yes, let's. I only pray we'll find some toast."

The hall was half filled with families and groups sitting at long tables. There was a counter at one end with an open kitchen, food in trays for people to take. There was a rather alarming amount of meat, both cooked and raw, but to his relief Randall spotted fruit and toast and a large pan of scrambled eggs. Every wolf was different—Edwin, for one, was happy enough with several raw, bloody steaks piled on his tray and a rather large glass of milk—and it was nice to see the pack wasn't trying to force a specific eating choice. He had been hoping to get breakfast for Anthony before the stubborn wolf had made his painful way across the camp, but clearly he'd dawdled for too long. Randall kept shooting concerned glances at Anthony as they waited in line, silently standing just close enough that he could ease a shoulder in under Anthony's arm, to be his support, while pretending he was doing nothing of the kind.

Between the two of them, he and Edwin got Anthony's tray handled, despite Anthony's insistence that he could do it himself. Randall got him a slice of toast and some fruit with a pointed look—some went on Edwin's tray as well in an attempt to get him to eat more than the meat—and Edwin piled on sausages and chicken legs.

Randall's own plate held a modest sausage alongside toast and eggs. The fruit was a welcome addition. He did enjoy something refreshing first thing in the morning. He and Edwin juggled the trays toward the tables, Anthony between them, searching for a place to sit.

"Hey! Furbutts! Over here." Jed's strident tone called them over, and they made their way to one of the tables in the middle of the room. Jed was sitting with Redford on his lap, the two of them reading the paper over their coffee and breakfast. Jed's chin was resting on Redford's shoulder, and they didn't seem to care at all that they were an interspecies couple in the middle of a very tight wolf pack. Then again, none of the wolves around them seemed bothered either. The few who had chosen to sit by them were obviously of the open-minded sort. Knievel was sitting on the table next to them, her own tray in front of her with some bits of chicken and a small pile of raw meat and what looked like a bit of squash that she was happily gnawing on.

"Morning," Edwin greeted with a huge smile, setting down his tray next to them and slinging himself into the seat to immediately start on his food. To Randall's exasperation, he didn't use utensils, instead picking up the slab of meat with his hands and chomping a rather large bite. "They have venison," Edwin told Redford enthusiastically. "Fresh too. It's really good, did you have some?"

"I don't know if I like venison," Redford said contemplatively, glancing back toward the food.

"You had the liver, remember?" Edwin grinned at him, bloody and unrestrained, like some mix between a cherub and a horror film. His brother, the next Miss Manners, everyone. "It was good, right?"

"Yes," Redford acknowledged, sounding reluctant. "But I'm not, you know." He hesitated before leaning in, and for a horrible moment Randall was quite sure Redford was going to share the location of a particularly disgusting mole or some such, from the way his eyes were darting around. "A wolf right now."

Anthony, Randall, and Edwin all exchanged looks. Randall found it very hard to not laugh, which was dreadful, he knew, but still. That would be adorable if it wasn't so very sad. "You *are* a wolf," Randall pointed out, attempting to be delicate. "Your form is simply not at the moment."

Blinking owlishly a few times, his gaze inevitably going back to Jed, Redford responded only, "Oh."

"And that means it tastes good now too." Edwin was surprisingly polite about it. "Seriously, you'll love it."

Victor was staring at Edwin. "Aren't you going to get E. coli or some other dreadful disease, eating that raw?"

Edwin stared down at his plate, nose wrinkling. "Cooked meat is gross. I mean, I'll eat it if I have to, but it tastes all bland when it's not raw." Chewing as he considered the matter, Edwin amended, "Ant's stew is good, though, and he makes these dumpling things with chicken I like."

Randall sighed as he prepared Anthony's coffee. "I'm sorry." He would apologize, because God knew Edwin never would think to. "I know it's a little... off putting, for people to watch him eat. Wolves are all different in what we like, but Edwin's always preferred his food to be as fresh as possible. He was an impossible child." But his tone turned fond at that, and Edwin shared a grin with him, sticking out his tongue.

"You love me," Edwin said, cutting off a piece of the meat and sliding it onto Redford's plate for him to try.

"Yes, well, you are very demanding," Randall replied blandly, squeezing Edwin's shoulder as he finally sat. He'd found some tea, and he took an experimental sip. Not fantastic, but at least it was drinkable.

Anthony slowly tipped over to lean slightly against Randall's shoulder. He never did that; he never let himself appear weak. Randall knew all of them were keeping it together by pretending the worst wasn't actually happening. That if they simply didn't talk about the nightmare, that meant it wasn't occurring. But Anthony looked tired, his fingers shaking as he tried to cut his meat. He wasn't even jumping into the conversation to tease Edwin about his eating habits. Without a word, Randall pulled Anthony's plate over in front of himself and sliced the sausage into bite-size pieces, then pulled the chicken off the bone.

With a thick lump in his throat, he slid the plate back into place like nothing had happened. Turning, he pressed his lips to the top of his brother's head, taking a slow, shaky breath. It was going to be okay. Everything was going to be fine now. The Gray Lady had decided to let them stay. Randall had done everything his research told him to do, so it *had* to be fine now.

"Thanks," Anthony muttered lowly. He sounded frustrated—not at Randall's help, but the fact that he needed it. "You weren't in the cabin when I woke up. Where'd you go?"

Randall looked over at Victor, a quick glance, before going back to his breakfast. Edwin was pretending he wasn't listening, but he'd moved his chair close enough to bump knees with Anthony, cutting little looks over at the two of them in between bites. Even Redford and Jed were watching Randall over the top of their newspaper. Randall shrugged off his sweater and wrapped it around Anthony's shoulders. "It's cold," was all he said.

"You two fucking?" Jed asked casually, waving his fork between Victor and Randall.

"What?" Randall spluttered, color hitting his cheeks. "No! Why on earth—"

"You just looked hella guilty." Jed shrugged, returning to his eggs. "Figured it was that or you did something your big brother wouldn't approve of. Wash lights with darks or something."

"Your mind goes straight for the gutter," Victor said blandly. "Not every situation involves someone's genitals. Really, Journey, keep your nose out."

"Don't call me Journey." The protest seemed so automatic that Jed wasn't even paying attention when he shot it back at Victor.

Redford was tentatively trying the raw venison, clearly intrigued by his own taste for it. Randall would admit that fresh meat had a vastly superior flavor. He just wasn't comfortable eating it in mixed company. It seemed rude to be bloody around those who might not find such a look appetizing. Knievel seemed just as content with the uncooked food, however, purring loudly as she attacked her own serving.

Jed poked his fork at the raw meat on Redford's plate, glancing up at him. Then Jed cut himself a bite and shoveled it in. Edwin chuffed out a laugh at Victor's horrified expression. Jed, though, calmly chewed and swallowed, shrugging. "Not bad. Had worse."

"I dread to think what you mean by that," Victor sighed. He reached over the table to snatch the newspaper away from Jed. "Now let Randall tell everyone what the Gray Lady said."

"Wait." Edwin stopped trying to get Redford to eat more of the venison. "You went to see her?"

Randall shifted in his seat, looking over at Anthony. "Um. Yes. I did."

"What did she say?" Anthony sounded cautiously hopeful. "Has she made her decision yet?"

Taking a slow breath, Randall gave his brothers a small smile. He reached out to squeeze Anthony's hand. "She said we could stay. She's going to have her healers take a look at you, Ant, see what they think." He wasn't going to tell them about the Gray Lady's cautionary words. There wasn't a point. Anthony needed hope right then; he needed to believe this would work. So did Edwin. So Randall would keep all that fear and worry to himself. It wouldn't do anyone else any good. "It's going to be okay."

"I take it that means the cure isn't a certain thing." There was a look in Anthony's eyes that Randall couldn't bear, a fraction of lost hope that Anthony quickly covered. He drew himself up and straightened his shoulders, taking a deep breath. "Okay. Did she say when I'm to report to the healers?"

Randall wanted to insist, to *promise*, that it would be fine. That a cure was just that easy, that everything was going to go back to the way it had been. Edwin was staring at him, waiting for just that. For his brainy older brother to recite some factoid that meant Anthony was going to walk away from this perfectly healthy.

He couldn't do it. All that was left was to squeeze Anthony's hand tighter, to force a smile. To promise himself that, no matter what the cost, he'd find a way. "We can take you in today. I wanted you to get some food in your system first, but we'll go after breakfast if you want."

"Yeah, I should get started as quickly as possible," Anthony agreed. "You guys don't have to sit around to watch, though. It'll probably be boring." He gave them a smile. "Why don't you wander around the camp some, talk to the wolves here?"

"You're an idiot," Edwin told him. "We're coming with you." He turned to the rest of the group. "You guys can come too, if you want." Like it was a pool party. Randall honestly didn't understand his brother sometimes.

Jed had been watching them all silently, eyes darting between them, some look on his face halfway between total fear and longing. Mostly the fear. The tightness in his shoulders made it readily apparent he would love to be running in the opposite direction. "Thanks for the offer, Lassie, but I think I'm going to go do something productive."

"Oh? Like what?" Victor asked. "Helping Knievel sharpen her claws so she can chase more wolves?"

Jed grinned. "That's my girl," he cooed at the cat, who was very happily cleaning off Redford's plate, purring rustily. Redford, for his part, was staring despondently at his now empty plate. Then, to Victor, Jed said, "Nah. Everyone keeps talking about these hunters. It's got me all curious. Figure I might poke my head in where it doesn't belong, see if I can drum up anything interesting."

"Do you believe they're human?" Randall asked him, interested.

"Sweetheart, that's kind of my default setting," Jed responded. "I know you guys are all freak flags flying, but in my experience, most things are definitely human." He shrugged. "Besides, I was talking to some people this morning, and they're pretty sure, whoever they are, they're using guns. How many creepy crawlies you know use assault rifles?"

"They may not be human," Victor said mildly. "Even minority 'creepy crawly' groups can be racist against one another, Jed. And I think you'd be surprised at the number of them that do use guns." He glanced over at the wolves. "Not all of us have built-in weapons."

Absorbing this, Jed leaned back, fingers drumming absently against Redford's side. "They got two more taken a few days ago," he mused. "Younger wolves, apparently, who went for a run and didn't come back. Everyone's saying they haven't really hit the pack yet. Just picking around the edges. Lone wolves or small groups that hang around the fringe, but nothing in this area. Everything's about fifty miles northeast, best I can gather. Gotta get my maps from the van to see what's up there."

"Taken?" Anthony looked unhappy. "Or were they killed?"

"No bodies." Jed frowned, rubbing his chin absently. The man clearly hadn't shaved. He had stubble and was wearing the same clothes he'd had on the day before. Randall wondered why he was doing this. Maybe the answer lay in how his arm was looped around Redford's waist, possessive and protective all at once. "This is all second and third hand, though. Stragglers from hit camps that come in, looking for help, saying that there was gunfire and blood and they ran. Could be kidnappings. Could be something's eating them. Shit, I don't know. That's why I want to go take a look."

Anthony made a growling sound under his breath as he sipped at his coffee. "I want to help," he said decisively. "If there's anything I can do, just say the word. Are you going to look for information today?"

Jed snorted. "Yeah, hotstuff, you and me'll talk about it when you don't need cardigan over there to cut up your food."

"I'm not an invalid," Anthony said. He was obviously struggling to keep calm, a snarl under his words.

"Maybe." Jed leaned forward, holding Anthony's eyes. "But you're weak. Right now, you're weak. Maybe you'll get better. I don't know. But if you go running around after these guys and they find you, we'll just have one more missing wolf to talk about over breakfast. And you know it."

If Jed was going to say anything further, he didn't get a chance. Anthony's eyes were yellow in his anger, his teeth bared—but instead of jumping over the table like Randall half feared he might, Anthony instead stood and walked away, every line of his body tense.

Randall turned to Jed, to give him a piece of his mind, to bite his stupid throat out, to do *something*. But far from gloating or being a snide asshole, Jed looked quietly regretful. "Your brother's a hell of a guy," he said quietly. "But he'd get himself killed. And I'm not having his blood on my hands just to spare his feelings."

Silently, Randall jerked the chair back, rising. Edwin's teeth were bared, and he was growling at Jed, angry and tense. "You're a fucktard," Edwin proclaimed. Randall didn't much feel like correcting his profanity. Edwin stalked away after Anthony, and Randall sighed, resting a hand on the back of the chair.

"He's not weak," he told Jed lowly. But then, even quieter, "Please, don't ever let him follow you." Because Jed was right. It killed Randall to admit, but he was right—if Anthony went out now, like he was, he'd die. And that was simply not something Randall could accept.

He left then, not looking back at the three of them sitting there. At the odd little group they made, the almost wolf, the half blood, and the human. He followed his nose to find his brothers, Edwin sitting next to Anthony on one of the low benches surrounding the dormant bonfire in the center of the camp. Edwin's shoulder was pressed against Anthony's and he was talking, so quietly Randall couldn't make out the words until he got closer.

"And then we'll go running, Ant. As fast and as far as we can. You can smell the woods, can't you? I bet there's lots of squirrels and rabbits to chase. You and me, we'll chase them together, just like back home. And swimming too, in the stream, just like you like. Where the water's so cold it makes you sneeze and we get all muddy and Randall makes that cross face at us."

Edwin was telling Anthony a story. The story of a healthy brother, of woods with no hunters, of the life they'd had up until a few months ago. Silently, Randall sat down on the other side of Anthony, listening as well.

"When the moon's all big and the stars look like ripe berries, we'll go howling. It's your favorite, I know. We'll all howl at the moon just like Dad used to do. You told me about it, remember, Ant?"

Anthony laughed lowly, bumping his shoulder against Edwin's. "If you howl at the moon and listen very closely," he teased, reciting the story one more time. And Randall, if he half closed his eyes, could almost hear their father's voice in the lilt of Anthony's. "Sometimes the man in the moon will howl back."

"But it's not true." Edwin had always said the same thing at the same part. It was almost a ritual now. A way Anthony had kept their parents alive for them, the bits and pieces they could hold on to.

"Maybe not," Randall said, very quietly. "But I howl at it sometimes. Just for him."

"Me too." Anthony's smile was sad. "He'd probably be proud. Or laughing his ass off, either one."

"You're going to get better." Edwin searched Anthony's face. "Right? That's why we're here. That's why we joined this pack. So you can get better."

"That's right." Randall made his voice firm, in control. Like the know-it-all brother they both teased him about being. "No time at all and we'll forget this even happened. Like a bad dream."

"In the meantime," Anthony said, hesitating slightly. He rubbed a hand over the back of his neck, sighing. "Jed's right, for now. Have you seen how he holds himself? He's military. He knows what he's talking about. So I'm going to try and concentrate on helping the healers."

"He slept outside on the ground last night for no damn reason," Randall grumbled. "He's not a sage or anything." He nudged his shoulder against Anthony's, letting out a slow breath. "But I think that's a good plan."

"Yeah, well, he's a human. They do weird things." Anthony laughed. "Although he gets points for trying the raw venison."

"If you told him that Redford needed to paint himself pink and dance naked under the moon, I think he'd join in and add a feathered headdress." Randall smirked. "He's kind of stupid. But sure. Points for effort."

Edwin was leaning against Anthony, head resting on his shoulder. "Let's go find these healers," he sighed. "Might as well get it over with."

They made their way to the other side of the camp, all three of them huddled together as they walked, as if they couldn't stand the idea of being separate. The rumble of an engine drew Randall's attention. Across the way he could see the van leaving, Redford and Jed off to go hunting. Maybe they'd even find something. Randall hoped it was humans. Some easy problem with a simple solution. It'd be nice if at least one thing was.

The healer who greeted them was an older wolf, her hair done in a long silver braid that hung down to the middle of her back. She greeted Anthony with a hug, informed them that the Gray Lady had already let them know they were coming, and hustled Anthony into the long cabin that served as the medical facilities. That left Randall and Edwin alone outside, sitting on the steps of the porch, waiting.

Edwin lasted all of ten minutes before declaring himself so bored he was going to die, shifting into wolf form, and curling up to go back to sleep, leaving Randall with a lap full of his clothes. Randall sat in silence, wishing only that he'd brought one of his books with him. It would help the time pass a little less painfully.

At least Edwin's side made for a semidecent pillow. Randall lay back on the wooden step, head resting against Edwin's haunch, staring up at the sky. The morning sunlight had dimmed. Instead of warming the earth from the earlier chill, it seemed to be retreating. A line of dark clouds was pressing in against the horizon. Lifting his nose, Randall took a deep breath. Rain was coming.

He marked the time by watching the approaching storm. It was still just a threat on the distant sky when Anthony finally emerged from the healer's cabin, looking a bit worn out but not too much worse for the wear. Edwin shifted back with a happy yelp, and Randall was forced to chase after him, holding out his jeans and shirt.

"Edwin, come on. At least put your pants back on." He dumped the clothes into Edwin's arms and fixed him with a look until Edwin was dressed again.

"You're such a prude sometimes, Rand." Turning to Anthony, Edwin searched his face. "Well?"

"How did it go?" Randall asked, taking Anthony's arm and leading him back to the bench. "How are you feeling?"

As Anthony sat, Randall saw he was holding a small pot of what looked like green paste. Anthony was staring at it in confusion. "I have to rub this on my hands every morning."

Oh. Well. Perhaps it was some sort of magical wolf remedy? Randall took the pot and sniffed it, immediately wrinkling his nose. It smelled like death. "That's great," he tried to enthuse. "I mean, mornings are bad for you, right? So this must be to help that."

Edwin poked his finger in the paste and promptly stuck it in his mouth. And then proceeded to gag. "Oh, man, do *not* eat that," he managed around dry heaves.

Anthony took a dubious sniff of it. "It's supposed to have stuff like flaxseed oil, nettles, apple...." Trailing off with a wince, he admitted, "All I can smell is the ginkgo oil. I'm sure they know what they're talking about, though. They said it'll relieve the symptoms."

Gripping Anthony's shoulder, Randall met his eyes. "Then it'll work. These are wolves, Ant. They know how to handle things like this. Besides, I've read that flaxseed oil is used all the time for joint pain. Clearly, they know what they're doing. Trust me." They had to know what they were doing. There simply wasn't another option.

"Well, I'll give it a shot." Anthony smiled at Randall and Edwin. He put a hand on the bench, pushing himself to stand. He hesitated as he looked at the pot. "Should I try it now? It's not really morning anymore, and they specified morning."

"Sure," Randall said confidently, taking the pot. "It's more of a once a day application, I bet. We'll put some on now."

Anthony gave a small sigh. "No wolf is going to come within fifty yards of me, with this on," he muttered.

"Good thing fish have shit noses then, huh?" Edwin chuffed a laugh. Randall had Anthony's hand between his own and was gently smearing the paste onto the joints. He didn't pause in his work, but his eyes flicked up to Anthony's as he felt his brother's hand twitch in surprise.

They didn't really talk about Vilhehn. Not directly.

Anthony just snorted faintly. "Good thing he'll never be around to smell it in the first place," he said lowly, taking over for Randall to smooth the paste onto his own joints. "Now, don't we have better things to do than stand outside the healer's cabin?"

At least Edwin had the good grace to look sheepish for bringing up topics they really didn't want to dwell on. "I was going to go running," he offered, giving Anthony an apologetic grin. As if either of them could stay mad at him. One big, sunny grin from Edwin and they'd find it impossible to deny him anything. "Feel up to it, old man?"

Edwin got a swift punch on the shoulder. "Old man?" Anthony said slowly, his eyebrows raised. "*Old man*? You still haven't beaten my record running between our house and the lake. Don't you talk to me about being old."

"Fine," Edwin laughed, ducking under Anthony's arm and half tackling him in a hug. "You and me. We'll find a new race. Bet there's *loads* of things to smell here too."

"It's going to storm," Randall pointed out practically.

"So put your clothes inside," Edwin returned, sticking out his tongue. "Fur dries, Rand. Come on, it'll be fun!"

Anthony had his hands halfway raised to his shirt, as if he'd been about to take it off. He paused, flexing his fingers in a way that looked stiff and painful. The excitement at the prospect of running faded from his face. "You go, Edwin," he said gently. "How about we have a run later tonight?"

107

Something flickered across Edwin's expression, behind the smile, the teasing. Something weary and worried and *old*. So strange to see on his brother's face. Edwin was the heart of them, was their innocence. It hurt more than Randall would have expected to catch a glimpse of that fading. "Yeah." Edwin nodded, hauling Anthony in for a rough hug. "I need to go check out the best places to run anyway. Haven't even poked my nose around here yet. I'm slacking."

With one last smile, just as bright, as if the cloud that had passed was already forgotten, Edwin kicked off his clothes and shifted. He barked cheerfully at them, nosing into their legs. Then, with a streak of blond fur, he was gone.

Anthony and Randall started walking back toward their cabin. Anthony never explicitly stated that he was going to take a nap, but Randall knew his plans nonetheless. Even the short medical consultation seemed to have worn Anthony out. For as long as Randall could really remember, it'd just been the three of them. And for several years, it really had only been Randall and Anthony taking care of things. Edwin had just been a toddler when their parents had been killed. Randall had spent nearly every day with Anthony, considered him to be something more than a brother, something deeper than a friend. He was half of everything Randall had in his life.

And, walking back to their cabin, for one of the first times in his life, Randall didn't know what to say to him.

Anthony seemed to pick up on his awkwardness. "You should go join Edwin," he encouraged as he palmed open the door to their cabin. "You know how he gets. He never likes to discover new things alone."

Fussing with Anthony's bed, smoothing out blankets, Randall shrugged. "I'm not good at the running around in the woods parts. You know that. Besides, it really is going to storm. Don't worry. I saw a big group of wolves come out of the school and head the same direction as Edwin went before you came out of the healer's place. I'm sure he'll make new friends before we know it."

That brought a faint smile to Anthony's expression. It fell off in a second, though, as Anthony put a hand on Randall's arm, stopping him from further fussing with the blanket. "I'm not an invalid," Anthony reminded him softly. "I can adjust my own blankets." However soft and friendly his voice was, there was a thread of frustration under his tone, an anger that was fighting to crack through the surface.

Randall's hands stilled. "I know." The words came quietly, Randall's head down, staring at the faded comforter. "But you are sick."

He honestly wasn't sure if he'd ever just *said* that to Anthony. There'd been talking around it. There had been a lot of assurances of getting better, insistence that everything was *fine*. But Randall's voice shook, just a little, as he forced the words out. "You're sick, and you need to stop pushing yourself so hard."

"I'm only pushing myself to be *normal*, Randall," Anthony said.

"Being sick isn't *normal*," Randall snapped. "You are not *normal* right now, Ant. I am not normal, *Edwin* is not fucking *normal*." Lips tight, he drew himself back. He choked down all the fear and anger and worry that was spilling out from the neatly packed little box he kept it in. Drawing in a shuddered breath, he shook his head, arms folded across his chest. "I'm sorry," Randall murmured. "You're fine. I'm just tired. I should let you sleep. Excuse me."

"No. You're right." Anthony's low words stopped him from leaving. "Nothing's normal about this." He rubbed a rough hand over his face, pushing his hair back, trying to get himself under control. He smiled then, a tiny curve at the corner of his mouth. "Compromise? I won't push, and you won't coddle?"

Despite himself, Randall felt the tense line of his shoulders ease. "You are not an egg," he agreed. He'd told Anthony the same thing about Edwin many times when Edwin had first wanted to go running on his own.

He wasn't an egg. He didn't need to be coddled. He could take care of himself.

"I'm sorry," Randall whispered, dropping his eyes, frowning down at his shoes. They had mud all over them. He really should see to that before they were ruined. "You've taken care of us our whole lives. I guess I just am feeling a little helpless. I don't know how to take care of you, now."

"You don't need to worry about that," Anthony said. "Because I'm going to be taking care of this family for as long as I'm alive." He took on a casual sprawl against the bed, sitting back against the headboard. "So maybe you'll let *me* talk to the Gray Lady in the future, huh?" There was a note of fond teasing in his voice, but steel too, concern for his brothers doing things that Anthony felt he should be doing himself.

Randall winced at the tone. Yes, he'd known this conversation would happen, should Anthony find out about his early morning trip. Just as the Gray Lady had said—it really was Anthony's place to handle those types of things. "You're my brother," he replied quietly, raising his gaze to meet Anthony's. The same reason he'd given her. "You shouldn't ever have to beg."

"Yes, I am your brother," Anthony replied, amusement touching his expression. "Your *older* brother, so it is still my God-given right to boss you around." He made a move, hooking an arm around Randall's neck and hauling him in to pull Randall into a headlock.

Squirming in Anthony's grip, yelping in a most undignified manner, Randall tried to wrestle his way out. Anthony's hand grabbed Randall's forearm, tightening to haul him back in. For a moment, all he could feel was shooting pain, the phantom memories of Cairo, of blood and fangs. Randall turned away from Anthony, putting up the playful struggle still, refusing to react. And then Anthony let go and they were rolling on the bed, and it was so easy to forget it. To shove it away like he always did. Randall did his best to squirm around and try to grasp at Anthony's ticklish spots, hoping for an upper hand. He failed quite utterly, but he was laughing by the time Anthony took pity on him and released him to wobble his way into sitting on the bed, the shadow memories locked away and ignored. As they should be.

"Yes, fine," Randall sighed heavily, nudging his shoulder against Anthony's. "You are still able to kick my butt if you so choose. Point taken." He glanced over, smiling slightly at Anthony. "You know I'm just doing this because I love you, right?" And he was worried. God, he was just so *worried*, all the time. Telling Anthony something that obvious, though, would be like pointing out he had brown hair. "I'm going to do whatever I can to get you well again. It really is going to be okay." Randall had to believe that. He just had to keep telling himself that, telling *everyone* that, and working as hard as he possibly could to make it true.

"I know. And thank you." Anthony had a corner of the blanket between his hands, twisting it in his fingers, apparently unconcerned at getting the paste all over it. "For your help, I mean. I just don't want you doing things for me because you think I can't." He smiled ruefully.

There were a lot of things Randall wanted to say to that. To point out the fact that Anthony shouldn't *have* to do things that were painful, that were hard, just because he could. To beg his brother to slow down, to not push himself, and the disease, past this point. Because that was what was going to happen. If the treatment didn't work, this day was going to be the best one he had left. And then the next day, he'd be a little worse, and that day would turn into the new best. And so on, further down, until the ability to walk, to run, to shift, were all forgotten. Until the new *best*, the new normal, was one of twisted, unmoving pain.

Until there were no more good days at all.

He just wanted Anthony to never see that day. To not have to feel pain that wasn't necessary. But Randall looked over at Anthony's face, the grim determination, the pride—God, so much *pride*, like Anthony was only asking to keep his identity, to keep the one thing that defined him. All Anthony had ever done, all he'd worked for, was to take care of him and Edwin. Randall couldn't take that away, even a little. He couldn't imply that there'd ever be a moment when Anthony couldn't be the man he'd wanted to be, because that would break Anthony faster than the disease ever could.

"Okay, big brother," Randall sighed, giving him a little smile. "No more mama wolf."

"Good." Anthony looked satisfied with the answer. He shuffled himself farther down on the bed, sighing as he got comfortable. "If I nap, you won't get too bored, I hope?"

"Nah." Randall had to resist the urge to smooth the blankets. "I think I'm going to go for a walk. See some of these woods Edwin is so enamored with."

Anthony sounded halfway to sleep already when he answered. "Make sure he doesn't start chomping on squirrels again. We all remember the time he couldn't eat for three hours because he had a squirrel tail stuck in his throat."

"He nearly starved," Randall agreed somberly, a smile twitching at the corners of his lips. "I'll warn the squirrels away. Sleep well, Ant." He left, closing the door as silently as possible behind him.

The wind had picked up, rattling branches, rubbing leaves off into desperate whirls of scattered color. Randall started walking in his pressed sweater, in his tie, in his muddy shoes. He was neat, he was contained, glasses firmly on, every inch a *man*. Every inch civilized.

He didn't want to be that. Right then, it felt as though if he stayed contained he would go mad. Without thinking, Randall kicked off his shoes. He shucked off the sweater and his perfectly creased slacks. He dropped them all into a pile, and he changed.

It was like the whole world came alive. He could smell leftovers from breakfast, the scent of the rain in the air, oranges and tea and parchment. There were wolves everywhere, and he smelled them too. He felt them like a hum in the back of his mind, an *awareness* of them that seemed so much more immediate now. Randall took off running, darting around trees, ears back, body sleek and low to the ground. He didn't think, didn't worry, didn't feel. He just ran.

The first raindrop that hit him was ignored. Randall was pounding through the woods, breath a harsh pant, senses alight. Then there were two raindrops. Then a dozen. A mist turned into a downpour, and the world cut off into a curtain of gray rain as the skies opened.

Skidding to a halt, Randall gave a start, a jolt running through him, ears twitching. Slowly, he came out of the run-haze to realize he had absolutely no idea where he was. The late morning sun was long gone, hidden behind black clouds and a downpour. It was dark, the trees around him creaking, shaking, shadows darting around him. A crack of lightning made him jump, jerking backward, whining in fear.

Randall didn't much like the dark these days.

He turned tail and started to run, desperately hoping he'd picked the right direction. The thunder chased him. Randall's ears were flat against his head, his tail between his legs, as he raced back toward camp. Finally, he could smell it. He could pick out the twinkle of lights from cabins through the dark. Heart racing, he threw himself onto the porch of their cabin, shivering and soaked.

Anthony was still sleeping. Randall hesitated, paws on the windowsill, looking in. The last thing he wanted to do was wake his brother up from a rare decent sleep. Randall glanced around, eyes landing on the cabin next door. Redford's cabin. Redford, who was out with Jed. That would do nicely.

Randall jumped off the porch and ran across the short distance to the other cabin, shifting back on the porch so he could work the latch. Shivering, soaked, and naked, he ducked inside.

Only to find Victor sitting on the bed, reading a book.

Ah.

For a few long moments, neither of them said anything. Victor just blinked at Randall, and Randall didn't miss the way Victor's gaze dipped decisively downward. If anyone else might have flushed or looked away or apologized for the blatant staring, Victor simply lifted his eyebrows in appreciation. Which was somehow so much worse. Flushing a deep red, Randall tried to not lunge for the nearest blanket, instead attempting a calm he certainly did not feel.

Gratefully wrapping the fabric around himself, he stammered an explanation. "I didn't realize you'd be here. I'm so sorry. I was running, and it began to storm." And he'd gotten scared like some stupid child, lost in the woods. "I'll go," he managed with the remaining tattered shreds of his dignity. "Again, I apologize."

"You're quite welcome to stay," Victor offered. He took off his glasses, cleaning them on his sweater. "I was caught briefly in it too. It's horrid out there. You'll catch your death." A brief tone of amusement touched Victor's words. "I am only borrowing the cabin, myself. The, ah, watch cat was very gracious." Randall caught sight of Knievel under the bed, curled up on what looked like a T-shirt, sleeping through the storm.

Ducking his head, Randall stared at his bare feet, at the little darkening spots from the water he was dripping. He felt so exposed, in a way he hadn't during the full moon. But that was exactly the difference, wasn't it? During the moons he was confident; he couldn't help but be. Now it was just him, none of the adrenaline flush buoying him up.

And all at once, Randall realized that Victor was able to see his scars. The horrible knotted mess of them in the lower crook of his neck, the jagged white jumble of them in his elbows and up his arms, and the long, stretched ones on his ribs, where the vampires in Cairo had decided that knives were fun to play with. He'd hidden them away for so long, under long sleeves and collared shirts, that he almost didn't know what to do with them so vividly on display. The full moon, once again, was not there to make him feel so *wolfish* that he forgot, to hide them in a softer light.

Jaw tight, Randall tied the blanket off around his waist, finding another on the bed to wrap tightly around his shoulders, until it was just his head poking out from a mound of fluffy pink covers. He sat gingerly on the edge of the bed, willing Victor to not say anything about what he might have noticed.

Apparently luck wasn't on his side.

"Cairo?" Victor said softly, his tone neither disturbed nor overly curious, but sympathetic nonetheless. "I didn't see those when I visited you in the hospital."

"I had a lot of bandages," Randall said flatly, not looking up. "And I was under the covers. It's not a big deal." A terrible parody of a smile touched his lips. "I'm one of the fortunate ones, after all, aren't I?" Mimicking the words that had been said to him over and over, by his brothers, by the doctors. He was lucky. He wasn't dead. He should focus on that. So he had. It was just so much easier when no one talked about it, when no one could see what had been left behind.

"In a manner of speaking." Victor was absently rubbing his own scar, a lot neater than Randall's, placed much higher up on his neck, though his attention was firmly on Randall. "Everybody seems to forget the lasting impact of those kinds of scars."

"Ah." Randall's eyes followed Victor's hand, again feeling that little drop of jealousy in his gut for the one who had put them there. For the man who made Victor's voice go so sad and so fond whenever he spoke of him. "But were you a willing participant in yours?" One corner of Randall's mouth edged upward in a vain attempt at a smile. "I imagine that would make quite a difference."

"That is a good question, isn't it?" Victor mirrored the same smile that Randall attempted. He didn't get very far with the effort either. "But I speak of aftereffects. Do either of your brothers know how it feels when the scars are touched?"

Startled, Randall's head jerked up, and he stared intently at Victor. He'd never told anyone. Not his brothers, not the doctors, not anyone. "How did you know about that?" he asked, voice hoarse. How could Victor possibly know? And then it hit him. Everything he knew, Victor would know. Every dark, secret part of his life had been gift-wrapped and handed to Victor, topped with a migraine bow. Of course Victor knew. Randall had no more secrets from him.

For a moment, Randall understood completely why the medusa had been run out of ancient towns as heretics and witches. How terrible, to be so utterly exposed.

After a beat, he slowly slid his arm out of the blanket cocoon he'd constructed. "It's like they're here," he muttered, eyes searching Victor's face. "Like it's happening all over again, if I touch them. I thought...." Randall breathed out a helpless laugh. "Well, I thought I was crazy."

Victor made a noise that Randall couldn't quite identify, something between sympathy and agreement. He was sitting on one of the single beds, his back against the wall, and as Randall watched, Victor tipped his head back against the windowsill, eyes focused on the ceiling, deep in thought. "I don't want to use the word *imprinting*, but it's somewhat the case," Victor said. "The science isn't exact. If you're bitten for pleasure, the pleasure remains. If you're bitten for pain, well, the example follows as is logical."

He tipped his head back down to look at Randall. "It must feel like the knives all over again," he continued in a murmur. "I almost want to congratulate you on your apparent extraordinary skills of concealment, if your brothers never noticed."

"Their teeth," Randall corrected softly. "It feels like they're ripping me apart all over again, like they're eating me. The ones on my sides don't hurt. Just...." He gestured toward his neck, his elbows, shaking his head. "Of course they haven't noticed. There's no reason for them to notice. It's just a bunch of scars, and there's no need for anyone to know."

"Randall." Victor's voice was a quiet protest. "There is *every* need for your brothers to know. The healing process is hardly one that can be done in isolation. You don't want to spend the rest of your life studiously avoiding touch, do you?"

"It's not a bad plan," Randall shot back, feeling that damn heat hitting his cheeks again. "No one needs to touch them. I've become quite adept at avoiding it, and if my brothers do by accident, I can control my reactions."

"It's a *terrible* plan," Victor corrected, "if you ever want to have a normal relationship. Don't understate the effect of things like those scars. Before you know it, they could start poisoning more aspects of your life than you want them to."

He was tracing his fingers over his own scars again. Instead of watching his fingers this time, though, Randall studied his face, his expression. He wondered if Victor was speaking every bit as much to his own scars as to Randall's. They were two sides of the coin, perhaps. The different ways that vampires could leave their marks.

Or, from the way Victor's long fingers were still lovingly outlining the neat, pale scars, maybe not.

"What relationships?" he snorted, trying to swerve away from the topic. "It's fine, Victor. They are just scars. I don't know what kind of poison you're speaking of, but clearly you haven't dealt with yours and you're fine. I need to focus on Anthony right now, on taking care of Edwin. I don't have time for silly nightmares about things that go bump in the night."

"Then apparently my powers of deception are just as extraordinary as yours." Victor gave an odd laugh, a near-silent huff of air. "A word of caution, Randall, nightmares only grow stronger as you ignore them."

Randall curled his fingers into a fist to hide their shaking, his head bowed, hair uncharacteristically messy as it dried, falling in his face. His blankets had slipped as they spoke, his shoulders bare and his skin prickling with a chill left over from the rain. "I was weak in Cairo," he finally said, so quietly he didn't even know if Victor's nonwolf ears could hear him over the sound of the rain pounding on the roof. "I'm a wolf. Vampires shouldn't have been able to get a jump on me." He snorted softly. "You can smell them from a block away. I was distracted and weak and they caught me. They tied me up. They called me *good dog* as they fed from me. I *want* to ignore them." The snap of his voice cracked just as loudly as the thunder. There was rage under his calm expression. There

113

was frustration and guilt hiding just beneath the tense line of his body. "I don't want to be weak again. This is my fault, and I'll handle it. Alone."

Victor didn't reply right away. A flash of lightning, followed by a crash of thunder, rattled the cabin. Then Victor was putting his book down and crossing the room to tentatively sit next to Randall. He smelled like rain, his hair still damp with it.

"That," Victor said carefully, his voice more gentle and kind than Randall had ever heard it, "is nothing to be ashamed of. You were never trained to expect such things would happen to you."

"Bad things happen." Randall found himself staring at Victor's hands, the slim strength of them, at the way the man held himself just a little bit apart from the world. Studying him, like if he looked deep enough he'd find the magic answer that would make Victor see him. "That is the one thing I have learned to expect. No matter what, bad things always happen."

The thunder rumbled again, and Randall shivered. He drew his legs up to his chest, still wrapped in the blanket, resting his chin on his knees. Dropping his eyes away from Victor, he ignored the ache in his throat, the way he wanted nothing more than to lean closer to Victor. He knew Victor didn't feel the same way he did, that his crush was one-sided. It was rude to want more. It was unfair to think that any of this was anything more than Victor being kind.

But then Victor, the man who consistently kept at least two feet of distance between himself and anybody else, reached out and touched Randall's arm. His fingertips pressed lightly on the skin just below a ragged scar at the inside of Randall's elbow.

"Bad things may always happen, but that does not mean you should simply roll over and never move past them," Victor said.

Under Victor's hand, Randall's arm jumped, and he found he was shaking, tiny tremors working their way through him. His eyes were locked on Victor's fingers, waiting for them to move. Waiting for the pain to start. "What are you doing?" Randall whispered, fear threading through his voice.

"I'm showing you that this could cripple you, Randall," Victor said lowly. "I'm not even touching the scars, yet I'd hazard a guess that you can barely think right now."

But in counterpoint to his words, Victor's hand was far from a threatening presence. Instead, he seemed to be curiously shifting his fingertips in fractional movements, as if he were more interested in feeling Randall's skin. Drawing in a shaky breath, Randall found that his muscles were tightening under the touch for a very different reason. Not in fear, but in anticipation.

"I can't ever think when you're around," Randall admitted throatily. "That's hardly a fair example."

Victor hadn't flushed when he'd seen Randall naked; he *did* color slightly then. "Well, I suppose my point just missed the mark," he muttered, but he didn't sound upset about it.

Randall hadn't meant to say that out loud. Truly, Victor being this close, touching him, threw off his thinking into fanciful circles and a logic-barren flight. He never should have admitted such a thing to a man who had no interest, who had clearly and quite politely shown exactly that. But Victor didn't move away, as Randall expected. His hand didn't leave Randall's arm. In fact, Victor's thumb made a soft arc against his skin, sending a shiver down Randall's spine.

"What would you do?" Randall asked, leaning closer until his breath stirred Victor's hair, until he could feel the warmth of Victor's arm pressed against his side. "If you were me?" Not just about the scars. Not just about the nightmares.

Victor looked startled at the question, his mouth opening and closing a few times as if he had no idea what to say. Not exactly typical for a man who, at the drop of a hat, gave lectures about the bi-gendered deities of the Norse pantheon. "I'm not sure I'm the person you should be asking for that sort of advice," Victor admitted. "I don't know."

At that, Randall gave him a very soft smile. There was a warmth in his gaze as he studied Victor that he struggled so hard to hide most of the time. "Not words you or I are fond of," he acknowledged. But it was fair. Perhaps no one could tell him how to proceed—after all, there was hardly a support group for vampire torture. "You don't want to move on from yours. And I wish, sometimes, I could cut mine out of my skin. So we're quite the pair."

"That we are." Victor sounded rueful. The normal indifferent mask he wore had softened slightly. "I doubt even my books would be particularly useful on a subject like this."

That was who they were. They were men of research, of dusty tomes and stacks of notes, of the fervent belief that every answer was able to be found by the one who was willing to do the work to unearth it. Admitting that there *was* no book, no solution, that they were forging a path that was unknown, was something of a big deal. Randall should be more worried.

Instead, he was absorbed in the sensation of Victor's fingers absently sliding along his forearm. Chalk it up to being young, but this once, Randall's heart was shouting far louder than the logic of his head. Which was more than likely why he caught Victor's hand, why he brought it up to press a kiss to Victor's palm. "Then perhaps we'll have to write our own."

Victor stared at him like he'd never seen Randall before, like he was some new kind of fantastic creature that Victor had stumbled across a picture of once but was only just now seeing in the flesh. He looked like he couldn't quite believe what he was seeing and hearing. "That is quite possibly the nicest thing anyone has ever said to me," Victor said slowly. Victor took Randall's hand in a tighter grip.

There were moments. Randall knew that because he'd read the old stories, he'd grown up on fairy tales and history books. There were *moments* when a single action sent ripples out, cascading into a thousand more possibilities. There were moments.

And this was his.

He leaned in, heart crashing in waves, hand rising to cup Victor's cheek. Before he could talk himself out of the action, before logic could supersede daring, Randall drew Victor in, their lips meeting in a soft exhale.

For a few seconds that felt like an eternity, Victor didn't move, clearly too surprised to reciprocate. Victor's response, when it came, was as tentative as the touches to Randall's arm had been. There was no surge of passion, no swelling music or bells on any hills. It was a kiss, nice but perfunctory, as if they were passing acquaintances who happened to get their lips in the same general vicinity.

Pulling back, horrified and struggling not to show it, Randall managed, "I apologize." Shame hit him, hard, and he began fighting with the blankets, trying to stand, to get away. "I am so sorry. I shouldn't have done that."

Listening to one's heart had always been something his brothers excelled in, not himself. Randall should remember that his brain was the only organ which should be making decisions in the future. It would avoid all of this. Victor did not want him. That was a fact that had been made clear. Misreading some kind attention and soft touches was not going to change that.

"No, it's...." Victor trailed off, touching his fingers to his lips.

Randall hardly had any sort of precedent for recognizing the look that came to Victor's face, but right then, he could almost *see* the visions swimming in Victor's mind, all the possibilities of the future that Victor had seen making his eyes look distant and his expression torn.

And then Randall realized what was going on. Why Victor had behaved so kindly and why the kiss had gone nowhere, they both had the same answer. Victor had seen inside his head. The memories, yes, but also the present, the possibilities of the future. He knew Randall had feelings for him. He knew what paths his future might take, in very specific detail. And he was picking and choosing from those paths for Randall.

Running hot and cold, yes, but the reason behind it was not as confusing as Randall had been assuming. "You're orchestrating this. You've seen something in my head, and you're trying to.... I don't know, steer me away? Steer me toward?" Frowning, Randall stood, torn between anger and hurt. "Hard to tell when you're the only one that knows the answers. One second you're being so *kind* that it's like you're really seeing me, and the next it's as if I don't exist."

"Randall—" Victor tried to protest, but Randall didn't stop. He wasn't going to be the polite little wolf, not now.

"If you actually felt that way, that would be one thing, but that's not it, is it? You're picking things from my brain and deciding which ones you want to become real."

This time Victor waited a few seconds to make sure Randall had finished saying his piece. He drew in a deep breath and took off his glasses, fussing with them and cleaning them on his sweater. "It's not just *your* future I saw," he said, his voice tight. "The future of any one person is not an island. We affect so many other people's lives with our decisions—"

"That's bullshit," Randall spat. "God, Victor.... If you're not interested, that's fine. I'm a grown man, not a kid with a crush. You can be honest. But every time I think we're going somewhere, every time I think I see *something* in how you look at me, you put up a wall six miles high and I'm left feeling like a dumb pup. So at least give me the respect of reacting to *me* and not some possible *maybe* you found in my head—"

"I saw us getting married!" Victor blurted.

Oh.

Blinking, Randall let the words hang there for a long pause, filling the space between them. They just kept growing, those words, and Randall honestly wasn't sure what to do with them. *Married.* They were going to get married? That was....

"With children," Victor added. "Or... wolf cubs. Though I suppose it's the same thing."

"How would we get cubs?" Randall asked faintly, feeling as though he ought to sit down. He did so immediately, waving off the question just as fast. "Never mind. I... oh, dear."

"Quite." Victor's voice was muted. He looked like he wanted to respond to the question Randall had asked, but he obviously held his tongue. "I never tell people this, Randall, but then again I have never seen *myself* in their futures. But yours...."

He shook his head, lifting himself off the bed to go stand at the window. The rain was finally starting to calm, and from the sound of the thunder, it was distant now, moving farther away. "About half of the possibilities had us getting married," Victor continued. He sounded as distant as the thunder, clearly trying to remove himself from emotional attachment to what he'd seen. "And I never saw myself as the marrying type." He laughed weakly, scrubbing his hands over his face. "But we were so *happy*."

"You sound like you're describing some horrible thing," Randall said very softly. He studied his hands, laced together in his lap, holding on tightly, as if that simple act would keep him from melting into some puddle of useless emotion. "Like you saw a train wreck you're desperately attempting to avoid." Marriage, children, *love*—none of that sounded so terrible to him.

But perhaps that was the problem. Victor saw *him*, had seen him, and the mere idea that he might actually wind up with Victor was apparently very distressing. "It seems as though you've dodged a bullet," Randall pointed out with a strangled little laugh. He rubbed his hands across his face, feeling a bit as if he was waking from a long dream. "By seeing the possible future, you've now the means to ensure you're never trapped in something so horrific."

"That's not what I meant," Victor said lowly. "Imagine you saw a future in which you never went to college. You wound up working a small office job where all you do is type budget reports every day. But you're *happy*. You see yourself happy and content with every aspect of your life." Victor looked back at Randall with a very small smile. "I imagine budget reports would be the *last* thing you want to do in your life."

"Any time you want to stop comparing *marrying me* to an eternity stuck in a cubicle doing budget reports, that'd be great," Randall said dryly, giving Victor a sideways glance.

"I'm getting to the point," Victor said, scowling.

"I see. This is the scenic route. I apologize. I didn't realize." Despite himself, despite every other emotion pinging around in his head, Randall felt one corner of his mouth twitching up in a very faint smile. "Please, do go on. I'm very much looking forward to the moment when you use an endless trip to the dentist as an analogy for our possible sex life."

"Oh no, I saw that as being *very* fulfilling," Victor said. He then seemed to realize what he'd said and quickly looked out the window again.

Now Randall really *was* smiling. "That's because you were with a wolf," he intoned seriously. "But unless you'd rather switch to that topic completely, please continue."

"Of course," Victor said, his tone as dry as Randall's. "As I was saying. You have seen a future which you at the present moment never wanted for yourself, but you see

117

yourself being deliriously happy with that future. It has little to do with specifics or people—you did not want your life to be an office job."

He finally slipped his glasses back on, turning to properly face Randall as he leaned against the window. Victor then seemed to think of better of it, frowning as he pulled away from his lean, smoothing down the wrinkles in his shirt. "But you have not seen *why* you are happy with it," he continued. "You have absolutely no clue how you got to that point, and all you see is this thing, this life situation, that is the complete opposite of what you presently want. It's… confusing, to say the least."

Bowing his head, Randall let out a slow breath. Yes, he supposed it would be. None of that made Randall any more settled in the situation. Victor had jumped to the end in every possible way. Instead of getting to know each other, seeing if there was any chance of something more, Randall was left at the starting gate while Victor read ahead and already knew how it all ended. Whatever beginning Victor had seen them having, it was gone now. All that was left was this—and most of *this*, Victor decidedly didn't want.

"So that's it, then?" he asked, looking over at Victor. "I'm never going to know if you are attracted to me or if you hate me, because you looked in my head and saw one thing that *might* happen?" He shook his head, running a hand through his hair. He probably looked completely unpresentable, chest bare, hair standing out at all ends, damp and curling from the rain. "I get that it's tough for you, Victor. I don't want to diminish that. But you've changed it all now." Randall's lips edged upward in a grim smile. "Observation, by its very nature, changes the path of the observed object. That future was yours too, and by looking in on it, you're already behaving differently toward me than you ever would have before. And I don't know, maybe it still could come true. Maybe not. Maybe it never would have." Philosophical theories of fate and destiny were always so much easier to debate in the abstract. The reality of it, something like this impacting his daily life, was not something Randall was equipped at the moment to deal with.

Maybe he should just be blunt. It had always worked for his brothers. "Look," he started, leaning forward, arms on his knees, searching Victor's face with an almost painful earnestness. "I'm just…. I'm just a guy who has a crush on an amazing, brilliant, handsome man. I'm not good at that anyway, Victor. I never would be smooth or polished or sure of myself. Add in the fact that I can't tell if you want me around or you wish I'd disappear completely, and maybe it's best if I just keep my distance. It certainly seems like it'd make you happier."

"Of all the things I saw, of all the things I can't picture myself being happy in, Randall, *you* were the one thing that actually made sense," Victor said. He was looking at Randall with the softest expression Randall had ever seen on the man.

"So why can't you just see what's right in front of you?" Randall asked, very quietly. "I don't want to get married right now either, Victor. And if you show up with a wolf cub, I'm going to check you for a brain injury. I just…."

There weren't *words* for what he felt around Victor. It was like running in a full moon, it was like howling, lungs full, the sound echoing through the night air. It was deep in the bones of him, and he'd no more asked for it than he'd asked for his tail. It just was, and he didn't know how to explain that to Victor. It was the most illogical he'd ever been, over a man who seemed to have no use for such emotions. "I don't want your envisioned futures," he wound up saying, voice hoarse and desperate for Victor to understand, "I just want you."

The wolfish side of Randall, the side that longed for the woods around him, the ground under his paws, the sun on his back, it hated the words. They hung there in the air, and they didn't encapsulate everything they should. And while Randall the wolf was a very quiet one, he was no less of a wolf for that reserve. In two steps he was across the room. In one more he was pressing Victor back, his fingers finding their way into that strawberry-blond hair that had taunted him since the first time he'd caught sight of Victor. Randall hauled him in, meeting him in a kiss that wasn't soft or hesitant or unsure.

He kissed Victor fully, wolfishly, to try and *show* him what words didn't seem to capture. And Victor responded. Still tentative, but there was palpable emotion underneath his movements, in the way he put his hands on Randall's arms, in the way he tilted his head so they fit just right.

It wasn't perfect. Randall didn't believe in perfect kisses, in sweeping, grand, love at first sight romances. He believed in this, though. In good matches, in love that built, in the way Victor's lips parted, in how their bodies pressed together. In how a shiver worked its way under his skin, heat flashing through him. Want and need and a sense of *rightness* he'd never experienced. When he pulled back, gently teasing a strand of Victor's hair from his forehead, he was smiling. Victor looked dazed.

"Just because you can see the future, medusa, doesn't mean you have to live there all alone," Randall murmured.

The rain had turned to a soft whisper against the window. Randall saw the confusion still in Victor's expression, the hesitance. But their lips met once more, so gently it ached through him, before Randall pulled away, wanting to cup his hands around that moment and keep it just so.

He let the blanket fall for the few moments it took him to shift back into his wolf form. As soon as Randall was on all four paws, Victor knelt down, one of his hands resting lightly on Randall's back. "Thank you," Victor said, so quietly even Randall barely heard it. "Just...." Victor shook his head. "Thank you."

Nudging his head under Victor's chin, Randall sat there for a few long seconds. They were warm, Victor smelled of tea and old books and, very faintly, like him. It was good.

But Anthony would be waking up soon, Edwin would be looking to warm up, and they both would be hungry. The real world was waiting outside. Randall had taken enough time away from it for now. So he nuzzled Victor's chest, tail wagging faintly, before he left the man there in the cabin alone.

Perhaps he didn't believe in perfect moments. That didn't mean he couldn't stumble across one now and again.

CHAPTER
7

Jed

SO HERE was the thing. Everyone talked about how great goddamn rain was. They sang in it, they skipped, they set fire to the damn stuff. Truth of the matter was, when you were out in it? It fucking sucked.

"Son of a *bitch*." Jed flicked his last match out into the woods, watching as it made a soggy arc and practically disintegrated under the deluge.

"I don't think that's working," Redford pointed out helpfully. He, like the aforementioned crazy people who enjoyed the rain, was goddamn *grinning* at him, wet hair plastered to his face.

"Yeah," Jed grumbled. "No kidding." They were about fifty miles up from the hippie wolf commune and had only gotten a mile into the hunt before the skies had opened up and dumped Noah and his goddamn fucking ark straight on their heads. They'd taken shelter under a small outcropping of rock, but the wind was making building a fire just about as hard as a cock in a glory hole. Jed's emergency pack of flares, a grenade, and matches hadn't been the most helpful things in the situation. Although, thank God, he did have his crisis stash of condoms, an extra tube of lube, and a chocolate bar. Just in case.

But it was clearly time for plan B. Squinting as the water poured down his face, Jed turned in a circle, trying to see their surroundings. But before he could scope out much, half of his vision was obscured by Redford's jacket being held over their heads. One of the wolves had given Redford a rainproof poncho before they'd left, and Redford had looked exceedingly proud of it for the whole drive. Now he held it above them, looking at Jed like he'd just solved the problem completely.

And yeah, okay, it was still fucking pouring and lightning was arcing across the sky, but Jed found himself grinning. It was nearly impossible for him to stay irritable too long around Redford. It was goddamn annoying, really. "Okay, we're going to need to get to a real shelter." The van was downhill, and the path behind them had turned to pretty much mud. Wading through that could take hours. So Jed grabbed Redford's hand and led him to higher ground. At least Knievel was safe back at the camp. She probably would have clawed his face off for daring to bring her out in the rain.

Quickly, Jed searched the surrounding area, picking out trees, rocks, dismissing each one as not what he needed. Finally he came across two large birch trees that had grown leaning into each other. "You stay here," he hollered above the crack of thunder, hauling Redford with him in between the trees. The whole "no trees in a thunderstorm" thing only applied to the tallest objects in the area. These birches looked plenty sturdy, but they were fairly young, sitting dwarfed by the larger growth. "I'm gonna go get us supplies."

He had a knife on him but no rope. Somewhere, his special ops director was trying to kick his ass from halfway around the world. Okay, so he'd improvise. Now *that* he had a lot of experience with.

Ten minutes later, he'd hauled a load of branches back to the birch trees. Most of them were thick and strong, but he had several very thin, flexible ones as well. Working quickly, rain streaming down his face, soaking him right down to his ass crack, he got the logs leaning against the birch trees, using the thinner branches to weave them together. He'd gotten lucky and found a pine tree. The long, thick-needled branches were perfect for a rain-resistant roof.

He left one corner mostly uncovered except for a thin layer of pine before ducking inside, hauling the few branches he'd found underneath trees with him, the dryer handfuls of leaves, and several stones. Kneeling, shoulders hunched over as he worked, Jed made a small circle with the stones in the corner under the hole. He used his body to shield it as he worked. The rain was still thundering down, but it was slightly quieter in here.

The kindling was laid out, then the sticks, cut down to the right length and made into a teepee. Jed took the stones and started striking them together, waiting for a spark. It took him a few tries. He was out of practice—it'd been a long-ass time since he'd had to do survival shit—but eventually he got a tiny tendril of smoke curling up from the leaves. He bent down, ear on the ground next to the fire pit, pursing his lips and blowing gentle, encouraging breaths to fan the start of the flames.

Several aching minutes later, they had a fire.

Sagging back, Jed ran a hand through his hair. "You okay?" he asked, turning to Redford, rubbing his hands briskly along Redford's arms. "Cold? Come on, switch me spots. Get closer to the fire."

Redford was too busy beaming at him, like he'd *invented* fire. "You're a genius," he told Jed, holding his hands out to the flame. He didn't look especially bothered by being soaked, instead leaning up close against Jed to share their mutual shivers. "Can you predict the weather too?"

"If I could do that, we'd still be in the damn car," Jed grumbled. He hauled Redford into his lap, frowning as he kept up his brisk rubbing down Redford's arms and then to his chest, trying to get him warm, to stop him from shivering. "Seriously, Fido, let's focus on getting you warmed up."

Redford shifted, getting comfortable in Jed's lap, hooking his own arms over Jed's to keep both wrapped tight around his waist. "In those books I'm reading, everybody always warms up using body heat," he said, so matter-of-fact. "You know, in *Her Lovelorn Wolf*."

And that was the last time Jed let Redford have free rein of the library. The guy totally judged all books by their covers—and once he'd seen that title, the wolf on the cover, the Fabio look-alike, there'd been no talking him out of it. Cheesy, bodice-ripping romances weren't exactly Jed's thing, but Redford had devoured it with the same enthusiasm as he'd ripped through Chaucer and that really big book of sexual positions.

Apparently, Redford was the pansexual of the book world. If it had writing, he'd read it, and then earnestly quote it to Jed for the next week.

He shouldn't find that as endearing as he did.

Jed nipped Redford's shoulder with a low, rumbling sigh. "That is a terrible title," he said for the umpteenth time. But Redford did have a very interesting point. First Jed dug his gun out of the holster, his knife out of his boot, checking both. They'd stayed nice and dry, thankfully. Jed never bought a holster that couldn't stand up to a flood.

After peeling off his shirt, he found a twig to hang it on. He did the same with Redford's. Hopefully they'd dry out a bit. Hauling Redford in close, arms wrapping around him, Jed rubbed his chin along the slope of Redford's shoulders. "This more like what you're imagining, darlin'?"

"It's not exactly what the books describe, but on the bright side, neither of us has potential pneumonia." Redford laughed, taking Jed's hands in his. "And that is a *great* title."

"You're crazy," Jed murmured, far more interested in tracking kisses along the back of Redford's neck. "Are you going to tell me what we're missing?"

"Well," Redford said thoughtfully, "at that point in the story, the protagonists aren't certain about what they feel for each other. But they realize, by being vulnerable, that they really do love each other. And then there's declarations of love." He paused, leaning his head back against Jed's neck, and said, perfectly genuinely, "I love you, Jed."

Well, who was he to argue with that? Jed huffed a laugh, trailing fingers across Redford's cheek. "I love you too." And then, with absolute sincerity, "Please stop reading romance novels."

Redford's laugh was a rusty purr of a noise, louder and freer than Jed had often heard from the man. When he'd pulled Redford out of the cage of his dead grandmother's house, he hadn't looked like a man who even knew what laughing *was*. Now his shoulders shook with it, the corners of his eyes crinkled in amusement. "Never," Redford said solemnly.

God, Jed loved that laugh. He wished he could bottle it, could wrap it around himself like a comfortable coat. If he could hear just one more thing before dying, just one last sound, it'd be those words—*I love you, Jed*, said like he mattered, like he meant something—and that laugh, it'd be Redford's voice surrounding him.

Which is not to say he didn't hitch up an eyebrow at Redford before very deliberately flipping them over. Blanketing Redford, Jed leaned in, biting his lower lip. "Never?" he asked, threatening. Really, he was very threatening, as he slowly rolled his hips against Redford's.

"Never," Redford promised, a light of mischief—and heat—in his eyes. "We'll have a pile of them on our bedside table until we're eighty."

There was an emotion choking in Jed's throat at that, some intense vulnerability that Redford always seemed to draw out of him. "Eighty?" he asked, rubbing his thumb along Redford's jaw. "Promise?"

"I'm actually planning for us to live longer than eighty," Redford said, leaning into Jed's hand. "But I'll get rid of the romance books then. I'll spare you a few years of seeing me read them." His teasing expression softened. "I promise."

Leaning in, Jed caught those words in a kiss. He pressed them between them, fingers threading through Redford's hair, a smile lost against Redford's lips. "You're not going to get sick of me before then?"

"Never," Redford murmured. He reached up to cup Jed's face in his hands. "Since you'll still be trying to do these jobs when you're eighty, I'll be close behind every step of the way." That mischievous little smirk came back. "Except then I'll be trying to nag you sit down instead of handing you your gun."

"You like to handle my gun," Jed returned, grinning. He leaned in to nuzzle kisses against Redford's throat. Their fingers laced, and he guided Redford's hand down to cup the front of his jeans, laughing against Redford's skin. "See? It's just your size."

He felt Redford turn his head, pressing his nose to Jed's throat. "You smell like other wolves," Redford muttered.

"Yeah, probably." Jed frowned, turning to sniff his own arm. He just caught a faint whiff of deodorant and the slightly earthy scent of mud and rain. Then again, he didn't have Redford's nose. "Kinda surrounded by them." This was not really the topic he'd been going for, so he smirked, lightly nipping at Redford's jaw. "Not a lot of room in here, but I think we could try for some of that body heat if we're careful."

Redford shifted under him like he wanted to roll them over—Jed recognized that movement of his shoulders, the way his expression would get a little stubborn—but there was a tree on one side and a fire on the other. Instead, Redford hooked a hand around the back of Jed's neck, bringing him down again so Redford could kiss his throat, inhaling deeply. "Telling you to stay away from other wolves would probably be weird, right?"

"Maybe impossible," Jed agreed, voice dipping down to a rumble. He turned as much as he could, back now pressed against the tree and the logs, lying on his side to face Redford. There was a flare of yellow in Redford's eyes, a flash of instincts rising to the surface. "I'd say we just go home but.... I don't know. I guess I feel kind of responsible for the furry idiots. And the princess. Something stinks here, for sure." Jed paused, frowning, thumb touching the corner of Redford's eye. "You okay, sweetheart?"

There was that saying, leopards changing stripes or whatever. Spots. Whatever the fuck leopards had. In any case, in Cairo, he'd seen that look on Redford's face. Some mix between hurt and insecurity and the *possession* he craved. His instincts craved. Whichever—maybe there wasn't a difference at all. Point was, Jed knew that expression, and he used to think he knew what caused it. He'd gotten so used to flirting with every older guy with a fat cock he'd kind of forgotten how to *not*. But Redford had hated it. Never really said much, a few things here and there, but Jed had put enough pieces together to realize that it was hurting Redford.

He was hurting Redford. The one thing he'd never wanted to do. He did it without even thinking.

So he'd stopped. Hadn't been that hard, really. He didn't want anyone but Redford. But Jed didn't let himself get into that mindset anymore, that weird headspace that had him turning himself into who he'd been before Redford. Before he'd gotten found. And now Redford had that look on his face again, something deeper, something that said he wasn't happy, and Jed couldn't even begin to imagine what had put it there.

"Hey, babe?" he murmured, cocking his head, studying Redford's face. "Talk to me."

123

Redford wasn't listening. Jed could tell that much from the way Redford's eyes were fixed on his throat instead of his face. His only answer came in the form of Redford's grip around the back of his neck tightening to near-bruising strength, and the sharp bite of teeth against his throat, right against where Redford had been sniffing earlier. A strangled little moan escaped Jed, his head falling back, giving Redford the entire long curve of his neck.

"I know it's illogical," Redford rasped lowly, his teeth worrying what would definitely be a bruise into Jed's skin. "I know it's stupid. I know you haven't gone near any wolves in a… you know, *bad* way."

He dragged Jed yet closer, moving an inch up so that he could get to a new patch of skin, seemingly determined to make another mark. Jed was whimpering, he realized dimly. Redford was claiming him so thoroughly and Jed couldn't even think for how turned on he was. A few stupid little bites, the steel in Redford's throat, and he was ready to come. Maybe Victor wasn't so dumb after all.

"But you're *mine*, and people have to know it," Redford continued. He sounded half possessed, his eyes bright yellow now.

"God, all yours," Jed agreed dimly. As Redford pulled him in closer, Jed wound up on his back, Redford hovering above him. Jed was just clinging to Redford's upper arms, legs spread for him, hitching moans and whimpers in his chest. "Tell every-damn-body if you want."

For a second, there seemed to be a brief hesitation in Redford, the pressure of his teeth lightening up slightly as if he was apologetic—but that moment didn't last very long once he got a look at Jed's face and saw that Jed was definitely enjoying it. He met Jed's eyes for a long time, the harsh panting of their breaths underscored by the thunder of rain outside, the feral yellow so unlike the Redford that Jed was used to. This wasn't the shy, soft-spoken man he spent his evenings with, the one that kept trying to make him play Scrabble instead of cleaning his guns.

This was a wolf.

And that thought was only reinforced by the hard movement Redford made, pushing his hips down against Jed's as if he'd forgotten their pants were even there. He moved with a feral grace, an abandon that happened so rarely with Redford. Jed met him with a low groan, wrapping his arms around Redford's shoulders, breathing kisses along his jaw. "Jeans," he reminded Redford lowly, word caught up in a moaning laugh. "Hang on, babe. We need to take them off."

He was met with a growl.

Okay, maybe Redford didn't have time for removing clothes right then.

Redford's teeth sank into Jed's throat again, one of his hands grasping Jed's hip and pulling him up close. What would ordinarily be painful as fuck—and okay, maybe it was, Jed was wearing *tight* jeans that didn't leave much room for Margaret Thatcher or Rambo, much less Winston Churchill at full salute—he didn't care so much about right then. Not with Redford showing this side of himself, the side that didn't care they were in the middle of a thunderstorm on the side of a mountain, the side that had no time for anything other than getting closer to Jed.

Their hips ground together, Jed's cock practically begging for release. Jed heaved in a breath, fingers digging into Redford's shoulders. Every time he tried to get a hand between them to at least unzip, Redford pinned him harder, sucking and biting down his neck, rocking down onto him and sending sharp jolts of friction rocketing through his body. Jed was begging, he realized, in soft little gasps. Not for it to stop, hell fucking no. His legs spread wider, his body lifted to meet Redford, and he just kept asking for more.

It took him even longer to realize that Redford was speaking too. Just a single word, every once in a while, in between pants. *Mine*, he was saying, mumbled against Jed's throat, barely audible.

And Jed had to reply. *Yours*, in every moan, every shuddering breath. Fucking right he was Redford's.

He kept meaning to get his pants off. To find the lube, to get Redford's cock in his mouth—*something*. Instead he was completely taken over, Redford grabbing his ass and lifting him up, fucking them together like their jeans didn't even exist. Every rock together, every movement, every *bite*, only drove him higher. He came as thunder crashed overhead, as he moaned Redford's name, fingers digging into Redford's arm, grasping at the dirt, spread out on the ground and completely *Redford's*.

Redford hadn't reached the same peak, but he stilled as Jed did, the bites turned into gentle nuzzling, the occasional growl turned into a happy-sounding rumble. Holy fuck. Jed smirked faintly, running fingers along Redford's shoulder, kissing his neck, and....

Fuck. He'd come in his goddamn jeans.

Wincing, Jed kicked his boots off before he reached down and managed to wiggle out of his pants. With a sigh, he tossed the denim out into the rain. Nature's washing machine. "Haven't done that since I was a teenager," he sighed, flopping back down and hauling Redford in close again.

Redford's eyes were still that bright, feral yellow, but instead of growling, he *grinned*. "Is that a compliment?" His voice was rougher than usual, and not just in an *I made Jed come really hard in his pants* way.

"Hell, yeah." Jed smiled, arching his neck up to catch that beautiful grin with a kiss. "I am going to be so pissed later when I have to walk around in wet jeans. That is how good you are." His neck ached with the bruises, and Jed loved the feel of them. He wanted to wear them always, like badges, like a sign that someone wanted him *that* fucking much. That Redford loved him. Rubbing his thumb along Redford's hip, Jed's smile grew. "Get your pants off," he murmured. "I want you to come on me."

"I know I've said I like it when you smell like me, but isn't that a bit overkill?" Redford made a sound like a laugh, mostly a rumble of noise, rising up to his knees to smooth his hands over Jed's chest, smiling down at him.

Well, that line had apparently worked better with the over-fifty and married crowd. Jed couldn't count the number of times some thick-waisted older guy would pound his ass and then come all over his chest, like he was marking a prize. He was, frankly, a little surprised that the wolfish side of Redford wouldn't want that.

Then again, the way Redford was looking at him, no one had ever even come close to that before. Yellow eyes or no, instincts or no—and these days, honestly, sometimes Jed wasn't sure what to think about all of that—this was his Redford. And he didn't need some porn set show to prove he'd had Jed. "Then get your pants off so I can suck you so hard you fall over," Jed amended in a lazy drawl, tugging Redford close. Mouthing kisses

125

along Redford's stomach, Jed murmured, "You're so goddamn beautiful. Best I've ever had. I don't tell you that enough."

Sitting on Jed's hips, Redford leaned down, tugging Jed up to meet him halfway for a kiss. He traced his fingertips so lightly over the bruises that Jed barely felt his touch. "You could help me get them off," Redford suggested. "If I try I'm likely to put my elbow in the fire."

Jed kissed him first. Simply, intently, they kissed, Jed's hand slipping into Redford's messy hair, sprawling out near the warmth of the fire. They kissed, and Jed forgot his jeans were outside getting soaked or there was now dirt in his ass. It was just Redford, and how could he really want to change anything about that?

Fingers fumbling, Jed managed to get Redford's jeans unsnapped, the zipper tugged open, and, finally, the pants shoved down Redford's hips just enough that Jed could get his cock out. "Hello, darlin'," he all but purred. Ducking down, he ran his tongue along the length of Redford's dick, sucking lightly on the head. If he sprawled out, Redford kneeling above him, there was just enough room for Jed to get the right angle for Redford to fuck his face.

Digging his nails into Redford's ass, he jerked him in closer, swallowing around Redford's cock and managing not to grin at Redford's surprised little noise. They'd had enough lead up, as his own jeans would attest. He just wanted Redford to come hard and fast.

Redford was apparently as wound up as Jed had been, though there was no growling this time, no bruising grips. Instead, Redford was gently carding his fingers through Jed's hair, following Jed's lead, and Jed guided his hips, his moan muffled around a bitten lip. When he came, he dug his fingers into the dirt beside Jed's head, head thrown back in ecstasy.

And when he promptly collapsed in a puddle of contentment over Jed, his hip was digging into Jed's shoulder. Jed couldn't even find it within himself to protest the odd position for the moment. He painted kisses along Redford's thigh, his side, whatever skin he could reach, hands smoothing along Redford's legs.

He could sleep. Just like this, he could sleep for days. Last night had been more watchful wariness, only drifting off to a troubled sleep sometime before dawn. But now, despite the slightly uncomfortable angle, Redford was here, and he was warm enough that Jed really did think about dropping off.

Redford started moving, pushing himself back so he was more properly lying on Jed, his cheek resting on Jed's chest. "The storm's clearing up," he murmured, sounding drowsy, like he was thinking about dropping off right here too.

Fingers tracing odd patterns against Redford's back, Jed hummed a distant agreement, eyes sliding half shut. For a long time, it was just that. The two of them, skin to flushed skin, Jed's idle touches, Redford's soft breathing, and the light drumming of the rain easing off into silence.

"You okay?" Jed broke the quiet, rousing himself back to wakefulness. Napping on the job, while okay for office types, wasn't so much allowed on his sorts of assignments. "You went all wolfy on me. I, uh, I gotta admit, I'm never really sure what I should do when that happens." Jed huffed a laugh, dropping a kiss to Redford's head. "Not that I'm complaining. I like it when you let go."

When Redford turned his head slightly to look up at Jed, the only yellow remaining in his eyes were dim rings around Redford's normal gray blue. He sounded hesitant when he replied, as if he already knew the answer but needed to hear it again anyway. "You do?"

Pressing a kiss to that worried crease in Redford's forehead, Jed wrapped his arms around Redford, hauling him in closer. "I like it when you don't feel like you have to hide shit from me," he murmured. "And, hell, you've been working with the headshrinker on accepting that side of you, right?"

"Yeah." Redford tucked his cheek back against Jed's chest. "It's just…." He gave a soft exhale. "Never mind. We've got hunting to do."

It took some maneuvering, but Jed managed to reach one arm out to snag his pants back inside. They were soaked from the rain, and Jed sat up, still holding onto Redford, to hang them near the fire. "Can't go anywhere, my pants are all wet," he told Redford with an innocent look. "Might as well spill."

Redford just smiled at him. Jed's innocent looks never worked on him anymore, sadly. Then the hesitant expression came back. "You remember how in Cairo I had a lot of trouble with the, um, violence?"

Christ, there went that damn look again. The one that had Jed wanting to grab every gun he owned, every goddamn explosive, and build a wall a thousand feet high around Redford so that nothing bad could get in. It was a childish wish and he knew it, but that didn't stop Jed from hauling Redford into his lap, from kissing his shoulder and resting his hand over the dog tags and whistle that were hanging against Redford's chest. "I remember," he said, giving Redford the space he needed to work out what he wanted to say.

Yeah, Jed remembered. He remembered a Redford so far gone he'd been ripping out vampire throats with his fangs and howling as he threw himself against a door, desperate for the chance to get back inside to kill some more. He remembered being fucking scared—not *of* Redford, but for him.

"It's different here," Redford sighed. "All these wolves, all this *space*. It's like I want to go running through the forest and never stop." He glanced up at the bruises still darkening on Jed's throat, then leaned in to press a gentle kiss to them. "They're all so in tune with themselves and their instincts, it's kind of weird. Their lives are so different from ours."

Because a wolf wasn't supposed to be confined. It was funny, the first time he'd seen that damn cage in Redford's bitch of a grandmother's basement, when he'd seen the chains and the muzzle, the scratches on the wall, he'd hated her. He'd wanted so badly to give Redford something *better*. To have him be free. And he'd been patting himself on the goddamn back for doing so.

Why? Because Redford wasn't tied up. Because Jed brought him *hot dogs* and played Frisbee in the apartment and rubbed his belly until he passed out every night. Because Jed held him through the change.

Because his cage was so much nicer.

Jaw tight, eyes distant, Jed ran a hand through Redford's hair, struggling to keep his expression from breaking. *Their lives are so different from ours.* Because they were free. Because these wolves weren't shut in with a stupid fucking human who, after a year, hadn't figured out that someone like Redford needed to not be held prisoner.

Those voices in Redford's head, that split personality mumbo jumbo, maybe it wasn't all that bastard Fil's fault. Maybe they were because of Jed too. Because Jed was putting Redford in a cage just as sure as his grandmother had. Maybe Redford wouldn't ever get better around Jed, because what was Jed going to do? Open a fucking window?

"I like our apartment better, though," Redford said. "At least there I don't need to sleep on the opposite side of the fence from you."

"You didn't need to do that here," Jed pointed out mildly. "There was a whole cabin, just for you. Bet Knievel thought you were giving up the bed because she demanded it."

"She could have it." Redford shrugged, tucking his head in under Jed's chin. "I wanted to be close to you. I *needed* to be close to you. Everything in me was screaming about it. Including the, you know, the instincts."

"Maybe that's not such a good thing." Jed didn't want to be cuddling. He didn't want Redford anywhere near him. Because by being *near him*, Jed was just continuing this idea that Redford had to be a tame wolf, that he had to fit into the world Jed knew. But that wasn't the right place for him, was it? That was why everyone back at hippie wolf central was looking at them like they'd sprouted two heads. They knew. Wolves and humans didn't mix. "Tonight you should, you know, sleep in the cabin thing. Like the other wolves do."

Redford gave a shudder at the idea. "No," he said simply. "If you have to sleep outside again, I'm sleeping with you. And if it rains or if it's muddy, then I'll sneak you in." He paused. "Maybe I'll do that anyway. That way you could sleep on an actual bed."

Jed was a stubborn man. He knew that. And, more than nearly anything, he wanted Redford. His list for Things Jed Needs To Survive was actually pretty damn simple. Redford, Knievel, his gun, some beer, a brick of C-4, and a window to see the sky from. That was it.

But loving someone the way he loved Redford wasn't as easy as he'd thought it'd be. It made him want Redford to be happy a fucking lot more than he cared about his own interests. "Nah," he lied so easily, kissing Redford's forehead. "I'll go to the hotel tonight if Miss Priss doesn't let us in. You should bond with the wolves. Make furry friends."

He'd stay. Of course he would. But Jed was beginning to think, to *know*, that for Redford to be happy, he'd need a lot more than what was on Jed's list. A window wasn't enough. Redford deserved the whole fucking sky.

What he sometimes tended to forget was that Redford could be as stubborn as he was.

"Then I'll come with you." Redford lifted his head, bringing a hand up to cup Jed's cheek. "Wherever you go, I go. No matter what, right?"

Well, if Redford needed to run, maybe Jed would just have to figure out how to keep up. Letting out a slow breath, Jed turned his head to kiss Redford's palm. "I just want you to be happy," he admitted gruffly.

"I am happy." Redford twisted their fingers together and bent down to kiss Jed's knuckles. He gave a rueful little smile. "Besides, I'm not sure I'd want to stay here too long. Communal living isn't really my thing."

"Yeah, well." Jed leaned his forehead against Redford's. He hated thinking about this shit. He hated the idea that there'd be a morning or an evening or anything in between where Redford wouldn't be there. So maybe they'd be okay. Maybe Jed would just... buy a house. With a big-ass yard. People had houses with yards; it wasn't an impossible thing. "What do you think about maybe getting out of that apartment? We finish this job, go fishing, get Knievel into that flotation vest, and when we get back we can look for something with some more room?"

"But you love that apartment," Redford protested, "*I* love that apartment, and—"

He cut himself off, turning his head to face in the direction they'd climbed up the side of the mountain from. He blinked, and then his eyes were yellow again, lip pulled up in the start of a snarl.

"Hunters," Redford said briefly, moving off Jed so he could get his pants back on. "Come on. I know where they're hiding."

Well, the whole wolf thing just wasn't getting any less hot, that was for sure. Jed managed to shimmy into his jeans, even though they were still mostly wet. He had to crouch to pull his boots back onto his feet, nearly toppling over twice before bracing his hand on a nearby tree for balance. They ducked into their shirts, and Jed tugged on his holster before kicking out the fire, moving the branches of their makeshift roof aside to let water spill down to sodden the ashes. It only took Jed a few minutes to disassemble their shelter, shrug on his jacket, and grab Redford's hand. "Quiet," he murmured, though he probably didn't have to say that to Redford, not when he was like this. "Show me where they went."

Redford was hiding his mouth with a hand, though Jed could catch the smile in his expression from the crinkles at the corners of his eyes. "You're... squeaking." Redford's gaze darted down to Jed's soaked jeans.

Growling under his breath, Jed just stalked off. Yeah, he was fucking squeaking. "*Someone* wouldn't let me get my *pants off*," he grumbled, shaking one leg and then the other as if he could flick off the excess water.

"I only barely heard it," Redford reassured from behind Jed, following him. "Wolf ears." He then took Jed's shoulder, turning him forty-five degrees to the left. "This way."

Adjusting his gait but never losing the irritated tic of his shoulders, Jed led the way down the muddy bank, back into the thick of the woods. The craggy face of the mountain swept downward, and they picked their way over rocks and fallen limbs, shoes sucking in the wet undergrowth. Jed's gun was out, both hands on the butt as he eased around the trees, gaze constantly sweeping the area around them.

"Tell me when we're close," he whispered.

"They're good at masking their sounds," Redford replied, equally as lowly, sounding frustrated. "I haven't heard anything from them since that first noise. But this is where it came from."

Pausing, Jed frowned, holding up his hand to keep Redford back. Everything looked exactly like the rest of this goddamn forest, all towering trees and the drip of water from soaked leaves onto the ground. But there was something *off* about the dense thicket ahead. Jed eased forward carefully, making almost no noise—except, apparently, *squeaking*—as he picked his way through the underbrush.

There were bent branches on a bush he passed. Some of the leaves were disturbed. No animal tracks, though. Carefully, Jed made his way around a large tree, stopping cold as he got past the pine's branches.

It was a clearing. Small, well hidden, but just enough space for the roughly built cabin. Jed immediately backed up, heart pounding as unexpected adrenaline surged through him. Minutes ticked past, though, with no gunfire, no one rushing after him, no one calling out. Jed moved slowly back around the tree trunk he'd taken shelter behind, gun aimed at the windows, looking for a hint of a sniper's barrel.

Nothing.

The porch of the cabin creaked under his foot, and he froze again. There were footprints in the mud leading away, clear tire treads going in the opposite direction. The marks had to be fresh. The rain would have washed anything previous away.

He eased the door open, teeth gritted with the expectation that it might creak, though it never did. Inside was one big room, bunks in one corner, a stove in the other. It was empty. Sticking his head back out the door, he whistled sharply once and waited for Redford to join him, watching the woods for any sign of the hunters' return.

Redford padded silently out of the forest, with—Jed noted, as a point of pride—his gun held loosely in one hand, muzzle pointed at the ground. He joined Jed just inside the doorway, taking in the room.

"Can you smell anything?" Jed asked, interested. Redford was so much better at this shit than anyone would expect, and the whole *nose* thing was so fucking cool. In Cairo, Redford had seriously gone full-Lassie-mode and followed Randall's trail based on nothing but a shirt.

"They left maybe ten minutes ago," Redford offered, though he sounded unsure about the time. "About that, anyway."

Wandering the room, Jed paused in front of a pin board. It held a map covered with thumbtacks and sticky notes. Leaning in, he scanned over them, memorizing the positions of the tacks, absently running his fingers along the notes.

Sm. pk. 2 d.

Feed. ground. 3 d.

Followed 2, tkn.

"They're hunting," Jed agreed after a pause, voice distant. Frowning, he tapped his finger against the map. "Where are we? About here, right?" There was a blue tack there, three other ones spread across the map. "These must be their base cabins. And these...."

Red tacks and yellow. "Red for kills, yellow for something else. Potential hunts? Where they'll hit next?"

Redford was studying the blue tacks, eyes narrowed. "Jed," he said slowly, "This is *really* long-term, isn't it? This isn't just random humans running around to kill wolves they're scared of."

"They're not just hunting wolves. They're hunting... well, yeah, wolves. But not *normal* wolves. You wolves. Human wolves." Jed pointed to the notes. "This isn't some wildlife special gone wrong. Look. Small pack, two dead, maybe?" Deciphering bad handwriting and shorthand wasn't easy. Jed squinted at the next two, centered around a cluster of yellow pins. "This looks like they were following two. Taken, maybe?" Taken where? For what? "They have to know what they're hunting. If it was just wolves, wouldn't there be, shit, more red marks? Regular wolves are pretty plentiful up here, and they're not exactly Houdini."

When he went to look over at Redford, the man had wandered off to the other side of the cabin. Nose twitching, Redford was running his hands along the rough wooden walls, pausing every so often to knock lightly. His knuckles rapped against the walls at odd intervals, and Jed paused, just watching him, completely confused. Until, that is, Redford hit a hollow-sounding board. Leaning in, Redford took a deep breath before stepping back, eyes going over every inch of the wall carefully. Then, just that easy, he reached out and pressed on a seam Jed wasn't sure he would have even noticed on his own.

A door swung open, revealing a tiny, cramped room. There were rows of semiautomatic rifles and long knives hanging from the walls. Several of the spots were bare, the weapons obviously taken out by the hunters. In the center was a wooden table with box after box of bullets. Redford picked through them, letting out a low noise as he flipped open the lid of one. "I don't think people just trying to hunt regular wolves would have these."

He held up a silver bullet.

Jed's jaw tightened as he moved to Redford's side, taking the bullet and holding it up to the light. The way Redford had Nancy Drewed the room was definitely going to be mentioned as fucking cool. Later, though. Right then, Jed was busy studying the bullet like it could tell him all the answers he needed. Silver knife with sacrificed blood or whatever the shit—that had killed Filtiarn. But he'd been special. Old. Regular bullets had worked just fine on Fil's pack, whether they'd been werewolves or full wolves or something in between. So why the silver?

"This shit's got to be expensive," he murmured, turning the bullet over in his fingers, squinting to see the faint markings on the bottom. "And specially made. See that? It's a marking telling us the manufacturer." Jed tipped the bullet toward Redford, letting him look closer. The letters *B* and *C* were etched there in brackets, and he felt like he should know this. Like he'd seen that before.

Redford picked up the box that the rest of the bullets were stored in, taking a sniff of it, and turned his head aside to sneeze suddenly. "This smells like... cow?" Redford wrinkled his nose in confusion. "But also kind of familiar?"

"Well, we did have burgers last week," Jed pointed out. He grabbed a bag from the corner, loading up one of the guns that had been left behind, a box of bullets, and then started carefully taking down the maps, working extremely gently as he rolled them so as not to lose the place of any of the pins. "Help me grab this stuff. We need to get out of here before Tweedledum and Tweedle-murders come back." He'd love to take all the goddamn bullets, but even he, with his He-Man like strength, couldn't lug that much back to the van.

There were a few books they jammed into the pack, another half a dozen maps with writing on them Jed didn't bother to stop to read. Wherever the hunters had gone, they might not stay away much longer. Jed wasn't exactly in the mood to have a face to face.

Not yet, anyway.

They ducked out of the cabin, Jed urging Redford into a run for the cover of the trees. Once they were out of the clearing, Jed looped the strap of the duffel bag across his chest and dug in his own bag to find his compass. "We need to get back. Whoever these chucklefucks are, they're packing enough ammo to start a very small, very bloody war." He had the urge to blow the whole fucking cabin to kingdom come. Sadly, he didn't travel with his C-4, and he hadn't spotted any in the armory itself. Which might be a good thing. Starting a forest fire would get Smokey the Bear on his ass, not to mention Jed had no idea who these bastards were. More information was probably needed before he started exploding things.

Too bad. Would have made him feel better.

The air was still damp with the aftereffects of the storm, and the crack of very distant thunder told Jed that some other poor bastard was having to deal with the torrential rain now. As long as it wasn't him. He shook the compass, hitting it with his palm a few times to get the needle working. Redford just lifted his chin and sniffed, then pointed to where his nose must be picking up their own trail. "That way."

Oh. Huh. "Have I told you in the past hour how awesome you are?" Jed asked with a grin, hefting both of his bags up to settle their straps more firmly across his shoulders and chest before setting out in the direction Redford had indicated at a brisk jog. They had more than two miles to go, and Jed wanted to cover it as quickly as they could.

"I still don't understand why *you* have to carry everything," Redford said beside him, keeping pace. For someone who had never been properly trained in stealth, he did a damn good job of avoiding dry twigs and rocks that would tumble.

"You're the brains," Jed reminded him with a smirk. "I'm the brawn." He flexed his arms as if to prove his point. Ducking under a low-hanging tree branch, Jed grimaced as his boot hit mud. Going this fast through regular wooded terrain was bad enough. Add mud on top of it and it was a fucking picnic right up Satan's asshole.

Redford just sighed at him, eyeing Jed like he was thinking about forcibly trying to take one of the packs off him. He shook his head, a small, fond smile lighting his expression. "So what do we tell the Gray Lady?" he asked.

Pausing by a rock outcropping, checking their twenty, Jed glanced over at Redford. He had a bag full of weapons that were definitely not made for hugs and sunshine, a bunch of silver bullets, and maps that made the Unabomber look like a teenage prom princess. He shrugged, giving the only answer there really could be.

"Shit just got real."

IT WASN'T that he didn't just fucking *love* having mud getting really nice and cozy with his balls. Really, the whole thing was goddamn super. That and the smell of wet dog was doing just *loads* to improve his mood. Standing in the Gray Lady's den of hippie incense, Jed tried to subtly remove wet jeans and about six feet of dirt from his ass crack only to get a far too haughty look from Victor for his efforts.

Whatever. Jed would just stop being subtle. It was hard enough doing that while sitting, he'd just stop caring about everyone's delicate sensibilities.

The drive back to the Gray Lady's camp had gone uneventfully, but once they'd gotten inside the gate they'd picked up their very own guard dogs, who hadn't been amused when Jed had told them to sit and stay while he grabbed a shower and a fresh change of clothes. Which was why he was standing there, damp and muddy-assed, waiting for the great goddamn Gray Lady to stop futzing around with some big-ass candle and get this show on the road. Knievel jumped up on the table, meowing loudly and head-butting Jed repeatedly. Apparently she was displeased with how long he'd been gone. Jed leaned his arms on the table, giving the cat a place to curl up, her head resting against Jed's wrist, tail flicking absently as she completely ignored the proceedings.

"Why are we here?" Randall asked, confused. The Lewises and Victor had been escorted in shortly after Jed and Redford had arrived. "What did you find?"

"Your balls," Jed told him with an entirely earnest expression. "They must have dropped. I'm just so proud. You're all grown up now."

Randall's expression didn't change. "Funny, I could have sworn I had an enormous pair right here," he mused. "Those must be yours. They look rather shriveled, but I hear humans do that when it gets cold." Jed didn't miss the way Victor tried to get a surreptitious glance in.

Jed just laughed. "Okay, fine. We'll agree they're Victor's tiny balls and be done with it."

Victor just sighed faintly, apparently not even dignifying that with a response. Randall darted a look over at him but didn't say anything. Great. Nerd awkwardness. That was just going to be so much fun to deal with.

"Once you're done comparing dick sizes?" Anthony's voice cut in.

"*Ball* sizes, sweetheart," Jed corrected with a wink. "Very different thing. Makes a whole world of difference."

Anthony didn't look entirely amused. He looked over to where the Gray Lady was preparing tea, then back at Jed. "Would it kill you to show a little respect?"

Eyebrows winging up, Jed barely restrained a laugh. "For what? Hocus pocus? Look, I went out and I did a hell of a lot more than I'm being paid for out there. I got forest gunk in places you've never even seen. So if you think I'm going to sit here and play reverent for no goddamn reason—"

"I didn't say *worship* her," Anthony said. "I said *respect* her." He looked like he wanted to say more, but he took a deep breath and shook his head. "Please. The last thing we want is to get kicked out because you lot are too busy talking about your balls in front of the most powerful wolf alive."

"That's a load of—"

"That's enough." The Gray Lady's voice was like thunder just before it crashed, the low rumble that almost ached in Jed's chest. She sat at the head of the table, nodding to the woman on her left to begin pouring tea. "I appreciate your intervention, Anthony Lewis, but I hardly need you to keep my ears pure." If Jed didn't know better, he'd think there was a faint twinkle in her eyes. "I have been alive long enough to know what *balls* are, and I have never met a man who could match my own."

Jed kind of thought he was in love.

Anthony shrank in on himself, his shoulders hunching. "Sorry, ma'am. I was just cautious about the, er, duration of our stay."

"I have accepted you into our pack." The Gray Lady waved one elegant hand, the bracelets around her wrist clinking like bells. "You are to stay here. So long as you abide by the code of the wolves, you will not be asked to leave."

Jed felt a nudge against his shoulder. It was Redford, leaning over to scoop Knievel into his own arms, giving Jed a meaningful look. His gaze went to the tea being poured, meaning the Gray Lady was obviously ready to hear them speak, then down to the bag Jed had placed by his side. Huffing out a breath, Jed slung an arm around Redford's waist, turning his attention back to the Gray Lady.

"You went hunting," she murmured before he could speak.

Which kind of took the wind out of his sails a bit. "Yeah," he muttered, deflating slightly. "I haven't blown anything up in days. I get itchy when I'm bored."

A faint smile touched the Gray Lady's lips, and she inclined her head. "Tell me what you found, human."

Said like he was an armless man at a circle jerk—just taking up space and getting nobody off. It still struck him as so fucking weird, how *human* could be an insult. Like everything he knew about how things worked was, in fact, just the inane ramblings of the dumbest kid in class. Everyone else had read the book, and Jed was busy picking his nose. There was a whole goddamn *world* that he not only wasn't a part of, he wasn't even invited into.

"You're being hunted," Jed confirmed. "But it's not by Cletus and the good ol' boy crew. This isn't a bunch of guys with a six-pack and some time to kill. They're organized, and they're specifically hunting *you*. Not just wolves." Four faces stared blankly back at him. The Lewises and the Gray Lady all looked like they were patiently waiting for some idiot to realize he was being insulting. "I mean, they're hunting *wolves* wolves. Not... you know. Wolves. They're... it's not wolves. It's wolves like you, not wolves like...." Jed waved his hand helplessly toward the woods. "Those wolves."

He heard Victor's muffled laugh in the resulting silence. Jed scowled. "Oh, fuck, you know what I mean. Jesus, what am I even supposed to call you?"

"The correct term is *Canos*," Randall piped up, looking all too amused. "Werewolves and Canos and then the common wolf."

Oh. Well, that made this easier to talk about. "What about Redford?" he asked, curious.

Randall hesitated, eyes flicking over to Redford. "Redford is...." Randall smiled faintly, voice kind. "Redford is something else entirely."

Hell yeah he was. Jed rubbed his hand along Redford's arm, looking as proud as a fucking peacock. "Werenos," he decided. "That sounds badass enough for you."

"That's linguistically appalling," Victor said witheringly.

"It certainly doesn't make sense," Randall agreed, stifling a laugh. "Werewolf comes from the Old English *werman*, which used to simply mean 'man,' as opposed to the female *wifman*. It turned into *were* and *wolf*, man-wolf. So you just named Redford a man... well, *nos* which doesn't actually mean anything. Man nos." Apparently that was a joke in dork-speak, because Randall was practically giggling.

"It's absolute gibberish." Victor still sounded personally offended by Jed's attempt to make up new words.

"I like it," Redford reassured Jed in a whisper.

"I like your man nos." Jed winked at him. "I could take your *nos* all night."

"Jed," Randall said, exasperated. "You can't just make random words mean your penis."

"Try and stop me." Jed was grinning, pretty damn proud of himself. Anthony looked like he might start knocking heads together, and as amusing as that was, Jed figured he should get to the point. "Okay, so the hunters are definitely going after the Canos variety of you furry fuckers." Pulling out the bag, Jed laid out the guns and the bullets, watching as the Gray Lady's eyes got wider.

That was practically a fainting fit from the likes of her, who had patiently sat through their naming conversation with barely a blink. "Where did you get these?" she asked, half rising, reaching out to pick up one of the bullets.

"Redford found the hunters' cabin. Well, one of them. These were in a hidden room. They've got a shit ton more. More than enough to make life very difficult for your pack." Jed frowned, reaching out to grab his own bullet, turning it over to examine the etching at the bottom. It still was vaguely familiar, even though he couldn't quite place it. "Don't know why they're all silver, though."

Anthony took the same line of thought that Redford had. "Why does it smell like cow?"

Edwin grabbed a box, practically burying his nose in it. "Not cow," he corrected his brother. "Not... exactly. Steer, maybe? Kind of, it smells a little bit like when we went to the fair and I was in the livestock tent."

Jed could just imagine how well that went over. "Stampede?" he guessed.

Edwin flashed him a self-satisfied grin. "Who, me?" He looked so innocent. Jed didn't believe it for a second.

"It was like a meat grinder," Anthony sighed. "But to get back on topic." He gave them all a significant look. "What does this mean? All of these bullets and maps? Are we dealing with just a few little groups of hunters, or a *war*?"

"War." Jed didn't even hesitate. He knew war; he knew what gearing up for it looked like. He sure as hell knew that those guns weren't peashooters. Eyes flicking to the Gray Lady, he arched an eyebrow at her. "You're awfully quiet down there."

"Yes," the Gray Lady agreed. Her voice was distant. "I am." She set the bullet down, frowning at it. "Were the hunters all human?"

"I couldn't smell any traces of anybody not human, ma'am," Redford said. "No half bloods or vampires."

"So," she mused. "Someone is telling fairy stories."

Okay, that didn't make any sense. Jed looked around the table, scowl deepening when no one else seemed confused, except for Redford, who shared his bafflement. "What the fuck does that mean?"

"It means that needing silver bullets to kill a wolf is a myth, Jed," Anthony explained. He glanced at the Gray Lady, looking like he was making sure he wasn't stepping on any toes by speaking. "Werewolves, Canos, we all die from regular bullets."

"That I know," Jed snorted. Which, maybe he shouldn't talk about the wolves he'd killed in Fil's little shop of horrors, because the Gray Lady gave him a look, the kind of expression Jed normally reserved for deciding which side of the burger to bite into first. "So, uh, what does that mean?" Changing the subject seemed wise. Too many things with teeth in the room and his pants were starting to stick to his ass, meaning his gun would be harder to draw. Also that he'd probably walk funny.

"A long time ago, when humans were just starting to move about and explore the dark, we started telling stories about ourselves." The Gray Lady's eyes had dropped back to the bullet, one long, graceful finger running along the length of it, like she was touching a sacred object. "Those stories grew as they did, fitting the times. Silver bullets were ours. They made us seem harder to kill, and most humans were content to stay inside and leave us be. But someone is feeding into those old tales."

Randall was leaning forward, attention rapt. "They're not all stories, though," he pointed out quietly.

"No," the Gray Lady acknowledged, tilting her head. "Silver, iron, holy water, all of these things have their places. But not for most."

"Why silver?" Jed found himself asking. "I mean, the silver knife thingy worked on Fil. You guys got a hard-on for mining or some shit?"

The Gray Lady looked at him, eyes flaring yellow. Once again, Jed thought that perhaps rubbing the whole *I killed your ex* thing in her face might not be wise. He wasn't afraid of her, but shooting his way out of this place wasn't exactly on his to-do list. "There are many reasons. The silver comes from deep in the earth, from the purest heart of it. It will kill many of the older ones if smelted properly and mixed with sacrificial blood."

"And the bullets wouldn't do anything to you," Randall said slowly, puzzling through it. "They'd kill a lesser wolf or a were simply by virtue of being a projectile weapon, but for you they'd be nothing at all."

"True. At the time of the first telling, silver was rare. Expensive. Telling the humans to make bullets out of it ensured we would have some peace." The Gray Lady shrugged. "A little truth mixed in with the lie."

"So all this means is that the hunters have bad information," Anthony said. "Did they stumble across that myth on their own, or is, as you said, someone telling them fairy tales?"

"These bullets are made special." Jed turned it over, facing the flat end of the bullet toward Anthony. "That's the maker's mark. We figure out who's supplying these and we know who's bankrolling the whole operation." He shot a glance down toward the Gray Lady. "One thing that hasn't changed, your royal furriness. Silver is still going to be fucking hard to come by for your average redneck. Especially enough for as many bullets as we saw. Not to mention the cash someone splashed for those guns."

"Of course." The Gray Lady examined the bullet a final time, then rolled it back over the tabletop to Jed. She took a breath, looking like she was gathering herself—her shoulders straightening, her expression hardening. "And how long do we have before this war arrives on our doorstep?"

Everyone always wanted to know that. Like they could avoid it. Like it was a dust storm in the desert and you could just roll up the windows and wait for it to pass. "Oh, sweetheart," he sighed, shaking his head, looking at the table. At the map with its little markings, at the bullets and the guns. "That shit is happening right now. They're picking off the little packs around you, see?" He jabbed his finger at the map. "Some of them killed, some taken, I think. They're looking for you." Jed looked up, meeting her eyes, holding them. And for once, just once, he almost didn't see that dismissal, like he might actually be worth more than a chew toy. "They will find you. It's just a matter of how long your luck holds out."

Silence descended around the table. The Gray Lady was looking down, clearly lost in thought. Jed felt Redford's hand steal into his, their fingers lacing together. Jed squeezed lightly, glancing over to catch Redford's gaze—he looked worried, even with Knievel standing on her hind legs to bat gently at Redford's cheek. Jed gave him a reassuring look. This was always the shitty part. Waiting for the client to realize he was right.

"Well, little human." The Gray Lady's voice broke the quiet. "I think you should stay with us for the time being. It seems that now is the time for closing ranks."

"Sister," Jed said, "now is the time for a hell of a lot more than that. You've got people out there *hunting* you. Right now it's a small group. Probably some ex-cops, private security types. Good, but not great. Someone is bankrolling this, and it ain't a cheap bill. Which means when they don't get results, they're going to step it up and hire guys like me. And let me tell you"—he leaned in, expression deadly serious—"you really don't want someone like me coming after you."

"We have been hunted before." The Gray Lady dismissed his concerns with a wave of her hand.

"Not like this."

"*Yes,*" she barked, eyes blazing into that inhuman yellow. "In all years, in all ages, your kind has sought to wipe us out. I know how to protect my pack, Journey Walker."

"Don't call me Journey," Jed gritted reflexively, half rising. "Look, I get it, you're all high and mighty, but—"

"I am my pack's leader." The Gray Lady was standing as well, both hands braced on the table, tension practically vibrating around her.

"*But,*" Jed continued, louder, as if he hadn't been interrupted at all, "this is not the time to sit in circles and hold fucking hands. We know where their bases are. We go out and we blow them all to fucking kingdom come. And then we find the fucker who's supplying them and we blow *his* ass to the sky too. Come on, you guys are goddamn *wolves*, not a bunch of fucking rabbits. Act like you've got some teeth and *attack.*"

Anthony gave a bark of a laugh. "We are not *animals*, Jed." There was a growl underneath his voice, his eyes as bright as the Gray Lady's. "We are not aggressive for the sake of violence."

Without missing a beat, eyes locked on Anthony's, Jed picked up one of the semiautomatics on the table. He took it apart, then put it back together, hands flying and snapping everything into place, like it was some deadly dance. He didn't even have to think about it; his gaze never wavered from Anthony's face. And before anyone could react, before one fucking person could even think to stop him, he put the gun to Edwin's head, and he pulled the trigger.

The empty chamber clicked with a deafening sound. Jed threw the gun on the table and sat. "You might not be, cupcake," he told Anthony. "But the men who are going to come? The men like me? They are."

Anthony was just shaking his head. He stepped closer to Jed, standing at his side, and picked up the gun, turning it over in his hands. "Don't ever do that again," he said simply, without a hint of threat in his voice. He didn't need to vocalize it so obviously. Whereas Randall had a look of such unrepressed rage on his face that Jed was kind of surprised he still had his throat, Anthony simply stared him down.

Edwin was white, staring at the pile of weapons in the middle of the table, uncharacteristically still. Randall had scooted closer to his brother, shoulder nudged against him. Jed felt bad for a minute, for scaring the kid, but in the end he just shrugged. "You don't think I would kill him. But here's the thing. I'm not a good guy. If Randall hadn't paid me to come with you, if the job was instead to hunt a bunch of wolves for cash? I'd have taken it. End of story. I'm not some hero riding in to save your asses. I'm just a professional who's telling you what the goddamn score is."

"Jed," Redford whispered urgently, tugging on his hand.

"You should probably shut up now." Randall's voice was hard. Redford had on those ridiculous eyes, the ones that meant he wanted Jed to stop talking and possibly stop insulting people. Which was usually the right call, but in this case, Jed didn't know how to say it any plainer. People with big guns were trying to kill this little commune. They should fight back. He wasn't going to just let them think the world was rainbows and magnum condoms.

"No," Anthony said. "Jed's right. Not about the explosions or blowing people up. He's right about the men that will be sent." He looked at Jed, his eyes faded back to their usual blue. "For what it's worth, I'm glad you're on our side, and I hope it's more than the money that's keeping you here."

"They've got a mean continental breakfast." Jed's lips twitched upward, but the sharp tic in his shoulders relaxed a little. He nodded at Anthony, accepting his support. "Trust me. Your brother didn't pay me nearly enough to be here. Besides, no one hired me. I'm Red's plus-one. This is just free advice." He turned to the Gray Lady. "And I can count on one dick the number of times I've given that out. So maybe listen to me."

Randall had deflated a bit, Edwin was still looking rattled, but the Gray Lady didn't seem calmed down at all. Still, she nodded sharply, sharing a look with Anthony. "We need time," she finally said, sitting elegantly. "Despite your impetuous nature, these things cannot be decided in a moment. Can you give us that?"

Jed considered it. "My rate's five thousand a day, plus expenses."

"Jed!" Redford looked scandalized this time.

"Oh, right." Jed looked a little sheepish, slinging his arm around Redford's shoulders. "Ten thousand. You're getting both of us." Knievel yawned, stretching and hopping up on the table. "Twelve," Jed amended without missing a beat. Knievel obviously counted too.

"That's not what I meant, Jed," Redford sighed. He leaned in close, hissing in Jed's ear, "They build their houses out of logs. How much money do you really think they have? We're not out to *bankrupt* them."

Eyes widening, Jed looked at Redford, raising his eyebrows as if to protest. Redford's expression didn't waver, so, with a heavy sigh, Jed sulked back in his seat. "Fine. Pro fucking bono. But you try and make me sleep on the goddamn ground again, I will blow so much shit up that you'll think it's the Fourth of fucking ass July."

"That would be one of our stipulations," Redford said, a lot more diplomatically. "That Jed be granted a cabin for the nights."

"Also, would it kill you to have some whiskey?" When Randall shot him an exasperated look, Jed pointed to Knievel. "It's for her! She likes a cocktail before bed."

"I think that can be arranged." The Gray Lady's voice was that dry, annoyed tone Jed remembered none too fondly from his school days. He'd practically majored in detention. "Any other demands?"

"No," Redford said, jumping in before Jed could open his mouth. "Food and a roof over our heads are all we ask." He put a hand to Jed's back, patting him consolingly. "As for advice—first you'll need to post at least twice the amount of guards you currently have around your perimeter, at all hours. If you need more time to make a decision, we'll find more information for you. We'll try to trace the bullets back to the manufacturer, and hopefully we can give you something to make a more informed decision on."

Redford was so goddamn hot.

Jed was just staring at him, that ridiculous little smile tugging up one corner of his mouth. And if they hadn't been in the room with prudish, overstuffed professors who would probably faint, Jed was pretty damn sure he would have kissed the hell out of Redford right then. Or gotten on his knees and begged. Maybe both. In any case, he had to content himself with drawing Redford in closer, nodding to everything he said, and being so proud he really wasn't sure how to begin to show it.

"And hopefully the increased guards will make the hunters think twice about attacking before they bring in the big guns," Redford continued. "We saw on the wall that the hunters had made notes about smaller packs in the area. They should probably be informed too."

"Do you guys have a network?" Jed asked, peering around the table. "Like in that Dalmatian movie? You go howl and the next pack gets the message?" Perking up, he added, "Or, like, virtual buttsniffing? E-mail for the ass focused?"

The Gray Lady did not look amused. Jed almost felt offended; that was *hilarious*.

"We have a system in place," she said, serene as ever.

And apparently she wasn't going to share with the class. Naturally. Jed shrugged, arms folded, leaning back dangerously in his chair. "Fine. You spread the word. I'll do some research, see if I can follow the money."

"Fine." The Gray Lady stood, nodding at them all. "I will anticipate a report soon, Jed Walker. Please, do not fail me." As if he needed a reminder of how high the stakes were. She swept out of the room, ramrod straight and elegant, like a willow branch refusing to bend in a windstorm. In all his life, Jed didn't know if he'd ever met anyone who mixed that much classy with balls that big. He found himself grateful that, at least for now, it looked like they were all on the same side.

"You smell like Anthony's sheets did when Veronica used to come visit." Edwin was standing close, leaning in to sniff Jed, nose all twisted up in a grimace. "It's sour. What is that?"

"Come, mud, rain, and ball sweat," Jed answered easily. "Welcome to the glamorous life of the mercenary for hire."

"ASSFUCKING DONKEY balls in a *fucking sewer*." Jed threw his phone across the cabin room, followed by the pile of maps and his half-empty bottle of beer. "Jesus *Christ*." Dragging his hand through his hair, he slammed his ass down on the chair, scowling at the dripping mess in the corner. "Fifteen calls, Red. *Fifteen fucking calls*. I might as well have shoved my hand up my ass and spun for all the info I got."

He'd been at this for hours now. After the painful act of peeling his jeans off—and the unexpected Brazilian wax he'd gotten from the mud and other assorted grossness drying and sticking to his short and curlies—he'd showered, changed, and gotten to work. This part should be easy. But one by one his contact list dwindled without a speck of new information to show for it. Hell, even the hardest cases he'd done were easier than this.

Turned out, everyone he knew still thought vampires sparkled and werewolves were in London. Not even whispers of silver bullets were going around the usual circles. Hell, in desperation he'd tried a couple of David's old numbers, only to come up against a disconnected message every time.

No one knew a damn thing that was useful. For the first time in his life, Jed found himself at the end of his rope with nothing to show for it but a limp dick.

Redford looked up from where he'd ensconced himself on the cabin bed. As Jed had been making calls, Redford had migrated his way under a pile of covers, curled up on his side with his nose in a book. Now he was looking at Jed with a faintly concerned frown. "You don't have anybody else you can call?"

"Well, I'm waiting for the Tooth Fairy to get back to me," Jed growled, eyes narrowed as he stared up at the ceiling. "But other than that...." Heaving out a long sigh, Jed scrubbed both hands across his face, desperately trying to massage some blood into his brain. "It's fine," he muttered, the chair thumping back down to four legs as Jed swung himself up again. He passed by Redford, dropping a distracted kiss to the top of Redford's head before he gathered up the maps and his phone, dumping them back onto the table.

He arranged the papers again, smoothing them out carefully. He'd just start over. And if that didn't work, he'd start one more time. Over and over again, he'd go over this until a pattern emerged or he got the info he needed for the next step.

"I guess most of your contacts don't really know about all this," Redford said. "Can you pass me the papers we got from the cabin? I want to have another look over them."

"You should sleep, babe," Jed protested, but he gathered up the papers and spread them out on the bed for Redford. God knew what time it was, but he was pretty sure they were rounding assbutt-o-thirty. Cracking his back, Jed took a moment to stretch, stifling a yawn and peering outside. It was still dark, but he swore he could see the first cracks of dawn lightening the sky beyond the trees to gray. "I need coffee," he mumbled, frowning. "I wonder if they have coffee."

"They do in the kitchen." Redford's reply was absent as he shuffled through the papers. "I think I heard someone mention the kitchen is open all hours. Do you want me to get some coffee?"

Blinking, Jed rubbed his eyes before sitting himself back down and picking up his phone. "I want you to sleep," he told Redford. "I'm fine. I can go for days. I think I've proven that on more than one occasion." His usual leer was more exhausted than normal, and he scrolled through his phone's contacts, looking for someone, anyone, who might give him a clue.

Redford looked like he was on the verge of disagreeing, but he relented. "Come here, then. Get all your stuff so you don't have to move." He patted the bed, shifting over to make room.

He wanted to say no. He was working. This was a job—even though he was getting paid fuck all for it—and when he was on a job, that was all he was. It was what he was good for. This and giving head were pretty much his only useful skills. So he should be able to *solve this*. Make the calls, do the research, track this shit down, and take care of the problem. It was who he was.

Only none of his contacts meant jack. Jed's whole fucking network was worthless. They dealt with gun smuggling and drug lords and kidnappers, they were the ears to the ground in a world where wolves were on the Discovery Channel and the biggest danger was a trigger-happy amateur. He didn't *get* this place, these people, and neither did any of his contacts.

So basically, he was worthless.

"Jed." Redford's soft call broke into his thoughts. Jed blinked and looked up to see Redford now standing in front of him, his hands outstretched. "Come on. You can keep researching if you really want to, but just come to bed."

Heaving out a long exhalation, wishing to God he still smoked when he was stressed, Jed gave a jerk of a nod. Redford took his hands, and they gathered up maps and books and the phone, Redford smiling so damn sweet as they arranged themselves in the bed. They wound up under the covers, Redford curled up against his side, under one arm, as they paged through the notes one more time, Knievel a warm weight on their feet.

Pressing his lips to Redford's temple, Jed breathed slowly, letting himself relax into him. "Okay," he said, flipping through his phone again, "we'll start at the As." Again.

Punching in a number, Jed's voice cracked into a boisterous, manic pace, his grin to match. "Artie! How are you, you stupid fucker? Yeah, I know, I called earlier. Well don't shit on me. It's not my fault it's six in the morning. Look, I got a question about bullets."

CHAPTER
8

Redford

THE SOUND of yelling woke him up.

Jed was up before Redford even opened his eyes. "What's going on?" Redford managed to mumble, rolling his way out of bed to find his pants. He couldn't pick out any words in the yelling, but the stench of fear was obvious.

As soon as Redford had a shirt on, he tumbled after Jed out the cabin door, eyes barely open—Jed had a gun out, his posture relaxed but alert, moving quickly with his body half turned toward the source of the yelling to present less of an easy target. Jed hadn't bothered to find clothes, not that he seemed concerned about standing in the chilly early morning air in nothing but his boxers. The sun hadn't even started to get close to the horizon.

There was a half circle of wolves already gathered around a young girl who looked no more than thirteen, terror making her mouth thin and her eyes wide. She'd fallen to her knees, drawing in desperate pants of air. Mallory was there already, standing protectively over her, one hand on her shoulder. She smelled subtly different than the rest of this pack, a wolf, but from a different family.

Since Jed wasn't even half-dressed and was brandishing a gun, Redford grabbed his arm to stop him from getting too close. "She's from one of the smaller packs," he murmured to Jed.

Jed didn't even glance over at him, just giving a tight nod, jaw working. "The goddamn hunters," he breathed, eyes narrowing. Redford could almost see the wheels spinning in Jed's head as he put pieces together, watching the girl as she was practically engulfed by the worried pack. "You go sniff out some details. I'm getting the supplies."

As Jed left, Redford edged closer to the group. He'd never been good at stealth, but in this case everybody was too distracted to notice him. It worked well enough. In the chaos of noise and questions he could see Mallory turning to another wolf, speaking lowly under his breath about the girl's pack: ten miles to the northeast, about twenty wolves.

Jed was right. The hunters had hit. Some members of the pack were wrapping a blanket around the girl, giving her water, making a place for her to sit on the benches around the fire. None of them were asking questions. In fact, no one at all seemed in much of a hurry.

"What happened?" Edwin was next to Redford, looking sleep tousled and only half-awake. Randall was after him, clucking his tongue and handing Edwin a sweater to wrap around his bare shoulders. "Who's that?"

"I don't think it's any of our business, Edwin," Randall started, but Edwin didn't seem to be listening. He darted around the bustling wolves, going to the girl. He was in pajama pants and Randall's gray sweater, looking ridiculous, but he smiled at the girl, took her hands, asking her questions in a low voice Redford couldn't quite make out.

"What is this, a party?" Jed had arrived, bag slung around his shoulder, dressed all in black. "We going or not? Who's got details?"

"It was hunters." Edwin appeared back through the crowd, normally cheerful face thunderous. "Tala, that's the girl, she was asleep when her dad woke her up. The pack smelled them and sent her for help. At least five of them, she thinks, and they stank of metal and gunpowder."

"Where they at now?" Jed was rifling through his pack, checking his guns again. It was a ritual, Redford knew. Jed liked to be prepared. "Gunfire yet, or no?"

Edwin shook his head. "She got away clean, and the pack apparently has a fallback cave they use when people get too close. It's by the river, about ten miles up."

"Northeast," Redford chimed in. "I heard Mallory talking about it. We can run there in twenty minutes or so."

"Maybe you can," Jed grumped. "Two hours for me. Remember, I've got half the legs."

"Drive it?" Randall had come closer, dark eyes serious behind his glasses. "Those maps you've got, they show all the forest roads, right? There has to be access points. If I remember correctly, that direction has the fire trails, so there'll be something drivable for most of the ride. We can run, you can follow."

"We?" Jed's eyebrow raised. "You too, specs?"

Randall snorted. "Edwin is already planning on going. I'm hardly going to stay here and let him go alone."

"Hell yes I'm going," Edwin practically growled. "And we're running out of time."

"Give me a gun." Victor had appeared at Jed's left flank, holding out his hand. "I'm coming too."

Redford could probably list about twenty reasons giving Victor a gun was a very bad idea. Jed seemed to agree with him because he held his bag a little closer, as if protecting his weapons from Victor's hands. "Am I being pranked?" Jed asked, looking between Victor and Randall. "Seriously, is this nerds gone wild?"

"Just give him a gun, Jed." Anthony's voice came from behind Randall. He'd approached them after sniffing around the edges of the pack, hovering just outside of the range of where Mallory and the Gray Lady were talking together. "An unloaded one, if it makes you feel better."

Victor went to protest, probably on the verge of giving Anthony a very stern lecture, but Anthony was already in the middle of shifting. He butted his head against Jed's knee, a clear *we're heading out.*

143

Redford could see Jed glancing at the girl and then back at Victor, obviously having a very brief, very intense mental war. Finally he handed over one of his precious guns, gently wrapping Victor's hands around the butt. "Safety," he murmured, coming closer to Victor to give him a quick lesson. "Trigger. Keep your finger here, on the guard, until you're ready to shoot. Safety on until I say so. It's loaded and ready, so don't aim at anything you don't want shot off, no matter what. Holster's in my bag." He handed said pack off to Victor. "Keep close, keep your head down, and for fuck's sake, princess, don't get shot."

With that, Jed took off toward Mallory and the Gray Lady. Randall and Edwin had followed their brother's lead, shifting, Edwin keeping close by Jed's side. Redford shot Anthony a sideways look, searching for stiffness or signs of pain. If he was feeling it, he was better at hiding the symptoms than Redford expected. Then again, he suspected adrenaline might be playing a part in that. Redford contemplated changing as well but decided against it—his shift would only take up time. Instead, he went to Victor and dug around in the pack for his gun, buckling the shoulder holster on.

"I don't know what you think you're going to do," Mallory was saying. "We can't go running after every wolf in trouble. Put the guns down."

"These people are getting attacked, possibly as we're all standing around, jerking each other off." Jed's voice was rising to a shout with every word. "Are you seriously telling me you're just going to let them die? Ten miles away, and you're going to what, shut your doors and pretend it isn't happening?"

"Every pack looks after itself," Mallory argued. "We're in danger enough as it is. We don't want to piss these hunters off even more and bring retaliation down on our heads. We're not ready for that."

"What about you, sweetheart?" Jed turned to the Gray Lady, hands spread in supplication. She stood slightly behind Mallory, likely through no choice of her own— Mallory looked every inch the guard right then, standing tall, shoulders squared. "Tell me this bozo isn't speaking for you too."

"There are laws, human." Her voice was low and sad but firm. "You wouldn't understand."

Jed paused, glaring at both of them. His guns were strapped to his hips, a long machete across his back, standing so at odds with the soft, unarmed dress of the Gray Lady. She was fierce and restrained, but Jed looked like barely contained fire, like a storm just about to break. His fury was nearly palpable in the line of his shoulders, the scorch of his glare. "Yeah. That's me," he gritted. "Just a goddamn human."

He turned away, going to where the rest of the pack was mingling. "Listen up." Jed raised his voice to be heard, ignoring any incredulous looks from the rest of the wolves. "If I wanted to let people die while I sat around and pretended I didn't hear them screaming for help, I'd have stayed in my old job. As it is, I've got a bag full of guns, enough explosives to take down a building, and a direction to point both in. If you want to come, fall in behind tall, dark, and furry over there." Jed motioned to Anthony. "He's going for a run. I'll be your friendly neighborhood backup van. If you'd rather stay here, well, fuck you."

The pack around them fell silent. Jed didn't wait for a reaction. He was already striding across the field toward their van, whistling sharply at Anthony. "Let's go, Lassie."

Anthony didn't look impressed, but he turned, looking back over his shoulder at the gathered pack. One of the wolves, a young woman with dark hair, stepped forward to incredulous murmurs, shifting smoothly and falling into line alongside Anthony. Then another did the same, and another, until five of the younger adults of the pack were grouped with the Lewises.

They didn't waste another second. Anthony raised a howl—a call to arms—and they started running, streaking out of the camp. Redford followed suit, making a quick pace toward the van, joining Jed and Victor there. They didn't speak, and Jed only gave them two seconds to buckle up before he hit the gas.

"Need that big, beautiful brain of yours, Fido," Jed muttered, pushing the van faster, the old vehicle rattling dangerously. Once they got off the main trail leading to the camp, the road to the northeast was little more than a well-worn dirt track. "You got those maps memorized?"

"Well enough, I hope," Redford replied. He'd gotten himself into the backseat, and he nudged Victor to move so he could lean over the back to sort through their bigger equipment, one hand holding on to the seat to steady himself with the bouncing of the van. "Do you think you'll want your grenade launcher? Or are we going smaller?"

"Big Bertha definitely should come out to play." Jed's voice was grim, and as he banked a sharp turn, the van practically bounced up onto two tires. "I'm not feeling in a subtle mood."

"You have a *grenade launcher*?" Victor squawked.

"You'd actually be surprised how useful they are," Redford said. He tugged Big Bertha up and laid it over two empty seats. "Jed, I've got explosive rounds, hollow points, and jacketed. The jacketed's probably a bit overkill. What do you need to know about the maps?"

Their exchanges were rapid-fire, Jed not even having to look up from the road to check on Redford's work. They knew each other now, they knew how to anticipate the other's thinking, what the other would need or where they'd go. It was a partnership that Redford hadn't even realized was fully forming until it gelled so easily. "Best route," Jed shot back. "River or mountain."

There were two main fire trails. One followed the meandering path of the river, sticking close to water, and the other went up onto the mountainside, getting the higher ground. Both headed in the right direction, and both wound up by the lake a hundred miles up, but if they took the wrong one, they could wind up too far away to get to the wolves in time. Trying to think of the best route was a little difficult when Redford was hanging over the backseat. Closing his eyes, he pictured the maps in his head, seeing his finger slide along the trails, zooming through both of them in his mind's eye. "The river."

He didn't need to explain his reasoning, and Jed immediately turned in that direction. Low-hanging tree branches were starting to smack against the roof of the van, and Victor was clinging to his seat for dear life, paler than usual. Remarkably, perhaps in respect to the situation, he didn't bitch at Jed's driving.

Every so often, Redford thought he could see flashes of wolves through the dark tangle of tree branches. Edwin's blond fur stood out against the shadows, Anthony little more than a dark silhouette, the chase of fur and paws darting through the underbrush like it was a dance. Then the trail curved away, no longer making a straight line toward their destination, and the wolves were gone.

"Shift?" Jed asked. When Redford looked up, Jed's eyes met his in the rearview mirror.

Redford glanced at the clock. They had a few minutes before they arrived. Time enough.

Damn it. He didn't *want* to shift, but it was the better option. He'd be faster, he'd have better senses, and no matter how much time Jed had spent with him at the gun range, he still didn't shoot with the same natural effectiveness. As little as he wanted to admit it, Redford's best weapons were his teeth and the brutal instincts of his wolf form.

"Yes," he confirmed, hurriedly tugging off his necklace and dropping it in the cup holder. His bracelet went the same way, and Redford didn't have time to worry about Victor's sensibilities as he stripped. Jed, however, seemed to have that covered.

"Look away, princess," he growled, threatening.

If Victor had a response, Redford didn't hear it. The rush of blood was too loud in his ears as he closed his eyes to try to focus, to shove aside all the external stimulation and concentrate on the change.

It hurt. It always did.

But Redford didn't have time for recuperating in the aftermath. He got himself into the passenger seat and shoved a paw against the window button to get the air rushing in. The eight wolves—the Lewises plus the five from the pack—were making better time than the van, which had to stay out of the thickest parts of the forest, and it looked like they'd arrive a few minutes earlier.

He thumped his tail against Jed's leg twice, for two minutes, and pointed his nose in the direction of the wolves. They'd worked out a whole silent communication system. It had had some failures, like the time Jed had misunderstood *unknown criminal coming from behind* as *you should come in my behind*. That hadn't been a good conversation to have in the middle of a job. By and large, though, it was an incredibly useful tool for when Redford didn't have proper vocal cords.

Jed's fingers pushed lightly through the fur at the back of Redford's neck, gently hanging on as he pushed the van even faster. The whole vehicle rattled and shook, the three of them bouncing around painfully inside. All of a sudden Jed swore loudly, jerking both hands back to the wheel and slamming so hard on the brakes that the van fishtailed, skidding on the dirt path and spinning nearly completely around. Redford only narrowly dodged as Big Bertha made an appearance between the front seats.

A large tree blocked the road. The van was stopped, facing back the way they'd come, inches from the trunk. Jed didn't waste time, though. One quick glance to make sure everyone was still in one piece and he floored it, driving a ways down the road before stopping again.

"Bertha," he snapped at Victor. Victor handed over the grenade launcher. Jed dove out of the car and took off at a run, shouting back, "Cover your ears!"

There was several beats of silence, Victor's eyes going wide. "Tell me he's not."

Redford just whined softly and ducked his head, paws over his ears as instructed. A count of ten later and there was a fizzing sound, a whiz through the air, a bright burst of light, and a very loud explosion. Scraps of wood rained down on the van, but nothing threatening, and Jed climbed back in. Despite the hurry, he still somehow managed to look extraordinarily pleased with himself.

The van ricocheted forward down the newly cleared path. Jed seemed to be pushing it twice as hard, the engine grinding in protest at the speed. If the engine gave up completely, Redford wouldn't care, as long as it did it *after* they got to the pack.

All at once, Redford could smell it, the concentration of wolves, the peppery tang of gunpowder. He nudged his nose against Jed's arm, and Jed stopped immediately, skidding to a halt and throwing on the parking brake. He left the engine running as he grabbed his bag. "Lead the way, Red," Jed muttered, quickly climbing out of the car, barely managing to fit Bertha in his duffel bag, gun already out. "Get to the wolves and tell them to stay back. You guys are going to get the pack to the van, got it? Victor, you're in charge of survivors."

Since the door wasn't easily opened with paws, Redford had to leap across to the driver's seat and out the door that Jed had opened. He lifted his nose to the wind to figure out where the other wolves were—a brief bump against Jed's legs and they were off. The acrid stink of the explosion was still lingering in the air, the stench of burnt wood and the sweeter smell of gunpowder overlaying the whiff of gunmetal and other wolves. They were close. There was no way the noise of Jed's blast wouldn't have alerted everyone to their arrival. Jed was running flat out, jumping over downed branches and underbrush, gun at the ready. His urgency spurred Redford faster, his ears flat against his head, the ground blurring underneath his pounding paws.

Everything in him wanted to stretch his muscles and run, to *soar* across the ground like he knew he could, but he couldn't leave Jed and Victor in his dust, even if part of him *wanted* to leave Victor. Either that or nip him on the heel for being so noisy, crashing through the forest like an asthmatic elephant.

A sharp yip of pain rose in the air, an angry howl following behind. At the bark of gunfire, Jed cursed, digging somehow deeper and increasing his speed. Redford could smell his sweat, could hear the deep gasps for air, but Jed didn't let himself rest. As they rounded the bend and came upon the cave, wolves racing through trees, the flash of guns after them, Jed didn't hesitate even a moment.

He climbed up onto the top of the rocky crevice, the cave under him, and he started firing. "Red," he bellowed, aiming for where the hunters seemed to be, laying down cover fire. "Get them out of here!"

If Redford ever wondered how Jed had been before, how the man who kissed him so gently, who smiled with genuine joy at silly things like a home-cooked meal could have done the things he casually referred to, he got his answer then. Jed was hard, unflinching. When the hunters began firing back, he coolly ducked behind a rock, reloading and continuing on as if this was just another day at the office. He trusted Redford to find the wolves, to start directing them back toward Victor, and he never once lost focus from what he was doing. Redford had only seen a glimpse of Jed like this back when they'd first met. *This* was truly Jed in his element.

When one of the hunters broke free of the rest and went after the wolves who were forming the front line, Jed left his birds-eye perch and went running, sniper rifle left behind in favor of his beloved pistols. "Get back," he barked at Anthony. "Victor's got the van. Now *move*."

One of the hunters was down, several of the wolves were bleeding, there were howls and shouts and the constant bray of guns. How Jed was keeping track of everything in the semidark, in the thick of the trees, Redford didn't know. Jed was constantly moving forward while trying to give everyone else room to fall back, like he really did think he was bulletproof.

There were a few steps in the undergrowth to Redford's left, the noise barely loud enough to be noticed above the gunfire. Someone was approaching Jed's left flank.

Jed was in danger.

Redford kept low to the ground, running behind Jed so he wouldn't distract him. Grass tickled against his belly, his paws barely making a sound against the dirt. The hunter was coming closer, shotgun raised, aiming straight for Jed's head. Redford could see the man's finger tightening on the trigger, the muscles in his arm tensing as he prepared to fire.

Jed could *die*.

Redford didn't think. He didn't stop to debate the morals, because right and wrong had been washed away in the howl of fury that rose from his instincts.

With a guttural growl, Redford leapt. He landed heavily on the man, knocking him back, the shot firing off into the woods. Under him, the hunter twisted and turned, hands closing around Redford's muzzle, fingers caught between his teeth. With a snap, Redford ripped his hand open, and when the hunter brayed in pain, Redford took the opening and tore out the man's throat. Blood gushed over his tongue and soft skin parted easily underneath his fangs, and for a few moments, Redford was lost.

Kill, his wolf chanted, the throb of his heart beating to a primal frenzy. *Kill hunter, protect pack.*

The roar of a semiautomatic caught his attention. Anthony growled. Redford didn't look at Jed. He didn't think about all the times they had trained for this kind of scenario, all the times they had gone over the fact that if Jed had a clean shot, Redford should stay out of the way.

But Redford could smell the blood in the hunter's veins just waiting to be spilled, and all the danger of potentially getting hit with a stray bullet didn't matter. He ducked past Anthony, coming up on the back of the hunter, and closed his jaws around the man's knee. The bone shattered easily under his bite. Redford used the grip to drag the man down onto the dirt, his snarl an undercurrent to the hunter's scream.

Pain blossomed in his temple. He turned on the attacker, jaws wide, teeth flashing. A forearm was thrown up, and Redford latched on to that instead of the throat he'd been aiming for.

He bit down, going to crack the bone, but he stopped on his next inhale. Gunpowder. Pine.

Jed.

A strong hand on the scruff of his neck dragged him back, away from Jed. Anthony, human now, was growling at him, threatening and deep. That growl said, *get down and stay down.*

Jed's arm was painted in red. The one remaining hunter lay still on the ground, Jed's gun aimed at him, never wavering. Some of the other wolves gathered in a loose circle. Jed was talking, voice like steel. Bodies were lying around, strewn carelessly like fallen autumn leaves. The hunters. Redford could count four, including one whose throat was a bloody, gaping wound, eyes glazed and staring sightlessly up at the leaves above.

Jed knocked the last hunter out with the butt of his rifle, one sharp movement across his temple. He stood with his left arm hanging uselessly by his side, dripping blood down the tips of his fingers to leave a trail. "Everyone accounted for?" he asked Anthony lowly.

"Everyone's fine," Anthony replied. Redford could smell injury on him, but not much. Slowly, the wolves filtered back in, most still shifted. Edwin's muzzle was bleeding. Randall was limping, blood winding its way down the fur of his back leg. Victor, pale and shaken and reeking of fear, was crouching near Randall, his quiet words a meaningless buzz to Redford's mind.

"Okay, princess, start loading up the van. Anyone who shouldn't be running goes there. We can probably fit everyone, if they don't mind sitting close." Jed's voice.

Victor smelled confused at first, then resolved. "You heard him. I don't want anybody playing macho and trying to run back if they shouldn't." The wolves started making their way to the van, and Redford growled under his breath, staying close to Jed to make sure none of them attacked.

Would they attack? Redford didn't know. All he could smell was blood and death. The lack of immediate danger calmed his racing heart some, but every movement was still suspicious.

Randall, dragging his injured leg, stayed behind with Anthony. Edwin was sitting close to Redford. Victor glared at them. "You three, in the van. I won't tolerate people not being sensible here."

Anthony gave a sigh but followed the order. He trudged toward the van, Edwin trailing behind him. Randall gave Victor a perfectly calm stare and sat at his feet, at which Victor threw up his hands in exasperation and moved toward the van himself. Randall limped after him, looking just a bit like a sheepdog herding a wayward lamb back toward the pen.

Redford blinked slowly, wondering if he should follow suit. He didn't feel injured, but a strange numbness was creeping into every muscle, every breath of air that carried the scent of blood making him feel dizzier.

Some of that blood was Jed's.

He'd bitten Jed, he started to realize. He'd hurt Jed.

He'd done it once before, when they'd been playing harmlessly and Redford had lost the battle against his instincts. It had been a human bite then, blunt and only deep enough to warrant a few stitches.

This was infinitely worse. If he'd bitten any harder he would have ripped Jed's arm off.

It looked like Jed was wearing a red glove, his entire arm bathed in it, the wound a gaping bite on his forearm. Jed was moving like he didn't feel it, grabbing his weapons, shell casings, cleaning up the scene. "Get in the van, Red," Jed said quietly. He was checking the bodies for ID. "I'll be right there."

Redford didn't know what to do. He wanted to prowl the woods and hope to find something else to attack. He wanted to lie on Jed's feet and beg him for forgiveness. He wanted to guiltily slink off and hope they wouldn't talk about it. None of those options was going to help, so he wound up going for the practical choice. He shifted, the change feeling easier when the wolf instincts were so close at hand, and retrieved Jed's bag.

Jed's good hand was immediately cupping his jaw, the worry that pinched at Jed's face almost unbearable. "Jesus, babe. You didn't have to turn back here. Are you okay? You—"

"*Don't.*" The snarl was ripped from Redford's throat, so harsh it was painful. Jed immediately stumbled back, eyes widening. With angry movements, Redford dug through the bag, going for the medical kit. His heart pounded again with that frenzy, but now it was directed inward too. "Don't ask if I'm okay, Jed. Don't you dare do that *now*, when I nearly ripped your fucking arm off!"

Jed looked stunned as he stood, bathed in the barest light of dawn, bleeding and dirty. He was cradling his arm to his stomach, absently holding it close, staring at Redford like he didn't know what to say. "It doesn't matter," he started, shaking his head, concern curving his lips downward. There were bodies strewn around them, one of them that Redford had put there, Jed's arm bearing Redford's teeth marks, and Jed didn't appear angry. He just looked so lost. "I'm okay. Just... are you.... Shit, I mean, I should get you back, right? You need...."

Redford had never heard Jed so hesitant.

He didn't reply. It would be more accurate to say that he *couldn't* reply. He felt some of his conscious mind start to return to him, but it was weak, only what he needed to be aware enough to help Jed. Nothing else was important.

In a daze, Redford got what he needed out of the first aid kit and walked the short distance to the van to give the rest to the wolves inside so they could start patching themselves up. When he returned to Jed, he still couldn't speak. He just gently took him by his uninjured arm and led him to the nearby river.

Blood was still flowing freely enough, but Redford could smell the high copper tang of it start to muddle into old as it clotted. Jed's skin was pale, dark circles under his eyes. Not dangerous levels of blood loss, not yet, but he was clearly beginning to feel the pain.

Redford wrapped a towel around Jed's arm, attempting to stop the bleeding for the moment. Tending to this couldn't wait, not even the half hour it would take to get back.

He'd done this. He'd given Jed an injury so severe it needed immediate treatment.

"We can't do this now," Jed was telling him, voice soft but remote, that clinical tone he got when he was on a job. But Redford wasn't listening. There was a hunter not far from them who was still alive but unconscious. His breath was rattling wetly in his lungs, every gasp of air a tortured struggle, and every exhale carried with it a short groan of pain.

Redford couldn't find it within himself to care. *Got what he deserved*, his wolf snarled in triumph.

Jed's voice filtered back into his hearing. "Flannel shirt *número cinco* over there is going to wake up soon, and we need to be long gone. There'll be a cleaning crew that comes out here. I got enough information to start tracking down these sons of bitches, but we have to go."

Redford just kept holding the towel around his arm. "Do we need that hunter alive?"

"I already got what he knows." Jed shrugged, wincing slightly as he moved his arm. "It wasn't much."

"Okay." Redford nodded. He looked away from Jed's arm to the hunter, the sound of his pained breathing seeming to grow louder. The hunter was useless now, nothing but dead meat.

But he was the reason Jed was insisting they leave before treating his wound. If he lived, he would continue to be a threat to Jed. Redford couldn't let that happen. He could not just sit by and let someone live when they endangered his pack.

Redford reached into Jed's shoulder holster, withdrew his gun, aimed carefully, and shot the hunter in the head.

The part of him that was still human started weeping, but Redford didn't have time to listen to it.

"What the *fuck!*" Jed's reaction had been too slow to stop him. He grabbed the gun out of Redford's hand. A thousand emotions seemed to flicker across Jed's face. Strangely, the one he settled on was guilt. Randall was running toward the hunter, shifting in midstride, skidding down to his knees before Jed could pull away. After a moment, he stood, looking over at Anthony and shaking his head grimly.

If Jed wanted to go to the hunter, Redford didn't let him. Flushed with satisfaction and the knowledge he was keeping Jed safe, he just dipped another towel in the river, making sure he kept it clean of the silt at the bottom. He removed the now-bloody towel from Jed's arm and started cleaning the drying blood off as best he could.

It was curiously hard work. His vision was blurry, and he was starting to feel a little short of breath. There was an odd warmth on his cheeks, but Redford didn't have the time to worry about that. Someone was making a strange, hitched sobbing noise. Was that Jed? It didn't sound like Jed.

"Redford," Jed barked urgently, grabbing Redford by the shoulder and shaking him. "Stop, babe, please. *Please.* Look at me. Baby, please, I'm sorry, I'm so, so sorry."

Redford just shook his head. He had no clue what Jed was apologizing for. Redford had killed the hunter and eliminated the threat. There was nothing left to worry about right now. "Hold still. I need to stitch you up."

"Stop *fucking taking care of me.*" Jed's voice was like a whip. "Jesus...." Jed's good arm folded around Redford, Jed seemingly not caring at all about his injuries. He just grabbed hold of Redford, hauling him in tight, whispering again and again, "I'm so sorry."

It didn't make sense. Jed had nothing to say sorry for, and Redford should tell him that. But all he could do was go limp in the circle of Jed's embrace, his cheek pushed hard against Jed's chest. The instincts retreated a little, content and reassured of Jed's

151

safety, and that minor retreat was just enough of a crack in the wall for Redford's humanity to break through.

That horrible sobbing noise was *him*.

He'd hurt Jed. He'd killed two humans.

He was lifted into Jed's arms, despite the pain Jed must have been feeling. Redford was only vaguely aware of being carried to the van, of Jed carefully climbing inside, Victor driving them out of the forest.

Jed didn't stop talking. His voice was so quiet it was barely more than a whisper murmured into Redford's ear. He apologized so many times, his voice breaking with every one. He told Redford he loved him until the words slurred together into a never-ending stream. Jed's injured arm was taken by Anthony so he could work to bind up the wound as best he could in the moving van with wolves pressed in so tight there was barely room to breathe. Jed never let go of Redford, though, not once during the whole trip.

The drive back was a lot more gentle than the way there. Victor, as opposed to Jed's more combative methods, seemed to prefer driving *around* the trees instead of blasting through them. Redford vaguely noticed Anthony tending to Randall. Redford was on Jed's lap, and he wondered if he should be embarrassed about the fact that he was naked.

Someone opened a window. The fresh air did a little to boot Redford's brain into working properly, and by the time the van was trundling through the main gates of the pack compound, his thoughts were starting to get back in order.

When they stopped, Jed jerked open his door and climbed out, Redford still held tightly. When their feet hit the ground, Redford was already in the middle of changing back to wolf, noting all of the people gathered around. Furry was a lot better than naked right then, and he barely even noticed the usual pain of the shift. Jed let him gently down, though he kept one hand in Redford's fur, which Redford was glad for. Neither of them wanted to break the connection.

"Everyone with me. Now." Jed strode across the camp, wolves trailing behind him like an army, Victor bringing up the rear. The door to the Gray Lady's cabin was unceremoniously kicked in. Her guardian wolves growled, but Jed bared his teeth and growled right back.

"Do you mind?" The Gray Lady was at her long table, several wolves with her. "We're in the middle—"

"Shut the fuck up." Jed was bloodstained and fierce-looking, anger radiating from every word, seemingly more wolflike than any of the actual wolves standing close. "You're in the middle of a *war* is what this is. And you don't get to press a dainty hand to your nose and ignore the goddamn stink. So this is how this is going to go. I am going to find the sons of bitches who are hunting you, and then you and I are going to find a way for your pack to stay alive."

The Gray Lady blinked at him, obviously torn between showing her own teeth and agreeing. In the end, her eyes went to the cluster of new wolves from the smaller pack, the injured and the young, and she nodded. "Very well," she said, raising her chin. "We will talk. Later."

"And I'm staying in a goddamn cabin," Jed rumbled as he turned, stalking back out of the building. "I'll stay in every damn cabin you've got. If you don't like it you can *kiss* my human *ass*."

At the doorway, the group dispersed. The wolves from the smaller pack were taken by members of the Gray Lady's in the direction of the medical house. Anthony cast a look at Jed and Redford, concerned. "I'm going to take Randall and Ed to get some proper treatment. You should come with us. I'm not the best at stitching, especially not in a moving vehicle, so all you've got is a bandage. You need more care than that."

"I don't want any voodoo herb smusher to touch my goddamn arm," Jed bit out. "I'm fine. We're fucking *fine*."

"Yes, we can see that." Randall was still heavily favoring one leg, the gash more visible now that there wasn't fur covering his upper leg. Victor was at his side, giving Randall an arm to lean on. "Anthony, you need to get looked at as well."

"Yeah, we're going." Anthony looked back at Jed again, like he wanted to insist Jed get properly treated, but he shook his head. Redford almost smiled to himself. Even Anthony had realized it was difficult to out-stubborn Jed. "Jed, just please get some attention if you feel like you need it. Victor's right, this isn't the time to be macho."

"This ain't my first rodeo, sunshine." Jed's hand had fallen again to rest on the nape of Redford's neck, fingers buried in his fur. "I've had scratches worse than this shaving."

"You think anybody's buying that tough talk?" Anthony huffed a near-silent laugh. But he was watching Jed with admiration starting to dawn in his eyes now that the adrenaline was dying down. "Thank you, Jed. For what you did. That pack wouldn't be alive without you."

Visibly uncomfortable with the gratitude, Jed cleared his throat. "Yeah, well. Good talk. And, uh, nice job out there. You aren't half bad to have around, even if I do probably have fleas now."

Edwin nudged his head against Redford before he started pushing at Victor's legs, encouraging him to start walking with Randall. The slash across the bottom of his muzzle gave Edwin a vaguely rakish air. He didn't appear all that traumatized by his first encounter with violence.

Redford envied him. So much was going on around him, there was so much to talk about, and he could scarcely think about any of it.

If Jed wasn't going to see the proper healers, then Redford would have to take care of him himself. He started to go for his usual tactic—gripping the bottom hem of Jed's jeans in his teeth to drag him in the right direction—but the second his teeth got shown, Jed flinched, and Redford drew back, ears down and tail between his legs.

He'd have to settle for just walking next to Jed, then. It was only right, Redford figured. Of course Jed didn't want Redford's teeth anywhere near him. Redford didn't want to make Jed react like that ever again. Still, he had to get Jed back to the cabin, so he went for a small nudge of his nose against Jed's ankle.

Knievel was waiting for them, curled up in the middle of the bed. She cracked an eye open when they walked in, deciding that it was worth leaving her cozy blankets to come and curl herself around Redford's legs. Redford, having expected Knievel to claw at his nose in revenge for what he'd done to Jed, relaxed slightly, and was faced with the odd situation of trying to pat their cat while he was lacking opposable thumbs.

Jed immediately tugged off his shirt, going into the bathroom to examine Anthony's handiwork. Apparently he was satisfied, because he just kicked off his shoes and collapsed facedown onto the bed. Knievel immediately abandoned Redford to hop up and requisition Jed's back as her new bed, kneading against his shoulder before she curled up and yawned her way back to sleep.

"Get up here," Jed told Redford, voice hoarse and rough.

Guiltily, Redford wondered if he should, if he even had the right anymore. When they'd first started to fall for each other and Redford had told Jed about his grandmother, Jed hadn't been happy. He'd yelled, called her an evil, abusing bitch, announced that he would very much like to resurrect her just for the pleasure of killing her himself.

But if Redford had hurt Jed twice now, didn't that make him as bad as his grandmother?

He loved Jed. He loved him more than anybody else Redford had ever had in life, and he'd never imagined feeling that way about somebody. He was fairly sure he'd never feel that way about somebody again. He wanted to leave the cabin out of shame and hope Jed realized how terrible it was that Redford had bitten him, but even as the guilt tried to push him into that action, Redford found he couldn't leave.

He shifted. It took a little longer this time, it hurt a little more, with the instincts being further toward the back of his mind, but finally Redford was able to cross the room and sit on the edge of the bed, gingerly placing his hand on Jed's shoulder blade.

"I'm...." Redford couldn't think of the proper words to say. "I'm so sorry, Jed." His voice broke on Jed's name, but Redford drew a deep breath, trying to keep himself composed.

There had been so much tenseness in Jed's body, like he was waiting for something, preparing for some terrible thing to happen. But the second Redford touched him, all of that melted. He turned, dislodging Knievel, grasping at Redford's hand. "Why?" he asked softly, eyes searching Redford's face. "God, babe, *I'm* the one that's sorry. I never.... I never meant for it to be like that. Not for you. You shouldn't...."

Sitting up, Jed had to pause, his voice cracking at the edges. "God, you're so... you're this innocent, amazing person, and I broke you." Jed's face shattered, a deep, heaving sob working its way through Jed's body. "Christ, I ruined you. I'm so sorry, Redford. I'm so, so sorry."

That wasn't what Redford had been expecting to hear. In fact, it was such a polar opposite of his own thoughts that he was taken aback for a long few moments, staring at Jed in shock.

"Jed," he protested, alarm flashing sourly in the back of his throat. He'd never seen Jed like this. On pure instinct, he raised his arms to wrap around Jed's shoulders, pulling him in close. "Jed, please don't apologize," he continued, his voice thin. "I *hurt* you. And that's not the first time I've hurt you."

"I don't care" was Jed's immediate response, forceful and sure even as his eyes were wet, even as he choked back another sob. "Jesus, Red, I *don't* fucking *care*. That wasn't... you're not *beating* me or some shit, okay? You were wolfed out, and I got in the way. I just didn't want you to…. I didn't want you to come to and realize you'd killed someone else. That's what I do, that's my job, but not you. You're better than that."

It still didn't excuse what Redford had done, but Jed seemed focused on a completely different issue here, one that Redford hadn't even been thinking about.

"I killed those men for you, Jed. That first one was going to shoot you in the back."

Even as he said it, Redford felt dawning realization at his own words. He'd spent the whole drive home feeling sick that he'd killed those men—and he still did feel that sour clench of guilt, the terrible churning shame of it—but now he started to realize there had been a point to it. They hadn't been needless murders. In fact, it was what any of them would have done. It was what Jed *had* done. Three of those bodies had been brought down by his bullets. Those men were trying to kill them, and Jed's first rule was that, if someone was coming after you, you had to live. Whatever that entailed, you just had to survive. And they had.

"I killed them for you," he repeated. "You taught me how to take care of myself and the people I love, and I did." He pulled back from Jed a little, showing him his arms, his chest, the way he didn't have so much as a scratch on him. And despite his lingering guilt and misery, Redford found himself smiling. "I don't even have a mark on me, Jed. Everyone else got hurt in some way. You taught me how to fight and look after myself and be independent."

Those were good things. Those were things that didn't involve him hiding in his grandmother's basement, afraid of the world. But Jed wasn't smiling. He looked vaguely sick, staring at Redford like he'd seen something horrifying.

Never once had Jed looked at him like that. Not when he changed, not when Redford was so lost in the competing instincts he chased the paper guy or wolfed down an entire plate of meat. Jed had accepted him, every part of him, from the day they'd met. But now he just seemed so *sad* and so afraid, and Jed's gaze dropped away, refusing to meet Redford's.

Redford's smile died. Every part of him had been accepted, except this part, apparently. The instincts had gone too far, maybe, or perhaps Jed wasn't being entirely truthful when he said he didn't care that Redford had nearly ripped his arm off. Either way, Redford wound up leaning back, losing contact with Jed.

"We should get some sleep," Jed mumbled, getting up, tugging off his jeans, and searching through his bag for pajamas. "You look exhausted."

Jed was the most stubborn man Redford had ever met, and if he didn't want to talk any further about this, then all attempts to do so would be absolutely useless. Redford wanted to grab him by the shoulders and make him realize: Redford was strong now, he was independent and useful, he had a purpose. Jed hadn't ruined him. Jed had *made* him.

But that lingering guilt over hurting Jed made him hold his tongue. He could see the fear in Jed's eyes, the sadness, and Redford could only assume both were his fault. There wasn't exactly anybody else in this room who could be to blame.

So instead of trying to talk more, Redford just got under the blankets. He expected that Jed would go sleep in the other bed, but Redford took his usual position anyway, the side farthest away from the door because, despite Jed's usual insistence on having a wall at his back whenever possible, he refused to sleep anywhere that wasn't directly between the outside world and Redford, like he could be a human barricade against any possible threats.

The thought that he might now consider *Redford* a threat made him feel sick.

But then the mattress dipped as Jed returned, and Jed wrapped his arm tight around Redford, the bandage scratching lightly against Redford's skin. He felt Jed's nose nuzzle into the nape of his neck, a soft exhale as Jed let out a breath. It didn't feel the same. There was a quietness in Jed, a stillness and brooding that seemed so out of place. But Jed wasn't pulling away. He kissed Redford's scar just like he did every night, settling back in and holding Redford close.

Right then, it was enough to know that Jed was still willing to be in the same bed as him. Redford took his hand and held on tight.

And he tried not to think whether or not Jed would leave him in the morning.

RESTLESS SLEEP didn't make anything better.

Jed was still there when he woke up; Redford was at least incredibly grateful for that. But they barely spoke as they got ready except to exchange the acknowledgement that they were going to do more research on the bullets they'd found and the ones Jed had recovered from the woods. Jed seemed certain those were their best lead. Redford considered breakfast, but the anxiety and guilt churning in his gut were enough to make his appetite abandon him completely.

A few times, he found himself reaching out to Jed while Jed was turned away, extending an arm to him with the intent of putting a hand on his shoulder, but he always drew back at the last second, remembering the flinch Jed had given yesterday.

He just had to turn his mind to research, Redford decided. Once he was dressed and washed up, he went over to the table where they had set up all their maps and their findings from the hunter cabin. Jed came to stand on the other side, and they went to work.

Time seemed to stretch on, where the only interruption to the silence was the sound of a map rustling or a notebook page turning.

It was the most awkward Redford had ever felt with Jed, and that included their very first meeting where Redford had thought he was a plumber come to fix his pipes. Every once in a while he went to say something, an apology on the tip of his tongue, a question, but he could never seem to get the words out. He kept worrying that he would say the wrong thing or drive Jed deeper into fear. So Redford said nothing and felt the uncertain hunch of his shoulders grow more pronounced with every minute that passed.

The knock at the door was so loud in their silence that it made him jump. Jed practically turned over his chair, leaping to answer it. He jerked open the door to find Randall and Victor on their porch, arms piled high with books, a laptop, and to-go cups of coffee. "Uh, hi," Randall said, peering around Jed toward Redford, giving them both a shy smile. "I hope we aren't interrupting."

Victor's eyes were barely visible above the pile of books. "We went to the library to—"

"Holy shit, princess, am I glad to see you." Jed practically threw his arms around both of them, dragging Randall and Victor inside. "Nerd boy and batgeek, here to save the goddamn day. Look, Redford, we have company." He was so desperately happy to have *anyone* else in the room, like he thought Victor and Randall would be able to shatter the silence between them.

Jed's relief at their company—at the company of *anybody* that wasn't Redford—just made Redford want to sink through the floor and vanish, but he managed a polite, if hesitant, greeting wave.

Victor looked more shaken at Jed's hug than he'd looked at the fight. He put the books down on the table so he could adjust his glasses, peering suspiciously at Jed. "As I was saying. We went to the library to procure books on bullet types, more detailed maps of the area, anything we could think of that might help you in your venture to discover who is behind this."

"Look, Red, books!" Jed picked one up and handed it to Redford like he'd found a magic talisman. "You love books."

Redford took it, but his smile felt a bit curdled. Jed's far too eager grin faded away, the manic enthusiasm crumpling.

Randall gave them both a look, one eyebrow rising, but he didn't comment. "Right. Anyway, we thought we'd volunteer our services. I am not good at much, but research is right up my alley."

"We even decided to be magnanimous and provide coffee." Victor pushed the to-go cups into Jed and Redford's hands. "There. Now sharpen up, both of you, we have research to do."

"You sure you've been laid before, princess?" Jed muttered, taking the offered coffee and sniffing it suspiciously. "Because you sound *way* too fucking thrilled at that prospect."

"What on earth does one's sexual experience have to do with the level of interest in studying?" Randall asked, obviously put out. "I don't think that if I had sex, I'd suddenly stop wanting to read or—" His words apparently caught up with him, and Randall stuttered to a halt, plopping down in a chair and noisily flipping through a book. "So, who wants to study bullet types with me?"

Victor eagerly sat down next to Randall with no comment on Randall's embarrassment. He reached out to get the box of silver bullets that was on top of one of the maps, and together they bent their heads over Randall's book.

Redford took a surreptitious sniff of the coffee and pretended to sip it. He didn't want to seem rude by putting it aside, but he'd never liked the taste much. While Victor and Randall read together, a bottle of water was pressed into Redford's free hand. He looked up to find Jed, wordlessly taking the coffee from him. Redford never really drank anything but water if he could help it, no matter how many times Jed tried to get him to taste different beers.

Hope and relief hit him hard. It was such a little thing, and he should probably be focusing on research, but if Jed was still thinking about him then it meant that Jed probably wasn't going to leave. Redford's smile was a lot more genuine then, and he silently mouthed a *thank you* at Jed.

Redford would swear most of the time that Jed wasn't nearly as closed off as he pretended. Every emotion he had, everything he kept so close to the chest, Redford could read in his eyes. It wasn't any different now. He saw love there in Jed's gaze, but it was underscored with a heavy, indefinable emotion that didn't seem to allow Jed to stay too close to Redford. Jed closed his fingers lightly around Redford's, just for a moment, before slipping away again.

That hope and relief dimmed somewhat but didn't die entirely. The smile didn't immediately slip off Redford's face—as upset and as guilty as he was feeling, Jed still loved him. He had to hold on to that.

"Have you looked into the etchings at the bottom of these?" Randall's voice broke into Redford's thoughts. "This symbol isn't one of the major manufacturers."

"And I don't think this would be any sort of do-it-yourself type build. They would need to have specialized equipment to make these silver bullets, not to mention the effort needed to produce the quantity you observed," Victor added. "But I highly doubt that a major manufacturer would do such a small, specific order. Thus, we can infer that—"

"Okay, Professor Hard-on." Jed cut Victor off, kicking his chair back to wander over to his bag. "Yes, Nancy Drew and her gal Friday have figured out that Sierra isn't going into the werewolf-hunting line. Good for you." Jed found a small flask and dumped half of its contents into his coffee. Downing a large gulp, he hissed in appreciation. Redford could smell the whiskey from where he was sitting. "It's a custom job. Someone—"

Jed stopped, eyes going wide. "Oh," he said lowly, before, louder, "Son of a *bitch*."

"What?" Victor still sounded irritable at being interrupted, but curiosity touched his expression. "Do you know someone that would be capable of custom-made bullets?"

"Sweetheart, half my rolodex would fit that bill." Jed was digging through his bag one handed, tossing clothes every which way. He unearthed a battered tin box and brought it over to the table. Dumping it out, he sent bullets rolling over the maps, all different shapes and sizes.

"One from each job," he explained, sorting through them. "Call me sentimental."

"Or a serial killer," Randall muttered, picking up one and frowning at it. "What does this very disturbing display of your trophies have to do with this?"

"Everything." Jed held out one bullet, longer than his finger and twice as thick. On the bottom, *[BC]* was etched into the brass.

"Holy shit." The curse seemed strange coming out of Randall's mouth. He leaned forward, eyes wide. "You know our supplier."

"More than know," Jed agreed. "Worked a few jobs for him. He likes custom-made toys, big guns, and blow jobs in the backseat of cars."

It didn't take more than that for Redford to understand who Jed meant. There was the etching on the bottom of the bullet, the fact that Jed had met him before. And then the references to big guns and custom made toys—Redford had heard Jed speak about those things to an ex-client before. There was only one person it could be.

Buck Cambridge. Redford had met him not long after Jed and Redford had first met, and Redford recalled distinctly disliking him even then. That's who the box of silver bullets smelled of.

"Are you going to be helpful and tell us exactly who it is?" Victor said witheringly. "Or shall we stay suspended on the edge of our seats?"

"Better if you don't know, professor." Jed was standing, moving around the cabin, grabbing shoes and a shirt and a gun with a kind of nervous energy. "This is not something you can lecture to death. I'll just go have a nice, friendly conversation, see if I can't figure out what's going on."

"You'll need to talk to the Gray Lady first." Victor looked like he wished he didn't have to say it but felt like he should nonetheless, a frown settling in at the edges of his lips. "She'll want to know what's going on."

"Bitches in hell want ice water," Jed shot back. "Doesn't help them either." He shrugged on a jacket. "Come on, Red, suit up. It's probably a few hours' worth of driving, and I want to get back before dark."

Redford had started getting ready before Jed had even finished speaking. He strapped his shoulder holster on and made sure his gun was properly loaded before he tucked it away, and started putting Jed's bag back together for transport. It didn't matter that things were awkward between him and Jed right now. He had Jed's back during jobs now and always, and neither of them were going to let a fight get in the way of that.

"I'm coming with you." Randall was standing, favoring his wounded leg, jaw set defiantly.

"That's a no," Jed replied, barely even giving him a look. "You're hurt, and I've already got all the backup I need."

"What you need is someone this person doesn't know. What do you think you're going to do, just burst through the front door?"

Jed shrugged. "The thought had occurred to me, yes."

"That might get you a fist fight for your trouble, but I hardly think it will give us the information we need." Randall took a step forward. "Put on nicer clothes, present yourself as a potential business client, and you'll get a lot further."

Snorting, Jed finally glanced over at Randall. "This guy ain't interested in my clothes."

"Yes, but *this guy* isn't who you need to get past. Secretaries and assistants run the world. They're the ones you need to be able to charm your way through." Randall's eyes darted between Jed and Redford. "Take me with you. I look harmless, which is to your advantage in any situation, and you know you can rely on me."

Jed looked like he very much wanted to protest. With a heavy sigh, though, he waved his hand. "Fine, whatever, come along. Keep your mouth shut and do what I say." Jed seemed to be sizing up Randall's outfit, the neatly tied tie, the buttoned up cardigan, the pressed slacks. With another irritated exhale, Jed dug through his own clothes, pulling out one of his few dress shirts and a pair of trousers. "Fucking hate dressing up," he muttered, flinging off his clothes and tugging on the nicer outfit.

Jed, Redford thought, should really dress up nicer more often. They'd done a few cases before where Jed had worn a suit, and while he'd bitched and complained about it the whole time, when they'd gotten home, Redford hadn't wasted any time in getting that suit off him. Jed definitely hadn't complained about that.

He supposed he'd need to be in nicer clothes too, so he set about retrieving the appropriate shirt and pants from his bag. Redford didn't think he cleaned up nearly as nicely as Jed. He figured it had something to do with the scar on his face, or his hair, that he'd never managed to force into a style that wasn't messy.

"Just be careful," Victor cautioned them all, but he was looking at Randall in particular. "The last thing any of us need is for you to wind up dead."

"Well, if I do bite it on this perfectly safe mission where there is a high likelihood that I won't even draw my gun, you can't have my stuff." Jed grabbed his bag and checked it over. No matter how many times Redford had packed for him, no matter even if *he'd* done his own packing, Jed always double checked. There was some story Jed would tell about Budapest and having to make his own knife out of a soda can, but the point was, Jed was slightly paranoid.

"Pity," Victor said dryly. "I was so looking forward to inheriting a gun collection of such enormity that no one man could ever hope to use it all."

"I'm sure we'll be fine," Randall agreed. He was giving Victor a sideways look, as if unsure if he should pay attention to the concern in Victor's voice. "And you do know that guns are often used as a compensation for smaller genitalia." .

"Yes, I was aware." Victor didn't even need to look at Jed to make his words pointed.

"They're also often used as payment for smaller jobs," Redford said, feeling the need to defend Jed. Not that Jed really needed any defending—the last time someone had inferred that he was compensating, Jed had pulled down his pants right then and there.

This time, though, Jed just gave a faint snort, ducking down to tie his shoes. "We ready?"

Redford was still holding his nicer clothes in his hands. "Um. Give me a second." He closed the bathroom door behind himself as he hid from sight, and got changed quickly. A glance in the mirror revealed that he looked, as usual, completely out of place in more formal clothing. But it would have to do.

When he emerged, he instinctively looked over at Jed for confirmation on his outfit choice. Despite Jed being strangely quiet and despite the strain between them, Redford still caught that familiar flare of heat in Jed's eyes. The corner of Jed's lip barely curved upward, but he nodded, hesitantly meeting Redford's gaze.

It made Redford want to call the whole investigation off so he and Jed could get some alone time together. Surely if they just *talked* about this, then they could figure it out. Redford could promise he would get some more help for his instincts so Jed didn't have to be wary of him. He'd go see Dr. Alona every day, if Jed wanted.

But time was of the essence here. There were hunters gathering around the pack, and they needed to find who was giving them orders. If Redford called time-out to sit down and talk to Jed, that was another few hours more that the pack was in danger.

"Ready," Redford said.

Randall had been fussing with the books, standing closer to Victor and asking his advice on various things that didn't seem entirely relevant to what they were doing now. Like how he'd categorize some of the research and if he preferred footnotes or references on the back page. "Hm?" He looked over to find both Jed and Redford standing at the door, waiting. Knievel wound her way around their legs, chirping at them before making a beeline toward Victor. "Oh, right. Yes, I, um, I'm ready as well."

"Let's head out, then." Jed led the way to the van, Randall's limp not preventing him from keeping up. The van looked beaten up, and that was about the kindest thing Redford could say about it. He hadn't noticed yesterday, but there were still chips of burnt wood stuck in the windshield wipers, heavy dents along the side where branches had hit. As long as it still ran, though, it didn't matter if it looked pretty. That was what Jed had always told him.

They piled in, and Jed pulled out onto the dirt trail. There were wolves running alongside them for a few moments before they vanished off into the woods. A few turns later, they passed the gate, and then it was like there wasn't anything out there but trees and silence. It took them a while to even hit the main road, though Redford was grateful when they got back onto pavement. It'd been so long, it felt, since he'd ridden in the car on anything but overly bumpy rough trails that driving down the highway was like being on a cushion of air.

Over the next two hours, Redford contemplated turning the radio on several times, but they were so far out of major civilization that the only two stations available were a talk show and a country music station. Redford quite liked country music, but Jed hated it.

About halfway into the drive, Jed had to stop for gas. He didn't ask either Redford or Randall if they wanted anything when he got out of the van, but when he came back he had a plastic bag. For Randall he'd purchased a glass bottle of iced tea on the basis that Randall clearly liked British things—Randall had given Jed a *look*, needless to say. And for Redford he'd bought Pixy Stix.

Even when things were tense between them, Jed still brought him his favorite gas station snack. This time Redford didn't feel that same relief and hope in him, not after an hour of sitting in tense silence. He was already exhausted from his thoughts running around in circles, desperately trying to figure out the situation and ways to solve it.

After eating one of the Pixy Stix and getting a blue tongue, though, he did lean over and lightly press a kiss to the corner of Jed's lips. It was a rule in their household, although the rule—and Jed—usually tended to demand much more intense kissing.

This time, however, Jed didn't immediately haul Redford back for something more. He did, though, gently take Redford's hand, bringing it up to kiss his palm so lightly it was almost no contact at all.

The next hour of the drive passed with less mental exhaustion for Redford as he tried to get his mind on track. They were going to talk to the man who was manufacturing silver bullets for these hunters. He couldn't afford to be distracted. And more than anything, he couldn't afford a repeat of yesterday, so he had to keep his instincts locked up tight.

He wished he'd had time to call Dr. Alona. He wished he'd *thought* of calling him earlier. Even if the man would just sit and quietly listen, he always seemed so calm. Redford could do with a little bit of calm right then.

When they pulled up in front of a tall, bland office building, Jed didn't immediately get out of the car. He peered up at it through the windshield, fingers absently drumming against the wheel in a nervous rhythm.

Randall had spent most of the drive with his nose buried in a book. He marked his page and stretched, looking around them curiously. "Are we going to go in?" he asked. "Or just sit out here and think real hard at him."

"I'm formulating a plan," Jed growled.

"Nothing like thinking ahead." Randall sat back in his seat, idly fiddling with his tie. "I don't suppose you could just call and make an appointment."

"Doesn't work like that." A few more long moments of quiet stretched over them, Jed muttering under his breath, lip caught between his teeth as he thought. Finally, though, he nodded sharply and opened the door. "Okay, kids. Everyone in the pool."

Jed had taught Redford a few things about body language. He straightened his shoulders, tipped his chin a bit higher, and did his best to look like he truly belonged in the clothes he was wearing. He wished he'd put on a tie; everybody looked respectable in ties.

The interior of the building was just as bland as the exterior. The lobby was decorated in whites and grays, chrome against marble, but it looked cheap, as if whoever decorated it had been trying to make it look like the home of a millionaire with a quarter of the budget. Jed went straight to the receptionist, a woman who looked exactly like the decoration—tastefully made up, but her earrings weren't real silver, and her scarf was *trying* to be silk but clearly failing.

Redford took a deep breath. Showtime.

"We're here to see Buck Cambridge," he said to her.

Out of the corner of his eye, Redford saw Jed giving him a questioning look, silently asking him how he'd figured it out. Redford waited until the secretary was looking away and tapped his nose. Jed's lips quirked, and he ducked his head, but Redford didn't miss the look of pride that had broken through his indifferent work expression.

"Do you have an appointment?" The receptionist's voice was bored, and she hardly seemed impressed with any of them, her gaze on her computer.

Randall gave the woman a slight, apologetic smile, rolling his eyes as if he was just *so very over* everything that was going on. "It's a last minute thing," he explained, sighing. "I am so sorry. I know he's probably booked, but is there *any* way?"

The receptionist softened, just slightly. She clearly didn't like the look of Jed, and Redford was getting the same suspicious glance, but Randall looked almost boring, completely harmless with his glasses pushed up and his bow tie. "He's got a small window, but...." She hesitated.

"Could you tell him Jed Walker's here?" Randall asked with another smile. "I would *really* appreciate it."

The name would definitely get Buck's attention, although Redford hated the very idea of using that ploy. The first time they'd met Buck at a gun show, Buck had pawed at Jed like he'd been contemplating dragging him around the back of the stall for a quickie. And Jed hadn't entirely been against the idea, either. That had been before Jed and Redford's relationship had been solid, but Redford still hated the memory.

The woman sighed at them, lips pressed tight together, but apparently Randall had thawed her enough that she turned to the phone and punched in an extension. "Melody? I have a Mr. Jed Walker and company here for him." A long moment of silence and then the receptionist nodded, eyebrows rising slightly. "Okay. I'll send them up." She hung up the receiver and gestured toward the elevators. "Third floor. He's waiting for you."

Jed muttered, "I'll bet he is," under his breath.

Randall stepped in with a quick smile, nodding and cutting Jed off. "Thank you very much." Redford was glad for his tact. He wasn't feeling very gracious himself, not with the thought of seeing Buck and Jed together in the same place again.

The elevator was playing some kind of classical music as they stepped in. Redford wrinkled his nose and traded a glance with Randall. The smell that had been all over the box of bullets was stronger here. It was even worse on the third floor. It wasn't an offensive smell; it was just odd for a box and now this building to smell like a cow. Randall actually coughed, lightly pressing his sleeve to his nose, like he was offended by the stench but too polite to point it out.

Buck's office was at the far end of the third floor hallway. They passed a few other closed doors, each with their own nameplates. Redford still hadn't managed to figure out what this building was even for—he hadn't seen a company name outside, and there were no immediate clues inside.

"What do you think he does here?" he said lowly to Jed.

"He fixes things," Jed said quietly. "He makes bad situations go away."

"By hiring people like you?" Randall asked.

Jed's jaw tightened, his eyes darting over to Redford. "Yeah," he sighed. "By hiring people just like me."

They reached the door. Redford had a brief vision of putting his fist through the glass. It would certainly be satisfying to ruin something of Buck's. Instead, he knocked as politely as he could. There was no sense starting the meeting off with carnage.

"Come in." The voice sounded the same as Redford remembered, and when he opened the door, Buck was sitting behind an expansive desk, raising his gaze from his monitors to the three of them. He brightened when he saw Jed, immediately standing up to greet them. His suit was ill-fitting, the jacket straining to fit around the bulk of him. "Jed!"

"Buck." Jed extended a hand to have it engulfed in both of Buck's. "Thanks for seeing me. I know it's sudden."

"Nonsense." Redford and Randall might not have even been there for all the attention Buck was paying them. "I always have time for you, Jed, you know that." Buck still hadn't let go of Jed's hand. He was beaming at him as if a particularly fat fly had wandered into his web. "Sit, sit, please. What can I do for you?"

Redford drew in a deep breath, reminding himself that they needed information, not for him to break Buck's computers. They hadn't talked about their strategy, but Redford knew what the right play would be here. People like Buck liked to feel in control. They liked to know that people needed them and their help.

So, he'd start with that.

"We need your help, Mr. Cambridge," Redford said. From the way Buck looked at him, the man clearly didn't recognize him, which worked for Redford. "We found this bullet. From the etching on the bottom we can tell that it's yours, but we're trying to track down the people that are using them."

He withdrew the silver bullet he'd stashed in his pocket and handed it over the desk to Buck. It looked tiny in Buck's grip, so he obviously wasn't crafting them with his own hands. He wouldn't have the dexterity to do so.

"I know how much you like your custom-made toys." Jed's voice was a low rumble, shoulders held in a tense line. Where Randall and Redford had sat in the chairs on the other side of a low table, Jed had been drawn in next to Buck on a couch. Buck's hand rested on Jed's leg, squeezing lightly as Buck examined the bullet.

"I bet you do," Buck hummed, giving Jed a look. "You quite enjoyed my natural accoutrements as well, as I recall."

Redford struggled not to growl at the man, turning the very start of the sound into a cough. "Sorry," he mumbled, waving at Buck to continue. Randall took Redford's hand, holding on to him. Redford wasn't sure if that was weird or really nice, considering that Randall's strong grip was a solid reminder to not go wolf and rip Buck's throat out.

"These yours or not, Buck?" Jed's voice didn't hold any of the lasciviousness or fondness he'd had last time they'd encountered Buck. "And don't bullshit me. If you remember my preferred positions, then you sure as hell remember what I did to Johnny. I'm not a fan of liars."

The threat was there under Jed's bland expression, but Buck just laughed. "Hands and knees, with me buried inside of you," he murmured with a wink. "Oh, yes, I recall all of that very clearly."

"The bullet, Buck," Jed prompted.

"You are so much less fun now, Walker," Buck grumped. "Last time you didn't mind mixing business with pleasure."

"Yeah, well, this time I'm not under the impression that getting fucked by you would be pleasurable," Jed all but growled. "Damn it, Buck, stop jerking me around. You're not as good at it as you think."

Redford's eyebrows shot up in surprise. If he took away their current worries and tension, he would swear by his and Jed's relationship. They were the most steady, most reliable thing he'd ever had in his life. However, Jed still casually flirted with other men. Redford knew him well enough to know it wasn't completely serious, but the instinctive reaction was there.

So he would have sworn that Jed would flirt with Buck to ease the flow of information along. Redford hadn't liked the idea, he would prefer to go with any other way, but he bowed to Jed's superior experience.

Jed looked absolutely disgusted at Buck's flirting.

Buck's hand clenched tighter on Jed's leg. "You certainly didn't seem to mind," he hissed.

Jed's lips twisted into a smirk. "Yeah, well, I've gotten fucked by a proper cock now, so. Call it inexperience."

Randall slouched in his chair, sighing. "Charm, Jed," he muttered under his breath. "We were going to go with charm." Redford couldn't find it within himself to make the same protest. He just rubbed a hand over his mouth to hide a little smirk.

Buck spluttered ineffectively, standing up and looming over Jed. It occurred to Redford that it was a position Jed must have been in before—sitting there with Buck leaning over him, his mouth at just the right height for Buck to take advantage of it. But instead of leering or making a comment to point out that fact, Jed rose to his feet, jaw jutting out in stubborn anger. "I want to know who ordered those bullets, Bucky," Jed pressed, voice hard. "Or I'm going to get really irritated. You don't want me irritated at you, do you? You remember how very, very creative I can get."

Going faintly pale, Buck tried to glare Jed down. When that didn't work, he swiveled his scowl onto Randall, who was calmly examining his nails, and then to Redford.

Redford just glared back, lifting his lip in a hint of a snarl. He still wasn't sure that he made for a very threatening figure, but he did his best.

When Buck turned back to Jed, Jed just gave him a huge grin, the manic edges of it more disturbing than any scowl Jed could work up. "Chop, chop, Bucky."

"Please don't make him explode something," Randall sighed, straightening the front of his sweater. "This is a new cardigan."

Deflating a bit, Buck seemed to know he'd lost. He could call for security, but Redford had seen Jed in action. It was highly likely there'd be some serious injuries and property damage before it was all said and done, if Jed didn't just kill Buck where he stood. And apparently Buck had seen Jed work as well, because he silently went to his desk and opened a locked drawer. In it was row after row of neatly organized flash drives. After a moment of searching, Buck pulled out one and held it out to Jed.

"Everything I have. It isn't much." Buck smirked faintly, taking pleasure in that fact. "It's an umbrella holding company. You'll never get past that."

Jed examined the flash drive. His expression revealed nothing when he said, "This'll tell me the how, but not the why. Why are they kidnapping the wolves?"

"You think I give a shit *why*?" Buck shrugged carelessly. "They could want extras for dance parties for all I know. I just supply, I don't ask."

"Yeah, well, fuck you." Eloquent as always, Jed tucked the flash drive into his pocket for safekeeping. "You must get *paid* somehow. You got hired somehow. Don't play the blushing virgin now, Bucky. You're shit at it, and I know how the business works."

"As I said." Buck smoothed his hands down the front of his shirt fastidiously, a scowl creasing his broad face. "It's all on the drive. But if you must know, I'm paid in cash via courier after every new shipment. I hire the hunters through the usual channels, ads in the right papers or on the type of message boards they prefer. Low-end muscle for hire at best, but they do the job. I pass on instructions that are e-mailed to me and pay the men when the time comes. That's really it for me, Jed. I'm a middleman, nothing more."

"You're a goddamn parasite is what," Jed growled. For a moment Redford could see the indecision on his face, the tenseness in his arms that usually preceded violence. In the end, though, Jed just clenched his jaw and nodded at Redford and Randall, before turning to go. "Oh, and, Buck? You call your meathead security, try to follow us, so much as *sneeze* in our direction, I will give you a replay of San Francisco that will make you wish you'd gone into another profession. We clear?"

"Crystal." Buck spat out the word, sitting back down heavily. "Now get out of my office."

That was one order from the man that Redford was entirely too happy to follow. He rose from his chair just after Randall did and followed Jed to the door.

"Oh, and, Buck?" Redford turned back to face him. "Jed's favorite position isn't hands and knees anymore. He likes to see my eyes."

With that, he closed the door on Buck.

Jed urged them to walk just a little faster. Clearly he didn't entirely trust that Buck's common sense would outlive his ire. They reached the vehicle without incident, Randall immediately climbing inside. But before Redford could open his door, Jed had grabbed his wrist and spun him around. Redford was pressed back against the van, Jed kissing him, hard, both hands cupping Redford's face. It was one of their hungry, deep kisses, the kind where it felt like Jed was trying to sink into him, their tongues twining together, their breaths lost in an endless moan.

It probably didn't solve anything. It didn't wipe out their tension. But it still felt amazing, and when Redford drew back he was smiling.

"You're incredible," Jed told him hoarsely, holding his gaze.

And you didn't flirt with him, Redford wanted to say. He wanted to tell Jed just how thankful he was for that, just how relieved. But he should probably save that for when there wasn't the distinct possibility that Buck's security would be coming after them.

Instead, he said, "I love you." The raw honesty almost hurt a little, but he wanted to say it. He *needed* to say it.

Jed's expression was agonized. His eyes searched Redford's, his thumb tracing an arc against Redford's cheek. "I love you too. I'll always love you, Fido."

They got back into the van, and Redford grasped Jed's hand tightly for a moment before he released it to let him drive. He felt a little lighter now. Jed still loved him, and they had information from Buck, which would be incredibly useful for the pack. Maybe, just maybe, everything might work out.

"So"—Randall's voice broke into the moment Redford and Jed were sharing—"did anyone else notice he was a minotaur?"

CROWDING SIX people into Jed and Redford's cabin was a tight fit, but they managed to make it work. Victor, Randall, and Jed were standing around the table, studying the contents of the flash drive on the laptop Randall had brought. Edwin and Anthony were slouched on the unused bed, a game of cards between them. Every once in a while they'd look up toward the intense research going on and get a look on their faces like they just might die from boredom.

Redford had curled up on his and Jed's bed, back against the wall. From there he had a decent view of the laptop without taking up important space around the table.

"A minotaur half blood," Victor mused. "That's incredibly fascinating. I've seen mentions of them in records, but they're apparently quite rare."

"Because they're stupid," Randall pointed out. He was hunched over the laptop, fingers dancing across the keys. "And slow. And *God*, they stink."

"So… he's got *bull* balls." Jed had said that a few times already, but he repeated it again with an amused smirk.

And, like every time since the first, Randall sighed at him. "No. Those are not bull balls. Please stop."

"Like, he's a bull. He has balls. They're bull balls." For some reason, Jed found that incredibly funny to say. "Buck's bull balls."

"He's not… a minotaur is not literally a bull," Randall tried, for the twelfth time, to explain the difference.

"I am going to *literally* die of boredom," Edwin piped up.

"Figuratively, Edwin." Randall turned to snap at his brother. "You cannot *actually* die from not being entertained."

This was apparently a fight they'd had before, because Anthony immediately rolled his eyes.

"You don't know that!" Edwin insisted. "What if I'm the first?"

"Then you are a medical miracle. Can you please just hold it together for two more seconds—"

"That's what you said an *hour* ago, but Jed keeps making the same bad nonjoke and Victor is giving you googly eyes and it's boring."

"Okay, children," Anthony said loudly, lightly cuffing the back of Edwin's head. "Sooner or later there'll be something you can help with, Edwin. Just be patient." He turned to Randall. "Do we have anything useful Edwin and I can do?"

Despite his admonishment of Edwin, Anthony too looked absolutely desperate for something to do that wasn't sitting around while other people parsed through information.

Jed took pity on them. "Why don't you guys go for a run? That clearing, I'm betting someone went to clean up the bodies. Sniff around, see if anything smells interesting?"

"Oh, thank God," Anthony said in relief. "Great idea, Jed. Come on, Edwin, we'll go check out that site."

Edwin was shifting before Anthony's hand had even hit the door. He stopped to butt his head against Randall's legs. Randall crouched down, rubbing behind Edwin's ear, whispering lowly to him and then watching, expression fond, as Edwin charged out the door. Randall's annoyance seemed to have faded as suddenly as it came.

Redford didn't know what it was like to have siblings; it looked nice. He found himself almost smiling at the sight of them. Victor had already forgotten about the whole thing and was once more intently studying the laptop.

"So how, exactly, are we going to find who's giving orders to Mr. Cambridge?" Victor turned to face Jed.

"Follow the money." Jed stretched, arms to the ceiling, arching so that his back cracked. "It's all we've got. If we can figure out who is bankrolling this little escapade, we can get some traction on this whole thing."

With a faint sigh, Victor looked at the laptop. "Well, it's not my area of expertise, but I suppose I can figure it out." He frowned down at the keys he was tapping, muttering under his breath, "I hate computers."

"Yes, they can be quite distressing." Randall leaned over, easily sliding the laptop to himself with a little smile. "I don't think this is going to be found in the card index. Perhaps I could drive?" His fingers flew expertly over the keys as Randall hunched in over the computer. Victor looked immeasurably relieved.

"Wolves have Wi-Fi?" Jed didn't look like he quite trusted Randall with technology. "You guys are out in the boonies."

"We've had satellite for a few years. We're not quite in the dark ages." Randall flicked his gaze to Jed, amused. "I also used to stay late at school to do research, and we had an extremely small library. I've gotten quite good at finding obscure information. Really, the Internet is the best library there is. See, Victor? Here there's a cataloged index of all the medieval texts written between the ninth and eleventh centuries, concentrating specifically on the medicinal uses of animal parts."

Victor looked fascinated, despite his wary frown. "And how do you know someone hasn't just made all that up to trick people? People can just write whatever they like on those sites."

"Because look, there are references here." Randall seemed to be enjoying his stint as teacher; he scooted a bit closer to Victor. "You can click these links, and they take you back to the source material."

"And there are also pictures of cats playing the piano and a whole lotta porn," Jed interrupted, scowling. "But none of that is helping us. Come on, nerd squad, focus."

Victor cleared his throat, giving Jed a pointed look. Redford just picked up the maps he'd been studying again, quite happy to leave Victor and Randall to the computer. Since living with Jed he'd figured out his way around technology fairly well, but computers didn't smell nearly as nice as books did.

"Give me what you have," Randall sighed, holding out his hand for the information. "I'll see what I can track down." Jed passed over the thumb drive, and Randall retreated to the nearby bed, curling up around the laptop and pushing his glasses more firmly up on his nose, getting to work.

With the laptop occupied, Jed, Victor, and Redford took to their own avenues of study. Redford occasionally passed a map with added notations over to Jed and pushed a note in shorthand that needed translating to Victor. There wasn't much to do with the physical information they had anymore—Randall was doing the most pertinent work—leaving Redford feeling a little antsy, determined to squeeze every last drop of information they could out of what they'd retrieved from the cabin.

The sun had long since set, and Redford found himself struggling to keep his eyes open. Victor had succumbed to sleep some time ago, his head down on the table, glasses pushed hard up against his face. Randall looked like he was going the same way, his head tilted back against the wall he was leaning against. Jed was still awake, but even he was starting to look sluggish as he and Randall passed the laptop back and forth.

Redford had the vague idea that he should probably go over to help. But Randall was better with computers than he was, and Jed was smarter than he was, so his contributions likely wouldn't be any help at all. Their low talking was unfortunately soothing, making Redford's eyelids heavier as he struggled to keep the map in focus.

He wound up slumped to one side, still valiantly trying to hold up the map. From over it he could see Jed's face, not focused on the screen as Redford had thought he would be, but watching him. Redford couldn't make out his expression, just the deep forest green of his eyes lit to a more pale color in the luminescence of the computer, the light bathing his face like a blue-tinged fire.

Redford wished he could go over there and curl around Jed so he could fall asleep properly. He knew he *could*, too, but hesitance and near-sleep left him staying right where he was, finally closing his eyes, secure in the knowledge that Jed was at least near him, if not directly next to him. He started to drift, smiling at the sensation of a blanket being tucked around him, a gentle kiss being pressed to his forehead.

"Sleep, Fido. I'm here."

And so he did.

CHAPTER
9

Victor

"I FOUND it!"

Victor was dragged to wakefulness with a startled grunt and then a quiet groan of pain as he dislodged his glasses from his face. He sat up, bleary-eyed, confused, peering at Randall, who was in the middle of eagerly thumping Jed on the back.

It seemed that Randall hadn't fallen asleep like the rest of them. *Disheveled* was probably the kindest word that could be applied to him right then, but Victor found himself smiling stupidly at the stubble on Randall's jaw, the way his hair was sticking out everywhere, the tiredness on his face that was only barely edged out by the excitement.

"What the fuck?" Jed was eloquent, as always. He'd apparently fallen asleep on Randall's legs at some point. Now he was blinking groggily, scrubbing his hands across his face in some vain effort at waking up.

"The holding company. I found it." Randall thumped the laptop down on the table, climbing into the chair next to Victor, grinning. "I traced it back through stockholder reports for the past ten years. See? If you follow this company back, it only came into existence eight years ago, right? And that year, the first annual report, there's a huge number of stocks that got passed back into the company the following year."

"And you found out who owned those stocks." Jed nodded. The news seemed to be doing wonders at getting him out of his half-dead state. Behind Victor, Redford was crawling out of bed with a grumble of protest. He stomped across the cabin and pitched himself across Jed's legs with another grumble, curling up on him and going right back to sleep. A brief look of surprise crossed Jed's face, pulling his concentration to Redford. His face softened, and he combed absent fingers through Redford's hair, shifting to make himself the most comfortable human pillow possible.

"Exactly." Randall was too focused on what he'd found to pay attention to the interpersonal drama. Victor envied him. He couldn't help speculating on what was happening with Jed and Redford. "And I found out *that* was another dummy corporation, though this one wasn't nearly as elegantly constructed. It's…." Randall paused, a frown creasing his face.

"Out with it, kid," Jed rumbled, voice quieter, thumb making light circles under Redford's ear.

"Far be it from me to point out that I'm not a genius," Randall said, rubbing a hand through his hair, sending messy waves everywhere. "But I probably shouldn't have been able to find out what I did."

Jed's lips pursed in thought. "Too easy?"

"More than likely, yes." Randall sat back, rubbing his eyes.

"Good." Jed nodded.

This whole conversation was far too technical for Victor this early in the morning. He'd mostly tuned them out, but kept part of his attention on their discussion as he shuffled his way toward the sink. His mouth felt as dry as the Sahara. He just hoped the reason for that wasn't excessive drooling.

That apparently was not the reaction Randall had been expecting. "We want them to want to be found? Isn't that the very definition of a trap? Meaning a thing we don't fall into?"

"If someone's setting a trap, that means they're expecting us to come nosing around." Jed leaned back against the headboard of the bed, looking entirely too smug. "They're going to be on guard."

"Again, none of this sounds ideal," Randall said dryly.

"They're going to be expecting normal reactions. Us to nose around or try to gather more info or shit like that."

"And we're... not going to do those things?" Randall shot Victor a baffled look. Victor didn't really know how to respond to that. He shrugged. Half of what Jed said never made sense to him anyway.

"Hell no. We're just going to ram straight at them. Best way to take them off guard." Jed seemed quite satisfied with his plan. "They won't be expecting it."

"Most people don't expect crazy," Randall agreed. But he was apparently ready to let Jed handle the planning. Randall brought the laptop to the bed, bending over so he could show Jed what he'd found without Jed dislodging Redford. "See? This is the parent company. Ashes Ltd."

"Do we know who owns it?" Redford's voice was little more than a mumble. "That'd be useful."

"Their CEO is listed as a Leonard O'Malley." Randall shrugged. "I don't know if that means anything."

Jed had gone still. Redford woke up properly then, staring in disbelief at Randall. "Leonard O'Malley," Redford repeated.

Victor frowned at them both. "You know who that is? Please don't tell me you've worked a job for him. That would be distasteful to the extreme." From the guilty look on Redford's face, Victor didn't need to ask again.

"Fuck you," Jed summarized neatly. "I go where the pay is. But yeah, we've worked a couple of things for him. Last one was, what, months ago, right? Just before Cairo. It was a simple recovery gig."

"So you could make contact with him," Randall prompted, shooting Victor a look.

"Maybe," Redford hedged. "Jed, um, wasn't very nice when he tried to not pay us in full. He might not be very happy to see us again."

"He's just an art dealer, though. A collector." Jed sounded baffled. "Why the fuck would he be bankrolling supernatural wolf Ghostbusters?"

"You should probably work on that name," Randall commented absently. "Doesn't exactly roll off the tongue." He'd brought up a new window on the computer and soon was turning it around, showing a picture that appeared to be from some kind of corporate brochure. The man was average looking, dark hair, gray eyes, something hard about the face, but overall totally forgettable.

"That's him," Jed agreed, peering at the monitor.

"We should tell the Gray Lady. See what she'd like us to do next." Randall was up, gathering the papers and the maps. He hesitated, rubbing a hand along his chin and grimacing. "Well, first I should shower. Shave, maybe. Definitely change my clothes."

"Whatever happened to your brothers?" Redford asked, looking around the room for them.

Randall gave him a slight grin. "You and Victor dozed off before they came back. Nothing all that earth-shattering. We can get them too, make a proper meeting of it."

A shower and a shave sounded like a fantastic idea to Victor, who still felt like he hadn't properly woken up yet. "We'll reconvene in half an hour?" He rubbed a hand over his nose to muffle a sneeze and leveled a glare at the cat that was currently sitting perched on the table. Knievel completely ignored him, grooming herself primly. The antihistamines he'd taken before he came over were starting to wear off.

"Make it an hour." Redford had levered himself up to sit upright. "We need breakfast first."

Since Victor's cabin was only two over from the Lewises, he glanced at Randall, lifting his eyebrows. "Shall we?"

Randall paused, freezing in mid-paper-shuffle. Eyes going rather wide behind his glasses, he looked up at Victor, and Victor swore he could see the start of a blush on Randall's cheeks. "I…. I'm sorry?"

"I'll walk you back," Victor clarified. "Your injury must be causing you some bother. I wouldn't want you to slip and fall."

Apparently that answer wasn't what Randall had been expecting. His expression was a strange mix between relief and disappointment. But he nodded, giving Victor a brief smile. "Right. Yes, of course. That's very thoughtful, thank you." His limp was less pronounced, but he was still moving stiffly as he headed toward the door.

Victor peered back at Jed and Redford as he left, but he shut the door on them as quickly as possible. There was entirely too much drama going on in that room for Victor to be comfortable, and he was rather glad to get the chance to leave. Not to mention the fact Jed seemed to take a perverse kind of pleasure in getting unclothed around Victor. He hardly wanted to stay and give Jed another chance to walk about naked. As much as he thought Jed and Redford were good for each other, he didn't want to see their issues right there in the open.

"You don't need to walk me back." Randall was walking alongside him, foot dragging slightly as he moved. "I really am quite all right, and I'm sure you're sick of the sight of me by now. I certainly would be." He looked down at himself, grimacing faintly as he rubbed a hand across his jaw. "God, I look terrible."

"I'm walking you back and that's final," Victor said sternly. "Goodness, Randall, it's the least I can do."

He still didn't remember much about that specific moment in the altercation with the hunters yesterday. Victor had never been good around blood or violence, and though he'd been determined to help in some way in the fight, all he'd managed to do was hang around the sidelines and anxiously watch the action. He hadn't felt brave enough to lift his gun once.

Apparently he'd made a vital error in not watching his back. All Victor had seen was a flash of a blue jacket—a hunter—and the blur of dark fur as Randall had sped toward him, knocking him down and out of the way of the bullet. Jed had taken care of the hunter shortly after that. Until Randall had shifted back, Victor had had no idea that the man had even been injured.

Guilt wasn't something he felt a lot of in his life. Victor found the emotion wasteful. But he was feeling guilty now.

"I never thanked for you yesterday," he continued, watching Randall closely for signs of a stumble as they walked. The grass underneath their feet was crisp with frost, entirely too easy to slip upon. "You saved my life."

Randall's head was down, as though he was carefully watching his step. Despite the limp, however, he still moved with the grace that seemed to characterize most of the wolves Victor had observed. Anthony and Edwin's was more an aggressive fluidity, a predatory gait, and one couldn't help but see the wolf beneath their skin. In Randall it was tightly contained, an almost hidden smoothness under the glasses and the messy hair and the too large sweaters. It was more readily apparent now with Randall disheveled and only half-awake, like he was forgetting to keep himself proper and prim.

"I didn't think you were one for overdramatics, Victor," Randall half teased, voice hoarse. "I didn't do anything. There really isn't any need for you to thank me."

"Overdramatics is what's happening in that cabin back there," Victor sighed. "I am merely grateful." And still feeling slightly guilty that Randall was limping because Victor couldn't use a gun. "And I would like to request that you let me get shot if that situation ever happens again."

"Not even the slightest chance that's going to happen," Randall told him very quietly, still refusing to look over at Victor. "But don't worry. I'd do the same for anyone. You don't need to feel obligated, Victor, please, I…. I really don't want that."

That took Victor off guard. He wasn't entirely sure how to feel about that or respond to it, so he simply fell silent as they continued walking. In one breath, Randall had dismissed his actions as completely impersonal, then had made it personal once more with the tone of his voice. Randall, needless to say, was confusing, and made even more confusing by the fact that Victor couldn't stop thinking about the kiss they'd shared.

Randall had told him he needed to stop living in the future, which was very good advice, if Victor could manage it. Unfortunately there was no way to simply switch it off, so he had to concentrate on the here and now and the recent past.

"Besides—" Randall huffed out a near-silent laugh, though it seemed to be lacking substantially in mirth. "—didn't you already know I was going to do that? Can't be that big of a surprise to you."

"Oh, er, not at all," Victor said, flustered. He still wasn't used to talking so freely about his visions. That Randall just openly asked about them was something quite new. "Of the dozens of possible lifetimes I see, it's difficult to remember every minute of each."

He caught Randall looking at him, an expression on his face that, for lack of a better descriptor, was entirely wolfish. Not threatening, but more as if the resignation that had been worn was forgotten, as if all that intelligence had been focused at once on Victor in expectation. "So," Randall mused. "I can surprise my medusa. That's good to know."

Victor didn't anticipate the warm flush that settled low in his chest at those words. *My medusa.* He wasn't one to get in a tizzy about flirtation or possessiveness, but that had been rather attractive. "The very knowledge of possible timelines can disrupt them," he said, taking off his glasses to clean them on the edge of his sweater, still feeling faintly flustered. "So I dare say we're venturing off into unseen territory here."

They'd paused in their walk, Randall studying Victor intently. "I wish I knew if that would make a difference," he murmured. "I'm afraid it's too late, though. You're always going to be afraid of what I might force you to become." A sad half smile touched Randall's lips. "Too bad. That was one hell of a kiss." Before Victor could respond, clearly wanting to leave so that Victor didn't feel obligated to, Randall nodded at him. "Thank you for the walk back. I'm sure I'll see you shortly." Another brief nod, another smile that wasn't quite full, and Randall turned and made his way the short remaining distance to the Lewises' cabin.

Which left Victor staring at his retreating form, even more confused than before.

With a short sigh, he went to his own cabin. It was on the smaller side but perfectly serviceable. As he showered quickly, he contemplated Randall—to say the man was baffling was putting it lightly. He had expressed clear interest, but now seemed to be blowing hot and cold by turns.

David had been far simpler. David had pursued him, Victor had reciprocated that interest, and they had gone from there. David had been very clear in his intentions. Randall was far less so, it seemed.

This whole situation was getting more muddled than Victor was used to. On one hand, he knew his own feelings. He knew that the thought of marriage and children and settling down was not something he was particularly interested in, and he was aware that Randall would want those things. With David, Victor had known those things were not on the table. Their intentions for their relationship had matched up nicely.

David had not required a *partner*. He had had baggage, but that baggage had rarely seen the light of day. Randall, on the other hand, had a whole life that Victor would be jumping into if he reciprocated in kind—a life that included a family with an ill brother, with Randall trying to deal with becoming the head of the family and giving up his own future to do so. It was a messy, heavy situation that Victor would find himself in the middle of.

It didn't help that Victor was starting to feel rather pleased when Randall showed interest. The man was not at all who he seemed to be half the time. He was the very essence of a wolf in sheep's clothing, and that wolf was far more attractive than Victor had realized. He'd seen it in the way that Randall had kissed him, in the way that Randall had protected him during the fight.

The shower started to run cold, and Victor cursed his overthinking, shivering his way through drying himself and getting dressed. If this situation were simpler, his mind would be so much clearer. The path forward would be clearly marked. Unfortunately, *simple* did not seem to be in the cards.

He got himself properly put together and exited the cabin. Wolves were starting to move around the camp, getting things ready for the morning. Victor might not have a nose like theirs, but even he could smell the coffee starting to brew, the meat being fried in preparation for breakfast. His stomach gave a growl, but he'd never been in the habit of eating big breakfasts. It could wait until after their meeting with the Gray Lady.

The thought made Victor laugh. What was he even doing here? He was a researcher by trade, a teacher, and here he was getting himself involved in a possible *war*. He honestly had no clue why Jed had even consented to bring him along.

The walk to the Gray Lady's house was thankfully short. The chill of the morning was starting to evaporate as the sun rose, at least, so perhaps the four layers that Victor had put on were not entirely necessary. Redford, Jed, and the Lewises were gathered outside the Gray Lady's house when Victor arrived. Edwin was a short distance away, lying on the grass, while Randall and Anthony were sitting on the edge of the porch.

Victor eyed Redford and Jed. He had absolutely no clue what was going on with them. They too were sitting together, but had a few feet between them, where normally they would be all over each other.

"Good morning," he said cordially to all of them, half distracted by the thought of the tea the Gray Lady would serve. He needed *something* to wake him up. "How are you feeling this morning, Anthony?"

Anthony had his hands clasped tightly together, his nose wrinkled. Victor caught a whiff of something vaguely herbal smelling, though not nearly as pleasant as any herbal remedy he'd ever been near before. "Absolutely fine," Anthony replied with forced cheer. "The doctors here gave me stuff for my hands, and it feels like it's working."

Victor may not be able to look anybody in the eye, but even he could tell that for a lie. Still, for the sake of not bringing the mood down, he smiled. "I'm glad to hear it."

Randall shifted slightly, rubbing his hands on his knees, but he said nothing. He'd shaved off the stubble, his hair was slightly tamed, and he'd changed into a sweater and tie. There was something raw about him still. Victor wondered if it was something to do with how Anthony's hands still shook, how tightly his fingers were clasped together to hide it.

Before he really thought about it, Victor reached out to clasp Randall's shoulder, hoping to give him some measure of silent support. He couldn't very well say it out loud, not with Anthony right there. He felt the slight jump of Randall under his touch, but then the man relaxed into him. Randall's hand stole up, long, cool fingers lightly brushing across the back of Victor's hand in wordless thanks.

The opening of the door caught Victor's attention. Mallory gave them a quick look, quietly assessing, and jerked his head in the direction of the door. "Go in. She's ready for you."

175

Anthony was the first to jump up and enter, followed shortly by Randall and Edwin, then Jed and Redford. Victor took the last place, as he was fairly sure he wouldn't need to speak at all during this meeting, so it was less vital that he get a good spot.

They had met with the Gray Lady a few times before, and Victor still found her to be a fascinating figure. Thus far he'd managed to restrain himself from asking a multitude of questions, but he wasn't sure he'd be able to hold off forever. It wasn't very often that one met a figure out of the books, after all.

She was as regal as always, sitting cross-legged at the front of the long room that served as her meeting room. Today the silk drapes covering the windows had been pushed aside to let the light stream in, and the whole place smelled of green tea. Not the kind of tea that Victor had been hoping for, but it would do.

He let the others take more central positions in front of the Gray Lady and seated himself off to the side. It meant that nobody saw his embarrassing half slide onto the floor when he accidentally encountered the edge of a cushion he wasn't expecting, which was just fine by Victor.

Edwin sprawled out next to him, shoulder budged up against his, giving him a lopsided grin. "Randall made me wear pants," he informed Victor. "And I'm not allowed to shift. He's cranky."

"I appreciate the wearing of trousers too," Victor said dryly. "Thank you kindly for your consideration."

Jed's voice rang out, signaling the start of the official meeting. "So, sweetheart, we gotta stop meeting like this." He dumped an armful of papers, books, maps, and the laptop onto the table.

"I concur." The Gray Lady arched an eyebrow at his mess. "What have you been up to, human?"

"We found out who's behind the hunters coming after you." Unlike his usual tone, under the necessary bravado that seemed to keep Jed Walker ticking, he almost sounded weary. "It's not good news."

"I have been discussing options with my people." The Gray Lady steepled her fingers, considering Jed. "We've reached out to any other packs that may be in the area. At this point, I assume stray wolves are a danger to us all."

"Pretty much." Jed unrolled a map, standing so he could mark out a few points. "Look, here's how I see it. These guys are being bankrolled by a Leonard O'Malley. He's rich. Like, let me buy an island rich. I don't know *why* he's doing this, but I do know his type, and this isn't going to just go away if you sit quiet and pray."

"What other choices do we have?" The Gray Lady glanced around the room, shaking her head. "We are too many to simply disperse back into the human world. There are several who wouldn't be able to cope."

Jed angled the maps toward her. "You run or you fight. Those are the only two options there ever are. I've found a coupla spots that might do you for hiding."

"Nearby?" The Gray Lady sounded intrigued. She leaned over the maps. "We've scouted this area numerous times, and this is the best place we've seen for our pack."

"Not nearby." Jed shook out the map in question and pointed to a large blank area flanked by mountains on one side and a lake on the other. "Think seven states over. This isn't a day trip. I'm talking complete *Brigadoon* here. You gather up everyone, every pack, every stray wolf, and you go deep underground. We'll rent a train or a fucking bus caravan, whatever, and we head out. Set you up someplace so far off the grid that O'Malley'd have to crawl up his own ass to catch a whiff of you."

Victor had to take a moment to figure out exactly what that meant. After a few seconds of contemplation, he was forced to admit that he had absolutely no clue.

"Or if you want to go on foot," Redford joined in, "we've plotted out a path that would do it. It, um, wouldn't exactly be ideal, though."

"Yeah, that could take weeks. Months, depending on if you're carrying anything with you. It's risky, and, frankly, there'd be some of you that wouldn't make it." Jed sat back, watching the Gray Lady. "I'd splash the cash and get a couple of semis, load them up and go as close as you could. Finish it on foot, but that cross-state trip would be a bitch."

The Gray Lady studied the maps, resignation dawning across her face. "So," she murmured, "it comes to this."

"Jed and I really think it's the best option," Redford said softly, apologetic. "We've worked with O'Malley before, and we know his kind. He's incredibly dangerous. He'll have well-trained people on his side, better than the army could do. Even if the pack outnumbered them ten to one, it would still be too dangerous for you all."

"People would die. A lot of them," Jed agreed bluntly. "This is the best shot you've got to prevent that."

A long silence filled the room. Edwin fidgeted next to Victor, leaning forward to tap the back of Randall's leg. The brothers exchanged a look, neither one of them seeming happy. It hit Victor then, that this was the pack the Lewises had come to join. This was where they'd sought out what they believed to be Anthony's last, best hope. If the pack moved seven states over, then they would be forced to choose between staying or uprooting their entire lives.

"I will have to consult with the elders." The Gray Lady was standing, dismissing them. "Thank you for your work, Journey Walker. I would appreciate if you would stay with us a while longer. We will need to formulate a more solid plan."

Randall frowned as the rest of them started to stand, moving as if to leave. "That's it, then?" His voice broke into the muted conversations. "We're just going to turn tail and run? Just like that?"

"Kid, trust me, there's not a lot of choice—" Jed started.

Randall cut him off. "You said there were always *two* choices. Run or fight."

"Fighting would be suicide." Arms folded, Jed shook his head wearily. "I applaud the balls behind the idea, but trust me, it's not worth the bloodshed."

For a moment it looked as if Randall was going to let it go. The Gray Lady was watching him, gaze intent, weighing his words. Jed, however, had already dismissed him and was rising again to leave.

Randall stood up, pushing aside the map. "And what do we do when this guy finds us again? Do we pick another remote spot? Do we live the rest of our lives in fear? Because that's what it'll be. Constantly watching our backs, constantly waiting for the day when stray wolves start disappearing again." He turned to Jed. "Are you telling me that if we're real quiet, if we hold really still, that O'Malley is just going to get bored of looking?"

Redford looked like he was on the verge of defending the idea of running, but he faltered before he spoke, looking to Jed—who was shaking his head, tapping his fingers against his arms. "That's a great speech," he rumbled. "But if these guys find you, they will shred through whoever is in their way. That includes you. Dying bloody is never a good option."

"Answer the question," Randall shot back. "Are you seriously telling us that O'Malley and the men like him are going to get bored and give up? That's our great hope? We are going to go hide and pray, *pray*, that no one comes looking. That he'll assume this big pack he's hunting has suddenly disappeared."

Jed's jaw jumped. He rolled his head on his shoulders, looking for all the world like he wanted to bark an order or force Randall to shut up. But in the end he muttered, "He won't stop. Not until he thinks he got what he was aiming for."

"So train us," Anthony said, standing beside Randall. "We might not be soldiers, but we can be taught. We can give ourselves a fighting chance."

"I'm not going to...." Jed paced away, blowing out a curse under his breath. He turned back to the Gray Lady, almost pleading. "You will die. *People* will *die*. What they're asking is for me to arm them for suicide. I can't do it. I cannot stand here and tell you that this is going to work. It won't. What's going to happen is you're going to be standing out there with a gun in your hand, bullets raining down on you, and you will be listening to the people you trained beside, the people who were alive and whole and *fine* that morning, you will listen to them screaming. You will hear them begging a God who sure as fuck ain't listening as they are mowed down around you. *That* is what is coming. That is war. It's not going to be some goddamn inspirational movie about the plucky underdogs who stuck it to the man. It will be your friends, the people who you handed those guns to, bleeding out while you can do *fuck all* to save them."

In the resulting silence after Jed's words, Anthony sighed. "If life isn't a movie, Jed, you're sure good at giving dramatic monologues."

Victor internally braced himself for the fallout.

"Yeah, that's all it is, kid." Jed's face was tight, his whole body tense. Victor was vaguely worried Jed was going to punch a wall. Or perhaps one of them. "Just a pretty story I'm telling."

"I'm not dismissing you, Jed," Anthony replied. "You're right. You're completely right. It's not a nice option. People will die no matter how well they're trained. But it is *their* choice, and you can't save them from it."

Jed all but growled. "I don't *save* people. I'm not a goddamn hero. I'm here to tell you your best shot. That's it. I'm not training up a bunch of fucking hippies to be soldiers." He tossed the maps toward the Gray Lady, who was watching the exchange silently. "There you go. Listen to me, don't, I don't fucking care. I'm out."

Anthony made no move to stop him, though he looked like he wanted to. Mostly, he just looked sad, like he'd thought Jed had more loyalty than that. Victor wasn't sure where he'd get that idea from—Jed had loyalty to himself and Redford, and that was about it. He had hoped Jed might find some friendships here. It seemed that might not be the case.

Or perhaps Jed was just angry and desperate to stop them all from getting themselves killed. Victor could certainly relate.

"Do you know anywhere that we might order guns from, then?" Anthony asked Jed. "Just in case we need them."

Jed didn't answer. He turned on his heel and marched out, trailing curses behind him. Redford was right behind him, though he kept darting apologetic glances back to the Lewises. As the door slammed shut behind them, Randall turned to Anthony, about to continue talking.

"That will be all." The Gray Lady spoke at last. "I need to speak with my elders. It seems we have much to discuss." She glanced over at Anthony as she added, "Perhaps no orders of weaponry should be made just yet. Not until we have determined the best course for the pack."

Anthony shrunk under her glance, embarrassed. "My apologies, ma'am," he said. He looked horrified at himself. Perhaps, Victor thought, because all the dominant personalities in the group kept trying to make decisions on behalf of the pack, and he was one of them. "I won't do anything before you have made your decision."

The Gray Lady simply nodded. Victor had the very distinct feeling they'd just been dismissed. One by one they filtered out. Edwin was oddly morose as he hung back by his brothers, and Anthony looked deep in thought. Mallory passed them, giving Anthony a nod as he headed out, presumably to gather the wolf elders.

Victor shivered as he transitioned from the warmth inside the Gray Lady's house to the chill air outside. Off in the distance he could see Jed and Redford standing by their cabin. Going by Jed's gesticulations, they were having a rather spirited conversation.

Anthony bumped Randall's shoulder with his own. "Morning appointment with the doctor," he said. "I'm heading over, and I'm told I'll probably be a few hours, so go do something fun. You too, Victor."

"Ah, yes. Fun. I think I've forgotten what that is," Victor said dryly. More likely he'd be attempting to do more research, or figuring out how to approach this Leonard O'Malley person and get him to stop this encroaching war. "Good luck with your appointment."

Edwin was tugging off his shirt almost as soon as they'd gotten out of the cabin. "I'm going for a run. I'll be waiting for you after, okay, Ant?" He shifted, a graceful leap forward, lean muscle and smooth skin changing to fur. He barked at them, tail wagging furiously, weaving between their legs before taking off like a shot toward the woods.

"I have fun," Randall told Anthony, hands in his pockets, watching Edwin as if to make sure he was all right. "How about I stop by and meet you after you're done at the healer's?"

"All right." Anthony fondly ruffled Randall's hair and smirked when Randall scowled and tried to duck away. He glanced between Randall and Victor, his expression lighting up. "Hey, so I heard some of the younger kids talking yesterday. Apparently there's a waterfall in the northeast of the camp that feeds into the river, and it's a real romantic spot for a picnic or a swim."

There was a beat of silence, Randall so deliberately *not* looking at Victor it was almost painful. Victor, for his part, merely stared at Anthony, dumbfounded. "Did you meet someone?" Randall asked Anthony, overly casual. "That's great. About time. Why don't I pack you a lunch to take?"

In all his life, Victor had never met someone he could accurately describe as having a *hearty* laugh. Anthony, he discovered, now fit the bill. "Playing dumb doesn't suit you, Randall," he said. "I'm covered in stinky goo, and none of the healers—who are pretty much the only people I see, by the way—are my type." A brief tenseness crossed Anthony's face, a tilt to his lips that didn't seem to match his casual tone. "Besides, I don't have the best luck, waterfall or no."

Victor didn't miss the flash of emotions over Anthony's face, though he didn't know how to begin interpreting them. Randall's expression immediately fell, and he reached out and squeezed Anthony's shoulder. "I'm sorry," he whispered to his brother, lips etched downward into a regretful frown. "I didn't think. That was incredibly rude."

Anthony just gave a shrug and looped his arm around Randall's shoulder to pull him close. "Don't worry about it," he said, his smile genuine. Just like that, the indescribable emotions on his face had gone, replaced with cheer. "Now seriously, have some fun so you can tell me about it later. I need to live vicariously through you so that my sole experience here isn't smelly ointments and being poked by a healer."

Hugging Anthony close, face pressed into his neck, Randall's shoulders shook slightly. But his voice was painfully calm when he spoke. "I promise. Lots of fun. And we'll go swimming together later, okay? You're going to be fine, Ant." It was said so fervently, as if his words invoked power.

It pained Victor to be a witness to a moment so emotional. As a man not normally inclined to be overly demonstrative himself, he felt more than a little awkward standing around while Randall desperately tried to reassure both himself and his brother that Anthony would be fine. In some small nod to courtesy, he turned aside and pretended to be intently studying the pack of wolves near the constant bonfire.

"Of course I am," he heard Anthony say. "I'd better go; they'll get annoyed if I'm late."

And then Randall was left standing there alone, watching his brother make a slow, agonizing shuffle across the camp toward the healers' cabin. It was worse in the morning, Victor had observed, particularly on chilly mornings such as this. The tense line of Randall's shoulders, the way he was leaning forward, clearly spoke to how much Randall itched to go help Anthony. But he held himself still, jaw so tight it looked like Randall might shatter.

Victor wished there was something he could say that wasn't pithy platitudes. Telling Randall everything would be okay felt like a farce, because he couldn't promise that. Telling him that Anthony was a fighter would just sound ridiculous out loud.

Then again, some people did feel reassured by such empty sentences.

In normal circumstances, he might ask if Randall wanted to hear some of those platitudes, because Victor was perfectly capable of saying them if it might help. But Randall didn't look to be in the mood for such a discussion. Instead, Victor said, "So. We've been ordered to have some fun. Have you any ideas, because I certainly don't." He peered into the distance. "Perhaps we could sidle up to Jed and Redford and listen in on their argument."

Randall snorted faintly. "That's your idea of fun?" But he didn't disagree. Shooting Victor a sidelong look, he nodded toward where Jed and Redford appeared to be very much absorbed in their own conversation. Jed was gesticulating wildly, pacing back and forth, clearly still upset.

"I'm not going to get a bunch of fucking *ass sniffing furry hippies* killed, Red!" Jed's voice was decidedly louder than necessary. Victor and Randall had hardly needed to get within ten feet before every word was heard crystal clear.

"But it's their choice!" Redford replied. Victor struggled to recall a time when he'd ever heard Redford speaking at a volume above a hushed murmur, and couldn't think of one. "You wouldn't be *getting* them anything, Jed."

Jed stomped away, all of a few feet, before turning back around, waving a finger at Redford. "I've been here before. I'm not doing this, not here, no fucking way."

Even from ten feet away, Victor could see Redford's eyes nearly cross as he attempted to focus on Jed's finger, looking faintly offended that he was getting it shaken at him. "They're not asking you to lead them into war," he said. "They're not actually asking *anything* of you, just your opinion. And you saw what happened back there. You advised them to run, and they might pick the war. Nobody's death will be on your head."

"Yes they *will!*" Jed actually turned and threw the laptop at the side of the cabin. Randall flinched as it smashed against the wood. "Jesus fuck, it's going to be *on me*. If I stay, it will be my fucking fault if they die."

Randall moved closer to Victor, their arms pressed tight together. Randall was watching Jed and Redford worriedly. This was his life they were debating, Victor realized. His future. Victor would go home and back to his house, his classroom, but if the wolf pack decided to run, it would mean the Lewises picking up and leaving with them. If they fought, it could be Randall who died.

"Actually," Redford said softly. "It will be on *me*. I'm the one Randall hired, remember? I'm the one in charge of our business presence here. You said it yourself."

"We are so far beyond that, Fido, and you damn well know it."

"We're not idiots." Randall's voice was so quiet, for a moment it didn't seem anyone had heard him. Jed dragged his gaze from Redford over to Randall, scowl deepening. Victor gave an awkward half wave, attempting to look like he wasn't hiding behind a bush and listening in. "We are wolves. We might not know this fight, but if you think we don't know what hunters mean—"

"This ain't your business, kid," Jed muttered. "You and the professor go back to making kissy faces at each other and leave us alone."

"Jed!" Redford's eyes had started flickering toward yellow, even as his shoulders rounded in embarrassment at Randall's presence. "That's *exactly* his business. That's his life, the future of *his* people. Don't you think he gets a say in that?"

"I'm not talking about *him*." Jed had dismissed Victor and Randall again, moving forward toward Redford, voice lowered to a desperate hiss. "Jesus, Red, come on. I'm not talking about what they do, I'm talking about *us*. You and me. I'm not going to stand around here and let you get turned into *me*."

Victor was glad nobody was looking at him, because he gave such a momentous roll of his eyes that he nearly permanently flipped his eyeballs.

"Jed, that's...." Redford sounded like he was struggling to catch up with the new topic. "I don't care about me right now. This pack is facing a war, and we need to decide if we're going to help or not."

"That's what I'm telling you. I don't care about one damn thing *but* you." Jed's hands landed on Redford's arms, gripping lightly. "I'd help them relocate, but—"

"*Us.*" Randall interrupted again, this time with a low growl. Jed's fingers immediately slid away from Redford, the distance between them all that much more obvious. "You're talking about us. And fine, you don't want to stay around here, you want to take off, fine. I'll find someone else. I'll get someone in here who *will* teach us how to fight these men. Or we'll figure it out on our own. But, Jed, I don't want to run. We *shouldn't* run. And you know it."

"Where the fuck do you get that idea?" Jed bit back.

"Because you're fighting it so damn hard." Randall squared his shoulders, meeting Jed's eyes boldly. "If you really just thought we were idiots and it was a bad idea, you'd insult us, get in your van, and go. But you're actively arguing for the other option. You're scared."

"Fuck you." Jed folded his arms tight across his chest. But he also didn't deny it.

"I'm scared too," Randall murmured. "I don't want to fight. That's not who I am. But it's the logical choice. Running will only prolong this."

Redford only had eyes for Jed right then. He took Jed's elbow, getting his attention. When he spoke, it was so low that Victor barely heard him. "I know why you don't want to do this. I know it's hard. But if we leave without helping them, they *will* die. By being here we can help make sure they survive."

Head bowing, Jed let out a slow breath. "What are you going to do when they die, Red? How am I going to look you in the eye when I force you to kill someone? That's what *I* do, babe, not you."

"I've already killed," Redford said gently. "And it hurt. And I felt bad about it. But then I remembered that I did it for us. Because I love you, and because I'm not the guy stuck in my grandmother's basement anymore. I'm free, and I chose this, because you showed me a better life."

Once again, Victor was starting to feel supremely awkward. Did he have a talent for walking in on intimate conversations?

"And when these wolves go to war," Redford continued, "some of them will die. And I'll be upset about that too, but at least I'll know that we *tried*."

"It's not better," Jed muttered, stare firmly fixed on the ground. "Doesn't matter how right it was to kill those guys, there shouldn't ever be blood on your hands. Not yours. Jesus, Red, it's not *better*. It's a cage. I'm keeping you in a goddamn cage, just like...." He broke off, rubbing a hand across his face, all but biting back the rest of that sentence. "Fine," he sighed, louder, refusing to look at anyone. "Fine, I'll fucking train the Lassie squad."

"*We'll* train them," Redford corrected. Victor noted that he didn't bring up the cage comment again.

"Yeah, great. We'll train them." Jed's arms were crossed tightly across his chest, brow furrowed.

"Thank you," Randall attempted, only to have Jed growl under his breath and stomp off in the direction of his and Redford's cabin. Randall looked a bit deflated, but he turned to Redford, sincerity in his voice, and tried again. "Thank you. For what you're going to do."

Redford looked uncomfortable at the praise, but he did smile slightly. "We're all wolves, right? Wolves should stick together."

The first time Victor had met Redford, the man had practically hidden behind anything bigger than he was to avoid seeing other people. The fact that he was smiling at Randall and tentatively including himself in a group was a rather big improvement.

"Although I don't know how much gun training would really help," Redford admitted, rubbing the back of his neck. "Everybody here would rather fight as a wolf."

"Then you and Jed can teach them that." Victor nodded over at the group of wolves lazing around near the fire. "See them? They may have hunting instincts, but that isn't knowledge of what to do in a fight against someone with a gun."

"You are going to save us," Randall said, so fervently, so absolute in his belief. "Think of the security, the patrols, all the dozens of tiny details that no one here considers. Those are what's going to be the difference between survival and being wiped out."

Redford seemed even more uncomfortable now, his gaze firmly fixed on the ground. "It's... um. Just—it's nothing," he stuttered, unable to get words out. "You're welcome? It might not even be an issue. The Gray Lady still hasn't decided what she wants to do. But if she decides to fight, we're, um, we're glad to help."

Randall took an awkward step forward, arms going half out, almost as if for a hug. Redford gave him a startled glance, and Randall wound up patting Redford's shoulder, looking highly uncomfortable and very much like he wasn't sure what to do with his body. "Yes, well. Right. Just in case. Thank you again." A beat and he sighed, shoving his glasses farther up on his nose. "I'm sorry. My brothers are so much better at this sort of thing."

Victor rubbed a hand over his mouth to hide his amused smirk. This was the third awkward thing he'd seen so far today, but this one was actually quite endearing.

"It's okay," Redford told Randall. "I'm not very good at, um, hugs either. But you are welcome. I don't think I could stand by and do nothing to help. Even if I have to drag Jed, kicking and screaming, with me."

"Redford!" The dulcet tones of Journey Walker came floating back toward them. "Come on. I ain't doing this alone. Let's look at some goddamn maps."

Redford ducked his head, but Victor could see the curve of a pleased little smile tug at his lips. "I'll see you two later," he said and took off at a quick pace toward Jed.

Victor still wasn't entirely sure what was going on between Jed and Redford, but as long as they were willingly working together and not gouging each other's eyeballs out, he frankly didn't care all that much. He watched Randall as Randall's gaze followed Redford, a small tinge of what might have been longing touching his expression.

"I should probably let you get back to... well, whatever it is you were going to do today." Randall didn't look at Victor, purposefully keeping his eyes anywhere but Victor's face. "I'm sure that watching paint dry would be more interesting to you than following me around."

"I rather think following you around would be the highlight of my day." Victor said the words before he really thought about them, and was surprised to find himself genuinely meaning them. "Have you had breakfast yet?"

Blinking rapidly, Randall fumbled off his glasses to clean them aggressively on the edge of his shirt. "Uh. No. I haven't yet." Shyly, he glanced over at Victor. "I suppose I did promise Ant to have fun. And I don't think that counted."

"Awkward hugs don't count as fun?" Victor lifted his eyebrows, pretending to be surprised. "I'm shocked."

"Yes, well, I am out of practice." Randall's mouth twisted up into a half smile. "Usually I leave the emotional displays to my brothers. I'm a sorry excuse for a wolf, I'm afraid."

"Who said that wolves have to be emotionally open?" Victor wasn't entirely sure where *that* particular myth had come from. "Is there even a basis in reality for that stereotype?"

They'd fallen into step beside each other. Victor couldn't remember if he'd moved first or if Randall had, but their gaits were in easy sync. "Not really." Randall rubbed the back of his neck. "I mean, I suppose the idea comes from the fact we're all supposed to be wild creatures, howling at the moon. But in my limited experience, wolves are pretty much like people. We have personalities. We have different opinions and emotions. We feel things... more intensely than humans, I think. And there are certain things, like the idea of mates or pack, that I think might be unique. But not being rough and tumble doesn't make me any less wolfish, no. At least, not in my opinion."

From anybody else, Victor would—rather hypocritically, he was aware—get bored of the lecture. From Randall, however, he found himself listening intently to Randall speak, wanting to ask him for more information. "Not in any opinion, I should hope," Victor replied. "It does make me feel thankful that medusas are quite rare. We have no stereotypes."

Other than eventually going crazy, but that was less of a stereotype and more of an absolutely certainly. And this conversation was rather pleasant. Victor didn't want to make it morbid.

"I have observed that you wolves do seem to feel things rather intensely," he then agreed. "But I must admit I've never understood the 'mates' thing. Isn't that just... falling in love, the same way everybody else does?"

Randall huffed out a little laugh, as if amused by Victor's assumption. He didn't answer straightaway, though. They climbed the steps to the dining hall, slipping in easily with the last stragglers of the breakfast rush. The room was nearly empty when they found an out-of-the-way table to sit at, their trays filled with tea, muffins, and bowls of fruit. Randall had a small plate of sausages, thankfully cooked, but he ignored them in favor of sipping his tea first. He kept glancing at Victor, as if trying to decide how much he should say.

"It's like...." He paused, taking off his glasses to fiddle with them, long fingers twirling the earpiece like he needed something to do with his hands. "It's the difference between a paper cut and breaking your arm." Randall cut a quick look over toward Victor. "Both are injuries, yes, but the degree between them is enormous." Again that little huffed out laugh, almost embarrassed, and Randall took a sip of his tea. "I think, from my interactions with humans, that wolves feel things so much more intensely. We hold onto them so much more tightly. My brother, for example. Anthony fell for this guy who used to live near us. Vilhehn. God, Anthony was head over heels. Never knew he was into men, and maybe he isn't. Maybe it was just Vil. But then Vil's family moved away and him with them. This was something like eight years ago? And Anthony still isn't over it. Sure, he's dated a couple of times, but nothing... nothing at all like that again. Maybe not ever."

"That," Victor said, feeling the need to be perfectly honest, "sounds horrifying. You mean he's incapable of moving on?"

"It is horrifying," Randall sighed, meticulously cutting into his sausage. "I don't know. I don't know if he *can't* or he *won't*. I've never been in love like that. I don't know what it does to lose it again." He very quickly looked up at Victor before redirecting his gaze firmly back to his breakfast. "I've heard of wolves pining for dead mates for decades. For the rest of their lives, even. It's just... a *mate* isn't something you simply get over. Once you find someone you're compatible with, once you fall that deeply, you want to bring them into your pack. All you want is to make them a part of your life, to protect them. Pack, for wolves, is more than family. It's more than blood. It's a survival instinct. We have a biological need to surround ourselves with those we care about."

Victor would point out that the biological need for family wasn't limited to wolves alone, but he knew the distinction Randall was attempting to make. "So wolves are a lot closer to their ingrained biological instincts than humans are," he concluded. "Does that play into exactly who you fall in love with? It's not star-crossed or predestined, surely?"

Randall snorted loudly. "Oh, yes. We smell them from afar." A quick grin crossed his face. "No, we date, we break up, just like humans. Just like medusas, I expect, though I don't have evidence to support that. But once we fall, we fall so much harder than it seems like others do. We...." Randall seemed to be struggling to find the right words. "We *ache* for them. We yearn. It burrows down into our bones. To mate means a lifetime commitment. A wolf is very particular about who they're going to spend time with, because if we fall in that kind of love, it's difficult to find our way out again."

Victor fell silent as he digested that information, picking at the fruit salad he'd gotten. It was all rather fascinating, and he was glad that Randall was so willing to discuss it with an outsider. "I have no clue if anything about my medusa blood determines how I fall in love," he said, amused at the idea of it. "Likely not, and I'm grateful for it. Can you imagine if it did? I'd probably turn people to stone or become a raging snake."

"I don't think that's a medusa's true ability." Randall said it blandly, as if they were discussing an academic matter. His expression, though, was warm as he studied Victor's face. "You know people. You pluck the future from their heads, the past from their hearts. You share that with them. For one who keeps himself so alone, Victor, you are a very intimate, entwined being. It's confusing."

"I'll agree with you there," Victor said wryly. He didn't aim the wryness *at* Randall. Instead, he included him in it, giving him a smile as they silently acknowledged the trouble with everything that Victor had seen in Randall's mind. "I'm actually rather lucky to not have a stronger strain of medusa blood than I do. They never turned people into stone, but they did hollow them out and remove them of all feelings and memories." He stabbed a strawberry with his fork, frowning. "I'm not sure I'd feel comfortable even going out into public if I did *that*."

"Do you regret it?" Randall spoke after a long moment of silence, chasing a grape around his plate. "Seeing me?"

"No." Victor didn't even have to think about that answer. "I've never regretted it with anybody. I fear what it one day may do to my mind, yes, but it's…." He trailed off, for a moment unable to think of a suitable way to say it. "It *is* intimate, and I miss out on a great deal of intimacy by never being able to look another person in the eye."

Quiet for several beats, Randall reached out to take Victor's hand. He lightly guided it up to rest Victor's fingers against the corners of his eyes. "You've seen me," he pointed out, very softly. "Would you see it all again if you looked?" Victor could feel the gentle crinkle of his smile under his fingertips. "Don't risk it. I'm just curious."

"I'm not sure," Victor admitted. "I have a theory that I'd see nothing, if nothing had changed since the last time I looked at you. But there's no way to be sure of that, and I've never tested it." He'd never been able to find any accounts of it either. Medusas were notoriously bad at writing down things for later generations, seeing as they all went insane.

Randall's hands dropped away from his, but Victor was a little slow in removing his own hand from Randall's face. He had one cupped around Randall's cheek, his thumb brushing the very edge of Randall's eye. For a long few seconds, Victor didn't move, feeling Randall lean against his palm.

The urge to look into his eyes again was incredible. Victor had to close his own to make sure he didn't, forcibly dragging his hand back and wrapping it around his mug of tea.

"What are you doing, Victor?" Randall asked, voice low, strangled, and hoarse.

"I'm telling myself that I am the very last person you want in your life," Victor admitted. "Because if you are worried about Anthony now, it will only be worse when you have to worry about me going insane. That is why I don't want marriage and children, Randall. Because I would inevitably check out and leave whomever I am sharing that with to shoulder the burden of my insanity alone."

As soon as he said it, Victor went bright red. He hadn't intended to be nearly so honest, especially not when he hadn't even fully admitted those things to *himself.* Damn Randall for forcing the truth out of him.

"Victor…." Randall sounded utterly confused. "What are you talking about?" His hands immediately closed over Victor's, and he moved closer, their knees bumping together under the table. "I don't understand."

"I'm talking about this." Victor motioned between them. "You and me. The thing that I have been utterly unable to stop thinking about since I saw it in your eyes."

Letting out a slow breath, Randall seemed frozen. But only for a moment. Randall's hand hooked lightly around the back of Victor's neck, pulling him into a kiss. It was soft at first, almost a question, Randall's fingers sliding up into the short strands of Victor's hair.

It was one of the best kisses Victor had ever had. There was no agenda in it, no forcing the issue about wanting anything more. It was simply Randall kissing Victor because he wanted to.

Victor forgot all about his hesitations for the duration of it. He forgot about the inevitability of losing his mind and the burden that would put on any long-term relationship, he forgot about the fear of jumping into a close-knit family, and all that mattered, for that moment, was Randall. The hidden sides of him that Victor had been slow to notice, the kindness in him, the strength, the wolfish nature of him that had no business being *that* alluring.

Unfortunately, once they broke apart, all those things he'd forgotten came rushing back.

"Kissing me isn't going to make the issue go away," Victor said, his voice unsteady. Where he normally focused on the eyebrow of the person he was talking to, or over their shoulder, he found he was staring at Randall's lips—they were rather a pleasant thing to be paying attention to.

"I know." Randall hadn't pulled back. His thumb was making a slow arc against Victor's cheek, his words thick, tone so much lower than normal. "But if this was going to be my last chance, I didn't want to miss out. You've obviously decided that I don't get a say in my own future. And, honestly, I'm tired. God, Victor, I'm so *tired*. So if you're bound and determined to ignore me, I just.... I wanted to kiss you again, one more time."

Victor drew back properly then, though he was reluctant to break contact. Any answer he might have wanted to say right then was drowned out by the swirling of *too many* potential answers, some apologetic, some defensive, some hopeful. The indecision was honestly starting to give him a headache.

He needed to clear his head. Mere fresh air wasn't going to do it.

"Well, don't write me off just yet," he said, managing a faint smile. "It's only been a week. After all, this isn't 1268. I'm not the voting cardinals of the Vatican, and I won't take three years to make a decision."

That got a quick laugh from Randall. "Yes, well, I promise not to starve you out or rip off the roof." After a moment, though, when it seemed as if Randall wanted to say so much more, he simply stood. "You've already made your decision, Victor. You told me before. You don't want this. You don't want what I would be. I.... I just need to respect that." Very lightly, Randall's fingers touched the back of Victor's hand. "I'm going to go check on my brothers. Have a nice day, Beatrice."

Once again, there was so much Victor could say to that. He said none of it, though. All of it was contradictory, and he needed to sort his own thoughts before he spoke them to Randall. He didn't want to confuse the poor man, since Victor had done a bang-up job of that already.

Before Randall could leave him, Victor twisted his hand, catching Randall's fingers between his own. He wasn't going to give Randall a long speech about his feelings and how he needed time. Instead, he just squeezed his hand, hoping to convey that what he felt wasn't all that platonic anymore.

If only Victor had been born in the early 1900s. His flirting methods would be much more apt for that time period.

"Say hello to your brothers for me," Victor said. He released Randall's hand.

Randall flexed his fingers, staring down at his palm for a moment as if it would suddenly give him answers. "Yes. Yes, absolutely," he murmured, clearly unsure. But he nodded and took off, walking quickly, disappearing around the corner and leaving Victor alone.

Victor needed a drink, and he didn't care that it was still morning.

To do so, he needed the van. Neither Jed nor Redford were in their cabin, and since Victor needed the keys to the van to go anywhere, he felt absolutely no guilt in sneaking in and taking them from the table. A mission to the bar was a very important thing. Victor knew Jed would understand.

The van rattled and protested when he started it up. It wasn't looking its best right now, with the mud and the chips of wood still stuck everywhere they could find a purchase, but it was serviceable. All it needed to do was get him to the nearest town.

As he turned out of the camp and got onto the dirt path that led to the main road, Victor tried to find a radio station that wasn't a bad talk show or farming reports. He wanted music, something that would distract him—all he got was a local station and a man with a voice more boring than drying paint. It didn't help.

Victor was not a complicated man, he liked to think, and this situation with Randall was incredibly complicated. On one hand, he had visions that told him exactly where this relationship would end up if he went through with it.

And on the other hand, he'd never considered himself the marrying type. The fault in his blood was a large part of it, but it had also been something he'd never seen himself doing. Before David, his relationships had been extremely casual. He had dated David because he had been a wild, dangerous man who was thrilling to be around, a man who was the complete opposite of afternoon tea and dry academics and a living room full of dusty couches and no sound other than a ticking grandfather clock. If his sanity was on a timer, Victor wanted to live life to the full.

But then he'd seen Randall at the airport on the way home from Cairo, and domesticity and peace hadn't sounded so bad.

Victor cursed his thoughts under his breath, gripping the steering wheel tighter and determinedly staring out the front window, pushing his anxiety and worry out of his mind. It wasn't as easy as it sounded.

Fortunately, a bar wasn't too hard to find when he reached the closest town. It looked to be one of the only two bars available, and the only thing that made Victor go with The Roundhouse was the bright-red wagon wheel outside it, marking it as slightly more visually interesting than the other choice.

It was completely empty at this time of day, which Victor counted as a minor blessing. The Roundhouse was more a pub than a bar, with old wood furnishings and creaky tables, exactly the kind of bar that Victor liked, and it was even better that he was the only one there. He ordered a beer, pulled a book out of his bag, and sat down in a corner booth to read.

After an hour, he wound up wandering the town a bit, the fresh air and new sights helping to clear his head. Victor poked around in small antique shops and hotly debated the specific origins of Chinese teapots with the shop owners. He sat in the park for only twenty minutes after discovering he'd sat too close to a particular genus of flowers that made his nose itch, and by the time it was starting to get dark he had wandered his way back to the bar.

To his irritation—although it wasn't unexpected—there were a few other people in there now. The after-work crowd had clearly started arriving, populated with thick-armed tradesmen and loud-voiced shop workers. The noise level wasn't too bad, though, so Victor reclaimed his former corner booth and resumed reading.

When he finally looked up from Jeeves and Wooster's antics—P. G. Wodehouse was a favorite of his—there were people much more horrifying than tradesmen and shop workers in the bar.

There were *youths*.

Even worse, one of them was walking his way.

Victor cringed back in his seat, but that didn't stop the red-haired young man from holding up a hand. "Dude, high five, ginger pride," he announced. "I'm, like, the only one in this shit heap. Now there's two!" Victor glanced with trepidation at the young man's hand. "Aw, come on man, don't leave me hanging."

Victor did his best to contain his grimace as he delivered the most unenthusiastic high five that had ever been given. That didn't seem to deter the young man, who beamed at him and slung himself into the opposite corner of the booth.

"Name's Dylan." A waitress approached the table and put a glass of milk in front of Dylan. A rather odd thing to be drinking in a bar, Victor thought. "Are you new around here?"

"No. Well, yes, I suppose, but I'm only a visitor." Victor supposed that Dylan didn't seem all that bad, as far as *youths* went. "Is there any particular reason you're sitting at my table?"

Bluntness typically scared most people off, which worked in Victor's favor, as he was not a great fan of socialization when he could avoid it. Dylan seemed to not notice it at all. He only grinned and tapped the side of his nose. "Thought I'd say hi to my own kind, man."

"I'm not *that* ginger," Victor muttered. "Only a little bit. It's—" Dylan didn't mean gingers, Victor suddenly realized. "Oh. Er. How could you tell?" He looked around the room and surreptitiously darted a glance at his own clothes, attempting to figure out if he was somehow looking particularly medusa-like.

"I see things most people don't," Dylan said. Victor couldn't tell if he sounded wise or just constantly stoned. Perhaps a bit of both. "I'm an ùruisg."

Thankfully, the music in the background would muffle their conversation enough, but Victor still kept his voice low as he said, "A brownie? Interesting." That explained the milk, at least.

"Yeah, man, it's awesome." Dylan beamed. "So what's your dysfunction?"

Victor found himself faltering as he tried to reply. As much as he knew about half bloods, he didn't tend to speak with them all that often, other than maintaining important contacts in the community. Speaking to more of them would require the very thing he dreaded: conversation. "Medusa. A weak enough strain."

"Damn," Dylan drawled, giving him a wide-eyed look. "Sucks, man."

"How kind of you to say."

"So, like, what's up? What's got you looking so down, huh?"

Victor decided then that Dylan really was stoned. "The sorts of things that make people feel down."

Dylan seemed completely unaware of Victor's withering tone. "Like what? You can tell me! I'm an awesome listener, I promise."

He just wasn't going to give up, apparently. Victor sighed and finally closed his book in acknowledgement that he wasn't going to escape this conversation any time soon. "I looked into someone's eyes and saw their future," he replied. "There were a great many futures, but one main theme was him and I getting married. He has told me that he has feelings for me. I had some mild interest in him before the visions, and I think that interest may be developing into something stronger."

Dylan gave him an uncomprehending look. "So what's the problem?"

"I'm a medusa, and he's a wolf." Victor felt that summed it up nicely.

"Ah." Dylan nodded thoughtfully.

"If he properly falls in love with me, well, you know how wolves are," Victor continued. "And it's inevitable that my mind will fracture at some point in my life. He already has so much to deal with in his family right now, I couldn't possibly burden him more."

Dylan was just nodding as he sipped at his milk. "So does he love you? Or, like, what do wolves call it? Has he called you his mate?"

"I don't know." Victor buried his head in his hands. He'd never intended to speak so personally to a complete stranger, but now that he'd started, he couldn't stop. "I never wanted to get married or have a domestic life. And part of me is angry at him—some small part of me is angry about this choice that I have to make. Either I be with him, or I make him lonely forever, if he really does love me as a wolf does. How is that fair to me? I cannot be responsible for someone's happiness, and yet I am. It almost leaves me no choice at all. If I choose to not be with him, I come off looking like an absolute asshole, even though it *should* be a decision I can make freely."

"Heavy, man," Dylan said.

Victor squinted at him. Where was he from, the seventies?

"Well," Dylan continued. "Is he, like, weak or something? Or really bad at coping with shit?"

"No," Victor said defensively. "He's one of the strongest, most capable men I've ever met. His brother is suffering from a degenerative illness, and Randall handles it with grace."

"So," Dylan mused, "why do you think he couldn't handle you?"

That gave Victor pause.

"He shouldn't have to," he eventually replied after a long few seconds of silence.

"Man, I shouldn't have to put some pants on to go to the door to get the pizza I ordered, but I still do. You know why? Because pizza is so fucking worth it."

Victor couldn't help but laugh. "So in this metaphor, Randall is pizza?"

"Yeah, man," Dylan said enthusiastically. "Good shit is always hard work. And sometimes there's some danger of bad shit along with the good shit. Like, you could get bad pepperoni and get food poisoning. But you never know it's a certainty, and there's no point living in fear of bad salami, so you may as well get that fucking pizza, right?"

"You make it sound so simple," Victor said dryly.

"That's because it is. Okay, hit me, give me another problem, I bet you I can make it real simple for you."

Victor wasn't sure why he was still talking to this kid, but he had to admit, he'd been given some good perspectives so far. Surely it wouldn't hurt to try for more. "All right. I've never been the marrying type. All my life I've seen married couples and their lives, and it seems so dull. There's no excitement, no danger, no thrill."

Dylan steepled his fingers. He had an easy look about him, soft features, but right then he looked to be concentrating hard. "Okay. Well, first of all, married life is what you make it, right? If you don't want it to be dull, then do interesting stuff. And he's a wolf, how boring can that really be? I know they're not all *vampire* dangerous, but they've still got big teeth!"

Victor sighed to himself. "That sounds easy in theory but wrong in practicality."

"What, so he's boring?"

"No. Not at all."

"Then you just have some kind of serious problem with the idea of settling down, man," Dylan said sadly. "There's nothing wrong with it."

Victor supposed Dylan had hit the nail on the head there. The problem wasn't Randall, it was his perception of how a married, settled life would look. He had been with David because the man would offer him the very opposite.

"I suppose I have a lot to think about," Victor muttered. He'd only half finished his beer, and he had no real urge to drink the rest of it. Beer had never been his drink of choice anyway.

Dylan leaned over the table to pat him consolingly. "Well, you'll never figure it out sitting in a bar. Hey, you said he's a wolf, right? Does that mean he lives with the nearby pack?" Dylan brightened. "Phoenix is talking there on summer solstice. A few of us half bloods in the area have been invited."

"Yes, that's where I'm staying," Victor replied, surprised. Phoenix, the half blood who was trying to rally the various supernatural groups together for solidarity, was speaking at a wolf gathering? He supposed Edwin would like that. He recalled Edwin being quite into his ideals.

"Cool," Dylan said cheerfully. "I'll see you there, then."

Dylan was right—sitting in a bar wasn't going to solve any of his problems. "Thank you for the advice," Victor said politely. He rose to stand and held out his hand for Dylan. They shook. Dylan grinned at him.

"No problem, man," Dylan said. "Anytime."

Victor left. The cool air outside was a welcome touch against his overheated skin, and he remained for a moment outside the bar, letting his eyes adjust to the light. He took his time to get back to the van, contemplating everything they'd just talked about.

In the end, it seemed like he might have been overcomplicating things. He liked Randall, and in the present that was all that mattered. Victor was aware that he had a bad habit of living in the future, of weighing his actions in the present against the visions he had seen. But Randall had told him he should try living in the present, and perhaps that was some more advice that Victor should take.

He got back into the van and started driving home. His gaze caught on the book he'd placed in the passenger seat—P. G. Wodehouse. Victor needed to make some sort of gesture to show Randall that he did indeed reciprocate his feelings.

And he thought he might just have the perfect way to do so.

CHAPTER
10

Jed

JED DIDN'T do fights. Not like this. He didn't get involved in domestic shit, he didn't have long hours of awkward silences, and he sure as fuck didn't spend half a day working while pretending not to see Redford's ridiculously upset face. That was why he'd always done one-night stands. They weren't messy, they weren't demanding. He didn't even have to know the other guy's name. And even if they were a repeat, it never *meant* anything. It was just sex.

Redford wasn't *just* anything, though. Redford was the goddamn moon and the hook it hung on, and up until two weeks ago, Jed would have said they were doing just fine. Sure, Redford was having some issues. Sure, sometimes things got a little wolfy and Jed lost Redford for a bit. But Redford had always come back. And Jed just figured that was a side effect of Fil.

Now he wasn't so sure.

This place, these wolves, none of them lost control. None of them woke up in the middle of the night desperate to get out and chase squirrels. None of them ripped the throats out of people and barely seemed aware afterward. Jed had thought he was helping. He'd thought they were fine.

He was pretty damn sure he was wrong.

And God, he wished they'd just gone fishing. He didn't want to do this; he didn't want to fight with Redford. He didn't want all the things he *should* say to get stuck in his throat every damn time Redford looked at him.

It was his fault. He was part of the cage Redford lived inside, and it was *his fault* that Redford wasn't happy. That he was cracking apart at the seams.

Redford was asleep beside him. They'd plotted and planned half the day yesterday about what they'd need to do if the Gray Lady decided to stay and fight. Redford had gone scouting so they could start work on a more accurate map of the pack's territory. Jed had made phone calls for supplies. They'd acted like nothing was wrong. They'd acted so damn hard like everything was *fine*.

It wasn't fine. Jed was fucking this whole thing up. From the day he'd met Redford, he'd just made the guy worse. All that time, Jed thought he was *saving* him. He thought he'd found Redford and Redford had found him, and, what, it was a goddamn fairy tale? He should have known better. Fairy tales, they weren't real. And people like Jed were a cancer. They spread and they corrupted every damn thing they touched.

Redford had been so fucking *innocent*. He'd been good, genuinely good. And now he was killing. Now he was part of some fucking war.

It was Jed's fault.

Sitting in bed, staring into nothing, Jed didn't notice the time pass. The stars and the moon trailed faint gray light across the floor of the cabin, Redford rumbled a whimper in his sleep and curled farther into the covers, but Jed still didn't move. At the first light of dawn, Redford shifted in his sleep again, but this time his eyes opened, automatically seeking out Jed.

Redford had never been a morning person. Unlike Jed, who had long trained himself to be up and alert immediately, Redford never liked waking up and moving out of bed. There had been many mornings where Jed had been tempted to let Redford sleep in, even when they had a job they'd needed to get to in an hour.

Now Redford just rubbed a hand over his eyes and rose, pushing the blankets aside. He kept glancing at Jed as he got dressed, shivering through the chill of the morning air until he'd wrapped himself in three layers. Then finally, when he was done, he said, "We should go get coffee."

Jed had plans for the morning. He hadn't anticipated Redford getting up at dawn. "You should go back to sleep," he mumbled, voice an exhausted rasp. Scrubbing his hands across his face, Jed sighed. "It's early. You can get a couple more hours in before anyone's really up."

Redford smiled slightly and spread his arms to show Jed the layers he was wearing. With a T-shirt, a light jacket, and a heavier jacket on top of that, Redford resembled a marshmallow. "I'm dressed, Jed. And I'm not going back to sleep in this, so we may as well go."

"Redford," Jed started. He didn't want coffee. He didn't want to sit at a goddamn table and pretend everything was *fine* anymore. Jed could only sit back and think about shit for so long. It was time he got some answers. And none of those answers would be found in Lassie's cafeteria.

But then he looked over and caught Redford's expression. That very stubborn, very determined look that silently said: *Jed, get your ass up off that bed because we are going to get coffee whether you like it or not.* Jed knew that look. It meant that any arguing Jed might do was simply wasted.

So, with another heaved exhale, Jed slid out of bed and tugged on his jeans, searching through his bag for a sweatshirt. "Fine," he muttered, teeth clenched. "Coffee. Great."

Redford made a little noise under his breath that Jed couldn't discern, either irritated or acquiescent. Once Jed had gotten dressed, they left the cabin and walked silently toward the kitchens. Redford tugged the fake-furred collar of his heavy jacket up around his chin to ward against the cold before shoving his hands firmly in his pockets.

Jed hated how they were. He hated that he was so goddamn fucking *useless* he couldn't even think of something to say. Over and over Jed nearly blurted something out, some desperate grasp at conversation or yet another apology. But every time he'd look over at Redford, and he'd just go mute.

193

There was something wild about Redford, Jed had thought that from the first time he'd met him, something so achingly beautiful, something strong and innocent and free. Something Jed both wanted to gather up and protect and wrap around himself like a shield. And everything in Jed, every fiber of him, only wanted to make Redford happy. To give him everything he deserved.

So why did he fuck it all up so badly? He'd shoved Redford into an apartment in the city. What kind of life was that for a wolf? What kind of person shoved something so beautiful in a cage? Jed was so goddamn selfish, he'd never even *thought* that the life he lived might not be what Redford needed. But now he saw, now he'd gotten example after fucking example of what a wolf should be. How could he possibly begin to make things right now?

The dining hall was nearly empty. Breakfast wasn't out yet, but Jed could hear the clank of pans and the low hum of voices from the back. There was an enormous pot of coffee, though, and Jed poured himself a cup, finding a bottle of water for Redford and carrying both carefully toward a table in the corner.

On the way, he passed Anthony—he hadn't even seen him there, tucked into a side table, out of the line of direct sight from the door. Anthony had both hands wrapped around an enormous mug, his shoulders hunched, head down so that his hair partially covered his face. When he looked up at them, though, he grinned. "Morning, guys. You're up early."

This was as good a table as any. Jed put Redford's water down, slinging himself into one of the chairs and taking a long gulp of the coffee. "Yeah, well, someone got a hankering to go for a beverage he doesn't actually drink."

There was no response from Redford, and Anthony just lifted an eyebrow. The look he gave them was patiently amused, but there was a hint of concern there too. "Wolves tend to have more sensitive tastes than humans." Anthony shrugged. "Ask Edwin why he never eats green vegetables. He keeps complaining that they're too bitter."

"It's not the lack of coffee drinking I was...." Jed sighed. "Yeah. Never mind." Another drink of coffee, then, just to have something to do with his hands. Jed was hunched over the table, jaw tight, too many thoughts in his head and not enough things he even remotely knew how to say. Looking at Redford was fucking painful right then. It was like staring into the face of every damn failure he'd ever had.

"So," Anthony said brightly, clearly seeing the need for a change in topic, "I don't actually know much about you two. When did you become mates?"

Blinking, Jed pulled his gaze up from contemplating his coffee. "Uh. You mean how long have we known each other? Isn't *mates* more of a British slang thing?"

Anthony laughed. "No, I mean how long have you been mated to one another," he clarified. "It's obvious enough from your scents. They're all over each other."

Jed couldn't help but look at Redford, who was giving Anthony nearly the same clueless look that Jed was. "Okay, explain it real slow for the dumb human," Jed prompted, leaning back, gaze darting between the two of them. "Because I'm not following."

Anthony frowned in complete confusion. "How can you not know what I'm talking about? Redford, you're a wolf."

Redford shrunk down in his seat. "Not really," he mumbled. "I didn't grow up like you guys, remember?" Jed had to bite back a very real urge to punch Anthony right in the throat for making Redford get that expression on his face.

"Right." Anthony apparently had to take a moment to get his thoughts in line, because he took a breath, shook his head slightly, and peered at them in amusement. "Sorry. I'll rephrase. How long have you been together?"

"Almost a year?" Jed tried to do the math in his head. "Something like that. So mates are, like, wolf boyfriends?" That kind of made sense, he guessed.

"Not really." Anthony was looking at Redford more than Jed, still faintly confused. "I guess the better analogy would be marriage, but even more than that. I'm sure Randall could explain it a lot better than I could."

"Whoa, whoa, hold on there, tiger." Jed gave a nervous half laugh, practically shoving his chair back as if to give himself distance from the *terrifying* m-word. "There's not... we are *definitely* not married. I don't think that is something you just want to be *saying* to people. You don't... you can't just throw that word out there, man, that's not cool."

"Of course you're not married," Anthony huffed, "I can see the lack of rings. But you've got to be mates, you smell like it. And that's even better than married." He grinned at them both, pleased. "It's a good thing, Jed. I'm happy for you, and I think it's totally okay that you're one human and one wolf."

Jed could feel the irritation seeping in, a scowl tightening the lines of his forehead. "What the fuck does that mean?" he growled.

Anthony didn't seem to notice Jed's irritation. He leaned back in his chair, taking on a wistful smile. "It's difficult to explain, but I'll try. We call our partners mates. I'm sure Randall could go on a whole lecture about it, but I guess the main difference is, wolves tend to feel things a bit stronger than humans. Or at least we have more trouble letting go." Anthony grinned. "It varies from wolf to wolf, how we find a partner. But in the end, we nearly always find our mate—someone that we could never think of leaving, someone that makes our life so much more whole than it ever was."

He leaned forward, elbows on the table, studying them both. "And it's the best thing that can ever happen to you."

Jed didn't want to hear this. Because then he'd start thinking about if he was that stupid *mate* thing to Redford, and what it'd mean if he wasn't. What it might mean if he *was*. And why both answers scared the living hell out of him. "Yeah?" he smirked, cocky and disinterested, to hide everything that was behind the expression. "If it's so damn great, where's yours?"

If he was intending to insult Anthony enough to make him back off, Anthony didn't take the bait. He just sighed into his coffee. "Somewhere that's not here. I know he's still alive. I think I'd feel it if he died. But he's been for gone for a while."

It struck Jed then that Anthony looked like a man who was missing his other half. Like there was something very lopsided about him when he sat alone, as if there should be someone sitting at his side. Jed didn't want to know what that felt like. More than anything, he never wanted to find that out.

Chewing the inside of his cheek, Jed looked down, shaking his head. "We're not mates," he muttered roughly. "End of story."

Because if they were, then he was going to wind up just like Anthony.

"Well, um," Redford hedged, "it sounds fairly accurate to me."

Before Jed had the chance to reply, Anthony brightened again, beaming at them. "I knew it. Jed, you just don't have the instincts, you probably can't tell. And that's okay! But I think after a while even a human will start to get it, so if you've been together for nearly a year, you'll get it soon."

"Yeah, 'cause I'm not wolf enough, right?" Jed nodded sharply, a far too wide grin on his face. "I don't *get* a lot of stuff about him. Like what he needs. Like how to even handle a wolf or full moons or any of that shit that just comes *so* goddamn natural to everyone else in this freak show. Right?" He stood, kicking his chair back, nearly upsetting his coffee. "You know what, I think I'm going for a walk."

Anthony had gone wide-eyed, like he was appalled at himself for saying something that could be taken as an insult. "That's not what I meant," he protested. "It's not a bad thing that you just need a little longer to learn this stuff, Jed. Hell, if Randall and Victor do wind up getting together, Victor will need to learn all this too."

"Please, for all that is holy, do not fucking compare me to the goddamn *princess*, all right?" Jed threw his hands up in surrender. "Fine. It's great that I'm ruining Redford's life, you're right. Goddamn adorable."

He didn't want to talk about this anymore. Especially not with Redford looking at him with those big eyes, those endless depths he'd gotten lost in so many times. It made Jed ache. It made him emotional and weak, because he got so afraid of losing Redford that he couldn't think about what was best for him.

"Jed." Redford sounded unsure and unhappy all at the same time. Jed felt Redford take his hand, reaching out for him. "You haven't ruined my life. You've made it so much better."

Staring down at the floor so he wouldn't have to see Redford, so he wouldn't have to make eye contact and pull up a fake smirk and pretend, Jed just gave a quiet nod. "Ask Anthony over there if that's even remotely true." A sad, quick smile touched his lips. "Hell, ask anyone. Ask them what they think of me shutting you up on full moons. On the fact that the only hunting you've ever done is stalking the hot dogs I throw around. How about the fact I taught you to kill, huh? Isn't that so much *better*, that I took you, that I took this perfect guy, and I twisted you? I shoved you into a fucking *cage*, and I let you fester in there because I was too *goddamn selfish*—" His voice had risen to a shout, a self-loathing bellow, and Jed choked back the rest of the words. Jaw tightening, lips trembling into a sardonic smirk, he turned away. "I'm going for a walk. Don't wait around for me, Redford."

There was no reply from Redford, and Jed was glad his back was turned. He didn't want to see whatever expression Redford was wearing right then: understanding, anger, sudden realization, he didn't know. He just knew he didn't want to see it. Because no matter what, it wouldn't change where they were.

He slammed the door of the cafeteria shut behind him. It wasn't as satisfying as it should have been. Hands in his jacket pockets, head down, Jed walked quickly across the camp. The dew on the grass under his feet soaked his jeans. The air held his breath in a trail of fog.

She was waiting for him. Maybe she'd known he was coming; maybe it was inevitable that he wind up there. Either way, when Jed knocked on the Gray Lady's door, she opened it immediately, gesturing for him to come in.

This time, Jed didn't bluster or bellow or fight. He simply sat, waiting as the Gray Lady made tea, waiting as she settled in opposite him. Waiting with his mind racing, with a sick drop of dread in his stomach. Why had he said all of that? Why had he told Redford *any* of that? He'd just ruined fucking everything.

"The Council has come to a decision." When the Gray Lady finally spoke, it took Jed several moments to figure out what she was talking about.

He didn't care. Christ, that made him a bastard, but he didn't. This whole fucking camp, they could go, stay, fight, turn into goddamn chickens and roost and he *didn't care*. All he could think about was Redford. But Jed scrubbed a hand through his hair, he sat up a little straighter, and he did his damn job. That was what he was, anyway. Just the job. He was an idiot for forgetting that. "Yeah? What's the verdict?"

"We will run." Jed couldn't read the Gray Lady; she was all smooth voice and grace. But he kind of thought she sounded sad. "As soon as possible. The potential loss of life if we stay is too great."

Jed nodded. "I don't think that's a bad idea—" There was a yip from the corner, a quick patter of paws, and then an unsteady fluff ball of a wolf pup came charging out from under a pile of cushions. It was all huge paws and a tail waving like an energetic flag. The puppy crashed into Jed's knee and barked happily at him before making its wobbling way over to the Gray Lady. She picked it up and smiled at it, cradling the pup in her arms.

"My apologies." The Gray Lady smiled. "This is my daughter. She usually sleeps much later than this."

"Loss of life," Jed nodded, understanding. Apparently the Gray Lady still had some game, if she was popping out kids. He wondered how old she really was. "Your kid."

"They are all my children, in a way." The Gray Lady rubbed her hand behind the pup's ears, settling her down. "But yes. We have young here who wouldn't be able to fight. Running might be the best way to keep them safe."

"Probably." Jed drummed his fingers against the table. "Well, I'll make some calls. Arrange transport, that kind of thing."

"We will be appreciative." The Gray Lady nodded.

Fidgeting, Jed nearly said more. He nearly asked all the things he'd wanted to. But the stupid fluff ball was wiggling in her arms, and Jed found he really didn't want to know. He couldn't even think of where to start.

"You have something on your mind," the Gray Lady commented, her eyes on her daughter. "Speak it. We owe you a debt, and I will give my counsel if you wish it."

Crap. Jed heaved out a breath, staring up the ceiling. "Look, I know you don't approve of the whole human-with-wolf thing."

"I do not." The Gray Lady said it so damn calmly.

It would have been nice for her to be a *little* less blunt, but whatever. "Okay, fine. But Redford... he's going through something. He's got these... voices, I guess? Or

197

instincts. Something going on in his head. And I thought I was helping, I thought I *could* help. But he's getting worse. He goes into this kind of blood haze, I guess, sometimes. And I lose him." Jed's voice cracked. His eyes dropped to stare at his hands, refusing to look up at the Gray Lady. "I mean, he's just... *gone*." His bandage itched under his shirt, the pull of the wound still painful. "And it's getting worse. One of these days, I'm pretty sure he's going to go wherever it is he goes, and I'm not going to get him back."

If he'd expected shock from her, he clearly wasn't going to get it. She just studied him, one of her hands absently smoothing over her now-sleeping daughter. "And have you bonded? Is this more than just a series of dates for you?"

Christ. Jed had denied it in front of Anthony. He'd shout from the rooftops how he wasn't anyone's fucking *mate*, that this wasn't what they were trying to turn it into. But the Gray Lady was just staring at him, infinitely calm, infinitely patient, infinitely a gigantic bitch waiting to rip his head off for lying. And Jed found himself nodding slowly, biting the inside of his cheek so hard he tasted blood. "I don't know about bonding or whatever the shit," he muttered hoarsely. "But I love him. Yeah. I... fuck, I love him. So whatever that means in your furry mumbo jumbo."

"That's unfortunate." The Gray Lady wasn't even looking at him now, apparently too busy fussing over her daughter. "Had you replied that you merely liked him, I would have cautioned you against getting too involved. In all my years, I have seen very few instances of wolves truly managing to live happy lives with humans. You are simply too short-lived."

"But what about his...." Jed circled his finger beside his ear, eyebrows rising. "I mean, that's not normal, right? Other wolves or whatever, they don't have problems with their instincts like Red does."

"No," the Gray Lady answered. For once, there was a hint of something other than complete calm in her tone. "That is Filtiarn's fault. The others that he turned received the full procedure; they were transitioned completely. Redford was not that lucky, and I have never before seen someone stuck halfway between a werewolf and a true wolf. It is a state of being that is simply not meant to happen."

Expression falling, Jed rubbed his hand across his face. His fingers were shaking, he noticed absently. That was fucking embarrassing. He wished they'd stop. "So there's nothing that can help him?"

"The voices you speak of, and the way he loses himself, those are products of confused instincts," she replied, a faint sigh underneath her words. "Werewolves were Filtiarn's first attempt to create more wolves like him. They are an abomination. What Redford is going through is a clash between those instincts and the ones of the true wolf. His mind cannot pick one, so there is chaos."

"Okay, I think you have me confused with the professor." Jed couldn't help the desperate growl in his voice, the needy way he was searching her face for the answers she seemed so intent on keeping from him. "I don't care *why*. The whole stupid history, I don't give a fuck. I'm just looking for a solution. Is there a way he can get better?"

"Yes." It sounded simple, said in her patient tone. "He would need to be with his own kind. He would need to be free to roam where he wants when he feels the need to turn. That is what would help him."

Jed wasn't unaccustomed to pain. He'd gotten things broken or burned or bruised more times than he could ever count. He'd been tortured, he'd been torn apart and put back together and stepped on Legos in the middle of the fucking night. Jed knew pain. And he'd insulated himself against it, in some respects. It was part of the job, it was expected, so he got used to the sensation of hurting.

That hurt more. More than anything he'd ever experienced, more than anything Jed knew how to handle. The blunt assessment that *he* was part of the problem, that the answer to Redford's issues lay in everything he wasn't, it felt like more than a punch to the gut. Jed was fairly certain that he had a gaping hole where his chest used to be.

"He should stay here," Jed managed in a whisper, gaze locked firmly on the table in front of him, staring sightlessly down at the wood grain. "That's what you're saying. He needs to be with other wolves. Not me."

He wanted her to say no. He wanted her to change her mind and say that, no, she thought it was completely okay that a wolf and a human be together. There had to be *some* kind of silver lining on this shit cloud, and Jed kept desperately hoping it would appear. Something he could do, some clear course he could map out and arrange so that everything would be fine. So that he could take Redford goddamn *fishing*.

"Exactly," she replied. "You are a good man, Jed, even I can see that. You make a fine partner. But you are a *man*. Not a wolf."

"I love him," Jed whispered, hating how much of a plea was in his voice.

At least she didn't look unsympathetic. "Then that will be hard for you. But wolves know what is better for wolves, and living with this pack would be the best thing for Redford."

"I could stay here." God, he couldn't think, he could barely breathe around the ache in his throat. "With him. I'd go native or whatever the fuck I had to."

The Gray Lady gave a short sigh. Her eyes were once again on her daughter. When she spoke, her tone was kind, but firm. "And what happens when you start to grow old and he does not? True wolves do not live as long as I, but much longer than humans. What happens when you can't run with him, when he really wants to run? What happens when your knees start creaking with the cold, and while you attempt to hide it, Redford runs circles around you, never quite understanding why you can't keep up. And what of yourself? Do you really think you could live here, among a people that are not your own? Would you be happy, hiding away? Would you be able to provide for him, give him a family, give him a *true* mate?"

Shoulders hunching in on himself, every word as calmly given, as skillfully aimed as a bullet, Jed didn't move for a long time. He couldn't. He'd come here for answers, for a solution, and he had one. It was simple.

He'd have to leave.

"Thank you," Jed managed to whisper, wanting to shoot her right in the fucking face for being right. For not having another way. But he stood, back straight, jaw tight, and chin lifted. He nodded at her. "Take care of him for me."

Turning on his heel, steps measured and precise, Jed marched back to the cabin. Knievel was still asleep on the bed, and he carefully loaded her into her carrier despite her meows of protest. He didn't have much there, thankfully; shoving all his clothes into

199

a bag didn't take long. He left his maps and his weapons, his burner phone with his lists of contacts. They'd need all that in order to finish the plans for the move.

Jed was going home.

Redford almost looked happy when he stepped inside. He'd gone wolf, with a big stupid wolf grin as he turned to shut the door behind him, shaking his fur out. When he saw Jed, Redford shifted back with more ease than Jed had ever seen. Normally his change took at least a full minute. It was painful, and frankly goddamn horrible to watch.

But the shifts seemed easier now. And Jed couldn't help hearing echoes of the Gray Lady's words—Redford was more at ease with the wolf side of himself just from being in the pack. He'd made more progress here than Jed had ever managed to help him with.

"You wouldn't believe how energetic wolf kids are," Redford said, a laugh underneath his words as he tugged his jeans on. "There was a lady taking a big group of them for a run, but they all collided into me, and I wound up having to play with them for—" He paused. "Are you packing?"

His voice sounded so distant. Jed zipped up the duffel bag, hooking it over his shoulder. "I, uh, I left what you guys will need. You know who to call for transport and shit when the pack wants to do their moving, so just give them my name and they'll treat you okay." Jed kept his eyes on the floor, away from Redford, expression remote. "I'm taking the van. Tell princess that he'll have to find his own ride back."

"What?" All of the happiness just dropped right off of Redford's face. "Jed, why are you leaving? Why are you leaving *alone*? I thought we were going to train the pack."

Shit. This would have been so much easier to do, fuck, in a note or hieroglyphs or smoke signals or some shit. Not face to face. Not with Redford looking beautiful and worried and with that crease in his forehead that made Jed want to kiss away every line. "I gotta go, Fido," he managed, voice breaking. "This place, this is where you belong. And I didn't want to see it, I didn't, but come on. Who are we foolin'?" Jed forced his lips into an aching smile. "I can't be what you need. You should stay here. And I.... I have to go."

He brushed past Redford, heading out the door, keys to the van clutched so tightly in his hand he could feel them cutting into his palm. Knievel was crying in her cage, nails scratching at the sides of the carrier as if to try to get out. Jed knew the feeling.

Redford followed him. "You're leaving *me*," he concluded. "Jed, why—where did this come from? I love you, and I know you love me. The only reason I like it here is because you're here with me." With two quick steps, Redford bounded his way in front of Jed, stopping him in his tracks. "Why do you have to go?"

Shoulders straight, eyes fixed somewhere over Redford's left shoulder, Jed couldn't help the broken little laugh that escaped. "How was that shift for you?" he asked quietly. "Didn't seem like it hurt as much."

"It was... okay?" Redford looked like he didn't know if he was giving the right answer. "I mean, I think I'm getting better."

"I think you are too." Damn it, his voice cracked again. Jed just clenched his teeth, refusing to give in to the yawning agony starting to eat through his veins. "I think that this place is making you better. I'm not. That's why I have to go, okay? I've got to give you your best chance. This is it. Not me."

"That's not—" Redford broke off, frustrated. "Jed, can we just sit down and talk about this? Please? I can't think straight when you're packed and wanting to *leave*."

"There's nothing to say." He had to keep walking, he had to get the fuck out of here, because if he looked at Redford, if he had to really *look* at what he was going to be leaving, Jed didn't know if he'd be able to stand it. "You need someone who can be there for you—"

"You're there for me!" Redford insisted. "You've always been there for me."

"I *corrupted* you." Christ, he was not going to fucking *cry*. "I turned you into something you shouldn't have been. You're good, Redford, you are really, *really* fucking *good*. And I'm… not." Jed started walking again, hitching his bag up farther on his shoulder. "You need someone who's not going to put you in cages. Or who will keep up with you, or not get old, or, fuck, just… not me, okay? It's never going to be me."

"Jed." Oh, fuck, Redford had gotten that pleading tone in his voice. Jed hated that tone, because he could usually never resist it. "Please don't leave." Redford was following him still, light footsteps accompanying his words. "Whatever horrible things you think you did, it's not true. You're just being hard on yourself. You don't have to leave."

Redford caught up again. Jed saw him move out of the corner of his eye as Redford reached for his arm. Redford's fingers closed on the bandages, where the bite wound was, and Jed hissed in pain, instinctively jerking back. They both stood there, guilt flushing Redford's face, resignation souring in Jed's gut. "You bit me because you couldn't even think straight," Jed intoned quietly. "You ripped out that guy's throat. You were covered in his blood, and you would have killed me too. You would have killed anyone who got in your way. That's not on you, Redford. That's not your fault. It's mine. Instead of figuring out how to help you deal with shit, I just…. I treated you like you were me. Like you were a hardened son of a bitch instead of who you are. And I made it worse."

"So you're leaving me because of that?" Anybody else would have sounded angry or incredulous. Redford just looked miserable. "I never expected you to solve my problems, Jed, but—but I'm sorry I got them all over you. I'm sorry I wasn't strong enough to solve them myself."

Jesus fuck. Jed dropped his bag, he set Knievel's carrier on the ground, and he turned to grasp Redford's shoulders. "Shut up," he spat miserably. "Jesus, *shut up* and listen to me. You are *strong*. You are… fuck, you're perfect, you are brave and sweet and *everything* that I…." Jesus fuck, he really was crying. Goddamn it. "I am leaving because I love you."

Jed's voice was thick and tight, like a string pulled back almost to the breaking point. "Because everywhere I look, the facts are piling up that I'm nothing more than a pile of shit for you. You're going to have a good life here. You're going to figure out how to be who you are. I can't be here for that. Wish I could. God." Jed brushed his fingers across Redford's cheek. "God, you have no idea how much. But you and me, that's not good for you. So it's time I stopped being selfish and I walked away."

"If you love me, then you should *stay*," Redford begged.

"It's not that simple anymore, Fido." Jed picked up his bag, Knievel's cage, and made his weary way to the van. He threw his stuff inside, getting his cat settled in the front seat. "Tell the professor I'm sorry about stranding him." Pausing, swallowing hard, Jed dared a look back over his shoulder. "Good-bye, Redford."

"Jed," Redford tried, but his voice broke off and it seemed like he couldn't find any more words to say. His expression was just as effective as anything he could have said. Jed could read him like a goddamn book, and he only needed a glance to know what he was feeling. That frown was guilt, that crease at the corner of his eyes was upset, the way his eyes were wider than usual was hurt. Redford tried again. "Jed, please. Don't leave me."

Damn it.

It only took two steps to be there, to be cupping Redford's cheek and to draw him in for a kiss. It was hard and desperate. Jed thought he could taste his own tears on Redford's lips, or maybe those were Redford's on his. It didn't matter. He drew back, carefully neutral expression completely broken. "I'm so sorry," he whispered, pressing his forehead to Redford's for a moment. "I love you. God, Red, I love you so damn much."

Which was why he had to go. Everything in Jed was fighting against it, but he wanted to do something good. To give Redford the chance he hadn't before. So Jed turned and got in the van, refusing to look back. He started the engine and drove toward the gate. He couldn't look back. If he did, if he caught one more sight of Redford looking so goddamn hurt, Jed didn't know if he'd be strong enough to keep going.

There were a few wolves at the gate, part of the pack's patrol. They let him through, and thank God no one commented on how wrecked Jed looked. He wasn't in the mood to play nice.

The nearest town was nearly two hours out, which was enough of a drive for Jed to realize he needed alcohol. Lots and lots of fucking alcohol. He hadn't gotten really blackout drunk since he'd met Redford, but now seemed like an excellent time to pick that habit back up. He found a little liquor store already open despite the early hour and stocked up. Jed didn't want to start the drive back to his place just yet. The apartment was going to be covered in Redford's things, was going to have his pillow on the bed, his clothes in the closet. Every inch of it would remind Jed that Redford was gone. So no, he was in no rush to get back there.

Instead he got himself a hotel room. It was tiny and shitty and it smelled like mold. He didn't give a fuck. Jed locked the door, he did a sweep of the room, set up his weapons in easy to reach locations, and he started drinking.

He didn't stop until he'd passed out, curled around an old shirt of Redford's he'd accidentally packed with him, sobbing his damn eyes out.

CHAPTER
11

Redford

REDFORD RECALLED a movie that he had once seen wherein the protagonist, upon leaving home, had abandoned his dog. While driving away, the protagonist had watched in the rearview mirror as the dog grew farther and farther away, looking back at him with pitiful hope and growing disappointment. It had been as if the dog's expectations of the protagonist returning had vanished with every inch of distance.

Redford felt like that dog. He was sure Jed would laugh at the comparison.

He waited for half an hour. And with every minute, his hope that Jed would turn the van around and come back quickly withered.

When he eventually looked at his watch and saw how much time had passed, Redford supposed he was forced to accept the fact that Jed wasn't going to come back. Not right now, anyway. He still held out hope that Jed would return later. Surely Jed couldn't actually leave him forever.

"What are you doing?" With a start, Redford looked over to find Edwin standing next to him, looking off in the same direction Redford had just been pensively staring. "What's over there?"

Over Edwin's shoulder, Redford could see the pack moving around in the camp with a greater sense of urgency than he'd previously seen—the Gray Lady had made a decision, it seemed. A few wolves were moving from cabin to cabin, and although Redford couldn't hear what they were saying, the scent of alarm was evident.

Jed probably knew what that decision was. He just wasn't here to tell Redford.

"Um. Nothing," Redford said awkwardly, his words coming out slow, like he had to spend great effort to drag them from within himself. "Jed's gone."

Edwin didn't seem to feel the need to comment on that. He continued staring where Jed's van had disappeared around the corner, shoulder to shoulder with Redford, letting the silence envelop him. It was probably the longest Redford had ever seen Edwin be still. "Do you want to tell me why?" Edwin finally asked, glancing over at Redford, shaggy blond hair falling across his eyes.

No, actually, Redford didn't particularly want to talk about it. But he bit back the upset and replied, "I lost control and bit him, and he left." It was a concise enough summary, even if Edwin probably wouldn't know the context.

"Well, that seems stupid." Edwin didn't seem to grasp the enormity of the situation. "He knows you're a wolf, right? If Anthony left every time I bit something I wasn't supposed to, he'd be halfway to China by now."

"I'm not really a wolf," Redford said softly. He dropped his gaze from the working wolves to the grass underneath his feet. "Not like all of you."

Another long moment of quiet. This time, Edwin was squinting up at the sky, contemplating a flight of birds streaking past them. "I wonder if they all have different-colored feathers," he mused. "I mean, they all look kind of alike to us, though, right? They're just all birds. We don't know if one of them learned how to fly late or if one has the ugliest beak or if all of them have different-colored feathers. They just are birds."

"Or if one of them loses their mind every once in a while and attacks people?" Redford said wryly.

Edwin gave him a lopsided grin, totally unaffected. "Yeah. Or that." He leaned in close to Redford—and however far Redford leaned back in startlement, Edwin leaned with him, getting in to nuzzle his nose under Redford's ear, taking a deep breath. "You smell like wolf to me. So that other stuff, that's just what you have to figure out. Doesn't change that you're one of us. You're pack."

It was both the most comforting thing anybody had ever said to him and the absolute last thing Redford wanted to hear.

"That's kind of why Jed left," Redford admitted. "He said... that I needed to be here to help myself, but he didn't want to stay here with me."

Edwin's lips tugged downward into a frown, and he sighed sympathetically. "What do you think?" he prompted. "Do you think you need to be here?"

Honestly, with everything that had been happening lately, Redford hadn't had the time to think about that. He could see why being with the pack could help him—it certainly seemed to have helped already, just being around people who were completely comfortable with the nature that Redford still feared inside himself. But as a permanent solution, he didn't think he'd want to live with them.

He liked his apartment with Jed. It had been *his* idea to spend the full moons in the apartment, after Jed had convinced him that his grandmother's basement wasn't doing him any good. He liked spending his full moons with Jed.

But he had to admit, the latest one had been his favorite. There had been nothing but the woods and the dirt under his paws, and Jed beside him as much as he could manage. Redford had never felt so free.

"I think it's probably been helping me more than my psychologist," Redford said, giving a mental apology to Dr. Alona. Sitting in his office or speaking with him over the phone had certainly been informative, and Redford would be forever grateful to the doctor for at least helping him keep his mind together this long. But it didn't compare to actually getting outside and feeling free.

Edwin crouched down, picking up a stick to poke at a line of ants walking past. He let the insects march onto the wood, watching as they accepted the new obstacle and kept moving. "So do you want to stay?"

"If Jed was still here I'd say yes." Redford crouched down next to Edwin, picking up a stick of his own and laying it across the path of the ants. If nothing else, it was certainly interesting to watch and a decent distraction. "I've never been good at being anywhere on my own, though."

"You're not alone," Edwin pointed out practically. He was busy gathering bits of wood and small rocks, building a fortress around the anthill. "You have us, now."

Redford didn't want to say, *that doesn't count*. He didn't want to be rude about it. But with Jed gone, Redford once again felt like he didn't fit here. The Lewises were nice, and they'd made every effort to make Redford feel at ease with them, but they weren't his family. They weren't his pack.

They weren't Jed.

"I'm not sure I even know how to be in a pack," Redford said honestly. "I... you and Anthony and Randall, you've been really nice, but I only met you a week ago. I don't know if it's true that wolves need packs. I've only ever needed Jed."

Edwin just smiled at him, still as friendly as ever, like nothing really could be that wrong about anything Redford was saying. "He's your mate," Edwin surmised with a nod. "Even if he is human."

"I think so," Redford replied, tentative. "I didn't really know what a mate *was* until this morning. Anthony explained it to Jed and me. It sounds right."

"Well, you want to be with him, right?" Edwin was busy fashioning a tiny flag out of a twig and a leaf. "Like... not just kind of. You *need* it. When he's not around, you get all achy, right here." He rubbed a hand over his chest.

Redford couldn't help a quick huff of a laugh. "Yeah," he agreed. The voice that his instincts had made inside his head had once called Jed *mate*. Redford still did think it was a slightly silly word, though. "Exactly like that."

"He's not a good match, you know," Edwin commented casually, propping his little flag on top of the barricade wall he'd made around three sides of the anthill. "I mean, I like Jed. But he's human. And that gets tough. I get why he'd leave, a little. If I thought that Ant or Randall would be happier without me, I'd go too. Even if it'd hurt."

That wasn't exactly making Redford feel any better. What was he supposed to do, just *accept* that Jed had left? Condone it, even? He couldn't do that. He could never be okay with the idea that Jed wouldn't be in his life anymore.

"Why does it get tough if he's human?" That notion, at least, was the one thing Edwin had said that didn't make Redford feel horrible. "He's always been even stronger than me."

"That's not true." Edwin rocked back on his heels, nose twitching as he watched the ants make their way into their fortified home. "I mean, I don't know, Jed looks like he could lift a lot of heavy things, but that's not all that makes you strong."

"I meant personality wise," Redford said. "He's confident and determined and smart. More than I am, in any of those things. Why does his being human change anything?"

"Still not what makes you strong," Edwin said, voice a happy little hum as he laid his hand down for the ants to march across. "But humans are... tricky." He looked up, a smile touching the corners of his lips. "Anthony and Randall are both better at this than I am. They'd probably get mad at me. I mean, Ant always told me that we're all equal. But we're kind of not too, you know? I've heard what some of the naturals have said, the half bloods and stuff, and I don't know, some of it makes sense. Jed's not going to live as long as you, for one. But you age slower too. So in twenty years, he'll be old, and you'll be not even in your prime. You'll want kids. I mean, not every wolf does, but I bet you will. And Jed can't really do what a pack needs to do. He can't run with you on full moons, not like another wolf. He can't hunt with you. And he doesn't get your instincts." Edwin's attention returned to the ants. "It just seems like it'd be really hard."

Redford couldn't help but remember, back when he'd first met the Lewises, how Edwin had used none-too-kind language toward humans. He didn't seem like he genuinely wanted all the humans gone, but he did possibly believe that they weren't equal, and that the supernatural creatures came out on top of that equality argument.

He could kind of see where Edwin was coming from. Some of that was true—Redford would age slower, and Jed wouldn't forever be able to keep up with him. But the rest of it, frankly, just sounded like personal issues. Jed was smart; he would get his instincts if they were properly explained. And the need for a pack? Redford had never felt it. He'd grown up alone, and while he'd longed for company, Jed fulfilled every single need for family and love.

"And what happens when one half of a mate pairing isn't around anymore?" Redford asked glumly. "Anthony told us about his, um, well, what happened to him. He looked miserable."

"He is." There wasn't a smile hovering around Edwin's lips at that. He slowly drew his hand back, making sure the ants were all in place and undisturbed. "Sometimes I honestly think that if it hadn't been for me and Randall, Ant would have just stopped. Or gone after him. Either way, he wouldn't be here." Edwin shrugged. "Maybe that's why everyone says not to fall for a human. It's too scary to think about them being gone."

Redford couldn't exactly go back in time and prevent himself from meeting Jed, and even if he could, he wouldn't want to. Jed had made his life so much better. Nobody other than Jed had showed even the slightest interest in caring about him.

Jed hadn't been the first person to visit Redford's house after his grandmother had died. Distant family had turned up at his door, mailmen with packages delivered to the wrong address, repairmen, next-door neighbors. None of them had even looked at him twice. But Jed had. Jed had *looked* and had seen him, and Redford had fallen in love so quickly it had made his head spin.

And he couldn't just simply make himself *stop* loving Jed, could he?

There wasn't much he could say in reply to Edwin. Yes, it was scary to think about Jed being gone, but that wasn't going to help Redford right now.

Instead, he twisted around to look back at the camp. The wolves were out in full force now: belongings were being carried to and from cabins; wolves were talking to one another in huddled groups. The whole place was beginning to smell like worry.

"In any case, I'm still going to stay and help with whatever decision the Gray Lady has made," Redford said, trying to sound calm and collected. "Although without Jed, I'm not sure I'm really going to be much help." Jed had taken the van, which meant he had every single scrap of equipment with him, other than what was left in the cabin. So that left Redford with a few guns, some maps of the area, his own bag, and the silver bullets they'd found. It wasn't exactly the beginnings of Fort Knox.

"Do you really love him?" Edwin asked, curious. His hands were resting on his knees, and he was staring up at Redford, head cocked to the side. "Even though he's human and it's scary?"

"Yeah," Redford murmured. "Everything that you and Anthony said about whatever a mate is, that's Jed for me. The thought of life without him...."

He couldn't bring himself to finish that sentence, because attempting to imagine it wasn't something Redford wanted to do.

Edwin stood, brushing his hands off on the sides of his jeans. "Okay." He tugged his shirt off, kicking his pants to the side next and shifting. The blond wolf nudged his head against Redford's knees, barking up at him twice, tongue lolling out one side of his mouth.

Redford stared at him, uncomprehending. Okay? What was he supposed to take from that? He wasn't sure if that was a dismissal or a real answer that he just hadn't figured out the deeper meaning of yet. Did Edwin want him to run with him?

"What does 'okay' mean?" he asked.

Edwin chuffed, running happily in little circles around Redford's legs. He nudged his nose into Redford's stomach, taking a deep sniff, backing up to bark once more. As if that was supposed to make it clearer. Before Redford could ask any more questions, however, Edwin took off running, a long, pale blur against the ground. He rounded the corner and disappeared into the woods, leaving Redford behind with the ant fort.

Redford still had no clue what any of that was supposed to mean. It would have been so beneficial for wolves to evolve telepathy or some form of communication that didn't involve barking and random body movements. He hoped Edwin didn't expect Redford to join him, because going for a run was the last thing on Redford's mind right then.

He stood with a faint sigh, carefully brushing stray ants off the bottom of the jeans. He wanted to ask someone what was happening, but all of the wolves looked busy, and Redford wasn't sure that the Gray Lady would appreciate a visit from him alone. He thought he could see Anthony and Randall in the distance, and Victor was bound to be around somewhere.

Redford just wanted Jed.

If he wanted to leave, he would have to make his way to the main road, well away from the camp, but that was doable. He could call a cab or find a bus station or something.

But then where would he go? If Jed didn't want to be with him anymore, then Redford doubted he would be welcome in Jed's apartment. They kept all their money in joint accounts, so at least he'd have funds. He hoped.

So. No home to go to. No Jed waiting for him.

It was enough to make Redford want to sit down and not move for a very long time. The panic that was starting to gather in his gut would be all too easy to give in to. But it wouldn't help anything, and Redford had promised to be of use to this pack.

With great effort, he shoved the anxiety aside and forced himself to stop thinking about the future. All he could focus on was the present, and while the absence of Jed was still a hole in his heart, Redford at least had something he could concentrate on while he desperately hoped Jed would return.

With newfound determination, Redford marched his way toward the Gray Lady's house. He was sure he could be of use—he might not have an arsenal at his disposal anymore, but he still had his mind, and he would be able to aid them in security planning if they had indeed planned to stay and fight.

Mallory stopped him at the door, his features as stern as ever. "She's not in right now."

"Oh," Redford said awkwardly, the wind taken out of his sails. "Um. When will she be back?"

"I don't know." Mallory stared at him. There was a hint of a crinkle to his nose, a very faint dislike for Redford's scent. "Why did you need to talk to her?"

"I wanted to find out whether the pack is staying and fighting, or running."

"We're leaving." Redford couldn't tell whether Mallory liked the idea or not. "As soon as possible. We estimate in a week or so."

Redford didn't immediately blurt out the answer that came to mind. He had been in synch with Jed's approval for running at first, but when Anthony and Randall had argued in favor of fighting, he'd had to admit they had a point. The hunters wouldn't get bored of looking for them, even if they did move seven states over. O'Malley wouldn't simply declare that it was too far away, he'd just relocate the hunters.

But it wasn't his decision, and he had wanted to help the pack in whatever way he could. So he thanked Mallory and left, unsure about what he should do. He supposed he could help them gather their belongings, but Redford doubted that anybody would want him going through their things.

At a loss, he made his way toward the bonfire, picking his way through the wolves moving through the camp.

Randall had apparently spotted him, because he was making his way to Redford, Anthony trailing behind. They dodged around huddled groups of wolves, Randall pausing to take Anthony's elbow casually when Anthony started to slow his step. "Hello." Randall smiled at Redford, finding a log around the bonfire for Anthony to sit on. "Did I see Edwin over here just a bit ago?"

"Um, yeah, he ran off that way." Redford pointed in the direction of the woods near the gate. "I don't know what he was doing."

"Wolf or human?" Randall asked, seemingly not disturbed at all at the idea of his brother randomly running around.

"Wolf," Redford replied.

Anthony just sighed. "He'll be back eventually. I do wish he'd take his phone with him, or I could attach a GPS to him or something."

"Maybe a pink collar with a jingly bell." Randall gave his brother a quick smile. "He'd like that."

"He'd chew it off after an hour," Anthony snorted. "And you know he'd just bitch about the bell all the time for making him unstealthy. Which he still somehow thinks he is."

Randall was watching Redford, a crease appearing between his eyes. "Hey." He nudged Redford's foot with his own, head cocked in a way that distinctly reminded Redford of Edwin. "Um. Are you all right? You look… not so much."

That was an apt way to sum it up, Redford supposed. He had been listening to Anthony and Randall, but he realized now that he'd been staring at the gates, waiting for some sign that a van with Jed in it was going to drive back through them.

There was no sign yet.

He didn't want to tell them. Redford had already had that conversation with Edwin, and he had no desire to repeat it. But they deserved to know, at the very least because Randall had *hired* Jed, even if Jed had already fulfilled the original request. "Jed's gone," he said succinctly. "I'm sorry. But I think I can still be of use to the pack, so I'm staying for as long as I'm needed."

Randall blinked, surprise flitting across his face and then something quite a bit like the opposite. As if he'd been expecting that. "Seems to be a theme." He offered Redford a slight smile. "I am sorry. Don't worry. I'm sure you're going to be massively helpful."

Redford wasn't so sure, but he appreciated the thought. Anthony wore the same look that Randall did, a faint resignation, though Anthony looked more disappointed at Jed's leaving. "Did he say why—" Anthony cut himself off. "You don't have to answer that, sorry."

Redford couldn't bring himself to say it out loud again anyway, so the apology was just as well. Instead, he changed the topic. "I just heard that the pack is leaving. What are you guys going to do?"

Randall took off his glasses and cleaned them on the tail of his shirt, staring at the ground as if it was suddenly very interesting. Perhaps all the Lewises had a fascination with ants. "We hadn't discussed that yet. But Anthony's treatment is ongoing, so I don't suppose there's much choice."

Redford grimaced in sympathy. They would have to uproot their entire lives to continue staying with the pack, and though Redford didn't know too many details of Anthony's medical treatment here, all he'd seen was some weird herb gunk that Anthony was using on his hands. It wasn't exactly advanced medical treatment, at least, not what Redford would imagine.

"If there's any way I can help, just name it," Redford offered. "I know I've technically exceeded what you originally hired me for, but you've been.... I haven't exactly had a lot of friends in my life."

Randall gave him a slight smile. "Nor have I. It's nice to count you among them."

Having the Lewises as friends still wasn't enough to make Redford feel completely content about a possible future with the pack without Jed, but it did help.

Anthony pushed himself up to stand, and before Redford could react, Anthony had engulfed him a hug. Redford froze, not sure what to do. "From one wolf who's had a nonwolf mate run off to another, we're here for you," Anthony assured him, the very picture of earnestness.

Redford couldn't help but notice that Randall looked sad too. He had to wonder if it was something to do with Victor.

A small, very spiteful part of the back of his brain said, *do relationships ever actually work out?* All three of them were currently upset over the loss of them. He couldn't hold on to that spite for very long, though, not when the ache of Jed's absence made itself known again.

"Well, aren't we a fun trio." Randall forced a smile, shaking his head. "Maybe I should go try to date one of these wolves here, since apparently all the horror stories I've read about dating half bloods and humans are right."

"Apparently so," Anthony said wryly, drawing back from Redford, who took the opportunity to collect his breath. Anthony hugged with the grip of an octopus. "If you want to make me happy, you and Edwin will find some nice wolves and settle down with a nice pack."

Randall's smile faded slightly, but he nodded, once more cleaning his glasses that, to Redford, didn't look to need the attention. "I suppose I should go get busy, then," he murmured in a faint voice, clearly attempting to sound teasing. "Before all the good ones are taken."

"Of course, what would make me even happier," Anthony continued, "is if I could find Victor and growl at him until he pulls his head out of his ass and dates you." He glanced around the camp, seemingly seeking out Victor, and frowned when he couldn't see him. "You two are perfect for each other. I have no idea why he's being the way he is."

A frown curled Randall's lips slightly, and he fidgeted in his seat, seemingly wishing he hadn't even brought it up. "Not so perfect," he corrected softly. "And we're dropping it, Anthony. I've imposed on the poor man enough."

Anthony gave a doubtful snort. "He'll realize you're good for him soon enough. He'd have to be an idiot not to, and he does seem really smart." He grinned suddenly. "He wrote all those books, remember, Randall?"

"Yes. I remember." Randall rubbed a hand through his hair. "I remember how long I've had a crush on him, Anthony. I also remember him acting as if I was an amusing little boy who followed him home. One moment we're kissing, the next he's acting like being with me is horrifying. So perhaps we could focus on Redford, whose mate *actually* loves him, hm?"

"Do you want me to go find Jed and growl at *him*?" Anthony asked hopefully.

Despite his mood, Redford smiled a little. "I don't think that would help. But thank you."

"It'd be a perfect world where it *could* help," Anthony sighed.

Redford decided he would wait three days. If Jed didn't come back by then, then Redford would go looking for him. He wasn't about to give up on this relationship after one argument, even if it had been the worst argument of Redford's entire life. "I'll give him some time," he said. "Maybe he just needs some time away to... do whatever he needs to and think things out."

It was a shot in the dark, a desperate hope. But Redford knew Jed loved him, and he also knew Jed was ridiculously stubborn. He didn't give up on things easily.

"Humans are ridiculous sometimes," Randall agreed. "But Jed cares for you, Redford, anyone can see that. He can't just walk away. I don't believe it works like that." He looked vaguely embarrassed to be voicing such a sentimental view.

"I wonder who's more ridiculous, humans or half bloods," Anthony mused. "So far we've got a count of two half bloods and one human. Really, wolves must be the only sensible lot around."

"Anthony," Randall said lightly, almost a warning in his voice, but then seemed to reconsider. With a sigh, he shook his head. "Oh, I can't even argue with that. Honestly, I don't know how to *read* him. It's as if he's speaking another language half the time."

Anthony just laughed, but he seemed more distracted by watching a pack of wolves walk past. As Redford watched, Anthony's expression took on a resigned tone. "I guess we should think about the fact that we're moving," he sighed. "Sitting here feeling sorry for ourselves is all well and good, but...."

"If there's anything I can do to help," Redford offered again. "I can lift heavy things, I think."

"Thanks." Randall gave him a little smile. "Why don't you come find us around dinner? I'm guessing Edwin will be back by then; he never misses food. We'll all go together."

"He'd *better* be back by then," Anthony grumbled. "Seriously, GPS tracker."

"All right." Redford nodded, sticking his hands in his pockets, suddenly at a loss for what to do. "I'll see you then."

There was a quick flicker of sympathy in Randall's expression. He reached out to gently squeeze Redford's shoulder. But Anthony was struggling to stand, knees obviously stiff, and whatever Randall might have said was left in favor of him going to his brother's side and casually slinging an arm around Anthony's waist. They both nodded to Redford, making their way back to their cabin with slow, shuffling steps.

What was Redford supposed to do now? His only plan had been to help the Lewises pack, except they'd come here with already packed bags, unlike the wolves that actually lived here, so their packing would take all of two hours. Less, if they were efficient. He didn't know anybody else here except the Gray Lady and Mallory, and not even very well.

His thoughts wound up turning back to Jed. Jed would know what to do. Jed would be announcing himself as Camp Packing Instructor and corralling everyone. That was the difference between them, Redford supposed—Jed was a natural leader, and Redford was not.

He ended up wandering the perimeter of the camp. A short distance behind the Gray Lady's house was a waterfall that fed into a lake, which in turn started the river that edged around the east side of the pack's territory. Redford stood and watched it for a while, trying to think if he'd ever actually seen a waterfall in real life before. His and Jed's jobs didn't often take them to particularly scenic places.

If Jed was there, Redford would be holding his hand and asking him if he'd ever seen a waterfall bigger than this one. He'd be pointing the fish in the lake out to Jed, trying to see if he could figure out what species they were and speculating if those were the fish that the wolves caught for lunch and dinner.

Redford heaved a short, hard sigh and left the waterfall. Three days. If Jed wasn't back by then, Redford would find him. Maybe Jed just needed space and time to think about things. He'd seemed so horrified by the fact that Redford had killed now, and was losing himself in his instincts. Surely, if Jed thought about it, he'd realize he'd never forced Redford to do anything, he'd never corrupted him, he'd merely shown him a better path, and Redford had been free to pick and choose what he did.

And maybe Jed would find some way to be okay with Redford's dysfunctional instincts, if Redford worked really hard to get them in line. Other than the episode with the hunters, they'd been relatively quiet for the last few weeks. No voices in the back of his mind, no getting up in the middle of the night to growl at shadows. Redford *was* getting control, he swore.

But wandering around aimlessly and thinking in circles wasn't going to help anything, so Redford made himself look at the wolves as he passed by them, searching out something he could help with.

There were families and couples, single wolves and young men and women, friends helping friends. They all seemed incredibly close knit, casual with physical affection. Finally, Redford wound up sitting at the bonfire, facing outward, trying not to frown and feel incredibly useless. It would probably be helpful if he could work up the courage to talk to complete strangers, but his thoughts were in enough turmoil as it was.

His eye caught on a family moving around the outside of their cabin. The mother and father, Redford assumed, were busier keeping their two young children in line than they were with packing, exasperatedly running after the two young girls in their attempts to keep them in line of sight.

Redford couldn't help but smile. Wolf children were energetic, it looked like. He wouldn't know—he'd been bitten when he was very young, but he didn't recall having the same kind of energy. His wolf had been a nightmare, not something he'd ever felt in tune with. He'd dreaded the change, the thing that made him different, the reason his grandmother had kept him home from school, had locked him up in the basement on full moons. But watching the kids play, it seemed that here, all the parts of Redford that had been held up as a *monster* were celebrated in the younger members of the pack.

He didn't remember much of his parents, Redford realized as he watched the family. He had a faint memory of his mother's hair, how she'd always kept it long. His father had had a mustache that he'd shaved off. That was, for whatever reason, a big event in Redford's young memory. They had been kind, he thought, and they had loved him. Redford was sure of that, at least.

Of the camping trip on which they had died and he had been bitten, Redford also didn't recall much. He remembered howling and his parents' fear, their attempts to reassure him that wolves wouldn't attack. He remembered their screams, the crackle of the campfire as a dark shape leapt over it, the pain of a bite on his arm and claws across his face. From then on, Redford's memories of his youth were dominated by a dry, dusty house and what felt like endless years of full moons and the chafe of metal.

The parents that he was watching would never confine their children like that, for which Redford was glad. The kids looked cute and completely at ease with their wolfish nature. As he watched, one of them went from two legs to four in a sudden collapse of the flowery dress she wore, and a wolf cub struggled out from under the fabric to charge once more at her sister in friendly play.

Redford was so absorbed in watching them that he didn't hear the footsteps approach him until they were mere feet away, at which point he hunched his shoulders, looking at the stranger with mild alarm.

"You look like you've got a decent pair of arms on you," the man said. He looked about fifty in age, which of course meant he was much older, though Redford wasn't sure exactly how old.

"Sort of," Redford answered tentatively. "Do you, um, need... arms?"

Six months ago he and Jed had done a job for a man who kept referring to people's body parts in really creepy, very culinary ways. Redford had been sure he was a cannibal. He wondered the same of the man in front of him now, though he was sure it was just paranoia.

"I need someone that doesn't have arthritis flare-ups in cold weather," the man said. He peered at Redford as if he were calculating exactly how much he wanted to socialize with him, which Redford could empathize with. "And you seem less busy than everybody else here."

It was only when the man started to look impatient that Redford recognized him. He was from the pack they had helped rescue the other day. Redford distinctly recalled the man gathering the younger wolves together and looking very exasperated when they took more than thirty seconds to line up.

"Um, yeah, sure," Redford said, hurriedly standing up. "What do you need help with?"

The wolf just walked off, clearly expecting Redford to follow. Redford was fairly sure he'd heard someone call him Cedric. He was led to a communal building on the side of the camp near the tree line, where the refugees had obviously been put up for their stay. Redford recognized some of the wolves they'd rescued mingling with the Gray Lady's pack—they seemed to be integrating well.

Cedric stopped at a door at the corner of the building and waved Redford inside. "I scavenged some boxes from the healers here. Just old things that they don't use, equipment and the like. Unfortunately, the people who brought it along for me had the gall to put it on the highest shelves."

Redford took a quick look around the room. It was Spartan and mostly bare, though some bags with what he presumed were Cedric's belongings were lined up against one wall. The boxes on the shelves were about shoulder height, and they looked heavy. He figured they were most likely full of herbs and salves, considering what the healers used on Anthony.

When he took a closer look, though, he saw the edge of a scalpel and plastic wrapping jutting out of the box closest to him. Redford couldn't resist flipping the lid of the box to peek inside. "This is actual medical equipment," he said, stunned.

"Yes, I did say that." Cedric frowned. "Unfortunately this pack seems to think proper medicine is how the devil gets inside you."

Redford had to smile at that. "Are you a doctor?"

"A properly trained one with a degree, yes, unlike the soothsayers here." Cedric, it seemed, had no patience at all for herbs and natural remedies. Redford liked him already.

"There's a wolf here," Redford started tentatively, "who has a degenerative condition. He's not from the pack, but we came here in the hopes that they'd be able to treat him. It's canine Parkinson's, I think it's called. But all the healers have been doing is giving him some really awful smelling herbs to put on his hands."

Cedric snorted disdainfully. "Did they chant around him too? Good God, I have no idea how any of them survived with this primitive approach to medicine. It's a wonder they're not all crippled or dead."

"So, do you think you could maybe take a look at him?" Redford asked. He wasn't sure if it was really his place to ask such a thing for Anthony, but a second consult couldn't hurt, right?

"If they're not busy with packing, then I'd be all too glad to have something else to do." As if on cue, a series of loud thumps came from upstairs, the sound of laughter and what sounded like playfighting. Cedric scowled. "I cannot abide the company of young people in such close quarters for too long."

Redford made a mental note to introduce Cedric and Victor. He had a feeling they'd probably get on well in their misanthropy.

"Thank you." Words couldn't contain his gratefulness. Instead, Redford got a good grip around one of the boxes and pulled, grunting with the strain as he balanced it close against his chest. "Where do you want these?"

He put the box where Cedric directed, alongside the bags lined up against the wall. Redford worked in silence, all the while telling himself that peeking in the boxes wasn't polite. He did have to wonder exactly what kind of medical supplies Cedric had, though, and if he'd be able to do something more for Anthony than foul-smelling herb concoctions.

Somewhere around the third box, Cedric had sat down in an old chair in the corner of the room, and by the fourth box, Redford realized that Cedric was staring at him—not in a rude way, simply watching closely.

"I imagine you're getting a lot of odd looks," Cedric said carefully. "I may not have been in the pack life for very long, but even I can smell that you're not like everybody here."

Redford worked hard to contain his embarrassed flinch, but unfortunately he wasn't all that successful. "It's a long story," he mumbled. "Mostly I get weirder looks for being in love with a human."

Cedric frowned. "Is that a bad thing?"

"Apparently." Redford set the sixth and final box on the floor, but he couldn't bring himself to fully face Cedric, afraid of the judgmental expression he might see on the wolf's face. "I keep getting told that wolves and humans shouldn't be together. And I think my…. I think Jed got told the same thing too."

"That is the most fatuous pile of bullshit I've ever heard in my life," Cedric said bluntly. "You may as well say that two women can't be together because they can't have children without medical help. Or that two people from different races can't be together because they have different cultural backgrounds. What a bigoted, asinine thing to say."

Taken aback by Cedric's tone, Redford had to struggle for a response. That was certainly opposite what every other wolf had been telling him. "You, um, obviously think differently."

"I had a wife of sixty years." Cedric smiled as he said it. "We met when I was thirty and she was twenty-five. She passed away seven years ago, and I don't regret our relationship at all. We had sixty years of the best relationship I'd ever had. She understood that I would age slower and outlive her, and that didn't matter to her."

"I'm sorry," Redford said, unable to think of anything properly useful to say.

Cedric snorted. "Don't apologize, boy. Why should anybody apologize for what we had?" He pulled his wallet out of his pocket and flipped through it until he found a photo, which he handed to Redford.

It was a picture of Cedric and his wife. Redford couldn't pinpoint Cedric's age in the photo, but his wife looked about forty. They looked completely and totally in love. Redford couldn't help but smile at the picture as he handed it back. "Was she your mate? I've been told that... wolves don't recover from that loss."

"She was," Cedric confirmed. As Redford was about to apologize for his loss yet again, perceiving that Cedric might be utterly heartbroken and alone, Cedric continued, "But I am also fine. I miss her every day, but we had sixty years together, and I am content with what we had. It doesn't mean I will be a sobbing wreck for the rest of my life. Wolves can recover from loss just as well as any other." He paused, scowl softening as he glanced at the photo. "We might feel things more deeply, but that means the good as well as the bad. Grief, yes, but also every happy memory, every moment of loving her, I've got that too. And I wouldn't trade any of that to spare myself losing her."

"Oh." Redford had to take a moment to wrap his mind around that. He couldn't imagine losing Jed and *not* being a wreck every day after that, but perhaps some of that grief would be eased by having a lifetime with him. "That's just really not like what I've heard."

"Everybody is different," Cedric said. "But is eventual pain a good excuse for *not* trying for happiness?"

Redford wasn't good at philosophy. To be fair, Jed was even worse at it than he was. Redford had just never managed to be very good at thinking about things like life principles or vague *what if*s. "No?" he guessed.

"No, it's not," Cedric agreed. "There will always be pain, whether you try for it or not. Happiness is not guaranteed unless you grasp for it. So whatever those wolves have told you about being with a human, you tell them to shut their mouths, and you do what *you* like. We're not clones. You least of all."

It was one of the grumpiest motivational speeches Redford had ever heard, but he still felt strangely uplifted. "Thank you," he said with dawning realization. "You're right. You're absolutely right."

"Of course I'm right." Cedric clearly hadn't considered any other option. "So you go find your mate and tell him that it is within nobody's right to give you shit about your relationship."

"I would, but he... left." Redford felt a piece of that motivation chip off, but it didn't die entirely. "I promised myself I'd go find him in three days if he didn't come back."

"What is he, Jesus Christ?" Cedric snorted, unimpressed. "You're not in high school, pup, and you definitely should stop acting like it. Grow some balls and talk it out."

Redford stared at him, wide-eyed. "Yes, sir," he said uncertainly. "I'll, um, get on that right away."

"Good. Go get him, or the next time I see you I'll whack you around the head," Cedric grumbled, but there was a smile touching the corners of his eyes. "Don't think I won't."

Redford thanked him and felt a little overwhelmed as he left. He wasn't sure what to do with all this new hope. He'd had faith before that he would find Jed, but he hadn't been sure they'd be able to work out their problems. He still didn't have a clear answer to that, but nothing changed the foundation of the matter: Jed was the man he loved, and nothing was going to get in the way of that.

He made a mental checklist as he went back to their cabin.

One, he had to work hard at getting his instincts under control. Though the clash of aggression and fear had lessened slightly in the recent weeks, from a combination of Jed's help, Dr. Alona's therapy, and the full moon spent properly in the wild, Redford still had work to do.

Two, he would have to convince Jed that Redford hadn't been corrupted by his influence. Redford wasn't sure where Jed had gotten the idea that Redford was *better* than Jed's job, but it was a notion he would have to help Jed get rid of. The hunters he had killed were human, yes, but killing them wasn't anything anybody else there wouldn't have done in a heartbeat. Redford had chosen to help Jed in his job, and it was better than his previous life in every single way. Redford *liked* their job.

Three, he needed to let Jed know that his being human didn't harm their relationship at all. That one was going to be slightly tougher, Redford knew, especially surrounded by a pack that thought humans couldn't possibly meaningfully understand them. But Redford was sure Jed did.

Checklist made, Redford determined that he would set off to find Jed at first light the next morning. As much as he wanted to rush off to find him now, contacting the appropriate people would take time, and they wouldn't be able to drop everything to come pick Redford up.

He also thought Jed really might need some time to himself. Jed had never been good at talking about his problems. He faltered and said things badly and nearly even stuttered, obviously embarrassed to be talking so openly about his emotions and misgivings. He especially hated being taken off guard by conversations he wasn't prepared for. For someone who *felt* so deeply, Jed was bafflingly unwilling to admit to it, as if he thought his emotions were a soft spot someone would use against him. Whatever the situation, when it came to the hard things, the important things, Jed was always better able to wrap his mind around them when given time to process through his knee-jerk reaction of shoving everyone and everything away as hard as he could manage.

So Redford would give him the night. He imagined that Jed would drink a lot and maybe smash some things, but problems were always clearer in the morning.

He knew Jed would come back. He had to, because Redford honestly couldn't imagine a life without Jed in it.

CHAPTER
12

Jed

SOMEONE WAS knocking on the fucking door.

It was still dark out, the flickering red light of the motel sign outside barely illuminating the room. Everything seemed to be moving in slow motion, the shit ton of alcohol Jed had poured down his miserable gullet sloshing inside his head with every throb of his heart. He knew his feet were still attached to his legs, he knew his eyes were somewhere between open and closed, and he knew the knock on the door meant there was a person, or possible people, outside wanting to get in. But unfortunately, owing to said *shit ton of alcohol*, he wasn't exactly up for moving. Or breathing too loudly. Or anything that required action beyond moaning in pain.

Unfortunately he hadn't suddenly developed psychic skills, because when he thought about all the ways he wanted to skin and burn whoever was pounding on the motel door, said person didn't stop. Eventually, Jed managed to get wobbly legs under him, half rolling off the couch, gun held loosely in his hand as he staggered across the floor.

"What the fuck do you fucking want, you fucking ass licking bastard?"

Whoever said he didn't have charm coming out of his goddamn ears was just fucking lying.

"You stink like the floor of a bar bathroom." It was goddamn Edwin Lewis standing there, naked as a freaking jaybird, nose wrinkled, as if Jed had offended his delicate sensibilities.

Eyes bleary and bloodshot, Jed blinked at him, brain struggling to figure out what the hell was happening. "How the fuck do you know what a goddamn bar smells like?" he grunted, scratching his chest and looking around. Were there hidden cameras? Some sort of prank where more people would jump out and surprise him? Because he had a gun, he *would* shoot. "Aren't you twelve?"

"I'm twenty, and I'm not exactly an idiot." Edwin didn't seem to care that he was pantsless. Jed would, because he really wasn't too keen to see all that, but he was too busy wondering why the room was rotating. "Let me in."

"No." Jed frowned petulantly. "You go away, unless you're bringing more booze. Even then, put some fucking pants on."

He moved to shut the door, but Edwin stopped it with a hand against the cheap wood, eyebrow raising. "Yeah, the last thing you need is more stuff to drink. Seriously, you look like you fell into a beer bottle and then got swished around."

Jed decided he wasn't up for a fight with some naked-ass wolf. So he just turned and stumbled back inside, face-planting onto the bed with a grunt. He could hear Edwin locking up behind him, but Jed decided it was much better to fish around on the nightstand through the empty bottles, looking for anything that might be left to drink.

Edwin was poking around, sniffing things, sneezing loudly at the dust he found on the chair. He sat anyway, on his heels, crouched there and still looking like he was half a wild thing. Jed just grimaced and averted his eyes. "Seriously, Cujo, get some fucking pants."

"I must have left my clothes in my other fur," Edwin replied with a slow grin. "Humans are such prudes. What does it matter? Do I have something you've never seen before?" He looked down at himself. "I think we're pretty similar."

"I am not discussing cock size with you, kid." Jed found a beer that was only half done, gulping the warm, disgusting liquid like it was nectar. "Even I'm not drunk enough for that."

Snorting, Edwin at least consented to dig through Jed's bag and tug on a pair of sweatpants. He went back to perching on the chair, watching Jed, blue eyes bright with interest. "Why are you drunk?"

Knievel sashayed out of the bathroom, where she'd been perfectly content to sleep in the sink. Upon seeing Edwin, she chirped out a happy purr, padded over to him, and leapt gracefully up to insistently nudge her head against his knees. Edwin wound up with a delighted cat curled up on his shoulders, gnawing at his hair and flexing her claws into his chest. He didn't seem to mind at all.

"Because," Jed answered with a grunt, fishing out the empty whiskey bottle and staring into it mournfully. "That's fucking why."

"You're not a very chatty alcoholic." Edwin reached up to scratch behind Knievel's ear.

"Why the fuck are you here again?" Jed glowered at him, sprawling back in bed, a heated buzzing in his ears as he choked back the insistent urge to vomit. Maybe later. Or maybe on Edwin if he didn't stop talking. It was way too goddamn loud.

"Because you're an idiot who left your mate."

Jed cracked an eye open, peering over at Edwin. For a moment, no words came. It took way too long for the meaning of that to filter in, anyway. In the end, though, Jed didn't protest. He didn't bitch.

He did surge upward and fumble his way to the bathroom, falling down twice and slamming his shoulder painfully against the wall. As everything he'd eaten in the past two days came back up again, he thought he might have been crying. Maybe not. Maybe it was just how fucking sick he felt. In any case, passing out on the cold tile of the bathroom floor felt pretty damn good.

Jed woke up in bed, face mashed uncomfortably into a pillow. A damp feeling on the pillowcase let him know he'd been drooling, which just made the whole situation ten times worse. And there was a goddamn half-naked wolf picking around his room, sniffing the empty alcohol bottles. Jed tried to turn over, he really did, but the bed was rolling, and he wound up half propped up on his side, grunting painfully. He hooked a hand onto the side of the mattress. At least stabilizing himself made the room stop spinning a bit.

"You're awake." Edwin sounded way too fucking cheerful. Jed wondered if he could shoot him. No, better not. He'd have two angry wolves on his ass. "You slept a long time. And you snore."

"If you don't stop talking, I will do something that will make you stop." It wasn't his best threat, Jed would admit, but he didn't hurl or fall off the bed while saying it, so he'd count it as a win.

"Like what? Drink me?" Edwin laughed, obviously not realizing that Jed was one loud noise away from dying. Bastard. "You drank everything else, might as well."

"You're a judgmental asshole." Gathering up all his strength, Jed hauled himself into a sitting position, clutching at the blankets for a handhold. Squinting, head throbbing, he peered over at Edwin. Who was... in his hotel room. Had they covered that yet? Jed honestly couldn't remember. There had been drinking and puking, and somewhere between Edwin had shown up.

And before that there'd been Redford standing there, whole fucking camp swirling around him, so goddamn beautiful. A willow tree in the middle of the desert. And Jed had left him there, had driven away, because it was the best thing to do. Because he had to.

He hated himself for it. Of course he goddamn did. But Jed had been in plenty of situations with his back against the wall and no way out. He knew what it felt like. He wanted Redford to be happy. To have a shot at being *whole*. As much as it pissed him off, apparently he couldn't do a damn thing to give that to him.

Edwin pressed a mug into Jed's hands. The sharp scent of coffee hit Jed, and he practically moaned in relief. Taking huge gulps of the liquid, burning his mouth and not caring at all, he swung his legs around to the floor. Baby steps. At this rate he'd be walking by the time he was sixty. "There's pills in my bag. Side pocket." For good measure, Jed swiped a mostly empty bottle of Jack and tipped the last dregs of it into the coffee—hey, hair of the dog worked wonders.

Redford would have already had them out. Then again, Redford had a freaky way of knowing exactly what Jed needed before he'd gotten around to realizing it himself.

And he was going to stop thinking about Redford right the hell now, or else he'd just drink himself stupid again and not care about the consequences. Thinking about Redford made him bring up the mental image of Redford's goddamn upset face, and even the *memory* of that face made Jed want to do whatever Redford asked. It wasn't fair.

"I'm here because you left your mate." Edwin sat on the bed beside him, looking at him like he was some curiosity. But he had the pills, so Jed just snatched those, shaking three directly into his mouth and washing them down with the fortified coffee.

"What, you want to take a fucking picture?" Rubbing his fingers across his stubble, Jed scowled deeply.

"No." The exasperation in Edwin's voice was practically visible. "I'm here to take you back."

Okay, either he wasn't sober enough or wasn't drunk enough for this conversation, and Jed honestly wasn't sure which. "You're the one who told me we wouldn't work," he pointed out, finishing the coffee and looking sadly down at the bottom of his too-small crappy hotel mug. The ancient coffee maker was all the way over on the other side of the room. It was like God was punishing him for past sins. "So what, now you're changing your mind? Did you forget I was a dirty, stupid human?"

"Nope." Edwin took pity on him, going to get the pot of coffee and pouring him a refill.

"So, what? 'Cause I gotta say, Rin Tin Tin, I'm kind of talked out." Another long gulp of coffee and Jed felt fortified enough to stagger upright, going to the bathroom. He gratefully brushed his teeth, doing his best to wash out the nasty fuzz from his tongue. It made the shitty coffee taste even worse, but Jed really didn't care. "I get it. Redford's a wolf, I'm a goddamn human, I hold him back. Not to mention I turned him into a killer. Trust me, kid, you're preaching at the fucking choir."

Edwin was watching him, crouching in the chair again, head cocked just like… well, just like a dog who was trying to parse out what a human was babbling at it about. "Did my brothers ever tell you why my parents left the pack?"

"Uh." Shit. Pop quiz. "Bad food? Too many Lassie reruns during movie nights?"

"Probably." Edwin gave him a quick smirk. "They didn't agree with the pack anymore, apparently. I don't know. I never got a chance to ask them."

Sheesh. Was he really pulling out the dead-parents card? "Yeah, well, that sucks," Jed said flatly. "But that still doesn't tell me why the fuck you suddenly want me to be with Red."

"I'm just saying, I don't know why they left. But they did. They decided that what everyone else said pack had to be didn't work for them." Edwin wrapped his arms around his knees, shrugging. "They were afraid of humans. I mean, they had to be, right? They took us way out in the woods. I, uh, I don't really remember them. I remember… my mom laughing. And I remember dad had this beard that was scratchy when he hugged us good night."

Jed sank down to sit on the bed opposite the chair Edwin had commandeered. "You were just a kid when they died, right?" he asked, rubbing a hand through his hair.

Nodding, Edwin smiled slightly. It was dimmer than his usual ones, worn down by years of borrowed grief. "Yeah. They died, and then it was just Ant and Randall and me. And that's not normal either. I mean, Anthony was way too young. Now he's sick, and Randall is starting to take over and… look, my point is, we're not exactly poster kids, you know? Maybe that's why I like listening to Phoenix. I don't really know how I feel about humans." Edwin's eyes flicked to Jed, and he amended, "Other humans."

"Thanks," Jed grunted.

"Yeah, you're okay. But, you know, other humans, they might be like those hunters in the woods. Or the ones that killed my parents. Phoenix doesn't just talk about them, though. He talks about how it's okay to be different. It's okay to be a half blood, it's *better* to be what we are, and we shouldn't be ashamed of that. He wouldn't think my family is strange or broken just because we're not like everyone else."

Slowly, Jed nodded. "Thinking you're better, though." He drummed his fingers against his mug. "Gotta admit, I'm not a fan of that. A lot of bad shit seems to go down when one guy wants to raise himself up at the expense of everyone else getting knocked down."

Edwin, surprisingly, looked a little sheepish. "Maybe," he agreed. "Sometimes it seems like we have to be better, you know?"

"Why?" Jed snorted quietly. "Because you can turn into a wolf? Baby, I knew a woman who could hit a target from half a mile away in a windstorm. I knew this guy, part of my team, he could get you into any safe, any locked door, in five minutes flat. Go to a museum, read a book, hell, just listen to goddamn Metallica, you tell me that we're inferior just because we can't do your kind of tricks. We're not. You might live longer, you might run faster, you might have a pert little tail or suck blood or, hell, do *whatever* the fuck Victor does, but that just makes you different, junior. Not better."

After a moment of Edwin staring back at him, wordless, Edwin began to laugh. Not loudly, just almost-silent little chuffs of air, a grin spreading across his face. "Yeah, okay," he agreed. "I guess you aren't *entirely* worthless."

"Damn straight," Jed grumbled. "Just because there's some shitheel hunters out there, don't write the whole bunch of us off. I mean, come on, there are bad vampires, you know that. Ask your brother. There's got to be bad wolves. Having asshole members of your group is kind of universal."

"So if you're not inferior, why did you leave?" Edwin asked, sounding genuinely curious. "I mean, you don't think you're somehow less than, so...."

Heaving a sigh, Jed leaned forward, arms resting on his knees, staring down at his once again empty mug. "Because I'm not good for *him*," Jed answered finally, quietly. "He deserves better."

"Why do you think you're not what he needs?"

Rolling his eyes, Jed grimaced. His fingers wrapped more firmly around the coffee mug, as if that could hold him together. He was fucking hungover. He did not have it in him right then to be having this conversation. "You saw him out there," Jed muttered. "Running around, being who he is. He's better with you guys than he was with me. I'm.... I'm a cramped apartment and shitty processed dubious meat products. The only sky I see is some sliver between buildings. He should be free." Something broke in Jed's expression. He rubbed a shaky hand across his face. "I thought he was. I honest to God thought he was, until I saw him out there. Shit, I didn't even know."

"You couldn't," Edwin told him. He sounded almost kind, eyes softening with sympathy. "You're not a wolf. You gave him what you thought he needed."

"I gave him what *I* needed," Jed shot back, voice cracking.

"That's the kindest thing you could have done." Edwin gave him a barely-there smile. "Look, I.... I know I sounded harsh, before. During the full moon. But I've never had to be cooped up. Hell, my brothers took me out of school because I cried all day to be let out of the room. Being indoors too long makes me feel like my skin is too tight, like I need to just... *climb* out of it. That's who I am, and my brothers have worked hard to make sure I get to be who I am."

"So you're saying I tortured him, basically." Jed sighed, gaze dropping again toward the floor. "Fantastic."

"No. I'm saying you gave him what you thought he needed. You gave him *your* freedom, what you think that means." Edwin paused, searching for words. "You gave him the sliver of your sky. That's kind, Jed. It's not right, but it's kind. And that's more important than getting it perfect your first time."

Jed just shook his head, jaw tight. He'd locked Redford up. He'd locked him up, and he'd exposed him to a life of blood and violence. Which was the life Jed knew, the one he was soaked in, but he shouldn't have sullied Redford with it. He shouldn't have rubbed his dirt all over someone so clean.

"I can't stand to be cooped up," Edwin said again, and Jed wanted to scream at him. He got it. He got that he'd fucked up. He didn't need some idiot kid telling him all over again. But then Edwin went on. "But Randall can. He wants to be inside, in a library, just as much as I want to run. And he's not less of a wolf. He's not being forced. Honestly, he just... he likes it. I don't get it, but he's my brother. So I'd go to the library with him, I'd stay outside on the steps while he picked out books. And he always brought back one to read to me. He'd go down to the lake with me, we'd sit there and he'd read me a story while I ran around and chased butterflies."

Confused, Jed looked up to meet Edwin's eyes, calm and blue, wiser than he should be. Wiser than anyone who went around naked as much as Edwin ever should be allowed to become. Maybe the eyes of a kid who'd grown up fast and still clung, as much as possible, to the things that gave him the most joy. "So you're saying I should read Redford a book?" Jed asked, voice low and hoarse.

"I'm saying, stop trying to dictate what kind of wolf Redford is." Edwin's lips curved upward. "Just sit outside with him. Read to him while he runs. Don't try to make him into what you think he should be, Jed."

"Yeah, well, I can only read the books with the big pictures, anyway." Jed forced a quick smirk, studying Edwin's face, the haunted look still lingering in his eyes. "Look, my line of work... it ain't pretty. And I've made my peace with what I do. Hell, I'm good at it. But Redford, he's better than that."

"He's also an adult." Edwin wrinkled his nose, obviously confused. "I mean, unless I missed his traumatic brain injury."

"Shut up," Jed muttered.

"Seriously, come on. Give him a choice. But don't walk away if he picks staying with you. Come on, martyring yourself for his happiness is kind of ridiculous. He knows what you do. Maybe you can just tell him what you're thinking and talk about it?" Edwin's eyes cut to the table full of empty bottles. "Without drinking yourself stupid."

Jed had the good grace to look a little rueful. "It's a coping method." Usually he'd drink and then go get fucked by a stranger. Funny, this time he hadn't even thought about that as a possibility.

"It makes you stink," Edwin told him bluntly. "I don't know anything about being a... whatever you are."

"Security consultant," Jed deadpanned.

"Yeah, sure." Edwin laughed at that, leaning back in his chair. "Whatever. All I know is, I'd be pretty pissed if someone decided they got to make all kinds of decisions for me. I might be young, but I'm not stupid. I can figure out what I want, what I should stick around for, and when I should run. I'm guessing Redford can too."

Yeah, he really could. That big, beautiful brain of his was definitely better than the walnut Jed was toting around. Redford was strong and brilliant. He could make his own decisions. "I think...." Christ, was he actually going to admit this? Jed swore he'd never fucking drink again. "I think I'm just afraid that I'm going to be just like his grandmother. I'm going to shove him in a cage, and he's going to take it because he thinks he has to."

Edwin was quiet for a minute, staring up at the ceiling. His fingers had started to tap restlessly on his legs, his foot jittering absently. "Get a yard," he advised solemnly.

Jed couldn't help but snort a laugh. "Thanks, Socrates."

"Get a yard, get some room, and stop thinking you get to tell him what it means to be free." Edwin pinned Jed with a look. "I've seen the way Redford looks at you. *You're* his freedom, Jed. You're part of what makes him feel like he can run forever, like he just *has* to howl because his body isn't big enough to hold everything in. That's what it means to be a mate, I think."

"We're not mates." The disagreement was almost automatic, but Jed's voice trailed up at the end, a question seeping in.

Edwin scoffed, apparently not interested in listening to his denials. "You have his mark on your arm. Trust me, I can smell this stuff." He tapped the side of his nose. "You're mates. Or you could be. If you let yourself."

Jed stared down at his arm, Redford's bite marks still standing out angry red and scabbed over. He'd noted the other day, idly, that it would definitely scar. And while it still ached, Jed had to admit, some small part of him didn't mind. Sure, he'd rather *not* get mauled, and he didn't want Redford to ever get so lost again that he couldn't find his way out, but if he had to add to his collection of scars, he was halfway glad it was from Redford.

"How'd you get so damn annoying?" he grumbled at Edwin.

"Daytime television." Edwin gave him a wolfish grin.

It didn't make a ton of sense yet, no. Though that could partially be because his head was still throbbing. Jed was pretty sure a bunch of nice words didn't suddenly make it okay that Redford was going to age a hell of a lot slower or need to be taken for regular walks. And Jed wasn't sure where he fit in with the hippie clan of four-legged idiots. Maybe he didn't. Maybe neither of them did.

Maybe he should just get a fucking yard.

"We gotta go," Jed decided, lurching to his feet, weaving his way to his bag to start shoving his stuff back inside. Christ, the whole world was playing Tilt-A-Whirl. Jed was kind of amazed that he didn't just go crashing to the ground. But he managed to hold himself upright long enough to get his stuff packed and a protesting Knievel back into the cat carrier.

They were a two-hour drive away. If they stopped for the world's largest coffee and maybe a greasy burrito, Jed could be moderately sober by the time they got back to the camp.

"Sure hope you can drive, Lassie," Jed said, tossing the keys to Edwin. "We gotta get back."

Edwin stared down at the keys, a slow grin working its way across his face. "Awesome."

SO IT turned out, Edwin could *not* drive. He could not at *all* drive, despite his protests to the contrary and the fact that he could sing "The Wheels on the Bus" with dirty lyrics. Jed just thought it was damn lucky he was so hungover, because if he'd been sober enough to get behind the wheel he might have left Edwin to run home after he nearly took out the drive-through speakers and then started laughing hysterically.

After a very quick lesson about what the gas and brake pedal did, Jed settled back with his coffee and burrito and tried to not notice how close they were to dying at every moment. Luckily, the road was near deserted, and no one was there to honk at Edwin when he drove ten miles under the speed limit and drifted all the way over to the white line.

When they finally were bouncing down the long dirt road that led back to the camp, Jed was feeling marginally more clearheaded. He was half leaning out the window, stomach cramping into knots as he mentally urged Edwin to go faster. He just wanted to *get there*. Redford was there, was alone, Jed had *left him alone*, and even though Jed knew all the reasons why, he still wanted to cut off his own balls.

He didn't have a fucking clue what he was doing. How they'd work. But he couldn't bear the thought of not figuring it out together.

As they rounded the last bend, Jed spotted a familiar figure standing by the side of the path.

Redford. Framed in the waving grass, he was almost achingly beautiful. Jed barked, "Stop," but didn't give Edwin much of a chance to comply. Before the van had done more than slow down, he was diving out of the door, rolling and landing flat on his back, wind knocked out of him. But he was up again in the next beat, shoving himself forward and running toward Redford.

Turned out they had the same idea, and their collision had more force than Jed had intended it to. Redford saved them from toppling into the grass by grabbing Jed's shoulders. He wore the biggest smile Jed had ever seen him with.

"I'm so glad you're back," Redford said in a rush. "I was just going to come find you. I rang that contact of yours that lives near here, um, Burns or something, and he was going to come pick me up, and I was going to scour every hotel in a hundred mile radius. Are you okay? You don't look so good. Did you get into trouble?"

"Red?" Jed pulled back enough to study Redford's face, to drink him in like he was a fucking well in the middle of the goddamn sun. "Shut up."

Just like that, Redford yanked him in close, Jed tangled his fingers in Redford's hair and tugged him in, and they met in a hungry, desperate clash. Their lips met, tongues pressing and taking, Jed completely breathless as Redford kissed him back so hard he couldn't think. If it had been possible to melt right into Redford, to give up the entirety of his physical existence just to sag into everything Redford was, he would have right then. He needed him, *needed*, with an ache Jed couldn't even begin to articulate.

So he kissed Redford, wrapping his arms around him tight enough to ensure there wasn't even an inch of space between them.

"I'm sorry," he was whispering between every kiss. "I'm so sorry. I'm sorry, Red."

"You don't need to apologize," Redford fervently replied. "It's okay. I don't care that you left. I just care that you're back." He pulled back from Jed so he could properly look him in the eye, doubt touching his face. "You are back, aren't you? You didn't just forget your toothbrush or something?"

Heaving out a broken laugh, Jed shook his head, studying Redford's face, sliding his fingers along those three faint scars on Redford's cheek. "I shouldn't have left," he told Redford seriously. "I mean, I thought.... I thought I had to. I just want you to be happy, babe. I need you to be happy."

Redford got that little crinkle between his eyebrows, the one he wore whenever he was thinking hard about something, weighing everything in his mind. "When you left, you said you were doing it to make me happy," he murmured, confused. "It definitely didn't make me happy, but did you change your mind?"

"I just...." A frown flickered across Jed's face. He leaned up to kiss away the wrinkle on Redford's forehead, nudging his nose in alongside Redford's with a quiet sigh. "I'm scared," he admitted heavily. Two times he'd said it in the same day. The world was probably going to end.

Redford glanced around them, which led Jed to do the same. Edwin had obviously taken the van back to camp at some point, and they were utterly alone in the long grass and trees beside the dirt road. Redford took Jed's hand and tugged him over to a fallen tree, where they sat—which was nothing short of absolute relief for Jed's still hungover brain.

"Are you scared of me?" Redford asked. "Or scared of my instincts? Or something else?"

Redford looked so damn *worried*, so pinched and guilty, that Jed couldn't help but pull him in close. Nothing should ever make Redford look that way. Jed wanted to burn down the world, knowing it was his fault. Cupping Redford's cheek with his hand, he sighed, thumb making a slow arc against Redford's skin. "Never of you," he said softly, holding Redford's gaze. "Not ever."

"I know you said you left because you thought you'd turned me into a bad person." Redford's worried look took on a touch of confusion. "But if you're not scared of me, and I know you still love me and you don't love bad people, then I just.... I don't get it." Redford paused. "But we don't have to talk about it if you don't want to. All I need to know is that you're back with me."

It was an out. And if there was one thing Jed Walker was good at, it was taking the goddamn out. Playing their fingers together, resting their joined hands on his knee, Jed found it easier to stare down at them rather than hold Redford's gaze. "I'm scared," he tried again, tone thick, "that I'm your grandmother." Shit, it sounded stupid when he said it out loud. "That I'm forcing you into a different kind of cage and that I'm the reason...." Fuck, did his voice actually crack? Goddamn it. "I'm the reason," he continued, clearing his throat, "that your instincts haven't settled down."

Redford shut him up by kissing him. Jed did have to agree that it was the more pleasant option, so when Redford drew back, Jed frowned, missing the contact already.

"I don't know why my head is screwed up," Redford admitted. "But I know it's *not* because of you. Don't you get that, Jed? When I was with my grandmother, I was young, and I didn't know any better. I'm strong now. I can think for myself. Do you think you'd be able to force me to do anything I didn't want to?"

225

Still resolutely looking absolutely anywhere but Redford's face, Jed shifted slightly, wanting to keep protesting. It was easier to just blame himself. Hurt like fuck, but it was easier, because he could control that. He could bundle up all that self-loathing and have a nice, handy outlet for his grief. But Edwin had been right. Redford was right. Redford was a man, a very intelligent, very strong man. He wasn't the scared guy Jed had found hiding in a dead woman's house.

And even then, *even then*, Redford had been beautifully strong. Even then, he'd been a better man than Jed ever would be.

"I'm not a good man," he said lowly, jaw tight. "I don't have... good things in my life. Just you. You're the best goddamn thing I've got going on, Red. What if I ruin you? What if my filth gets all over you? I think I'd just put a bullet in my goddamn brain, because you're... fuck, you're the goddamn moon, you know? And I'm just this.... I'm this shit-stain who doesn't deserve you."

However much the words hurt to say, Redford looked even more wounded by them than Jed felt. "If you keep going, I'm going to hit you, because you're talking about the person I love," Redford protested. "And I don't like it when people insult you."

Christ. Jed could feel his face crumple. Maybe it was all the booze still sloshing around somewhere in his system. Maybe it was the lack of proper sleep or the hangover pounding his head like a hippo doing tap dance. Maybe it was just Redford, the sweet sternness in his gaze, the strength with which he was holding on to Jed's hand. Maybe it was that he still felt safer here, with Redford, than he ever had.

Jed chased a lot of monsters. Real now, and the all-too-human kind. He'd *been* a monster; he still was sometimes. He was brash and he was bold, and he never flinched. He never backed down.

Redford was the one goddamn thing that made him feel safe.

One minute Jed was just sitting there, still reciting all the reasons why not, still not entirely sure. He'd been sure a few hours ago, but the drive had given him more time to think and for old fears to resurface. So he sat there and he thought, and he wondered if Redford was right. If there was a chance. Or if he should listen to reason and just leave. He was thinking. He was caught between the two. And the next minute, he was leaning into Redford's shoulder, hot tears burning at his throat, caught there when Jed refused to let them fall.

"Yeah?" he managed, voice almost gone. "Well maybe I should listen to you, then. You are the brains of this operation."

He could feel Redford smile against his hair as his arms came up around Jed's back, gently rubbing over his shoulder blades. "I am," Redford replied, holding him tight. "And I'm an expert on the subject of Journey Walker. So when I say you're the best man I've ever met, you should listen to me. I have footnotes and citations and everything."

Huffing a laugh, pretty damn glad no one had seen his chick-flick moment, Jed just pressed his face into Redford's neck, feeling all that sick tension ease away. "Yeah?" A low breath and he was sliding his lips along Redford's skin, aching to feel him. God, it felt like forever. "I love it when you talk nerdy."

"That's not nerdy, that's just well-sourced research." There was a hint of a laugh under Redford's words. He bent his head, tucking his chin over Jed's shoulder. They were so wrapped up together, a knot of limbs and sighs and smiles, that Jed wasn't sure they'd ever untangle. What he did know, though, was that he never fucking wanted to.

Eventually, they did make it into their cabin. As much as Jed wanted to stay curled up in Redford's arms forever, they probably shouldn't turn into the crazy woodsmen who lived on a fallen log. Hand in hand, they walked back toward the camp, shoulders pressed tight together. They passed the van, which was parked... interestingly. Points for effort to Edwin, in any case. Probably having the van half up on a small hill of dirt was not the *best* choice, but at least it was right side up.

"I let Edwin drive," Jed told Redford with a slight laugh. "Holy crap, I nearly died." It all hit him then, and he started to laugh, cheeks hurting with how wide he was grinning. "He showed up *naked*, Red, and I was so drunk I passed out, and then I let him drive home. That was the weirdest goddamn night."

Redford just smiled at him, squeezing Jed's hand tighter. "I'm guessing you'll never let him drive again?"

"I am pretty sure I let him pop his driving cherry," Jed snorted. "So no. Never, ever again." They reached their cabin. Jed was only distantly surprised to find Knievel sitting on the porch, waiting for them. He probably should have let *her* drive home. It would have been safer, and she had two fewer thumbs than Edwin.

The cabin looked exactly the same. Jed had almost been expecting some kind of significant change, but it had only been a day. And Redford didn't tend to get drunk and throw alcohol bottles everywhere like Jed did. Redford shut the door behind them and flicked on the light, his gaze never leaving Jed.

"Hey," Jed whispered, tugging Redford into him, a faint smile crinkling the corners of his eyes. Redford came easily into his arms, leaning his weight on Jed to topple them onto the bed, where Redford seemed to have a moment of thinking he was some kind of octopus in wrapping every limb around Jed.

"Do you know what I learned when you were gone?" Redford asked lowly.

"How to do origami?" Jed guessed, trailing kisses along his jaw. "The secret of the universe?"

"Close," Redford huffed. "I learned that you're my pack. And some wolves need lots of pack members, and some don't. And some need to be outside, or to be with another wolf, and some don't." He lifted up on his elbow to look at Jed. "But that first realization was the most important one."

Rubbing his thumb along Redford's cheek, Jed studied his face, throat oddly tight. "You think I'm your pack?" Two years ago, he was pretty sure he would have laughed right out loud at the idea. And the terminology. But now he could feel warmth spreading in his chest, a terrifying sense of *rightness* at the thought. "Isn't that kind of a big deal for you?"

Redford frowned. "A big deal in admitting that, or a big deal, period?"

"Kinda both." Jed let his fingers trail lightly through Redford's hair. As far as he knew, the whole *pack* thing meant... family. It meant something a lot bigger than Jed could handle. He wasn't anyone's *family*. He wasn't that guy.

"It's not." Redford bumped his chin against Jed's chest in an affectionate gesture. "I liked saying it. And you being my pack is probably the most *right*, natural thing I've ever felt. You're everything I need."

227

Silent for a few moments, rubbing his hand absently up and down Redford's back, Jed struggled to come up with a response. Redford just said it so *easily*. He honestly wasn't sure what to do with that. "Have I ever told you about my family?"

Redford blinked at him, startled, and an eager look started to light his eyes. "No, you haven't. I'd love to hear about them."

Grimacing, Jed just kind of shook his head. Yeah, he didn't have many Walton family Christmas stories. And he honestly couldn't remember the last time he'd talked about them. Maybe sometime in his early army days. When he'd enlisted, he'd had to write down his family's medical history, and he hadn't even known if he knew their latest address. "I, uh." Sighing, half hating that he'd brought it up, Jed shrugged. "I've got an older brother and sister. Two parents." He trailed off, scowling. Christ, how did he even talk about this?

Redford started to look concerned. "If it's bad, you don't have to tell me about them."

"No, no, fuck, it's not… *bad*." A lot of people had assumed Jed came from some horrifying background. The truth of it was probably a lot more mundane than one might guess. "They were just… they were nice." Jed sighed, flicking his gaze away from Redford to stare up at the ceiling. "They were all really nice. Normal. I just…. I don't know. I never fit. Ever. I grew up feeling like I was some tacked on piece of a puzzle that didn't belong there. I hated it, not because they were bad people, they weren't. Just because I never felt like I should be a part of them."

It made him seem like an asshole, Jed knew. He'd known it back then. His parents had loved him, probably. They'd certainly never abused him. He'd had food and clothes and a roof over his head. All common sense dictated that Jed should have been grateful. He should have stuck around. And he hadn't. Even as a kid, he'd been the guy who ran away when shit got too hard. Give him a war any day. He'd never figured out how to handle family.

Redford rubbed Jed's arm. "That sounds like it was hard," he said sympathetically. "Are they all still alive?"

Snorting a little laugh, Jed shook his head helplessly. "I don't know." Christ, Redford was going to hate him. "I, uh. I left home when I was sixteen. Haven't talked to them since. I don't even know where they are." The guy who could find anyone, and he didn't have a fucking clue if his parents were dead or alive.

Redford looked like he wasn't sure what to make of that. Jed hadn't told many people about his parents: a few army buddies, way back when, when he'd been so drunk he couldn't control his words and someone had brought up the topic of family. It'd never gone over well, saying he just *didn't talk* to them. For some reason, it was assumed that whatever unit you were put into—by fate, design, a broken condom, or some adoption agency—you were supposed to like them. Hell, you were supposed to *love* them. If they didn't beat you, if they fed you, took care of you, it was a biological imperative that you have some kind of emotional connection. And Jed just… didn't.

Redford, who really had had it bad, finally just nodded and smiled at Jed sadly. "Okay," he said simply. His hand stole up to find Jed's again, and when they were joined, Redford brought them up to rest under his chin. "Do you think you'll ever want to contact them, someday?"

Jed had to admit, he was still waiting for Redford to react differently. To realize that if Jed couldn't even hack it with the people he'd been born into, how the fuck was he supposed to make anything else work? "I don't know," Jed answered, fidgeting a little.

That was a lie.

"No," he sighed, eyes still locked somewhere above Redford's head. "Shit, Red…. I know, I know that I should be different. But it always felt like they were strangers. I'm sure they loved me, I don't doubt it. But I never could figure out how to be a part of something like that. I don't do families. I don't know how."

"And you don't have to, if you don't want to," Redford replied softly. "You didn't pick them. You didn't get on with them, and that's okay." He hesitated, bumping his chin against Jed's knuckles. "You can choose me to be your pack, if you want."

Jesus Christ. It wasn't even a conscious decision to finally lower his gaze to Redford's. He was drawn like a goddamn magnet. "I'd pick you a hundred times over," Jed whispered, the words sinking down into him. They were true. He knew they were true. For the first time in his life, he honestly felt like he was home. "I don't know how to do this, Red, but you make me want to figure it out."

"Me too." Redford smiled. "We can figure it out together."

A very slow smile started curling across Jed's face. "Now that sounds like something I can handle." They were a team. They were partners. Jed trusted him. He trusted Redford with his back, his guns, his life. He sure as hell could trust him now. His slid his hand down, bumping fingers over the dog tags and whistle Redford wore. "You and me?"

"Always."

CHAPTER
13

Randall

IT WAS the summer solstice.

As the longest day of the year, it was a traditional day of ceremony and marked observance in numerous cultures. In some places, it was a holy day. In others it represented an instance of celebration, mirth, festivals or grand parties. It was a day out of time, one where bacchanals and fertility goddesses danced together. It was a day where one was encouraged to step outside the normal grind of planting and harvesting to give thanks to the sun that grew their crops, to the ground that held them.

To wolves, it apparently meant an absolutely obscene amount of food and an even larger bonfire.

Sitting on the porch of their cabin, watching the preparations, Randall couldn't help but marvel at how some traditions never changed. The pack was preparing to move, furnishings being packed up, arrangements being made. A small group of scouts had even been sent out yesterday to check out the possible spots Jed had found for the pack to settle. But today, it was all about the celebration.

Edwin was out there, chasing after a platter of freshly butchered meat, trying to charm a predinner snack from the women carrying it. Anthony was hovering nearby, eyes firmly fixed on Edwin. After their brother's little disappearing trick the other day, Randall was frankly surprised Anthony hadn't put Edwin on a leash.

If he squinted, he could just make out Victor hovering on the other edge of the gathering, some kind of package in his hands as he scowled at everyone. He looked like he was trying to make his way through the crowd, though he wasn't being very successful.

Phoenix, the half blood, was scheduled to talk at the celebrations today. Later, Randall had heard, a few local half bloods from the nearby area would show up, granted access for one day only. Rumor had it that the Gray Lady had initially refused them, but since she planned to move, she obviously felt safe enough to give out their location to a select few. The knowledge would cease to be relevant in a week, after all.

Randall wasn't sure how he felt about the whole thing. Moving, leaving everything he'd known, *Phoenix* being there… he just didn't know. Maybe it didn't matter. Anthony needed the pack, and that was the most important thing.

Good thing he'd already dropped out of school. Not that his brothers knew that, but moving several states away would have put a huge cramp in his commute.

"Randall!" He looked up to see Victor had finally made his way through the crowd, his free arm held in front of him like a barrier to stop overly friendly wolves from bumping into him. "I wanted to catch you before Phoenix spoke. I think after that happens, the alcohol will start to flow freely and I'll have to hide in my cabin."

Randall had to admit that he stared blankly for far too long. Victor seeking him out was not a normal occurrence. And with everything that had happened, with all the confusion and the *really* good kisses and the fact that Victor had looked terrified after both, Randall had assumed the man would take the pack moving as an opportunity to leave and never see him again. "Is something wrong?" he asked, half standing, frowning. Of course that had to be the reason. Why else would Victor come find him?

"No, no, not at all," Victor assured. "I wanted to give you something."

He held out the package to Randall. It was tidily wrapped in brown paper, and from the shape of it, it had to be a book. Stunned, Randall reached out, taking it and staring at it like it was something he'd never seen before. He looked back up at Victor, unsure. "You brought me a gift?"

"It's merely something I wanted you to have." Victor looked faintly embarrassed. "It's not in the best condition, I'm afraid."

Randall could feel the smile starting on his lips. He ducked his head to hide it, carefully tearing the paper from the package. It was, indeed, a book. *Carry On, Jeeves*, by P.G. Wodehouse. It was, as stated, in somewhat rough condition, the edges of the pages yellowed with age and use, but it was obviously not suffering from neglect. This was a cherished tome. Randall could see the love that had gone into turning the pages. The grin on Randall's face couldn't possibly be masked as anything but delight now. With reverent fingers, he opened it, caressing the well-worn paper. He leaned down and took a deep breath, delighting in the unique scent of a carefully handled old book. "I love it," he told Victor honestly, eyes rising to him. "Thank you, Victor. I will treasure it."

"It's my favorite," Victor replied, still sounding a bit awkward but obviously relieved that Randall liked his gift. He reached down to turn the pages back to the start, revealing the carefully handwritten notation on the inside cover: *Victor Rathbone, age 6.* "Have you read Wodehouse?"

It wasn't just a book. It wasn't just a nice title that Victor enjoyed, that he'd picked up in some used-book shop and passed on. This was *his* book, Victor's, and Randall knew how people like them felt about such things. It was a nice gift, to share a story you had enjoyed. It was an intensely intimate, completely amazing gift to give away a book you'd grown up owning. Victor's hands had touched this cover, had turned these pages, countless times before. He'd fallen asleep with this book, he'd woken up and reached for it, he'd carried it with him and read it over and over, delighting in the places and characters it held.

It was a part of him. It was a piece of who he was, of what made up the man he'd become. To receive a bibliophile's book was like sharing in their soul.

Randall wasn't easily impressed by material goods. He didn't understand the point of jewelry. He thought flowers were nice but could be overdone. Chocolates were a decent dessert. *This*, though. This was the most romantic gift he could imagine receiving.

"I haven't," he managed, torn between staring at the pages and at Victor, stunned. "This will be my first."

Did Victor intend for this to be so important? Perhaps it was simply an extra copy, or maybe Victor didn't put such a hefty weight on his books. Maybe it was a consolation gift, given out of some sense of pity. Randall couldn't tell. Victor couldn't meet his eyes directly, the nuances of Victor's scent were unfamiliar to Randall, and he hadn't realized how much he relied on those things until they were taken out of the equation.

"I'm glad." He could see Victor's smile, though, the way it touched the corners of his eyes. "This book has always been the one thing I'd literally take to the grave with me, but… it's helped me through some difficult times. I'd hoped it might do the same for you."

Throat tight, Randall studied Victor's face, feeling as though he should say something, do something, *be* something more, something worth receiving a gift like that. "Thank you," was all he could think to say, his voice low and thick with emotion. He stood then, reaching out to lightly touch Victor's arm before he forced his hand to fall away. "I truly can't think of anything I could cherish more."

Even if it meant nothing to Victor, Randall knew he would treasure the book. Even if Victor never felt the way Randall did, it didn't diminish Randall's own emotions. It just made them a bit lonelier, was all.

"Good." Victor smiled tentatively at him again. "May I sit, if you're looking for company?"

Randall really was trying not to read too much into this. He'd pushed twice, he'd kissed Victor, and while both times had been amazing, it had been abundantly clear that Victor was… well, *confused* at best. Randall had decided to step back and let Victor have the easy out he obviously wanted. But he was smiling at Victor as he nodded, gesturing to the steps of the porch and taking his own seat again. He was cradling the book carefully, absently rubbing his thumb along the spine.

"I feel a little useless," Randall said, forcing himself to stop staring at Victor. "All this activity and I'm not doing much to help." Their knees were budged lightly together. Randall stared at the point of connection, raising his eyes to Victor's face as heat flushed his cheeks. He was being ridiculous. He really needed to stop overreacting to everything. "Have you ever participated in a solstice celebration?"

Victor gave a muted chuckle. "Only once or twice. I'm afraid parties aren't really my thing." Even from this distance, the light of the bonfire flickered over his features, reflecting off his glasses. "The celebrations I'm invited to tend to be quite different than this."

When Randall looked back at the partying wolves, Edwin was dancing with one of the women he'd been trying to charm earlier. The food was out, and there were clusters of wolves coming in to eat, a small group of people with instruments playing a light, springy tune. The preparations looked to be finished, and now the party was beginning.

"Oh?" Randall wasn't much interested in joining in. He'd much rather sit and get to know Victor. Which might be incredibly lame, but Randall thought if the pack really was going to be leaving in a week, he should take this chance. "I've never really been to, uh, anything like this. The group I went to Egypt with had a bar crawl the night before we left, but I didn't last very long." He gave Victor a sheepish look. "Not a big drinker, I guess." He'd actually wound up singing bad karaoke and then passing out after kissing the bartender. Randall referred to that night as *the time we do not speak of.* There was a reason Randall didn't go out drinking.

"Neither." Victor was smiling, from what Randall could see of his face. "This is very wolfish. The solstice celebrations I keep getting invited to year after year are actually through contacts and friends that my parents had. I was never interested in joining that particular group for partying, but they keep insisting."

Out of the corner of his eye, he saw Edwin take the arm of another girl who was walking past, pulling her into the growing group of wolves dancing around the fire. It was, indeed, very wolfish. The stars were barely visible, the sun still hovering on the horizon, the smell of meat along with the smoke of the bonfire. Randall caught Anthony's eye across the way and smiled at him, nodding to Edwin. Anthony grinned back. In that moment, Randall felt perfectly content. "Are your parents still with you?" Randall asked, turning back to Victor.

"Oh no, they died quite some time ago," Victor replied. "They were good people, but I do despise their friends." He turned his head slightly to look at Randall, and, as if knowing what he was going to ask next, said, "My mother was the one with the medusa blood. I was very young when they died, and I'm not sure if their car accident was the result of her mind letting go, but I suspect that was the case."

A frown flickered across Randall's face. "I'm so sorry, Victor," he murmured, his hand, almost of its own accord, going to rest lightly against Victor's arm. There was nothing more he could say, so he just sat there, turned toward Victor, fingers gently wrapped around his arm.

"Thank you." To Randall's surprise, Victor placed his own hand over Randall's. "They maintained connections in the half-blood world. There's a sort of, er, pretend high society where some of them are considerably snootier than other half-blood breeds. I want nothing to do with it, but the invites keep coming. Though I'm not a fan of parties, I must say I appreciate the honesty of wolves much more."

Marveling at how warm Victor's hand was, how dry and smooth his fingers were, Randall dared to hook one of his fingers around Victor's. "They are rather enjoying themselves, aren't they?" he half laughed, turning to watch. The food was a big hit, half the meat being cooked, the other half laid out fresh and raw. Edwin ran past with the two women, chasing after a man in a wild dance, catching the male wolf and swinging him around with a happy laugh. The four of them danced together, Edwin happily flinging his arms around whomever was closest.

"There's food," Randall pointed out, throat a bit dry, not sure what one did in circumstances like this. He desperately wanted to point out they were all but holding hands, but at the same time, he was certain that making an issue of it would mean it would end. "Should we try some?" He gave Victor a shy, hopeful smile. "I'll be brave if you will. I'm sure they have to have something you'll like."

"I'm sure they will."

Randall only barely picked up the murmured words, but before he could ponder too long about what sounded like a double meaning in them, Victor was standing beside him, using his free hand to dust off his pants. Victor released Randall's hand but offered his crooked arm instead. Randall couldn't even begin to stop his pleased grin. He tucked the book safely by the doorway, and, standing himself, he slipped his arm through Victor's, laughing again lowly as they made their way together down to the celebration.

The drums started to thrum in the air as the bonfire grew ever larger, feeding on the wood underneath it. Summer solstice was a day more potent than the full moon.

Edwin was now with a huge group that had turned into one of the most primal, raw dances Randall had ever seen. They all looked more wolflike now than they did in their actual fur, eyes gleaming yellow in the dying light, toothy grins and casual touch. Edwin danced with Mallory, a woman with bouncy blonde curls behind him. He raised his chin to the sky and howled. The others echoed his cry, and Randall felt a surge of heat through him, a sudden wish to *run*, to strip down and dance under the moon, to greet the summer with fur and teeth and a full-throated yell.

Randall stumbled to a halt, eyes closing, taking in a deep breath. His heart was echoing the beat of the music. The howls that reverberated around them thrummed through his veins. Even on the moons, he'd never felt a pull *this* strong. He knew his eyes would be yellow, his voice dropping to a low growl as he shook off the sudden thrill through him. "Sorry," he murmured, rubbing a hand through his hair. "That's.... I don't know what that is."

Victor had come to a stop beside him, watching him curiously, a strange light in his eyes. "Er. Yes, no, that's quite all right. Absolutely all right. You—yes. Carry on."

Randall took another deep inhale, smelling meat, smelling wolves, but above all he could smell *Victor*. Tea and dry scales over rock, books, power, and cinnamon, all the things Randall knew as Victor, only *more* somehow. More immediate. More urgent. Randall's hand slid up Victor's chest, heat flushing through him as he tangled his fingers into the hair at the base of Victor's neck. "Come on," he murmured, more daring as the music rose higher, as the sun disappeared and the half-full moon slipped into her rightful place.

Tugging Victor with him out into the throb of wolves dancing, Randall grinned, moving with the music. He wasn't graceful, no, but God it felt good. "It's the solstice," he said, leaning in close to Victor's ear to be heard. "I think we should participate. For research purposes, of course."

"You want *me* to dance?" Victor looked nothing less than terrified at the idea. "I'm not sure that's a very good idea. Not unless you want to unleash chaos."

Randall just laughed. He wouldn't normally be doing this either, except there was the beat of the drums, the high thrill of the music, the sound and scents of an entire pack of wolves welcoming the solstice. He felt so *wolfish* that *not* participating seemed impossible. "Come on, medusa," he teased, arms wrapping loosely around Victor's neck. "It's not a ritual dance. The old gods won't be displeased if we're terrible. Unless you'd rather I stop bothering you and let you go back to your cabin?" It was a legitimate question, Randall waiting, unsure, for the answer.

He could see his own yellow gaze reflected back at him in Victor's glasses, the man's downcast eyelashes providing only the smallest peek at Victor's actual eyes, blue lit brighter by the fire. And although he still looked horrified at the idea of dancing, Victor started to relax. He put one hand on Randall's hip, unsure of his movements.

"If there's dancing to be done, I cannot think of a more ideal partner," Victor said.

Randall's smile was softer. He rested his forehead on Victor's, closing his eyes so that Victor wouldn't have to worry about meeting them by accident. "You confuse me so much, my Beatrice," he murmured. "And yet I've never been happier to not know the answers."

They moved together, somewhat slower and definitely more restrained than the wild whirl of wolves around them. But it was perfect. Randall relaxed into Victor's arms, laughing as they experimentally spun around. Randall caught sight of Jed and Redford at the edge of the group, swaying together, completely caught up in each other. He nudged Victor and nodded toward them. Apparently someone had finally made up.

Victor made an amused noise low in his throat. Where he might have speculated, he instead just turned his attention back to Randall. Even when Edwin spun by in the arms of yet another partner, dragging Mallory behind him, Victor didn't seem to notice. All that was happening around them, and Victor was focused only on Randall. He had to admit, he wasn't quite sure what to do with the attention.

They gravitated closer without conscious thought, at first only their knees and arms brushing together, then more, then closer still until there was no space between them at all. Victor pressed his cheek lightly against Randall's, his arms hooked low around Randall's back. Every inch of Randall responded, every part of him feeling as though it had been formed only to fit in against those parts of Victor. Taking a low, shuddering breath, Randall turned his head, nudging his nose in under Victor's ear.

It was an intensely personal thing, to smell someone's neck. To get that close, that intimate, to such a vulnerable place. Randall shouldn't; he didn't have the right. But Victor just held him closer, and Randall gave in to the thrill of his scent. "If we're not careful," he murmured, lips catching against Victor's skin, "I might kiss you again."

He felt a nudge against his own neck, Victor mirroring his actions. "Who's to say I'd want to avoid that now?"

Eyes closed, Randall felt every throb of his heartbeat, every surge of heat through his gut at Victor's breath on his neck. He'd never had anyone do that to him before. Not like this. And Randall honestly hadn't expected such an immediate physical reaction. It was like he was suddenly acutely aware of the arch of his own neck, the shiver of muscles under taut skin. Slowly, Randall pulled back. There was that breathless beat, he and Victor standing still in the middle of the wild dervish of movement and sound.

And then they leaned in, the both of them together, Victor's hands sliding up to cup Randall's cheeks. They kissed, and it wasn't hesitant, it wasn't Victor holding back. Not this time. Randall heard himself moan loudly as Victor teased his tongue against Randall's lips, as they sank further into each other with a spark of heat.

When they broke away, Randall biting at Victor's lip, Victor ghosted the faint promise of a kiss against Randall's mouth as they panted in a breath. Stunned, Randall wasn't even sure what to do. He'd never had a kiss like that before.

"Randall, I—"

The murmurs of the crowd grew into a roar around them, the crackle of a microphone audible above the cries for a speech, the applause, and the excitement.

Phoenix must have arrived. Randall had never hated anyone more than he did Phoenix in that moment. Whatever Victor had said was lost, the dance breaking up in favor of the pack sprawling out with food and company around what appeared to be a large tree stump turned into an impromptu stage.

"Victor." Randall turned to him, searching his face, trying to catch the moment again. Victor's fingertips touched Randall's cheek.

"To be continued?" Victor said, raising his voice to be heard over the cheering.

They made their way closer, finding a spot to sit. Edwin was curled up in a pile with at least four other people, his head lying on the lap of some man whom Randall vaguely remembered seeing around and the blonde woman sprawled out next to him, using him as a pillow herself. Randall had to laugh. Yeah, that was definitely his brother. Anthony was just a little ways off, a blanket tucked around him, looking content.

Nearby, Randall spotted Jed and Redford. They were sitting together, Jed resting with his back to Redford's chest, Redford's arms around him, and their fingers laced tightly. Jed was kissing Redford's chin, the two of them whispering and smiling, intensely intimate. It was... nice, to see them happy again. Randall hadn't realized how good they were for each other until they'd started fighting. Jed had a plate piled high with grilled meat, and he fed Redford a messy bite after eating his own, both of them laughing at their joint attempts.

As for himself, his hand was still entwined with Victor's. They were sitting together, Victor's shoulder pressed against his own, and Randall didn't care what else happened. This was one of the best nights of his life.

Above the crowd, Randall could see Phoenix stepping onto the huge tree stump, the portable speaker by his feet and the microphone in his hand. Randall realized he could smell other scents mixed in with the wolves now, a few scattered half bloods who had arrived with Phoenix.

Phoenix himself was a tall, willowy man with angular features and an effortlessly crowd-commanding presence. Blond hair fell to his shoulders, and pale eyes watched them all calmly. Randall wished he could pinpoint the man's scent. He had to admit, he was curious to know what kind of half blood he was, considering that he was doing rallies for them. Some of the breeds of half bloods had natural leadership instincts, but Randall couldn't pick up the scent of any of those types right now.

"Good evening," Phoenix said. He didn't shout into the microphone or motion them all to be silent. He merely waited for the crowd to quiet down before he continued. "I trust you're all having a good solstice?"

The roar of the crowd was deafening. Randall leaned in to whisper to Victor, lips catching the curve of his ear, "I can't tell what he is. Too many scents." It wasn't important information to share, perhaps, but it was an excuse to move a little closer.

Victor leaned into the contact. "Well, looking at his height, I'd feel safe in saying he's not a dwarf," he joked.

Randall laughed loudly. Unfortunately, it was during a lull in the crowd's noise, just before Phoenix began to speak. Heads swiveled around toward him, and Randall flushed hotly, wondering if it was possible for a wolf to dig a hole to hide in. He heard Edwin laugh then, louder, and start to clap, chanting Phoenix's name. It worked. Most of the wolves turned back to the stage, cheering again, the attention diverted from Randall. Randall sagged back, embarrassed, covering his face with his free hand.

Phoenix inclined his head, half smiling at the encouragement. Once again he waited for the noise to taper off.

"I'm honored to be able to join you here today," Phoenix continued. "I can think of nowhere I'd rather be on the solstice than with my brothers and sisters." He paused, as if to let that sink in. "I call you that because, though you may be wolves and I may be a half blood, we are united in one thing: our superiority over the humans that are so destructive to the world they think they rule."

Randall noticed that some of the wolves didn't cheer. There seemed to be no rhyme or reason in who did, though. The majority of them raised their voices in agreement, both young and old, men and women. Randall shifted uncomfortably, exchanging a glance with Victor, flicking a quick look over at Jed. Though he was still lounged back against Redford, Randall could see the sharpness in his gaze, the way his whole body had tensed. His hand had gone down to rest at his hip. Randall realized it was on his gun.

Jed was the lone human in a very large, very rowdy crowd. And now someone was talking about human inferiority. Randall couldn't blame him for being concerned.

"I'm here tonight to reach out." Phoenix seemed to look at each and every one of them, even though there were hundreds in attendance. "We are isolated. With our wolf packs and our half-blood dens, we only make ourselves weaker against the humans. Many of you know my philosophy, but for those who don't I will gladly bend your ear. Believe me. I can talk all day if you'll let me."

The crowd laughed, and Phoenix gave an easy, self-deprecating smile. Randall didn't buy it. There was something a little too calculating about that smile.

"I believe that we are superior. I believe that we are strong." Another cheer from the crowd. "And I believe we have so much in common that we should acknowledge more than we do now. We realize the Earth we live on is a precious, sacred thing that should be cherished and protected, not destroyed like the humans so carelessly do. We understand that history is also sacred, that we are intimately connected to our past and our bloodlines. We understand that the family we choose is everything. The humans? They waste such things, they forsake their bloodlines and their history, they forsake their planet, they forsake their family."

Jed was sitting up then, tenseness practically radiating off of him. Randall pleaded silently with him to keep his mouth shut. Up on his stage, Phoenix paused to give a faint sigh, then continued. "We are better than that. Unfortunately, right now we are the minority. We must still keep ourselves hidden. We must shield our true natures from the humans so that their fragile little minds do not break under the strain of true knowledge. I am sick of it."

This time Randall winced at the sheer volume of the agreeing shouts of the wolves around him. He caught sight of Anthony, who was shaking his head, looking disgusted. And then he heard a low, rolling growl, a steady rumble of noise. He knew the sound of it. Looking around, he found Edwin sitting up, eyes narrowed at Phoenix.

Giving a low bark under his breath, the noise nearly hidden in the applause, he nonetheless caught Edwin's attention. Edwin looked over at him, gesturing up at Phoenix. Randall just shook his head. Yes, he knew that what was being said was unbelievable. He also knew that trying to do anything was suicidal. At the very least, it'd start a fight that wouldn't solve anything.

"Know that at this time I am not advocating war, or violence, or attacks on the humans," Phoenix said. "They may be pitiable, but they do not deserve to die for their ignorance. Nor am I advocating walking plainly around the human cities as your true selves. I am here for other reasons. One, to share in your magnificent celebration. And two...."

Phoenix trailed off and held out a hand to his left, palm up. There was a moment's pause. The Gray Lady came through the crowd, wolves parting around her. She took Phoenix's hand. He bowed low, kissing her knuckles in reverence. Randall took a sharp intake of breath, eyes going wide. That, he had not seen coming.

"My lady," he murmured, still loud enough for the microphone to pick up. "You look absolutely stunning tonight. I did not ask you to dance earlier, and I will never regret any inaction more."

The Gray Lady smiled at him. Randall couldn't tell if she looked sincere or if she was just humoring him, maybe a mix of both. "Are you going to continue charming me, Phoenix, or should you continue your speech?"

Phoenix gave a melancholy sigh. "If only I had the time to do both." The Gray Lady's smile was genuine then, small but privately pleased at the flattery. Phoenix turned back to the microphone, still holding the Gray Lady's hand. "I propose a union," he announced. "Of half bloods and wolves."

The shocked murmurings of the crowd were respectfully quiet, but Phoenix still paused to let them speak to one another for a few moments.

"To ease your fears, no, I would not be suggesting that this camp suddenly be overrun with half bloods." The murmurs turned into laughs. Phoenix smiled briefly. "A diplomatic union, of sorts, though I would be privileged to call it a family union. We would continue our lives as we do today, but with the added benefit of knowing we have allies everywhere. The half bloods in the cities, the wolves in the country. Wherever we would go, we would feel safer. We would feel even *stronger*."

Phoenix shared a silent look with the Gray Lady. "I have been told that human hunters threaten your home here, and that you are relocating. With this union, I would offer allies at your new home, as well as added protection for the smaller packs who might remain here."

"He's offering them everything they could want," Randall murmured to Victor, eyes locked on the stage. "I don't know about you, but I stopped believing in Santa Claus when I was three."

Victor looked pained. "I wish I could believe him," he whispered in reply. "Not about the superiority. But half bloods have never been a very solid community, not like wolves. A union would *make* them a community as they banded together to help the wolves here."

"It is a good idea," Randall agreed, squeezing Victor's hand, voice low, head tipping toward Victor to keep their conversation private. "I wish it could happen. Maybe someday. But not from him. I don't know why, but I don't trust him."

Phoenix seemed to have fallen silent to let the wolves discuss what he had said. Victor shook his head. "Neither," he sighed. "Wasn't Edwin a fan of this man? He didn't seem to be too happy earlier."

"This is much more inflammatory than what I'd heard him speak of earlier." Randall frowned. "I don't know what Edwin's heard, but I went to one of Phoenix's speeches shortly after I got back from Egypt. He talked a lot about half-blood and full-blood unity, but not about humans."

"Full-bloods," Victor mused. "Notice how he hasn't mentioned vampires at all here. Smart of him, the wolves would second-guess the union if they thought vampires were going to be involved."

Phoenix was now chatting with the Gray Lady, the crowd muttering among themselves. Randall noticed that Phoenix kept his distance from all of them, aloof without being obvious about it. Eventually he waved at the gathering to thunderous applause and then stepped down. A few men emerged from the shadows and gathered Phoenix's things, the group walking quickly back toward the road and the cars parked there. The Gray Lady turned to her pack and the half bloods who had joined them. "I think the food is not quite gone," she said with a welcoming smile. "And there are drinks and music yet aplenty. Happy solstice to you all."

"Happy solstice," the crowd returned, clapping, stretching and moving once again. Edwin darted around people to go to Jed and Redford, leaning in to speak with them. Anthony was shortly after, the four of them gathering for a moment before breaking up. Edwin looked slightly reassured, and Jed had lost the tight look to his face. Apparently they were happy that none of them had bought Phoenix's speech.

"We never did get that food." Randall turned to Victor, giving him a small smile. "I believe we got distracted."

Victor still looked thoughtful, his eyes on the crowd where Phoenix had vanished. Randall's words brought his attention back. At once, that tender expression that had been on Victor's face while they danced made a return. "That we did. And look, I can even see some food on those tables that isn't meat."

Victor stood and held out his hand. Randall took it, and Victor tugged him up with a smile. Such a simple, stupidly *domestic* action, but it had Randall all but beaming. He took Victor's arm, and they walked to where the food was spread out. They loaded up plates with some beautiful vegetables and thickly crusted bread. Randall didn't even try to resist the delicious looking meat. There were even pies, hugely deep with flaky crust and plump berries. Plates weighed down with food, big cups of what had to be some form of wine in hand, they made their way back to the porch steps of Randall's cabin.

"I love eating outside," Randall admitted as they started to eat. "There's something about having the stars as your chandelier or a beautiful afternoon as your lamplight." He laughed, poking his fork into the steak. "Probably the most wolfish thing about me."

Victor smiled as he ate. "I think medusas must have lived in caves," he replied. "I'm at my happiest in dimly lit libraries. Then again, it may just have something to do with the fact that I attract mosquitoes by the flock."

"I had my first kiss in a library," Randall informed him, grinning, ducking his head. "I was, uh, sixteen I think. There was this boy in my class who I think might have been sent on a dare. I was back doing research in the history section. He came up and gave me a peck on the cheek and then ran away. We never spoke again."

"I have a library at home." Victor was giving Randall a look out of the corner of his eye. "With a far superior collection than you'd normally find in public libraries."

A beat passed, and Randall could feel a flush starting on his cheeks. "Oh?" he managed, trying to sound casual. "That sounds very interesting." Darting a quick look over at Victor, he tried to control his smile. "Do you have a history section?"

"An extremely thorough one," Victor replied. "I even have a few books on subjects like Sarah Tarrant."

"Oh, I have recently discovered how thorough you are," Randall murmured. "I think I'd like to see further evidence of that fact."

Victor flushed, though the hesitance he'd once worn didn't make an appearance. "I'd like that too. Would you like to dance some more? You were...." Victor paused, maybe to gather his thoughts. "You were stunning out there."

Taking in a slow breath, Randall stared down at his plate. No one had ever said anything like that to him before. His mind scrambled through every book he'd read, all the stories, trying to think how to respond. Nothing came to mind. No tale he'd ever read, nothing he'd experienced, prepared him for the exquisite jolt of warmth through him, the nervous flutter in his stomach, the way his whole being seemed attuned to the tone of Victor's voice, the slight hitch in his words, the breath he let slide out as Randall remained silent.

Setting the food aside, Randall took a large gulp of his wine—it was stronger than he expected, and he coughed, wincing. But it gave him a little shot of courage, enough to stand, holding out his hand to Victor. Their fingers laced, and Randall pulled him in close, arms sliding around Victor's waist. The music from the celebration was softer now, slower, with a raw throb through each of the notes. Randall rested his forehead against Victor's as they swayed together, the red light of the fire bathing Victor's skin.

"You are so beautiful," Randall murmured. "I don't even know what to say to you half the time. I'm certain you think I'm a complete idiot."

"I think you're the smartest man I've ever met." Victor curled his fingers into the hair at Randall's nape. "I went out to a bar last night. I wound up having a conversation with a brownie half blood. He managed to simplify things, about my feelings for you, for me in a way that I hadn't managed in my own mind."

"You met a brownie?" Pulling back, Randall searched Victor's face. "Really? What was he like? Did you know, I read a theory once that the alleged English and Scottish versions are actually their gender divisions? The English are the females and the Scottish are the males. Well, their equivalent, it's actually not certain how they reproduce, and one book I read heavily implied that they don't actually have two separate genders at all."

Victor laughed lowly and turned them slightly so Randall was looking over Victor's shoulder to the bonfire. "You could ask him yourself. He's right there."

There was a redheaded man talking with Edwin, the two of them laughing and dancing together in a loose-limbed sway around the fire. Randall grinned, shaking his head. "Leave it to my brother," he murmured. "I swear, he'd fall in love with anyone and everyone." His gaze returned to Victor. "I think I'm fine right here, though. I've found a much more interesting topic of study."

"As have I." Victor huffed in amusement. "Besides, you wouldn't want to go near him unless you want a secondhand high. Never in my life have I met someone who was that much of a stoner."

Crap. Randall started to laugh helplessly, watching Edwin and the brownie dance. "Well, then. Oh, Edwin. I hope Anthony stays close by. I shudder to think of Edwin on a munchie bender." But it seemed innocent enough. The two of them collapsed in a heap together, Edwin happily cuddling and staring up at the sky. Randall's attention was caught by Victor's fingers lightly playing through his hair. His eyes half closed and he sighed, rocking into the touch.

"A terrifying thought," Victor agreed in a hum. He sounded distracted. There was more focus in the movement of his fingers than in his words. Every stroke seemed to pull Randall in closer, like the sensation was a hook straight to his gut, and he found he was making a low rumble of noise in approval.

Around them, the music turned into a slow drumbeat, every pulse of it in the air seemingly matching the heartbeats of those around them. Randall could feel it in Victor's chest, pushed close against his, could hear it whenever Victor swayed closer. Some of the wolves around them had turned, playfully chasing one another or slumped over one another in piles of fur.

"What was simplified?" Randall asked, blinking the heavy, languid pleasure away so he could try and focus on words and not the feel of Victor's body pressed tight against his own. "You said... before, you said things were made simpler. What did you mean?"

"I'd be happy to tell you the specifics, if you like. For now, I'm not sure details matter." Victor smoothed a hand down Randall's spine, coming to rest at the small of his back. "I was very confused about how I felt about you. Now I know."

Strange, how so few words could completely stop his heart. Randall wished desperately he could look into Victor's eyes, just for a moment, to search out the meaning without having to hear the almost certain rejection. Victor's hand was like a brand on his back, their breaths all but intermingling, but Randall couldn't let himself believe this was happening. He didn't want to feel the disappointment again. "What do you know?" he finally dared to ask, gaze dropping away. "Or... no, don't tell me. This night, it's perfect. And I don't have many perfect nights. I can just pretend, if you don't say it."

"Now I'm not sure if I *should* respond." Victor chuckled. "Isn't it obvious, Randall? I'd hardly be dancing with you if I didn't want to, and believe me, I've done some very out-of-my-way things to get out of dancing." Their movements slowed as Victor looked up, his eyes coming so close to meeting Randall's that he must be staring mere millimeters away from Randall's pupil. "I can't say for sure whatever our future would hold. But I do know that I'd like to see what happens."

There was a long beat of silence, and Randall was careful, so very careful, not to move his gaze downward to meet Victor's. Instead he just tried to parse out all Victor's words, sifting through each syllable, each inflection and drop of tone, trying to make sure he understood. Trying to convince himself it was real.

241

"I've never been, uh, with anyone before," he murmured, voice low and hoarse. "I want.... I want to. With you. If you do. I mean to say...." It was a lot harder to say this than Randall had been expecting. "I'd like it if you were my first."

Victor obviously hadn't been expecting that so quickly. He blinked, clearly startled, and had to close his eyes—maybe because he was afraid of instinctively looking into Randall's. "Inexperience doesn't matter," he said, a smile tugging at the edge of his lips. "And I'd like that too."

Relief hit Randall, and he grinned, giddy, so incredibly thankful he hadn't said something horribly wrong. Fingers hooking into the front of Victor's shirt, he lightly tugged Victor in, their lips meeting. The kiss unfolded with an aching slowness, a flame of want slipping in under Randall's skin, hooking down into his gut, shuddering through him with a groan. "Your cabin?" Randall mumbled between kisses, hands sliding down to curl around Victor's hips. "Please, Victor."

"You're sure?" Concern wasn't an emotion immediately evident in Victor's face, but it was there. "It doesn't have to happen immediately, Randall. If you'd rather wait—" He broke off as a howl lifted in the air. "—that's okay with me."

The night was wild around them, the moon dancing with the stars. The fire burned brighter, painting the world in golds and reds. As the howl lingered in the air, Randall felt the surge of it in his blood, the answering sound tickling at his throat. Wolves around him lifted their own response, and Randall tipped his head back, his full, aching howl joining the chorus.

When he dipped his head back down again, Victor was looking rather flustered. "Now is good," Victor agreed hurriedly.

The grin that stretched across Randall's lips was positively feral. Lightly pushing Victor back against the wall of the cabin, Randall followed quickly, blanketing him, biting his lips, his jaw, nuzzling into his neck. "Now," he murmured, voice a hoarse growl. "I like now." The scent of the pack was difficult to ignore, the untamed celebration whispering to him, urging him to give in. To let his instincts run free. Randall was beginning to think that might not be such a bad idea. Victor certainly didn't look like he minded.

"Perhaps my cabin would be the better idea," Victor attempted to suggest. His hands were raised to Randall's shirt, white-knuckled. "Otherwise I'm going to start removing clothes right here."

No matter how much Randall's instincts were pounding in his veins, howling in the back of his mind, he definitely had no desire to be caught out on a porch with Victor taking his clothes off. So he managed a nod, forcing himself to step back and running his hand through his hair. "Quite," he agreed, straightening his sweater, pushing his glasses back up on his nose. "Please, lead the way."

Randall stooped to pick up the book, cradling it close to his chest while they quickly made their way the short distance to Victor's cabin. Alternating between unrestrained need and his own painful awareness of his inexperience, Randall was practically vibrating with nerves and want.

He needn't have worried that Victor would be put off by that. As soon as they were inside Victor's cabin and the door had been shut, Victor was hauling him close for another kiss, fingers working at Randall's buttons. Neither of them had bothered to turn on a light. The flickering glow from the bonfire, streaming in through the windows, served as illumination enough.

"I have to say, you're quite attractive when you're all… *wolfish*," Victor said lowly. "Not that you're not normally attractive anyway. But there is a certain something when you are so truly yourself."

The book was put down on whatever flat surface they happened on first, Randall fumbled off his glasses, blinking as the world swam into slightly softened edges, and his shirt was half unbuttoned before he could even begin to think. "I'm always myself," he murmured, tugging Victor's sweater off over his head, smoothing his hands down the broad stretch of Victor's shoulders. "And you are truly stunning." There was no point in talking about *him*, Randall thought. He was awkward, unimpressive. Victor, though, hidden under layers, had an absolutely magnificent form.

It seemed like Victor might be thinking the same thing of him. When Victor managed to get Randall's shirt off, he stared like Randall had recalled he'd done on the night of the full moon. The smile that came over Victor's face was the closest to a pleased grin as Randall had ever seen on him. Victor didn't even seem to notice the vampire-given scars. His gaze skipped right over them as if they were just regular skin. Randall would have covered them up again, his hands were even moving to do so, to pull his shirt back up over them and hide, but Victor was right there, kissing him, smiling, as if there was nothing to be ashamed of.

"Bed's right there," Victor said, his usual thoughtfulness in his grammar and wording completely vanished. He ignored his own words, though, hands drifting down Randall's sides as he kissed him again, the edge of need in their actions heightening with every touch. Randall pulled Victor's T-shirt off of him, sucking in a breath when, at last, he had acres of skin bared for his consideration. Slowly, he dragged his fingers down Victor's chest, bumping over his nipple, down to the dip of his stomach. Randall's mouth followed, slow, sucking kisses mapping his trail. Randall hooked one hand into the belt loops of Victor's trousers and tugged him back toward the bed.

Randall sat on the edge of the mattress, Victor standing between his legs, at the perfect height for Randall to do more exploring. He bit lightly at Victor's side, tracing his tongue back up to the hollow of Victor's throat. He stopped there, though, pulling back, unsure. "Can I?" he murmured, hand absently sweeping up and down Victor's stomach. "Your throat. I…. I don't want to overstep." Because there was sex, yes, but baring a throat? That was something else entirely.

Victor had flushed a pale shade of red, his eyes glazed. He opened his mouth to reply and seemed to be unable to. Instead, he nearly met Randall's eyes again and very deliberately tipped his chin back. "You can do absolutely anything you like," Victor said lowly, his voice more breath than sound.

The permission sent a vicious thrill through him. Randall didn't realize how *much* he'd feel that desire, how deeply Victor's bared throat would affect him. With a rumbling, possessive growl, Randall wrapped his hands around Victor's hips, yanking him in closer, rising up to stand with Victor, to press closer, stealing his warmth. He nipped at Victor's shoulder, his chest, leading his way to his neck. Taking his time.

When Randall finally closed his teeth around that beautiful, pale arc, he had to stop, all but trembling, the growl deepening in his throat.

His. It was thrumming through him, whole body pulsating with it. Victor had tangled a hand in his hair, his grip tight, almost on the verge of pain, keeping Randall exactly where he was. *His*. Randall bit down harder, just enough to dimple the skin with his teeth, to send a flush curling along the skin from his action.

With a sharp bark, he turned them, Victor sprawled out on the bed, Randall following. He blanketed Victor's body with his own. Victor clutched his free hand at Randall's back, nails digging into skin. Randall returned to his neck, peppering kisses and soft, sucking bites, marking him. Claiming him.

Until his nose brushed up against the scars. Pulling back with a frown, Randall was panting, eyes blazing yellow, the light of the flames outside flickering across his bared skin. He didn't like that scar.

Victor didn't let him think about it for too long. He rose up to meet Randall, using the hand he still had buried in Randall's hair to pull him back in. "I'm sure there's a more eloquent way to say it, but I was rather enjoying that," Victor panted. His eyes were darker now, his breath shorter. "Forgive my ignorance. Do I do it in return? I'd like to."

Blinking, Randall rubbed his thumb along Victor's cheek, a smile easing across his face. Some of the overwhelming possessive instinct faded, and he nuzzled in soft kisses to Victor's jaw. "If you want. It's a sense of claiming. It means… it means you're mine. Right now, in this moment, you're mine."

Victor nodded slowly. "And do I get to make you mine at this moment in return?"

The surge of heat that rippled through him at that question was utterly surprising. "Yes," he whispered. Begged, almost. He tipped his chin back, baring his throat completely. Giving Victor every intimate part of himself. "Yes, I'm yours. I've been yours." It wasn't a permanent thing. It probably didn't even register to Victor what submitting meant to a wolf. But for this moment, in this place, they were both giving themselves to each other. And that mattered. The marks would fade, the moment would pass, but for now, they were as vulnerable with each other as a wolf could be.

He felt Victor's hand clap around the right side of his neck, and Randall had a moment of pure panic, of freezing entirely. The mess of scars left by the vampires' bites was low on his throat there, and Randall was sure Victor was going to touch them, to send all this gentle pleasure into remembered pain. But Victor's fingers stayed up by Randall's jaw, far away from the knotted, pale marks. Then the gentle contact of Victor's teeth on the other side made Randall forget them entirely. He felt the blunt pressure of a light bite, teeth barely sinking into the skin, not enough to even ache, but the meaning was clear. He had bared his throat to Victor, and Victor wasn't ripping it out. The shared bites were just a light reinforcement of power, of being equals. Randall moaned softly, fingers threading into Victor's hair, riding the wave of intense, sudden pleasure the bites gave him. "God," he managed in a shaky exhale. He'd had *no* idea that it could feel like that.

The pressure of teeth released, much to his disappointment, but Victor made up for it by moving up to kiss him. "I quite like that ritual," Victor said lowly, wrapping a hand around Randall's hip. "It's a shame I don't have one of my own to share with you."

Laughing softly, Randall moved to lie on his side, watching Victor, sharing slow, deep kisses. "You could teach me what to do next?" he suggested. "I'm afraid that there is a rather large gap in my knowledge. I have been told, though—" He lightly sucked on Victor's lower lip. "—I am an excellent student."

"So I've observed," Victor said, rising up to kneel over Randall, hands trailing down his chest. "I must admit I'm spoiled for choice as to where to start." He leaned down, stealing one more kiss before he shifted, hooking his fingers around Randall's belt. "May I?"

Yeah, like he was going to stop now. Randall lifted his hips, helping Victor tug his pants and boxers away, flushing once he realized how exposed he was. Being unclothed before and after shifting was somehow very, very different than this. He distracted himself by painting curves and whorls against Victor's arms, watching as goose bumps chased his fingers.

Randall had obviously guessed right earlier about contact to the stomach feeling good; Victor did it to him in return, his lips tracing soft paths over Randall's collarbone down to the jut of his hip bones. Eyes fluttering shut, Randall arched up into each press of Victor's lips, a surprised moan torn from his lips.

By the time Victor had gotten to his thighs, Randall was starting to feel a bit short of breath. Victor looked up at him. "Is there anything you'd like me *not* to do?" he asked, ducking down again to rake his teeth over Randall's left thigh. His next words were murmured against skin. "I want to make sure you enjoy yourself."

"Don't stop," was all Randall could think to say. His legs had spread automatically, heels digging into the mattress. Randall's wide eyes stared down at Victor, completely unsure of what might happen next. His body felt like it was burning from the inside, want a constant pressure, itching under his skin. "Just... please, don't stop."

He felt Victor's lips curve in a smile against his skin. "Stopping is the very last thing on my mind right now." Crouched above him, his eyes dark and a smile on his lips, the firelight flickering over pale skin, Victor looked as wolfish at that moment as any of them dancing outside.

Victor's hand traced a path from Randall's knee upward; he was obviously enjoying taking his time. Every touch was frustrating in the best kind of way, so when Victor's fingers finally smoothed over Randall's cock, curling around it, Randall's breath left his lungs like he'd been punched. Victor only glanced up at him briefly before looking back down, heat and need flushing over his skin.

"I have to admit I did stare quite a bit, on the full moon." Victor's voice had gotten huskier. "I attempted to not be a *complete* pervert and stare below the belt. I should have. I was missing out on quite a lot." As if to punctuate his point, his fingertips slid lightly from the base of Randall's cock to the tip, exploring so gently it almost seemed it shouldn't affect Randall so profoundly. And yet.

Muffling a stunned whimper, biting his lip, Randall's head fell back. He'd touched himself on occasion, of course, but this was nothing like that. This was so intense that Randall honestly wasn't sure if he should move his hips up, hold still, or just beg for more. He wound up doing some awkward roll upward, a strangled groan lost in his panted breaths. "Please," he managed. He wanted something more, something he couldn't even begin to try to articulate. So he just asked again, "Please, Victor."

He had the presence of mind to note that Victor looked rather pleased by his lack of ability to speak coherently. Victor leaned over him, a forearm braced on the bed next to Randall's head to hold himself up, their lips inches away from each other as they shared breath. Victor's hand on him curled around him properly then, his grip tightening. Randall wasn't even sure *what* kind of noise he made right then, but the pleased look on Victor's face only grew stronger.

Then, as Victor started moving his hand with long, slow strokes, Randall had to make a conscious effort to not lose it right then and there. Victor ducked down to kiss at Randall's throat again with another gentle bite. Randall wrapped his legs around Victor's hips, eyes glazed as he got lost in the slide of Victor's hand, the friction of his palm, pleasure nearly overwhelming as it tightened in his gut.

"I think...." Randall's voice cracked, a desperate whimper trailing after the words. He moved up into Victor's hand, one hand fisted in Victor's hair, body moving out of pure instinct and need. "I think I might be... close."

In response, Victor slowed the movements of his hand to a standstill. The loss of friction made Randall groan in frustration, but Victor swallowed the noise with a kiss. "My apologies." There was a gentle laugh under Victor's voice, not directed *at* Randall, but a fond noise. "I did want to do a few more things before you finished. While I'm sure your stamina is excellent, I do like variety."

"What else is there?" Randall said, too stunned to censor himself. Yes, fine, he had *some* knowledge of other things, but honestly, that had felt perfectly good. He couldn't imagine anything being *better*.

"Some things I'd like to save for a later date," Victor said. He was just holding Randall now, but even then the contact still felt incredible. "But believe me when I say there are *many* more options." He moved down again, his teeth catching on Randall's hip for a moment before pressing his lips lightly to the base of Randall's cock.

Jerking backward, Randall stared down at Victor, eyes huge. "What... that's not sanitary." Which was probably the most idiotic thing ever said during sex, but Randall was honestly a little too surprised to gather his wits correctly.

Victor lifted his eyebrows at Randall, then very deliberately pushed his tongue against Randall's cock, running a path around the head.

The moan that lifted from Randall's chest was so loud, so drawn out, he was quite sure they would hear it over the music outside. Maybe he *really* didn't care about hygiene right then. Legs spreading wider, back arched, Randall panted, "Fair point."

Victor didn't seem to want to push him over the edge. His touches were light, the contact of his tongue brief but lingering. For far too short a time, Victor wrapped his lips around him and sucked, but backed off a second later, a positively fiendish look in his eye.

Randall was making noises he didn't even know existed. "That," he managed thickly. "That is good. Do that."

His vocabulary had apparently been reduced to caveman speak. Perhaps all that talk about blood flow and two heads was more than a joke. He felt as if his intelligence had been reduced to the way his body moved, the way Victor was touching him, not that he could imagine anything else mattering.

When Victor went back to what he'd been doing before—that incredible suction and the soft pressure of his tongue—Randall had to actively think about not coming. And again, Victor seemed to know just when he should back off, because he did so. Victor dropped his hands to his own belt, frowning as he tried to concentrate enough to undo it. Randall was suddenly obsessed with the idea of getting Victor naked, of touching like Victor had touched him. He sat up, fingers joining Victor's to pull his belt open. Randall eagerly tugged Victor's pants down, biting his lip, eyes wide as he finally freed his cock.

"God, you're perfect," he mumbled, happily wrapping a hand around Victor. He stroked slowly, mimicking Victor's movements, dragging his hand up to the head, thumb lightly tracing over the slit. Randall watched Victor's face to try to study his reactions. Apparently he was right on target. Victor sucked in a sharp breath, and his head fell back, baring his throat once more.

"You certainly are a quick learner," Victor said, watching Randall through heavy-lidded eyes. Randall liked that expression.

"I have a very good teacher," Randall responded, pressing kisses to Victor's throat, tightening his fingers as he stroked faster. "Tell me, professor, is there an advanced move? Because I seem to recall hearing something about, uh, penetration. That sounds very interesting."

"Would it be strange of me to want to save that?" Victor looked oddly hesitant in the jumping light of the fire, as if he wasn't sure that Randall would agree with him. "I'd like to at least make you dinner first."

Laughing, Randall gave in to the impulse to kiss Victor softly. "Are we dating now?"

"I'd like to." Victor gave him a hopeful smile, which clashed oddly with the heat in his eyes and the flex of his fingers over Randall's cock.

They were moving together then, stroking each other in matching rhythms. They shared air, kisses, soft little moans. "Yes," Randall agreed. "I would too." He grinned then, sharply, biting Victor's lip hard enough to see it flush. "Now stop teasing me."

"As you wish." A sly smile took over Victor's expression. He leaned his weight on Randall, bearing them both back down onto the mattress, Victor's body pinning him down. They shifted just slightly, Victor burying a pant of breath against Randall's shoulder when their cocks came into contact. Victor lifted him, bracing himself above Randall as he pushed his hips down, rubbing them together. "Is this more to your liking?"

"Victor, I am twenty-four and a virgin. *Everything* is to my liking, you prat." But Randall was moaning over the sound of Victor's quiet noise of amusement in reply, hips rocking upward into Victor's, the friction driving him mad. Randall's hand slid down Victor's back to grasp the curve of his ass, hooking him in closer.

Victor apparently wasn't in the mood for slow anymore. They grasped at each other, rocking together, the bed squeaking under them. Randall pressed his heels into the mattress, thrusting upward, every rub of their bodies together sending sparks of beautiful friction through him. The sound of the drums outside had slowed to an intimate beat, seeming to throb in the very air around them.

They kissed once more, softly at first, their urgency growing with every press of movement. Randall dimly noticed the pop and crackle of someone adding new wood to the bonfire. It sent the flame flaring brighter, red and gold and yellow light pulsing in through the window to flash over their skin.

With a shaky breath, Victor reached between them, and Randall bit down on a sharp moan at the feel of Victor's hand wrapping around both of them. Coordination became a thing of the past, both of them driven by blind need. Randall's hand joined his, fingers tangling together, kisses so messy and desperate they became nothing more than sharing pants of air.

He felt it start as if his body were a coil, wound so tight it was vibrating. Randall gasped Victor's name, rocking forward one more time, coming in a sudden flash of release. Randall sagged back, head pressed against the pillow, gasping in low, dragging whimpers. Dazed, he rode the wave of pleasure until all he could do was sprawl out under Victor, completely spent.

Victor went still, nearly trembling with the effort of it. He lifted a hand, trailing his fingertips down Randall's cheek. When he spoke, it wasn't in English, rather in a rolling language that Randall managed to recognize as ancient Sumerian. He wasn't nearly fluent in the language, but he knew enough—particularly the piece of the poem that Victor said right then, a rather dirty few lines about the size of Randall's cock and the beauty of his release.

Laughing then, feeling an exalted sense of connection, of bliss that seemed far too big for his body to contain, Randall flipped them over. Victor on his back under him, Randall nudged their foreheads together, hand tightening on Victor's cock. "Come for me," he murmured, stroking him faster, twisting his wrist to hear that one beautiful moan. Randall nuzzled kisses down Victor's neck. As Victor lifted his chin to bare his throat, Randall bit him softly, then harder, sucking at the skin to leave it flushed. "My beautiful medusa, I want to see you fly."

Victor grabbed at his arm, squeezing hard—Randall took the action as permission to bite down a little harder on Victor's neck, so that the skin dented under his teeth. Not enough to give a black-and-blue bruise, but hovering just at the edge of marking. Under the skin his teeth was gripping, Randall felt more than heard Victor moan, his muscles trembling, arching up underneath Randall as he came.

He was breathtaking. No one would ever look at Victor like this and think he was anything but magnificent, Randall was sure. He pulled back to watch him, slowly stroking him through the orgasm until Victor shivered under his touch. "But, like a sad slave, stay and think of nought, save, where you are, how happy you make those. So true a fool is love, that in your will, though you do anything, he thinks no ill." The words came out almost without Randall realizing he'd said them. He paused and smiled, sliding his thumb along Victor's lips. "I once did a paper on that sonnet. I didn't understand it until now. How you could want someone so completely that even the pain doesn't matter as much."

Victor just looked back at him, blankly dazed and still flushed. "Do you expect me to be able to understand Shakespeare when I've just had a frankly phenomenal orgasm?" he said breathlessly. "You think too highly of me."

The grin Randall had as they kissed was absolutely impossible to restrain. "My poor professor," he murmured, nudging kisses against the marks he'd left on Victor's neck. "You are amazing. And absolutely beautiful. I should tell you that every day."

"You sound rather coherent," Victor said, his voice slow, dragging at the words. "Should I be insulted that I didn't do a good enough job?"

"Am I not supposed to be?" Randall entertained himself by kissing down Victor's body, dragging his lips down the dip in the middle of Victor's chest, the soft expanse of his stomach, the length of his side. "You did incredibly. I have never felt anything that good. Ever." Randall grinned wickedly. "I am very much looking forward to further lessons."

Victor's chest moved with a silent laugh. "We're men, even if we are a half blood and a wolf. There's a stereotype about men, where after we've come we roll over and start snoring." Victor tilted his head in interest at Randall, his eyelids drooped low with contentment. "Perhaps that doesn't apply to wolves?"

"I don't know," Randall admitted, circling his tongue around Victor's belly button. "I know I want to devour you." He lightly bit at Victor's hip. "But if you'd rather I sleep, I think I can manage that for you."

Victor gave a wordless hum, stroking his hand along Randall's arm. "My body says sleep. My mind says I'm good for another round," he mused, his fingertips reaching Randall's shoulder in slow exploration.

"I wonder if I can change your body's inclination," Randall murmured. He traced his tongue experimentally down the length of Victor's cock. Even soft, he was so beautiful and perfectly large. "What do you think?"

"I think that sounds like a very good idea." Victor's voice had dropped into a husk again. Randall lightly pursed his lips over the head of Victor's cock, eyes locked on his face, watching as Victor bit his lip at the sensation, hips arching up into it. "Christ, Randall."

Yes, he definitely enjoyed that reaction. He wanted more of that. Slowly, Randall lowered his mouth onto Victor's dick. He couldn't manage much, but he definitely liked the feel of Victor starting to harden against his tongue, the way Victor's leg shook when he sucked a little harder.

The gunshot outside was not really part of his fantasy coming true.

Randall jerked upright, eyes widening, ears pricked. Silence pounded around them, throbbing with every wild beat of Randall's heart, and after a moment, he'd nearly convinced himself he was hearing things. Victor was motionless underneath him, breath caught in his lungs in fear. Randall looked over at him, hand finding Victor's, shaking his head. Surely it was nothing. He almost believed it too. Until there was an even louder burst of gunfire and a high-pitched wail of a howl.

He knew that voice. "Edwin," Randall gasped, surging off the bed and scrambling for the door. As soon as he'd jerked it open, he was shifting, changing. He leaped from the porch on two legs and landed on four, skidding on the loose dirt and powering his way toward the bonfire, ears laid back and body a low streak against the ground.

There were hunters.

Anthony was at his side in a second, fangs glinting in the bonfire light. They shared a wordless look, then ran toward where Edwin's howl was still echoing. God knew where the hunters had come from. Edwin came tearing back into the camp, the redheaded brownie in front of him. Edwin was herding him with bumps of his head, shoving the brownie into a nearby cabin with a growl.

Relief hit Randall. He and Anthony charged toward their brother, meeting Edwin halfway. More gunfire, another howl, and the wolves were panicking. Randall looked at Anthony, crowding around Edwin as if to protect him, but what could they do? He couldn't even tell where the hunters were. The half bloods that had traipsed through the camp earlier had confused the scents, and now it was taking him longer to pick out where the humans might be.

The wolves around him were having the same problem, noses lifted to air, and huffs of confusion filled the camp.

Until Jed came storming out of his cabin, gun in each hand, Redford as a wolf by his side. "Anthony, you gorgeous bastard," Jed hollered. "Get your pert ass over here." He clicked the safety off, striding toward the woods. "Get behind me. I'm going to lay down cover fire; you're going to take three wolves to the right. Redford? You get three more and go to the left. Circle around. We're pinning these fuckers to the goddamn ground."

Redford bumped his side against Jed's legs in acknowledgement, his head turning to seek out wolves. Silently, three stepped forward to stand by his side. Mallory joined Anthony, Randall and Edwin standing shoulder to shoulder with their brother. Redford tipped his head back, letting loose a long, hoarse howl before he and his three followers darted into the woods. Anthony followed suit. They kept their bodies low to the ground and their paws away from twigs and loose rocks as they silently slipped into the forest. Jed was smart, not drawing the hunters out. It was dark in the woods, the firelight and the moon doing nothing to pierce the dense leaves overhead. Wolves could see just fine. The humans, however, would be limited.

There was a rapid burst of gunfire from the camp, aimed high over the wolves' heads. Then return fire, indicating exactly where the hunters were clumped together. As Jed kept them busy, Randall followed Anthony, the four wolves moving rapidly toward the humans, silent and deadly.

There were six of them, hunters in camouflage gear, guns spread out and ensconced behind a barrier of fallen trees. They had a clear view toward the camp, and Randall watched as one of them took aim and fired at Jed, nearly hitting him. Jed kept moving, strafing back and forth, firing nearly unceasingly, keeping himself as a difficult target to pin down. Across the other side of the hunters, Randall could see the other group of wolves approach.

None of the hunters noticed the wolves until one of them—Redford, Randall thought it might be—leaped forward, jaw snapping down on his arm. There was a flurry of movement, cursing, gunfire. One of the wolves jumped at the hunters, only to be cut down in midleap. Randall knocked a hunter over, ripping at his arm, tearing the skin open and leaving him lying there, unable to grip his weapon.

It was chaos, howls and whimpers of pain, shouts and bullets and blood. Randall tried to keep his eye on Edwin, but he lost him when a hunter rushed at him, kicking him aside and aiming a gun at his head. For a moment, it was all over, Randall struggling to get his legs under him again, the bullet one squeezed trigger away from hitting him.

The hunter didn't see Anthony leaping at him until it was too late. The gun went off, the bullet hitting a tree a few feet away from Randall, and the hunter screeched in pain as sharp fangs bit into him. Randall managed to get himself up, joining Anthony, thumping the hunter's head back and knocking him out.

Jed had arrived, and he was calmly, efficiently finishing off the last of the hunters. All except one. He hauled the last one up by the throat, baring his teeth and aiming a gun directly between the hunter's eyes. "Go home," Jed told him roughly. "Piss your pants, thank your fucking lucky stars, and *go home*. And when you're there, you call your boss and you tell him to back the fuck off. I mean you're done. All of you. If I see one more fucking hunter here, I will personally track everyone down and I will slaughter you. Name's Jed Walker. You don't believe me? Look me up."

He shoved the hunter back to the ground, watching impassively as the man scurried away into the woods, one of the wolves chasing after him for good measure.

Randall nudged his nose against Anthony, checking that he was all right. He was moving slowly, but there was no blood on him—a long night and dancing probably meant that his joints weren't as fluid as they should be. Anthony leaned his side against Randall, and they trotted over to Edwin.

Who was standing over a corpse. The man's throat had been ripped out. Edwin's muzzle was covered in blood. Edwin wasn't moving, didn't acknowledge them. He was staring down, horror evident in his eyes, the way his tail was tucked between his legs.

Edwin had once cried over a bird he'd accidentally knocked from a nest. They'd killed to eat before; they'd killed what they needed. Edwin was too kind to harm anything for any other reason. And now there was a human lying on the ground, bloody and ravaged, and Edwin had put him there. However justified, however much it'd been in self-defense, in protection, Edwin couldn't seem to see that right then. He was whimpering, Randall realized, low in his throat, a heartbreakingly ragged sound.

Anthony nudged his nose against Edwin's neck, pushing down slightly. He waited until Edwin had lain down, and very carefully started grooming the blood from his face. Randall remembered Anthony doing that countless times to them as children—when Randall had broken his leg after slipping in mud, Anthony had just pinned him down and groomed him until Randall had fashioned a splint and set the bone. It was a comforting action, a reassurance. Randall went to lie down next to Edwin, grooming his other side, nudging his nose in behind Edwin's ear. Surrounding him with family.

Jed came over, studying the scene and sighing heavily. "Oh, Lassie," he murmured, shaking his head. He grabbed the dead hunter's arms, dragging the body away to lay it with the others. There were two men still alive and unconscious. The rest had been taken down by wolves or Jed's guns. Randall wondered what Jed would do with the survivors.

Nudging his face against Anthony's, Randall pulled away and shifted back. The pine needles of the forest floor were cool under his feet. "What are your plans for those two?" he asked, moving toward Jed.

"Haul them back to the camp, bind up whatever's bleeding, and drop them off at the nearest town before they wake up." Jed's eyes flicked over to Randall. "I'm not a monster, kid. I'm not going to kill someone I don't have to. At this point, there's no reason to kill anybody else. Won't send a message we haven't already, and they're sure as hell not going to be shooting back anytime soon."

Randall nodded. "I'll help." He and Jed muscled one of the wounded men up between them, carefully carrying him back toward the camp. An older man was waiting for them, a black bag in his hands. No herbs there, just actual medicine.

"Cedric," Redford greeted gratefully. He'd shifted back to two legs, and looked as unconcerned as any of them about being naked. "You have no idea how glad I am to see you."

251

"Get this guy good enough to travel. Can you keep him unconscious?" Jed lowered the hunter to the ground, Randall gratefully dropping his end of the burden as well.

"I could keep him down with a sedative. Or I could paralyze him and let him feel the pain of his wounds." Cedric seemed positively gleeful about that last idea. "Your choice, Mr. Walker."

Jed was just studying the hunter, jaw working. "Sedate the bastard," he muttered, stomping back toward the woods, Redford on his heels. "He was just doing a job."

Randall found himself pinned under the weight of Cedric's gaze. "You, there. Are your wits intact enough to hand me equipment?"

"My wits are fine, thank you." Randall crouched next to him, studying the man. "You're a doctor, then? Not, uh, someone who uses odd-smelling pastes?"

Cedric made an irritated grumbling noise under his breath. "I have a degree and decades of hospital experience. Pastes are for cavemen, and we are in the twenty-first century." A snort rumbled through him, reminding Randall rather vividly of a warthog in an irritated slump. "Not that all their ideas are bad, mind you. Had a nice conversation the other day about natural painkillers. Sometimes the old ideas are the best. But broken bones and cancer, now. Those need something more than incense waving. At least, that's this old doctor's opinion." He looked at Randall, his hands paused above the hunter's body. "Are you one of the Lewis brothers? Redford spoke to me about your eldest brother."

"He has canine Parkinson's," Randall said quietly. "Human doctors are out of the question. We came here for help, but.... I honestly don't think they're doing anything. I had hoped alternative medicine might lend us some sort of relief, but...." Randall hadn't wanted to admit any of this. How profoundly he'd failed. How *wrong* he had been. This was supposed to be their great cure, their last-ditch effort. And nothing was working. "I think he's getting worse. He's in a lot of pain right now. Do you have anything that could help him? Even getting a full night's sleep would do wonders for him."

"I can do my best," Cedric said gruffly. "Now for God's sake, stop talking so that I can treat this hunter and we can all go back to our warm beds."

Randall just gave him a brief smile, biting back a laugh. "Yes, sir." He'd had a professor his first semester that made Cedric seem like a cuddly teddy bear. He could handle a bit of grump. "What do you need?"

Jed arrived then with Redford, carrying the second hunter between them. "I've got some of the guys digging graves," Jed said, sounding unusually somber. "We'll bury them where they fell. I took their wallets. We'll leave them with these two so they can take care of notifying whoever the fuck needs to be."

"I'll get started on that," Redford murmured to Jed. "You go with Cedric and the hunters back to the camp, just in case they wake."

Jed gave Redford a quick kiss. "Be safe, babe. I'll be back in two hours."

Randall and Cedric worked together to wrap bandages around whatever wounds the hunters had, with Cedric wrapping and Randall lifting whatever limb Cedric needed him to. It didn't take more than a few minutes before Cedric declared them ready to travel, and glared at various wolves until they shifted back to help carry the hunters. Randall watched as Jed finished loading everything in the van. He and Cedric climbed in and took off, their taillights disappearing around the bend.

And then it was over. An hour ago he'd been wrapped up in Victor, in slow kisses and hands sliding on skin. And now he was dirty, he had blood smeared in odd places, and three men were dead. Rubbing his hand through his hair, Randall sighed and took off to find his brothers. Nothing like a perfect end to a perfect evening.

Anthony was still next to Edwin. The blood had been cleaned off Edwin's face, but they hadn't moved. Randall carefully sat, and Edwin rested his chin on Randall's knee, looking up at him with huge, sad eyes. Ever since he'd been a kid, Edwin had felt safer in his wolf form. It was unsurprising that now he'd stay shifted, even if it meant that a conversation was going to be distinctly one-sided. Randall gave Anthony a helpless look, rubbing his hand across Edwin's face, scratching absently behind his ear.

Well, they couldn't stay out in the woods for the rest of the night. So Randall stood again, scooping Edwin up and holding him close to his chest. He'd done this all the time when Edwin was a puppy. He was distinctly heavier now, but Randall just shifted his weight and started the slow walk back toward their cabin.

They managed to get inside, Anthony jumping up onto the bed where Randall put Edwin. Edwin curled up in a ball, his tail over his nose, watching Randall and Anthony quietly. Anthony shifted back and pulled on some sweats, then went to sit beside Edwin.

After what felt like an eternally long stretch of silence, Anthony said, "It's sad that you had to take a life, Edwin. But I'm proud that you saved lives by doing it."

Edwin whined lowly, turning to nudge his nose into Anthony's side. Randall quietly went and found a pair of loose pajama pants to pull on, grabbing a blanket for Edwin. "You did good, Ed," Randall told him, crouching by the bed and carefully covering Edwin up. "If you hadn't killed him, he would have killed us. You did what you had to."

After a long moment, with a sigh, Edwin shifted back. He wound up curled on the bed, his head resting on Anthony's knee. "You didn't kill anyone," he pointed out quietly, tears brimming in his eyes. He looked so *young*. So vulnerable. Randall felt a spasm of guilt for letting Edwin be a part of that, of all of it, of a war that seemed so determined to shatter their quiet, sheltered lives.

"Redford did," Anthony replied, smoothing his hand over Edwin's hair. "Jed did too."

"I would have," Randall told Edwin. "To protect you guys, I absolutely would have."

"But it's okay to mourn." Anthony looked pained, the corners of his lips pinched with guilt. Randall knew what he was thinking. Anthony was wishing he'd been the one to kill that hunter, not Edwin. Their whole lives, Anthony had been protecting them, had been taking on the hard stuff so they didn't have to. Of course he'd wish he could take this too. "It's okay to feel sad, Edwin."

"Taking a life should always be something somber." Randall wasn't nearly as good at this sort of thing, but he tried. "Like when we thank the earth for giving us meat to eat. You protected your pack. There's nothing to feel guilty about. But taking a life is something worth feeling remorse over. It would have been better if we'd never been in that position. The fact that we were doesn't change that it sucks."

Edwin sighed, but at least he was looking at both of them, less frozen and remote. "Can you guys stay with me tonight?"

It wasn't until Edwin asked that Randall remembered Victor. He'd left him in the cabin; surely he'd be worried by now. "Yeah, Ed," Randall said, gently rubbing Edwin's shoulder. "How about you take a shower? I'm going to go, uh, use Victor's shower, I think. I'll be back as soon as I'm not covered in mud." He very deliberately did not meet Anthony's gaze at that, trying to sound casual. He wasn't sure if he succeeded.

Despite the heavy mood, Anthony smirked suddenly. "So *that's* why I can smell medusa all over you. Have fun in *Victor's shower*."

"Shut up, Ant," Randall grumbled, but he couldn't help his smile. One last hug to Edwin and Randall eased out of the door, making his way back to Victor's cabin. He hadn't bothered to put on a shirt or shoes. He really did need to wash, and he could put on his clothes after.

He knocked lightly on the door, cautiously poking his head in. "Uh, Victor? Are you still awake?"

He was grabbed in a hug before he could really react. "Good *God*, you're all right," Victor breathed in relief. Randall's arms slowly went around Victor's waist, pulling him in closer. "I'm sorry I didn't join the, er, attack force. After my last attempt I thought it prudent to stay out of the way." Victor drew back, cupping Randall's face between his hands. "*Are* you all right?"

A very faint, rueful smile touched one corner of Randall's mouth. "Edwin killed one of the hunters. He's... understandably not doing well. And Anthony's in pain, even though he'd never admit it. But I think they'll be fine with a night's sleep." Randall rested his hand over Victor's heart. "I'm glad you stayed inside. I don't know what I'd do if something happened to you."

"I'm glad your brothers are okay." Victor raised an eyebrow. "But I did ask about you, specifically. You're not injured?"

Blinking, surprised, Randall glanced down at himself. "I don't think so, no. I nearly... one of the hunters nearly...." Randall pressed his lips together, shaking his head. "I'm perfectly fine. Not hurt at all."

Victor nodded. "Is there anything I can do to help?"

Randall simply wrapped his arms more tightly around Victor, nudging his nose into Victor's neck and taking a deep breath. "This. This is extraordinarily helpful." After a moment, though, he pulled back with an apologetic wince. "I'm sorry. I'm a mess. I, uh, I don't suppose I could use your shower?"

"By all means, use away," Victor said. He looked reluctant to step back from Randall, but he did so in order to gather Randall's clothes from where they'd been carelessly tossed. "There's everything you'd need in there. I hope my shampoo doesn't smell horrendous to a nose of your caliber."

A faint grin crossed Randall's face, and he pulled Victor back in to sniff enthusiastically at Victor's hair. "No, I think that's good," he informed Victor innocently. "I quite like how you smell."

There was a quick knock at the door, interrupting them. Randall went to it, cautiously pulling it open to find Mallory. "Sorry to bother you," Mallory said, giving him an amused look with a glance back at Victor. "We're setting up a heightened patrol around the camp for tonight. The Gray Lady wishes to speak with you and your group in the morning." It wasn't phrased as a request.

254

Randall nodded. "I'm about to head back to my brothers. I'll let them know."

"Good. We're asking everyone to stay inside until morning as well. Just for security." Mallory nodded at them both before taking off for the cabin Redford and Jed were sharing.

"Well, that's going to be an interesting meeting." Randall shoved his hair back, sighing wearily. He shuffled toward the bathroom, taking his clothes from Victor. He hesitated, their fingers barely touching, searching Victor's face. "Have you... thought about it at all? What you'd do if the wolves really leave?" Perhaps this wasn't the right time to ask. Maybe there was no good time. But the question was out there, hanging between them, and Randall knew he couldn't take it back even if he'd wanted to.

"If you'd asked me a few days ago, my answer would have been very different," Victor sighed. "Now? I have to admit, I don't particularly like the thought of never seeing you again. I'm not sure what that means for my plans."

It wasn't a definite answer, but considering they'd only barely started, and Victor would have to uproot his entire life and his job the same as them, Randall figured he couldn't expect much more. Randall took Victor's hand and lightly kissed his palm, eyes closed. "That's what I think too," he murmured. He couldn't leave his brothers. Anthony needed the pack. After everything Randall had done to get them there, he couldn't just walk away.

So what could that possibly mean for him and Victor?

"I'm going to shower and then go back to my brothers," he said quietly. "Edwin needs us there tonight. I was thinking about reading him some P.G. Wodehouse." Randall gave Victor a slight smile. "I don't know how you feel about things like that, or if you'd even want, but I thought I'd mention... my bed there is plenty large enough for two. If you were thinking about going to sleep soon and thought company sounded nice."

"That depends on if your brothers snore." The arch tone of Victor's voice was softened by the squeeze of his hand on Randall's.

"Oh, we all do. Very loudly." Randall's teasing smile just barely crinkled the corners of his eyes. "It's a wolf thing."

He left Victor to consider if he wanted to risk such a task, taking a quick shower and gratefully washing dried blood from his side, mud from his hair. When he came out, towel wrapped around his waist, he felt moderately more himself. A good sleep would take care of the rest, he was sure.

"Not much of an afterglow, was it?" Randall quickly tugged on his slacks, pulling on his shirt and trying to find where he'd set his glasses down. "I have to say, though, as far as first times go, I can't imagine anything better."

"I'm sure we'll get a chance to try for a better aftermath." Victor pressed Randall's glasses into his hand. "Are we going back to your cabin now?"

We. Randall smiled. Picking up the book Victor had gifted him with, he reached out with his other hand. "Yes. I think that sounds like a plan." They walked together, Randall leaning his shoulder against Victor's, feeling at that moment like there was very little he'd change in his personal life. However confused he might be about his and Victor's future, he had this moment, and that was worth quite a bit.

"Edwin, I hope you have pants on," Randall said as they entered. "Victor is going to sleep with me." He said it boldly, chin out, almost defying his brothers to refuse Victor entrance.

"As long as I don't hear anything below the belt going on," Anthony grumbled. He seemed preoccupied with Edwin, who was in bed, fussing over his blankets. Randall got a spare pair of pajamas from his bag and handed them over to Victor.

"You can change in the bathroom, if you like." He smiled at Victor, lightly touching the marks on Victor's neck, wanting very much to kiss them. He contented himself with squeezing Victor's hand. "There's a couple of spare toothbrushes in my gray bag on the sink too. Help yourself."

Edwin was watching them quietly, but even he didn't seem to be much in the mood to comment as Victor went to the bathroom. Anthony had shoved all three beds together so it was one huge mattress to sleep on. Edwin curled up against Randall when he'd changed and crawled in, book in hand. "Are you going to read to me, big brother?" Edwin asked, sounding weary.

"I thought I might, yes." Randall left the far side of the bed for Victor, slinging his arm around Edwin, squeezing Anthony's shoulder. "Does that sound okay?"

"It better not be some textbook," Edwin grumbled, but he settled himself under the blankets and seemed quite content to stay, regardless of the reading material.

"Hey, don't complain," Anthony snorted. "A textbook would send you right off to sleep, and that's the aim."

"Besides, you might even learn something," Randall teased, laughing when Edwin poked him in the side. "Oh, hush. You'll like this." He honestly had no idea what the book was about, but anything Victor had cherished since he was a child Randall was absolutely certain he'd love. As Edwin settled in, Randall met Anthony's eyes. "The Gray Lady wants to see us in the morning."

Anthony just nodded, curling up under the covers. He looked exhausted. Randall didn't blame him for not wanting more to worry about. Randall turned the pages to the start of the book, smiling fondly at Victor when he emerged from the bathroom. Randall had to admit, he quite liked the look of Victor wearing his clothes. As Randall started to read, he pulled down the covers next to him, waiting for Victor to slide in.

Victor looked a little awkward as he got in, obviously not used to the idea of sleeping in one big bed with three siblings. Randall hadn't thought it odd. They had done it a lot, especially when they'd been younger or the one winter their fireplace had gotten stopped up and they hadn't been able to heat the house. He nearly apologized to Victor, but Victor settled soon enough, curled up on his side facing Randall. Randall liked this far more than he knew how to express. His pack was there, was close and protected. It soothed him.

As he read, Edwin's eyes slowly drooped until he was asleep, curled up on Anthony's shoulder, his legs sprawled across Randall's. Randall paused, smiling, exchanging a glance with Anthony. "I guess that went as well as could be expected." He honestly didn't want to stop reading, he was quite enjoying the story, but Anthony looked a few moments away from sleep himself. Randall closed the book and carefully reached across Victor to set it aside, along with his glasses.

"Do you like the book?" Victor's voice was soft with sleep, nearly a slur. "It's nice to hear you read it out loud. You have a good reading voice."

Curving his arm around Victor, Randall smiled, letting his own eyes slide shut. "I do like it quite a bit. I like thinking about you reading it too. It makes me feel like we're connected." He moved around in the bed, getting as comfortable as he could with Edwin half on top of him. He wound up with his face pressed against Victor's shoulder, arm slung over Victor's chest. "I am glad you're here." He yawned, nuzzling in closer.

"Me too." With a sigh, it sounded like Victor had dropped off to sleep. Randall kissed his chin, watching him for a few moments. Anthony was asleep now too, he and Edwin warm at Randall's back, Victor's arms around him. His pack was whole and safe and right there. For that moment, Randall couldn't imagine anything better.

"Good night, Victor," he murmured. And as sleep claimed him as well, Randall knew one thing for certain. There was no room at all in his mind for nightmares.

CHAPTER
14

Victor

WAKING UP to the sounds of three other people breathing in close proximity was not something Victor was used to.

He squeezed his eyes closed in reflex. He didn't know where the other people were, and he couldn't be sure they weren't staring directly at him, just waiting for him to open his eyes and accidentally meet theirs.

It took a few moments for memory to filter back in. It was Randall lying next to him; beyond him would be Anthony and Edwin. Victor still wasn't sure why he'd agreed to sleep on three pushed-together mattresses with three wolves. It probably had something to do with the quietly upset look on Randall's face last night, the pain of seeing violence and his younger brother hurt by it etched into his expression.

Randall was also right: they did indeed all snore.

Judging by the brightness beyond his eyelids—or lack of it—it wasn't nearly time to wake up. It was, at best guess, the normal time most people got up, perhaps around six or seven in the morning. That was horrifyingly early in Victor's book. So he didn't open his eyes. He dragged a pillow over his head instead, hoping to block out the buzz-saw snoring. Edwin seemed to be the main culprit.

When he couldn't take it anymore, Victor grunted quietly and dragged himself out of bed. Randall reached for him, arm across Victor's abandoned pillow, murmuring in his sleep but not quite waking. Victor dragged the blankets a little farther over Randall's shoulders before leaving, squinting heavily as he left the cabin.

He was torn. On one hand, he didn't want Randall to wake up and think Victor had had second thoughts and left. On the other hand, if he'd stayed in there much longer, he might have throttled Edwin in his sleep.

It was at least somewhat warmer than it had been recently this morning, allowing Victor not to shiver too much as he walked back to his own cabin in Randall's borrowed pajamas. He took a quick shower and got dressed, attempting to make himself presentable. When he looked at his watch, he grimaced. If Mallory had wanted them to meet with the Gray Lady, he likely meant now, or at least soon. Most wolves seemed to have a horrible preoccupation with getting things done early.

Victor returned to the Lewises. Once he'd shut the door behind him, he gently shook Randall's shoulder. The man looked so peaceful that Victor hated to wake him.

Randall stretched languidly, hair in his eyes, skin flushed with sleep. He blinked blearily and looked around, obviously confused.

"What—" Frowning, Randall tried to sit up, elbowing Edwin when Edwin tried to drag him back under the blankets like a human pillow. "What time is it?"

"Time for you to shut up." Edwin's mumbled reply came from where he'd buried his face in his pillow. "What are you doing up?"

"Hush, Ed," Randall sighed. "Go back to sleep."

"It's nearly seven," Victor said, keeping his voice low—God only knew why, seeing as he *was* trying to wake them all up. "We have a meeting with the Gray Lady."

"Shit." Apparently Randall cursed in the morning. Fumbling for his glasses, he nudged Edwin again. "Get up, Ed. Come on, we need to get dressed."

"I'm giving up my wolf membership." Edwin yawned so widely his jaw cracked.

"Too bad. Up, Ed. I need to go get Ant some coffee." Randall managed to haul himself out of bed, pajama pants half slipping off of his hips while he searched for clothes. Victor could help, but he was too busy appreciating.

Anthony gave an incoherent groan from the bed. "Oh my *God*, you guys, why are you moving around and talking?"

"We have a meeting with the Gray Lady," Victor repeated for Anthony's benefit. That didn't seem to cheer Anthony up any.

There was a loud pounding at the door, and Edwin wailed, trying to burrow his way under the covers. "I will eat whoever is trying to blow down our house," he shouted.

"Little pig, little pig" came Jed's voice from the other side. "I brought coffee."

Randall sagged back on the bed, apparently giving up in his search for matching socks. "Christ, come in. You're my savior."

Jed and Redford walked in, both juggling several to-go mugs of coffee. Jed stopped, staring at Anthony and Edwin still under the covers, Randall looking for his clothes, and Victor standing there next to them all. "Jesus, princess." Jed whistled, eyebrows winging upward. "*All* of them? I don't know whether to congratulate you or get you tested for steroid use."

"Ha, ha," Victor intoned. "Make yourself useful and give me caffeine. For once I don't care what it comes in."

Redford handed out the coffee, Edwin was finally prodded out of bed, and the Lewises got dressed. Randall was standing there, watching over Anthony while trying to not look like he was doing so, hands cupped around his drink. "Did you sleep well?" he asked Victor out of the blue, turning toward him. He flushed slightly, shifting from foot to foot, looking embarrassed. "I think that's what one asks, correct? How you slept?"

Victor had slept like utter shit. He recalled waking up often, startled by the noises of other people in the room with him, confused about why the bed was moving, too many things that alarmed his brain enough to wake him up. He felt like he'd been hit by a truck and then sat on by an elephant for good measure.

"Well enough," Victor replied. It was officially The Morning After. Though Victor had more experience with this sort of thing, he still felt a little awkward. "Your voice is a wonderful thing to fall asleep to."

259

Apparently that was exactly the thing to say, because Randall's insecurity faded, a smile replacing the worry. "I'll remember that," he said, reaching out to lightly take Victor's hand in his own.

"Okay, while this tea party is nice, I'm missing valuable beauty sleep for this." Jed was herding Edwin toward the door, Anthony walking after him. "Let's get moving."

Victor internally groaned at the sunlight once again as he got outside. He felt hungover, though he hadn't consumed more than a few sips of wine last night. Redford and Jed were talking lowly as they walked toward the Gray Lady's house, while Victor cast his gaze across the camp. Wolves were already all around, tending to the fire pit and cleaning up the tables and food scraps from last night. Some, he noticed, were hanging together rather closely. Apparently the summer solstice was fairly potent.

The thought made him smile. He looked over at Randall, who looked tired but alert, his gaze on his brothers.

Victor hadn't imagined he'd ever come to a conclusion about his feelings for Randall. They'd been so enormously confusing, so complex, and too tied in with too many variables, too much history, and Victor's own preconceptions about what he wanted for his own future. The visions had clouded his normally straightforward thinking, as had Randall's deep interest in him while Victor had only been at the stage of intrigue with the wolf.

But Dylan, the brownie half blood, however stoned he was, had been surprisingly wise. He had managed to simplify everything for Victor, and once Victor had been able to look at the situation clearly, he'd known what he'd wanted. For better or for worse, he wanted Randall.

As for how that played out compared to his visions, Victor would have to take Randall's earlier advice: one day at a time. Stop living in the future when nobody else could see it. It wasn't easy to do, but it was manageable, at least right then. As if reading his thoughts, Randall glanced over at him, gaze softening slightly. It was easy then, for both of them to move a little closer, for the brush of fingers to turn into hands held between them.

The house of the Gray Lady loomed ever closer. Victor had no idea what the meeting would be about. They had already decided to move, and the hunter attack last night hardly had anything to do with them. He wondered if the Gray Lady was changing her mind about her plan to move.

Victor didn't let himself hope for that option. It was terribly selfish, to hope for a fight just so that Randall wouldn't have to move seven states over.

Mallory was waiting to greet them. He pulled open the door and wordlessly gestured them inside. Randall gave him a slightly worried frown, but he also didn't let go of Victor's hand, despite the look Mallory was giving them, despite the fact the Gray Lady was watching them as they walked in and found seats around her table.

"I don't think you have a week." Jed spoke first, reaching into his bag and pulling out maps. "What we did last night is either going to buy you a few days, tops, or it's going to get an even bigger group of hunters in here tonight for retribution. I'd guess the former, but honestly, there's no way to tell."

"Yes, that is what I assumed." The Gray Lady nodded at them all, sitting back in her chair. "We need to move up our evacuation."

"You're still planning on leaving?" Randall's voice was heavy with disappointment. He was obviously trying to not sound combative, but Victor saw his gaze flick over to his brothers and then back to Victor, a frown creasing his forehead. The same heaviness felt like a weight on Victor's chest. "Do you really think we'll be safer there?"

"It might be a temporary solution, but at least it is one that will cause a minimal amount of bloodshed. For now. Tomorrow is not something I have the ability to see." The Gray Lady paused, her eyes very calmly going over to Victor.

Victor felt his heart jump into his throat. He didn't need to be told; he knew what she was thinking.

"But I can," he said, resigned.

"No." Randall and Jed spoke at the same time. Jed shot Victor an irritated look, then took his maps and unrolled them on the table. "Let's talk turkey," Jed continued, pretending that the Gray Lady's innuendo hadn't even been spoken. "The scouting parties e-mailed me last night, and this looks to be your best bet." He tapped one of the locations. It was surrounded by mountains, in a hidden valley, with a large lake at the center. "It's easy to keep unseen here, and it's defensible, if it comes to that."

Victor kept his head down, hoping Jed's distraction tactic would work.

"What good is having a medusa around if we cannot use him to our advantage?" the Gray Lady said, her voice delicate and tempered steel at the same time. "Mr. Rathbone?"

"He is not a tool to be pulled out and used." Randall's voice was more firm this time, a growl under his words. "It's too dangerous."

"One life for the lives of many?" The Gray Lady shook her head. "That is not the way of the pack, and you know it, little wolf."

"He is not part of your pack," Randall replied, chin raised defiantly. "And he is not meant to be used."

"Of course he is," the Gray Lady returned. "That is what medusas are for. To tell the future. Why else would they exist?"

"Do I get to have a say in this discussion?" Victor asked dryly. As much as he hated to admit it, the Gray Lady had a point. If he didn't look into her future, then half the pack could get killed in an attack because they had no idea when it would happen.

Besides, he was going to crack someday. He may as well do something *useful* with his ability before then.

Randall had turned toward him, the worry in his face easy to see even without meeting his eyes. "Victor, you can't do this," Randall said lowly. "This isn't looking at a human. It's not even looking at *me*. This is a near immortal. If anything would break you, don't you think this would do it? It's not worth the risk."

Victor grimaced. Everybody in the room was watching him now, which made for a very uncomfortable feeling. "I don't think the breaking works like that," he replied. "At least, I'm not sure it does. It's nothing specific like *who* I look at."

To be honest, he had no clue what really did it. He could have researched. He'd collected the journals and accounts of various medusas through the ages, though he'd never been able to bring himself to read them to the end. Perhaps if he had, he would have actually found a pattern.

"It's worth it," he told Randall, hoping to make him understand. "It's worth it to help an entire pack."

"It's *not*," Randall bit back, concern turning his voice into a growl. "That isn't how lives are weighed. You are important, you are too important to throw away without need. Knowing what might happen is no guarantee that our very actions won't *lead* to it. This isn't a promise of safety. It's not worth the risk." He reached out, laying his hand on Victor's. "Please," he asked, voice cracking. "Don't."

"I disagree," the Gray Lady said smoothly. "There *is* a need here, and any information we could get outside of what is normally available to us would be of great help."

This decision, Victor knew, would be a lot easier if he didn't have two people arguing about it right in front of him. If it had just been him and the Gray Lady, he likely would have said yes and not thought twice. But with Randall asking him not to....

"May I take a few minutes to think about it?" he asked.

The Gray Lady looked a touch impatient, but she inclined her head. Victor took that as permission and exited her house, suddenly feeling the need for fresh air.

There was every possibility that Randall was right, that a medusa broke according to how much they had seen. If that was true, then looking into the eyes of the Gray Lady would surely do it. He could barely comprehend how much history she had, let alone how much future he would see. If looking into the eyes of vampires and wolves knocked him out, then her eyes would surely do worse.

But how could he live with himself, if wolves got killed when he knew he could have done something to help prevent it? Redford and Edwin had recently suffered upset from killing hunters. At least they had done it directly, to prevent harm to those they loved. If wolves died because Victor refused to see the future, they would die from his inaction, from his *fear*.

And then there was a small part of the back of his mind that *wanted* to look into her eyes, for no reason other than to see. To absorb. To share in that knowledge for himself. A part that didn't mind if he went crazy, craved it, even.

Victor might have never been able to read to the end of the accounts of medusas, but they all had one thing in common. Curiosity killed the cat, and it drove the medusas insane.

Randall emerged from the cabin and quietly sat down on the steps next to Victor. Hands laced together, arms resting on his knees, Randall just stared out over the pack. Under the surface of wolves waking up, cleaning up after the solstice activities, having breakfast, was a very real thread of fear. There were groups of wolves patrolling the perimeter, the cubs were being ushered by three or four adults, and no one seemed willing to stay alone for too long. The wolves were worried.

"I don't know what to say," Randall admitted quietly. Slowly, he let out a long breath. "You shouldn't do it, Victor. There are some risks that simply aren't worth it."

"Not even if it could help your brothers?" Victor asked.

"I don't believe it will." Randall didn't answer the question directly. Then again, perhaps it wasn't a fair question. Victor felt a little guilty about it already, but he didn't apologize.

"I can't be sure that it *won't*," he replied. "Any scrap of information here is going to be useful, Randall. I can't ignore that."

"Oh, that's bullshit." It was a sudden exclamation, sounding rather odd coming from Randall. But he scowled down at his hands, not shying away from the message. "You know better than anyone that your glimpses into the future can be as harmful as they are helpful. This isn't you doing it for the very small chance that you will not only see a possible future that will be helpful, but that by telling us about it you won't then *change* that future. It's because you want to." Randall turned to him, pleading. "The thrill, the knowledge, whatever it is, Victor, it's not good enough to chance losing you."

Victor frowned and looked away, oddly hurt by Randall's words. "Are you implying that I wouldn't do whatever I could to help people? That I am only selfish and doing this for myself?"

"I'm telling you that this isn't helping people." Randall had turned back to staring down at his hands, obviously tense. "Everything I've read about medusas tells me that they crave knowledge. I wouldn't blame you for wanting to see the Gray Lady's past and future. If I could, I know I would. But it will hurt you, Victor. It could hurt you permanently."

"So could skydiving," Victor said, suddenly frustrated. "So could driving a car. So could walking along a road, and people do those things every day. I have the smallest chance to be *helpful*, Randall. I'm not like you. I'm not strong. I don't have good senses—"

"Clearly," Randall shot back. Victor withered where he sat, the wind taken out of his sails. Randall immediately reached over, apologetic before the word had died between them. "I'm sorry. I just…. I'm scared." Randall leaned forward, resting his head on Victor's hand. "You are like me. You're *better*. You're brilliant. You're strong. You don't need to do this in order to help."

"Let's take a poll of where we both were last night." Victor sighed. "I was hiding in the cabin, hoping desperately that a hunter didn't sneak up on me."

"Victor," Randall started. He stood, pulling Victor in, resting his forehead against Victor's temple. "That doesn't matter. I nearly got shot. If Anthony hadn't shown up, I wouldn't even be here. Should I go do something stupid to prove that I'm not worthless?"

"At least you *tried* to do something," Victor said.

"I can't lose you." Randall's voice was low, desperate. "Please, Victor. There's other ways. Please, don't do this."

The last time Victor had deliberately looked into someone's eyes, they had been David's, and David had merely sighed at him and set his glasses aside so Victor didn't break them when he fell. Randall's pleading was new to Victor.

But it would be a lie to say he didn't know what he was going to do. His mind had mostly been made up the second the Gray Lady had asked him.

"I'm sorry," Victor said gently. "But I have to do this."

He turned and walked back into the house as quickly as he could, unable to bear the thought of Randall pleading with him more. He had reasons—good reasons, Victor thought—for doing this, and if he was going to help at all, this would be the one way he could do it. He could not fight or protect or even research Jed's kind of work very well.

But he could use the one inborn talent he had and hope that it would be at least *some* help.

"I'll do it," he said as he reached the Gray Lady. There was a quick spasm of relief at the corners of her mouth, in the tense line of her shoulders. She stood gracefully and inclined her head to him.

"My gratitude, then, medusa." She gestured for Victor to sit. "There's no reason to waste time, then."

Randall had come back in, Victor saw out of the corner of his eye, taking a place next to Anthony. He was staring steadfastly down at his hands, refusing to watch. Victor shoved aside the twinge of guilt.

"I'm not sure how long I'll be unconscious, given that I've never looked at somebody with your lifespan before," Victor said, taking off his glasses. He knelt on the cushion she had placed on the floor near her chair. Someone behind him put a steadying hand on his shoulder. Redford, Victor confirmed as he looked back. "I will make every attempt to give you an answer before I pass out, though."

Victor wasn't sure what to feel about the silence behind him. Randall, he knew, wasn't happy with him doing this, but he couldn't help but wonder if everybody else was just bored or didn't care. It was an entirely self-centered thought that he immediately struck down. He had a job to do, and if he succeeded, then perhaps he would finally be useful.

He felt an arm around him and looked over to find Jed on his other side, bracing him, jaw set. He gave Victor a little nod, clearly ready, with Redford, to catch him when he fell. That made Victor feel somewhat better, at least.

He cleared his throat and turned back to the Gray Lady, who had knelt in front of him. She grasped his face in her hands, gentle but as firm as steel, and their eyes met.

She actually had quite beautiful eyes, Victor noticed, somewhere between a light hazel and the permanent gold of a wolf's eyes. He didn't even need to fall into the visions to know she had a long past.

What little sound there was faded to nothing, deafened by the noise of blood rushing in his ears. Everything else but the Gray Lady's eyes blurred out of focus. Victor felt an odd warmth trickle from his nostril, but he didn't take the time to wipe it away. A bleed, already? That was new.

And then he was gone.

Heat and dry ground were the first things she remembered.

The buzz of insects much larger than now, the stampede of hooves and paws all around. She didn't know what she was. She was new. She had no name for herself. Her mother was not like her. All her mother seemed to notice was food and danger.

She noticed much more.

A blur of time. Days fading into nights and weeks and years. Her mother died in an avalanche, and the only real word she could get out of her was a soft, low whine of pain. No thought for her cub, no higher consciousness to understand what was truly happening, only barely intelligent enough to recognize the agony of crushed organs.

She finds another that looks like her, and is surprised to find that he thinks like her too. She is relieved, and so is he.

They learn to turn into the strange sort of evolved monkeys they see around, but neither of them likes it much. That shape is too soft and unbalanced. The one advantage of the evolved monkeys is their intelligence, and the wolves have that already. The strange creatures do not talk in anything other than grunts, but they have a name for themselves.

The name changed. Grew, as they did, evolved. It all came to mean the same thing, though.

They became humans.

The wolves learn too quickly that humans are not friendly to them when they appear on four legs, and they are loath to spend much time on two legs. They run instead, and keep to themselves, though they never stray too far from human groups. The humans learn at a fascinating rate, and the wolves learn from them, though the tool use of humans is something they do not mimic, having no need for it.

They see their own kind evolve, but at first they do not understand why the wolves that look like them cannot talk to them. They begin to understand. They are not even like those which resemble them. They are something else entirely.

Thousands of years pass. The humans evolve, as do the wolves. The humans have long since spread out of Africa, and the first real settlements begin.

Languages become complex. The humans begin to understand the world around them. Tool use improves so quickly the wolves have trouble keeping up.

They see the start of the animal wolves staying close to humans and becoming domesticated. It disgusts them.

They have their own children. After thousands of years of trying to find others like them they have had no luck, and come to the conclusion that it is their responsibility to foster more like them. Their children are happy and live for two hundred years before they die of old age. The first two wolves are devastated. They have lived for thousands; why do their children die at mere hundreds?

They take on different names, depending on where they live and travel.

Their species grows in number as humans do. They see the first manipulation of metal, the first rolling mechanism, the first machinery. The first written word, the first true city, the first large-scale war.

Victor, through half-closed eyes, was dimly aware of having fallen onto his side. Everything *hurt*. He usually only experienced pain afterward as a result of the seizing, not *during*. There were strong arms circling him, a slim body pressed tight to him, soft hair falling against his cheek. He heard his name dimly, concern and so much fear there, but he couldn't seem to form a response.

The visions pulled him back.

The present. Her worry about her pack, her children, *her bloodline. The species would not die out if this pack were to be eradicated, but she loved them nonetheless.*

She wanted to run. She did not want a fight. But if she needed to, she would make a stand.

Another blink. There seemed to be a small puddle of something red under his nose and chin, streaked messily across the floor from movement. Victor dimly saw his hand, stretched out in front of him. Bruises bloomed randomly under the skin.

Odd. His blood vessels must be breaking.

A flash of yellow eyes. Dark hair. Randall.

And then the future.

The only way to accurately describe it was an explosion.

Even in the middle of the visions, Victor felt pain. He wished it would stop.

Threads arcing off into the distance, many different colors. Some ended soon, some ended so far into the future that even Victor couldn't comprehend the flashes he saw there.

The pack stayed where they were, and O'Malley hired every gun he had. The entire pack died.

The pack ran and were gunned down nonetheless.

They stayed and Jed trained them, and most of them lived.

They ran and stayed hidden.

She outlives all of them, and in the end the survival of this pack doesn't matter in the grand scheme of things. She dies and the wolves continue on without her. She dies and the wolf species dies with her.

In every possibility, there is a war. Wolves, vampires, half bloods, and humans. It starts slowly, murmurs in back alleys and whispers and half-spoken fears. But it always starts. It always happens. There is always death.

Except for one thing. A tiny glimmer in one thread of something that was thought would never happen. An old expectation fulfilled. A random happenstance that leads to hope in the war, a possible end instead of nothing but destruction.

A spark of light, a blaze of the sun against polished steel.

A hope... an end to....

Victor opened his eyes.

"There's a war," he choked out, blood smearing over his chin. "There's always a war. It doesn't matter if you run or fight. There's something so much bigger coming."

A cool washrag was smoothed across his forehead. He was cradled in someone's lap, arms curled around him, a body hunched over him protectively. A bottle of water touched his lips, encouraging Victor to take slow, shallow sips. He only managed three before he started coughing it up again, his head feeling like it was on the verge of splitting.

Was anybody listening to him? Could he just do what his body wanted and pass out?

"We will speak more later." The Gray Lady's voice coming from a short distance away. "Thank you, medusa."

"Take these." Randall's voice. It was Randall holding him carefully, a low, growling threat rumbling almost continuously in his throat. Randall gently held pills up to Victor's mouth, followed by more water. "It's okay, Victor. I have you. It's all right."

Victor managed to grab Randall's arm. In the vague realization that he hadn't gone insane, he tried to filter through what he'd seen for any clues on Anthony's well-being. But there was too much, and he'd been told it was okay to pass out.

He did so with a small sigh of relief.

CHAPTER
15

Randall

UNTIL EGYPT, Randall had never seen anyone die. Finding his parents' bodies when he'd been young still haunted him, but they'd already been gone by the time he and Anthony had come home. Actually watching the life drain from someone, seeing those final choking moments, it was something else entirely.

The first time he'd watched a person perish, it had been while chained up and muzzled in a stinking factory somewhere in the bowels of Cairo. It would be nice to be able to say he'd struggled, that he'd tried to get to the man, tried to save him. But there had been ten vampires with gleaming teeth and bloodthirsty gazes, so Randall had simply hung there and watched, helpless. He hated himself, still, for that moment, that decision. Intellectually, he'd known he couldn't do anything different. A wolf might be able to take on a vampire, but not that many. Not when he was bound.

The second person had been thrown at his feet, the vampires laughing at him, calling him *puppy*. Biting him and spitting his own blood in his face. They'd offered him a bite of the corpse, of the body that, ten minutes before, had been a living, breathing person. Randall had choked down his bile, his fear, and stayed silent.

That hadn't lasted long. The vampires seemed to enjoy making their new pet scream.

Randall didn't like to think back to that part of Cairo. He didn't want to remember. There hadn't been any point, he'd thought, in explaining what had happened to his brothers, in telling them why he hid his bite marks, why he didn't much like the dark now. And he was better. He was. There was no point in letting himself dwell.

Holding Victor, though, while blood choked him, while he seized, Randall honestly thought he was back there. His Beatrice had saved him, had pulled him from hell and led him back to the living. Surely only that nightmarish place could hold a moment when Victor was taken from him.

Victor was going to die. Randall was certain of it. Right there in his arms, he was going to die.

Hours passed with Victor still unconscious. Randall had carefully carried him back to Victor's cabin, refusing any help. Jed had followed him, making sure he had what he needed, silently worrying like an overlarge German shepherd. Randall hadn't spoken, though, and eventually Jed had gone back to the Gray Lady. Anthony checked on him later still, sharing the news that the pack was leaving at first light. Randall barely acknowledged him.

He counted Victor's breaths. He checked his pulse every few minutes, reassuring himself that Victor's heart was still beating. Eventually he changed Victor's clothes. He washed the dried blood from his nose and mouth. He had to find a new shirt for himself as well. Somewhere along the line he'd gotten covered in Victor's blood.

Staring at the red patches staining the white cotton, Randall realized his hand was shaking. In a few stumbled steps, he got to the bathroom and emptied his stomach into the toilet in a noxious, rolling clench of fear. Victor was alive, yes. Despite everything Randall's senses had told him during Victor's vision, he was still alive. Randall wasn't sure how much difference that made.

The pack was leaving. Anthony was growing weaker, though he was doing his best to hide it. A war was coming, a war Randall desperately wanted to avoid. But because of Anthony, they were going to be walking straight into the middle of it, following the Gray Lady despite the apparent target on her back. All Randall wanted to do was go *home*. To go back to school, to dust off those plans he'd had for his life.

He'd been dreaming of being a historian since he was ten years old. When he'd been twelve, he'd plotted out a map for how to achieve that goal. He'd had his walls covered in college brochures and class schedules since he was thirteen. And every step of the way, he'd known exactly what he wanted.

Now none of that would ever happen. He'd left school to focus on Anthony, telling himself that as soon as Anthony was recovering, he'd be able to go back. Now they were going to some remote location states away from all his carefully made plans. There was no more college in Randall's future. Anthony wasn't ever going to get better. Even Cedric's approach with real medicine could only possibly be a stopgap, if it was even possible where they were going, with what would more than likely be a lack of actual medical supplies. One day, perhaps sooner than any of them wished to believe, he would be holding his brother exactly as he'd held Victor, watching the last bits of life flicker and die in his eyes.

And then what? Taking care of Edwin was the only thing Anthony would ever ask of him, and Randall couldn't drag his brother back into a life of schools and regular jobs and the dreaded requirement to wear clothing. Edwin would be miserable living Randall's chosen life.

Quietly, Randall packed up Victor's things. Jed had left the van keys. Of course Jed was going to go with the wolves. He might bluster and rant, but he was a good man. He was utterly devoted to Redford, and Redford wanted to help. Of course Jed would go. So Victor would take the van and drive back to his own life, and Randall would go on with the pack. It was the only thing that could happen.

Once upon a time, he'd thought Victor his Beatrice. His savior. Victor had chased down vampires, had helped to haul Randall out of their den. Randall had thought it the act of an extraordinarily brave man. He'd hero-worshiped Victor, he'd read his books, he'd idealized him.

And now Randall was forced to acknowledge he didn't actually know him at all.

There was a noise from the bed. Victor was waking up. Randall went and got a fresh washcloth, soaking it in cold water. He replaced the one that was currently over

Victor's eyes with the new. "Stay still," he murmured very quietly. "You're in your cabin."

The only movement Victor seemed capable of was a twitch of his fingers. "Randall?"

"I have your pills." Randall carefully shook out two more and put them into Victor's hand, making sure a bottle of water was next to him should he want it. "You should probably take them."

Victor's fingers curled around the pills, though he made no move to take them yet. "Is my pack safe?" he asked groggily. "Are my children safe?"

A frown flickered across Randall's forehead. "You don't have children," he pointed out. "You—" Yes, of course. He was still caught in the Gray Lady's memories. Nearly half the day had passed, and Victor was still processing.

Randall wasn't sure if he wanted to shout at him or just leave. Neither one was truly an option, though, so he simply sighed and shook his head. "Those aren't your memories, Victor."

Victor just made a confused noise, but he didn't ask about "his" pack anymore. A few moments of silence passed, with Victor painstakingly lifting his hand to pop the pills in his mouth, swallowing them dry. "Yes. Right, of course. My apologies."

Feeling as though he'd aged ten years in one day, Randall found all of this was easier if he simply didn't look at Victor—if he didn't remember what they'd done on that bed, how it'd felt to have Victor finally *see* him. Finally want him the way Randall had since the moment he'd seen Victor. It had been a foolish crush, a pipe dream based on a man who didn't exist. Victor wasn't a hero. He was someone who chased after reckless things, who put himself into harm's way for reasons Randall couldn't understand.

And maybe, if he'd been someone else, if this had been another time, another place, it wouldn't matter. Maybe Randall would figure out a way to be what Victor needed to feel whole. But none of Randall's life right now would allow for that. The time was coming, closer every day, when he would lose Anthony. There was a war approaching, already here, and they would be in the thick of it.

"Your things are packed." Randall finished zipping the last bag. "The pack is leaving at first light. Jed left you the keys to the van, so you are free to go whenever you wish."

"What?" Victor managed to raise a hand to drag the cloth from his eyes, squinting blearily at Randall. "Why am I not coming along?"

There were a thousand answers to that question. Perhaps if he'd been someone else, a better man, he could have voiced even one of them. All Randall could think, though, was how Victor had dismissed him until he'd seen Randall go wolf. How his interest peaked when Randall was closer to his instincts.

How there were scars on Victor's neck so very much like Randall's. Only Victor had sought his out. He'd *wanted* them.

How perhaps even the small glimmer of light Randall had been clinging to, the hope he'd so carefully kept warm to give him strength enough to give up everything else, was nothing more than another one of Victor's risks.

"You aren't a wolf," was all he said, though, his voice thick and painful. "This isn't your fight. It's time for you to go home to your own life."

If possible, Victor just looked even more confused. "But I thought we...?" He trailed off, his words obviously not coming very easily to him. Instead, he waved a hand between himself and Randall. "What happened?"

"I think we both know I'm not going to make you happy." Randall paused when his voice threatened to crack, the words weighing him down. "So thank you. For everything. Good-bye, Victor."

The one thing that had scared Victor, the one thing he'd been so damn frightened of, was not Randall's wolf instincts. It wasn't the coming war, the vampires, looking into an immortal being's life. No, the thing Victor had shrunk from was the idea of a *normal life*. Of marriage and children, of a quiet existence. The one thing Randall longed for, and Victor simply couldn't bear the thought of it.

Gently, saying good-bye less to the man he didn't know and more to the possibilities that were never going to exist, Randall kissed Victor's forehead and silently turned to leave.

"Randall," Victor protested hoarsely. "I don't understand. We were both completely ecstatic last night."

Last night, when Randall had been half drunk on the wolf pheromones, feeling his instincts surging with every beat of the drums. God, he had to stop thinking about this, he had to stop going over every word Victor had said, every glance and touch, or he'd go mad trying to figure out if any of it had ever been real. "You want something I can't give you" was his answer. It wasn't good enough, Randall knew that, but he couldn't figure out how to explain everything in his head. If it'd been a thesis paper, a dissertation, he could go into every nuance with perfect clarity. Here? He felt completely out of his depth, as if his vocabulary had been reduced to the ache in his throat and the angry longing he was trying desperately to repress.

"You can't mean to tell me that you don't want this, the day after I finally got my act together." Victor's voice had been reduced to a whisper. He sounded like he was trying to move but wasn't having much success with it. "What have I done to make you turn away?"

Christ. He wasn't good at this. Randall wished horribly that Anthony was there, or Edwin. Either one of them could have articulated his feelings far better than Randall ever would. "You don't want me. You want someone who will make you feel the same way the vampire did. I can't do that." Grabbing his jacket, Randall moved toward the door, frantic for an exit. "Have a good life, Victor. I hope you find what you're looking for."

The fresh air was cool on his face. The pack was a whirl of activity, wolves hauling boxes and bags outside, a few large trucks backing up to the middle of the camp for easier loading. They would be working well into the night, with how much they had to do. Randall ignored all of it. He headed back to his cabin numbly, an almost deafening buzzing his ears.

Anthony was alone in the room when Randall came in. Wordless, Randall sank onto his bed, drawing his knees up to his chest, wishing that, for once, Anthony wouldn't be kind to him. He couldn't bear the thought of anyone asking how he was, being concerned, much less Anthony. He was holding himself together now. Any show of kindness would break him, he was sure.

That wish must have been written all over his face, because Anthony only observed, "You look like you're about to seriously hurt the next person that says anything stupid."

Nodding, throat too tight to speak, Randall just curled up further on himself and stared blankly at the floor. He heard Anthony's mattress creak, footsteps, then his own bed dipped as Anthony sat next to him. "Everything okay?"

And just like that, the dam burst.

He listed over into Anthony, head buried in his shoulder. He didn't cry, because Randall was quite certain if he started, he wouldn't stop. But he pushed himself into Anthony's arms as if he was a child again, clinging to his brother after a bad dream. "No," he whispered, voice shattering.

With a quietly sympathetic sigh, Anthony wrapped his arms around Randall's shoulders. "Let me guess. Victor?"

He nodded, clenching his jaw as tight as he could to hold back sobs. He couldn't break. Anthony had enough on his plate, enough *real* things to worry about. Randall couldn't let himself go in front of him. "It's okay," he managed. "It's not a big deal."

"Randall, come on," Anthony admonished. "It's you. You're one of the two biggest deals in my life. What did he do? Should I go kick the shit out of him? Did he change his mind about being with you?"

Anthony, gods love him, had a tendency to be a complete mother hen when he saw that Randall or Edwin were hurt, physically or mentally. Randall dreaded the inevitable day that Anthony really felt he *would* need to go kick the shit out of a problem, because he had no doubt Anthony would give it a good attempt.

"It's nothing, Anthony." And the very *last* thing Anthony needed to be doing was expending energy on Randall's problems. "I'm sorry. It really doesn't matter." He sat up, taking off his glasses to clean them, trying to carefully control his expression.

"You can say that all you like, but we both know that's going to end up with me just asking the same question all night." Anthony curled the arm he had around Randall's shoulders, tugging him in closer. "Do I need to keep asking?"

"It's nothing," Randall repeated. But one look over at Anthony confirmed he had that stubborn set to his jaw. There was literally no way to get Anthony off a topic once he'd sunk his teeth in like that. Randall might as well save himself several hours of nagging and give in. "He's going home. Like he should. I packed his things and told him to go home. That's it."

Anthony peered at him. "Something tells me that he wasn't the one to make that decision. You'd be reacting a lot differently if he had."

Randall shrugged, trying to appear disinterested. "He'll be happier this way."

Anthony looked just about as confused as Victor had been. "Do we need to talk about this? Or...." He frowned in even deeper bafflement. "I don't understand. He was perfect for you!"

Jaw tightening, Randall shrugged Anthony's arm away, then pushed himself off the bed. Desperate for something to do with his hands, he grabbed one of their bags and started to pack what few belongings they'd brought with them. He took a moment to mourn his books, back at their home. There was no time to go back and get them. Maybe

271

someday. "He is an adrenaline junkie, looking for something dangerous. Which I am most definitely not."

"*Victor*? An adrenaline junkie?" Anthony stared at him. "That guy probably just drinks an extra cup of tea to get a thrill."

"Or dates a vampire," Randall said, words coming short and brittle as he jammed clothes into the duffel bag. "Or chases after a pack of wolves. Or looks into an immortal's eyes. Or sleeps with a goddamn *wolf*."

Anthony didn't look surprised at the mention of Randall and Victor sleeping together. He did, however, sigh very faintly. "I still think you're perfect for each other. But it's your decision. I just wish you had an opportunity to work things out." He paused, a gleam in his eye. "What if we didn't—"

"No," Randall said bluntly. Even if there'd been hope, Randall wasn't about to stay simply for himself.

Anthony frowned. "Is there any way I could talk you into letting Victor come along?"

Teeth gritted, Randall finished fishing Edwin's socks out from all the random corners where he seemed to toss them. "Victor is a grown man. He can certainly do whatever he wishes. But I doubt he will have any reason to come with us. He has a job, Anthony. A life." One-night stands to continue. "It's not like he's my mate. I'll get over it."

"Okay." Anthony didn't sound thrilled to let the point go, but he did it nonetheless. "I'm so sorry, Randall. I wish things had worked out better." He sounded about as miserable as if *he'd* been the one in Randall's situation. Anthony had always been too empathetic for his own good, especially when it came to his brothers. "You need anything, you know you can just talk to me?"

"I am perfectly fine, Anthony." Randall zipped up the bag and tossed it toward the door. "And we're packed. So how about we go round up Edwin and find some dinner?"

"Perfectly fine my ass," Anthony grumbled under his breath. He leaned over the mattress and slid something off the nightstand. "Just one thing more to pack. I think there's room in my bag."

It was the book. The one Victor had given him. A tight ache settled into Randall's chest as he reached out to take it, lightly running his fingers along the cover. "No, it's all right," he whispered, voice wavering. "I, uh. I'll take care of it."

Gently, carefully, he slid it into his own messenger bag. He tucked it away next to all those possibilities he'd extinguished, all those hopes he'd let grow only to watch them wither away. For a little while at least, his Beatrice had been a very nice dream.

It was time to wake up now.

CHAPTER
16

Jed

THREE WEEKS later, and they'd finally finished setting up the new camp. There were tents for shelter, outhouses far enough away to not make the wolves gag, and a tarp-covered space for the kitchens. It wasn't pretty, but it kept the rain off while cooking, and that had turned out to be goddamn crucial. All in all, everyone had a place to eat, sleep, and shit, so that had to count for something.

Whatever the fuck Jed had thought about how hard planning a goddamn vacation was, getting a couple hundred furry-assed wolves packed up and moved cross-country? Yeah, that was some serious shit. Fuck knew how Jed had managed to get enough trucks there with a day's notice, but once the hunters had found the camp, they'd had days, not weeks, to get their asses in gear.

And the travel had been the fun part. Actually setting up camp had been a fucking nightmare.

It'd rained for a week straight, turning their carefully picked clearing into mud soup. Setting up any kind of semipermanent structures had turned into a dirty, dangerous job. More than one person had gotten injured by shit sliding where it wasn't supposed to, falling when no one could catch it, and plain bad luck. When the sun had finally broken through, Jed had thought he'd never seen anything better.

Redford had helped him set up a training program for any of the wolves who wanted to learn how to fight. They had regular patrols and what was shaping up to be a pretty decent militia, even if half of them didn't want anything to do with guns. The Gray Lady had named Jed an honorary pack member, which as far as Jed could tell meant he had a lifetime membership at the gym, and nobody tried to sniff his ass anymore when he went out walking the perimeter of the camp.

The new camp was set in a valley between two steep mountains, trees crawling over every surface except for the one decently large clearing Jed had found on the map. It had everything they needed: a water source from a nearby lake instead of the river they were used to, and thickly wooded areas at the north and south of them with more than enough territory for hunting.

It hadn't been easy. They were low on food, the hunting parties were still learning the lay of the land, and it'd be weeks before any of the newly planted crops were able to be harvested. Instead of nice cabins, there were tents and plywood buildings. The kids had school around one of the campfires, and the adults got their meals at the communal

273

space, a tarp thrown over several tall posts to make some kind of half-assed shelter. But everyone had survived the trip, and, in three weeks, they'd seen no sign of the hunters.

In short, Jed was putting this one in the win column.

Shotgun slung over one shoulder, Jed tramped back from the woods. He'd been doing an inspection of the sentry points and was pretty pleased with the design Redford had instituted. They'd taken their cue from deer hunting blinds, set high up in trees and camouflaged, practically invisible to anyone below. They were watching all possible entry points, and Jed was determined that when he and Redford went back home, the wolves wouldn't have one damn excuse for being taken by surprise. Effective, and also hilarious to hear wolves bitch about how they didn't belong in trees. Jed had taken to calling them Fur Pigeons.

Knievel was trotting next to him, tail in the air, chirping happily at the wolves they passed. When they spotted Redford across the way, the cat took off like a streak of fur, only to stop short and begin aggressively grooming herself just shy of Redford, like she didn't even notice him. Jed had no such illusions of aloofness. With a grin, he covered the distance between them in a few long strides and grabbed Redford for a long kiss. "Hey, babe," he murmured, wrapping one arm around Redford. "I missed you."

"Jed, you've been gone two hours," Redford pointed out practically. But he was smiling, and that was what counted.

"A very long two hours," Jed insisted, eyes wide with pretend earnestness. "The longest. I practically wasted away."

"Of missing me, or of hunger?" At Redford's question, Jed braced himself. In the past few weeks, Redford had gotten it into his head that Jed didn't eat enough, and three times a day Redford now appeared, seemingly out of nowhere sometimes, just to shove a meal at Jed. "Because you skipped lunch."

"I was working!" Jed protested. "It was very important."

"So is food." Redford frowned at him, taking Jed by the arm and leading him to one of the campfires. There was no big bonfire in this new place, but a series of smaller ones that would be less visible from a distance. Redford leaned down and picked up a tray just in time to save it from Knievel's paws. "One of the hunting parties had some good luck today, so there's plenty for everyone."

Settling down onto a bench, Jed's first priority was serving a good chunk of the unidentified meat on his plate to Knievel. She immediately dragged it a short distance away, gnawing on it, tail swishing contentedly. Jed then tugged Redford down to sit on his lap, ignoring the rest of the meal for a moment in favor of kissing Redford's shoulder. "So, how did the training session go? Anything interesting happen while I was chasing Fur Pigeons up trees?"

Redford snorted. "They had a fifteen minute long discussion, trying to come up with a good name for themselves to avoid letting you have the honor. Some of them aren't happy with the idea of using anything but their teeth, but they're getting there. I just keep emphasizing that it's good to be prepared in any form."

"And they have an excellent teacher," Jed informed him. Absently, he took a bite of the food, raising his eyebrows. "This isn't half bad. What'd we catch this time?"

"Mule deer, they said." Redford leaned back against Jed then, getting comfortable. "They all looked really happy about it. They also said they saw mountain lions, but they wouldn't eat them."

"That's 'cause they know cats are superior. Isn't that right, 'Nievel?" Knievel, for her part, had rolled over and was now vigorously attempting to catch her own foot, which was kicking hyperactively, seemingly independently of her body. Jed paused. "Okay, maybe not."

Redford laughed lowly. "Hey, you haven't seen the hunting party get bored and chase their own tails."

It was simple out here. Sure, hard to get to, and Jed was desperately missing television and a really good beer, takeout food or going down to the gym for a game of basketball. But there was something kind of nice about eating food that people he knew had gone out to hunt hours ago. That his whole day was Redford and training and watching the stars at night. Jed would be happy to go home, but he'd admit, part of him wouldn't mind staying.

There was a thump next to him, and Jed didn't even need to look over to know it was Edwin. The kid was ridiculously easy to spot when he wasn't trying to be stealthy. He approached everything like it was some game he was thrilled to be playing. Edwin was also pretty decent at the whole sentry thing that Jed had been working on with the wolves. He had a good nose and wasn't afraid to follow it.

He also refused to use a gun. Oh, he'd tried. He'd even approached Jed asking to be taught. But after an hour shooting makeshift targets, Edwin had handed Jed the pistol and declared it *too noisy* before running off to do whatever the fuck he did during the day. Chase butterflies or wash his clothes with talking birds or whatever. Jed would give him this, though—Edwin was goddamn lethal in wolf form.

"Do you like the deer?" Edwin asked, flashing them both a grin. "I got to take it down. It was awesome. We tracked this herd for miles. Normally only the older wolves actually do the kill, out of respect for the animal, but this time they let me and then we gave honor to it and I got to say the blessing and it was *awesome*." He was practically wiggling in excitement. "Redford, you should come next time!"

"I'm not really much of a hunter," Redford mumbled, embarrassed. "I'd prefer to do the cooking. I'm much better at that."

And there was another thing that was going well—Redford hadn't had an "episode" for the last three weeks. He hadn't been overcome by the instincts or lost himself. A few times he'd looked like he'd come close, but every time he'd forced himself to breathe slowly and beat back the yellow in his eyes. He'd also become more comfortable around every aspect of the pack. He still wasn't running around on all fours at the drop of a hat, but he seemed a bit more willing to participate in some of the pack dynamics, and Jed was trying his damnedest to be supportive.

"You could come anyway," Edwin assured him. "Randall isn't that great either, but he came last time. I think he just wanted to be helpful."

Or get out of the camp, Jed figured. Jed wasn't exactly Oprah, and God knew he *really* didn't care, but even a blind eunuch could have figured out that Randall and Victor had gone through some kind of pissing match. Which, oddly enough, hadn't stopped Victor from coming with the pack.

Yeah, Jed didn't get that either. A week after they'd arrived, Victor had come huffing and puffing into camp. He'd driven the damn rattletrap van as close as he could and hidden it in the woods only to make the hour-long ascent up to the camp. Hell, Jed was just impressed he hadn't passed out or died. Victor didn't strike him as the hiking type.

But since Victor had arrived, Randall hadn't said two words to him. Which was probably weird, but honestly, at least now Jed only had to deal with one nerd at a time. Victor had thrown himself into helping set up the school and was, at that moment, surrounded by a bunch of kids, half of them in wolf form, teaching them the history of their people around the campfire. It had been funnier when Victor had looked terrified of anyone younger than twenty-five. Now he was actually *smiling*—if a bit awkwardly—at the kids. Weird.

"Randall isn't that great at what?" Randall had appeared, pausing to give Knievel a scratch just in front of her tail. "My ears are burning."

"Hunting," Edwin replied, flopping down on the ground to stick his nose in Knievel's face. The cat touched her nose to his and then rubbed her cheek against his jaw. "Red was just saying he wasn't good enough to go with the party next time, but you went!"

"Yes, well, it was educational to be sure," Randall replied dryly, taking a careful seat next to them. "I think I'll stick to helping out here in the future."

Anthony was incredibly involved in getting everyone settled and helping the sentries train. Edwin was a hunter and learning how to fight. Randall, though... well, there wasn't much call for the bookish type out here. He didn't seem to have a place to fit in. Normally Jed would tell him to go do the school thing, but since he very much did not want to know what was going on there, he decided to keep his damn mouth shut.

Redford shifted on Jed's lap, casting a glance at the still half-full tray and then a frown at Jed with a silent reminder for him to keep eating. "Maybe I'll try going out with the hunting party tomorrow," he said, phrasing it more like a question.

Obligingly popping another bite of the meat in his mouth, Jed nodded. "That sounds awesome. I'm going to do a few training exercises I think, see if the Fur Pigeons can spot me sneaking into camp. Going hunting sounds like way more fun than crawling in the dirt for four hours."

"It probably is." Redford smiled. "Oh, and Anthony was looking for you earlier. He said he wanted to talk to you, but I don't know why. I think he's with Cedric at the moment."

Nodding, taking one last bite, Jed kissed Redford's cheek and regretfully dislodged him from his lap. "Duty calls. Want to come with?"

"I promised I'd help clean up after cooking." Redford didn't look too happy at the prospect—he'd always hated doing dishes, and Jed had never managed to get the hang of it. Between them, they were just grateful to have a dishwasher in their apartment back home. "I'll see you after?"

Kissing him, ignoring the exaggerated gagging sounds Edwin was teasing them with, Jed smiled. "I think that's a plan. Our tent. Tonight. I have plans." Plans involving driving Redford so out of his mind with pleasure he forgot to try to be quiet so no one would hear them. Tents had thin walls; that wasn't Jed's problem.

"It's the full moon tonight," Randall pointed out. He'd brought out a book, the same book he'd been carrying around since they'd arrived at the new camp, and was half absorbed in the well-worn pages. "I think you might need to take a rain check. I've never been around this many wolves during one before, but I kind of think it's going to be a little more intense than usual."

Redford stared at Randall, worry pinching the edges of his expression. "Intense how?"

"Remember the summer solstice when everyone started howling?" Randall glanced up, arching an eyebrow at Redford. "That was probably not even close."

Redford had gone bright red. "I can't imagine," he said faintly, darting a worried, but also fond, look at Jed. "The summer solstice was already, um, crazy."

Jed just grinned widely back. "Oh man, I am clearing my schedule tomorrow for sure." Forget his plans. "'Cause I think I'm not going to be able to walk once you get back." Goddamn, that was a happy prospect. Redford would go out and do his running thing and then come back all naked and blissed out and fuck Jed into the ground. That was definitely the new plan of action.

Snorting quietly, Randall returned to his book. "I need to find earplugs."

"I'm just going to sleep in the woods tomorrow," Edwin decided. "You guys are *loud*."

"Hey, it's not my fault you aren't getting laid," Jed informed both of them smugly. "My boyfriend is hot as hell, and I refuse to restrain myself." With that, Jed tugged Redford in for a slow kiss, biting his lip lightly before he headed off to find Anthony.

He found him in the new medical center, which was actually just a single room plywood hut that Cedric had claimed as his own. Anthony was seated with an IV in his arm, staring out the window while Cedric made notes and fussed over a stack of books on the desk. Plopping down on one of those rolling stools, Jed grinned at Anthony, sliding his way across the floor. "What's going on, fur butt?"

It sucked, that Anthony was sick. More than sucked. A guy like that, full of life, he shouldn't have to worry about medicine and getting weaker. But crying about it wasn't going to do a damn thing.

"Hi, Jed." Anthony sounded tired but pleased to see him. "Have you got a free minute?"

"Well, I did have a pedicure scheduled," Jed drawled, spinning idly in half circles on the stool. "But hey, I can get my french tips later."

At least Anthony laughed at his jokes, unlike some people. Jed wasn't going to name and shame, but, well, Victor. "Okay, I won't beat around the bush, then. Cedric says it's too early to tell if his treatment is going to do anything. I wanted to ask you for something."

Eyebrow rising, Jed stopped fidgeting. "Updated reading material? 'Cause I gotta tell you, as much as I love the one copy of *Home & Garden* from 1958, it's getting kind of old."

Anthony frowned contemplatively. "Was *Home & Garden* even being published then?"

Jed shrugged. "They had homes back then, kid. And gardens. And words."

"I don't know, that's pretty far back. Did they even have the written language then?" Anthony teased.

"I was not even a glimmer in my father's eye back then, so for all I know they had fucking dinosaurs." Laughing, Jed shook his head. "So, what do you want me to get? I've got a trip to town scheduled. I can pick up some gossip mags for your secret boy band crush stalking."

Anthony smiled, but that time he didn't get distracted. "I wanted to ask you a favor. I know this might sound pretty dramatic, and I'm not asking you to seriously commit to anything. But—" He drew a deep breath. "—if I die, I want to know that there'll be someone looking out for my brothers. Just checking in on them every once in a while to make sure they're okay. And I can't think of anyone better for the job than you."

Well. That was one good way to get Jed focused. A frown crept over his face, and Jed instinctively shook his head, wanting nothing more than to get up and run. "I'm pretty sure you must be taking the good drugs, then, Rin Tin Tin." Jed didn't do *family*. He'd never been good at it. Redford was... a massive exception to the rule. "I'm not your guy."

"I'm not asking you to live with them and hold their hand, Jed. Just a phone call every once in a while. Help, if they need it." Another wolf ability, besides the senses and the glamorous fur coat, must have been the ability to give irritatingly good pleading eyes. Redford had it down, and now Anthony was giving him the same face.

Jaw tight, Jed just shook his head more determinedly. "You want Red," he grunted, staring somewhere over Anthony's left shoulder. "Or, fuck, *Victor*. Anybody but me. I'm not the person someone wants checking up on them. They get in a tight spot, sure, I'm there. But everyday stuff isn't my thing."

"I'd ask Victor if I didn't think Randall would hang up on him," Anthony said wryly. "And since Randall would, Edwin would. Can I ask both you *and* Redford, then?"

Leg jiggling, Jed tried to think of a really good excuse. Like he was allergic to hugs or he was pretty sure he turned into a wolf-eating maniac on full moons. A were-man of some sort. In the end, though, Jed just heaved a sigh and nodded. "Fine. Redford does the emotional shit, though." He nudged Anthony's shoulder. "Not that this conversation matters. You're going to be fine."

Before Jed could protest, Anthony had reached out and gotten an arm around Jed's shoulder, dragging him into a hug. It was, needless to say, a bit awkward while both of them were sitting down. "Thank you," Anthony mumbled against Jed's shoulder. "Really. Thank you. I can't tell you how much that means to me."

Patting Anthony's back, floundering more than a little, Jed cleared his throat. "Yeah, well. Good talk." Christ, he hated stuff like this. Who just went around *hugging* people? It was weird. Anthony didn't even let him go after the allotted two seconds. He just kept hugging him.

After an excruciatingly long time, Anthony said, laughter under his words, "You really hate being hugged, don't you?"

"I like naked hugging," Jed grumbled, arms now stiff at his sides, completely unsure what he was supposed to be doing. "That's the only kind of hugging that counts."

Anthony scoffed. "Regular hugging is good too. Here, I'll give you a tip. Lift your arms and put them around me. You will have then successfully hugged me back and I'll let you go."

Well, that didn't sound like a viable option at all. Wincing, Jed held still, hoping Anthony would give up. The bastard just tightened his grip, and Jed swore he could feel him laughing silently. Finally, letting out an exasperated breath, Jed raised his arms and gave Anthony another quick double tap on the back. "There. Fucking hell, you freaking muppet."

Anthony was a man of his word. He let go and sat back in his chair. "Now, was that so scary?"

Glaring at him, Jed rubbed the back of his neck, feeling as awkward as some teenager after their first date. "Whatever. You need anything else while I'm in here? Should we do each other's makeup and talk about boys?"

"We totally should." Anthony was so deadpan Jed found he couldn't tell if he was being serious or not. His heart sank. Shit. Was this like a Make-A-Wish thing? Did he now have to follow through for the sick guy?

Fuck that. "You come near me with mascara and I will kick your ass, I don't care how many needles the doc has got in your arm," Jed grumbled, scowling. "My lashes are perfect. I don't need a goddamn thing on my face."

Anthony's expression split into a grin. "So you've spent time thinking about your eyelashes, huh?"

Jed swore he was going to hit him. Jed rolled his eyes heavily, flopping back in his chair. "You are an asshole," he declared.

"A loveable one," Anthony corrected. "So, have you got anything planned for this night's full moon?"

"That's debatable." Going back to making lazy circles on the stool, shooting Anthony the required scowls as he turned, Jed shrugged. "Spend as much time with Red as he wants. Sleep. Get fucked into the ground when Red gets back." A slow smirk spread across Jed's face. "You know, nothing big."

Victor would have scowled at him. Hell, most people would have protested that was way too much information. Anthony simply slapped him on the shoulder and said, "Good luck. You'll need it, especially if Redford is getting more in tune with his instincts."

The smirk turned into a full-on grin. "Any tips?"

"Eat a lot of carbs and try not to pass out," Anthony laughed. "Wolves are more energetic than most."

"I've never had a complaint." Snorting out a laugh, Jed waggled his eyebrows suggestively. "I think I can keep up just fine."

"I'm sure you can." Anthony half turned in his chair as Cedric bustled over to do something with the IV in his arm. "Okay, Jed, I'm sure you have something better to do than watch me get treated. But thank you." Anthony looked up at him again, a teasing light in his eyes. "For a human, you're pretty good to have as a friend."

279

He'd been released from sticking around with the threat of future ninja hugs, but Jed didn't move. "How's that going?" he asked, nodding toward the IV. "Better than the smelly paste shit?"

It was Cedric who answered him. "I can't say there will be any improvement just yet." He sounded grumpy. Then again, the guy always sounded grumpy.

"But I think I am starting to feel better," Anthony said optimistically. "Not *improved* yet, but less worse, if that makes sense. My hands don't shake as much, at least."

Nodding, Jed glanced over at Cedric—who, frankly, scared him a little—and rolled his shoulders forward, unsure. "Look, seriously, if you need something... just ask. Supplies or better drugs, some weed, whatever." That was a good way to show support, right? Besides, pot would totally help with the pain.

"Are you angling for another thankful hug?" Anthony raised an eyebrow at him.

"Please, God, no," Jed returned, arms folded. "Just, you know. Jesus, don't give me the goddamn puppy eyes. I'm just saying, okay?"

Anthony's expression softened. "I know. And thank you, again. I'm not sure weed will ever be on my shopping list, but medicine might be one day."

Nodding, Jed sat in uncomfortable silence for a few more beats before standing. He felt like something else needed to be said or done, but, at a loss, he wound up sticking out his hand for Anthony to shake. "Good stuff."

Anthony, the asshole, smirked at his awkwardness. "Have a good full moon, Jed."

Back out in the main flow of the camp, most of the busy work seemed to have eased. This was the first full moon at the new camp, and it seemed a little bit like the hours before some kind of government holiday. There were people cooking, a few doing some wash by the stream that came off of the lake, but most people seemed too jittery for mundane tasks. Even the kids Victor was teaching were practically vibrating out of their seats, restless and obviously done with whatever Victor was teaching.

Jed wandered over, hands in his pockets, smirking as one of the kids shifted into a plump dark gray wolf and took off toward the woods, howling its little head off. Three more followed him, and just like that, half of Victor's class was chubby, on four legs, and wrestling with one another in mass chaos while Victor closed his book in resignation and looked like he was trying to figure out if he should stop them biting one another.

"You look like you could use a drink," Jed informed Victor cheerfully. One of the roly-poly wolf cubs ran straight into Jed's leg. He stooped down to pick the kid up, carting him under one arm while he took a seat and tugged a flask out of his jacket pocket. Rubbing behind the wolf's ears, grinning when it nipped at his fingers with a playful growl, Jed tossed the flask toward Victor. "Happy full moon, princess."

Victor only glanced at the flask before passing it back. "I've decided not to drink in excess anymore," he announced. "But thank you for the offer."

Well, next thing he'd know the sun would be coming up ass backward and shitting rainbows. Blinking, surprised, Jed took his own drink and put the bottle away. "What's gotten into you?" he asked, wrestling lightly with the wolf pup, smiling when two others ran over to help. They were rolling on the ground with little growls that shook through their bodies, tails wagging happily while Jed attacked their stomachs with both hands.

"It's a long story of contemplation that would no doubt bore you to death," Victor said dryly. "But if my medusa blood is going to kill me someday, chancing liver disease is only adding to my problems."

"You're thinking ahead?" Jed smirked, shaking his head and watching as the wolf kids decided that chasing one another around trees was far more fun. They waddled off in a run, and Jed kicked back, watching them play. "Seriously, Vickie, it's like I hardly know you. What's going on?"

Victor sighed as he turned to the makeshift table that he'd obviously hauled out for the class, for the sole purpose of bearing ridiculous numbers of books. As he began getting them into order, he replied, "Before the pack moved here, I was told that I exhibited a number of self-destructive behaviors. Though I initially thought it was ridiculous, I'm beginning to see the truth in it."

"Everybody's self-destructive," Jed dismissed, taking another long drink. "Wouldn't have thought you the type to get your panties in a bunch over something like that."

"You only think that because you constantly rush headfirst into things that would happily kill you," Victor pointed out dryly. He paused then, staring at Jed oddly. "Is there something you wanted?"

Yeah, he wasn't exactly someone who sat down and chatted it up with random people. Especially not Victor. But he'd been surrounded by wolves for a month, and even though he'd be the last damn person to admit it, Jed felt... well, like he was something *else*. And yeah, he knew, Victor wasn't human either. But he also wasn't wolf, so maybe they were *something else* together.

"Anthony just asked me to look after the furry duo when he kicks it." Jed absently picked up a stick, drawing patterns in the dirt while Victor packed up his books. "Not really sure what I feel about that. I mean, he's crazy, obviously, but kinda couldn't say no."

Victor made a faint *huh* noise, obviously surprised. "And are you going to do what he asked?"

"You ever tried to turn down a pleading wolf?" Jed snorted, shaking his head. "Yeah, I guess. I mean, I'd rather the big lug just *lived*, you know, but I said yes. Redford and I will play mommy and daddy if he can't." God, just the thought of it was close to giving Jed a panic attack.

Victor was trying, and failing, to contain an amused smirk. "What an entertaining thought."

Rolling his eyes, Jed took another drink. He'd have to ration himself—he was running low on his booze supply. "So why doesn't the nerd talk to you anymore?" Christ, maybe there was something in the water. Jed *really* didn't want to know, but there he was, asking anyway.

Then again, Jed had watched Victor and Randall dance big fucking circles around each other for three weeks. Maybe somebody needed to point out that everyone knew they were idiots.

"Because of the aforementioned self-destructive tendencies," Victor replied, his voice clipped. "It's something I'm addressing."

281

Oh, well, he'd found a nerve. "Wait." Jed couldn't help the huge grin. "Are you telling me the virgin blushing geek boy *turned you down*?" That was *hilarious*.

"Oh, shut up, Jed," Victor said witheringly. But there was a hint of a returning smirk on his face. "Besides, he's not a virgin anymore."

Pausing, Jed waited for Victor to walk that back. Surely that wasn't what Victor meant. But oh no, Jed knew that smug look. He'd *had* that smug look. "You seductive devil." Jed grinned, raising his flask. "Come on, drink to that, at least. Virgin chaser."

Victor still refused the flask. "Well, none of it's any good if he continues to avoid me." He went right back to looking morose.

"Come on, princess, I know you've got some balls hidden under all those perfectly ironed slacks. Go after him." Smirking, Jed leaned back. "Try a little pursuit for a change. There's got to be something in those boring books of yours about how to woo, or whatever the fuck nerds call it."

Victor looked incredulous. "Are you trying to give me relationship advice?"

"Well, I am *in* one," Jed pointed out. "And he hardly ever tries to eat me. So yeah. I think I can give you a few pointers." He winked at Victor. "Don't worry, professor, no charge for this one."

"Jed," Victor said delicately, "I'm not going to say that you're a slut, but you've had more balls in your mouth than the Hungry, Hungry Hippos."

A beat of silence and then Jed started laughing. Oh, Christ. His stomach actually *hurt*, how hard he was laughing, head thrown back and eyes watering. "You're a little bitch," he told Victor, grinning broadly. "Come on. I'm going to go get some food. Let's find Red and get dinner before everyone gets all furry."

Though Victor seemed a bit startled at the offer, he nodded and said, "I should take these books back to my tent first. But I can catch up with you later?"

He and Victor had started to walk, pausing where their paths would split. "Sounds good." Just as Jed turned away, someone collided full on with him, falling back with a grunt. It was Randall, arms loaded with books and maps, everything going flying as he landed on the ground. His glasses were somewhere in the grass, and he blinked blearily up at Jed, looking dazed.

"Sorry," Randall automatically apologized, fumbling to find his glasses again. "I wasn't looking where I was walking."

"No problem. I wasn't looking where I was standing." Jed shot Victor a little encouraging smirk, shoving the man toward Randall. "Here, let us help you." This was like a fucking love connection. He couldn't wait to tell Redford. Pack gossip was almost better than soap operas.

Victor dropped his armful of books to go to Randall's aid. He found Randall's glasses and picked them up first, holding them out, close enough that Randall would see them. "Here," he said softly. "Are you all right?"

As soon as he realized who else was with Jed, Randall had flushed, gaze dropping away. "Yes, of course," Randall answered stiffly, but something in his expression softened slightly as he took his glasses back. "Thank you."

Victor started gathering Randall's books for him, wincing at the sight of dirt on one of the covers and doing his best to wipe it off. "You're sure? That fall looked painful."

Jed was, honestly, not really helping. He was standing back, giving Victor a huge shit-eating grin from behind Randall every time Victor looked over. Randall seemed flustered, unsure of what to do. His and Victor's hands kept getting tangled together as they tried to gather his books.

"Yes, well." Randall shot Victor a quick glance, obviously awkward. "I'm not really that breakable."

"That's a relief to hear." Victor picked up the last fallen book and handed it to Randall. He seemed to handle that tome with more caution than the others, making sure it didn't have any dirt or creases. Randall looked intensely embarrassed that he had seen that particular one out of the stack, but when Jed craned his head, it didn't look like porn or anything. Just an old book, one he'd seen Randall carrying before, with a weird title, something about Jeeves. A butler porn book, maybe?

"Thank you," Randall said again, softer, standing and cradling his armload closer to his chest, the butler porn held closest. "I appreciate the help."

Victor collected his own books off the ground, clearly unsure what to say. "I hope you have a good full moon," he wound up going with. Jed could have smacked him. Randall was obviously going to take the out, and then they'd just go back to being awkward.

So he shouldered Victor aside, grinning at Randall. "And by that he means you're joining us for dinner. Me and Red and Vickie."

Randall looked a little surprised, eyes darting over to Victor quickly. "I'm not sure—" he started.

"I'd really like if you did," Victor said in a rush. "We'll get the food together. All you need to do is show up."

Clearly hesitant, Randall fidgeted, foot to foot. "I just—"

Jed didn't give him a chance to say no. "Great." He beamed, slinging an arm around Victor's shoulders. "See you in twenty." And then he guided Victor off, sneaking quick looks behind them to catch Randall staring after them, utterly baffled. He'd show up, though. He was far too polite not to.

"Well, I hope you're in the mood for an awkward dinner," Victor sighed.

"Fuck that. Red and I are bailing five minutes after he gets there." Jed smirked widely. "It's the full moon. I have it on reliable intel that all the wolves are going to get *very* frisky. Why don't you take a little risk?"

"Your attempts to get Randall and I back together are hardly helping," Victor said crossly. "He'll spend the full moon with his brothers. If he can't look at me, I highly doubt he'll want to rekindle the one-night-long relationship we had."

Rolling his eyes, Jed gave Victor a little push toward his tent. "So make him want to look at you. Fuck, Victor, I don't know. But you two acting like the world is your fainting couch is getting old. Do something."

"What an inspirational speech," Victor said drolly. "Isn't all this talk on topics other than guns and explosions making you break out into hives yet?"

"Yes," Jed grunted. "So consider this the last time we're ever doing anything remotely like this."

"Duly noted." Victor looked like he might be almost smiling. Jackass.

Jed left him to go do his nerd thing and obsessively arrange his books, and went back to the campfires. Redford was busily grilling meat, Edwin already in wolf form and happily gnawing on a chunk of raw something. Venison, probably. Jed sprawled out on one of the logs next to Redford, leaning into his side. "So, Victor and Randall are going to be here for dinner too," he informed Redford, kissing his cheek. "Hey."

This close to the full moon, there was a hint of yellow beginning to show in Redford's eyes. But there was no menace there, no sign that he was anything but fully within his right mind. Redford budged his shoulder against Jed's in greeting. "You took a while," he noted, adding some more meat to the fire. "Is Anthony okay?"

There was something wild about Redford now, something just a little more confident in the set of his shoulders, a little more relaxed, like he was learning to be at peace with himself. This was the right thing for him, to be here. Jed might want to go home—and at some point, they'd have to—but right now, this was exactly what Redford needed. Jed could deal with tramping around in mud and being the only human to get to see Redford like this. Eyes darting to Edwin, Jed absently took Redford's hand. "We'll talk about it later," he murmured. Probably shouldn't discuss Anthony's big plans in front of Edwin. "But Victor's an idiot."

Though Redford looked concerned, he didn't push the topic about Anthony and focused on the topic of Victor instead. "Over Randall?"

Snorting, Jed hooked his legs over Redford's lap, curling up closer. He liked this. There was a fire, there was the smell of cooking meat, and Redford. He was pretty damn happy. "Yeah. So we're going to leave them alone once they get here, and hopefully the wall of stupidity will break."

Edwin gave a wolfy chuff, something that might have even been a laugh. Clearly he approved as well.

Redford snorted quietly. The meat was well on its way to roasting, and Redford left it alone for a few seconds to focus on Jed, curving a hand over his knee. "I bet neither of them were too happy at that plan."

"Like I care." He trailed his lips along Redford's jaw, happily teasing kisses across Redford's skin. "They're annoying." And he was done talking about them for sure. Edwin grabbed his dinner and took off, leaving them relatively alone. Smart kid.

With a low laugh, Redford turned to catch Jed in a kiss, more demanding than usual. "They are," Redford agreed. "But they're friends."

"Let's not get carried away." Jed slid his hand up under Redford's shirt, fingers sprawling against the warm skin. "Anthony asked us to take care of his brothers if he died. I said okay." There, now Redford was all caught up. "Should we go to our tent?" he asked hopefully.

Sadly for him, Redford was too busy looking pleased at the news. "You promised Anthony you'd take care of his brothers? That's really nice of you."

"I promised *we* would. We." That was very important. "And by we, I definitely mean *you*."

"You'll help, if we need to fulfill that promise," Redford said knowingly. "I know you will."

"Not a family guy, Red," Jed reminded him, arching an eyebrow. "Just the man with the weapons."

"You're a family guy when it comes to me." Redford kissed him again, smiling. "Trying to convince yourself you're an island isn't going to work much longer."

"You are different," Jed murmured against his lips, hooking him in closer. "Two-person island. Two people and a cat. That's it."

"I'd be okay with that." Redford paused in the middle of kissing him. Before Jed could complain, he heard two sets of footsteps approaching—one from the north, one from the west. Victor and Randall. They had *terrible* timing.

"Five minutes," Jed insisted. "Then I want you. Got it?"

Victor made a derisive noise. "Can you not talk about your sex life in public? Besides, you won't have time. It's getting dark quickly."

"You would be amazed what I could do in fifteen minutes." Jed reluctantly pulled back, grabbing a plate from the stack next to Redford.

"That is rather more information than I needed." Randall approached next, awkwardly, gaze constantly drawn back to Victor despite his best efforts to appear unaffected. "Er. Hello."

Redford started dishing the meat onto four plates. Jed caught a hint of his expression: somewhere between bemusement and worry for Randall and Victor. "Good evening," he greeted both of them. "I hope the meat's done enough for you. This is thicker slabs than I've worked with before."

"It will be fine," Randall assured quietly. He took a plate and sat, knees hunched almost up to his chest.

"That's not true, babe," Jed said, eyes widening. "You are used to *way* thicker meat than this." A grin slowly replaced the put-on innocent expression he had as he waited for Redford to get the joke and ignored Victor's scowl.

"That steak we got from the organic market was not cut nearly as thick as this," Redford corrected.

Very lightly, Jed took Redford's hand in his and casually cupped the front of his jeans with their joined fingers. "Much, *much* thicker," Jed informed him with a huge smirk.

"Jed!" Redford yanked his hand away, but he was laughing as he did so. "Yes, okay, I get your innuendo now. And you're completely right—"

Victor made inelegant gagging noises in the background.

"But," Redford continued, "we can talk about that later."

"I don't know if I'll be able to talk with your big, delicious—"

"Victor, why don't we take a walk." Randall had shot straight up, eyes wide, looking at Jed as if he was quite sure he was going to start taking off clothes right then. "Or... go find earplugs."

"God, yes," Victor agreed desperately. He yanked two plates away from Redford for himself and Randall. "Anywhere but here."

Hey, look. His master plan worked. "Go get yours, princess." Jed was enormously pleased with himself.

Redford just shook his head in exasperation as Randall and Victor took off in a hurry. "Did you plan that?"

"Nope." Jed shrugged. "But hey, it worked." Although, watching them, Randall was obviously standing farther away from Victor than people who wanted to fuck should. Definitely not his problem, though. Now it was all on Victor. God help them both.

Redford leaned into Jed's side again as they started eating. Despite his worry about not cooking the meat right, Redford had done a damn good job—better than Jed ever could. He'd never been able to figure out just how the fuck cooking worked. To his mind, Redford dropped a whole bunch of things in a pot and *bam*, a gourmet meal. It was pretty much magic.

"Do you want to come to the woods with me?" Redford asked. "Just while I turn. I, um, don't really know what the instincts will want to do after that. I think I'll go run for a bit and then I'll come see you?"

"Sure." Jed ran his fingers idly through Redford's hair, sharing bites of the spicy meat between them. "I mean, I'll run with you if you want, or just wait. Whatever you need." He still wasn't quite sure what the right thing to do was, but he was damn sure he was going to let Redford figure it out. If he wanted to go run all fucking night, Jed would keep up the best he could.

A glint of mischief shone in Redford's eyes. "You don't need to come running with me. I think you'll need to save your energy for the morning."

Now that Jed could agree with. He tugged Redford in for a slow kiss, lightly parting his lips, happy to let Redford take the lead. There was something intensely sexy about Redford's quiet strength on the average day. Now, this close to the moon, it was completely irresistible.

Redford turned his head to shove his nose against the side of Jed's throat, inhaling deeply. Words seemed to have lost all importance. Whatever Jed wanted to say, Redford could probably read off of his scent.

The sun was finally beginning to duck the last of itself behind the horizon, and wolves all around them were starting to vanish into the forest. Redford drew back from Jed, his eyes shining fully yellow now. "Sorry, I don't think we'll get that fifteen minutes beforehand," Redford apologized.

Jed just hooked him in for another kiss, hard, hungry. Redford's teeth nicked his tongue, his hands were demanding, and Jed just submitted to it fully. God, that was hot. "You are so gorgeous," he murmured. "God, I love you."

"Me too," Redford said lowly. He kissed Jed a final time, long and lingering, then reluctantly drew back. "Come on. Otherwise you'll wind up kissing a muzzle, and that would be really weird."

"I'd adjust," Jed teased, taking both of Redford's hands in his. They walked, wound up in each other, Jed kissing Redford's neck and shoulders. When they reached the woods, Jed lightly backed Redford up against a tree, smiling at him in the low light, helping him tug his shirt off.

"Sure we don't have time?" Jed asked in a murmur, sinking to his knees with a wicked leer. "I can be very quick."

Redford looked torn, but only for the briefest of seconds. Then he launched himself forward, bearing them both to the ground, where he pinned Jed with hands on his chest, ducking down to kiss him hard. "Time enough," Redford managed. "I can make time."

"You need to change," Jed reminded him, even if it had been his suggestion. Even though he was quickly pulling off Redford's pants, tossing them away, and eagerly wrapping his hand around Redford's cock. "Don't want you to hurt yourself." *God*, he'd never get over how good it felt to have Redford's cock in his hands.

"Then if I change in the middle of this, we can both be horrified and try to forget it," Redford muttered, scowling down at Jed's pants as he tried to undo them. "But right now, you smell *amazing* when you're turned on."

"Oh, God, don't change," Jed half laughed, half moaned. "I don't even know what I'd do." He kicked his jeans away, spreading his legs and groaning loudly as their hips arched together. "I've been turned on since you growled at me this morning for waking you up too early."

"I was having really nice dreams," Redford insisted, biting his way along Jed's neck. He shifted like he wanted something different, turned around, and without warning promptly took Jed's cock in his mouth, sucking hard. No patience for foreplay, no slow lead-up, just right to deep-throating.

Jed was not at all ashamed of the volume of the noises he was making. It took him several minutes of lying back on the ground, legs spread, hands digging into the dirt, to even begin to be able to think of anything but the delicious heat of Redford's mouth, the tight pull of his lips. When he did finally manage to get his brain working, all he could think about was touching Redford.

Grabbing Redford's hips, he pulled Redford in, arching his head up to take Redford's dick into his mouth, tongue sliding down the deliciously thick length of him. Muffling his moans, Jed pulled Redford in closer, bobbing his head fast and deep.

Redford's grip on his thighs was bruising—not keeping him down, just maintaining contact with Jed with a strength he couldn't think about holding back right then. It was completely and utterly hot as fuck. Jed did his best to keep up, wrapping his arms around Redford's hips, nails digging into his skin. They were moving together in a symphony of grunts and wet moans. Jed was fairly certain that his lips would be bruised and swollen with how Redford was thrusting down onto him. Not that he cared. Fuck, having his mouth full of Redford was better than just about anything in the world.

It wasn't long before he felt the telltale signs of Redford close to losing it. He had a pattern, one Jed had eagerly memorized: his grip would tighten, any noises he made would start to have an edge of a growl, and he'd double his effort of whatever he was doing. In this case, he was already close to blowing Jed's brains out—the extra need behind Redford's movements just about had him seeing stars. Determined to give Redford an orgasm he'd be shaky from all night, Jed tightened his lips, drawing Redford down farther, letting him use his mouth to push him over the edge.

Redford was the most unselfish partner he'd ever had, something that still surprised Jed sometimes. When Redford came, he didn't immediately disengage and roll over and wait for Jed to finish himself off. He just muffled his groans around Jed's cock and worked him harder, determined to make him come as well. It didn't take much.

Gasping, grasping at Redford's leg, his back, any part of him he could reach, Jed tensed, back arching up off of the ground. He came with a soft cry of Redford's name, sagging back down, panting heavily.

Holy fucking bouncing baby Jesus.

Only when Jed was starting to get ridiculously oversensitive did Redford back off, looking rather pleased with himself as he twisted to hover on hands and knees over Jed. Jed didn't lose any time pulling him in for a kiss, long and deep, hands roaming over Redford's back like he could somehow figure out a way to just sink into him completely. "God, that was good," he murmured against Redford's lips. "You're incredible."

Redford nuzzled against his neck, giving a contented noise. He'd said a few times that he liked it, right after sex, when Jed would smell like both of them. "We've got the morning to look forward to," he reminded Jed.

"I know." Jed let his head fall back, exposing the curve of his throat to Redford. It was a thing with wolves, he'd figured out pretty early on. And he liked what it did to Redford. "And you've got a whole night of running. It'll be good." He just wanted to give Redford something to remember.

"It'll be even better when I'm with you again." Redford reluctantly drew back from Jed's throat and started shedding the few remaining clothes Jed hadn't gotten around to ripping off. He'd lost some of the fear he'd had about turning, but there was still worry in his eyes—there probably always would be.

Jed just hauled Redford into his arms, sitting there, uncaring that there was a stick under his ass. "Everything's better when I'm with you," he agreed, kissing Redford one more time. "Come on, I can hear the rest of the pack running around. I bet Edwin can't wait to show you something gross he's sniffed out. I'll stay with you until you want me to go."

Redford nodded, tugging Jed in for one last kiss. Jed bit his lip lightly as they pulled back, grinning at him. No one in this whole damn world was half as beautiful as Redford was. Jed would lay down his last dollar on that fact. He sat back as Redford took his jewelry off, carefully handing it to Jed. Redford had theorized yesterday that he doubted he'd be able to completely control the shift on full moons, like the wolves here did, so when Redford tipped his head up to watch the moon, he looked like he was waiting.

When it happened, it wasn't quite as brutal as Jed had gotten used to seeing. There was still pain, still the awful noise of bones shifting and joints changing direction. It still wasn't as fluid and smooth as the pack managed. But it was better. It didn't cripple Redford with agony anymore.

It was still a weird sight, though. Jed wasn't sure he'd ever completely get used to it.

After he'd gotten his paws under him and looked steady enough, Redford budged his head into Jed's knee and held out his right foreleg. A week ago, Redford had gotten the idea to put a GPS tracker in his bracelet, just in case Jed ever needed to find him in the middle of the forest. One of the pack, a woman named Emily, was practically going out of her mind without any form of technology. She had been more than happy to take the tracker and turn it into something Redford would be able to wear.

"Be safe," Jed told Redford, kissing the top of his head. He slipped on the bracelet, making sure it was tight enough but not painful, and gave a good-bye scratch behind Redford's ear. "I'll be in our tent."

Redford got himself up on Jed's knees to give Jed a long, disgustingly slobbery lick to the side of the face. With a bark that sounded like a laugh, he took off into the forest, mere seconds passing before Jed couldn't hear him anymore. Wiping off his cheek, Jed remained sitting for a few more minutes, listening to the echoing howls, the sound of wolves running through the undergrowth. Finally, he got himself dressed again and headed back toward the camp. He passed a few of the sentries on his way in, all of them in wolf form, yellow eyes gleaming in the pale light. Everything seemed quiet.

Randall was standing at the edge of the camp, alone, eyes blazing yellow, still unchanged. "You're out late," he greeted Jed.

"You're not furry," Jed responded. "Have fun with Victor?"

"You're very lucky I don't bite you." Randall showed his teeth, but there was no real threat. "Don't play matchmaker. You're terrible at it."

Anthony, already wolfed out, trotted over to sit next to Randall, looking up at him with an exasperated huff. When he noticed Jed, he was promptly up again, affectionately throwing himself against Jed's legs. Jed immediately crouched, rubbing both hands on either side of Anthony's cheeks, behind his ears, laughing when he got a slobbery lick. "Yeah, yeah, you giant fluff ball," he murmured. To Randall he added, "Don't worry, sweetheart. That was my one and only interference. I think I got heartburn from caring."

"I appreciate it," Randall replied dryly.

"So why aren't you furry?" A cold nose budged into Jed's arm, and he turned to find Knievel, her tail swishing, curling herself around Jed's legs before she nudged her head against the underside of Anthony's chin. "Even Knievel's getting in on the party."

Anthony made a series of noises that sounded even more exasperated, directed at Randall. Randall rolled his eyes. "I'll be there. I don't know why you care so much. It's not as if you have any lack of people to run with tonight." He looked over at Jed. "I don't turn just because the moon goes up. I wait until I feel like going out."

The snort that Anthony blew out showed what he thought of that, but he nonetheless picked himself up—Knievel climbing around to lay over his neck like a scarf—and stared at Randall expectantly. Jed knew that look. Sure enough, Randall gave one glance down at Anthony before blowing out a heavy sigh. "Yes, yes."

He peeled off his sweater, his pants, making a neat folded pile and placing them on a nearby rock. Jed kept his eyes averted while Randall shifted. Randall nudged his nose against Anthony's side, tail wagging slightly. Knievel, much to Jed's surprise, didn't come back to him as the wolves headed off. She slid off of Anthony and kept pace beside him, streaking off at a run when Randall and Anthony increased their speed. Before Jed could call her back, she was gone.

Jed wanted to run after her. But after a few moments of pacing back and forth, distressed, hollering her name, he was forced to concede that she obviously didn't want to spend the night in the tent.

He swore to God, if she got eaten, he was going to explode something.

The tent wasn't nearly as warm or comforting without Redford, but it didn't take long for Jed to drop off to sleep. He slept soundly, the mountain air good for that, at least.

The first loud crash of noise, Jed barely woke for. Rolling over, burying his head under the covers, he drifted back off, only to jerk fully alert at the second report.

Gunfire. Accompanied by a sharp yelp he knew all too well.

Staggering out of the tent, Jed was strapping on his holster, grabbing his shotgun, all before he'd managed to shove his feet into his boots. His heart was hammering, his dog tags and whistle thumping against his chest as he ran. He wore them when Redford shifted. Jed fumbled for the whistle, putting it to his lips and blowing repeatedly.

Wolves were streaming into the camp, chaos mounting. Jed should be organizing them, trying to get a party together. But all he could do was stare at everyone as they passed, desperately searching for a familiar shape.

No more gunfire. That wasn't a good sign. That meant they'd hit something. Or they were dead, but since there weren't any triumphant howls, Jed wasn't betting on that scenario.

Most people couldn't tell wolves apart when they howled. They all kind of sounded the same, admittedly, but when you lived with a pack for a month, you started to be able to pick out the individual ones. And the howl that had risen from the forest was definitely Redford's. Without hesitation, Jed plunged into the dark woods, leaping over fallen trees, running full tilt toward the direction of the anguished noise.

He stumbled to a halt, heartbeat throbbing in his ears, spinning around and trying desperately to make out the shadowy shapes. His eyes weren't good enough for this, and he hadn't grabbed his flashlight. Stupid. Again he blew the whistle, holding completely still, listening desperately. "Come on, Red," he begged in barely more than a whisper. "Where are you?"

He waited. An agonizing minute passed by, every beat of his heart sounding like thunder in his ears. Other wolves passed him, none of them Redford. Just when Jed had decided he was going to turn this whole goddamn forest into woodchips, Redford burst out of the undergrowth, obviously frantic. He reared up and slammed two paws on the ground—their code for *hunter*.

Jed immediately took off, running in the direction everyone else was fleeing from. Shotgun in hand, he darted around trees, crashing through undergrowth, not caring how loud he was being. They sure as fuck better know he was coming. He caught a glimmer of light out of the corner of his eye. Immediately, Jed hit the ground, rolling, coming up to a crouch with the gun braced on his shoulder.

Nothing. He couldn't see anything. *Damn* it.

"Need a nose," he whispered, turning, expecting Redford to be right behind him.

Redford just shook his head. He pointed in the direction Jed had been going, but that head shake meant whoever had fired that gun was long gone, or at least gone long enough that there'd be no point in following them.

Fuck.

They'd come back in the daylight and track them to whatever bolt-hole they'd decided to crawl into. For now, at least, they needed to regroup and reassess. Jed absently wrapped an arm around Redford, pulling him in close. "God, my heart almost stopped when I heard you," Jed murmured, rubbing his hand absently through Redford's fur. "Glad you're okay."

His hand was wet. Sticky. Jed frowned and turned toward him. "What were you rolling in—" He held up his fingers, only to find them coated in red.

Redford was bleeding.

Jed stopped thinking. A rush in his ears, a roaring, was all he could hear. In one smooth movement, Jed scooped Redford up into his arms, abandoning his shotgun without a second thought, and started running back toward camp. He couldn't tell how bad it was, how much pain Redford was in, but it didn't matter. A scratch or something worse, the answer for everything was going to be *get him home*. So Jed ran.

Stumbling to his knees as he got near one of the fires, Jed set Redford down, shakily running his hands over him, searching for the wound. "I need the doc!" Jed hollered to whoever was nearby. "And a fucking light! Now, let's go, fucking *move*."

He couldn't be hurt. Redford *couldn't* be hurt. Jed simply wasn't going to let it happen. Someone handed him a flashlight, and Jed quickly switched it on, searching Redford for the source of the blood.

"The doctor's coming." Randall was next to him, in human form and dressed again, kneeling down and gently taking the light to aim it for Jed. "What happened?"

"Don't know. Hunters. Blood." The words came out of Jed like bullets, worry making it impossible for him to focus on anything else. Christ, what if Redford was dying right here? What if Jed had hurt him while he was running? What if he *died*? "Please be okay," he begged Redford lowly. "Okay? Hear me? Be okay."

Redford nudged against his hand, tail between his legs in a way Jed knew to be guilt, and turned so Jed could see his upper foreleg. That was where the blood was coming from.

Cedric was there a few seconds later, and after a cursory look, he sighed, "All right, Mr. Walker, you can stop tearing your hair out. It's just a graze."

Oh, thank fuck. Sagging forward, forehead resting against Redford's side, Jed took two breaths, just two, to let his heart start beating again. Okay. He was going to be okay. "Does he need stitches?" he asked Cedric, voice muffled by Redford's fur.

"Just a few," Cedric assured him, pulling a small kit out of his pocket. Redford laid his head on Jed's knee, still looking guilty. God knew why. "Can you change back?" That was directed at Redford, but Jed's answer was sharp and immediate.

"No way. We'll just, you know. Shave him or something." Redford's shifts were painful as it was. Jed didn't want him to chance one while he was injured. What if that made everything worse? What if he bled out because of all the goddamn muscles and bones moving around? It wasn't worth the risk.

Redford gave him a mournful look. Cedric, though, just sighed heavily and dug through his kit for a straight-edged razor. "Don't worry, kid," Cedric informed Redford gruffly. "I've been shaving my own damn face for longer than you've been alive. I think I can handle your bit of scruff."

Jed's fingers tightened in Redford's fur. He moved them around so he was holding Redford out on his lap, injured leg carefully supported. "He's going to be good, Doc, right?"

"I've told you, he's going to be fine. Now shut up and let me work."

291

"Okay." Right. Some fucking bastards had come into their woods, and now Redford was bleeding. Which meant Jed wasn't waiting until goddamn morning. "Okay," he said again, voice dropping dangerously. He rubbed behind one of Redford's ears, leaning in to press a kiss to the top of his muzzle.

Knievel had come slinking back from the woods, and she curled up by Redford, her back to his stomach, and dropped off to sleep. Strangely, that comforted Jed slightly.

He held Redford close while Cedric put the stitches in, ignoring Cedric's grumbles about damn fool wolves and their damn fool boyfriends. Anthony had arrived at some point, human again, watching everything with a dangerous glint in his eye.

Jed barely realized Anthony was talking. With some effort, he managed to pay attention. "Jed?" Anthony sounded like he was repeating himself. "Was it hunters?"

Dragging a hand across his face, Jed's jaw tightened. "Yeah." He glanced up at Anthony. "You feel up to a little playtime? Want to go pay them a visit?"

Anthony smiled grimly. "Absolutely."

Jed left Redford with Cedric and Randall, the latter looking very much like he wanted to protest. But in the end, he sat silently and watched as Jed and Anthony marched back to Jed's tent. Jed pulled out his crate of supplies, dug through, and found several carefully packaged blocks of C-4. He'd brought them here special a week ago, intending to try and set up some kind of perimeter. Now, though, they were going to get a whole different use.

It didn't take Jed long to set up ten charges. He packed them into a bag, gently settling it along his shoulders and grabbing his guns and some extra ammo. "You going to suit up?" he asked Anthony. "Or you going furry? Might need your nose, mine is worthless out there."

"Depends on what you think is best," Anthony said. "I've got no problems starting out wolf and going naked if I need to shift back to talk."

"Not anticipating a lot of talking," Jed replied grimly. He grabbed a flashlight and nodded toward the woods. Fuck, he wished he had his night-vision gear. Or his silencer. Or, hell, any of the gear he'd left back at home. A flashlight was going to give away their position long before Jed wanted it to. And if he was smart, he'd wait until first light, until he had a better chance of taking the bastards by surprise. One look back at the camp, though, at where Redford was lying there, stark white bandage shocking against his fur, had Jed turning toward the forest, jaw tight. Fuck *smart*. "Let's go."

Anthony nodded, and two seconds later he had dropped into wolf form, silently waiting on Jed's signal. When Jed nodded at him, Anthony put his nose to the ground, presumably following Redford's scent first, which would lead him to the hunters' trail.

They arrived at the point where Jed had found Redford in fairly short order, and Anthony only paused for the barest of seconds before taking off toward the east. Jed kept close on his heels, though he was pretty damn sure Anthony was holding back so Jed didn't get left in the dust. They kept going for another fifteen minutes, until Jed's lungs felt like they were going to burst. He came crashing to a stop, bracing one arm on a tree and half bent over, heaving in huge breaths.

Fuck. Goddamn wolves.

Even sick, Anthony moved with a grace that Jed just couldn't match. Jed could see the hesitation in Anthony's steps from time to time, the way he pulled himself up short, but honestly? If he hadn't known, he wouldn't have guessed the kid was slowly dying. He was just so goddamn determined to keep moving, not to let it stop him. Jed didn't know if he was stupid or brave. Funny, how those two things seemed to overlap.

Anthony stayed close while Jed worked his way through not vomiting. With a jerk of his head, Anthony motioned to just over a small incline where, if Jed squinted hard enough against the darkness, he thought he could see the top of some kind of tent. Jed dug into his bag to pull out the first charge.

"What are you doing?" Anthony shifted back to hiss. "You never mentioned *blowing them up*."

"What did you think we were going to do out here?" Jed asked in a near whisper, moving closer to the camp. "Hold hands and sing?"

Anthony grabbed him by the back of his jacket. "Jed," he said urgently. "You don't have to kill them. Look at them. They're not attacking anybody right now."

"They *did*." Jesus fuck, did he have to seriously do a paint by numbers, now? Crouching behind a half-fallen tree, Jed turned back toward Anthony. "And when they get up? They're going to skip merrily along and *do it again*. So yeah, Lassie, I'm going to blow their sleeping asses to kingdom come, and then I'm going to go back to the camp that they *won't* be attacking anymore and sleep like a goddamn baby."

"It won't change anything." Anthony sounded like he was only just managing to keep his calm. "I'm sorry that Redford got hurt, I understand how angry you are, but killing these men won't protect the pack. There'll just be more of them tomorrow."

"Then I'll *blow them up* too." Jed's voice rose into something not at all a whisper. "And I'll keep doing it, because they hurt Red. Get that? They hurt *my* Redford, and now I'm going to turn them into confetti."

"No, you're not," Anthony said firmly. "We can scare them off. We can send a message that will make them think twice about bringing more hunters in. Killing them obviously isn't deterring them."

"Why the hell did you even come?" Scowling, Jed stood, bag over his shoulder. "This isn't a damn tea party. Go home, kid."

Anthony promptly yanked him back down. "I came to stop you doing *this*," he growled. "We're not animals, Jed. We were given brains for a reason."

"What would you do, then?" Jed met Anthony's eyes, practically vibrating for how much he needed to *hurt* someone. Something. Punch a goddamn tree, he didn't care, just *something* needed to break, because Redford was bleeding. "Sit back and wait for them to pick you off one by one? These bastards only understand *one* thing, and it isn't reason."

"Playing by *their* rules isn't going to win this." Anthony laid a hand over the top of Jed's bag, curled under the strap. "I would blow up the perimeter of their camp. Scare them away, and once they're gone, we could look for more information in the camp. We could go higher up the chain of command, which would be a lot more effective."

But not *nearly* as satisfying. "You realize," he growled, holding Anthony's gaze, "that not one of those fuckers would hesitate even a second in blowing your head off. Or anyone else back at that camp."

Anthony just smiled. "I know. But that's why we're better than them, and that's why we're going to win."

293

"Son of a—" Sighing, rubbing a hand through his hair, Jed just glared at him. But the goddamn earnest wolf eyes were out in full force, and in the end, he wound up jerking his head in a nod. "Fine. *Fine.* We'll do it your way."

"Okay." Anthony tugged at Jed's bag. "Get your explosives. Maybe put them in the tree line near their tents?"

"Stick close." Jed nodded, starting out toward the tents again. "And try to keep your furry ass down." He made his way slowly toward the camp, doing his best to be nearly silent.

He and Anthony planted the explosives around the entire perimeter of the camp. Each one was on a timer, and as soon as they put down the last one, Jed grabbed Anthony's shoulder and hauled him up over the ridge again. They'd just barely got down, Jed sprawling over Anthony protectively, when the bombs went off.

Explosions sprayed up dirt and fire, a deafening thunder of noise. As soon as the debris started to rain down on them, Jed was up, gun out, watching the retreating backs of the hunters as they ran away as quickly as their legs could move them. Apparently picking off unarmed wolves in the dark was only fun if no one was blowing you up.

They waited. Anthony was just as tense behind him. Finally, Jed flicked the safety back on and, nodding at Anthony, picked his way carefully down to the empty camp.

Anthony caught up to Jed a few seconds later. "They're still running," he confirmed. "They won't come back."

They poked around the tents, finding more boxes of silver bullets. These had different etchings on the bottom. Buck was apparently no longer in the niche bullet manufacturing trade. But other than that, clues were scarce.

"You said you knew where he was? The man who employed Buck?" Anthony said as he rolled a silver bullet between his fingers.

He glanced over at Anthony. "I absolutely do. And I think it's high time we paid him a visit."

"Count me in." As he stood from where he'd been stooped over a tent, Anthony wasn't showing a single sign of his illness. None of the stiff movements Jed had been witness to, the shaking hands, the momentary spasms of pain. Anthony's expression was grim, his lips pulled tight, but if Jed didn't know better, he'd say he was just a healthy kid about to go on a murder spree. Apparently anger was enough to make him forget the pain. Jed'd bet fifty bucks and his last condom, though, that Anthony would be paying for it later.

"You sure, Lassie?" Jed gave him a quick smirk. "Not going to be a lot of hugs involved."

For once, Anthony didn't smile back. "I hate hunters."

Yeah, Jed could see where that'd be the case. Jed nodded, regarding him. "All right, then. Let's get going."

They trekked back to the camp, a lot slower this time, thank God. By the time they walked in, the wolves were huddled together, the Gray Lady standing in the middle of the group, obviously working on keeping them calm. She looked over as Jed approached, but he didn't waste a lot of time. "We're going to put an end to this," Jed informed her.

"The hunters?" she asked tensely.

Jed gave her a flat smile. "I wouldn't worry about them. They're not going to be your problem for much longer."

Redford, still curled up with Knievel by one of the fires, looked up at Jed. He saw no worry in Redford's eyes—only support. Jed nodded at him, his dog tags still around his neck. It felt strange to be wearing them, now.

"Jed," came Victor's disapproving tones, "you probably set half the woods on fire. Did you really need to use explosives? Not that I'm not happy the hunters are gone, mind you, but that was a bit excessive."

"The fires are out" was Jed's reply. He walked over to Redford, dropping the chain holding the dog tags and the whistle back around Redford's neck. A silent promise that he was coming back. "And yeah. I fucking needed to use explosives. They're damn lucky I didn't bring the goddamn rocket launcher. And don't you fucking tell me you'd do any different if you were me." They'd hurt Redford. They were a threat that constantly followed the wolves, yes, but *they'd hurt Redford*.

Victor grimaced, looking faintly embarrassed. "You're right," he said. Randall, helping to gather some of the younger wolves together, gave Victor a surprised look. "Good luck with what you're about to do next. If you need more weapons, I'm sure we can scrounge up some more."

"We're good." Jed clapped Victor on the shoulder and nodded toward the faint path leading down the mountain to where the few communal pack vehicles were stashed. "Come on, Ant. Let's ride."

While he'd been talking, Anthony had obviously gone to get clothes, because he reappeared next to Jed in jeans and a heavy jacket. "Do you know where we're going?"

"Yup. I always know where my employers work. Even if they don't want me to. Especially repeat customers." He'd made that a hard and fast rule after Filtiarn. They could maintain their illusion of privacy as much as they wanted to, but at the end of the day, Jed knew who was behind the mask or he walked away.

They reached the cave the pack had commandeered as a sort of garage after an hour of hiking. After tossing his bag of supplies inside the Jeep, Jed climbed behind the wheel. Anthony clambered into the passenger seat, and they took off toward the main highway.

"His name is Leo O'Malley. This guy is a snake," Jed informed Anthony. "Seems real slick, you know? But he's got his fingers in shit even I don't know about."

"You said you'd worked with him before?" Anthony asked, canting his head to one side, obviously genuinely curious.

"Couple of jobs." Jed nodded. "Nothing big. One was a retrieval job. Another just had me getting some info from a rival company. Hell, I didn't even use my gun. But one was a nice little piece of insurance fraud." Jed grinned, glancing over at Anthony. "Which means he'll definitely talk to us. And might try to kill us."

"Good." Anthony nodded. "Is there any way I need to act so that he doesn't kick us out?"

"Don't piddle in the corner." Jed shot Anthony a smirk.

Anthony rolled his eyes. "I'll do my best to remember that."

295

The drive was a few hours. They stopped for coffee, Jed let Anthony have control of the radio, and by the time the early morning sun was burning the mist from the roads, they were pulling in front of a nondescript office building. Unlike Buck's place, which was cheapness striving for an illusion of grandeur, O'Malley's place was quietly restrained wealth. The front was all glass, the lobby was marble and deep, rich mahogany wood, and the woman at the reception desk was wearing a suit that cost more than Jed's entire wardrobe.

"We're here to see Leo O'Malley."

The receptionist just looked at Jed, eyebrow arched. "Isn't that nice," she mused, turning back to her work. "Let me know how that goes for you."

Why didn't anyone ever take him seriously?

In response, the start of a low growl rumbled in Anthony's throat, and though he looked like he wanted to start threatening, he simply said, "Pick up the phone and tell O'Malley we're here. Now."

A very slow grin split Jed's face as the woman stared at him and then, with a quick, cross breath, turned to do just that. Goddamn, that was useful. Usually to get that kind of reaction he'd have to pull out his guns. "Tell him Jed Walker is here," he prompted, grin not diminishing at the woman's scowl.

It only took a few moments before they were gestured toward the elevators and instructed to go to the top floor. Far from looking tense like Jed had half expected him to, Anthony looked completely relaxed, like this was something he did every day. "You're kind of badass," Jed informed Anthony with a smirk as they watched the floors tick by.

"It comes from an unlikely source," Anthony laughed quietly. "Imagine Edwin as a toddler. Now imagine how stern I needed to sound to keep him from running off. It's really just that."

Snorting a quiet chuckle, Jed shook his head. "How you kept that kid from running off and joining the goddamn circus I'll never know. You must be a hell of a dad."

"Dad? Not likely." For a moment, Anthony looked sad, but he wiped any trace of that from his expression quickly enough. The elevator reached its destination with a quiet bell for an alert, and as they stepped out, Anthony said, "One day, if I'm lucky."

"Hey, you raise kids, they don't die, that's pretty much a dad in my book." Jed led the way down the hall, shoulders tight, eyes darting to every doorway they passed. He didn't like having this much unknown space at his back. But walking in here with guns drawn was a surefire way to get really, really dead. They'd have to play nice.

"Knock, knock, Leo." Okay, kind of nice. Jed pushed the office door open and strode in, not bothering to wait to be admitted.

He'd never actually met Leo in person. All of their work had been done over the phone or by e-mail. But Jed had not a doubt in his mind that the man behind the expansive dark wood desk was the guy he was looking for.

Leo wasn't tall or imposing. He had a handsome face, short, dark hair, but was utterly unimpressive. Until you met his eyes. They, behind the genial smile, were stone-ass cold. They were the eyes of a reptile, of something that would gladly unhinge its jaw and devour you whole. Jed had met a hundred men just like Leo. Every single one of them wanted one thing. Power.

So why the hell was Leo sending hunters after a bunch of wolves?

"Can I be of some assistance?" Leo asked, spreading his hands like he was welcoming them to a fucking tea party.

"Yeah. I'm gonna need some answers, here, Leo. Can I call you Leo?"

"I prefer Mr. O'Malley, as I hardly would classify us as friends, Mr. Walker." Leo gestured for them to sit. Anthony ignored the invitation and stood right in front of his desk instead.

"Let's talk about why you're sending hunters to kill wolves," Anthony said.

"I'm sorry?" Steepling his fingers, Leo arched an eyebrow at them. "Perhaps you are mistaken. I don't have any environmental holdings, as far as I'm aware."

"Cut the crap." Jed leaned back in his chair, grinning the whole time. It wasn't a pleasant look. "You're bankrolling Buck Cambridge, who is in turn funneling your money into silver bullets and hunters to fire them."

Leo tilted his head, studying them. "This is a nice fantasy. Why would I do any of what you're suggesting? It sounds a lot like madness."

"Listen here, sunshine. Why don't you get on your little phone and try to call the men you just sent out." Jed waved his hand. "Go ahead. We'll wait."

"Something tells me it wouldn't do any good." Leo sighed.

"Nope." Jed's manic grin grew. "I doubt they'll be answering. They're too busy running. And that? That was *foreplay*. So unless you want me to get balls deep in fucking you over, Leo, you are going to call them off."

"But first I want to know *why*." Anthony continued on where Jed had left off. "You're completely human. Why are you going after wolves?"

Leo shrugged. "They are a menace. A few interested parties asked me if I could eliminate the pest problem. I agreed. Simple as that."

"*Which* interested parties?" Anthony snarled.

To that, Leo just laughed. "Why, the vampires, of course. They want your flea-bitten race eliminated."

Anthony visibly reined himself back. When he next spoke, the snarl was only implied, instead of outright voiced. "And why is a human making business deals with vampires?"

"Because they paid me, little puppy." Leo stood, buttoning his suit jacket. "And they will continue to pay me. The men I sent out are cheap to buy and even cheaper still to arm, in the grand scheme of things. But do tell your lovely leader to try to run again. It's so much more *fun* that way."

"And why are wolves getting kidnapped? What are you capturing them for?" Anthony asked.

A very faint smirk crossed Leo's face. That arrogant kind of sneer that made Jed want to reach for his gun and just start blasting, because *whatever* was behind it, it sure as hell wasn't rainbows and unicorn farts. "I certainly never gave authorization for that," Leo all but purred, leaning back in his chair, looking for all the world like the cat that ate the goddamn canary. "But I have heard that, in certain circles, men of taste enjoy having luxurious rugs made of unusual pelts. That may be where your missing pups have gotten to."

Anthony, amazingly, still looked like he was keeping his temper. Jed was pretty sure he wasn't going to be able to say the same, shortly. Anthony glanced at Jed, then back at Leo. "And how many jobs have you worked with Jed, Mr. O'Malley?"

Leo paused, gaze darting between them, another smile creasing his lips and never touching the cold blue of his eyes. "Are you implying blackmail, wolf?"

"He might be implying it. I'm just fucking saying it." Jed met Leo's gaze without blinking. "I so much as smell one of your flannel fucking hunters sniffing around that pack again, I'm going to ruin you. Akron, Ohio, Leo. That's all I'm going to say."

Leo pursed his lips in thought, considering them both. "I am being paid quite a lot," he pointed out, like this was just another business transaction.

"Enough to be okay with the fact that there are a few hundred wolves that will shortly know your scent and where you do business?" Anthony said lowly.

"If I was afraid of the big, bad wolf," Leo smirked, "I wouldn't have let you in the door."

"Well, little pig," Jed growled, "I'm about to huff and puff and blow your fucking head in."

Leo rolled his eyes. "Crass threats are utterly boring." He sat again, pulling out a silver cigarette case. "Fine. Vampires are tiresome to deal with long-term. I will terminate their contract if it will get you both out of my office immediately."

Anthony nodded. "Let's get out of here, then, Jed."

Jed *really* wanted to punch Leo. Or shoot him. Nonfatally! Maybe in the kneecap. But he just fixed Leo with a glower as he stood and marched out the door, Anthony beside him. They had a silent ride down the elevator, neither one exchanging a word as they stalked out to the Jeep. Jed started it up and headed out onto the highway, fingers clenched tight on the wheel.

"Vampires," he grunted, darting a glance over at Anthony. "You think that's true?"

Anthony frowned. "It wouldn't surprise me. Do you think he'll keep his word?"

"He's a businessman." Jed sagged back in the seat, eyes itching with exhaustion. "I think he's going to do whatever gets him the biggest payday. Whatever the bloodsuckers are paying him can't be worth pissing the both of us off."

"Do you think he was telling the truth about the kidnapped wolves?" Anthony sounded skeptical. "Are they really getting... what he said?"

The thing about Anthony, Jed realized, was that he apparently couldn't comprehend that people would kidnap sentient creatures to skin them. Jed had seen a lot worse in his day, so he had no trouble imagining it. Hell, he wouldn't be surprised if there was a whole side business in it for Leo: exotic rugs and Murdering Fuckheads R Us.

"Nah," he lied easily. What would be the point in saying yes? Hunters going after the pack were enough of a nightmare. Jed didn't want to add to the pile. "Leo's an asshole. Probably just wanted to rile you up so he'd have an excuse to sic his goons on you."

"Right." Though he'd sounded skeptical before, Jed could hear a little bit of relief in Anthony's voice. "Getting wolves for rugs would be ridiculous, anyway. If you want a pelt rug, bears are way bigger."

"Exactly." Jed clapped Anthony on the shoulder, nodding. And he added another mark on his list of reasons to blow these goddamn hunters out of the water. Whoever was bankrolling them, whoever was pulling Leo's strings, they needed to go down. In a very bloody fashion.

Although avoiding war would be nice. Jed wouldn't mind not having an inter-freak battle on his hands.

"So he said that vampires are the ones calling for all this. I wonder if that's the start of the war Victor saw in his vision," Anthony mused. "Wolves versus vampires."

"I don't know." Jed shifted, dragging his hand across his jaw and wondering where he could get some more coffee. There had to be a drive-through somewhere. "Maybe? Does that sound like something that might actually happen? I mean, I know I'm the dumb human, but wouldn't you guys, you know, *not* want to kill each other?"

"I'm just as in the dark as you." Anthony shrugged. "I've never interacted with a vampire. I think wolves and vampires generally stay away from each other. You're right, nobody wants a war. But then you get cases like what happened in Cairo. It's not just the vampires that cross the line either. There's bad wolves out there too."

"So we're really not as different as people keep saying," Jed pointed out with a grunt. "Hey, maybe there's hope for us all yet." He took an exit and pulled into a fast-food place, got out of the Jeep, and stretched. "I need coffee or I'm going to fall asleep and kill us both. You want anything?"

Anthony answered by hopping out to join him, keeping his hands warm in the pockets of his jacket. "These places never have real meat, but I'm starving so I don't care."

"Yeah, their coffee is going to be shit too," Jed agreed. "But fuck, I'm about to give the Folgers can a blow job just to get some caffeine in my system, so it'll do." They walked in, shoulder to shoulder, and ordered a couple of breakfast sandwiches, Anthony's heavy on the sausage, and two large black coffees.

He and Anthony traipsed back out to the Jeep and leaned against the hood of the car while they ate. It was chilly, too early yet for there to be much traffic but late enough that they'd missed the morning commute. Anthony had started moving his hands too carefully again. Whatever determination or adrenaline that had allowed him to push past his illness was gone now. Jed shrugged off his jacket and unceremoniously wrapped it around Anthony's shoulders to help ward off the morning cold.

"You can sleep on the way back," he told Anthony with a grunt, hunched over his coffee like it was literally a form of lifeblood. "Give me a chance to listen to some decent music instead of the crap you pick."

"You've just got shit taste." Anthony smiled wanly.

"Watch it." Jed wagged a warning finger at him. "I'll make you walk home." Anthony's quiet laugh was reward enough, and they ate in silence for another few moments. Jed watched the passing traffic on the highway beyond the parking lot, mind nicely disconnected, weariness seeping into his bones.

"So," Anthony said eventually. Jed braced himself; he recognized that tone. A serious discussion was imminent. "Do you regret that we didn't kill those two hunters?"

299

Heaving out a breath, Jed concentrated on gulping down more coffee without burning his tongue off. "Honestly? I haven't even thought about it. Probably wouldn't regret it if we'd done it, either. I'm not really one to dwell on jobs once they're finished."

"I'm glad we didn't," Anthony murmured. "Edwin killed a hunter before. Do you remember?"

"Yeah." Jed folded his arms, squinting up at the sun. "Yeah, Ant, I get it." Civilians in combat were the worst fucking thing. They weren't trained for it, and they didn't know how to handle the aftermath. Like Edwin.

Like Redford.

"I just hope you don't regret it. Lot easier to sleep at night when you know the thing that's out there trying to kill you is dead."

"I told him that he shouldn't feel guilty," Anthony mused. "We were getting attacked, and he had to protect his pack. But those hunters that we scared off? They were sleeping. I don't think I could have lived with myself if we'd killed them."

After a beat, Jed glanced over at Anthony. This was a guy who'd raised two kids by himself, no help from goddamn anyone. He hunted his own meat, he dealt with a disease that was eating him from the inside, he was basically Superman. He had a code. Even men like the ones who killed his parents had some kind of worth to him.

He was a better man than Jed was. And, hell, Anthony wasn't even a man.

"Okay, Jiminy Cricket." Nodding, Jed finished the rest of his coffee and tossed the Styrofoam cup toward a nearby bin. "Lesson learned. Can we hit the road now?"

Anthony just smiled in reply. After they got rid of the rest of their trash, Anthony climbed into the Jeep and relaxed back into his seat, closing his eyes. Jed, despite what he'd threatened, didn't turn the radio on at all. He drove as Anthony slept, making the long trip back as quickly as he could. They parked the Jeep, and he woke Anthony to make the trek up to the camp.

They were greeted ten minutes out by one of the sentries, which made Jed want to practically burst with pride. As soon as the Fur Pigeon made sure it was really them, they were let through. Redford was waiting right at the entrance to the camp, visibly relieved that they were both in one piece. Jed went to him, immediately wrapping his arms tightly around him, burying his face in Redford's neck.

"You okay?" he asked, needing to hear it again. No matter what the doc had said, Jed needed to hear it from Redford.

Pulling up the sleeve of his T-shirt, Redford showed him the bullet graze. "Just four stitches," he reassured. "You've had worse cutting yourself shaving."

Yeah, like he cared. Jed pressed a careful kiss just below the bandage, silently apologizing for that wound as well. One more way he'd failed. He was racking up quite a count. "Come on," he murmured, arm hooking around Redford's waist as if he couldn't bear the thought of being too separate. "Anthony and I need to update the Gray Lady. Which means you're coming with me, because I am going to want to stick close for a while."

Redford looked like he wouldn't have it any other way. They made their path toward the campfires, numerous wolves giving Jed and Anthony curious, anticipatory looks as they passed. The Gray Lady was waiting for them by one of the larger fires, surrounded by younger wolf cubs. She raised her head to acknowledge them as they came close.

"Well?" she asked, as if their conversation hours ago was merely being continued now with no break at all.

"It's vampires." Jed didn't see any point beating around the bush. "They were paying O'Malley. I'm pretty sure we've convinced him it's no longer worth his while to continue that particular arrangement, but I don't know if they'd try someone else. Or if there's even anyone else for them to go to."

"*Vampires*?" Victor looked like he wasn't sure whether to be confused or horrified. "I know there's something of an odd rivalry, but I'd hoped...." He trailed off, staring hard at the ground.

The Gray Lady looked over at him. "Your vision?" A nod was the only response Victor gave. Jed glanced over, half frowning. This was probably a David thing. Most of the time when Victor got that look, the one half like he'd sucked sour grapes and half like he liked it, it was a David thing. Which meant Jed really, really didn't want to talk about it.

"In any case, I think we're in the clear. At least for now." Jed looked back at the Gray Lady. "If you have anyone in the vampire world you can talk to, you might want to. Because the last thing we need is both sides starting a goddamn war."

From her expression, he may as well have suggested she roll around in shit. "We don't keep contact with leeches," she sniffed.

"Maybe you should start," Victor said bluntly. "Jed's right. Diplomatic contact may be essential at this point." But even he didn't look convinced by his own argument.

It was a mistake. Jed could see that so clearly. If vampires and wolves wanted to duke it out like some cheesy B-rated horror flick, then fine. But people would get caught in the crossfire. Half bloods, humans, *Redford*, they'd get stuck in the middle, and that could get very bad, very fast.

But right then, Jed was exhausted, he was hungry, and he wanted Redford. None of those things would be helped by having a long debate on the merits of diplomacy. So Jed just nodded and took Redford's hand, breaking up the little meeting and heading back to their tent.

"You really need sleep," Redford told him softly, ushering Jed into the tent when they reached it. "Everybody else can handle the strategy talks now."

"I'm fine," he insisted, but it was habit now. Jed collapsed face-first into their bed of blankets and pillows, barely managing to kick off his boots before he burrowed into the warmth. "How's your arm? Does it hurt?" He cracked one eye open and peered up at Redford. "Shit, it does, doesn't it? I should have gotten you some pain pills." He tried to struggle back up, getting caught in the blankets around his legs. "I think I have some left in my bag."

"Jed." Redford put a hand on his chest, pushing him back down onto the blankets, then crawled in after him. "It hurts, but it just aches. I'm okay."

He still wanted to get Redford the pills, but his whole body felt too heavy to move. So Jed just wrapped his arms carefully around Redford's waist, pulling him in close. "I thought I lost you." The admission felt like he'd let out some agonizing weight that had been crushing him slowly since he'd heard the first gunshot. "I hate that feeling, Red."

"I'm sorry. I should have been watching my surroundings better," Redford whispered, getting that guilty look on his face again.

Wait, what? How had that happened? Jed frowned at the way Redford's lips were pulling down, touching his thumbs to the creases at the corners of Redford's mouth as if he could smooth them away. "Why are you saying sorry?" he asked, voice thick with approaching sleep. "It's not your fault."

Redford didn't answer right away. Instead, he leaned forward, brushing a kiss against Jed's forehead. He stroked his fingers through Jed's hair, knowing the motion always had Jed's eyes falling closed in relaxation. "It doesn't matter," Redford murmured. "Get some sleep, Jed."

"Not until you tell me it wasn't your fault." It was getting harder to string words together, but Jed struggled valiantly to do just that. He snuggled in closer to Redford, letting out a slow breath of content at the feeling of Redford's fingers. "'Cause it wasn't. It was their fault. I blew them up for it. They ran away like scared little rabbits."

He felt Redford smile against his forehead. "Fine. It wasn't my fault."

"Damn straight." Cracking a giant yawn, Jed buried his face into Redford's chest, relaxing. "Love you," he mumbled before he lost the ability to speak altogether.

"Love you too," he heard Redford say. And then he slipped into sleep completely.

CHAPTER
17

Victor

VICTOR HAD started to think Randall was perhaps right about certain tendencies of his.

It was all he could think about as he hovered awkwardly at the edge of the pack gathering around the campfires. The Gray Lady was speaking to her guards, Jed and Redford had just left to presumably get some sleep, and the Lewises were huddled around another fire. Edwin and Randall were paying particular attention to Anthony, who was warming his hands at the edge of the fire, shaking his head sharply. Victor presumed he was denying any symptoms, but even he could see them from this distance.

The treatment wasn't working, and all Victor could do was stare at the back of Randall's head, wishing he could find the right words to say.

After the pack had left their first camp, Victor had gone home for a week. Randall's words had echoed in his thoughts too loudly to let him do anything else—and Randall had been right, Victor wasn't part of the pack. He had come with them half for some need for a thrill.

Once home, Victor had expected to find little to truly interest him. His home was lovely, inherited from several generations of Rathbones, but it had always felt empty to him. It was dull in a way that seeped into his bones and made him fear the long days of tediousness that might encompass the entirety of his life until he went insane well before a ripe old age. But he hadn't been bored when he'd arrived home. He'd been *relieved*.

Where once he'd rather enjoyed a brush with life-or-death, looking into the Gray Lady's eyes had scared him. It wasn't just her life span or the dread of the upcoming chaos. His reaction had been what had made him most afraid, the bursting of his blood vessels and the shake in his useless limbs. He hadn't gone permanently insane, but it felt like he'd come dangerously close.

He'd realized, in that moment, that all of his desperate attempts to live life on the edge hadn't made him enjoy life at all. They had only made it more chaotic. Victor still hadn't quite come to terms with the fact that the potentially happy alternative was the very thing he'd been avoiding all of his life, though.

He had collected various supplies, and a week later he had driven to the new camp. And now his sole useful contribution was staring at Randall's back and wishing he were more eloquent or open. He should, he knew, at the very least try.

303

Picking his way through the wolves, Victor got close enough to hear a snippet of Anthony speaking. From the sound of it, he was trying to reassure his brothers that he was absolutely fine.

"Whatever treatment Cedric is giving you isn't working," he heard Randall say lowly. "And it's clearly not going to. We need to find a currently practicing doctor with access to a hospital."

"The treatment could still kick in," Anthony protested.

"And you could keep getting worse." There was frustration in Randall's tone and heavy guilt. "Cedric might be brilliant, but his supplies are limited here. Even he says so."

Anthony didn't look entirely pleased. "That means we'd have to leave this pack. And it's really good here. Edwin loves it."

"Love you more, idiot," Edwin muttered, leaning into Anthony's side. "I don't care about the pack. Just you."

"Okay, and what happens if we do manage to somehow find a doctor that can treat canine Parkinson's in something other than a dog, *and* has access to a hospital?" Anthony raked his hands through his hair. He was starting to look stressed. "I don't have the money to pay for that. All three of us together couldn't afford it."

"I have my school savings." Randall sounded so tired, like he was close to giving up completely. "I can get two jobs. Edwin too. We'll figure it out, Anthony."

"You need your school savings for school," Anthony dismissed.

There was a long, uncomfortable pause. "Anthony...." Randall took a deep breath, head bowing. "I dropped out of school. At the end of last semester."

The silence stretched on even longer then. When Anthony spoke, his voice was perfectly flat. "You did what?"

Randall rubbed a hand through his hair, practically curled in on himself. "I turned down the offer from the state college. I.... I'm not going back."

"You—" Anthony broke off, sounding so furious that Victor thought it was a good thing he'd stopped himself from continuing whatever he was going to say. "You're going back to school, Randall. I know you still want to, and—"

"If I may cut in," Victor said. He'd tried to sound smooth, but he was fairly sure all he achieved was awkward. "I have the perfect solution, if you're willing to consider it."

Randall's gaze darted up to him, a tense clench to his jaw. They'd spoken after Jed's frankly juvenile attempt to force them to spend time together, but it had felt uncomfortable and tense. Randall had made his excuses and left Victor soon after the conversation had begun. The entire time Victor had been at the camp, Randall had avoided him as much as possible, as if keeping his distance would somehow change everything that had been between them. Perhaps it was working, because now Randall simply shook his head, turning back to Anthony. "I am not going back to school," he told his brother plainly. "I have no desire to continue. I'll get a job, two if I have to. Edwin—"

"I can work," Edwin assured Anthony. "We'll make it. Whatever it takes."

Anthony ignored both of them to say, "Talk, Victor. What's your solution?"

After being so obviously dismissed by Randall, Victor was taken off guard by Anthony's address. "Oh, er, I was going to suggest that Randall could attend the college I lecture at for a greatly reduced fee. And I am, to put it bluntly, absolutely filthy rich. I could pay your hospital fees."

"Why would you do that?" Edwin asked, eyebrow raised. Randall was just busy staring at Victor as if he'd suddenly sprouted another head. "I mean, that's not something people just *give* other people, you know?"

"Perhaps the world would be a better place if they did," Victor sighed. He looked at Randall, finding himself unable to discern the emotion on his face. "I just want to help. There's no ulterior motive."

"We're just fine, thank you." Randall stood then, jaw jutted out defiantly. "We're not in need of charity."

"It's not pity money," Victor protested. "I simply—"

"Just stop, Victor." Anthony sounded weary. "It's really kind of you to offer, but we'll make our own way."

Feeling once again quite useless, Victor had no idea whether he should leave or stay. He could make a second offer, allowing them use of his house should they ever need to be close to the hospitals in the area, but he doubted that would go over very well.

Fortunately for him, the Lewises then seemed to completely forget he was there. "I want to continue giving this treatment a chance," Anthony said, his expression positively mulish. "We've just done a seven-state move. We can wait at least one more week before we think about another one."

"You don't have time." Randall's arms were folded across his chest, a stubborn tone to his voice. "This isn't working, Anthony, come on. You can barely stand sitting there, your knees hurt so bad."

Anthony looked torn. "If we go back, can I make you promise that you'll go back to school?"

There was a beat of silence, and Victor realized that Randall was looking at him, expression completely shut down. It was possible, Victor thought, that if he could see Randall's eyes, everything would be plain. As it was, the curve of Randall's lips, the set of his shoulders, only radiated tension and worry, with no nuances to be found. "I don't want to miss anything," Randall finally told Anthony very quietly, "I don't want to lose out on time with you. School can wait. For now, you're what I am going to focus on. That's my decision."

Anthony's shoulders sagged, and his head was bowed. "I'm just not sure I want to admit that finding this pack was for nothing," he murmured, so lowly Victor barely caught it. "I've completely wasted our time."

"You haven't." Randall sat next to him, taking Anthony's hands in his own. "We helped them. Imagine what would have happened if we hadn't shown up. And we know Cedric, who has contacts out there still. He'll find us someone we can go to. This... this was my idea. To come here. I thought it'd be your salvation. I was wrong. But it wasn't a waste."

The conversation was now becoming too personal for Victor to feel good about overhearing, so he sneaked away, though he was fairly certain the Lewises wouldn't have noticed if he'd stomped, as absorbed as they were with each other.

The Lewises, it seemed, were going to leave. Victor wondered what Jed and Redford would do—he wondered what *he* would do. Surely there was no call for him to stay. Then again, there had barely been a call for him to come along in the first place.

Randall had been wrong when he'd assumed that Victor only came here because he was intrigued by the thrill. Part of it had been Randall himself. Though Victor hadn't consciously acknowledged it at the time, he had already been very interested in Randall's company even back then. Before then, even, when they had met in Cairo.

Without Randall here, nobody else would particularly want Victor to stay. He supposed he should start packing, then.

"Victor." Randall had left his brothers and come after Victor, ducking around a group of wolves moving past them.

Coming to a stop—Victor had had no destination in mind anyway, only a direction that was away from the Lewises—he summoned up a smile for Randall. "Decision made, then?"

"What the hell was that?" Randall glanced at the people passing, arms folded, voice a low hiss.

His tone took Victor off guard. He'd never heard Randall sound like that before. "That… was an offer that you had the choice to take or decline?"

"I understand that I'm not my brother." There was a sick undercurrent in Randall's voice, his head bowed, tone barely higher than a rumble. "I know that I am not made to lead. But I can take care of my family without you coming in and throwing pity at me."

"I said that it wasn't pity, and I stand by those words. I never meant to undermine your leadership, Randall," Victor replied, appalled. But it only took a second more for him to realize that was exactly what he'd done. Damn it. "My apologies. I, er, I wasn't thinking of wolf etiquette."

"If it wasn't pity, then I honestly can't understand why you felt the need to step in, tell us how well off you were, and snap your fingers at our problems as if they were that easy to solve." Randall barely looked up at him, gaze firmly fixed on the ground. "You haven't spoken to me in weeks."

"That road goes both ways, Randall," Victor said thinly. "Do not put all the blame on me. And I was simply trying to help. Is it so surprising that I still have strong feelings for you?"

Randall shook his head, jaw tightening. "I don't know what you mean," he said. "It was a crush, Victor. It was foolish. You were right from the start. But it hardly matters. I'm over it."

Victor wasn't sure if he should believe that or not. On one hand, Randall had an odd tone to his voice, one that didn't usually make an appearance when he told the truth. On the other hand, Victor had made quite a few mistakes and had done more than enough to sour Randall's feelings for him.

"Then I suppose we are back to where we began, but with the positions reversed," Victor replied. There was something oddly funny about that, but he didn't smile.

There was a long beat, Randall swallowing quickly a few times before he nodded and lifted his head, a forced smile tight at the corners of his lips. "I suppose so."

"If you're trying to tell me that you feel nothing for me, you should probably try to sound less like you're forcing the words out," Victor said softly. "The honesty would be appreciated, since I cannot ask you to look me in the eye and say it like you mean it."

Something of the manufactured confidence fell from Randall's face. He looked away, and Victor watched his throat work, as if Randall was trying to make the words come. "I think you are a brilliant man," Randall finally managed thickly. "I'm only sorry I was never able to take any of your classes."

"The offer is still open," Victor replied. He hid how frustrated he was starting to get. He just wanted a straight answer on whether Randall still had affection remaining for him. "The college I teach at is excellent."

"Well, as soon as my brother dies, I'm sure my schedule will clear right up." Randall's jaw was so tight it seemed ready to crack. "If you'll excuse me, I need to go pack."

That took the wind right out of Victor's sails. He sighed, pinching the bridge of his nose. "Randall, I'm sorry, I didn't mean it like that," he said softly. "I'm sorry for how much stress I've caused you over the last month. I never meant—I never *wanted* to make your life harder than it already was. I can only hope that you're even slightly less stressed when you get back home."

"Victor...." Randall seemed to deflate, face turned away from him. "Please. Don't, please. I can't."

Though initially baffled, Victor didn't take long to get what Randall was asking. The man was barely holding it together as it was. He hardly needed Victor making it worse with his conversational fumblings.

"Sorry," Victor apologized again. "I'll, er, leave you to pack, should I?"

There was a pause, and Victor had turned to go when Randall's hand landed on his arm. With no warning, Victor was pulled back, and just like that Randall was kissing him, hard, messy and desperate. "Stop apologizing," he heard Randall murmur before his lips were caught again.

"I'm English, it's a compulsion," Victor said, baffled, before he was kissed again. That time he relaxed into it, tentatively grasping Randall's arm in return. For a few moments, that was all there was. Randall kissing him like he couldn't bear the thought of being apart, arms tight around him, completely cut off into their own world.

There was a laugh, a burst of conversation, the noise of the pack filtering back in. Randall pulled away, resting his forehead against Victor's. Again, so softly, he said, "I can't."

There were so many meanings to that that Victor was having trouble telling them apart. He supposed it wouldn't be too hard, though. Randall had made his reasons for not being with Victor quite clear, and however much Victor wanted to protest that he'd come to a few realizations, it wasn't nearly enough.

"I know." It pained Victor to have to pull back, but any more contact and he wouldn't want to let go. "I understand."

"I should go," Randall murmured, but for once, he wasn't running away from Victor. "Edwin is a terrible packer. I'll have to redo his bag or not everything will fit."

"That doesn't surprise me in the slightest." Victor smiled faintly. "And.... I know you already refused my offer of help. But if you ever do need anything, I want you to remember that you can call me."

"Randall!" Edwin came charging up, grabbing his brother's arm. "Come on. We have to go talk to the Gray Lady before we can go, and Anthony's trying to lift stuff."

A very tiny sigh escaped Randall, but he nodded, rubbing a hand through Edwin's hair and half smiling when Edwin immediately reached up to fix it. "Okay. I'm coming." He glanced back at Victor, and for an instant Victor was certain that there was something there, some moment that was nearly born. But in the end Randall just turned away and followed Edwin toward the other side of the camp.

That didn't mean Victor was going to give up on him, however.

Unfortunately, since the Lewises were leaving and Jed would most likely want to know about it, Victor was faced with the daunting task of waking Jed up to tell him the news. He hardly kept tabs on Jed's sleep schedule, but he was fairly sure Jed hadn't gotten a lot of it lately. Still, someone would need to wake him up.

He watched Randall walking away for a moment longer, then walked in the direction of Jed's tent. Unsure of what the proper protocol for waking people in a tent was, Victor awkwardly loitered outside for a few moments. Then, gathering his courage, he stuck his head inside.

Well, at least Jed and Redford were merely sleeping.

"Wake up, both of you," Victor said crisply. "There's urgent news."

"You had better be on fire." Jed's grunt came from where he was half buried under the blankets, wound around Redford like some form of octopus.

"The Lewises have decided to return home," Victor replied. "Permanently."

Redford gave a confused groan and just tugged Jed in tighter, apparently thinking he was dreaming some kind of horrible nightmare in which Victor was disturbing their pleasant rest. Victor did feel a bit sorry for waking them, but he could hardly let them sleep through the Lewises' departure.

"Are they on fire?" Jed muttered.

"No, Jed. Shall I light myself on fire to get your attention?" Victor was going to continue, but he was distracted by Jed throwing his lighter at him, hitting Victor in the chest. "Ow! Bloody hell, Jed, you needn't resort to violence."

Jed apparently accepted the fact, not very graciously, that Victor was not going to go away. Rolling over, he peered blearily over toward Victor, looking completely rumpled and out of sorts. "Okay, princess, what the fuck."

To say Victor sighed would be putting it mildly—to be more accurate, he released an exhale of pure exasperation. "The Lewises are leaving. The treatment isn't working for Anthony, and they see no need to remain."

Jed poked Redford's shoulder. "You get that, Fido?"

Redford made a pitiful noise that might have translated to *yes.*

"They're going to see the Gray Lady now, so you have some time," Victor informed them. He squinted in the dimness of the tent, frowning at the sight of clothes, supplies, and weapons shoved up against the edge of the tent walls. "Goodness, you're even messy in a tent."

He ducked out before he could get anything else thrown at him—objects or innuendo both. However, bereft of things to do, Victor wound up sitting a short distance from the tent, waiting. Jed tumbled out of the tent first, hopping up and down as he tugged on one boot, a toothbrush clamped in his mouth. Redford followed him a few seconds later, a thick jacket with a fake fur hood lining pulled up around his chin. Both of them still looked utterly exhausted.

Jed spat out his toothpaste, passing a bottle of water to Redford after he rinsed his mouth. While Redford brushed his own teeth, Jed ducked back inside the tent and emerged again with a heavy leather jacket.

It was so utterly domestic that Victor should have found it sickening. He *would* have found it sickening before. Now he felt a tug in his chest, a faint little spark of yearning. That was new.

Before Jed did anything else, Redford was pulled into a quick kiss, the two of them talking lowly, arms wrapped around each other. Victor could just hear Jed murmuring *good morning*, smiling at Redford's return whispers. Hand in hand, they walked over to Victor, Jed leaning against Redford's shoulder.

What would that look like for him and Randall, if Randall took him back? Victor couldn't help but try to picture it, tentatively testing out the idea. Perhaps he would bring them both tea in the morning. Maybe Randall would smile and point out the pillow creases on Victor's cheek. Maybe their Saturdays would be spent doing nothing but curling up on couches and reading or watching the television.

Of course, that was a very isolated view of it. Edwin and Anthony would be in the picture too. Victor couldn't quite imagine that right then, but what he'd pictured of just him and Randall seemed quite interesting.

"Are we trying to talk them into staying?" Jed asked as they approached Victor. "Or just throwing a bon voyage party?"

"The latter," Victor admitted. "They're right. They won't get the treatment Anthony needs, here. Cedric has apparently given them some contacts that are in the know and work for hospitals."

"Animal hospitals?" Jed smirked widely, apparently very pleased with his joke.

Victor didn't dignify that with a response. "Besides," he continued, "you know how well trying to talk a wolf out of anything goes: not very well."

A wide grin spread across Jed's face, and he leaned over to kiss Redford's cheek. "Damn straight."

"And what about you?" Victor asked. "With them gone, your original job is too, and you've trained the pack well enough. If O'Malley stays true to his word, they'll be safe. I suppose you'll be leaving as well."

Jed exchanged a glance with Redford. "We've been talking about it, yeah. Kind of up to Redford, really."

"I think it's time," Redford agreed. "I kind of miss our apartment."

"You sure?" Jed actually was actively asking Redford for an opinion. Victor wasn't sure if he should check the man for a fever or take video for evidence. "This has been good for you, babe. We can stay longer if you want."

Redford shook his head. "*Been*, past tense. I think I'm okay now. Or.... I'm getting to be okay. The rest is just up to me."

Jed just squeezed his hand, studying Redford's face in silence another moment. "Okay, then," he nodded. "We'll pack up and leave tomorrow morning."

Where that left Victor, he wasn't sure. He hadn't been here for a worthy cause like the Lewises, and he hadn't helped the pack like Jed and Redford had. But he had promised the children he was teaching that he would finish reading for them, and Victor did hate to stop halfway through a book.

"Is there any way you could give me the name of a contact that would be available for transportation purposes?" Victor asked. "I may not leave when you do, and I don't know anybody in the area."

"Why don't we leave you the van?" Jed wrapped an arm around Redford's waist. "I know an old army buddy coupla towns over, owes me a favor. He flies these little corporate jets around. I was thinking—" He grinned at Redford. "—if you wanted, we could fly back. Just you and me in an airplane. You can sit by every window in the place if you wanted."

"Really?" Redford's eyes went round in excitement. "What kind of plane?"

"Little private jet, probably. Depends on what he's got in." Jed's smile only grew wider. "Eight seater, maybe, where you can see right up to the cockpit. It flies so fucking fast, Redford, you're going to get to see everything."

Redford nodded rapidly, as excited as a kid in a candy store—when suddenly he faltered, the anticipation dropping from his expression to be replaced with doubt. "Wait, but you hate flying."

"Yeah," Jed agreed in a rumble. "But you loved it. I'll live. Flown in a lot worse before, and I trust Mac to get us there in one piece. Hell, he dropped me off in planes that were practically falling apart, rattling around us, dead of fucking night. I think he can get us home."

Victor was just glad he hadn't received that invitation. He wasn't as bad a flier as Jed, but he still hated it. Jed's description of bad flights had him nearly feeling nauseous. "Just don't get in a crash," Victor said. "Strangely, I've become attached to the two of you being alive."

Jed shot him a look but, thankfully, apparently didn't feel the need to mercilessly mock Victor. "We'll do our best not to die in a fiery explosion, princess." He looked vaguely green around the gills the longer they talked about flying. "Solid advice, because that actually was on the agenda."

"Maybe we could go see the Gray Lady with the Lewises, then," Redford suggested, patting Jed on the back to relax him. "We may as well tell her we're leaving at the same time."

"Hopefully, she doesn't try and make us take home a parting gift." Jed grimaced and rolled his shoulders. "Those little fur balls follow me goddamn everywhere. If one of them tries to stow away in our bags, we're taking it to the pound."

Victor snorted delicately. "You could just admit that you like them."

"Shut your dirty mouth, princess." Jed's grumbling and stomping protests did little to fool anyone, though. He'd been more than happy to hang out with the younger members of the pack. On more than one occasion, Victor had watched Jed play hide and seek with all the wolf pups, completely content to be the slow, smelly human that they all tracked so easily. He would miss them, despite his denial.

Victor knew the feeling.

They walked to the Gray Lady's tent, arriving just as the Lewises were speaking with Mallory about entrance. Victor wasn't sure if he could really bring himself to look at Randall with their most recent conversation still heavy in his thoughts. Instead, he let his gaze wander over toward Mallory, who looked more than a little exasperated at the new arrivals that would no doubt *also* be asking to see the Gray Lady.

"Oh, come on, Mal, just let us all in. You know she already knows we're here." Jed clapped Mallory on the shoulder and ignored Mallory's protests as Jed led the way into the tent. "Your Ladyship, you have guests. Hope you're not naked."

Ladyship? Victor silently disapproved. Next Jed would be referring to her as *mothership* and thinking he was the most hilarious man on the planet.

"You should be so fortunate." The Gray Lady's voice was dry. She was seated on a bed of pillows and furs, several wolf puppies playing at her feet. "You simply wouldn't be able to handle the sight, I'm afraid."

"Ma'am?" Anthony sounded rather single-minded right then, ignoring the banter. "Randall, Edwin, and myself are leaving. I can't thank you enough for the aid you've given us and for taking us in, but it's time for us to go back home."

After sitting silently a moment, the Gray Lady cocked her head. "So, I was right," she mused. "You are just like your parents."

"It's not that we don't like the pack," Anthony hastened to say. "We'd probably even be staying if circumstances were different. But we need things that the pack can't provide."

"The point is, you are leaving," she pointed out, tone inflexible. "You are endangering the pack. Lone wolves are never a good idea, little one. Look at what happened the last time."

"We're *not* lone wolves. We're a pack of three, and you let smaller packs live by themselves just fine near you," Anthony replied. He'd folded his arms over his chest, a distinctly defensive gesture.

"You were a pack of three before. Then four. Then five. And still the hunters came." The Gray Lady shook her head. "You would put us all at risk. You are sick, young wolf, and you will not last through a harsh winter. Every instinct I have is telling me to make you stay."

"I won't last *here*," Anthony said bluntly. "You don't have the medical supplies. I'm grateful for everything you and your healers have done, but it's become clear that I need a hospital and a proper doctor. By not letting me leave, you *would* kill me."

"Please." It was Edwin, taking a step forward, showing his throat. "Please, let us go. We just want Anthony to get better."

"That is why you came to us, if I recall." The Gray Lady stood, eyes snapping. "And I told you, did I not? That our help would extend only if you became part of this pack. Now you're asking to go."

Anthony twitched, like his instincts were telling him to back down when that was the last thing he wanted to do. "We're not asking," he said simply. "I'm telling. The healers here just don't have the capability to help me. It doesn't matter whether I'm *really* part of the pack or not."

Beside Anthony, Jed shifted a bit, eyes darting between everyone. It was a small tent full of very tense wolves. Even Randall looked as though his hackles were up. "Oh, we're going too," Jed added, raising his eyebrows. "Just, you know, while we're talking about it."

Victor raised his hand. "I'm actually staying for a few more days," he announced. Since the Gray Lady didn't so much as look at him, he assumed she didn't really care about him as much as she cared about the wolves.

With a low growl, the Gray Lady stopped any further discussion. Eyes narrowed, she glowered at all of them in turn. Edwin actually shrank back behind Anthony at the force of her glare. "I will not hold you here," she finally said, teeth gleaming in the low light, lip curled. "Go back to whatever is so important beyond our domain. But do not come here again unless I summon you." She stood, dismissing them. "And little Lewis?" She held Anthony's gaze. "For that, I would not hold my breath."

"I'm sorry," Anthony murmured. He backed away rather than turning and walking, his head bowed. Victor had never seen a wolf do that, but since he assumed he didn't need to do the same, he just nodded at the Gray Lady and walked out properly.

All three of the Lewises were looking rather miserable when they finally got outside. The Gray Lady's thunderous disapproval was clearly weighing on them. Redford had a touch of it in his own expression, but Jed looked completely unbothered.

"That went well," Redford sighed.

"It did," Jed agreed with a smile, arm around his shoulders. "No one's dead, maimed, or bleeding. I call that a win."

"I guess we should keep packing," Anthony said morosely.

"We'll be home soon." Randall squeezed his arm. "We'll be back in our own beds, at the lake, and you can lay out in the sun all day while we get you rabbits for stew. Just focus on that."

Anthony nodded, visibly attempting to gather his courage once more. "Right. Okay, if we get packing we can start driving home by midday."

Out of the corner of his eye, Victor saw Jed and Redford exchange a quick glance, Jed giving a quiet huff of air and an almost imperceptible nod to whatever Redford's pleading gaze was asking. "Jed and I are getting a plane, actually," Redford said. "You could join us? It'll be a lot faster."

"That would be great," Anthony said gratefully. "Really. When are you leaving?"

"Whenever you want. A couple of hours drive to get to Mac, but once we're there, he'll take us where we need to go. He owes me a coupla three favors, might as well cash them in now."

"I've never been in a plane," Edwin said, eyes going wide. "What's it like?"

"Don't ask me that question," Jed grunted. "I plan on being very drunk for it. Let's just put it that way."

"It's really fun," Redford assured. "You can see the tops of clouds, and everything looks really tiny."

"I liked it," Randall said quietly, hands in his pockets. "Um, on the way there it was kind of boring, really. The way back was... much nicer."

Victor smiled at the mention. On the way back from Cairo they had shared a flight, and Victor had found Randall's company entirely pleasant. Though they had both been battered and bruised and bandaged, they'd talked far longer than Victor normally spoke with people. He had not been in the best mood, considering that he and David had broken up in the parking lot, but Randall had lifted his spirits a little.

"All right, then we'll plan to be ready around noon," Anthony said to Jed. "Thank you again. Flying will be a hell of a lot easier than a seven-state drive."

Victor watched them disperse. The Lewises left for their tents, and Jed and Redford for theirs. He wasn't sure what he'd do all day without them to speak to. Perhaps he'd catch up on his reading, maybe even some of his research.

He had a collection of journals written by various medusa half bloods over the last few hundred years—Victor had retrieved them from home when he'd gone back for a week, and on a pure whim he'd brought the journals with him. At the time, he'd thought that perhaps he could finally get the courage to look for patterns as to how medusas lost their minds.

Perhaps it would also shed light on other things too.

He retreated to his tent and did some light reading, keeping an eye out for Jed, Redford, and the Lewises. At the very least he wanted to be able to wish them a safe flight. When noon rolled by, Victor caught sight of the Lewises making their way across the camp with their bags. Anthony was carrying one and kept moving it away from Edwin, who was trying to take it off of him. Randall was behind, more bags slung over his shoulders, his head down and a weary tilt to his posture. He straightened up, though, whenever one of his brothers looked back.

Victor had seen that before. It wasn't a major moment of life, not a turning point or anything particularly influential, so it wasn't the sort of future memory he tended to remember after looking into someone's eyes. But as he watched, he remembered multiple versions of how it could have happened. In one version, Anthony had died. The healers had unknowingly given him medicine which had hastened the degeneration of his condition.

In this version, though, the future-now-present that was playing out in front of him, Victor knew exactly how Randall was feeling, because he'd felt it himself. He didn't want his brothers to know how tired and stressed he was. He didn't want them to feel burdened with his worry. Acting normal had started to weigh on him. He had been so sure that if he'd done everything right, if he'd educated himself, then everything would have worked out.

But things had only gotten worse. Anthony hadn't been helped, and now Randall would continue having to move toward taking over seniority of their pack.

And he'd started to like a medusa, only to figure out that Victor had more than a few issues that he needed to deal with before he started to think about settling down.

Knowing all of that was enough to make Victor feel even more guilty, so much so that he contemplated avoiding seeing them off. Surely Randall didn't need more reminders of the things that were stressful for him. But before Victor could make any kind of decision, Edwin was beside him, wrapping his arms around Victor in a tight hug.

"You're coming to say good-bye, right?" Edwin asked, voice muffled against Victor's shoulder.

Victor still had no clue how to act when people hugged him, so he didn't raise his arms to hug Edwin back. He did, however, gingerly pat his shoulder. "Er, yes, of course."

Edwin grabbed his hand and hauled Victor over to where Randall and Anthony had gathered, near the entrance of the camp. The vehicles were stored a good half-hour hike down in a cave the pack had sought out to hide their transportation. So this would be the last chance Victor would have to see them. "Hey, guys, Victor is here."

Anthony looked over, frowning. "You don't have anything packed. You're not coming with us?"

Victor had really hoped to be able to avoid that question. He wasn't ashamed of staying. He did expect to get mocked for being useless or not fitting in, though. "I'm staying for a few more days. I have, er, certain obligations I need to fulfill."

Randall, Victor noticed, seemed more than a little surprised. It was Jed who spoke, though. "Honestly didn't expect that." Standing up from where he'd been crouched next to Knievel's carrier, Jed held out a hand. "Well, when you get back in town, look us up. We might even let you in the door."

Victor took Jed's hand and shook it. "I will," he promised. "I might even be civil."

Jed grinned then, clapping Victor on the shoulder and nodding his good-byes. Edwin was next, with another bone-crushing hug. "You still smell funny," he informed Victor. "But I like it."

"Thank you," Victor said dryly and was then engulfed in another hug from Anthony.

"You should come around for dinner again," Anthony told him. "I won't take no for an answer."

Victor glanced at Randall, who immediately looked away, caught in the act of staring. At least he didn't look disgusted at the thought of seeing Victor again, which was a step in the right direction. And, if Victor wanted to be bold, he might even say there was hope there, in the way Randall kept looking over at him when he thought Victor wasn't paying attention.

"I'd like that," Victor said to Anthony. "Let me know when you're free."

Then it was time to say good-bye to Randall. A dozen options ran through Victor's mind, each of them weighed for appropriateness and whether Randall would want that response or not. He settled on gently grasping Randall's elbow and leaning in to kiss his cheek.

There wasn't anything he could really say that summed up everything neatly. He knew Randall wouldn't expect to see him again, and wouldn't believe him even if Victor tried to say otherwise. He also knew Randall didn't think he could be with him, not right then. But Victor couldn't bring himself to let go, even if he did have many things he needed to sort out before he saw Randall again.

So he left his good-bye silent and reluctantly pulled away from Randall. Victor said to all of them, "Have a safe flight."

Randall was looking at the ground, feet shuffling side to side. He opened and closed his mouth several times, but no words escaped him. Randall finally nodded, giving Victor a brief smile and turning back toward his brothers. As Randall moved to help Edwin finish gathering all their things, Victor saw him grab his backpack and murmur to Edwin, "Hey, I forgot something. Be right back."

"What did you forget?" Anthony said. "I can go back and get it."

"It's fine," Randall assured him, slinging his bag over one shoulder. "It'll take me two minutes. Wait for me?"

Anthony clapped Randall on the back, and Victor tried not to watch Randall go. It wouldn't do to be creepy and stare. He looked away and stood by while the wolves and Jed strapped on the last of their bags, luggage and cat carrier in hand. Victor didn't want to be rude and leave, so he stayed, half listening to the idle chatter in the group as they discussed what it was like to fly on an airplane.

As much as Victor had come to enjoy their company, he thought that a few days on his own might do him some good. The wolves here respected his need for privacy, and perhaps the fresh air of the mountains would help to put some things in perspective.

By the time everyone was ready to start their hike, two members of the pack going with the group to drive the van back after dropping them all off, Randall had come running back, gaze studiously avoiding Victor's. And then there was nothing left to do but give one last round of good-byes and watch as they headed out, disappearing among the trees. A few members of the pack ran with them, all of them howling their good-byes until, at last, there was no trace of them remaining.

Victor spent the rest of the day in relative solitude, emerging from his tent only to eat dinner, after which he took a walk around the perimeter of the camp. He'd never been one to enjoy nature walks, but he'd decided to try one on a whim to see if he'd started enjoying it. He hadn't. He still hated insects and stray rocks that he tripped over.

He forced himself to sit down and read the medusa half blood accounts, finally making it to the very end of them. Most stopped suddenly, indicating that they hadn't continued to keep the journal after they had lost their minds. Some had attempted to continue writing, though their efforts had resulted in incoherent ramblings.

There was no way to tell if there was a pattern, since most of them stopped. It gave Victor no clues as to who their last visions had been for, and without that, forming a pattern would be impossible.

He put the last journal down with a sigh, pinching the bridge of his nose. Victor uncurled from the cross-legged position he'd been reading in. When his knee brushed against his pillow, it hit something hard. There was a book underneath it.

Mittelalterliche Liste gefährlicher und unerkennbarer Bestien. The medieval index that Randall had been reading in the van on the way here.

Victor picked it up and opened the cover. It was obviously well cared for, and on the front leaf was a neat, childish scrawl. *Randall Lewis, 7,* and then some very carefully printed beginner's German. *Das ist mein Buch.* This is my book.

As Victor flipped through the book, a page of notepaper dropped out. It had been marking the section of Canos lore. Victor picked it up and found Randall's script, messier but now somehow much more graceful than his seven-year-old self.

Victor, it started, his name in careful loops. *I want to start out by saying thank you. Thank you for finding me. Thank you for being kind enough to stop and speak with me in the Cairo hospital. Thank you for being the one good thing out of my nightmare. I called you my Beatrice, and that is very true, but I think more than that you are also my Virgil.*

315

You have been a light during a time when I have found it very hard to see forward.

I know that this is good-bye. I know that the ending is not what I would have wished. But I just wanted to tell you that even if I had known, if I had looked into your eyes and seen this moment, I would have fallen for you anyway. Because you were something wonderful.

Thank you, for what you gave me, for the memories I now have. I feel a little bit like a medusa myself, I think. I have a part of you that will always be with me.

I hope you enjoy the book. It was one of my first in German, and it has been a favorite. And now we are even, at least so far on the book front. I don't think I'll ever be able to thank you enough for the rest.

I will miss you, my (for a little while, at least) medusa.

Randall Lewis

But, like a sad slave, stay and think of nought
Save, where you are, how happy you make those.
So true a fool is love, that in your will,
Though you do anything, he thinks no ill.

Victor found he was smiling as he reached the end of the note, though it was a bittersweet expression. So, Randall truly thought it was over. That shouldn't hurt as much as it did. Victor had half known it already, and Randall had enough reason to want it to be over.

He had hoped that Randall might consider giving him another chance, but with what Randall was currently going through with his family, Victor knew he already had a lot on his mind. He was stressed, exhausted, and worried. The last thing he needed was a medusa with self-destructive tendencies.

Still, it wasn't completely over. Victor just hoped that Randall would perhaps be willing to consider what they could have together if Victor could figure out the mess that was his mind. So he would simply have to do that.

Unfortunately, sorting out one's mind wasn't as clear a mission as, say, doing the dishes. There was an objective but no obvious steps, and it wasn't something that could be done halfheartedly or forced. He couldn't hurry the process along, and he couldn't tidy the metaphorical dishes into the sink and pretend they were done.

Victor folded up the note and tucked it into his pocket. He didn't want to lose it.

He slept uneasily that night. Too many thoughts swirled around his mind, too many *what-ifs* and doubts. Every time he woke up, he spent half an hour lost in his contemplation again before managing to fall back asleep.

By the time morning came, Victor was so thoroughly grumpy he seriously considered the idea of attempting to sleep through the day. That, however, would not be possible with rowdy wolves constantly running past the tents and shouting to one another across the camp. He reluctantly got up, got himself dressed, and ended up nursing a mug of tea at a makeshift table near the campfires.

Further pursuing the medusa journals wasn't helping, and Victor was starting to get frustrated. Randall had theorized that his character flaw was linked to his blood, but while Victor saw the logic in that, he simply didn't have a clue how to fix it. He was well aware of the medusa love of knowledge, but it wasn't that, specifically.

He had his head in his hands in frustration when he felt someone sit next to him.

"Deep in thought?" The Gray Lady's smooth tone washed over him.

Victor didn't want to dismiss her, because he did respect her—even more after he'd seen her life and her future—but he didn't particularly want to speak to anyone. "One could say that," he sighed.

"You're not the first medusa I've known in my lifetime," she said. "I knew your distant ancestors, those who would hollow out the ones who dared meet their eyes. The bloodline has weakened, but the effects of the visions on the medusa are still the same."

It occurred to Victor then that the Gray Lady had the potential to be even more useful than the medusa journals, as she might have seen a pattern in their lapse of sanity. Before he could ask, she continued speaking.

"I know you have looked into Randall Lewis's eyes. But have you done that before? Have you looked into someone that you were involved with?"

That was an odd question, Victor felt. "Twice. I didn't love him, but I did very much like him. Before that the eyes I met belonged to people on the streets, casual acquaintances, people I barely knew."

She gave a thoughtful hum, studying him over the cup of tea she sipped at. "And did you realize that medusas tend to hold on longer to the visions of those they care for?"

"I didn't know that." He only glanced very quickly at her, unwilling to risk even getting close to looking into her eyes again. What she said held... interesting ramifications. Victor was so tired he didn't want to think about it right then, but he supposed he had to. "The last person I cared for was a vampire. I looked into his eyes twice."

The Gray Lady grimaced. "That must have been unpleasant."

It hadn't been. Victor had very much enjoyed looking into David's eyes. "I wouldn't say that."

"To feel that bloodlust, that cycle of craving blood and pain?" She shook her head. "As a wolf I cannot imagine anything worse. We are bound by the moon, but we are not forced to obey it. Vampires are destructive, obsessed creatures."

"It's hardly *their* fault," Victor protested. "They don't ask to be a slave to that. I'm sorry, but all you have to do is run around on the full moon. They have to drink *blood* from the living to even stay alive, when they were once victims themselves. Damning them for their instincts and necessities is not fair."

The Gray Lady's expression tightened, but she didn't reply right away. She and Victor sat in silence for a while, each drinking their own tea and watching the comings and goings of the pack. Victor began to feel that perhaps he'd been a bit too blunt, and he wanted to apologize, but he personally felt he had nothing to apologize for. So many people hated vampires and forgot that they had perhaps the rawest deal of all in the supernatural community.

Instead, he said, "Randall told me that I was self-destructive." Why he was telling her this, he wasn't sure. Maybe he just needed someone to speak to, much like the night at the bar when he'd met Dylan. "I have no idea how to fix it. I don't even know *why* I have that tendency."

She smiled. "You looked into the eyes of a vampire and now wonder why you crave a hurtful cycle of pain?"

"I was already looking for, er, *adventure*, so to speak." Victor shook his head. "I doubt it's related."

"Can you honestly tell me that you would have looked into the eyes of an immortal back then, though?" Out of the corner of his eye, Victor could see the Gray Lady looking at him. "I heard your conversation with Randall outside my house. He was right; you had every chance of losing your mind."

Victor let out a slow exhale. "No," he admitted. "I wouldn't have."

When he'd met David, all he'd been looking for was anything that wasn't a life of boredom. He had asked to look into David's eyes a month after being with him—Victor had dated before, but they had been humans, and therefore relatively easy to understand. David had been much more complex, and Victor had wanted to truly know him.

After that, he had started offering David his blood. He'd thought at the time that the two events had not been connected. Then he'd traveled to Cairo with him, into a situation he'd known full well was dangerous. He and David had broken up, but Victor had still traveled with a van full of wolves and an unstable mercenary to go see a wolf pack. And then he'd looked into the eyes of an immortal.

"Damn it," Victor cursed lowly.

She was right. Randall was right.

"You wouldn't happen to know if there's any way to stop feeling so close to someone's memories, would you?" he tried.

The Gray Lady had a touch of regret in her expression. "I do not. I may have known medusas, but none very closely. That is something you are going to have to discover for yourself."

"I'm surprised you're helping me," Victor had to point out. "I'm doing this so that I can be with a wolf. I thought you didn't approve of such pairings."

"I don't," she said simply. "But there is one thing I have learned with the activities of your group of friends. You are going to attempt to be with that wolf no matter what I say. I may as well help fix you so that you at least don't make him completely miserable."

"Thank you," Victor said dryly. "I'm touched."

The Gray Lady stood, looking down at him. "Then go help yourself, Victor. Make your own memories and try not to dwell on mine. I will be remaining in contact with you."

Victor blinked at her in surprise. "Why? You clearly don't like me. That's completely understandable, but you hardly need to call me up every once in a while."

"You have my memories." She narrowed her eyes at Victor. One long, graceful finger nudged gently at his temple. "There are a lot of people that want to know what I know. Now that you have that information, you would be considered the easier access point for that knowledge."

"Oh. Right, then." Victor really didn't like the sound of that, but there was nothing to be done about it. He couldn't exactly purge the memories from his mind.

"And, Victor? Don't go spreading around what you saw about the future." With that, the Gray Lady left, her retreat as silent and regal as her appearance.

Unfortunately, she had just left Victor with yet more things to think about.

VICTOR SPENT two more days at the camp before he went home. The wolf children had been glad to hear the end of the story and sad to see him go. He'd gotten enthusiastic good-bye hugs from a few of the wolves, even though they barely knew him.

The pack needed the van far more than Victor did, so he enlisted the help of Mallory to drive him to the airport. The flight was awful, as usual, and Victor spent the whole time drinking as much red wine as he could to be able to deal with the turbulence. No more drinking to excess was a wonderful thought, when both of his feet were on the ground. Horrid flights demanded alcohol. Baggage was a nightmare, though at least getting a taxi didn't require too much waiting.

He arrived home with much relief.

Victor lived two blocks from the college he taught at. The area was the nicest in the city, full of old mansions and modern townhouses. Victor's house wasn't a house. It was a two-wing mansion complete with gardens, a groundskeeper's house at the far edge of the lawn, and tasteful dark wood mixed with light stone.

The house had been in his father's family for six generations now. It was stuffy and drab, dusty in corners Victor never bothered to go into, with floors that creaked and groaned from age. He'd hated coming here on holidays from boarding school, and he had hated it even more when it was passed down to him after his parents' passing.

What was he supposed to do with all this room? Even when his grandmother had been alive, the place had hardly been filled with light or cheer. No, it was stodgy with Rathbone tradition seeped into every plank and board. They'd visited here once a year while Victor had been growing up. When he'd been off to school, his grandmother had passed, his grandfather had slowly curled in on himself as the madness took hold, and his parents had moved overseas to care for them.

Then the house had been the thing looming during every break. He'd sat in the library and read; he'd haunted the rooms, promising himself he'd never be stuck there.

And yet, here he was. The last of the Rathbones in the great, rattling Rathbone manor.

To be honest, he still loathed the place, though not quite as passionately. These days he just hated that he only regularly used about five rooms when there were forty-one of the damn things, and he had to bring in maids every month to keep it in shape.

The rooms he didn't use were mostly kept closed off, the furniture covered in protective sheets. The paintings were similarly covered, and all the antiques were locked away in dust-proof cabinets. Every day, Victor walked down the hallway that was filled with portraits of his family line, and every day he winced at the fact that he would be the last of the bloodline. He had no interest in having biological children. More to the point, the opposite sex held no appeal for him at all.

But now, as he walked through the empty halls and looked into long-disused rooms, Victor began seeing use in them.

He had offered the Lewises a place to stay. It was close to the best hospital in the state, and it would mean they wouldn't have to worry about household bills. Victor looked at a room that overlooked the gardens, the lawn stretching to a small wooded area at the base of the hills, and thought that Edwin would like this space. He poked around a room with high ceilings and a worktable that had once been used for carving wooden sculptures. Perhaps Anthony would like this one, given how much he liked working with his hands.

He saw the potential for Randall to fit into his own room. Victor didn't even use half the cupboard space; there was more than enough room for Randall. Victor thought he might like the antique furnishings and the small shelf of books Victor kept close at hand.

Victor sat on the edge of his bed and wondered if he should invite the Lewises once more. Randall hadn't reacted well to it, and in retrospect Victor could see how a wolf would understand that offer, especially a wolf who was trying to adjust to becoming the head of the family amidst his brother's illness.

Even as he thought that, he walked into the next room and started taking the sheets off the furniture. Victor retreated at the clouds of dust he brought up, sneezing violently and cursing himself for forgetting to call the maids in while he'd been away.

He retreated into his bedroom, scowling and rubbing his nose. Victor typically kept his room tidy, but there were a few photographs scattered over the top of a chest of drawers that caught his eye. They were photos he'd taken in Cairo. He'd gotten physical copies printed of some, since he preferred it that way, and he hadn't really looked at them since he'd picked them up in the tiny Cairo photo shop. Most of them were just images of the sights Victor had seen, the pyramids, the streets around the hotel.

One of them was of David.

Victor carefully picked up the photo. He had asked David if he could take a photograph of him staring directly into the camera lens—David had snorted a bit and called him daft, but he had done it. Later, Victor had looked at the photo on his camera screen, finally able to gaze into someone's eyes without fearing for his sanity.

He looked at it again now, studying the deep brown of David's eyes. And he was surprised to feel only the smallest twinges of emotion. Victor still missed David, but somewhere along the line he'd stopped wanting to be with someone like him. He just missed him because he honestly liked him and wanted to remain in touch. The last he'd heard of David, unfortunately, he was off in parts unknown. He hoped David was safe.

His and David's relationship had ultimately been too destructive for both of them. David had been addicted, and Victor had only made that addiction worse. Now Victor understood why he had been stuck in the cycle of self-destruction so strongly after David was gone.

Victor smiled faintly as he smoothed a finger over the photo. Now that he understood, he could overcome. It was time to put David's memories aside as best he could and move David himself into the category of *friend* more than *ex*. He opened the top drawer and put the photos on top of scattered old Christmas cards and other photos. Memories, all of them, that he now had to put in the past so he could focus on the present.

He wanted to help the Lewises. He wanted to be with Randall.

And maybe, if he was lucky, he could show Randall he could be a good partner.

CHAPTER
18

Randall

IN THE month since they'd come home, Randall really would have thought things would be... easier, somehow. That he would have figured out some kind of routine or solution. He'd gotten two jobs fairly quickly, working days at the library shelving books and evenings bagging groceries at the local supermarket. Edwin swept floors with a janitorial service at night, and, together, they were trying desperately to make ends meet.

It just wasn't working.

Anthony had tried to go back to his job as a mechanic. Before his illness, that was what his trade had been, and he'd been confident he could do it again in between treatments. Except he'd been let go after a week because he kept dropping equipment. He simply didn't have the strength in his hands anymore to work long days. Randall had shrugged it off. Edwin had gone out during the times when Anthony was napping to find cans and recyclables to turn in for cash. They told Anthony they could easily make up the wages. It was a lie. Randall was pretty sure they all knew that, but they smiled and nodded anyway.

Exhausted, Randall pulled up to the cabin, still wearing the stupid green apron from the grocery store. He hated it. He hated that he wore a *name badge*, he hated that it was mindless, brainless work and yet when he got home, he was so tired he could barely function, much less read. He couldn't remember the last time he'd done anything except work and take care of Anthony.

Most of all, though, Randall hated that he hated it. Anthony had given up his entire life, his whole childhood, to take care of them. To even have a moment of resentment seemed so selfish, Randall didn't want to think about it.

He plodded up the steps, rifling through the mail he'd picked up in town. Bills. A lot of them. Inside the cabin, he could hear Edwin and Anthony talking; he could smell dinner cooking. Sinking down to sit on the steps, Randall started opening the mail, reading them all by the porch light.

Past Due.

Final Notice.

Payment Needed.

A sour, sick feeling settled into Randall's gut. He'd been hiding bills from Anthony for weeks now, scraping together every penny he could to pay for the treatment.

Cedric had gotten them in to see a doctor who was friendly toward the nonhuman elements, but it wasn't free, not by a long shot. And first there had been tests, so many tests that Randall had begun to think that they'd run out of names for them all and just started slapping together random letters of the alphabet. They'd only just begun the attempts at treatment, to see what Anthony would respond to.

So that meant the bills were piling up, for the tests and the maybe treatments, for medicine, for basics like gas and food. He wasn't keeping up. Their savings—*Randall's* savings, the carefully collected college money—were all but gone now. Working as hard as he ever had, and he was still failing.

Randall honestly didn't know what else to do.

The moon was lighting the surrounding trees, the half-full flush of it tingeing everything in silver. The woods were lonely and quiet, almost shockingly still. From the smells coming from the kitchen, Randall assumed Edwin had spent his day out hunting. Randall hoped Anthony had joined him—spending some time out in the woods always lifted his spirits. It was grounding. Anthony was doing as much as he could around the house, but the treatments hadn't taken much of an effect yet, and he got so tired, was in pain so much of the time.

Randall just wanted to do something right, to actually *help* his brothers. But so far, all he'd done was fail. He'd dragged them to the pack, only to find out that there was no real help there. He'd come home, only to not be able to support them. Anthony had done this as a *kid*, and here was Randall, unable to do the most basic job of caring for his pack.

He should go inside. There was no way Anthony and Edwin hadn't heard him pull up. But Randall couldn't make himself move. He just sat on the steps in his ugly green apron with the name tag declaring him *Randal L,* staring up at the sky, willing himself to think of something. To come up with a plan.

Nothing came to him.

Then something did. A scent on the wind—gunpowder, another wolf, and above all that, sinking deep into him, calling to him like an ache he couldn't identify, old parchment and tea and dry snake scales. Randall raised his head, staring into the dark, heartbeat picking up despite himself. And then, around the corner, came the lights of a car, a Jeep pulling up in front of the cabin. The window was down, Redford's head poking out with a smile, Knievel's paws resting on the edge of the door.

"Hi, Randall," Redford greeted as he stepped out of the car. In his hands was a huge casserole dish wrapped in cloth to insulate it. "I, um, hope it's okay that we're here. We probably should have called ahead."

Randall stood, eyes going not to Redford or to Jed, who was getting out of the van, Knievel in his arms. No, it was to Victor, who had emerged from the back, looking... well, looking as he ever did. Cool and calm, utterly gorgeous, and out of reach. He reduced Randall, always, to a fumbling mess, like he was a teenager tripping over his own feet. "It's fine," he said faintly, all at once aware of how he was dressed, the deep bags under his eyes, the fact he was clutching a pile of bills. Not how he would have preferred to greet anyone, much less Victor. "Is something wrong?"

Redford and Jed looked like they wanted to answer, but they looked to Victor first. Then Redford shook his head. "No! But we're going to go inside now and leave you with Victor," he said, none too subtly. "Alone."

Taking Jed's arm, Redford hauled him inside, Knievel lightly leaping out of Jed's arms and following close on their heels. As he passed Randall, Jed rubbed his hand through Randall's hair with a grin. "Don't worry, kid. We'll keep your brothers occupied. Redford taught me how to make a pasta casserole, even. We're your very own Martha Stewart distraction." And then they went inside, the noise of the greetings muffled as the door swung shut behind them, leaving Randall standing on the porch, feeling completely stunned. He sank back down to the steps, wondering if this was some kind of dream. Nightmare, perhaps. All he'd need was to be naked with people laughing at him and it would be very close to some bad dreams he'd had.

Victor approached and eased down to sit beside Randall. "It's a beautiful night," he said in greeting.

Gaze locked on the papers in his hand, Randall carefully smoothed them out over his knee, trying to compose himself. "I...." What did he even say? "Yes," he wound up agreeing, almost helplessly. "I guess it is."

"I'd ask if you're well, but I can see how exhausted you are," Victor said. Randall saw his head turn, looking down at the envelopes in Randall's hands. "Things aren't getting better?"

Immediately tucking the bills into the front pocket of his apron, Randall shook his head, forcing a smile. "They're fine. We're doing just fine." He lied, of course. What else was he supposed to do? Victor... he was like the fragment of a hope that simply didn't exist anymore. It hurt to think about him, to wonder *what-if*. What if Anthony hadn't been sick, what if they'd met earlier or later, what if Randall had the energy and the time to be able to actually make things work? Victor was on a course that Randall simply couldn't follow. Knowing that and still seeing him, talking with him, was more painful than Randall could have anticipated.

"I want to do something to help." Victor sounded frustrated with himself. "If I offer you once again a place to stay and to pay the medical bills, it would still be taken as insult, yes?"

"Victor...." Randall sighed, finally turning to look at him. "Is that why you're here? You knew I'd be failing?" Maybe it'd been obvious from the start. God, Victor must think he was a horrible idiot, the petulant child who didn't know his own mind, who couldn't even take care of his pack.

"No," Victor protested. "That's not it. It's just the only thing I *can* offer, and I want to do *something*. I have stayed away this long to address certain personal issues, but the more time went on, I...."

Randall caught the edge of a little self-deprecating smile on Victor's lips, expressed in sharp relief from moonlight and shadow.

"I missed you," Victor said. "Staying away for even a month was difficult enough."

Randall wished he could just believe him. He wished he could take his hand and smile and let Victor make all their problems go away. "You don't owe me anything." As Randall looked down, he caught sight of the name badge. He ripped it off with a growl, barely restraining the urge to chuck it into the woods. "I don't want your money just so you can stop feeling guilty for fucking the virgin and it not working out."

Which was probably quite a bit harsher than Victor deserved. Shoulders slumping slightly, Randall found he couldn't bring himself to look at Victor, feeling as though he was careening out of control, a slow-motion train wreck, and everything he did only made it worse.

"I owe you more than you think," Victor said softly. "May I tell you what I've been up to, the last month? It might be distractingly entertaining, if nothing else."

After a moment, Randall nodded, jaw tight, head bowed.

"I found other medusa half bloods. I wanted to know how they lived," Victor said.

Now that surprised him. Randall looked over at Victor, eyebrow arching upward. A thousand questions crossed his mind, but all he ended up asking was "What did they say?"

"Some? Not much." Victor smiled wryly, and he didn't need to explain. It was easy for Randall to see he was talking about the ones that had already lost their minds. "Others provided me with perspectives on things that I hadn't considered before. Long-lasting effects from looking into minds that I hadn't even known about."

Randall was surprised to feel a light touch against his back. Victor had reached out, fingers curving over his shoulder blade. "Back when the bloodline was stronger, medusas used to take everything from the person they looked at," Victor continued. "Whatever past, present, and future they saw would become theirs, in a way. We're more diluted now, but the visions... what we see, it stays with us. Especially if we have an attachment of some kind to who we look at. It means we have a piece of that soul in our minds for the rest of our lives. I suppose it's not dissimilar to what wolves experience, just in a more literal way."

Randall's gaze dropped to Victor's neck, and he nodded to the two scars. "So the one who gave you those," he surmised. "You have a part of him." His instincts rose up at the thought, a low growl threatening to escape him. But Randall was too tired to fight for something he knew he couldn't have. There simply wasn't another pointless battle in him. So he gave Victor a weary half smile, looking down at his hands. Victor's touch on him was like a brand, like every part of him was caught up in that five-inch expanse of skin.

Victor hesitated, clearly weighing his answer before he said it. "Not anymore," he finally said.

"I'm sorry," Randall murmured, shaking his head, "I don't understand." Maybe he should have gotten what Victor was trying to say, but he felt as though his brain had been dipped in mush, as if he couldn't form any thoughts beyond an intense longing to sleep for a week.

"There were, er, certain parts of my behavior that came from a few different things." Victor sounded like he was struggling to talk so honestly. "The recklessness, I mean. Cairo, going to the wolf pack, looking into the Gray Lady's eyes, those decisions were partially made on something that I picked up from David, I think. I'm not sure how to fully explain it to a nonmedusa, but think of it as picking up a new instinct. It becomes natural to think that way."

Victor took his hand back from Randall's shoulder and clasped his fingers in his lap, tightly held together. "When I got home, I put my memories of David in the friend pile, so to speak. I then experimented and made risky situations available to myself, but… none of them held any appeal anymore."

"You can decide how to let the memories affect you?" Randall felt a faint flicker of curiosity, like something was trying to make its way through the vague numbness in his mind. "That's… fascinating."

"Probably not *that* interesting," Victor said wryly. "I did as anybody moving on from an old relationship does. I let go of David, and in doing so the memories I have, the little shards of him I have inside my head, lost their potency. It's just a little more literal for my kind."

"It's interesting," Randall disagreed. "You should think about a paper, Victor. Think of how little there is on the medusas. You could publish something for our kind. If it's anything like what you've done before, it will be the formative work on medusa theory." He paused, realizing that probably hadn't been Victor's point. It was just… wonderful to use his brain for something other than mindlessly alphabetizing or deciding what bag to put the bread in. "Sorry," he murmured, gaze dropping away again. "I'm glad you found a way to handle your ability with greater control. That's wonderful, it is. I'm just confused, I think, as to why you came to tell me."

Victor didn't answer right away. Though he didn't make any noise, didn't move, Randall knew he was trying to find the right thing to say. He had this way of letting out a sigh, of pursing his lips, that Randall had learned signaled his brain searching through possible responses.

"I just wanted you to know," Victor said. "And more importantly, I wanted to know how you are. I don't want you to deny everything and say you're fine, Randall. How are you, really?"

"I'm fine." The response was automatic, Randall still looking away, still refusing to yield. Victor didn't pry, though. The two of them sat quietly, Victor so close that Randall could feel the warmth of him along his side, the nearness practically begging him to soften. And it was *Victor*.

After a beat, Randall tipped his head back, a helpless laugh caught in his throat, an exhausted, almost hysterical smile just barely touching his lips. "I'm not fine at all," he admitted, throat tight. "God, Victor. I'm just…. I'm so *tired.*"

Just saying it out loud, admitting it, felt like a release. Randall laughed again, the sound breaking in his chest, and rubbed his hands through his hair. "And I hate it. God, I hate working every second and wearing"—he shook the name badge—"*this* and this *stupid* apron. And no matter what, I can't get ahead. Anthony's treatment is eating up everything we can make and then some. And I can't tell him. I mean, what kind of terrible person am I that I actually am resentful of this?"

"It doesn't make you a terrible person at all," Victor said firmly. "It makes you human. Or a wolf, however accurate you want that statement to be."

Randall just stared up at the sky, watching a plane winking overhead like a shooting star. "He never complains." Randall didn't know why he was talking to Victor about this.

No, that wasn't right. He did. Because Victor was the person he wanted to talk to about *everything*. But he also knew that he'd walked away, he'd decided that right then, all his energy needed to be on his family and not a medusa with a hard-on for self-destruction. So Randall frankly wasn't sure if he should be taking comfort in this.

Then again, maybe he got to have a momentary burst of weakness.

"Who, Anthony?" Victor asked.

"Not once." Randall laced his fingers together, shoulders hunched. "He was *eight* when our parents were killed. Edwin was two. He never missed a beat. Our whole lives he's only done what he needed to do to take care of us. He even let his mate go, because he couldn't leave us behind. And now that he needs me...." Christ, he actually felt heat prickle at his eyes, the sharp ache in his throat making it almost impossible to keep talking. "I'm standing at work today, *hating* how sick he is. Because I should be in school. I should be going to classes and thinking about tests. And I'm *bagging groceries*. Not only that, but I'm failing. All the work, all the sacrifice, and I haven't done one thing right."

Again, Victor didn't reply right away. He let the silence stretch between them, but before Randall could start to dread that Victor was sitting there judging him, he felt Victor's arm settle over his shoulders. Lightly at first, then more decisively, a tight, centering grip pulling Randall against Victor's side.

"If I learned anything about Anthony, it's that he doesn't complain for the same reasons you don't," Victor said. "He doesn't want to burden anybody with his stress."

The strength of Victor's embrace, the way their bodies fit together so perfectly, was the most restful thing Randall had felt in months. He let his head fall onto Victor's shoulder. He accepted, for the moment, the shared steadiness. "I am never going to be as good of a person as my brother," he murmured, the realization sinking guilt into his gut. "I just want to take care of him. Of Edwin. But we have nothing left. Anthony has an appointment this week, and I don't know how I'm going to pay for it." His eyes darted up to Victor's face, self-condemnation riding on him so heavily Randall could feel it in the turn of his lips, the lines of his forehead. "I've been hiding bills from him. He doesn't know how bad it is."

"You are already as good a man as your brother," Victor said. He lowered his head, pressing his cheek against Randall's hair. "It's not weak to admit that you're having trouble."

"It's always just been us." Randall, very hesitantly, let his fingers barely rest against Victor's knee. "We've never had anyone to rely on. If we couldn't do it ourselves, then it wouldn't happen. I.... I honestly don't know how to ask for help like this." The Gray Lady had been different. She'd been a desperate plea, throwing themselves on the age-old traditions of the pack. And in the end, it hadn't ended up being *help* at all.

"I know," Victor replied softly. He took a deep breath, holding Randall tighter. "I want you to know this. When I offer my house and my money for your use, it's not charity to make me feel useful. If you and your brothers were to move in with me, I would want you to move into my room so that it could be *ours*. I would renovate the house to cater to Edwin's need for open space and Anthony's health needs. I would—it would be something that I would do for *us*."

Something tight and sharp and *wonderful* clenched in Randall's chest. Hope. More than hope, an actual flutter of want, of confidence that desperately wanted to be set free.

He could see it so easily, the simple comfort of settling into a life alongside Victor. And if he reached out, it would be there. It was right in front of him.

"I thought that idea frightened you." Randall glanced over at Victor again. "You've seen all of this, Victor. You weren't thrilled at the prospect, if I recall."

Victor laughed a little. "I know. But do you know what frightened me more? The aftermath of looking into the Gray Lady's eyes. That normal excitement just didn't happen. And when I got home after all of you left, I began to…. I wandered around my overly large house and started imagining you in it. And it didn't scare me."

Feeling wrung out, like he had an elephant sitting on his shoulders and he was struggling simply to keep himself upright, Randall couldn't bring himself to give in. He wanted to. Just the idea of laying all this at Victor's feet was incredibly tempting. But that wouldn't be right. Not for Victor, not for himself, and definitely not for his brothers. He couldn't just force his weary brain into action and take the easiest way out, as much as he wanted to right then.

"I don't know what to say," he admitted quietly. "I feel like I'm underwater, and I can't make myself think."

"It's all right." Victor rubbed his shoulder. Randall felt the curve of a smile against the top of his head. "You don't have to make any major life decisions right now. I just wanted you to know the offer was there. How about we go inside? That casserole is probably getting quickly devoured."

Nodding, Randall nonetheless didn't immediately move. For a while, he and Victor just sat on the steps, staring up at the sky, the quiet noise of conversation and the clatter of dishes inside marking the time. "Thank you," Randall whispered into the silence. "For listening to me." Even if nothing else happened, he was grateful for that.

Victor pressed a light kiss to his forehead. He stood and offered Randall a hand up. "It was my genuine pleasure."

Hand in hand, not too tight of a grip, but steady, as if neither one particularly wanted to let go, they headed inside. Redford and Jed were at the table with Edwin and Anthony, passing around food and drinks, Knievel happily curled up on Edwin's lap. There were logs burning in the fireplace, laughter and smiles, and Anthony looked, for the moment, happy. Everyone was fed and content and safe, and Randall felt a sharp sense of satisfaction at that. Of relief.

"I'm going to go change," he said, smiling a little at everyone. "Save me a plate."

Victor squeezed his hand before he let it go to sit at the table, finding a space beside Anthony. As Randall left to go get into his own clothes, he could hear Anthony inquiring how Victor was, Jed's comment about how that was a wasted question because Victor did nothing but read books and bitch at people, and Redford's quiet laugh.

Randall was too tired to worry about what sort of clothes he wore. He just took his uniform off and put on whatever nearest clean clothes he had, going back to the dining table just in time to have Anthony hand him a plate piled high with casserole and the venison he and Edwin had been cooking earlier.

And the only chair left was pushed suspiciously close to Victor. He gave Edwin an exasperated look, only to be met with a totally innocent grin. Right. Some days, he swore he was going to start putting Edwin outside at meals. But he took his seat, knee bumping up against Victor's, sharing a quick, slightly embarrassed smile before he started to eat.

"So, not that it isn't awesome to see you guys," Edwin said, looking at Jed and Redford, "but what are you three doing here?"

"We're trying out something called 'socializing,'" Redford answered. Randall couldn't tell if he was serious or joking, he was that deadpan.

"And I couldn't remember where you lived, but I wanted to see you, so I tagged along," Victor added.

"*You* meaning us?" Edwin asked with a sly look over at Anthony. "Or you meaning Randall?"

"Shut up, Ed," Randall sighed, pushing the plate away, barely having touched the food. He was too tired to eat. "Just be grateful they drove all the way out here to put up with you."

"I did have something I wanted to ask Anthony, actually," Victor said.

Anthony glanced up from where he'd been concentrating on shoveling food into his mouth, surprised. "Yeah? Shoot."

"Er." Victor fidgeted with his fork. "Unfortunately, even after spending time with you and the pack, I'm still very ignorant about wolf customs."

All at once, Randall was pretty sure he wasn't going to like where this was going. Eyes wide, he looked up, glancing at Victor and then over at Anthony, praying that Victor wasn't about to attempt to do something wolfish, like challenging Anthony to a fight or offering to go sniff someone.

Victor continued, "If I wanted to state my intention to be with Randall romantically, would I have to, er, challenge you for him or something? Perhaps wrestle you to show my strength?"

Jed choked on his food, going red as he bent over, caught somewhere between a laugh and actually suffocating. Randall was still caught on the *state my intention* part of the conversation, and yes, while it was highly unlikely that any kind of physical altercation between Anthony and Victor would end with something other than Victor in a lot of pain, Randall found it rather.... Well, it was hot. Bottom line. It was hot, having Victor show some dominance.

Anthony, on the other hand, had his head down on the table, muffling his laughter into his folded arms. His shoulders were shaking, and his attempts to speak every few seconds were cut off by more laughter. Edwin wasn't even trying to hide the fact that he was completely howling in amusement. Victor looked highly put out, and Anthony eventually managed to answer, "You'd seriously fight me?"

Victor drew himself up, squaring his shoulders with every attempt to look tough. "I absolutely would," he declared, which just sent Anthony off into fresh peals of laughter. Victor withered where he sat. "I seem to have said something incredibly stupid."

"You ask me." Randall's answer was quiet, but he found he was smiling at Victor, some of the tenseness he'd held around Victor ever since Randall had walked away softening slightly. "That's all. I mean"—a quick, wolfish grin, then—"as much as I'd like to see you wrestling around with Anthony, you're not challenging him for his place in the pack or anything. If you wanted me, you'd ask me."

"Oh." Victor had gone red in his embarrassment. "Right, then. I'll do that after dinner, shall I?"

"I think we should talk about burial rites," Edwin said, attempting to be very serious. "I mean, if you're going to go around fighting wolves, we need to know your last requests."

"You should have a second," Jed agreed, a broad smirk on his face. "So that when your scrawny professor ass gets handed to you, someone can drag you to safety."

"I don't think that's what a second is for," Redford piped up. "Seconds take over when the challenger gets killed."

"Oh, well, then Victor will need two of those." Jed nodded. "Maybe three."

Victor sniffed haughtily. "I'm a medusa. I've had a will and a family tombstone since I was three. Since that's taken care of, I'll leave you lot to figure out the duel rules."

"And while you do that"—Randall stood, his mostly uneaten plate gathered up—"I think it's my turn to do dishes. And if Edwin didn't eat it all today, there might be a pie lurking somewhere. I'll get it and some coffee."

"I'll help," Victor volunteered. He started to gather up dishes, leaning over the table to collect three of them from Edwin.

Together they carted everything into the kitchen, where Randall collected the leftovers to put into the fridge. They fell into an easy rhythm to the murmur of conversation in the other room, an almost practiced dance around each other. Randall washed, Victor dried, their heads bowed over the sink as they worked in silence.

"You're not a wolf." Randall's voice cut into the space between them, a frown creasing his forehead as he scrubbed the plates.

"You're not a medusa," Victor replied, a smile in his voice.

With a noise that wasn't quite a laugh, Randall darted a look over at Victor. "I mean, you don't have to try to take on my instincts. My bonding to you, or not, that's my problem. Not yours."

"I know," Victor murmured. "The truth is, if medusas can be said to bond by looking into someone's eyes, I've already done that with you." He accepted a dish that Randall passed him. "But I'm not speaking of bonds. I'm speaking of dating."

Randall considered it as he started in on the last of the silverware. The suds made everything slippery, the bubbles catching in the fine hairs on his arms. "I'm worried I don't actually know you," Randall admitted. "Before, I thought you were someone other than the man who took risks simply because he wanted to. Now, though, I'm afraid you are, and I don't know who he is. You've become this… dream." Randall dared to look over at Victor. "What if we don't fit the way I think we do?"

Victor's expression didn't give much away about his thoughts right then. "I'd say that dating is the way to find that out. But if you've discovered that you don't like who I am, then you're free to say no."

Randall studied Victor intently as he dried off his hands. Before he could change his mind, Randall leaned in, burying his nose under Victor's ear, taking a deep, slow breath. "You smell the same," he whispered. He smelled like home. Like a promise of a home Randall had yet to find.

"I wasn't lying when I said that I believe I've changed," Victor replied quietly, lifting his chin a little to allow Randall greater access. "I know I can't expect you to

329

instantly believe me, but I'd like it if you gave me a chance. Go on a date with me, Randall."

He didn't have many more excuses, and all the ones that were left seemed so worthless. Pulling back, Randall briefly closed his eyes so Victor wouldn't have the worry of meeting his gaze, instead leaning in to nudge their foreheads together. "I missed you too," he admitted, and it was like a release, like that tightly coiled grief he'd kept buried was allowed to breathe. "Yes. I'd like very much to go out with you, Victor Rathbone."

A smile he'd never seen before spread over Victor's face: uninhibited, none of the usual caution or dryness that tinged all of his other expressions. "Good. Because I've been planning a date for two weeks, and I'd be very disappointed if I didn't get to do it."

"Two weeks, huh?" Randall couldn't help but return the smile, the two of them standing there, just barely apart, not touching but hovering there, giddy with the closeness. "Was this just general date planning? Because if I need to get on your schedule, just tell me and I'll move some things around. I wouldn't want you to use up all your good ideas."

"Oh no, all of my ideas were specifically for you." Victor's expression took on a hint of embarrassment. "I made a spreadsheet and gave the ideas a numerical value with how much I thought you'd like them, then ranked them accordingly."

And that was, hands down, one of the hottest things Randall had ever heard. "Tomorrow?" he asked, moving just a little closer, repressing the urge to ask to see the chart. Maybe after, if the date went well. "I have work until seven, but after that, I'm free."

"Perfect. I'll take you out to dinner," Victor said. He reached forward to take Randall's hand, grasping it tightly. Randall turned his fingers to catch against Victor's, smiling again at the simple touch.

"Where did dinner rate on the list?" he asked in a teasing murmur.

"Actually, third. But the first two ideas would require a whole day," Victor replied.

Surprise hit Randall. He couldn't even imagine Victor spending time thinking about *him*, thinking of things he might enjoy. "You planned a day with me?" Randall honestly couldn't believe someone so wanted to spend that much time with him that they'd purposefully plot out a way to fill the hours.

"More like eight," Victor clarified. "And that's just dates that take place in establishments around the city. I've yet to get really creative with my date ideas. I'm afraid I'm a bit out of practice—"

Pulling Victor forward, Randall caught his lips in a kiss. All his life, he'd had his brothers. The three of them had been everything to each other. And while Randall had dated on occasion, while he'd had friends, no one had ever put that much thought into *him* before. Anthony and Edwin, yes, but this was wildly different. So he kissed Victor, because he had a chart with *dates*, whole days' worth of plans. Because he'd driven all the way out here just to tell Randall he'd gotten better.

Because he was the most wonderful man Randall had ever met. And *that* part of him, Randall was beginning to see, hadn't changed at all.

When they parted, Victor brought his hand up to lightly touch the base of Randall's throat. "That biting thing," he said, "is that strictly for sex, or can I do it any time, with your permission?"

A shaky laugh escaped Randall, and he cupped Victor's jaw, thumb rubbing along his cheek. "Anytime," he managed, voice barely more than a rumble, "though I have to admit, I can't promise I won't simply start tearing clothes off." But he tipped his chin back, baring his throat, a surge of anticipation, of *rightness*, sinking into his gut just from the action.

Instead of the bite he expected, he felt the light touch of Victor's lips, then the brush of his nose, as if Victor were scenting him. "Then I'll keep it chaste for now," Victor said, a similar laugh under his words. "Because I should let you get an early night, if I don't want you falling asleep during our dinner tomorrow night."

"Coffee," Randall reminded him, his breath caught in his chest. "I said I'd make coffee." And something about pie. Though he was finding it hard to think about anything other than Victor.

"Then I'll help." Victor inhaled. "Sometimes I envy the wolf nose. It's so much more useful than what my blood gives me."

"I don't smell that great." Randall shrugged, his fingers tracing down Victor's neck to rest lightly on his shoulder. "And I think what you can do is incredible. *You* are incredible."

A shout came from the dining room. "Where's the pie?" Jed's voice interrupted the moment, sending Randall jumping slightly away from Victor.

Sagging back against the counter, Randall started to laugh a little helplessly. "It's coming," he called back. "Hold your horses."

Victor gave a sigh of exasperation. "I'll get the pie, you make the coffee? I'd be an awful barista, I'm afraid."

"Tea's in the cupboard," Randall said, going to switch on the coffeepot. "If you'd prefer that. It's not a very good brand"—he'd cut out that luxury weeks ago—"but it's… no, I'm sorry, it's terrible and weak. I can't say anything nice about it. Please don't have the tea."

"Coffee, then," Victor agreed, bemused. "And some decent tea at dinner tomorrow."

They worked together well, Randall noticed. It was in the simple things, like how Victor reached up to grab the cups before Randall could ask, how when Randall held out the sugar, Victor was there with the cream. It was simple and lovely, achingly so, domestic in the most warming way. They carried the plates and cups and the pot of coffee out to the dining room. Randall ignored the significant looks from everyone, choosing instead to serve dessert and take his seat.

He just had coffee. But it was nice to sit next to Victor, leaning just barely against his shoulder, the weariness of the day easing slightly.

"I haven't heard from the pack," Jed was saying, taking a huge bite of his pie. "But I'm guessing they'll have moved again by now."

"I thought you said you took care of things?" Edwin looked a little worried, carefully pulling all of the fruit out of his pie to pile it on the side of his plate so he could attack the crust alone. "Are they still being hunted?"

331

"Oh, we took care of things," Jed snorted. "Anthony and I showed Leo who was the goddamn boss."

"Jed was badass," Anthony agreed. "It was like every action movie I've ever seen, except with less motorbikes and slow motion."

"Hey, we could have had motorbikes, sweetheart." Jed waved his fork at Anthony. "Next time we will definitely have bikes."

Redford sighed, like he put up with ludicrous requests from Jed all the time. Anthony just nodded in satisfaction and added, "And cool leather jackets and sunglasses."

Jed, his arm slung casually around Redford's shoulders, pointed at Anthony. "Yes. Yes, exactly. There is no point at all to a cool bike if you don't have the right accessories." He gave Redford a pointed look, as if this was a conversation they'd had before.

Under the table, Victor's pinky finger brushed against Randall's. It was like a little shock of heat, a slide of skin as their fingers hooked together, and Randall had to duck his head to hide his smile. Out of the corner of his eye, he saw Victor look at him, seeming just as content as Randall was.

Jed grinned. "You should have seen your brother. *Growled* at this woman, got her to unclench right up and let us upstairs."

"Yes, and it was really rude and you should never do that to anyone, Edwin," Anthony said. Edwin snorted, giving Anthony a look.

"Fuck that, do it, it was awesome," Jed said, tipping back in his chair. "I would have had to pull out a gun to get that kind of response."

"So you're sure this O'Malley person isn't going to be hunting the pack anymore?" Randall asked. "Not that I'm doubting your manliness—"

"Damn straight. We were manly as hell," Jed informed him.

"I'm sure," Randall continued dryly. "But you think the pack is truly going to be safe now?"

Jed cut a glance over at Anthony and sighed, shrugging. "Maybe? I mean, I don't know how *safe* a big group of wolves is ever going to be, not with things being what they are."

"That's why they moved again," Randall surmised.

"I would have." Jed nodded. "Once someone finds you, doesn't matter if they stop hunting. Your cover's blown. You have to find someplace new. Leo might be done in the hunting business, but if he's telling the truth about the vampires, it probably won't be the end of it."

"It won't be," Victor murmured. "There's much bigger things yet to come."

There was a long beat of silence, all of them exchanging looks, the jovial mood dampened by a sense of very real dread. Randall let his hand slip farther into Victor's, tightening his grip slightly. Jed was the first to react, snorting faintly. "No offense, princess," he said plainly, "but I don't buy this whole *seeing the future* shit. There's no such thing as fate or destiny or whatever you want to call it. Bad shit is coming, because bad shit is always coming. But nothing's set in stone."

Instead of arguing the point, Victor just smirked and said, "I'm disappointed, Jed. I said 'much bigger things yet to come,' and you didn't make a dirty remark about it?"

"I just assumed you were talking about my cock," Jed returned with a grin. "Or maybe you were busy with your mind in the gutter. I'm surprised you two are back in here with your clothes on."

"Please." Victor snorted. "The last thing I want to think about is what's in your trousers."

"Too bad." Jed clucked his tongue in disappointment. "It's definitely worth more than a few thoughts."

"As fun as this conversation is," Randall broke in, surprised to find how hard he was scowling at Jed or how tightly he'd gripped Victor's hand, "it's getting late, and I have to be up at six."

"If you guys don't want to drive all the way back, we have a guest house, of sorts," Anthony offered. "It's out back."

Victor looked surprised. "Really? I'd never noticed before. I recall you mentioning that you'd built this place. Did you build that too?"

Anthony grinned proudly. "Every inch of it. The rooms are small, but there's two of them above the workshop. We can get it set up for you, if you want."

"Anthony's *really* good at that stuff," Edwin said, beaming just as proudly. "He made these chairs too. And this table."

"He's very talented." Randall gave Anthony a smile. "And his ego doesn't need inflating." That was said fondly, teasing, because Anthony should be given all the accolades he could get.

"You guys should stay," Edwin urged. "You can stay a few days!"

"Edwin," Randall sighed.

But Edwin just kept going, straight over Randall's gentle protest. "We can go hunting tomorrow! And there's a lake out back. I have to go into town tomorrow, but you guys can stick around with Anthony in the afternoon."

Jed, Randall suddenly realized, wasn't nearly as lazy or laid back as he'd been pretending. His gaze had been going over everything since he'd come in; now he pinned a look on Anthony. "How's the treatment going?" he asked, not a trace of his usual flippant attitude in his voice.

"It's fine," Randall answered. "We're doing fine."

But Jed just quietly waited for Anthony to answer, gaze unwavering.

"It's... progressing?" Anthony grimaced. He'd paused halfway in spearing a chunk of pie on his fork, suddenly looking like his appetite had been lost. "I'm still waiting on a verdict. But it's a hell of a lot more comfortable than Cedric's bad chairs."

Jed and Redford looked at each other, seeming to have a whole conversation without speaking. "Yeah, we'll stay," Jed decided. "Hell, I never did get to go fishing. We'll just use your lake." Jed nodded at Anthony. "That okay with you, Lassie?"

"As long as you're okay with catching tiny fish," Anthony snorted. "It's not as fruitful as it used to be." There was an undercurrent of sadness to Anthony's words. The fact that the lake had shrunk, that the fish were smaller and less numerous now, was not something they often talked about.

"Never caught any kind of fish." Jed shrugged. "Unless they were fried and slathered in tartar sauce. I won't know the difference."

Anthony nudged Edwin with his elbow. "Ed, can you get started on getting the guesthouse ready?"

"I'll do it," Randall said. And yes, maybe he gave Victor a little sideways glance. "I'll just grab some sheets and blankets."

"You've been working for fourteen hours today," Edwin pointed out. "You look like you're going to fall over, and you stopped sleeping, like, three days ago."

"It's making up beds, Edwin, not running a marathon." Randall got up, going to the hall cupboard and starting to pull out the linens. "I think there are pillows in the cedar chest over there. Do you need more than one each?"

Jed and Redford shook their heads, so Randall set about gathering everything they needed. Anthony looked like he wanted to help, but at a stern look from Randall he sat back down. Redford and Victor helped him carry everything over to the guest shed, as they called it, while Jed went out to the Jeep to gather up the few things they'd brought with them.

The first room had a queen-sized bed. Jed took the sheets from Randall's arms and very politely kicked him out. "We're going to sleep," he informed Randall. "And we can make our own bed." With a leer, he winked at Victor. "Get some earplugs, princess."

"Please don't have sex in our guest bed," Randall sighed. Jed did not look like he was going to listen, simply grinning at them both and shutting the door in their faces.

He led Victor to the other side of the attic area, the room that was directly above Anthony's workshop. "This room is smaller," he apologized, opening the door and switching on the light. "But it has a balcony." The bed was facing the double doors, the balcony overlooking the dark woods. There was a skylight above, the sky scattered with pinpricks of light.

"It's nicer than my house. And I live in a mansion," Victor said, admiring the room.

"Now I know that's a lie." Randall smiled absently as he spread out the sheets, setting about making the bed. "The bathroom is that door we passed on the right. Only one here, I'm afraid, so you'll have to share or come over to the main house."

"It's perfect," Victor assured, moving to the other side of the bed to help Randall with the sheets. "It was obviously built with love." He hesitated before adding, "Am I wrong in guessing that this place has something to do with Anthony's mate?"

A sad, rueful smile touched Randall's lips. He moved over to turn off the light, reaching out to take Victor's hand and lead him carefully to the balcony. When they stood outside, the lake was like a shimmering blanket spread out in front of them, the stars reflected in the inky black. "He built it for Vil. I think he really thought Vil would come back. It was going to be theirs, and Edwin and I would have the main cabin to ourselves. Originally, the whole top floor was the bedroom. The bottom floor was going to be the kitchen, a den with a huge fireplace lined with river rocks...." Randall sighed, shoulder rising in a shrug. "But he stopped. I think he realized that Vil was gone. We turned it into a workshop and these bedrooms. Ant always said if we got married we could live here, but I don't think either one of us could. It's not ours."

It was Anthony's. It was yet another dream he'd given up for his brothers.

"Come on." Randall gave Victor a slight smile, moving to turn the light back on, ruining the view in favor of finishing making the bed. "You look tired. I should let you get some sleep."

Victor approached him, reaching out to take Randall's hands. "Where shall I meet you for dinner tomorrow?"

"My room?" Randall squeezed his fingers gently. "I'll come straight home and change. I have to be at the library at seven tomorrow morning, and then I have a half shift at the grocery store, but I should be back home by seven at the latest. And then I'll have one of my rare days off for Anthony's appointments, so we don't have to worry about being out too late."

"All right. I'll borrow Jed's Jeep so I can drive us out." Victor leaned in to brush a kiss over Randall's cheek, the contact lingering. "Sleep well, Randall."

"Sweet dreams, Victor."

Dreams were not something Randall was on the best terms with. Before Cairo, his idea of a nightmare had been being naked in class without his homework. But then....

Well. And then he'd been collared like a dog, he'd been *fed from*, and he'd honestly thought, to the very bottom of his being, that he was going to die like that. Or worse, that he'd live, that he'd be broken down and used as a pet for the vampires' amusement. There was no one, he'd known, who could have saved him. His brothers wouldn't even know something was wrong until it was too late.

In those days, Randall had been utterly helpless. Shifting only got him more abuse. They didn't even *like* feeding from him, he apparently smelled terrible to them, but they'd done it. Not to slake their hunger, but to cause him pain. They thought it was funny.

Randall hadn't spoken about Cairo to his brothers. He saw no need to. They knew he'd been taken, that he'd been rescued, and now he was back home. They knew he covered his arms now, that he wouldn't appreciate someone commenting on his neck. And that was all. What was the point of dwelling on it? Anthony and Edwin had enough real problems without Randall's imagined ones. He was alive. That should have been enough.

That night, though, when he closed his eyes, when his brain put him right back into those moments, it didn't feel like enough. It felt like he was dying all over again, that fear eating him from the inside. He couldn't move, couldn't fight back. He was helpless.

Waking with a start, Randall lay in bed, panting, trying to get his racing heart under control. His shirt was soaked through with sweat, his sheets a twisted tangle around his legs. Slowly, he forced himself up, so exhausted it felt like every movement was lifting a mountain. He tugged off his shirt, grimacing at how clammy and overheated he felt.

It was four in the morning. He had two hours until his alarm would go off. Randall desperately needed the sleep, but he found himself utterly unwilling to risk another dream. He checked in with Anthony, who for once was sound asleep, tugging the covers back up around his brother's shoulders. Edwin was sprawled out in his bed on his back, limbs everywhere, Knievel dozing on his chest. Everything was quiet and still.

Randall shivered in the cool night air as he slipped outside, still shirtless. He made his way down to the lake, wandering aimlessly. The huge sky overhead reminded him that he was free, that he wasn't shoved into a dank hole to die. With his bare toes wiggling in the wet mud at the edge of the lake, Randall considered it. It used to be bigger, the lake, when Vilhehn and his family had been here. The fish had been huge and numerous; lush plants had grown at the edge. Now it was so much less.

But the water was chilly and clean, the half-moon reflected in the soft waves. Randall stripped off his pajama pants, waded into the shallows, and then ducked his head under the water. The sweat of his nightmare was washed away, the calm stillness of the lake soothing him. He swam out to the center with strong strokes and floated there, staring up at the sky, letting his mind still.

When he'd been younger, he'd believed that the lake was alive, that it protected them. Even though he knew such a notion was childish, Randall felt a little more comforted, just floating in the middle of the water, letting himself drift.

When he finally swam back to shore, he felt more relaxed than he had in days. It was temporary, he knew, it was nothing but a brief respite, but it was something. Nothing about his life had changed out there in the water, but at least now he felt a little less like he was being swallowed whole by it.

No one was awake when Randall left for work. The hours passed far too slowly, work sliding him into a kind of numb half awareness. He shelved books he didn't have time to read, far too many paperbacks with half-naked people on the covers, he ate half a peanut butter sandwich alone in the break room, and when he was finally released, he went straight to the grocery store to tie on his apron and attach his name badge. The navy-blue polo the store required him to wear was unobtrusive enough he could get away with it both places. Of course, the library thought him to have an extremely limited wardrobe, but Randall would hardly be winning any fashion awards regardless, so his wounded ego was easily mended.

Bagging groceries was possibly the most numbing job Randall could imagine. It was just engaging enough that he couldn't mentally drift off, while simultaneously being so repetitive that he couldn't seem to grasp hold of anything to challenge him. By the time he dragged himself out to the car, Randall wished he could just curl up in the backseat and sleep.

But Victor was coming to take him out. And that alone was worth forcing himself to stay awake.

He ran in the door, later than he'd wanted because of traffic, and went straight to the shower. No matter how little time he had, Randall was desperate to wash off the sweat of the day. When he emerged a few minutes later, toweling off his damp hair, robe wrapped tight around him, he found Edwin and Anthony waiting for him with big grins. "So," Edwin said, practically wiggling in excitement, "you have a *date*."

"Have you two just been waiting for me to walk in so you can point that out?" Randall headed past them to his room, digging through his closet frantically for something to wear. "If you're going to mock me, at least be helpful."

"Being helpful is for people with fashion sense," Anthony said sagely. "We don't have any."

Randall glanced over at Edwin in his ragged T-shirt and Anthony in his flannel. "You're right," he agreed. "Get out, you're both horrible."

He shut the door to the sound of their gleeful laughter. "Wear something that's not a sweater vest!" Anthony called through the door.

"Shut up," Randall responded. He looked down at the vest he'd pulled out of the closet, sighing and dropping it onto the bed. He chose a simple shirt instead, slacks, a tie. Dressing quickly, he glanced at himself in the mirror.

Oh, God, he was a mess.

He yanked open the door to find both Edwin and Anthony waiting for him, and gave them a panicked look. "This is bad, right?" His fingers ran over the tie, looking down at himself. "When did I get so fat? And I should just wear a bag over my head, right? God, why did I agree to do this? I'm not a date person. I look terrible."

Anthony gave him a pat on the shoulder. "You look great, Randall," he said. "I mean it. Victor's not even going to care what you're wearing."

"Because I look horrible," Randall agreed miserably. He turned on his heel and went back to the closet, digging through it, tossing clothes everywhere. "Maybe a different tie?" Or a different face.

Anthony was chuckling behind him, dragging Randall away from the closet. "No, because he's so smitten he only cares if you turn up," he corrected. "You think you're nervous about clothes? The guy turned up in a three-piece suit earlier today."

"He's wearing a *suit*?" Oh, God. Randall immediately started undoing his tie. "I don't know what I'm doing."

"Here." Edwin was standing there with a tan sport coat, a deep-green tie, and a dark-blue shirt. "Put this on."

"What—"

"Jed and I watched daytime television today." Edwin nodded sagely. "Trust me." He paused and wrinkled his nose. "Also, television is *boring*."

Randall took the clothes. "Why did you watch, then?"

Edwin shrugged. "Jed and Redford wanted to relax. We went for a run and then swimming and then tried to fish, only there wasn't anything biting and they had no idea what they were doing. Jed just kind of poked the water with a stick. I think they got tired." Giving Randall a grin, he shoved his shoulder. "Now go get dressed. Victor's been pacing outside for the past ten minutes." They left, and Anthony shut the door behind them.

Randall studied himself in the mirror after he got dressed again. He ran a hand through his hair, adjusted his glasses, and wondered if it was possible to be any more nervous than he was right then.

It turned out that yes, it was. Because when he heard Victor coming up to the door, all the butterflies that had been beating around his stomach turned into a cyclone that twisted him up completely. Letting out a shaky breath, Randall forced himself to wait for the knock, going over to let Victor in.

Victor was indeed wearing a three-piece suit, the perfectly tailored kind that only came with significant money. There was even the chain of a pocket watch hanging out of the pocket of the gray pinstripe waistcoat, a burnished silver to match the rest of the suit. Despite all of that, Victor looked just as nervous as he did.

He also looked incredible. In the middle of all his worry, Randall felt a smile start, a giddy little lift to his gut that made it impossible to not grin.

"Are you ready?" Victor asked. The once-over he gave Randall was obvious, his gaze darting up and down the length of Randall's body. "You look fantastic, by the way."

Randall ducked his head as he exhaled a laugh. "I think that word's being used up by you, actually. You, uh. Yes. You look very good."

"Oh my God, you two." Jed and Redford had apparently shown up to watch the show. Jed smirked widely at both of them, sprawled out on the couch with Redford's legs on his lap—Randall's door was only just visible from the living room, and they'd obviously deliberately placed themselves on the one couch with viewing access. "Just kiss or nerd bump or whatever it is you people do and get going."

Victor decisively took Randall's hand. "Do be quiet, Jed," he said carelessly and turned back to Randall. "Shall we take our leave of this rabble and go somewhere with good company?"

"I think that sounds perfect." Randall squeezed Victor's fingers lightly, and they walked down the hall and toward the front door. Edwin was grinning at the both of them, and he darted up to give Victor a big hug.

"If you hurt him, I have teeth, and I will rip your throat out," Edwin informed Victor cheerfully.

"Edwin!" Randall gave him an exasperated look, gaze going to Anthony. "Could you please, Ant?"

"What?" Anthony just looked deeply amused. "Oh, right. Edwin, don't threaten people. It's rude." He reached out to shake Victor's hand. "If you break his heart, we really will wrestle."

"Okay," Randall sighed. "That's enough testosterone for the day."

"Hey." Jed whistled, stopping Randall in his tracks. "Fur boy. You hurt the princess and I'll find my explosives. Got it?" He gave them both a charming smirk. "Have fun!"

"Dear God, can we leave now?" Victor groaned. "We're leaving. Come on, Randall." Still looking faintly perturbed at Edwin and Anthony's threats—and perhaps more especially at Jed's gesture of protectiveness—Victor tugged Randall out the door.

The moment they were outside, Randall started laughing. He couldn't help it. "You might not believe this," he told Victor, shaking his head, "but that actually went better than I'd expected it to."

"I don't doubt it," Victor huffed. In less of a hurry now that they'd escaped outside, they walked toward Jed's Jeep.

"The first boy who came to take me out, I was eighteen." They both climbed inside the Jeep, snapping on seat belts, getting themselves settled. "Edwin bit him. Twice. Needless to say, we never made it on the date."

As Victor started up the engine, he smiled. "I'll consider myself lucky that I remain unbitten, then."

"I wouldn't say that," Randall murmured, looking out the window rather than at Victor. "I wouldn't think a little biting this evening would be so bad."

"Neither would I," Victor agreed slyly. "Now, before I start driving in any particular direction, do you have a preference for type of restaurant? Are you allergic to anything?"

Randall shook his head. "We don't often eat out, so I'm afraid my input will be limited. I'd prefer it if some sort of meat was available, but it's not a necessity. I really don't expect anything, Victor." Randall relaxed back into the seat. "Fast food would be fine with me."

"Well, we're certainly not going to go through a drive-through." Victor seemed appalled at the very idea. "We'll have Italian, then. There's a place in town I'm quite fond of, and I think you'd like it."

"That sounds good," Randall agreed. His entire experience with Italian was when he tried to make pasta at home, only to have Edwin and Anthony pick out the meatballs and leave the rest. It would be interesting to have something authentic. "How was your day? I hope Edwin didn't annoy you too much. I think he gets lonely sometimes."

Victor seemed to hesitate before looking over at Randall, a small smile curling at the edge of his lips, different from the ones he usually wore. This one seemed more content. "Not at all. He finds Jed and Redford far more entertaining than me. I went back home briefly to get some things, but other than that my day was fairly uneventful. Yours?"

"Long," Randall admitted. He absently rubbed his hands together, watching the traffic out the window. "But not worth speaking about, really." They were headed back toward the city, and Randall found his gaze increasingly drawn toward Victor, the lights of the vehicles flashing across his face, lighting him in sporadic vision. "I've been looking forward to this, though. I, uh—" He briefly smiled. "—honestly didn't think we would ever be going on a date."

"Neither did I," Victor admitted. "Everything was… very confusing for a while. But I'm glad I got my head straightened out."

A smile touched Randall's face, and he daringly reached out to lightly brush his fingers along Victor's knee. "Well, here we are. I think we've had enough of talking about the past. I'm much more interested now in just you."

"Well, we're nearly at the restaurant," Victor replied. "Why don't I save that topic? I'm not actually that interesting, and I should probably save my good lines of conversation for the actual date."

"This isn't the date?" Randall asked, eyes crinkling in amusement. "My God, I am out of practice. I forgot the pre-date ritual."

"I suppose this could be counted as the date." Victor looked over at him briefly, obviously not wanting to take his eyes off the road for too long. "But driving in Jed's Jeep is hardly one of my good ideas."

"It's kind of bumpy," Randall acknowledged. "But our car sounds like the muffler is going to drop out. Anthony's fixed it a thousand times. It's really amazing it still runs. So this isn't half bad."

Victor turned the Jeep around a corner and leaned forward over the steering wheel, peering ahead to look for a place to park. "I hate driving," he said absently. "I have cars, but I never use them."

Randall glanced over, eyebrows lifted high. *Cars*. As in multiple. As in, yesterday Randall dug through Edwin's sock drawer looking for enough change to get a loaf of bread, and Victor was talking about more than one car. "You should hire a driver," he managed, wondering exactly how rich Victor was. Randall hadn't actually thought much of that before, but maybe it was relevant.

"Goodness, no, I live close enough to where I need to go that I can just walk. Any driver would be bored stiff for weeks on end." Victor grimaced as he pulled the Jeep into a parking spot, sitting up to try to see over the hood to make sure he didn't bump into anything. He looked relieved when he was done. "Right, then. Just in time for our booking."

The restaurant that Victor directed them toward looked small and tasteful from the outside, the windows glowing with low lamplight, vines crawling over the white stone walls. A waiter, impeccably dressed, greeted them as soon as they walked in the door. The outside, it turned out, belied what was inside. The interior was only just bright enough to see, lending it an intimate air. Every person dining, to Randall, looked like something out of a movie—perfectly made up without being ostentatious, their taste revealed in more subtle smaller diamonds and expensive cufflinks.

It was something he would have loved watching from a distance. Just seeing how people interacted had always been interesting. But walking among them, being led to his table, Randall was suddenly aware that his clothes weren't nearly that well fitted, that his suit coat was something he'd gotten from a clearance rack. He didn't fit in here at all. His hair was messy, he was awkward, and this was not a world he knew how to handle.

The waiter took them to a cozy corner table that overlooked a courtyard. Victor pulled Randall's chair out for him and sat down opposite him. Randall noticed that he unbuttoned his jacket as he did so, a casual motion by the very rich used to not wanting to crease their suits.

Victor looked satisfied with the restaurant, but when he looked over at Randall, that expression faltered slightly. "You're uncomfortable," he surmised. "Oh, Randall, I'm sorry, I should have picked better. We can go elsewhere, if you like."

"No, of course not." Randall looked down, frowning, fiddling with his tie. "It's fine. I just haven't ever been someplace this nice. I, um, I don't think I'm dressed right." He felt ridiculous. Worrying about his *clothes*, honestly. "I would just prefer not to embarrass you." Randall gave Victor a crooked, rueful little smile.

"Nobody minds what you're wearing, Randall," Victor said gently. He nodded to the other patrons, who all looked far more interested in their meals or their dining company. "Only the *snooty* rich would look down on you, and I don't socialize with that lot."

"Okay, this is going to sound terrible, but when you say *rich*"—Randall glanced over at Victor—"you don't just mean 'I have a savings account with more than ten dollars in it,' do you?"

"It's family money, mostly." Victor looked a little uncomfortable talking about it. "Built up over generations. My mother's family was one of the first settlers in America. My father's family is well established in Manchester—that was where I spent most of my youth. I've added some of my own through stocks, a few book sales, and a couple of properties I own. Let's just say that if I had children, neither they nor their children would have to work if they were smart with their money."

Okay, so more than ten dollars. Randall gave that a moment to sink in. He'd honestly never really thought about *money* like that. Not in anything other than the vague acknowledgement that he needed to have more. Especially now. But he honestly didn't care if Victor had a thousand dollars or a million or ten million.

Although he did wonder what it'd be like.

"So you want children?" Randall asked with a half-hidden smile, changing the subject and ducking his head to glance through the menu.

Victor's frown seemed unsure. He too was looking at the menu, but he only gave it a cursory glance, as if he'd been here enough to know what was offered. "I've never thought seriously about it," he admitted. "No further than being wary of passing on my genes."

"I don't know if that'd be a bad thing." Randall reached out to take a sip of his water, slowly starting to regain some of his self-confidence. This was better. This was just him and Victor, talking. He'd always enjoyed that. "Beyond the fact that a child having your smile could never be terrible, the part of yourself you're concerned about seems to diminish by further generations."

"Flatterer," Victor said fondly.

"Oh, I don't flatter," Randall assured him, a bit of teasing in his expression. "I only speak truths. That's one of my wolf qualities, didn't I tell you? Attractive men only get the truth."

Victor seemed bemused. "Really? Not even only after asking four times, like the Coyote of myth? I'm very lucky, then."

"You are," Randall hummed in agreement. They shared a smile, and Randall went back to perusing the menu, searching through the heavy parchment pages for something familiar. "Do you have any recommendations?" he finally asked, glancing upward, careful to keep his eyes below chin level so Victor didn't accidentally meet his. "I've had bad spaghetti before, but that's about all my experience with Italian food."

Victor waved the waiter over in response and ordered for them both in fluent Italian. His accent wasn't the best, but since Randall knew enough to be conversational in the same language, it was obvious to his ears that it was at least occasionally practiced. And there was something incredibly attractive about Victor at that moment, easily taking control of the situation.

"I thought we'd go with a number of smaller dishes," Victor said to him once the waiter had left. "So we can share, and you can get the full experience of how excellent these chefs are."

"In this moment, I am extremely glad you can't look into my eyes," he said, just barely audible to Victor, head bowed as he carefully arranged his silverware. "Because the expression I was giving you just then was most definitely not decent."

Victor smirked. "Perhaps I'll have to take a photograph for later reference."

It took him a moment to get it, but then Randall sat back, letting out a small huff of realization. "Because you can look into someone's eyes that way," he presumed, long fingers playing with the stem of the water glass. "A photograph, a movie, they're just images, and so you can look without seeing anything. How fascinating."

"Yes," Victor muttered, seemingly embarrassed. "I don't like to ask people for photographs, but... they're nice to have."

Randall simply held out his hand. "Let me see your phone."

Victor's rapid blinking had a startled twitch to it, but he didn't hesitate in finding his phone and handing it over. Randall flipped through it, finding the camera application and holding the phone up in front of himself. Normally he would avoid such things, but in this case, he simply looked straight into the camera and took a picture without worrying about how terrible he would look, how his hair was out of place or he had an odd smile. Then he removed his glasses and did the same thing, thinking of the same expression he'd had earlier, wanting Victor to see. When he was done, he handed the phone back to Victor without a word, slipping his glasses back on.

"I hope you ordered that garlic bread I can smell," he commented, looking around. "I bet it's fantastic."

Victor didn't seem to hear him. He was too busy cradling his phone in both hands, staring down at the first photograph Randall had taken. He switched to the second and stared at that for some time, before flipping back and forth between the two. His smile looked a bit wobbly as he said, "You have stunning eyes, Randall."

There was a sudden tightness in Randall's throat, a soft hook in his stomach that seemed to demand he reach out, taking Victor's hand in his own. "You are the most amazing man." His smile too was shaky, but he gripped Victor's fingers tightly. And for a moment, they just sat there, Victor staring down at his phone, Randall holding his hand. The restaurant didn't exist. The whole world just faded away, until they were the only ones left.

He wanted a thousand days of this. A thousand times a thousand. The realization hit Randall like a punch, inevitable and completely consuming. As if in that moment, he couldn't imagine a future that didn't include, in some way, exactly this. Victor holding his hand.

"I suppose it must seem a bit silly, getting overcome at seeing someone's eyes," Victor said ruefully. "I could look into my mother's eyes. Since we were both alike, our abilities cancelled one another out. It made it difficult to understand why, at a young age before I fully grasped the concept, I couldn't simply look at other people if I could look at her. On the day I was born, my father took a photograph much like you did, so that I could see him."

For someone who had grown up completely intertwined with family, Randall simply couldn't imagine. It seemed impossible to grasp growing up so isolated that your only time looking fully into your father's face was through a picture. He almost couldn't think of anything to say, the lump in his throat seeming to swallow his words completely. He pulled Victor's hand up to place a kiss against his palm. "I don't think it's silly," Randall murmured. "You found a way to connect. There's something lovely about it." Lovely and incredibly sad.

"They never looked into each other's eyes," Victor replied. "It was an agreement they made when they started dating. Father was much like Jed, actually, not in personality but in ignorance of the supernatural community when he met her, but he adjusted quickly enough. When I was still young, about three, I think it was, my mother had shielded me from other people up until then. She'd wanted my first vision experience to be with someone that I loved, so she had me look into my father's eyes."

Victor's slightly queasy expression said enough. "I wasn't old enough to grasp what I saw," he continued, "but I was told I wouldn't stop crying for days on end. I'm pleased I had the opportunity, though. I knew him so fully that I felt like I'd been around him for a lifetime."

There were tears in Randall's eyes, he realized at once. But he smiled a little at Victor. He laced their fingers together and brushed another kiss to his knuckles, resting his chin against them, trying to think of anything to say that might sound like more than a platitude.

"I'm sorry," Victor said hurriedly, before Randall could say anything. "That's not exactly pleasant date conversation."

"Thank you for telling me." Randall found he really didn't want to let go of Victor. "I just...." Letting out a slow breath, he shook his head. "I can't imagine." His thumb made absent circles against the back of Victor's hand. "What were your parents like?"

Victor seemed relieved for the question. "I take after my mother more, so I'm told. She grew up here in America, taken care of by my grandmother. My grandfather is the one who passed the medusa gene on. He's been in a nursing home for quite some time now. My father was a tailor. He was a very methodical man, and he didn't give up his trade even when he married into money. You would have liked them, I think. They certainly would have loved you." He tightened his grasp around Randall's hand. "What about your parents?"

"I would have liked to meet your parents." And he would have. To see if Victor's laugh came from his mother, if the way he would get so focused on his research made him look like his father, if he had his mother's strength and his father's kindness. Yes, Randall very much would have loved to meet them both. "Maybe, someday soon, we can go visit your grandfather. I don't know much about your family, obviously, or what happens to medusas as they age. But if you wanted to go, I would go with you."

Victor just nodded silently, letting Randall continue speaking.

His parents were a subject Randall didn't often speak of. He ducked his head, gathering his thoughts. "My father," he started, "had the worst sense of humor. I mean, absolutely wretched. He told puns. Terrible, horrible puns. And I laughed at every single one." He stared off into nothing as he thought back fondly and dredged up memories he'd thought had been shut away. "He was a woodworker. He would make the most beautiful things. I remember Edwin's crib had all of these carvings...." He frowned, head cocking to the side as he pulled up a remembrance he honestly hadn't thought of in years. "Fairy stories, I think. I used to sit in Edwin's room and trace my fingers over all the wolves and the fat, chubby sprites, and make up names for them all."

God, he hadn't thought about that in years.

"My mom was a lot like Anthony. She was strong and brave; she took care of us. She would go hunting and come back with enormous deer, and we would always get the best parts. But she saved the heart for my dad, because it was his favorite. Every time. And she'd put it on a plate and tell us how they met. Every single time. They never got tired of talking about it."

He realized Victor was half grinning as he listened. "And what was the story of how they met?"

"Once upon a time," he started, as his mother always had, and he couldn't help but smile. It was painful, yes, and his voice wavered, but he smiled nonetheless and buried a kiss in Victor's palm. "There was a brave wolf who was out hunting. Only this brave wolf got lost from her pack. And she couldn't find her way home." Randall paused, breathing out a quick laugh. "This is when Anthony would always ask 'but why couldn't she smell her way back?' And mom would tell him that sometimes, when you are very far away, everything will smell strange and you won't know which way leads home.

"So the very brave wolf began to howl. It was all she could think of to do. She howled up at the sky...." Hesitating, Randall laughed again, "Which I will not be demonstrating to you now, but she howled, and she asked the stars to show her the way home. When the very brave wolf looked over, she saw another wolf, the handsomest wolf in the world. His coat was silver, and he shone in the moonlight. When she howled, he howled too, and it was like their voices were as one. And do you know what the brave wolf smelled then?"

As often as he had heard this story, as many times as his mother had recounted it, Randall always recalled being utterly taken in by the telling. Victor looked just as entranced. "What did she smell?"

"Home." Randall gave a little shake of his head, *missing* them with an ache he thought he'd forgotten. "I'm sorry. It's such a silly story. She just loved telling it."

Victor was silent for a moment as he digested the story, his thumb making absent arcs over Randall's knuckles. When he spoke, he seemed hesitant, but like he had to know the answer. "And what do *you* smell now?"

A grin flashed across Randall's face, painful and sweet, and he breathed a laugh that caught in his throat. Carefully, he lowered his nose to Victor's wrist, taking a deep breath. Parchment paper and tea, the faint tang of his smoke, sunbaked scales over rocks, all the things that made up Victor. All the things that meant *him*.

"Home," Randall answered simply. "I smell home."

BY THE time they got back to the house, Randall was feeling fuller than he'd ever been, stuffed with steak and pasta and salad and warm with Italian wine. He and Victor had sat for hours, just talking, sharing bites of food and laughing. They had discussed favorite books, philosophies, even had a friendly argument over art styles, which they'd agreed to call a draw over a plate of tiramisu and cups of strong coffee. They had traded stories about university on the drive back. A story about Victor's student days and the time he'd wound up accidentally pledged to a fraternity had had Randall laughing so hard his sides had started hurting.

The evening ended, in Randall's opinion, far too quickly. Before he was ready, they were at the door of the guest cabin, hand in hand, dawdling there with comments about the weather. Randall must have said it was a nice night three times now, as if that was an excuse for not leaving.

And then Victor had suggested they admire the view from his room a bit, and they sat on the balcony overlooking the lake, comfortably ensconced in the twin chairs that sat side by side.

"I know I should let you get some sleep," Victor murmured over the sound of the lake brushing up against the shore. "But I'm afraid I don't want to let go of your hand."

"I know the feeling." Randall tightened his fingers on Victor's. Another few moments of silence, dragging out their evening just a little longer. But he could smell the night creeping onward into early morning, and no amount of dawdling was going to stave off time. "I should go," he finally said, regretfully.

Victor sighed, just as reluctant. He stood and gently tugged Randall out of his chair. "All right," he agreed. "This has been... this was wonderful, Randall. We should do it again soon."

He wanted to demand that they do it every night, that he and Victor simply go forward with their lives in good food and excellent conversation and never, ever let go of each other's hands. But, sadly, Randall knew such things weren't possible. If they were, he was fairly certain Jed and Redford would have done so by now. "It was perfect," he agreed as they walked slowly toward Victor's bedroom door. "I can't promise the food will be nearly as good, but maybe this week? I'm not sure if it's too pushy to ask for tomorrow, so—"

"Tomorrow," Victor agreed in a rush. "Definitely tomorrow."

A grin broke out across Randall's face. "Tomorrow," he said, lightly touching his fingertips to Victor's jaw. "I'll cook. Maybe a picnic, away from the herd?"

"Perfect," Victor breathed. He leaned in close to brush a kiss against Randall's cheek. "Good night, Randall."

"Good night, Victor." They smiled at each other, perfectly polite, perfectly chaste. It was the picture-perfect ending to a first date.

With a growl, Randall hooked his hands into Victor's shirt and hauled him in, meeting his lips in a hard, hungry kiss. They stumbled backward, back into the bedroom, Randall kicking the door shut as he shoved Victor's jacket off. The surge of heat that hit him was completely overwhelming, like he'd been waiting to touch Victor for *months*.

And now he could. Now he *was*.

"Thank God we're on the same page," Victor breathed, in the middle of doing his best to get rid of Randall's tie.

Biting at Victor's lips, Randall grabbed his hips and pushed him back toward the bed. "I thought you were just going to let me leave," he laughed, ducking out of his tie, kicking his shoes off somewhere in the corner. There was a confidence in his movements now, a want that he knew exactly what to do with. "God, I can't wait to get you out of that suit. I've been thinking about it all night."

"I had much the same sentiment," Victor murmured. He hooked his fingers into Randall's shirt, deftly getting the buttons undone. "You do look amazing in these clothes, by the way. I'm almost sad to get rid of them." He scowled down at one button in particular, looking like he was close to ripping it off just because it got in his way.

"If you want, I can keep them on," Randall huffed, a laugh caught up in another kiss. With a light shove, Victor was sprawled back on the mattress, Randall straddling his waist and leaning in to capture his lips, the wet press and pull of them absolutely intoxicating. Together their fingers finally conquered the last of Randall's buttons, and Victor slid his shirt off, letting it drop to the side, forgotten.

Victor paused, and though Randall couldn't look directly at his eyes, he could see Victor's eyebrows raised, as if in appreciation. "You are like nothing I'd ever seen before," Victor said, his hands sweeping up Randall's chest.

"Scrawny and pale?" Randall laughed, catching Victor's hands, kissing the tips of his fingers. "Nearsighted? Bad haircut?"

"Beautiful," Victor corrected. He curled his fingers around Randall's, holding on tight. But then he reared up suddenly to reverse their positions, pushing Randall down to lie on his back. "I'm sad that I didn't let myself think of you that way for some time, because by now I might have had quite the list of ideas."

Victor smiled down at him, but his touch suddenly seemed hesitant. Randall realized that his fingertips were dangerously close to the biggest scar that curved over Randall's collarbone, holding still, as if asking permission to touch. With a low, almost frightened exhale, Randall tipped his chin back, exposing the ugly knot of scars low on his neck, the lowest of which was closest to Victor's touch. He couldn't meet Victor's eyes and show him his trust. But he could believe that Victor wouldn't deliberately hurt him. He could demonstrate that in the most basic way he knew how.

He saw Victor lean down and felt the featherlight pressure of Victor's lips against those scars. There was that flash of terror, the drop in his stomach that made Randall want to do nothing but shove Victor away. It took everything in him to hold still through the sharp jump of pain, the phantom memory of teeth tearing through his skin.

Another kiss then, just as gentle as the first. Randall stared up at the ceiling, forcing himself to remain motionless, blinking back the hot ache in his eyes, refusing to let what happened before resurface and ruin this. The vampires that had hurt him were dead and gone. There was no reason to allow them to continue to have this kind of power.

Victor's lips ghosted lightly up to the base of Randall's neck, kissing him again, and again that jerk of pain shuddered through him. But it wasn't what was happening *now*. Now it was Victor's lips, soft and warm against his skin. *Now* it was a gentle touch, coaxing Randall to relax, to stay in the moment.

All the pain was nothing more than a reflex. A nightmare haunting him.

Closing his eyes tightly, Randall let out the aching breath he'd been swallowing back. He finally unclenched his hands from the sheets, one going up to lightly thread through Victor's hair. Victor slid his tongue along the marks marring Randall's throat, and he forced himself to see past the pain, to focus only on Victor's touch.

"Everything okay?" Victor whispered against the scar he'd been kissing.

"I think it's going to be," Randall managed with half a laugh, blowing out another shaky exhale.

"You truly are so beautiful," Victor said again. Randall could feel the curve of Victor's smile against his skin.

No one had ever called him *that* before. And Victor said it with such sincerity that Randall couldn't even find it in himself to doubt the compliment. To Victor, he really was *beautiful,* as impossible as that seemed. Arching his neck up, legs hooking around Victor's waist, Randall grinned as he bit sharply at Victor's lip. "How about you come up with some ideas now?" Another bite, Randall sucking on his lip to soothe away the sting.

"Pop quiz, professor. You have a very eager student in bed, half-naked. What do you do now?"

Victor muffled a laugh against Randall's jaw where he was busy kissing it, his lips trailing down to Randall's neck. "Is this a multi-choice quiz?"

"A," Randall's head fell back, a soft moan lost in his chest. "Fuck him. Hard."

"What about options B through D?" Randall could feel Victor grinning against his throat, then the slide of Victor's fingertips toward his belt, stopping on the buckle. A quick little inhale and Randall looked down, gaze lit up with pure *want*.

"B...." Randall struggled to think of what else could be done in bed. It was hard to think with Victor, positively devilish, between his legs, fingers playing along the skin above Randall's waistband. "Mouths could be involved. Preferably mine. And yours. Both sets of mouths are an option."

"Oh?" Victor deftly undid Randall's belt, sliding it agonizingly slowly through the loops on his slacks before dropping it over the side of the bed. Randall arched up into the next touch, a leisurely drag of Victor's hands over his thighs. "That could be taken a great number of ways."

Everything seemed so *heightened*, nerve endings Randall didn't even know existed suddenly alight. As if his body began and ended under the slide of Victor's palms, the hot pant of his breath. "I don't even know what that means," Randall admitted in a quick laugh, the sound teasing out into a moan. He instinctively spread his legs, his boxers suddenly feeling tighter than usual. He spared a quick flash of embarrassment over that. It seemed so... *rude* to be so on display, to be so obvious and in Victor's face. "But yes. Let's do all of the above."

After he spoke, he noticed Victor staring in a way that indicated he certainly didn't seem to mind Randall being, er, rather rude about things. Victor ducked his head to kiss Randall's throat, the briefest contact of his lips before he moved to Randall's collarbone. "Well, I could use my mouth *here*," Victor said. Going downward, he then gently scraped his teeth over Randall's stomach, an ever-so-slight ache that had Randall shivering in reply. "Or here."

Victor moved back up again, the contact of his lips gentle on the scarring on the underside of Randall's forearms. "Even here."

Randall's muscles jumped under the touch, but the expected pain was fainter now. A ghost of a memory, fading under the heat of Victor's presence.

Then he felt the warm, strong contact of Victor's hands decisively dragging his pants down to bunch them at Randall's knees. With wide eyes, Randall watched him, breath catching in short, shallow gasps with every touch. Victor was still smiling as he moved to Randall's thigh.

"Here too," Victor murmured, shifting aside to pull Randall's pants off completely. "I could spend hours listing every body part I'd like to get my mouth on."

"Well, very good," Randall managed, somewhat thinly. His hands had fallen to grip the sheets, fingers twisted up in the fabric, as if he needed an anchor to hold him down. "That sounds excellent. Good listing skills." Perhaps he was finding it a bit hard to concentrate. At least Victor didn't seem to mind his sudden incoherence.

Victor gave a hum of agreement, and if he said anything else, Randall didn't hear it, because he was too busy arching into the contact of Victor's tongue on his cock. He muffled a groan around a bitten lip, staring down at Victor.

"Turn over," Victor said, cupping one hand under Randall's hip. "I've only covered one half of you."

"What?" Dazed, Randall ran fingers through Victor's hair, desperate to have contact, to find a way to wrap himself fully around Victor and never let go. "What do you mean? There's nothing... back there."

"There's your back, which I have noticed to be quite well formed," Victor replied, giving Randall's hip another nudge. "It deserves attention too."

One last skeptical look, but Randall rolled over, feeling so much more exposed now. One's back was not something Randall particularly thought about in reference to these sorts of activities. Then again, he had quite liked running his hands along Victor's their last night together, so Randall assumed he just was lacking knowledge in this area. It did feel more than a little strange to just be sprawled out in bed, naked, while Victor was still clothed.

He felt Victor's lips press against his shoulder blade. It didn't make Randall squirm, but it was nice, an exploration of a part of his body he'd never considered an intimate one. Victor trailed his fingers down the bumps and curves of Randall's spine, as if cataloging each one and storing the feeling away for later. Then Victor's lips were again at the small of his back, dropping light kisses against the muscle that curved down to his hip.

Randall jerked a little in surprise when Victor's hand smoothed across his ass. "If at any point I do something that makes you feel uncomfortable, I want you to tell me," Victor said. Randall found it a little hard to think about that statement when Victor's fingers were tracing the curve of his thighs. Instinctively, he arched up into the pull against his skin, the soft skim of a touch leaving goose bumps in its wake.

Then Victor's lips were on his *ass*, biting lightly at the curve of it. Randall jumped slightly, shock making him flinch, but the groan that rumbled in his chest definitely wasn't a protest. "What—" was all he managed to get out, hips rising slightly, as if to encourage more.

Victor's laugh had an edge of a rumble to it. "I'm showing you option C," he replied. Randall could feel his tongue then, sliding over the back of Randall's thighs, moving up, a wet, warm trail. Randall shivered, biting his lip hard enough to dimple it, anticipation hooking low in his gut. He had no idea where Victor was going, but his body seemed tight and tense, waiting for it.

The gentle press of the point of Victor's tongue against his hole made Randall jump in shock again. He looked back at Victor, shaking his head, not to stop him, but in utter confusion. "I don't think that goes there," he tried to joke, voice low, hoarse, barely more than a whisper.

"No?" Victor's grin wasn't as big as before, but there was more of an edge of mischief to it now. "Then I must be lost. Oh well, I may as well explore while I'm here." He did it again, running his tongue once over Randall's hole. The odd sensation was slowly being replaced with tentative want. When Randall tried to answer, all that came out was a low, drawn-out moan.

Obviously encouraged by that, Victor kept doing what he was doing—first just gently licking over where Randall had sworn tongues absolutely weren't meant to go, letting him get used to the feeling and waiting until Randall was beginning to move back into it a little. Victor grasped Randall's hip, slipping around to grasp his cock where it was trapped between his stomach and the bed.

That got a whimper from Randall as he went up on his knees, not even remotely sure which way he needed to move—forward into Victor's hand, but then back against that delicious wet pressure of his tongue, both such slow buildups he barely remembered what it was to not be turned on. "Please," he managed, fingers digging into the mattress. "God, Victor." All he knew was he wanted *more* of *something*, whatever it could be.

It turned out that something more meant the point of Victor's tongue again, except this time it wasn't what Randall was coming to expect. This time Victor pushed his tongue inside Randall, a slow drag inside and then out, and then again, his hand moving over Randall's cock in time with his tongue. Yes, that felt... very good. So good that Randall abandoned all pretense of holding it together, legs spreading wantonly, back arched to raise his ass to meet Victor's thrusts. A steady stream of whimpers, of moans, was caught in his throat, buried into the pillow.

Victor gripped him harder, his stroking faster now, seemingly determined to drive Randall to the edge as quickly as possible, all the while pushing his tongue in as deep as he could get it. To Randall the sensation was still a little strange, but it felt so *good* that he'd completely stopped questioning it. He rocked his hips back against Victor, then forward into his hand, babbling senseless encouragement. Pleading with Victor for more, telling him how good it was, how deep he wanted it, how it felt like he was flying apart.

Victor only broke away briefly to dig his teeth into the curve of Randall's ass, murmuring, "You're so beautiful." And then he was back again, the shock of the slide of his tongue that much more pleasurable due to the few seconds of loss of contact. Randall's moans reached a louder pitch when Victor added a twist to his stroking, his thumb rubbing hard over the tip of Randall's cock on every drag up. Randall wasn't sure if he was supposed to maintain control, if he was honestly expected to ride this out without losing his mind in the wave of sensations. But he certainly didn't. His body tightened, heat coiling like a spring in his gut, desperate for release. Without a warning, barely before he realized it was happening, Randall was gasping Victor's name, legs shaking, overwhelmed with the force of his pleasure.

Victor kept fucking him with his tongue the entire way through, one hand grasping firmly at Randall's hip to keep him still. And when Randall started to lose strength in his knees, sagging toward the mattress, only then did Victor let up, moving back with a slide of his hands over Randall's legs.

Randall felt the mattress drop and dazedly opened his eyes to see Victor sitting next to him, looking extremely pleased with himself.

"Thank you," Victor said, his hand making absent circles on Randall's shoulder blade.

"I'm very new to this," Randall managed, words faintly slurred together, "but I'm pretty sure that's backwards. I think I should be thanking *you*. That was...." No words came to mind. There *were* no words. So Randall just tipped his chin back and howled softly, a long drawn-out, shivery sound that echoed deep in the very bones of him. That

349

was *perfect like a night with a moon and no rain,* that was *deep and hard like the frost under my paws,* that was *exactly right, exactly mine, mate and pack and full bellies and warm cave.* It was everything *good,* and Randall didn't know if there *was* a word to describe it.

"Well," Victor said, "I'm not very good at translating howls, but I'm to take it that was meant as a good thing?"

Turning to face Victor, reaching out to run his fingertips along Victor's sadly still-clothed thigh, Randall smiled loopily. "Oh, yes," he rumbled. "The very best thing."

"I'm glad." Victor's fingers trailed to the curve of Randall's neck. "I'm glad that we finally get to do this, as well."

"Me too." The lethargic bliss of his orgasm was fading, and Randall gave Victor an appraising look. "You're still dressed."

"That I am." Victor didn't look like he minded. Instead, the curve of his lips showed an amused, satisfied expression. "I was rather too busy to pay attention to my own clothes, unfortunately. Removing yours was much more pertinent."

That wouldn't do at *all.* With a quick pounce, Randall pushed Victor back, capturing his lips in a heady, deep kiss. Their tongues fucked together, sliding one with the other, and their fingers laced together as Randall pinned Victor's arms above his head with one hand. He rocked against Victor in cadenced rolls of his hips, loving the slow burn of arousal now, after the insistent, urgent heat. "Fuck me," he mumbled against Victor's mouth, burying any response into another hard kiss. "Please."

Randall went into eager pursuit of Victor's buttons, popping each one out in turn, rewarded by the growing expanse of smooth, pale skin, just barely dusted over in freckles. Victor paused him before he could finish the job, smiling at Randall's huff of frustration. "I'll be right back," he promised, and then he was getting off the bed, moving quickly to the door. Before Randall could further protest the absence, he could hear Victor going through a bag in another room. He returned victorious with lube in hand and tossed the bottle onto the bed. Victor then went to his wallet and pulled out several foil packets.

"Victor." Randall struggled to sit up from where he'd sprawled out on the bed. "Did you just steal sex supplies from Jed?"

"Er. I may have." Victor looked a little embarrassed at that, but not embarrassed enough to prevent him from getting back on the bed to come to Randall, catching him in a kiss. "He didn't have condoms, but luckily I believe in being prepared. Is that all right with you?"

Hand threading through Victor's hair, Randall slid back farther onto the bed, pulling Victor with him. "I'll write a proper thank you note in the morning," he mumbled, much more interested in the fullness of Victor's lips catching between his own. "Dear Mr. Walker. I am ever so grateful for your donation."

Victor laughed quietly at that, the eagerness of his kisses growing with every one. "I'm sure he'd appreciate it." Victor only broke away to pull his shirt off, dropping his hands to his belt next. Randall gladly went to help, gliding his hands down Victor's sides, easing his pants off and curling fingers around his hips.

Randall had to break away to stare, drinking in the sight of Victor. He was all soft, pale skin. The curve of his stomach, the lines of his hips, the way broad shoulders swept down to his chest, he was utterly perfect. Poems were written about men like Victor; songs were sung with the hopes of winning them. And here he was, in Randall's bed. A star captured in a wooden crate.

"You are the most amazing thing I've ever seen," Randall breathed, thumbs painting circles against Victor's arms. "I could live and die a thousand times over and I'd never see anything like you again."

Victor looked like he didn't quite know what to do with the praise—he kissed Randall, the contact sweet and gentle. They turned again, Randall hovering over Victor, the sky to his lovely expanse, kissing and touching as if they were the first beings born to do so. As if this was exactly what their lips and hands had been formed from clay to do.

"You're clearly far too coherent, if you can be poetic," Victor finally said, a fond tone under his words. Randall heard the quiet click of a tube, but he didn't look right then, far more interested in exploring the rounded curves of Victor's shoulders.

He felt Victor's hand trail over his ass again, then the light press of Victor's fingertip against his hole, slick with lube. "If you're sure?" Victor murmured.

Nudging their foreheads together, eyes closed, Randall nodded. "I trust you," he said quietly. "I want you, Victor. You're who I've been waiting for."

"Later, I will tell you exactly how honored I am. But right now I'm far more interested in fucking you." Randall could hear a smile in Victor's words, the corresponding press of his finger inching in deeper. It was different than his tongue, reaching in farther and a little uncomfortable at first, but Victor was so gentle that the faint ache soon faded. It started to feel wonderful again in short order when Victor began moving his hand slowly. Randall's hesitation faded as Victor whispered soothingly to him, rubbing the small of his back, encouraging him to relax around him.

Letting out a slow breath, Randall dropped his head to rest in the crook of Victor's neck, concentrating on breathing. The ache turned into heat, into friction that built up into, all at once, a small burst of pleasure. Randall rocked forward, startled a little, gasping, his lips catching against Victor's skin.

And then Victor's finger grazed over something that made sparks burst behind Randall's eyes. He dimly recalled hearing something about it, though he'd never experimented with it himself. Victor seemed determined to, though, rubbing hard over his prostate. Rocking back against Victor's hand, Randall's moan was lost in the tight clench of teeth, biting Victor's shoulder, his neck, hard enough to leave marks scattered behind.

The slight pressure of Victor adding another finger never turned into an ache, only a greedy anticipation that had Randall gasping. Time seemed to glaze over in a whirl of messy kisses and panted breaths.

"Ready?" Victor breathed against Randall's lips, sounding a little strained with the effort of holding himself back.

It took him a moment to gather the scattered whirl of thoughts, to force them into a neat little line that led to a moaned, "Yes, *God*, yes."

Victor rolled them over, and Randall flopped back into the bed in a boneless, pleasure-heavy sprawl. He watched through half-closed eyes as Victor fumbled with the condom, scowling at it before finally managing to get it on, then moved to kneel between Randall's legs, leaning over to kiss his chin. Victor's hands smoothed over Randall's

351

thigh, fingertips dipping down to briefly rub over his hole again before he started easing his cock inside.

Randall hissed in a sharp breath as he closed his eyes, torn between the mild ache and the approaching pressure. He grabbed Victor's arms, his grip tight enough to redden the skin. For a moment, a stomach-dropping moment, he panicked. He was so sure it wouldn't fit, that it would *hurt*, and a pained whimper escaped him. His head arched back, teeth catching his lip, and Randall barely restrained the urge to beg Victor to stop.

"It's okay," Victor said under his breath, going still, his hand rubbing over Randall's stomach. "We'll go as slow as you need. Just tell me when, Randall."

Focusing on his breathing, Randall dropped one hand from Victor's arm, going to grasp a tight hold on Victor's hip. "It's okay," he breathed, staring up at the ceiling. "I'm okay."

He felt Victor's fingers trace lightly over his stomach, then up the side of his cock, grasping it lightly. Randall arched into the contact as pleasure started to spark at his nerves again. Victor still wasn't moving, just gently stroking him, coaxing him back to full arousal. A low groan rumbled in Randall's chest, and he pulled Victor closer, muffling another low sound as Victor slid deeper inside of him. The rub of his cock pressing inward, the friction and the heat, was slowly melting away his tension.

"Victor," he murmured, keeping his eyes closed, not wanting to accidentally meet Victor's eyes. But that jump of fear again, soothed away by Victor's touch, and then another long stroke, and Randall was wrapping his legs more firmly around Victor's waist.

As if knowing exactly what Randall wanted, Victor leaned in and captured his lips in a hungry kiss. "Still okay?" Victor whispered, rocking his hips so slightly that Randall could barely feel it at first.

The ache had faded into heat and need, and Randall didn't so much answer as moan, leaning up to kiss Victor again, hand sliding up to fist in his hair, pulling him closer. He bit Victor's lip, his jaw, growling his want into his skin and the dip of his collarbone. God, yes, he was okay. He was more than okay. Any worry was gone now, any hesitation lost in the drag of Victor's cock, the friction that felt like it was sinking into his bones.

Victor paused again, making Randall give a groan of need—but then Victor did something Randall had not been expecting. Victor *growled*. It was a tentative little sound, unsure and thready. It was also *incredibly* hot. Randall growled back, surging upward to pull Victor into a hard kiss, hooking one leg up farther around his waist, as if he could simply tangle himself around Victor completely.

Snarling under his breath, biting Victor's lips, his jaw, Randall rolled upward into him, all but begging for more. And Victor obliged, only too happy to do so, rocking into him with smooth thrusts that took Randall's breath away. Their mouths met in a clash, teeth catching on lips. When Victor lost all of his hesitation, he started fucking Randall hard, braced over him and panting against his jaw, one hand shakily wrapping around Randall's cock.

Randall was howling, he was sure. His hands were digging into Victor's back, meeting him thrust for thrust, gasping with every deep slide of Victor inside of him. It was like riding a wave of white heat, of endless sparks against his skin. Randall wasn't sure where he began or where Victor ended. Their bodies were moving as one, writhing in pleasure, dancing in an endless, gasping reach for something more.

His second orgasm felt even better than the first, crashing through him, making him latch his teeth into Victor's throat and bite down as he came. Victor continued to move against him, low gasps and stuttered moans leading to a near-incoherent growl of Randall's name as he reached his own pleasure, trembling above Randall.

Victor slowed, then stopped completely, his muscles still shivering in the aftermath. Randall curled his arms around Victor's waist as Victor settled on top of him, their breaths coming at the same time, heartbeats pounding.

"I have no words," Victor managed, tucking his lips into the curve of Randall's neck.

"Now that is new." Randall tightened his hold around Victor, rubbing his thumb along the line of Victor's spine. "I think we should get some kind of award." All he could think of then was how badly he wanted to look into Victor's eyes. To see him fully to know if the satisfaction he felt on his own features was mirrored there.

Randall sat up a little, braced on an elbow, and Victor rolled off him to sprawl on his front next to him. Randall frowned as he looked around the room. Victor's pants were tossed over the edge of the bed, so he reached out, pulling them toward him and rifling through the pockets. Finding Victor's phone, Randall held it up over him, looking straight into the camera, not changing anything about how he looked—utterly spent, completely satisfied, disheveled and loving every inch of it.

"Your turn," he murmured, nudging Victor, who lifted his head from the pillow to reveal half of his face. Victor looked into the camera, a mess of red-blond hair and one visible blue eye. Randall took the picture and sprawled out next to him, both of them meeting the camera's gaze without fear. One of Randall kissing Victor, just because of the look on Randall's face as Victor pressed his lips to Randall's throat. All things they couldn't see themselves, set down into digital imprints.

Settling back beside Victor, head on his shoulder, Randall showed the photographs to him. "You look incredible," Randall murmured, placing a kiss onto his chest. And he did. There was a lightness in his gaze, an amazing languid power that made Randall's breath catch. "I could stare at this all day."

Victor gave an agreeing hum. "Likewise. Next time we should set up a video camera."

The idea made Randall snort a laugh, dismissive only for a moment. Then he gave Victor a considering look and curled up further around him. He took another picture, this time of him, a close up of his eyes, of lips swollen from Victor's kisses, a smile curving across his face. "I think that is an excellent plan," he said, handing Victor his phone. "Maybe I'll make a video just for you. I have some ideas, now. You can watch it after you leave."

"Now that is a good idea," Victor said. His eyes had fallen closed, and he rested his cheek on Randall's shoulder. Randall had to smile fondly—nonwolves seemed to get so tired after sex, he'd discovered, and it was strangely endearing. Right then Victor looked like he wanted nothing more than to drop off into sleep, so Randall shifted accommodatingly, getting them comfortable.

353

But before Victor was lost to the world, he seemed determined to do one last thing, even though his movements were sluggish with contentment. Victor smoothed a palm over Randall's hip, dragging upward to rest fully over the scars scattered across Randall's collarbone, his hand a warm weight on Randall's skin.

And it didn't hurt. Whatever lingering memories of fear and pain and helplessness were, for the moment, washed over with the present. Victor's touch had branded him far deeper than any vampire could bite. For now, Randall felt no part of himself caught in that hell. His Beatrice truly had led him out into heaven.

The pale light of the moon and stars painted the sky outside the room. The doors of the balcony were open, and Randall could hear the lake lapping lightly against the shore, the soft sigh of the wind through leaves. He was surrounded by everything familiar, by the scent of him and Victor combined, and it was the most at home he'd ever felt. As if all of what he knew *home* to be had just been magnified and expanded. His pack had gotten bigger, fuller, and it felt like this was exactly as it should be.

Victor was leaving in the morning. Randall shouldn't be so attached to the idea of falling asleep in his arms. And yet he was.

One more picture, then. Not for Victor. For himself. Victor half-asleep, strawberry-blond hair spread across the pillow in a messy tangle, Randall's darker head pillowed on his chest. The two of them, tangled together, like nothing on earth could find a way to pull them apart.

RANDALL WAS dragged out of sleep by a knock at the door, a muffled laugh, and Victor groaning, "Jed, for the love of God, go away."

"I know you stole my lube, you sex fiend." Jed was battering on his door, head poking around it to grin widely at them both. "Kinky, professor."

"Oh, I'm so sorry." There was a distinct dry tone in Victor's voice. "Do you want it back?"

"Nope. That was my extra supply. Just want all the dirty little secrets. Come on, breakfast, and we can have the sex talk over pancakes."

Randall buried his face deeper into the pillow, trying to figure out why all these people were in his bedroom.

Except it wasn't his bedroom. Bleary, he lifted his head and stared around, hair completely in disarray, totally confused. Very slowly, he woke up enough to remember what had happened. Victor. Victor was in bed with him. They were tangled up together, legs entwined. A smile eased across Randall's face, and, with a grunt of protest at the whole *waking up* thing, he dropped a kiss on Victor's shoulder. "Hey," he mumbled. "What time is it?"

"I have no idea. Let me look." Victor was without his glasses, but he attempted to peer at the clock on the bedside table. After a few moments, he said, "I still have no idea."

Randall decided he didn't care that much. He pulled Victor in for a kiss instead, winding his arm around Victor and nuzzling in close. "Hey," he whispered again, more quietly. "Good morning."

Victor turned into his arms, draping himself over Randall's side. "Good morning," he replied, eyes still closed, a smile at the corners of them. "Did you sleep well?"

Surprisingly well, actually. Randall blinked and stretched, biting back a yawn. "For one of the first times since Cairo, I think I did." He was more than a little shocked. Nuzzling into Victor's neck, Randall peppered kisses along the softly reddened marks he'd left the night before. "How about you?"

Victor seemed more interested in wrapping his arms around Randall, getting comfortable, like he wanted to go right back to sleep. "Very soundly," he replied. "Better than I do at home."

"Well, maybe you should stay longer." It was more than Randall would have suggested any other time, but he was still aching from the night before in the best possible way, they were all wrapped up and warm in each other, and it was so easy to whisper the words against Victor's skin. He eased kisses along Victor's collarbone. "Anthony's appointment is later today. Just stay over after our dinner tonight."

Giving a hum of agreement, Victor said, "Excellent idea. Do we need to get up right now?"

Randall really did have to squint at the clock then, attempting to get the numbers in focus. Nine in the morning. "The appointment is at noon," he yawned, half sprawled out over Victor. "And it's an hour and a half drive. So we have about a half an hour before we need to get up and start getting ready."

"Then how about we sleep more?" Victor sounded like he was already halfway there, his cheek resting on Randall's bicep. "That sounds good."

"Mmm." Randall contented himself with scraping his teeth lightly on the inside of Victor's arm. "We should sleep."

They drifted back into that hazy, warm space that lay halfway between wake and sleep. Randall's fingers slid in with Victor's, and he curled up closer, letting himself relax. Until, of course, there was a pounding at the door and a very loud, very strident voice calling, "Okay, lovebirds! Ten minutes before I come in and start pulling off covers."

"Fuck off, Jed," Victor shouted back. Even half-asleep, Randall was startled at his cursing. Apparently Victor only did it when he didn't have the brainpower to think of better words.

"Yes, Jed, do go fuck yourself," Randall agreed with a low growl. "We're sleeping."

"Nine minutes!" Jed was apparently not threatened at all. Jed's fist slammed several more times into the door, jerking Randall out of that pleasant doze. "Redford's making breakfast. Get your fornicating asses over there."

Victor muttered something under his breath that even Randall's ears couldn't catch, but the mattress shifted a moment later as Victor hauled himself up with a grunt. Randall felt a hand on his shoulder, rubbing gently. "Jed's probably right," Victor sighed. "Up we get."

Rolling over, Randall just studied Victor. The morning light was streaming through the windows, bathing everything in a soft golden glow, lighting Victor up like some ancient god. "You are so beautiful." Randall reached out, letting his fingers trail along Victor's arm. "I've never seen anyone half as gorgeous as you are."

Victor smiled down at him and teased, "Well, you do have your glasses off. I'm probably just a big blur to you."

Randall struggled to sit up, grabbing said glasses again and shoving them on. "Nope," he declared, tugging Victor back onto the bed with him, kissing his shoulder. "You are simply beautiful."

"You really are a shameless flatterer," Victor replied, braced on his hands to lean above Randall. He ducked down to give Randall a kiss, lingering, but sadly not as long as Randall wanted it to be, before Victor got himself out of bed. "Come on, Randall. Don't tell me I'm somehow more a morning person than you are."

"I just suddenly have a very good reason for lying around in bed all day," Randall returned, sticking out his tongue. But he got up to wrap his arms around Victor from behind, nuzzling his nose into the nape of Victor's neck. Sighing, he bit lightly at the soft skin there. "You need to go take a shower before I decide I really can't keep my hands to myself."

"Is that supposed to *deter* me?" Victor gave a quiet laugh, leaning back against Randall. He smoothed a hand over Randall's arm, every inch of his body language speaking of content. Burying a smile in his shoulder, Randall couldn't help saying it.

"I love you," he whispered. He just said it, hanging it out there like some hopeful prayer. He shouldn't have said it yet, maybe. He should have waited. But Randall felt strangely impulsive, like he couldn't bear to keep it inside. The emotion was too big for him to live with it inside his skin.

Victor's reply was low but utterly without hesitation. "I love you too."

After a low breath, Randall murmured, "Hold still." He fumbled and found Victor's phone, holding it out in front of them, taking a picture so that Victor could see his expression. So that he could see Victor's. Turning it around, he stared at it, at the pure joy in his expression, at Victor's sleepy-eyed content.

"I think I might have to start password protecting my phone," Victor huffed, bemused. "There's a few interesting pictures on there now."

"Just for you." Randall smiled, kissing Victor's neck, the spot just below his ear, his jaw. "So yes, please put a password on it. I don't want anyone else to see that."

Victor turned in his arms, kissing his jaw, then giving Randall a light push against his chest. "Now really, go shower and get dressed," he said, attempting to be stern. "Otherwise we'll be late for everything."

"You're really staying tonight?" Randall confirmed, catching Victor's hand.

"Yes," Victor replied. "Whatever we wind up doing, dinner or a picnic, I wouldn't miss it for the world."

Randall leaned in to kiss him one last time. "Okay, okay," he mumbled. "I'm going. Use the bathroom here. I'll be over at the main house."

Reluctantly, Randall got dressed and made his way back to the house. When he walked in the front door, it was to a round of applause. Jed was even standing, whistling at him loudly as Randall rolled his eyes and headed toward his room. "You are all children," he informed them.

"What?" Anthony grinned at him. He intercepted Randall at the doorway, arms out for a hug. "Does this mean you're mated now? Is he part of the pack? Can I do some kind of official ceremony just to confuse him?"

Ducking under Anthony's arms, Randall shot them all a scowl. *"Children,"* he repeated. "And no. No one is mates. Do not say the M-word to Victor when he comes over here."

He heard Anthony give an exaggerated sigh as he headed back to the table.

"Why not?" Edwin asked, following Randall into his room as Randall searched for clean clothes. "I mean, you slept with him."

"Sex does not mean mates, Ed," Randall told him, arching an eyebrow at him. "Didn't we have this talk with you?"

"I know that, but you're kind of old-fashioned." Edwin sat on the edge of the bed, picking absently at the comforter. "Are you going to get married?"

"Edwin, Jesus." Turning to face him, Randall fixed him with a look. "Spill. What is this about?"

"Anthony has an appointment today," Edwin mumbled. "What if it doesn't help again? Then he'll get worse and you'll move in with Victor, and I can't take care of Ant by myself." He stared down at his laced fingers, looking, all at once, like he was five years old again. "I'm not good at that stuff like you guys. I don't want to let him down."

Putting aside the clothes for the moment, Randall sank to sit down next to Edwin. "I am never going to leave you," he promised, nudging his shoulder against Edwin's. "That's who we are, remember? We're family."

Edwin almost laughed, a not-quite-there noise. "Victor's not a wolf," he pointed out, sounding miserable. "He won't want to stay here."

"Then I won't be with him." It was said so simply, as if it wasn't an instant stab of pain through him. "Ed, come on. You guys are the most important thing in the world to me. I'm not going to leave you alone, and I'll always be here to help with Anthony. Okay?"

Strangely quiet, Edwin chewed the inside of his cheek, foot wiggling in a nervous jitter. "Do you think Anthony's going to die?"

Randall wrapped his arm around Edwin's shoulders. Bright, beautiful Edwin, who lived life so fully and never seemed to get bogged down in the things that other people did. Apparently Randall had failed him too. "How long have you been worried about this?" Randall asked with a frown.

"Since you started hiding the bills and not sleeping." Edwin glanced over at him, knocking his knee lightly against Randall's. "I'm not stupid, you know. I can smell what's going on. And Anthony knows something's wrong too, only he just goes in his room and frets by himself."

Feeling a sharp sense of guilt, Randall hung his head. "I'm sorry."

"You should be," Edwin said quietly. Stunned, Randall looked over at him to find Edwin staring at him steadily. "You and Anthony both. Nobody's talking anymore. We used to do everything together, like a pack, but you started keeping secrets when you got back from Egypt, and Anthony pretends he doesn't hurt, and you both worry about money. Like if you talk about it somehow everyone is going to break down. Well, it's stupid."

"Edwin—" Randall started, but Edwin stood up, shaking his head.

"Don't, okay. Just… start talking. Tell Anthony what's going on." Edwin gripped Randall's shoulder before he turned to leave. "And go shower. You smell like snake."

Once left alone, Randall found he honestly didn't know what to do. He'd tried to protect his brothers from the worst parts of what they were dealing with now, only to find out they both knew anyway. So apparently he was the world's worst liar. He finally dragged himself into the shower, and by the time he walked back out, hair still damp, everyone was gathered around the table. Redford was just bringing in a platter of sausages to join the huge stack of pancakes and bacon.

"So you really drive an hour and a half to get to each appointment?" Victor was asking Anthony.

"It's not as if there's any closer hospitals." Anthony shrugged, looking tired as he curled his hands around his coffee mug to warm them.

"That's ridiculous." Victor was frowning, looking at everybody as if he wanted them to agree with him. "You're all busy, and as the weather gets colder you'll find it more difficult to drive yourself. Anthony, I've offered it before, and I will do so again. Come stay at my house. It's close to the hospital, and it's more than big enough to host you."

Randall caught Anthony's questioning glance. He didn't know what to say. His instincts were to say yes, to immediately start packing and move in and never leave. But he was aware that instincts were not a reason to make a decision. This was new. No matter how fantastic the night before was, they were only starting out. "You have three appointments in the next week, right?" he confirmed with Anthony.

Needless to say, Anthony didn't look thrilled at the prospect. "That's right."

The seat next to Victor was empty, and Randall, having fixed his cup of tea, sank into it gratefully. He nudged his knee against Victor's, a shorthand for checking in with him, rather than reading his expression. "Well, a week is not forever," he mused. "That might be nice, Ant, for the next week to be closer?"

"It would be," Anthony said, a rare hesitation in his words. "Are you sure you're okay with this, Victor?"

"Absolutely," Victor said.

Randall glanced over at him, trying to gauge more from the way his lips were curved, the set of his shoulders. "We'd just be guests," he pointed out, half for Anthony, half making sure that he and Victor were on the same page. He wanted to go at a normal speed. Randall *wanted* the dates and the anniversaries of first kisses. He wanted to build something that would last. Just because he had instincts that were pushing for more, just because Victor had seen the future, that didn't mean either one of them knew each other emotionally well enough for that.

Most of all, Randall didn't want to be David. Or any of Victor's other past relationships. If they were going to make it, they needed to grow into each other.

"I know." Victor didn't look at him, but he gently knocked his knee against Randall's. "We've just only had our first date, after all. Moving in permanently would be moving the schedule along quite quickly."

"So you're going to play wolf hotel?" Jed smirked in amusement, leaning over to steal a bite of Redford's pancakes. "You might want to invest in a carpet cleaner, princess."

"I have people that do that for me," Victor dismissed. "Or you could come over and do it, since you seem to have nothing better to do."

"Fuck you, princess, I've got *loads* to do. Redford and I just got another job. Sorry"—Jed winked at Victor—"no seeing me in a maid's uniform just yet."

"I thought you guys were going fishing?" Edwin asked. "Redford told me how much you were looking forward to it."

"It's getting too cold to do it local." Jed shrugged. "And helping out the furry clan took more of our resources than I would have liked. Just one more job and we'll be finding someplace warm and remote and jetting off."

Randall felt a quick twist of guilt—he was the reason Jed had done a job that had cost him more than he got paid. But Jed didn't seem overly worried about it, really, and there hadn't been anything *forcing* Jed to stick around. Maybe he'd wanted to do what he'd done for the Gray Lady. Or maybe Jed just honestly couldn't walk away from someone asking him for help.

"Right, then," Victor said, rising from the table. "If you're going to be staying for the week, we'll need to get packing. All you need is clothes. I can provide everything else."

"Do I have to stay inside?" Edwin asked, looking more than a little worried. "It's not one of those apartments up on some top floor where you can't see the sky, is it? Because I think I'd rather drive. It's the full moon soon, and being cramped up in a tiny place would suck."

If Randall looked closely, he could see the curve of a faint smile in Victor's expression. "Oh, no. Not at all. You have a choice of where in the house you stay, of course, and I think you'll like it more than a cramped apartment."

Edwin still looked unsure, but all it took was a look over at Anthony and he was nodding. "Okay, yeah. Sounds great." A little unenthusiastic, but Edwin had never been that great at hiding his emotions. "Are we going straight there from the doctor's?"

"Oh, yes." Randall sat up, looking at his watch. "It's just after ten. We need to get going in no more than twenty minutes. Pack fast."

"We'll tag along." Jed gave Anthony a look. "Might as well. Our place is closer to the hospital than here, so we'll just follow you up."

"Trying to make sure we don't run off the road?" Anthony laughed as he stood, gathering the plates away.

"Of course." Jed easily took the plates from Anthony, Redford getting the rest off the table. "I've seen you drive, Lassie. It's a miracle you're still alive. And don't get me started on Edwin."

"Go pack, Anthony," Redford said. "We'll take care of the dishes." Anthony looked reluctant, but he nodded and headed off to do just that. Redford immediately took the dishes from Jed, as if he didn't trust Jed to know what to do with them. Which, fair point, he probably wouldn't.

Randall headed into his room to gather his things, passing Edwin's, where Edwin was stuffing clothes into a bag and looking more than a little worried. Apparently he didn't much trust Victor's opinions on what a wolf would like. Alone in his room, Randall tried to pack, he really did. It was a simple enough task. Choose clothes for the week, bring along a few books, some personal items. Nothing too difficult.

But he was stuck, staring at the clothes he'd laid out on his bed, suddenly second-guessing everything. What if this ruined things? What if they carted Anthony to yet another place, yet another bed, yet another doctor, and it didn't matter? Was this the right decision?

Nothing he seemed to be doing was turning out the way he wanted it to. Why should this be any different?

Randall took a deep breath to steady himself. Right. This was what they were doing. They were packing; they were going to stay at Victor's for the week. Anthony was going to have his assessment appointments, and they would find a way to treat him. End of story.

Ten minutes later, Randall was ready and heading out toward the cars. Edwin was already in Jed's jeep, Knievel on his lap, his bag next to him. Anthony was with Victor, loading the rest of their things into the trunk of their own car. Once again, Randall locked the door of their house, hoping that this wasn't going to be the last time. That when they returned, it would be with an Anthony who had some kind of faith again.

"We should get going," he said, putting his suitcase into the trunk. "Don't want to be late."

Victor passed by him, briefly touching his back and giving him a reassuring smile. "It'll be okay. If you hate it, you can come back to your home."

Randall shook his head. "I'm more worried I'm going to like it," he admitted lowly. "And that you'll get sick of me being there too quickly. Or the fact that I come with two decidedly more rowdy brothers."

"I've had a lifetime of being the only one in that house. I think some noise would be more than welcome." Victor opened the door to Jed's Jeep. "I'll see you there."

"You're not riding with me?" A little surprised, Randall paused at the door of the car, looking over the roof at him. He didn't want to be the clingy one, really, but it was an hour and a half ride of knowing Victor was in the next car over. Which suddenly seemed very strange.

"I can." Victor seemed surprised at the offer. "I didn't particularly think about it, I suppose. Is there room in your car?"

"I'm over here so you two can kissy face at each other and I don't feel the need to puke," Edwin informed him cheerily, leaning forward to look out the Jeep door. "Poor Anthony, though. I'm leaving him behind."

Victor looked to where Knievel was perched on Edwin's lap and rubbed his nose with a mild grimace. "Yes, I think the other car would be much more pleasant."

"Come on, you two," Anthony called, sticking his head out the window of the Lewises' car. "You can even both sit in the back like I'm a taxi driver. Just get in, because we need to get moving."

Randall slipped into the backseat and gave Anthony a grateful look as he buckled his seat belt. Victor sat in the seat next to him, and just that easily, they tangled their fingers together, resting joined hands on Victor's knee. It felt so *good*, that simple gesture, the way they seemed to fit.

Anthony started the engine, which sputtered to life with a protesting groan, and they followed the Jeep out onto the main road. Randall watched the rearview mirror, their home seemingly growing smaller and smaller until it was swallowed by the trees.

CHAPTER
19

Victor

EVEN IN a mansion with forty-six individual rooms, two rowdy wolves somehow managed to make the place seem full. Once, Victor might have complained. Now he couldn't help but smile at Anthony and Edwin bickering over the dinner table, Randall sitting exasperated between them.

In the end, Randall had not moved into Victor's room—they'd agreed that doing so would be moving a little too quickly, though Victor had noticed Randall lingering in his room as if he wanted to get a feel for it, exploring every nook and cranny of the shelves and the adjoining office area. Randall had picked a room two doors down from Victor's bedroom, while Anthony and Edwin had taken their rooms a little farther down the main hallway.

None of them had really unpacked yet. Anthony's appointment had been entirely run of the mill. The doctor had told them that the real results would start to come in at the end of the week, and they just had to be patient. After that, the Lewises had seemed exhausted, listless even, more interested in crowding together in the living room than exploring the mansion. Victor just did his best to be a good host.

For dinner, Victor hadn't even tried to cook; he'd ordered in from a nearby steak house. The dinner table was packed with various dishes, and Anthony seemed determined to hoard the fries for himself, playfully growling at Edwin whenever Edwin's hand strayed too close.

Victor finally got himself sat down next to Randall and tried to decide if he was brave enough to join the food fray. He leaned in close to Randall and whispered, "Would I get growled at if I took that steak?"

A smile touched Randall's lips. Instead of replying, he reached out to take the piece of meat Victor had indicated. Sure enough, as soon as his fork touched the steak, Edwin growled at him. But Randall simply showed his teeth, growling back, before they both grinned at each other and Randall victoriously deposited the requested food on Victor's plate.

Victor clamped down on a laugh. It really was like living with, well, a wolf pack. He couldn't even bring himself to mind the mess and the noise. In fact, he rather found himself liking it. They were Randall's family, and as much as Victor didn't usually get on with people, he did like Anthony and Edwin.

"You have a yard," Edwin pointed out, happily cutting into his very rare steak. "And woods. I really wasn't expecting that. You seem too, I don't know. Stuffy."

"For a yard?" Randall gave Edwin a look, eyebrow raised. "I wasn't aware you had to be a certain type of person for that."

"No, I mean, there's just a lot of room to run. Stuffy people don't normally have room to run. That's why they're stuffy." Infallible logic dispensed, Edwin went back to his food, attempting again to steal some of Anthony's fries.

"My grandparents and their parents before them *were* stuffy," Victor agreed. "But they also liked to own a lot of land to show off their wealth, so in the end it's a benefit."

"I saw all those portraits in the hallway," Anthony said around a mouthful of steak. His eyebrows were drawn down, a question in his expression that he seemed hesitant to ask. But he finally said, "It's okay if I look at the portraits, right? A picture of an old-school medusa won't steal my soul or something?"

Well, that was a fear Victor had certainly never heard before. "No, they're just oil paintings." He started to smile, bemused. "Did you already avoid looking into their eyes?"

Anthony's answer was mumbled, but it still sounded distinctly like a *yes*.

"What if they already have stolen your soul," Randall intoned, completely deadpan. "How would you know? Maybe you're soulless."

"It could happen," Victor agreed easily. "Perhaps older medusas had that power, to steal souls when they're long dead. Maybe that's why my mother's family had the portraits made."

Anthony looked unsure, his gaze darting between them. "You are joking, right?"

"Oh my God, I looked at *all* of them." Edwin's eyebrows were beetled together in distress. "What's going to happen to me?"

Victor couldn't restrain his smile anymore. At the sight of it, Anthony immediately slumped in relief. "They're just kidding, Edwin," Anthony said, scowling at them both. "I was about to start checking myself to see if I'd begun to turn into stone. I've heard too many creepy old stories about medusas."

"There are just as many creepy stories about wolves." Randall's tone was mild, but Victor could see the protective tenseness in his shoulders. "We know better than anyone that old stories aren't necessarily true. Especially not ones written by humans."

Anthony looked apologetic and silently slid his closely guarded bowl of fries over to Victor. "Sorry," Anthony said. "That was really rude of me, especially when you're putting us up in your home."

Victor just waved a hand. "Think nothing of it. I'd actually be interested in hearing those stories later. They'd be quite helpful for my research."

"What're you researching?" Edwin, seeing the fries had been moved from their fortified position, decided to take a daringly bold approach and just lunge for them. Anthony smacked his hand away, and Edwin sighed, glowering. "You *are* one. Seems silly to research yourself."

"We're a quickly fading bloodline," Victor replied, not bothering to hide his smugness as he took fries without getting his hand slapped, "since many of us go insane before we have children. That, and we're just not all that cleverly evolved to hide and manage our abilities, not like wolves or other types of half bloods. I feel something of a sense of obligation to document us before we vanish completely."

"You should have kids," Edwin said, stealing another steak. "A lot of them. After you guys get married you could get one of those... what are they called, Ant?"

"Surrogates." Anthony looked like he'd had this kind of conversation with Edwin before. "But not everybody wants to have children, Edwin. And not everybody wants to have a surrogate, either."

"And not everyone who dates gets married." Randall's words were a little tense, his gaze flicking over toward Victor and away again. "In any case, Victor has a lot of years to decide that, and for now, I think it's admirable that he's assembling a work on medusas. They are a fascinating race."

A warm flush of pride made Victor smile. He didn't often feel that being a medusa was something to be *proud* of. Somehow, Randall made it sound like it should be. "Thank you," he murmured, privately pleased. Randall's hand found his, as it so often seemed to, squeezing gently.

They ate the rest of their dinner amidst chatter between the wolves, which Victor listened to but didn't feel the need to join in. Honestly, it was just nice having company in this big, old mansion, so much so that he really didn't mind that Edwin threatened to throw food at Anthony. He would have made them clean it up, of course, but it would have been amusing.

Victor was content to occasionally lean his shoulder against Randall's as they passed food between them, sharing bites of various dishes. He had never particularly wanted domesticity, but now that he had it, Victor was starting to find that he quite liked it. There was just something so peaceful about being by the side of someone he trusted unconditionally, sharing the smallest of things with them with no need for the usual small talk.

When everyone had eaten their fill, Anthony made motions like he wanted to start cleaning up, but Victor's stern expression stopped him in his tracks. "You are going to have a relaxing evening," he ordered. "There's a living room with a television at the end of the hall."

"We're going outside." Edwin looked determined, hands on Anthony's shoulders. "You were cooped up in that hospital all day. Even if you're too tired to run, we're going to go out in the woods, and you're going to get some fresh air."

"Thank God," Anthony sighed, glad for the offer. "Your mansion is lovely, Victor, but after the hospital, any four walls and a ceiling feel too close."

"Not at all. Go have fun. Just don't kill anything on the adjoining properties," Victor said. "The last thing I want is my irritating neighbors raising a fuss about predators in the woods."

Out of the corner of his eye, he saw Randall grin, quickly ducking his head as if to hide it. Victor gave him a curious look, but Randall was apparently trying too hard to bite back laughter to answer. At what, Victor wasn't sure.

"Okay, then we'll see you guys later," Anthony replied. "And hey, just so you know, we'll be out of earshot. So we won't be hearing anything that comes from this part of the mansion."

"Thank you," Victor gritted out around a smile. "That's very kind of you."

Anthony slung his arm around Edwin's shoulders, and as they left, he just grinned back at them before turning the corner. Victor had to wonder if Anthony was already anticipating that they'd go further than simply seeing each other. He seemed incredibly invested in keeping them happy and together.

Yesterday, when he and Randall had arrived home from dinner, they had agreed on another date tonight. Unfortunately, with the rush of the hospital appointment and getting their belongings to Victor's house, planning any grand ideas had slipped Victor's mind. They'd already eaten, so that was out.

He thought he might have a better plan.

"Would you like to take a walk around the gardens with me?" he asked Randall.

A slow smile spread easily across Randall's lips, softening the tense worry and exhaustion he seemed to be carrying around so heavily. "I feel very Victorian Romance in this, but I would very much enjoy that, yes."

Just to play up the theme, Victor offered his arm. "There's no time like the present, then, is there?"

Randall slipped his hand into the crook of Victor's arm. "Lead the way, good sir."

The gardens were never something Victor paid attention to. He appreciated them, but he had absolutely nothing resembling a green thumb, so he employed landscapers to keep them in shape. His mother, he recalled, had loved the gardens. She had spent a lot of time out there, clipping the roses and making sure everything was well structured and growing according to plan.

He took Randall to the outer east edge, leading him to the path that started a winding trail through the growing vines that twisted over trellises. It was not yet fully dark, the sinking sun lending an orange glow to the light.

"This is absolutely lovely, Victor," Randall breathed, his fingers going out to trail along the petals of the gardenia bush they passed. "It's like something out of a book."

"My mother loved it here. Every time I was here during school break, it seemed she would spend half her time in the garden," Victor replied. "She was very careful to cull out the ones I was allergic to. I unfortunately wouldn't know a cactus from a Venus flytrap."

Randall stooped down, studying the flowers that lined the path. The broad purple petals were spread out gracefully against dark-green leaves, and Randall seemed to choose one carefully, picking it and standing again. He tucked the flower into the buttonhole of Victor's jacket. "This is not a Venus flytrap," he informed Victor, teasing. "It's an iris. You have so many out here, they're like a carpet of color. It's beautiful."

"I didn't know what they were," Victor said, peering at the flower in his jacket. He laughed softly, pulling Randall in tighter against his side. "Apt, I suppose. My mother's name was Iris."

Randall pressed a kiss to his jaw. "We'll put vases full of them everywhere in the house. It'll make the whole place smell like out here."

Randall was making plans for the house. That made Victor smile to himself, though he didn't comment on it out loud. What they had was still tentative in many ways, and he didn't want to force Randall to stand by or discard those words. Instead, he just took Randall down a bend in the path toward the roses.

The roses were probably the part of the garden that Victor liked the most. There was every shade of rose imaginable planted together in clusters of color, framed with low-lying bushes to line the sides of the paths. In the middle of the circle where the paths came together there was a fountain, one that Victor hadn't switched on for some time, depicting a full-blooded medusa of old, her fierce gaze looking north, the stone snakes that made up her hair looking like they would come alive at any second.

"I always hated this thing." Victor chuckled as they stood at the base of it. "It used to make me fear that my hair would do that, no matter how much my parents reassured me it wouldn't. It always made me glad that I did not spend much time here when I was growing up—sometimes I would look out my bedroom window and I could swear that the statue was looking at me."

Breathing out a quick laugh, Randall leaned forward, inspecting the statue. He pressed his glasses up farther on his nose in an absent gesture, his whole expression one of intent contemplation. "I didn't know medusas could be men before I met you," Randall said lowly, musing as he circled the statue to see it from all angles. "They're always shown like this, a powerful matriarch figure, her hair, the symbol of her femininity, literally alive and full of dangerous intent. It's such a striking image, really. Taking back the traditional ideals of what women were in those times. I always was quite fond of them in myths. I thought they must be so lonely."

Victor was so absorbed in listening to Randall speak that he forgot to reply in kind for a good few seconds once silence had settled in. "Medusas usually are women," he agreed. "My grandfather and I are statistical outliers." He settled a hand on Randall's back, quite enjoying watching him study the statue. "I'm surprised you thought they were lonely. Most people thought they were monsters."

"Most people believe I eat children." Randall shrugged, head tipped back as he stared at the statue—meeting her blank stone eyes without fear, Victor realized. "I don't believe in monsters. At least, I don't believe it when the books tell me they are."

"You've got more common sense than most, then." Victor smiled. "Shall we continue? We've got half the garden to go yet, and the sun is setting fast."

"That should be on my tombstone," Randall hummed, taking Victor's arm once again. "More common sense than most."

"Only if you don't die of something extraordinarily stupid," Victor pointed out. "That would give contradicting messages."

"Only if I do," Randall decided with a laugh. "Here lies Randall Lewis. Dead of a toaster in the bathtub. He had more common sense than most."

Victor had to bite back the urge to suggest that it might one day be *Randall Lewis-Rathbone*. The very idea of it, where it had once sunk dread into his stomach, now made a little spark of hope in his gut, an anticipation for a future where that might happen.

They next went into the west side of the garden, which was dedicated less to structure and more to chaotically growing wildflowers which twisted around each other to form a carpet of color. The flowers crept up the sides of statues and walls, only held back from dominating everything by the monthly prune the gardeners gave them.

"So," Victor said, "about those eight other date ideas I have. Would you like to schedule another one?"

Randall tapped a finger to his lips, as if thinking very deeply. "Is it too forward to ask about your availability tomorrow? I have to work"—he looked extremely depressed by the very thought, some of the lightness fading back into worry—"but I should have a few hours free in the evening."

"What about the weekend? Are you available then?" Victor asked.

"I asked for double shifts at both jobs," Randall admitted, sounding disappointed. "The bills we have coming up.... I can't afford them as it is. I need the hours."

More than anything, Victor wanted to once again offer his money. He was living off the interest that accumulated in his accounts. He had *more* than enough money to easily pay for all the bills Randall was dealing with. He could, at the very least, give Randall a small amount to get him ahead of his current debts. But if he knew Randall, he knew Randall would never accept.

But then an idea began to form in the back of Victor's mind, and he nearly started smiling from the simplicity of it. Why hadn't it occurred to him before? He would have to do this very gently.

"Well, I may be a bit busy tomorrow evening," he apologized. "I'm due for a phone call with my research assistant, but they're always late and manage to take up an hour more of my time than I had scheduled. But if we manage to get some free time together, I would love to do something with you."

"Are you having them pull Galatas's *Evolution of Primal Fear*? It's incredibly boring, and please, don't get me started on the accuracy of his sections on water nymphs and wartime signals, but he has several excellent firsthand accounts of what I am quite sure are early half-blooded medusas." Victor was admittedly barely listening to the actual words. Randall's entire face lit up when he talked like this, his hands moving as if words alone couldn't capture what he was trying to express. "It talks about a small city in central Greece where there was a family whose women, it said, would steal the soul of their suitors. They'd have fits in the streets, and the men who came to ask for the daughters' hands were all strangely empty afterward, some even dying. Galatas calls them witches, but he's an idiot."

Victor had had a better plan for attempting to offer Randall a job. Instead, it came out more suddenly than he'd anticipated. After a speech like that, how could Victor *not* immediately want Randall working by his side?

"If I offered you my research assistant job, would you want it?" Victor asked. "Please say yes. You are so much better than any other person I've looked at for the job."

Randall stopped walking completely. "Me?" He was immediately shaking his head. "No, Victor, I'm not qualified. I've only two years of school. I don't even have a *degree*. You need someone with far more experience."

"I need someone who is interested in the work," Victor insisted. "I need someone who *wants* to be there, not some undergrad who spends most of his time chewing gum and texting. Randall, you would be absolutely perfect for the job. The pay would only be a little better than what you're getting now, but I would give the job to you in a heartbeat if you said yes."

Randall slid his glasses off, fiddling with the earpieces. It was a nervous habit, Victor had noticed, one that he used when he was stalling for time to think. "Is this because we're sleeping together?" Randall finally asked, a frown creasing his forehead.

367

"Or because you think you have to? Because I really don't want to compromise your work over... whatever feelings you might have about it. You don't have an obligation to me. What you're doing is far too important for that."

Victor sniffed, a little insulted at the insinuation. "I can promise you that I would be one hundred percent professional during office hours," he replied. "The work *is* important. I'm hardly going to play grabby hands in the middle of research."

Randall lifted an eyebrow. "One *hundred* percent?" he asked, a very slow smile starting to curve one corner of his mouth. "Now that just sounds dull, professor."

"I might be willing to negotiate it down to ninety percent, if you took the job," Victor bargained. "But if you didn't want our relationship to affect the work, then yes, I would keep my hands to myself. I promise."

"I think I could live with ninety percent." Clearly making a decision, Randall nodded, putting his glasses back on and smiling at Victor. "Yes. Yes, let's... do that. I'll be your research assistant."

"Good." That single word didn't express how relieved Victor was—both for Randall's sake and for the sake of his own research—but he found he couldn't come up with any better right then. "Excellent. When can you start?"

"Well, I hear that you have a meeting scheduled tomorrow," Randall said with a sly look over at Victor. "Perhaps I should prepare a few things for that?"

Victor took Randall's arm again, and they started walking through the rest of the garden, slowly making their way back to the mansion. "Then I suppose I should make a phone call to my old assistant," he mused. "Since I have a far better one coming along."

"And I think I need to quit my jobs." Randall stopped, pulling Victor to a halt as well, as if the realization had just hit him. "Oh my God, I get to quit my jobs." The *relief* on Randall's face seemed to take ages of worry away from him. "I can throw out the apron. And the *name badge.*"

"And I believe you'll find I'm a lenient boss," Victor offered. "If you need to take time to be with Anthony for his appointments, you're more than welcome to. In fact, I'll insist upon it." Though he knew he wasn't explicitly part of the family yet, Victor couldn't help but worry at the idea of Anthony going to the hospital alone. Hospitals were lonely places, even when surrounded by people going through the same situation as you.

"You wouldn't come with us?" Again Randall paused, this time turning to face Victor, the dying sunlight bathing his skin in gold and ruby. Quieter, Randall moved a step closer, their entwined fingers brought up to rest against Randall's heart. "I would understand if you didn't want to. But if you think that I wouldn't rather have you there, Victor, you're wrong."

"I'll come with you." Victor was surprised to realize he genuinely meant it. Not even that long ago, the idea of integrating with Randall's family had seemed something scary. Now he wanted to be there for them. He wanted to sit in the waiting room and bring bad coffee to Randall.

"Well, then." The words were said lightly, but Victor could see the relief in Randall's smile, the way he moved closer still, sharing Victor's warmth, the soft breaths mingling between them. "It is a very good thing my boss is willing to give me the time off."

Arm in arm, they exited the gardens. The mansion seemed looming in the not-quite darkness, but there were lights on inside, more windows lit up than there had been in years. He could see Anthony and Edwin going through the front door, Anthony's arm looped over Edwin's shoulders, their body language easy and relaxed.

For the first time in a long time, the mansion felt like *home*.

THE NEXT day seemed to blur between chaos and stillness. To Victor, it felt like highs and lows crashing from one to the other—first the high of Randall starting his first official work day, the way they meshed so easily together making Victor unable to stop smiling. Then the low of accompanying Randall and Anthony to Anthony's hospital visit, the weight of watching Randall's shoulders grow tenser and tenser in anxiety.

After that, the mixed relief and resignation when Anthony came out: not worse, but not better either.

They took Edwin to the nearby shops to buy enough food for all of them, and the sheer amount they wound up with left Victor wondering if he had enough fridge space. The whole time, he'd noticed Randall and Anthony eyeing the prices of things, wincing when they thought something was too expensive before putting it back. Every time, Victor then picked up what they'd discarded and declared that he was buying it for himself. If they tried to complain, Victor put on a huffy host act, insisting that his very soul would be dishonored if they didn't let him spoil them.

Dinner and a peaceful night passed, and the next day there was no hospital visit. Victor spent several hours properly showing the Lewises around the mansion. Edwin's favorite room was one on the far west side that hadn't been used in decades. It had once belonged to great-grandfather Sir Milton Braxton, and the room contained nothing but two dozen sets of armor on mannequins. Anthony had particularly liked the workshop at the end of one hallway, and had spent a long time looking at the old wood-carving tools.

Victor had guessed correctly that Randall's favorite would be the library. Long after Anthony and Edwin had wandered off to go collapse on the couch, Randall had meandered around the library, entranced, sometimes devoting half an hour to a single shelf.

When Victor had shown him the antique books, Randall looked like he might have a heart attack then and there. He studied the books in their glass cases like they were the finest treasures, which pleased Victor to no end. Not many other people he'd known had the same appreciation for such things.

He and Randall slowly learned how they fit into each other's lives. Randall washed the dishes; Victor dried. Victor retrieved the books from the shelves; Randall marked them at the appropriate pages. Randall, as Victor had known he would be, was the best research assistant Victor could possibly hope for.

Anthony rested a lot. Edwin went back and forth between being content to slouch in front of the television to raising hell around the mansion, tearing through hallways so fast that all anybody ever saw was a blur of wolf. Anthony joined him on the days he was feeling better, though at a somewhat more sedate pace. The wolves bickered over dinner and took up all the hot water, then thoughtfully repaired old cracks in the walls and cleaned out the garden shed.

Three days into their stay, Victor offered both Anthony and Edwin employment opportunities. Anthony loved driving and Victor hated it, so it seemed a match made in heaven, and Anthony had been only too happy to take the job. He'd found the cupboard in the service quarters that held some very old uniforms and had walked around the whole day with a driver's cap on.

To Edwin, Victor offered a gardening job. The previous day he had noticed Edwin absently strolling among the gardens and plucking off old leaves that needed to be pruned. Though Edwin couldn't name most of the plants in the gardens, he seemed to know how to treat them nonetheless, and the prospect of a job where he didn't have to work cooped up inside had made Edwin beam.

Four days into the Lewises' stay, Victor had to do something other than sit at home and research.

"Randall," he called. Hidden away behind one of the massive shelves in his library, Victor had no clue where Randall was in the room, as all he could see was his possibly too large collection of historic texts. "I'm going to go by my office today, if you'd like to come along?"

Edwin, in wolf form, leapt over the desk and scurried away, tail wagging. It had been raining for the past two days, which meant Edwin had been forced to entertain himself inside, as Anthony couldn't stand it when Edwin shook water everywhere, and Victor absolutely forbid him from it. Edwin had taken to sniffing absolutely everything in the house and giving them all detailed rundowns of what he thought used to happen in each room. Apparently this was his day on the third floor. "Edwin." Victor despaired. "Please don't knock over my work. I just got it in order."

It was the full moon tonight. Victor had learned in his time with the pack that in most cases, wolves didn't seem to feel the effects of it strongly until late afternoon. Edwin, however, always marching to the beat of his own drum, had been buzzed since the moment he'd gotten up.

Edwin just gave him a wolfy grin, tongue lolling out the side of his mouth as he trotted off to sniff the windows. Victor got up from behind the desk to stretch and check to make sure his tower of notes hadn't gotten pushed out of order. Randall had apparently taken up space in a huge armchair in the far corner, volumes with brilliantly colored sticky notes poking from their pages scattered around him.

"What?" Randall said, eyebrow raised, an enormous book spread out in his lap. "Are you feeling a little claustrophobic in here with all us big, bad wolves?"

Victor just smirked a little to himself. Yesterday the two of them had sneaked outside alone. They'd deliberately forgotten Victor's rule about not going out into the rain so that they didn't track it inside, and Victor had forgotten his usual hatred of dirt and twigs in favor of spending some time with Randall in the forest. Randall had jokingly suggested that perhaps Victor was afraid of the big, bad wolf, and it had led to a rather entertaining chase through the trees, ending with both of them muddy, soaked through, and satisfied.

"I need to pick up some mail from there, and speak to some of the other professors," Victor replied. Randall had something of a point, though. As much as Victor liked having company, it was difficult going from a house that had been empty for years to a house with rambunctious wolves. "I thought you might like to see where I work."

Standing, stretching his arms over his head, Randall collapsed back down on himself with a smile. "I absolutely would. Let me get changed. I'm a mess." He had dust on his nose, his hair was in wild waves, and his shirt was untucked. If Victor didn't have a schedule for the day, and if Edwin wasn't sniffing around under his desk, Victor would have enjoyed the chance to engage Randall in a repeat of yesterday's adventures.

Unfortunately, he'd put off going into his office for three days now. He probably shouldn't continue delaying. "I'll meet you in the garage. I have some work to collect," Victor said. He reached out to trail his fingers over Randall's nose, ridding him of the dust.

Said nose wrinkled under Victor's touch, and Randall lightly hooked his fingers into the front of Victor's shirt, pulling him in closer. "Yes, sir, boss," Randall murmured with a highly unprofessional grin.

"Is this part of our ten percent allotted unprofessional time?" Victor asked. "Do we have a schedule for that?"

"I really haven't done the math, professor." Randall tugged him in for a light kiss. Victor could feel Randall's smile pressed against his own. "Should I do extra work to make up for it?"

"Maybe we'll have to raise the percentage to fifteen." Victor kissed Randall again, forgetting about work for the moment.

"Ew. Guys, I'm still in here." Edwin's voice came from the corner. Neither he nor Randall even looked over.

"And you're naked. Shift back or put pants on, Ed," Randall sighed, shaking his head. Victor, for his part, raised an incredulous eyebrow at Edwin. The man was naked, and yet he was complaining about their incredibly chaste kissing.

"I had to change back so I could tell you you're gross." Edwin's logic was clearly infallible. But a few moments later, the blond wolf nudged past them, nipping at their knees as he trotted out into the hallway, leaving them alone at last.

"I'm getting him a collar with a jingly bell," Randall murmured, arms sliding around Victor, nipping lightly at Victor's lower lip. "A big, loud bell."

Victor restrained a smile and pressed a light kiss to Randall's nose before reluctantly pulling away. "Come on," he reminded him. "Work calls, and as much as I want to indulge in more of our ten percent of time, we should be on our way."

"Fifteen," Randall corrected, but he gathered up a stack of books, carefully marking his place in the one he'd been so intently studying. "I'll meet you downstairs."

Randall left, and Victor did the same after he'd found the paperwork he needed to take into the office. He got changed into clothes a tad more professional than the old shirt he was wearing and passed by the living room to check on Anthony. The television was on, and Anthony had fallen asleep on the couch, a blanket falling off his shoulders. Perhaps it was paranoid, but Victor took a few seconds to check that Anthony was breathing.

After he'd confirmed that and tucked the covers more closely around Anthony, he went down to the garage. Randall arrived at the same time he did, and they shared a smile as Victor found the keys to the car he liked the most. Though he wasn't big on driving, he did have an appreciation for vintage cars, and the black Rolls-Royce Phantom III that barely got any use was one of his favorites.

When Victor looked up from unlocking the doors, he found Randall standing, staring, expression extremely hard to read. He seemed a little torn, and Victor wasn't sure what could have affected him. "Is everything all right?" Victor asked him, frowning. "We can take a different car if you like."

"What time did you say we needed to be there?" Randall asked, voice a bit thin.

Victor checked his watch. "Er, about ten minutes ago," he replied guiltily. He abhorred being late, but sometimes it was unavoidable. "Why?"

Randall stalked over to him, his movements liquid and predator smooth. Without another word, he grasped Victor's newly donned tie and hauled him back, pushing him to sprawl against the hood of the car. With a growl, Randall pinned him there with a kiss, slow and deep, fingers already fumbling for the belt of Victor's trousers.

It seemed the full moon had effects on the wolf sex drive too.

"Then we're already late," Randall muttered, biting Victor's lower lip sharply. "Can you be quiet? I'm very sure sound will carry."

"Actually, the garage is soundproofed," Victor managed to say. His pants were getting dragged down while he lay on the hood of a very old, very expensive car, and Randall was flush with the effects of the moon. Victor was surprised he could even speak. "My grandfather used to fix cars down here. It's a very noisy business."

"Good." Randall sank to his knees, lips sliding along the outline of Victor's cock through his boxers. "Then I don't have to worry."

"Not at all." Victor's voice came out more like a squeak than the smooth tone he'd wanted to go for. Then his boxers were gone, and Victor had gotten hard so quickly it made his head spin. Randall didn't waste any time, didn't go for a slow buildup. His mouth was hot and wet around Victor, his fingers digging into Victor's hips, pushing him back farther against the car.

All worry about possibly denting or scratching the car flew from Victor's mind. If they damaged it, it might just be worth it for a memory like this.

Randall's cheeks were hollowed out, his eyes fallen half closed, lips tight around Victor's cock as he bobbed his head, taking Victor in deeper. And then he was pulling Victor toward him, moving with him with a hum of pleasure, like he was so desperate to get *more* he couldn't think of anything else. The physical sensations were of course amazing, but it was almost more the expression on Randall's face that drove Victor's arousal higher. There was nothing sexier than a partner who was absolutely in the moment, who went for things like this without fear or thought of anything else. With Randall's eyes closed, Victor could truly *look* at him.

He wound his fingers into Randall's hair, struggling to keep his own eyes open so he could take in every moment. Victor wanted to hold off on his orgasm, to enjoy this for longer, but Randall was almost ruthless in his attentions. He didn't slow down, he didn't take it easy, he just dug his fingertips into Victor's skin and sucked hard, his tongue rubbing over the underside of Victor's cock, employing all the little tricks he'd learned about Victor's body over the last few days.

It was an extremely good thing that the garage was soundproofed, because the volume at which Victor moaned Randall's name might have been a bit excessive for any other situation. He curled forward as the pleasure concentrated, teeth gritted around more utterances of Randall's name. The building arousal had all the mercilessness of an oncoming train, and Victor came so hard he swore he saw dots at the corners of his vision.

Panting, he sagged back over the hood of the car, staring dazedly at the ceiling. "Dear God," he said faintly. Randall's tongue was still moving, softly cleaning him off, and Victor twitched at the sensation, a rough groan sounding at the back of his throat. "Enough," he pleaded, laughing, gently pushing at Randall's head. "You utter monster."

He could feel Randall kissing his cock, which was just cruel, but then moving up his body, leaving behind traces of his lips against Victor's hips, his stomach, his arms, until Randall was leaning over him, nose burying itself against his throat. "You are so hot," Randall murmured. "How on earth are you so attractive?"

"I'm fairly sure it was the *car* you found attractive." Victor laughed again. "I had no clue what that look on your face was at first." He raised his hands to Randall's shoulders, curving them around the back of his neck, and brought him down for a kiss.

"I have never been much of a car person," Randall admitted, deepening the next kiss, hands sliding down to Victor's hips. "But God, you and the car and the whole thing, I wanted to beg you to fuck me over this hood. And then again in the backseat." Randall still looked a little embarrassed every time he stated something like that so openly. That hadn't stopped him yet, though. Even the flush that touched his cheeks was counteracted by the way he pulled Victor in closer, teasing bites down his throat.

Just the thought of that was almost enough to get Victor wanting a second round right then and there. "That's an idea we'll have to save for the next rainy day," he said instead, wandering one hand down Randall's chest. "And as much as I want to do so right now, I'm going to have to be a killjoy."

Very reluctantly, he pushed himself off the hood, but even as he knew they should go, he caught Randall in another kiss. Though Victor desperately wanted to return the favor, he also didn't want to be late and make his coworkers angry. "Rain check?"

"I will hold you to that." Randall kissed the corner of his mouth, hand wound in Victor's tie to keep him close. "But I think we just used up our whole ten percent with that."

Victor laughed under his breath as he pulled his pants back up. He put a hand to Randall's elbow, nudged him over to get him in the passenger seat, and made his way around the car to sit behind the wheel. Ten percent be damned, he certainly wasn't going to complain if that kept happening during work hours.

The engine started up with a finely maintained purr under them. Victor pulled it out of the garage with a glance over at Randall, who once again looked utterly distracted. Victor smirked to himself. Well, that was one use of this car he certainly hadn't intended.

It was only a few minutes' drive to the college, though it took Victor a few minutes more to squeeze the car into his parking space. The way he cursed the whole time was probably unflattering, but Randall just seemed bemused, sticking his head out the window to tell Victor how close he was to scraping the entire side of the car against the building wall. When he finally got it parked, Victor let out a sigh of relief and got out first so that Randall could climb over the middle and exit via the driver's side.

The college itself was old, built shortly after Victor's house. Carved from stone and brick and populated with wide parks and the occasional tree, it was one of the most beautiful campuses Victor had ever seen—which was at least part of the reason he'd chosen to work there.

When he began to walk, he realized Randall was no longer beside him. Turning, he found Randall staring around, expression one of pained longing, watching students walk past with books and bags in hand. It was only a moment and then Randall was smiling at him again, was walking quickly to catch up, but there was something on the whole *less* about him now.

Victor knew Randall had given up on college when Anthony had become sick, and although Randall had never said it expressly, Victor started to wonder if this was the college Randall had been signed up for. He'd mentioned working and saving to transfer to his chosen university. From the way he was looking at everything around them, absorbing everything like a child with their nose pressed to the glass, Victor couldn't help but think this was where Randall was supposed to be now, instead of running after wolf packs and working himself to the bone.

Victor didn't say anything. He just put his hand to Randall's back in what he hoped was a comforting gesture and walked them toward the building he worked in. He'd hoped that he would one day be able to help Randall go back to college, but Anthony would have to get better before Randall did that. It was, unfortunately, something out of Victor's control.

"That's where I work." He nodded at the two-story building they were approaching. It lay on the far side of a grassy park, the stone a dark gray in color, arches above the windows lending it an almost religious air.

"I changed my mind," Randall murmured, head tipped back to take in the whole structure. "I want you to fuck me *here*."

Victor almost laughed, until he realized they were in the middle of a campus. Wincing, he took his hand off Randall's back. It probably wouldn't do to have a professor and a possible future student getting cozy in the middle of everybody.

Immediately going red, that fragile confidence Randall had built up fading just as quickly, he muttered an "I'm so sorry, I don't know what's gotten into me," fumbling off his glasses to clean them on the corner of his sweater. "That was highly inappropriate. It—"

"That's not what I was reacting to," Victor said quietly. "Believe me, I'd like nothing more than that. But I'm a professor here, and you may be a student someday. I wouldn't want to jeopardize your chances of getting in."

"I'm not going to be a student, Victor," Randall sighed, straightening his tie. "But I am your research assistant. I should act like it. You're absolutely right."

Victor couldn't lean in close to whisper—he could, however, speak lowly enough that only Randall's wolf ears would pick it up. "You're just awfully distracting," he said fondly.

A smile touched Randall's face, and he ducked his head, clearing his throat. "Why don't you show me your office, professor?"

A few more steps took them to the entrance of the building. Victor scanned his identity card. They waited for the welcoming buzz before Victor pushed open the door and let them in. He led Randall down a series of hallways that twisted and turned, as confusing as any university building, until he finally came to his office. It was only a small one, little more than the size of two closets pushed together, but Victor didn't need very much space.

He hadn't decorated it with much, only books and papers. There were no photographs or mugs or posters. Now that Victor looked at it with new eyes, it looked a bit... pathetic.

"Well, this is it," he said to Randall, waving a hand at the room before getting behind the desk to go through the drawers. "It's not much, but the door locks, so I can avoid students when I want to."

As he had with Victor's bedroom, Randall slowly made his way around the room, fingers lightly sliding along book spines, nosing into the corners, inspecting everything. "You have a first-edition Nietzsche." He carefully lifted one of the books from the stack. "The chapters here on the basis of good and evil are stunning."

"It really is a lot better in the original German," Victor said absently. "Though still very dry to read."

"Viele Menschen warten ihr ganzes Leben hindurch auf die Chance, auf ihre Weise gut zu sein," Randall mused with a slight smile, glancing over at Victor.

Victor snorted at the sentiment—"'many people wait throughout their whole lives for the chance to be good in their own fashion.' I'm not sure if that's a compliment or an insult."

"A philosophy of sorts." Randall slid the book back into place, long fingers touching the cover lightly like a silent good-bye. "I think the idea of *in their own fashion* is fascinating. Good is such a slippery thing, after all. I don't know if I believe in heroes. But I can believe in the idea that we're all striving to be better."

"I think Nietzsche would agree with you." Victor closed the drawer he'd been looking through, hefting a stack of papers onto the desk. "I've also got some Aristotle there if you'd like to try your hand at ancient Greek. Not a first edition, sadly."

"I've always wanted to learn Greek," Randall said, immediately searching through the shelves eagerly. "Ancient, specifically, though honestly I'd be happy with anything. I could never find a class, though."

Gathering the last of his work, Victor tucked it into the briefcase he'd brought with him and joined Randall at the bookshelf. "I've taught a few classes on ancient Greek," he said, gaze caught on Randall studying the books. He was so in his element that it was impossible not to watch him. "I could arrange a few private lessons, I think, or I could just give you the textbooks. They're dense but easily understood."

"Anything," Randall agreed, his eyes devouring the Aristotle like he'd been starved for weeks. "I don't want to take up your time, so the books would be more than excellent. Thank you, Victor." A pause and Randall looked up, expression softening. "Really. Thank you." The words were said so gently, so *earnestly*, that it seemed one of the most intimate things Randall had ever told him.

Once again, Victor wanted to insist that Randall attend this college. He knew he could pull a few favors and get Randall in late, but Randall seemed to have given up on the idea completely, and Victor couldn't force him into it. One day, perhaps, he would offer and Randall would take the chance. He knew other things had to fall in place first— like Anthony's health.

"It's my pleasure," Victor said. If he could, he'd gladly spend all day in his office with Randall, but he'd rushed here for a meeting and he was still unfortunately late. "I need to go meet with the other linguistics lecturers," he said apologetically. "You can stay here if you like, or if you want to wander, I can just call you when I'm done so we can find each other."

"I'll stay here." Randall reached out, adjusting Victor's tie, absently smoothing his hands down the front of Victor's shirt. "I want to pull some more books for your personal research. And if you'll allow me, go through some of those notes you were telling me about? From your past books. I think there were some excellent points you made about the propensity of humans to project their own internal struggles onto the supernatural community, turning us into fairy tale monsters, as it were, that I think will really add to the current chapter you're writing."

Even though Victor was getting later by the second, he had to stop and kiss Randall on the cheek. How he'd ever gotten something fully researched before Randall, he had no clue. "Hiring you was the best decision I've ever made," he said. "Have fun."

Then he all but ran out of the office, wincing to himself as he looked at his watch. He wasn't normally late to these sorts of things, but there was so much else happening in his life that he was finding it difficult to multitask, especially when lecturing and research had once been the *only* things in his life.

His attendance at the meeting for the linguistics professors was largely ceremonial, as this semester was his scheduled time off. But Victor liked attending those sorts of things nonetheless, even if he had to stare at the table or the projection the entire time to avoid a room full of possible eye contact. It was supposed to go on for an hour, but since linguistics academics tended to favor the spoken word and embellish, it lasted for an hour and a half, a good portion of which was Victor's fault for eagerly vouching that the students have to ask questions in the language they were learning.

When they were released, Victor was stopped no less than five times by students. Some of them wanted to know when he'd be back—they apparently liked his teaching style, which Victor found very strange, as most did not. Some, it seemed, appreciated the fact that he was blunt and to the point, and didn't tolerate students sleeping or texting.

He returned to find Randall surrounded by books piled on the floor, various papers spread out around him. His office had been transformed into chaos, but if Victor had learned anything about Randall, he knew it would be an extremely organized chaos, one that could be cleaned up in a matter of minutes.

"You look like you're having fun," Victor greeted, carefully stepping over some books.

With a soft grunt as his only response, Randall frowned down at the page he was reading, lips moving as he silently worked through whatever language it was in. A quick glance showed that he'd found one of Victor's Sumerian texts. Difficult to get through, especially since, as far as he knew, Randall didn't speak it. But there was a translation guide open by Randall's elbow, and a page full of notes in his messy, cramped writing.

"I can't figure out the context of this verb," Randall finally sighed, sitting back. He'd pushed his glasses up on top of his head and pinched the bridge of his nose. "It's saying that the snake people were either worshipped or cooked, and I'd say that changes the ending quite a bit." But he smiled up at Victor, leaning back in the chair. "Yes. I am having a great deal of fun. Your office is a bit like my idea of a dream vacation."

"It's one of those verbs that depends heavily on context, unfortunately," Victor replied. He got himself over another pile of books to crouch down beside Randall. He pointed at the text that Randall was looking at, a few lines farther down. "See here? It lists ingredients."

"Ah." Randall wrinkled his nose. "So I'm guessing this is not a story with a happy conclusion." He turned, kissing Victor lightly in hello. "Fascinating, even if it is quite brutal. They apparently, from what I can gather here, thought that by, er, eating medusas, they'd gain all the souls the medusas had taken. Worship probably would have been less messy and just as effective."

"Exactly," Victor agreed. "And, on the bright side, should you ever want to cook me, you now have a very nice soup recipe."

"I have other ways of eating you that are far more pleasant," Randall returned with a huge grin, obviously proud of his innuendo. Another quick kiss and Randall stood, stretching, having loosened his tie and rolled up his sleeves while he worked. "Should I gather up what I think we should take? I believe we can make it in one trip."

Victor eyed the fairly impressive collection Randall had pulled from his shelves. "I think you might be a bit overconfident in my upper body strength. Here, give me a second. I'll enlist a minion."

He took two steps to the door again and stuck his head out of it. The student he asked for help was one of the best in his classes. She was currently working as a research assistant for one of the other professors and seemed all too happy to take a break from the offices. Between the three of them, they managed to get all the books out to the car, where the student farewelled Victor with a hug after making him promise he would be back for the next semester.

Victor handed the small pile of older books to Randall for him to keep on his lap as they drove—the last thing Victor wanted was to turn a sudden corner and have a pile of near irreplaceable books fall over and get damaged.

As they drove back, Victor kept watching Randall out of the corner of his eye. He had looked so at home at the college that it pained Victor to know Randall was denying himself the opportunity. He understood Randall's reasons, but he just had to ask. Just once more.

"Do you remember how staying at my place wasn't the only thing I offered, before we left?" he said, keeping his tone neutral. He didn't want to be too pushy in this. "I can pull the necessary strings to get you back into college as a very late enrollee, if that's something you'd be interested in."

Letting out a slow breath, Randall absently rubbed his hands together, staring out the window. "Victor," he started before simply shaking his head. "You know I can't."

Victor knew he had to be very delicate about this conversation. Unfortunately, he wasn't good at delicate. Nonetheless, he'd try, for Randall's sake. "Not going to college won't make Anthony get any better," he said, wincing as he said it. It was true, though, however indelicate it might be to point out that fact. "Denying yourself a future will not make Anthony improve, just as allowing yourself to go back to school won't somehow make him worse."

377

He could see Randall's jaw tightening, his profile difficult to read. "I know that," Randall finally admitted. "It just seems... wrong. It's a long drive from our house here, and that would be hours and hours I wouldn't be with him. I can't just go on like nothing is wrong, Victor."

"I know." Victor couldn't argue with that. He understood Randall wanted to spend every moment with Anthony he could, and to tell him otherwise would be nothing short of heartless. "I don't want to seem pushy, but if you all stayed at my place, things that like would no longer be an issue."

"A week is very different than an indefinite stay," Randall pointed out after several long moments of silence. "And as much as I would love to just say yes and move in, it's not that simple. Our cabin is the only place we've ever lived. We built it ourselves. Our parents lived and died on that land." Randall turned, studying Victor, obviously searching for the right words. "And what we have, what we've started, it means too much to me to ruin it by rushing. You say you want us there now, but you've not even had time to get sick of us. I'd rather go slow and have a lifetime to get to that point than to push it because of a few good dates."

In response, Victor reached over the seats and took Randall's hand. He wished it *were* a very simple matter of them just moving in, but everything Randall said was true. There were other factors in play here, ones that were big decisions.

However much he wanted to help Randall, he couldn't *force* that help on him. And he certainly couldn't get annoyed when Randall refused.

Instead, Victor nodded. "I understand." He gently squeezed Randall's hand. "I just want you to know that the offer is not on a time limit. If in five years you decide that's what you want, I will still gladly accept."

Randall pulled Victor's hand up and kissed his knuckles. "Do you think we'll still be together in five years, then?" he asked, tone light but something achingly sweet in his expression. Something so very hopeful.

"If we're not, I'll be very cranky," Victor replied.

"Well, then." Randall breathed out a quick laugh. "Anything to avoid that."

Victor's hand remained in Randall's for the remainder of the drive. Upon arriving back home, they had to enlist Edwin's help in bringing the books into the house—and Victor very carefully took responsibility for the older books himself. As soon as Edwin had dumped the textbooks onto the desk, he was gone again as quickly as if he'd just vanished into thin air.

He and Randall spent the rest of the day neck deep in research, only surfacing for cups of tea or water, or to stretch their legs. Over time, though, Victor started to notice that Randall's concentration was slipping. As time went by, he would, more and more, have to pause to put the book down to look out the window where Anthony and Edwin were working in the garden. They seemed jittery too, Edwin dropping his rake to chase a rabbit across the lawn, human form merging into wolf and then back again in shifts so quick they seemed almost unreal.

When Randall seemed completely incapable of focusing, Victor offered to cut their work day short—but as Randall got more restless with the proximity of the full moon, he also got more stubborn, so Victor was treated to a frown and a passionate insistence that Randall could continue reading. And Randall certainly did seem to try.

An hour before it got dark, the wolves corralled themselves into the kitchen for dinner, which was a rather more growl-filled affair than usual. On one occasion, Randall really did growl seriously at Edwin for attempting to steal something off Victor's plate, a protective note to the rumble that just made Victor smile. Victor spent the rest of the dinner with Randall practically forcibly dividing him from Anthony and Edwin. He clearly didn't think Anthony and Edwin were threats as such; he just seemed to be feeling possessive.

When Anthony and Edwin abandoned the dinner table to go outside, Randall lingered. Victor glanced at him as he finished the rest of his meal—he knew Randall often held off on the change, simply because he didn't want to be ruled by his instincts.

"What's your plan for the night?" Victor asked. He cast a look at the table and silently despaired. Wolves were apparently rather messy when they got jittery.

"Well." Randall turned toward him, even the simple motion so much more graceful now, a predatory stalk in the way he walked across the room to Victor. "I was thinking about how hard I could fuck you over the back of the couch." A slow smile eased across Randall's lips. "Which is less a *plan* than an *impulse*, really."

There was very little in the world that could make Victor speechless for even a few seconds. That, apparently, was something that could. "Oh? Well, never let it be said that I would have you deny your impulses."

With a growl, Randall moved, grasping Victor by the hips and all but tossing him toward the couch. Victor caught himself and kept his balance, one hand braced on the back of it. He looked at Randall over his shoulder, twisting his lips into a half smirk. He would admit to looking forward to their first full moon, though the anticipation of it had mostly slipped his mind in all the chaos of moving the Lewises in and having them stay. Even though he'd come to terms with David's memories and the echo of self-destructiveness, it didn't change the fact that Randall—when he was closer to his wolfish nature—was *very* attractive.

Randall stalked forward, stripping off clothes as he went. He carelessly tossed his sweater aside, kicking off his trousers, so much of his usual reticent nature now brushed aside in the brashness the moon seemed to give wolves. Randall confident under normal circumstances was one thing; this was a voracious *need* that Randall seemed unable to deny. For freedom, yes, for the ground under his feet, the wind at his back. But also for more carnal things—food, company, *him*. As Randall approached him, grasping Victor's shirt and easily ripping it open, bowing his head to suck biting kisses along his chest, Victor wondered if this was how all wolves treated their mates on such occasions. They should probably invest in soundproofing if that were the case.

Mates. It was a word that sounded so much more intimate to Victor than mere "husbands." If asked, he couldn't say *why*, only that the connotation of the word seemed more meaningful. He didn't know if he and Randall would ever get to that point, but he sincerely hoped they did.

Far from the hesitation of their first night, they fit together so much easier now, like they had been reaching out for each other their whole lives. Randall's fingers were deft on Victor's pants, slipping into his pockets to find the condom and the lube Victor had been carrying around in awareness of the full moon since they'd gotten home. He felt more than heard Randall laugh, teeth catching against Victor's throat.

"Someone's prepared," Randall murmured. He pushed Victor's shirt back over his shoulders, sending one of the half-torn-off buttons flying, too anxious to get to as much skin as he could. He paused, taking a slow breath, as if realizing what he was doing. "Do you want me to stop?" he asked, concern underneath the obvious want in his voice. "I've never... been like this with anyone on a moon. We're getting closer. I don't know what I'll be like."

"Don't you dare stop," Victor insisted. "And don't worry about it. You were perfectly considerate in the garage." Randall was already naked, which unfortunately meant that he didn't have the pleasure of attempting to do his own clothes ripping—it did mean that he had the benefit of not wasting time doing it, though.

They came together in a clash of a kiss. Randall let go at the permission, his eyes shining yellow again. His touch was hard but not rough, firmly grasping Victor's sides as they kissed. Victor's pants were shoved off, kicked aside carelessly, and Randall lifted him up to sit on the back edge of the couch, keeping Victor steady with an arm around his waist.

Randall slicked his fingers with lube, hand shaking a little with the force of his want, with the little muffled growls he was burying against Victor's skin. Jerking Victor forward so he was all but laid out on the back of the couch, Randall eased one finger inside of Victor, letting out a groaned, "God, you feel so good." Victor breathed in sharply and tried to remind himself that moving too eagerly against Randall would result in falling off completely.

Leaning over him, Randall bit sharply at Victor's shoulder, sucking hard at the skin, and added another finger. His movements were quick, hard, thrusting into Victor with an urgency that was mirrored in the tenseness of Randall's shoulders, the frantic breaths against Victor's skin. When Randall's teeth closed on Victor's scar, it was with a rumbling growl, a possessive sound that shook Randall's whole body. "Mine," he muttered, biting harder, sucking away the sting, pulling back only to go in again, worrying at Victor's flushed skin as if he could claim the scar completely. "*Mine.*"

Victor was only dimly aware that he was leaving clawed scrapes over Randall's back with his fingernails, his own version, perhaps, of the bite. He shifted, hooking an arm more firmly around Randall's shoulders for better balance as Randall withdrew his hand. Randall pressed inside him, and their simultaneous groans vibrated through Victor's chest.

Randall didn't go for a gradual buildup, a slow and steady increase in pace. He simply wrapped his arm around Victor and thrust into him fully, pulling back almost completely before rocking back into Victor, hard and fast, groans and growls alike pulled from his throat. They moved together at a frantic pace, until Victor was sure that the couch had become barely involved at all, and surely Randall must be lifting most of his weight himself. He twisted his head to bite at Randall's throat, sinking his teeth deeper than he'd ever done before, pleasure jolting through him at the resulting growl Randall gave and the way he moved harder in reaction.

It was desperate and primal, no thought spared for comfort, only raw need. Victor knew both of them would be covered with scrapes and bruises, and the thought only excited him further. Once upon a time he might have been already deciding to wear turtlenecks for the next week—now he liked the idea of proudly showing them off.

When he came, the force of it making him shake, he bit Randall's throat again, still moving with him as they both sought Randall's pleasure. Victor turned his head to catch Randall in a kiss that involved more teeth than usual, the clash leaving their lips bruised. "Mine," Randall was saying again, voice almost lost in rough moans. "Mine."

"Yours," Victor promised lowly, his words stuttering at the force of their movements.

That seemed to be what Randall was waiting for. With one last hard snap forward, buried as deeply in Victor as he could be, Randall came. He pressed his face into Victor's neck, he half howled in a guttural sound of release, and then, finally, he sagged down to the floor, taking Victor with him, both of them tangled up completely in each other.

Heaving breaths, they sprawled together, Victor still half on Randall's lap. He could see the darkening skin on Randall's neck from his bite, could feel the ache on his own from Randall's teeth. And Randall, eyes half shut, had his head tipped back, grinning at absolutely nothing. Or rather, at everything all at once.

"God, that was good," Randall murmured, running his hands up and down Victor's back absently. "You okay?"

"Absolutely," Victor replied, stretching his arms out from where they were still hooked around Randall's shoulders. He felt more satisfied than he could remember feeling in recent memory. The ache was perfect; everything that Randall had said was perfect. He leaned in and gently kissed one of the forming bruises on Randall's throat.

From outside there came the faint sound of a car door slamming shut and then a voice that Victor had not expected—Jed. He frowned, hearing Redford's voice a second later, then Anthony's.

"Apparently Jed and Redford have shown up to spend the full moon with you," he said, though he supposed Randall would have heard it much more clearly. Victor kissed the bruise again, reluctant to let Randall leave. He was warm and comfortable on Randall's lap. He didn't want to move.

"I smell them," Randall said, voice low, a rough tug to each of his words. He was busy sucking the bruises he'd left behind, laving the skin with his tongue. "Redford's excited to run." He seemed much less concerned with the prospect of moving very far from this spot, turning them over, Victor sprawled out on the floor, Randall hitching Victor's legs around his hips. "I'm excited for this."

Victor had to take a moment to contemplate exactly how lucky he was. He didn't take *too* long, though, because he was much more interested in grasping Randall's hips in encouragement. "That makes two of us, then."

Two rounds later—once on the floor, Randall pinning Victor's hands above his head and fucking him so hard that they'd wound up six feet away from where they'd started, and the second time with Victor pressed against the wall, Randall behind him, and probably a whole line of bruises down his back from Randall's eager bites—they finally stumbled out into the yard. Jed was sprawled out with Redford in the grass, an already shifted Edwin happily chasing a stick that Jed kept throwing for him. Randall was holding Victor's hand, jeans slung low on his hips, shirtless. It was pointless to get fully dressed, he'd explained, since he was just going to be taking them all off again.

And it nicely showed off his new marks, which Victor suspected might have had a bit more to do with the wardrobe choice. Evidently Randall got possessive on the full moons.

They apparently smelled very strongly of sex, from the way Redford wrinkled his nose at their approach. He was obviously holding back from shifting too, his face having taken on a more wolfish expression while he sat with Jed.

"I thought it was polite to call *before* one shows up at someone's house," Victor greeted, with no real bite to his tone. Two months ago he would have been irritated to see Jed. Now he felt... well, he still didn't have any inclination to be his best friend. But the man felt like family, in a strange way.

"Princess." Jed nodded, sprawled across Redford's lap. Redford lifted a hand in a welcoming wave. Jed was sporting his own bites, reddened skin easily seen above the neck of his T-shirt. He grinned widely, starting to laugh. "Welcome to the club."

"Thank you," Victor said dryly, lowering himself to sit against one of the low stone walls that surrounded the gardens. It was at times like this he was thankful for the tall fences surrounding his property and the sheer size of the lawns. Even if someone did, somehow, get a glimpse through the fences, all they would see of the wolves in the low light was vaguely dog-like shapes.

As soon as Victor sat, Anthony appeared with an exasperated rumble directed at Randall and then Redford, who looked to Jed. "I'm going to head out," Redford said. "Is that okay?"

Jed ran his fingers along Redford's jaw, leaning in to kiss him. "Don't have to ask me," he said lowly. His hands went to lift the dog tags from Redford's neck and place them around his own. The same was done with the bracelet Redford wore, the blue scarab from Cairo. "I'm going to be out here for a while yet. Probably will bunk down in the car. If you want me, you know how to find me, okay?"

"You will not be sleeping in your *car*," Victor said, appalled at the idea. "If you're staying the night, you're staying in the house."

Jed looked vaguely surprised when he turned to look at Victor. "You sure?" Jed's gaze flicked to Randall and then to where Edwin was chasing circles around Anthony. "Already got a full house. We just needed a safe place for Red to run, and he wanted to be with some other wolves. You don't need to give me a bed too."

"I'm not asking you to *move in*. It's just for the night so you don't freeze in your car." Victor waved a hand back at the mansion. "Do you really think it'll be crowded in there?"

Jed gave the house an appraising look, absently running his fingers through Redford's hair. "I've seen bigger." He smirked, but he nodded his thanks too. Kissing Redford's shoulder, Jed asked him, "That okay? Me inside for the night?"

"That's fine," Redford reassured. "Just try not to break all of Victor's antiques when you get bored."

"No promises." They stood, hand in hand, Jed watching over Redford with a gruff kind of protectiveness.

Randall sat next to Victor, scooting closer, lips brushing against Victor's shoulder, his jaw. "Come out," he asked lowly. "Just for a little while. You can spend some of the moon with me."

Victor glanced down at the shoes he'd put on—they would hopefully be adequate enough for a bit of running around. He stood too, as Redford started shifting next to Jed. It still looked painful and slow, but not nearly as much as it once had been. "Maybe I'll have to get a bit fitter so I can keep up with you on full moons," Victor mused to Randall.

"I think you kept up with me just fine," Randall murmured, brushing a kiss across Victor's lips, smiling. "Or do I need to remind you?"

Laughing softly against Randall's lips, Victor swatted his shoulder. "Oh no, no reminders will be needed."

"Get a room, you two," Jed called. He'd knelt by Redford, rubbing his hands through his fur, smirking when Redford returned the favor by licking his cheek. "Or, better yet, don't. I don't need to see Victor looking any happier. I might get cavities."

Rolling his eyes, Randall dropped his pants, neatly folded them, and left them behind on the stone wall. His turn was graceful, the sweep of fur over skin, the shift of muscles and bone to a longer, lean lupine form. When he was on four paws instead of two legs, Randall shook his fur out and trotted back to Victor to nudge his head against Victor's leg.

Victor raked his fingers through the thick fur at Randall's nape. "Shall I run?" he asked, bemused at the prospect. He had no idea how far he'd be able to run, but he was certainly willing to try.

Barking quickly, Randall crouched, forelegs flat on the ground with his tail in a playful wag. Though Victor still wasn't an expert on wolf body language, he'd picked up a few things from his time in the pack. That was definitely an invitation to go play.

"I should invest in a Frisbee," Jed said, half to himself, watching as Redford loped off in the direction Edwin and Anthony had gone.

"I don't think a Frisbee would last very long, with a wolf catching it," Victor huffed. He tugged at Randall's fur again, inhaled a deep breath, and took off toward the trees at a run. Randall was at his heels, then racing ahead of him, a dappled blur against the ground, before rounding back toward him. Tail wagging furiously, Randall kept pace beside him, tongue lolling from one side of his mouth. They headed under the trees, Randall breaking away to dart after a squirrel and then coming back again, seemingly not bothered at all by Victor's slower pace.

They came to a clearing, the brook that fed Victor's small pond rushing over rocks, barely deep enough to even wade through. But Randall splashed in the water anyway, with a strange huffing sound that Victor took to mean a laugh. And then they were off again, Victor trying to keep up with Randall's seemingly endless energy.

An hour later, he reluctantly had to call it quits, and hugged Randall before making his way back to the mansion on wobbly legs. He heard Anthony howl, and then Randall did the same as they located each other. Randall took off once he'd made sure Victor was back on the lawn of the house. In the semidark he was barely more than a shadow. Victor realized how very, very slowly Randall must have been going to accommodate him, and yet, he'd never once appeared as though he was anything but thrilled with their tramp through the woods. He'd even found a branch with a few faded blooms, the last of the late summer blush of color, and brought it to Victor, clamped between his teeth.

Victor carried that branch with him as he got inside. He passed by the kitchen, where Jed had his head stuck in the fridge. "I'm going to get some sleep," Victor said, taking his glasses off to wearily rub his eyes. "Do you need anything before I go? The rooms in the hallway to the left of here have made-up beds."

"Carb load" was Jed's response. He came out of the fridge with half a chicken and a bottle of beer. Victor honestly didn't remember purchasing *beer*, but Edwin had carted in several bags the other day. Perhaps he'd added to the shopping list a little. For some reason, Edwin and Anthony didn't appreciate wine. Either that, or Jed had some strange, magical ability to produce beer out of thin air simply by wishing it. "And protein. Oh, if you can get a nap in earlier in the day, preferably before one-ish? That helps. Pretty much once you hit afternoon, you're done for."

Victor stopped on the verge of a dry remark and instead watched Jed putter around the kitchen for a moment. "When I first met you, I had no idea that you would one day be giving *me* advice on how to deal with a supernatural species," he said, rather bemused at the situation.

Jed grunted. "Not telling you their history, or whatever fancy-pants stuff you study, professor. Just sayin', I nearly got killed from sex the first few moons. You kind of think it's going to be all nighttime furry howling, but Red seems to start getting jittery in the afternoon, and apparently part of that is wanting to fuck my brains out and mark me up as much as he can. He says it's like he feels like he needs to *claim* me." Jed grinned as he found bread and butter, making himself a chicken sandwich. "Not that I'm complaining. Just thought I'd share the wisdom."

Victor grimaced. "Thank you for your specificity." He hardly needed to be told that now, anyway. He knew it quite well.

Jed arranged pickles on the bread. The grin had turned into a contemplative frown. "You, uh." He cleared his throat, shifting his weight a little from foot to foot. "You seem happy," Jed finally managed in a rough growl, shoulders ticked upward uncomfortably. "Especially since the last time I saw you with someone. Just... you know, just saying. You seem happier now than you were."

Victor suppressed a groan. There were few things more awkward in his life than Jed attempting to talk about such things, but he did appreciate it on some level. It was hard for Jed too, and the very fact that he was attempting the conversation meant a great deal.

"I am happy," he said simply. "I found a way to reconcile my insight of the future with the present. I'm still working on some issues regarding my own bloodline and the craving for knowledge without caring about the danger, but it's going well. Randall and I are dating, and we're determined to move at a normal pace." Victor paused, thinking back over his summary. "Is that enough information so that we can cease having this conversation?"

"God, yes," Jed managed in relief. "I hate that shit." Turning, he gave Victor a short smirk. "Can I make fun of you for having nerd sex, now?"

In response, Victor tugged down the collar of his shirt, showing Jed the ring of bitten bruises around his neck. "Does this look like the result of nerd sex to you?"

Jed laughed at that, raising his beer to Victor in cheers. "Well done, princess."

There was a long, drawn-out howl, and both of them turned to the window, peering out over the rapidly darkening lawn. They searched the woods, Victor's heart pounding a bit louder, until they saw a streak of blond fur, Edwin darting out of the trees and then back in again. No immediate signs of danger.

They relaxed, and Victor sighed as he realized he wasn't feeling tired enough to sleep. He went to the fridge, absently listening to Jed mutter to himself about bells and emergency plans. Victor looked over the frankly ridiculous amounts of food in his fridge. Jed's voice had started to grow quieter. Victor tilted his head in Jed's direction, trying to listen better.

Everything was getting quieter.

Victor's heart gave a beat so hard it felt like it had the force to break ribs. "Jed," he managed, clutching the side of the fridge. He had no idea what was happening. He'd been looking at *food*, not at anybody's eyes. "Jed, I think I'm about to have a vision."

"What the—" He dimly heard the clatter of things falling, the distinctive crash of a plate breaking. But when Victor fell backward, Jed caught him, arms circling around him and easing him back toward the floor. "Talk to me, Victor. What the fuck is going on? You didn't see me. I know we didn't. I wouldn't do that to you. What is…."

His voice seemed to trail off, but Victor vaguely recognized it wasn't that Jed had stopped speaking, but rather his own hearing had shut off completely. He opened his mouth to try to reply, but no words came out.

His eyes *burned*, and then….

Nothing. A black expanse of absolutely nothing, a void that stretched on for an infinity. A nothingness that made Victor want to weep from the lack of warmth, light, and feeling.

Flame flickered at the corners of his vision—not around him, but seemingly in his eyes. They didn't hurt anymore. He blinked, and the flame spread over his eyelids while the void seemed to stretch and expand, flexing while somehow moving him.

There were things in the background that Victor couldn't see. Strings, much like the future threads he saw, that started from blackness and ended in blackness, too massive for him to see the beginning and end. Whispers reached his ears, terrible howls from the darkness.

One of the voices started to become more audible. It was a murmur at first, vibrating around one of the threads. Then it rose in volume until it became the piercing shriek of a wind that whipped at Victor from all sides, and the only thing that was important was listening.

Victor felt his body move, his hand casting about for something. Jed's arms shifted, though Victor couldn't hear him speak.

The howling voice rose to a fevered pitch, repeating its words.

Victor had no pen and paper. Instead, he touched his fingers to the warmth he could feel coming from his eyes. Slowly, he shifted from Jed's grip, sightless gaze fixing on the kitchen floor.

He began to write with red, bloody smears over white kitchen tile.

And once he was done, the voice stopped, seemingly soothed by the physical recording of the words.

His job finished, Victor pitched forward to land next to his writing, unconsciousness rising up to greet him like a familiar friend.

CHAPTER
20

Jed

OKAY, SEE, werewolves he could handle. Vampires, fine, whatever. All this crazy half blood, *the truth is out there* shit, Jed had made some kind of peace with. But this? This was bleeding from the eyes, seizing, writing messages in blood, *freaky-ass shit*. And it was *not okay*.

Holding Victor as he finally passed out, Jed stared blankly at the message he'd scrawled, wondering what the fuck he was supposed to do now.

> *When the Walker comes,*
> *Dark of eye and light of skin,*
> *From which blood flows,*
> *And blood denied,*
> *When the Walker comes,*
> *When solitude turns to many,*
> *The sword will be gained,*
> *Battle ne'er ceasing shall find its end,*
> *When the Walker comes,*
> *Raven's cry shall be o'er heard,*
> *Stones shall line the footpaths,*
> *And the flames from ashes rise,*
> *When the Walker comes,*
> *The lion's roar shall be silenced,*
> *The lamb's cry shall shatter bones,*
> *And the old ways shall be new again,*
> *When the Walker comes.*

The words were small, streaky, some of them only half-legible. Honestly, Jed had to resist the urge to swipe his foot across the whole damn thing and turn it into nothing more than a smudge. Because whatever the hell freaky-ass shit was going on here? Was not his department. At all.

Yeah, they were definitely going to table that discussion. Who the fuck knew what any of that meant, and right now, he had an unconscious Victor in his arms, blood a drying streak against his cheeks. So Jed hefted him up and carried Victor to the closest bedroom, cursing under his breath the whole time.

"Couldn't do your freaky *Exorcist* routine when someone else was here, could you?" Jed muttered, depositing Victor onto the bed and studying the man, hands on his hips. "Oh, no, Victor goddamn Rathbone has to pull that shit while everyone else is four legged and furry. Just fucking great."

Jed was going to kick someone's ass for this. He didn't know *who* yet, but an ass was definitely getting a kick.

After finding a rag and running it under warm water, Jed carefully cleaned off Victor's face, searching for a wound in his eyes. There didn't appear to be any obvious reason for the blood. Then again, there probably wasn't an *obvious* reason for any of this. People didn't bleed from the eyes just for shits and giggles.

Jed shone a flashlight into Victor's pupils, doing his best to look while not actually meeting them directly. Harder than it sounded, but in the end, Jed was pretty sure Victor didn't have a concussion or anything. He was just his normal, freaky self.

Fan-fucking-tastic.

A howl rose in the distance, the sound of it setting Jed's nerves on edge. Shit, he recognized the tone to that. That was a *something's wrong* howl, except it was getting closer. He had no idea how far wolves could smell—could one of them have smelled the blood from all the way out there?

There was the clatter of paws on the porch and then a *thud*, a heavy body physically throwing itself at the front door. Rolling his eyes, Jed headed out after giving Victor one last look. "Don't move," he told Victor. Probably unnecessarily.

When he opened the door, Randall streaked in, already half shifted. "What happened?" Randall demanded as soon as he could talk again. "Where's Victor?"

Randall's bare feet skidded to a halt in the kitchen, his nostrils flaring at the sight of blood. It wasn't just making creepy words on the floor, it was in odd streaks along the edge of the verse too, where Victor had braced bloody hands on the tile to keep his balance. Basically, it was a horror show, and probably not the best thing for Randall to stumble into. Eyes glowing yellow, a protective growl rumbling in his chest, Randall rounded on Jed. Jed was slammed back against the wall with an arm across his throat before he even had time to form words.

"Where is Victor?" Randall barked, teeth bared. "Tell me *right now*."

"He's in the bedroom. Jesus," Jed snapped, shoving Randall back. "He had a fit. I just got him cleaned up and—"

Okay, apparently they were done talking. Randall took off, thudding through the hallway and banging open doors, finding Victor where Jed had left him. Jed followed at a distance, fingers itching for the gun he'd left in his bag. *Stupid*, Walker. Never go anywhere without a weapon. Just fucking stupid. He was going soft.

Randall was sniffing Victor. Okay. Weird. But whatever he scented seemed to calm him marginally. Randall sat on the edge of the bed, holding Victor's hand, studying his face with worried eyes. After a beat, he ventured, "I… apologize. I just…. I smelled the blood, and I couldn't think."

Jed inclined his head. "Don't worry about it," he allowed grudgingly. "Probably would have done the same."

Randall hefted an eyebrow at him.

Jed amended, "Okay, definitely. And worse. So don't worry. I think he's fine."

"He's unconscious," Randall confirmed. "But I can't smell anything seriously wrong. My nose isn't as good as Edwin's, but I agree, I think he's okay." A frown puckered Randall's face, and he turned to Jed. "Did you meet his eyes? What happened?"

Shrugging, Jed went to the closet, rifling through what looked like a thousand years of bad clothing choices stored away before he found a drawer with what appeared to be old-man pajama sets. He tossed a pair of the pants at Randall, who gratefully tugged them on. "Don't know," Jed answered, arms folded. "One second we're talking, he's looking through the fridge, the next he's convulsing and writing shit in his own blood."

"Was he hurt?" Randall's fingers were combing lightly through Victor's hair. "I mean, I don't see a cut or—"

"His eyes." Jed grimaced faintly. "He was bleeding from his eyes."

Randall made a soft noise, somewhere between distress and something else, before he looked up at Jed. "There's a book, on the nightstand in my room. Third door on the left on the second floor. Can you get it for me, please?"

"You think reading to him will help?" Jed snorted, confused.

"No, but I think I might know what happened," Randall responded, a slight bite of impatience to his words. "And I'd go myself, but I don't want to leave him. So please, Jed. The book."

The sounds of a few more sets of paws came from the door, and Redford looked worried when he trotted in, though he gave a soft chuff of relief when he saw Jed. Redford didn't change back, but he did budge himself against Jed's legs, looking up at him questioningly. Edwin came howling in right behind him, still in wolf form, circling his brother in obvious concern before hopping up onto the bed and burying his nose in Victor's neck, his chest, snuffling around for several moments. Apparently he came to the same conclusion Jed and Randall had, because he collapsed in relief, nose resting on Victor's chest, eyes flicking from Victor's face up to Randall with a soft whine.

Anthony was last, back on two legs and in jeans. He was already frowning as he came in; he'd probably seen the kitchen. "What the hell happened?"

Nodding his head at Redford and Anthony, Jed headed out and toward the stairs. They followed, Redford close on his heels. "Fit. Blood, writing on the floor, crazy freaky-ass motherfucking shit. I don't know. Did you see?" The kitchen floor—or, more specifically, what Victor had scrawled there—was going to bug him.

"I saw." Anthony sounded as disturbed as Jed felt. "Did he do that after looking at you? What kind of weird things are in your head that would make him do *that*?"

"That's the crazy thing." Jed paused at the foot of the stairs, gaze darting back at the room, voice lowering. "He wasn't even near me when it started. Look, I'm careful around the guy. The princess is okay, sure, but I don't want him getting a free tour of Jed town, you know?" Jed tapped the side of his head with two fingers, raising his eyebrows. "So I make sure. But he was facing the whole fucking *other direction*. So it wasn't me."

He didn't like this. Life was weird enough without adding blood-written messages from the great beyond. Hesitating, voice dipping even quieter, Jed asked, "Do you think this is what it looks like? When snake people go crazy?"

Anthony exhaled slowly. "I have no idea," he replied, voice just as low. "But I hope not." The *for Randall's sake* was hanging there, unspoken. Jed got it. It would suck to tell the kid his boyfriend was probably going nuts. Then again, Jed wasn't sure Randall wasn't already thinking the same thing.

"He, uh, asked me for a book. Randall. Apparently he thinks he has an idea what happened." Jed gestured vaguely in the direction of the second floor. "I'll be right back." Though apparently he was not going to go alone. Redford and Anthony were right on his heels, Redford bumping up against his legs with every other step.

Randall's room was almost obsessively neat. Jed couldn't resist the urge to move pillows out of place, to disorganize the neat pile of books on the desk. There was only one tome on the nightstand, however, and Jed picked it up, flipping through it before grimacing. "It's in German," he sighed. "I hate German. Took me forever to get down the basics." And he'd probably forgotten most of it. He used to be able to order food, order sex, and pay for both. Oh, and *shoot here*, that was one of the first things he learned in whatever language they'd taught him. *Fire* and *kill* and *don't piss over there, there's snakes*. The important stuff.

Anthony took the book from Jed. From the way he frowned at it, he understood even less German than Jed. "Did Randall say what it was about?"

"Answers, I hope." Though what kind of *answers* could be found in some dusty old book in a foreign language, Jed didn't know. Unless it was the big German book of *my boyfriend is a creepy motherfucker who bleeds from his eyes and has fits, volume one*.

They headed back downstairs to find Randall hadn't moved at all. He was just sitting patiently, holding Victor's hand. With the moonlight streaming in the window and Edwin on the bed, just for a moment, Jed thought it looked like a picture in one of the fairy tale books his mom had read to him as a kid.

But then Randall turned toward them, Edwin got up to whine in their direction, and Jed shook off the cobweb of a memory, leaving it behind. "Here," he grunted, passing Randall the book. "What's it about?"

"It tells a story," Randall said, frowning as he paged through the book. "I think I translated it wrong originally. It's one of those weird lines that could mean one of a few things, depending, and I had put it aside to work on more later."

Jed leaned against the wall. Redford, his constant shadow in wolf form, rested against his legs, tail thumping a few times against the floor when Jed rubbed his hand behind Redford's ears. Anthony looked exhausted, and he checked his watch as he sat down, grimacing at the time.

"Got somewhere to be, Lassie?" Jed looked half-asleep, he knew, eyes barely opened. But he studied Anthony carefully, noticing the stiffness in his gait, the way he changed positions a few times, obviously trying to get comfortable.

"I've got my final hospital appointment in the morning." Anthony looked guilty for saying it, like he felt bad for mentioning he had shit to do while Victor was having a situation. He didn't say anything further than that, but he didn't need to—with the full moon making him too hyped up to sleep, and now Victor being creepy, none of them would probably get much rest tonight. And Jed knew from hard-earned experience that being in a hospital when you were exhausted was one of the most annoying things he'd ever had to do.

"Here." Randall cleared his throat, glancing up at all of them. "It's talking about witches. Or rather, what they thought were witches. Um, okay, here." His finger slid under the words, and Randall read with a slight pause before each word, working out the translation. "They were brought to the pyre, one after the other, the ones who saw what they should not know. The witches were brought forth, and we knew them by the red of their eyes."

"So…. Victor's a witch?" Anthony sounded just as confused as Jed was.

"No. He's a medusa. That's what I'm saying. I was having trouble here, because they keep talking about the *red eyes*, but I think they mean blood. These were beings convicted of witchcraft because they had visions. They saw things, the end of battles, of regimes, and when they prophesied against the royal family at the time, they were hauled out and executed." Randall pointed to the book, as if suddenly Jed was going to grow a German-speaking gene and be able to see what he was talking about. "They accused them of witchcraft because that's what they thought. But it's medusas. I'm sure of it."

"So how come Victor's never mentioned this?" Anthony glanced between Victor and Randall. "He told us about looking into people's eyes, but, you know, 'I might get visions and turn my kitchen floor red' is pretty big."

"Because this is literally the only mention of it I've found in three days of research." Randall shook his head, flipping through the pages of the book. "It was not common, even back then. And prophecies now are… well, they aren't. The last mention of a true prophecy in any form that I've ever seen is something like a hundred and fifty years ago. And in this country? Forget it. Revolutionary war was the last time anyone recorded any kind of seeing. I really don't think he knew, because none of the prophecies are ever linked to a specific species. They're simply recorded as *from the seer*."

"So what makes you think—" Jed started.

"Because I've been reading everything on medusas I can get my hands on," Randall cut him off, voice quickening in his urgency. "I know how they're talked about now. They're a secretive race. There's barely any direct documentation of the half bloods."

"So that's a *prophecy* on the kitchen floor?" Anthony dragged a hand over his face, obviously not quite believing it. "I saw something written about a battle. You think it's something to do with that war Victor saw from the Gray Lady?"

"Either that or we've stocked up on them at Shitstorms R Us." Jed sighed. "Okay. So, do we need to… write it down?" What the fuck did someone even *do* with a goddamn *prophecy*? "Are there crazy people authorities we need to contact? A who's who of freaky shit?"

Anthony pushed himself out of his chair with a faint grunt, then briefly rested a hand on Randall's shoulder. "I'll go take pictures, write it down, that sort of thing. After that, I…." Anthony paused, apologetic. "I'll need to get some rest if I'm going to be moving around at all tomorrow. Will you and Victor be okay?"

"We're fine." Randall nodded. "I'll stay with him. You go sleep."

"We'll drive you in the morning," Jed said. That decided, he kicked away from the wall, whistling lowly. "Come on, Eddie, Fido, let's go do some more laps before bedtime." He was fucking exhausted, but if he didn't take at least Edwin for one more walkie before he hit the hay, God knew the kid would be bouncing off walls all night.

Edwin and Redford had chased each other around for a few hours. Jed had lasted all of one before he'd spread out on the grass, dozing lightly, one ear cocked for trouble. By the time the wolves were done with their gallivanting, Jed was half-asleep. Both Edwin and Redford had collapsed on him in a happy pile of waving tails and tongues, and Jed had managed to drag them all into the house to finally fall face-first into a bed.

The morning came far too early. Jed and Randall organized everyone getting ready, showering, breakfast, the whole nine yards. Turned out that Jed's master skills in cereal pouring and Randall's quickness getting the coffee and tea up and going were a match made in heaven. They had everyone fed and out the door just in time to make the drive to the hospital.

And then came the waiting. Anthony had been whisked back behind double doors, leaving them all marooned in a waiting room, the sterile antiseptic stink forcing the wolves into trying to breathe through their mouths. There was the squeak of shoes in the hallway beyond, the low murmur of overly cheery voices on some annoying daytime talk show, things that should have felt normal but didn't, not at all. Even the paintings, generic landscapes and one of a boat on calm seas, only served to underscore how *wrong* it was to be there. How unnatural to shove someone into a box like this.

Jed fucking hated hospitals.

Victor, at least, had managed to wake up in time to come with them. Jed had heard him and Randall talking, with Randall trying to insist that Victor should stay where he was, but if Jed knew anything about Victor, it was that he was stubborn. He was pale now, slumped in the waiting room seat, a far cry from his usual proper stance.

"I suppose I'm going to have to clean all the blood off the kitchen, if we ever want to cook there again," Victor sighed. Jed saw him take Randall's hand. "I'm so sorry, Randall. I apparently have terrible timing. You should be focusing on your brother."

"It's fine." Randall kissed his cheek, leaning his forehead against Victor's temple. "I'll take care of it when we get back. I sprayed some bleach on it last night, before we went to sleep. It'll come right up with a good scrubbing."

Jed traded a look with Redford. Sometimes, Jed just had to reflect on how fucking weird his life had gotten, sitting next to a wolf and a medusa while they casually talked about cleaning the blood a fucking prophecy had been written in off the floor. Then again, at least the whole discussion on mop-up techniques for dried blood was one he had intimate knowledge of.

"Milk," Jed announced, leaning over toward them. "Sounds weird, but it works. Dab some on the stains and let it set for a bit before you start to scrub. A rust remover too, if the stain's set in."

"You're right, that *is* weird," Victor said wryly. "But thank you."

"So...." Jed glanced around, but no one else seemed willing to ask the question. Fuck it, he would. "What's up with you going crazy?"

Victor snorted a soft laugh. "I'm just thankful I *didn't*, actually." He seemed to tighten his grip on Randall's hand. There was a tenseness to his expression, a faint wrinkle between his eyebrows that spoke to how rattled he was by the experience, even if he wasn't saying it out loud. "I had no clue such a thing even happened to medusas. But Randall has shown me what he found, and it makes sense. I suppose now we have to...."

He trailed off, shaking his head.

"Don't say it," Jed warned.

"We'll have to figure out the prophecy," Victor concluded. "Yes, Jed, I am entirely aware of how fantasy-novel that sounds."

"Well, Princess von Smalldickton—" Jed scowled. "—unless the prophecy fairies are *paying* me to solve their little riddle, I'm out. I don't chase after roads that go fucking nowhere. Not unless someone is footing the bill."

"I think perhaps you most of all should pay attention to this," Victor said mildly. He didn't look directly at Jed, but the stare felt just the same as if he had. "There are some clues in the words I wrote. Walker. Blood flowing—you are involved in quite a bit of violence. Blood denied could point to you dating outside your species, or your family that you never talk about."

"You think that prophecy is about *Jed?*" Redford said in shock.

Victor made a contemplative noise. "Perhaps. There are certainly signs pointing that way."

Jed waited for the inevitable punch line. This was one of Victor's little jokes that Jed never caught because he wasn't a goddamn prissy nerd. Any moment now, he'd do that little snorting chuckle of *aren't I so English and clever* and Jed could roll his eyes and they'd move on. But instead there was just uncomfortable silence, Randall staring decidedly at the floor, Edwin pretending as though he was very interested in a magazine about women's health.

Finally, Jed actually had to say something. Because this was ridiculous. "You scrambled your goddamn brains, princess," Jed growled. "There might be a lot of things you can say about me. But none of it is going to be in some freaky shit prophecy. Not unless it's a dirty limerick."

"Well, I certainly won't jump to conclusions." Victor leaned back in his seat. "But I do have to ask, just in case. Do you know how to use a sword?"

Jed's eyes narrowed. "To chop off your tiny dick? Yeah, I think I've got a penknife around somewhere I can swing with enough force." Asshole.

Victor just smirked. "Perhaps you should look into lessons."

"Keep talking, professor." Jed rolled his eyes, since Victor had, thankfully, decided to veer off the serious talk about Jed being some kind of foretold hero or whatever. "Maybe the whole thing was about you, huh? You're the one who wrote it down. Isn't that a saying? He who smelt it has to carry the giant sword of destiny."

He felt Redford crowd in close against his shoulder. "It could be about anyone," Redford said, though he didn't sound too sure.

Jed turned to him, eyebrows raised in surprise. "Don't tell me you're falling for this malarkey too."

"No," Redford said defensively. He looked at Jed, and then his shoulders sagged. "I don't know. There has to be a reason that Victor got the vision, and not a medusa over on the other side of the world."

"Why should that matter?" Jed was now looking around the room, searching for *someone* who was still damn sane. "Hell, maybe he's supposed to post it on some website for freaks. Whatever he does, it's *not* about *me*, okay? I don't do swords, I don't... hell, I don't even know what it was *saying*."

"Yes, all right Jed, we know," Victor muttered. "Do try to keep your voice down. This is a hospital. We'll figure everything out later."

"What *does* it say?" Edwin finally decided to join in from where he was curled up in a chair, across from Jed and Redford. "I mean, I read it. It sounded like a bunch of gibberish. Maybe it doesn't mean anything at all."

"I bled from the eyes and wrote that damn thing out on my nice, clean kitchen floor. I'll be very cranky if it's meaningless gibberish," Victor replied with a scowl. "As best I can tell, it's about someone that must take up a sword to stop a battle. There's mention of several animals, possibly in reference to people or maybe just symbols. There'll be clues in the wording of it. I'll just have to study it closer."

Before Jed could point out that it was entirely possible Victor had intercepted an advertisement for a zoo opening and this whole thing was just the result of metal tooth fillings, the double doors swung open and Anthony's doctor walked out. Jed already knew this was going to be bad. There was a *look* doctors got, a particular kind of grimness they hid behind a professional smile. But it was there. And this guy had it all over.

"Are you the Lewises?" The doctor moved forward, holding out his hand for Randall to shake when Randall stood and nodded. "I'm Dr. Medena. Why don't you come with me?"

Jed wanted to offer to hang back, but they were all swept up and escorted through the hallway. Edwin was pressed close to Redford, Randall was holding Victor's hand, and apparently, in that moment, they were all going to be goddamn Lewises.

The office they were taken to was as coldly clinical as the rest of them, though the doctor had clearly attempted to offset that with personal knickknacks on his desk. Anthony was seated in the chair across from the desk, and he gave them all a wan smile when they crowded into the small room. "I seem to have collected three more brothers."

"Sorry," Redford said awkwardly. "We can go if—"

"No, you can stay if you like," Anthony replied. "I'd like that."

"Yeah, well, you needed a good-looking brother, so Redford and I stepped in." Jed collapsed into one of the chairs, hauling Redford to perch on his knee. Edwin stayed standing, while Randall insisted Victor take the only remaining seat.

Dr. Medena barely seemed to notice the crowd of them in his office. He sat behind his desk and shuffled some papers, then looked up at them. "We're down to two options," he finally announced, "and it's entirely up to Anthony, although he knows which one I'd strongly suggest. Without treatment, the illness would continue to get worse and he would deteriorate quickly. That option would leave him with about two years left."

There was a long, aching beat of silence. Jed, watching the Lewises, could see Randall suddenly deflate. It looked like someone had punched the guy in the stomach. All the color drained from his face, his jaw working as if to swallow back some horrible noise of pain. Edwin didn't move. He was standing by the doorway, half looking like he wanted to bolt, but, foot stuck in a trap, he was frozen. A look of pure anguish on his face, Edwin ducked his head, clearly trying to hold it together.

"You said there was another choice," Jed interjected gruffly, keeping one eye on Randall and Edwin. "Let me guess, we're going to like that one better?"

He saw Dr. Medena look quickly at Anthony, then back at them. "With treatment, we've had a lot of success in other wolves with canine Parkinson's. There would be some side effects, and it would never fully cure the condition, but it can be managed."

Jed noticed Anthony didn't particularly seem to like that option, though he couldn't take a guess as to why. The doctor continued, "The treatment would slow down the progression of the disease. We could help Anthony manage his pain, and if we're lucky, he'd be able to return to some aspects of his life. A part-time job, maybe."

"So why are we talking about this?" Randall asked hoarsely. "Anthony, you have to take the treatment."

"It'd dull my senses," Anthony muttered. "He said it might make it difficult for me to even *turn*."

"You know what else makes that difficult?" Jed said bluntly. "Being *dead*." After all this time, all the things they'd tried, Jed could not believe Anthony would sit here and start having second thoughts.

"It really is the best option," Dr. Medena said, clearly trying to school his voice into some sort of soothing tone. "It would add decades to your life expectancy if you don't push yourself too hard."

Anthony let out a short, explosive exhale. He scrubbed his hands through his hair and seemed to fold in on himself. "Fine," he said quietly. "Okay, I'll do the treatment."

Edwin threw himself at Anthony, practically knocking him over in a hug. "It's okay," Edwin was whispering fiercely. "I'll smell everything for you, I promise. And I'll go running with you no matter what. Okay? Just don't die."

Anthony put his arms around Edwin. He still didn't look happy, and Jed had no problem admitting he had no fucking clue what the issue was. Two years of pain versus decades of management didn't even sound like a choice to him.

"We'll get you started on the treatment right away, then," Dr. Medena said. He stood from his chair, getting some folders in order. "It's a regimen of pills, so you won't have to be in and out of the hospital much. Though I would advise you to come in for regular checkups, just in case we need to change the dosage around."

"Should we worry about any other side effects?" Randall looked like he wanted to fall over, like stress was just eating him alive, but he'd pulled out a little notebook that Jed could see was already half filled with a messy scrawl. "If you could just tell me any instructions I might need."

They sat with the doctor for a while longer, Randall asking questions, writing everything down, and Anthony looking increasingly more miserable. Jed honestly didn't understand. Yeah, it wasn't a cure, but at least it wasn't as big of a death sentence as Anthony had been walking around with. And any kind of pain relief had to be welcome.

As they walked out to the van in uncomfortable silence, Jed just kept looking over at Anthony, utterly confused. Maybe it just hadn't sunk in yet. "Hey," Jed tried, giving him a light punch in the shoulder. "At least you're not going to croak anytime soon. That's got to be a relief, right?"

Everyone just stared at him blankly. Apparently that wasn't the best way to lighten the mood.

Jesus. And people wondered why Jed didn't do *families*.

Eventually, though, it did make Anthony smile, so that was something. "Yeah," he replied after a few moments of silence. "It's good news." He rubbed a hand over his eyes, his expression still numb somehow, like he hadn't really had the chance to think about everything. "I'm sorry. I'm being a buzzkill. How about tonight we all cook up a massive dinner and celebrate?"

"Are we going home?" Edwin asked. "I bet there's loads of rabbits out in our woods."

"Yeah, we'll drive back once we get everything packed again." Anthony clapped a hand to Victor's shoulder. "Want to come for the night? You too, Jed and Redford. Pack gathering."

"What, we've been adopted?" Jed smirked. But what he'd thought would be a joke turned into Edwin hugging him, grinning as he looped his arm through Redford's.

"Of course. I can take Redford hunting. There's this *awesome* spot out west of the lake."

"Maybe you and Anthony could go fishing for real, Jed," Randall suggested. "We'll have rabbit stew and baked fish for dinner. And some roasted vegetables, for the noncarnivores among us."

Anthony gave a low laugh. "Hey, Victor, maybe you can hunt the vegetables for us."

Victor sighed, a long-suffering sound. "As long as they don't fight back, I'm sure I can manage."

"So, family dinner tonight." Randall nodded, arm tightening around Victor's waist. "And you're all welcome to stay over. I know it's a long drive back." He gave Victor a low smile, kissing his shoulder. "You could make a weekend of it? We'll bring the research, get some work done, if you're worried about being productive."

Victor kissed Randall's cheek in affirmative; then they crowded into the van. The mood was a lot lighter on the drive back than it had been on the way there. Having a death sentence averted would do that. Anthony still seemed a little quiet, but both Randall and Edwin, as the news seemed to sink in, were starting to act like they'd gotten a stay of execution.

Packing didn't take long, though it did require three trips to load up all the books Randall and Victor insisted were *necessary*. And even though Jed pointed out that it was highly unlikely they'd leave the bed for days, much less do heavy reading, no one was willing to listen to him. He did insist that they stop by his and Redford's apartment to pick up Knievel. His princess might be fine for a few days on her own, but any more than that and she made him pay for it later. Like all spoiled cats, she demanded attention in regular intervals. Redford worried that they were overreaching, bringing the cat along, but Jed just packed her and her toys up in the cage, putting Edwin in charge of making sure she didn't get lost under the seats.

The trip to the Lewises' cabin was getting really goddamn familiar. By the time they got to the house, Jed was ready to stretch his legs.

After Edwin and Randall insisted that Anthony didn't need to do anything to help, Jed spotted Anthony slowly making his way to the edge of the lake. There were fishing poles lined up neatly in the mudroom of the house, and Jed grabbed three, along with a tackle box. Redford behind him, Jed headed toward the water, finding Anthony sitting on a long log that had been pulled up close to the lake's edge, obviously purposefully placed and secured.

Wordlessly handing Anthony one of the poles, Jed got himself settled and set about baiting his and Redford's hooks. He'd at least learned that much in the fishing books they'd gotten, and Anthony had all sorts of interesting things in the tackle box. No live worms, though. Jed still wasn't sure how one would go about getting those.

His cast was... not good at all. The first few times Jed didn't make it in the water. Redford got all tangled up in his line and nearly cut his palm open on the hook. Anthony finally took pity on them and showed them how to send their hooks flying out into the water. Not with nearly as much grace as Anthony showed, but at least they weren't impaling themselves.

Redford sat close to Jed, their shoulders pushed up against each other, and in the break between casts he grinned over at Jed. "At least we get to go fishing," he said.

"This is practice fishing," Jed allowed, tongue caught between his teeth in concentration as he arced the rod over his head and sent the line flying toward the middle of the lake. "Real fishing comes with sun and sand and drinks with umbrellas in them."

"And real *fish* come from mountain lakes, not sand," Anthony snorted. "What kind of fish would you even catch on a beach, Jed? Sharks?"

Jed blinked, thinking. "Ones that go good with rum-based drinks?"

"I may have to give you some more tips before you try fishing for real," Anthony replied, bemused.

"I got this postcard once." Jed was focused on watching the steady swell of his bobber as it floated above the light ripples of the lake. No bites yet. "I was seventeen, I'd just left home a year before, I don't know, I was young. Stupid. Living on the streets, doing whatever. They wouldn't let me enlist yet, so I had to kill time before I turned eighteen. Anyway, I found this postcard stuck in a grate near where I was holed up. It was winter and fucking cold, but the card had this picture of these two beach chairs, fishing pole stuck in the sand, palm trees, table with two drinks. And it just said *wish you were here*." Jed snorted, reeling in his line again for another try. "All I could think was 'yeah, well, me too, fucker.' But I kept it for a long time. Always wanted to do that."

After a second of silence, Jed felt Redford lean against his shoulder. Yeah, yeah. Caring and sharing time. "Anyway," he muttered gruffly, scowling out at the water. "Probably not so much about catching fish."

"Probably not." Anthony patted the shoulder that wasn't being taken up by Redford. "But you'll get your beach fishing eventually."

"Yeah." Jed cast again, watching the bobber make a wobbly arc back out to the water. "Think I just like the idea of being on the ocean. Been around it a lot, but most of the time I didn't get to just relax or anything." Hell, most of the time he'd get dropped in someplace in the dead of night or get carted in after three days with no real sleep, do his job, and get out again. Leisure time was kind of a new concept.

Anthony made a noise under his breath that sounded like a laugh—one that he hadn't wanted to give proper voice to, but had made its way out nonetheless. "Well, if you ever need a water fix, we've got a little dingy you can take out on the lake. Fishing isn't great anymore, but the water's still there. For now."

"What, you afraid it's going to run away?" Jed gave Anthony a sideways glance. "Didn't realize that lakes were that mobile."

"It's drying up slowly." Anthony cast his line out with a casual ease born of years of experience. "The fish are nearly gone, and this year the water level has gone down half a foot. There used to be someone here that tended to it, but without him"—Anthony shrugged—"it'll be gone in five or ten years."

"Why?" Jed reached out a leg and poked the toe of his boot in the water, as if he could somehow see it retreating. "I mean, is that even normal?"

"It misses him," Anthony said softly. "It got used to his company, and now that he's gone, it doesn't want to stay. I tried everything, but water isn't my expertise."

Okay, that didn't make any sense. Jed exchanged a quick glance with Redford, who looked just as baffled as him, before figuring he might as well ask. "What the fuck are you talking about?" As far as Jed knew, water didn't have *emotions*.

Anthony only looked at Jed quickly before he started laughing. "I'm sorry, Jed," he said, grinning ruefully. "That probably didn't make a lick of sense to you. There used to be someone that lived nearby that I used to see all the time when I was a kid. He was a half blood, a selkie, and whenever they live near water, the water prospers. But he had to leave, so it's like… giving a plant some really good soil and then switching it to sand. So the lake is drying up."

"So these sookie people, they make lakes grow?" Jed frowned, again looking over at Redford. "Did you know that?"

"I don't even know what a selkie *is*," Redford said, apologetic.

"It'd be a long explanation. But the mermaid myth came from selkies," Anthony explained. "They don't make lakes grow, they just…. I guess it's difficult to explain." Even though Jed was trying to wrangle his fishing line into doing what he wanted it to, he couldn't miss the way Anthony's voice took on an edge of nostalgia. "Vilhehn would come to the lake about once a week. We'd go out and swim in the middle of it, and he'd say things to the water, he'd sing. I never knew what he was saying. But every time, we'd catch an extra big fish for dinner, or the water wouldn't be so cold the next morning."

"That's your guy, right?" Jed settled in, legs kicked out in front of him, looping his free arm around Redford to play his fingers along his side. "That Vil whatever. He's the one who left?"

Anthony let out a slow breath. "Yeah," he replied. "He had to leave and I had to stay. It didn't work out."

"Want to talk about it?" Jed asked bluntly, figuring he wasn't going to pry if this would send Anthony off into some sort of crying fit. Or, worse, make him start hugging people.

"I pretty much just said everything there is to say." Anthony patted Jed on the shoulder. "It's a short, sad story that I do my best to not really think about most days."

"So that's it, then?" Seemed kind of like a raw deal to Jed. "You liked some guy a thousand years ago and you're just stuck?"

"I've tried to date," Anthony admitted. "About a year back, I had a two-month relationship. Before that I managed to stay in one for about three months. It's not like I'm literally physically unable to be with anybody else, it was just... well, nobody else ever came close."

Jed looked over at Redford, who was oddly silent, staring out over the water, just letting the conversation wash over him. "You should go after him," Jed pointed out quietly, his eyes on Redford. "It's always worth it to go after them."

Anthony was one of the most openly emotional people Jed had ever met. Every single thing he felt expressed itself on his face, so seeing him nearly blank now was a little disconcerting. For a brief moment, a horrible, sick look passed over Anthony's eyes, but then it was gone again. "I can't now," he said flatly. "The doctor said no exerting myself too much. No long travel. No hiking across the mountains to a beach that no airplane goes to."

Jed nodded, considering things. "Want me to find him?" he offered quietly, gaze returning to the water. "Can't say I've ever tracked down mer-dudes, but I'm not half bad at finding people who don't want to be found." Unless they were pain-in-the-ass vampires. "He should know, Ant. You know he should know."

"No, he shouldn't," Anthony said. "He has a different life now, things he needs to do for the sake of his people. He doesn't need to hear about some sick wolf halfway across the world."

"Look, I'm not Oprah or some shit. I don't know much about anything. And I'm not an expert. Just... if you wanted." Jed shrugged, uncomfortable. "I'd want to know. For the record. So would you."

"Maybe one day." Anthony started reeling his line in—the first of them to catch a fish so far. The fish that came out on the hook was so tiny that nobody would bother with it, but Anthony took it anyway.

Jed reached out to poke it, fascinated. "Are you going to eat it?" he wondered. And then, frowning, "What part is the fish stick?"

"I thought I might give it to Knievel," Anthony said, smiling a little. "And there's no actual *part* that's the fish stick. Fish sticks are disgusting."

Redford fidgeted beside Jed—Jed recognized that movement. Redford was trying to gather up the courage to say something. "Anthony, um," Redford said tentatively, "I just wanted to ask. You didn't seem too happy at the cure."

The smile dropped off Anthony's face. "It's stupid," he sighed. "I know it's stupid. I *am* happy. It'll be expensive, but we'll figure it out. It's just... the side effects. And what I'll need to do. My senses will be dulled. I won't be able to shift much, the doctor said. I can't run. It feels like I won't even be able to be who I am. I won't be a wolf, not really."

"You'll be alive," Jed pointed out. "Nothing else fucking matters, man. I've seen some shit. Guys blown apart in front of me, legs ripped off, eyes popping like grapes, and you get down to the core of it, *who you are* is *alive*. Everything else you figure out. You get a peg leg or you wear a fucking eye patch, whatever. Long as you're breathing in and out, that's what's important."

"I know." Anthony's shoulders had slumped, his head bowed. "I do know. I'm sorry. I probably seem like the biggest asshole in the world right now."

"Nope." Jed nudged his shoulder against Anthony. "You sound like a guy who just got his legs blown off. It sucks. And you get to be pissed about it, because it isn't fair. I'm just sayin', don't go too far down that road. It gets real dark, real fast."

And then he was engulfed in a one-armed hug. What the hell was it with Anthony and hugs?

"Thanks, Jed. For everything." Anthony squeezed him tighter.

"You're a freak," Jed muttered, scowling. But he bumped their knees together, and maybe, *maybe*, he didn't mind it as much as he let on. Just because Anthony was an idiot and it was hard to stay irritated with idiots.

Anthony took pity on him and let him out of the hug. "Jed," Redford announced, excited, "Your line is moving."

"What?" Sure enough, it was. Whooping, Jed stood, prancing forward and then back, all but flailing. "What do I do? *What do I do?*"

"Reel it in," Anthony laughed, standing with him and putting one hand on the fishing rod. "Don't rush. Just wind it back steadily."

Tongue poking out from between his teeth, Jed tried to follow Anthony's directions. Nice and slow, he turned the crank and eased the line back. The fish jerked on it, pulling away, and Jed cursed loudly, surprised at the fight. Instinctively, he let go of the reel, and the line ran out, the fish swimming away. Anthony jumped in, helping him, and together they reeled it back again, slowly, sometimes letting the line out a bit more, sometimes fighting the fish as they brought it in. Finally, with one last hard turn of the reel, they hauled a giant bass out and onto the sand. Jed's eyes went round with shock as he watched it flop around.

"Holy shit! I caught Moby Dick!"

Redford looked positively gleeful beside him, kneeling down to help Anthony hold the fish still. "Jed, you probably caught the biggest fish in the lake," he enthused. "Do you have your phone? You have to take a picture."

Jed was grinning so wide it hurt, fumbling to get his phone out. "Oh my God, can we frame it? Like those big deer heads?" He took a picture of the fish next to Redford, almost dancing in victorious joy. "Anthony! Look how huge it is!"

Anthony didn't look as excited as they did, but his little smile was heartfelt. Jed noticed his gaze dart toward the lake, and he seemed to say something under his breath, though Jed didn't catch the words. "You can frame it if you want," Anthony finally replied. "But it looks to me like it'd make a *really* good dinner."

"Yeah, that," Jed agreed with a nod. "Let's eat it." He paused, hands on his hips, staring down at the flopping, scaly fish. "How the fuck do you eat it?"

IT TURNED out, you could roast the whole damn thing. Eyeballs and all. Jed found himself hovering in the kitchen, fascinated, watching as Randall cleaned the fish and put it in the oven, just like that. He was once again told that there was no *fish stick* portion, which seemed kind of sad to him, but they had that going and a rabbit stew, and Victor and Randall were happily working shoulder to shoulder to cook the vegetables. Randall even had some kind of apple dessert thing baking.

In short, everything smelled *really* good.

Knievel was happily chowing down on her minifish while the rest of them gathered around the table. Passing plates and drinks, the casual conversation petered out to nothing as they all dug in. The food was so damn good that they all were perfectly content to eat rather than try to come up with small talk.

When they were down to scraping their plates—or even licking them, in Edwin's case—Anthony took a deep breath and said, "We need to talk about the future."

"Good idea," Edwin agreed. "I think we should definitely take a vacation at Victor's when it gets colder. I bet his pond thing would freeze, and I *really* want to try ice skating."

"That's not what I meant, Ed," Anthony said gently. "I meant your future, and Randall's. Whether or not this treatment works, both of you need to start having lives, not just sitting around looking after me."

"Anthony...." Randall hesitated from where he was pouring coffee. "I'm not sure we need to talk about this. We're doing just fine how we are now. My job is going to help a lot with expenses, Edwin is going to go up to Victor's with me three times a week, and with that extra income we're going to be a lot better with bills."

"I didn't mean just money either." Anthony scrubbed a hand over his face, looking frustrated at himself. "I'm not saying this right. You should go to *college*, Randall. Edwin, you should figure out what your passion is, what you want to do for a living. If the treatments work and I can get out of bed, I'm going to go get my old job back. And if these treatments *don't* work, you need to start thinking about those things anyway so you can be properly set up for your futures."

There was absolute silence. Not a lull in conversation, not even a moment of thought before words started to flow again. Just silence. As if Anthony had suggested they all merrily skip off of a cliff. Randall looked blank, like he'd been shut down and put away. Edwin wasn't moving, staring at the table, lips pressed together tightly.

"I wish I didn't have to say this," Anthony said. "But you're my brothers. And I need to look out for you both, because neither of you seem to be doing it yourselves, lately."

A wince crossed Randall's face, but he still wasn't talking. Edwin stood up. "Shut up," he told Anthony, voice cracking. "Just *shut up*. We... we've done *everything*, okay? And I didn't say a word. We went and found the pack, we came home, you used *goop* on your hands, like, what the hell? Who actually thought that was going to work? But we did it. Because you are family and *that is what we do*. So don't sit there and tell me to start thinking about the future, okay? Because I don't want to. If there's any version out there where you're not in it, I'm not looking. I refuse. You can't make me."

"You're going to have to," Anthony said bluntly. It looked like even just saying the words hurt, but he did it anyway. "We all knew what loss felt like when we lost our parents. And there is every possibility that you both will have to go through it again. It's not nice, it's not *fair*, but it's *happening*. And if the both of you are at square one and have no prospects for your futures if I check out, I'll never forgive myself."

"If you die, then I'm just going to too," Edwin shot back. "So shut up and stop talking about this."

The snarl that Anthony gave made even Jed flinch back. "Don't you *dare*," Anthony said hoarsely. "You think it's funny, saying that? Jesus, Edwin, Randall's right there. You'd leave him too?"

"I'm not joking," Edwin gritted out. "You're giving up, so why the hell shouldn't I? You think I'm an idiot? You don't want to take the medicine. And if you stop, you're going to get worse."

"Guys," Randall whispered, but Edwin kept going, getting louder, shouting right over Randall's interjection.

"You don't get to tell me to *move on*, like you're some bad thing I need to get over! So stop being so... *stupid.*"

"I *am* going to take the goddamn treatments," Anthony growled. "And I am going to continue fighting this disease every step of the way, but I'm not going to pretend there's not a chance it might not work."

"*Stop saying that.*" Edwin turned and ran, shedding clothes as he went, knocking a glass over in his wake. The next moment there was a flash of blond as Edwin ran into the woods, wolf form blending into the shadows and disappearing completely from sight.

Randall sighed, staring at the table. After a beat he stood, moving to clean up the shattered glass. Anthony cursed under his breath and slumped back down in his chair. Beside Jed, Redford sounded like he had only just started breathing again, and Victor looked flustered, cleaning his glasses.

Then Anthony was up and out of his chair again, moving to the front door. Randall still wasn't trying to talk, barely even reacting as he carefully swept up the glass, as he mopped up the spilled water. In the distance was a long howl, an anguished noise that seemed to shiver through Jed, some primal reaction to something that wild.

"I'll go bring him back," Anthony sighed, shrugging on a heavy jacket that had been hanging by the door.

"Don't." Randall's voice was sharp, his jaw so tight it looked like one good push and he might just shatter apart. "Let him be, Ant. You know he needs to run when he gets like this."

The way Anthony's shoulders tensed looked like guilt. "If he's not back by midnight, I'm going to find him," he muttered.

"Or you'll let him be," Randall repeated, voice low. He took the broken glass into the kitchen to throw away.

Jed glanced around the room, fidgeting in his seat, uncomfortable. This was why he didn't do family shit. It all just got so... messy. Much better to not deal with it at all. "Do you need help in there?" he asked, starting to stand, to reach for half-empty cups.

"No" was Randall's firm response. And Jed sank back down again, sighing. There went his exit strategy. Victor, on the other hand, didn't even ask before he went to help Randall clean up. Randall's tense body language didn't ease, but at least he didn't snap at Victor.

Anthony sank back down into his chair, his hands clenched tightly together on the tabletop to ease the shaking. "I'll get the guesthouse ready for you guys in a minute," he told Jed and Redford, but his gaze was fixed out the window, his breaths deeper.

"Don't worry about it." Jed practically fell over his chair in an effort to get to the hall closet. "We know where everything is. You just sit there and think calming thoughts. Come on, Red."

Redford looked just as relieved for something to do as Jed did, and together they piled their arms high with pillows and blankets. After they picked their way across the yard, they made up Victor's bed first, before retreating into their room and getting the sheets on the mattress. "That was...." Jed shrugged, shaking his head. "Not exactly what I was expecting."

"Neither," Redford admitted. He tossed a pillow across the bed at Jed and straightened a corner of the sheets, fussing just to have something to do. "They've all seemed happier lately."

"I get it, though. Hell of a thing to sit there and listen to someone list out what you're supposed to do when they kick it." Jed bent over the bed, reaching across to grab the comforter and hauling it onto his side.

"Yeah." Redford heaved a sigh. But then he looked at the bed they'd just made, then up at Jed, and a quirked a little smile. "I never thought I'd see the day where you made the bed."

"Hey, come on now." Jed put a final fluff on the flower-dotted comforter. "This is manly as hell." Grinning at Redford, waggling his eyebrows up and down, Jed gestured to the mattress. "If you think I'm not getting enough practice, though, we really should mess it up. You know, so I can try again." The *messing it up* was really what Jed was most interested in.

"I'm just surprised you even know *how* to make a bed," Redford mused. Clothes and all, he crawled onto it and tugged Jed down with him, manhandling Jed around until Redford had him in a comfortable position. After ending up on his back, with Redford half lying on his side, Jed curved an arm around Redford's shoulders. "Did you learn that in the army and just haven't employed that knowledge since?"

Jed ran his fingers along Redford's arm, flashing a half smile. He could lie. It'd be easy to say yes, to roll them over and kiss Redford, to let the subject die. There wasn't any *reason* to talk about this, or to let Redford in any further.

"My mom."

But, for some reason, Jed was just full of the Care Bears today. He couldn't seem to help himself. "My mom made my sisters and I make our beds every morning, before school. If we didn't, we had to go to bed an hour earlier that night. It was a big deal, for whatever reason. Army just taught me how to do hospital corners."

"Yeah?" Redford sounded pleased, inching up so he could put his head on the pillow next to Jed's. "That sounds nice." Redford always got those dumb puppy-dog eyes whenever Jed mentioned his past. Like Jed was giving him a *gift* by talking about freaking bed making.

"It was annoying," Jed grunted. "Why make your bed *every day*? You are literally just going to mess it up twelve hours later. It makes no sense at all."

Redford gave a quiet laugh against his shoulder. "You make it because it looks pretty. And because it feels good to get into a bed that doesn't have the sheets hanging off the edge."

"I like my sheets hanging off the edge." Grumbling, Jed turned them so he was hovering over Redford, so he could drop a kiss onto the bridge of his nose and smile at the way Redford blinked, trying to bring him into focus. "I like you on my bed most of all. And that *really* tends to mess things up."

Redford rolled them again so he could use Jed as a mattress, bonelessly sprawling over him. "I think we should make the bed more often," he said. "It's nice, doing things that aren't blowing things up."

"There's nothing wrong with a good explosion," Jed mumbled, hop-skipping kisses against Redford's neck, hands sliding up and down Redford's back. "That's way more fun than bed making."

Redford caught Jed in a kiss. There was no hurry to it, no edge to either of their movements, just a leisurely connection. "And what if I disagree?"

A slow little smirk curled Jed's lips. "I'll have to change your mind." Slipping his hands up under Redford's shirt, he deepened their kiss, taking his time, a soft moan caught between them. He gently pulled off Redford's clothes, pants getting pushed away, his own jeans lost over the edge of the bed. They took their time, rolling together in exhales and grasping touches, the sheets bunching under Jed's back as Redford moved above him, the brilliant orange of the fading sun painting Redford's skin on fire.

And when they finally did collapse, when the slow pace turned urgent, Redford's gasps became quiet moans, and Jed grinned into the dark as he slid kisses along his skin. "See?" he whispered as they lay together, legs and sheets tangled all at once. "Explosions."

They fell asleep in a messy sprawl, Jed using Redford's bicep as a pillow, Redford's breaths evening out into a relaxing rhythm that Jed listened to until sleep claimed him.

They woke with the sound of gunshots splitting the air.

Jed jerked upright, heart pounding, a cold sweat making him shiver. At first there was nothing, the throb of his heartbeat in his ears, the sick sour stench of his own fear. A dream, maybe. A nightmare. He had those. But then a third shot rang out, followed by the high-pitched yelp of a wolf in pain. Jed was tumbling out of bed before he had time to realize he was moving, grabbing his jeans, shoving his boots on, tugging on a shirt even as he ran out the door.

"Get my bag from the Jeep!" he hollered to Redford, grabbing his Glock from the holster he'd left by the door and thundering down the stairs, out onto the lawn.

Another drawn-out howl, this one cut short by the staccato bursts of a semiautomatic. And then there really was nothing but silence.

Shit.

CHAPTER
21

Redford

REDFORD CAUGHT up with Jed just as Anthony and Randall did. He didn't waste time speaking. He threw the bag to Jed and ran by his side, the four of them sprinting in the direction the noise had come from. Redford's eyesight wasn't good in the darkness when he was still on two legs, but he had no time to shift, so he endured the thin branches whipping at his shoulders and face and ignored the sting of rocks coming up hard against his feet.

Anthony and Randall got there faster than he and Jed did.

"I smell blood," Redford gasped out, skidding to a stop. Anthony was circling a tree, his ears back in the universal wolf body language for anger. "Not enough for a kill shot, though."

Fumbling through the bag in the darkness, Jed found the flashlight and switched it on, frowning as he swept the light over the area. He crouched down, illuminating the trunk of the tree and the matted grass before letting the flashlight slide along a trail. "He got hit here," Jed muttered to himself. "Blood against the tree trunk, a slug there, so probably a through and through. But then he was dragged." Rubbing a hand across his mouth, Jed nodded. "Yeah. Yeah, they took him."

There was a far off noise of someone crashing through the forest with as much finesse as a herd of stampeding elephants—Victor, from the cursing Redford could hear. Anthony shifted back, though his eyes still blazed yellow in the dim light. "Jed, if you have explosives in that bag, I want to borrow them," Anthony said flatly. "I'm going to track these bastards."

"Explosions come with me," Jed returned. "It's a two for one deal. But yeah, I've got 'em. You, me, and Red, we'll go after them now. I can keep up."

Randall, still shifted, growled under his breath, fur at the nape of his neck standing up. Anthony held out his hand. "Give me the explosives," he said. "Will they kill the hunters if I put them close enough?"

"I'm not handing over a bunch of C-4 to a guy looking for revenge." Jed took a step back, gaze going between Anthony and Randall. "And yeah. You put a big boom-boom next to squishy things and you'll be in a whole world of red rain. *Including* yourself, because you don't fucking know what you're doing. Now listen. You aren't a goddamn killer. We don't know what's going on here, but I'm not going to lead another

405

untrained wolf into a slaughterhouse just because. How do you even know they're not a bunch of idiot kids who shot a wolf and have no damn clue?"

The growl that came from Anthony made Redford wince. Jed was lying, that was obvious enough to Redford—that gunfire had been from a semiautomatic, and idiot kids didn't wander around in dark forests with semiautomatics. And even if they did, they wouldn't drag a live wolf away.

Anthony didn't seem to be thinking that clearly.

"I don't care who they are; they took my brother," Anthony barked. "If you're not coming, you're welcome to stay here. Get some sleep."

Grabbing Anthony's arm, Jed didn't back down from the warning growl. "Fine. *Fine*, okay. I'm coming with you. And if you say we go in for the kill, we will. But I am handling the explosives. Okay?"

Victor chose that moment to burst into the clearing, bending over to brace his hands on his knees once he came to a stop. "What," he wheezed, "happened?"

Redford didn't want to interrupt Anthony and Jed, so he leaned over and whispered to Victor, "Edwin got taken." Just the thought of it made *him* want to tear into the woods after the hunters too. O'Malley had promised he would call off his operation, and they'd all thought they'd be safe. But now there were hunters on the Lewises' property. This might have just gotten far more personal.

Anthony's anger seemed to dissipate some. "Okay," he said, taking a moment to breathe deeply, getting himself focused. "You're right. You know more about this kind of thing than I do. But we're going *now*. If you tell me to wait until morning, I'll remind you of the time you tried to blow up that hunter camp because Redford got a tiny bullet graze on his arm."

"Yeah, well." Jed pulled his shotgun from the duffel bag, ratcheting off the safety. "You talked me out of it. I'm a cold-blooded killer. You're a nice guy who likes to fish. There's a world of difference between what I do and what you can live with." There wasn't time for this. For a big drawn-out heart-to-heart. And Jed seemed to feel that just as much as the rest of them. He met Anthony's eyes, holding his gaze, brilliant human green against feral wolf yellow. "You told me once that you weren't animals, that you didn't kill without reason. Was that true? Or only when you didn't have skin in the game?"

Anthony's upper lip lifted in a reactionary snarl, but he didn't voice it. Jed waited patiently as Anthony seemed to struggle through his thoughts, his gaze darting from Jed to the forest. "Everything in me wants to tell you there's a *damn* good reason," he said, his voice tight.

"Wouldn't argue with you." Jed darted a glance forward, tense. Redford knew he'd be trying to guess how much time had passed, how far ahead the hunters might be. "It's always easy to be a good man when nothing you love is at stake. I know. That's the only kind of *good* I ever am."

Jed's eyes flicked over to Redford, expression going grim. A thousand thoughts seemed to be held in that glance. Redford knew that if it had been him taken, Jed wouldn't stop to debate morality. He *hadn't*. But this seemed different. And Redford honestly wasn't sure if Jed was thinking of the time the hunters had shot him, or the way Redford had lost himself to the instincts and ripped out a man's throat. Neither memory seemed to fill him with any sort of confidence about this situation. Maybe there was more at stake now. Maybe there was something bigger than just himself to think about. Either way, Jed was standing between Anthony and men who didn't deserve the consideration. Something had changed.

"I am two seconds away from just ignoring you and running in there," Anthony replied. His shoulders were hunched up tight, but as Redford watched, they slowly drooped, leaving Anthony looking defeated. "You're right. And I wish you weren't."

"Story of my life, kid." Jed gripped Anthony's shoulder. "But I promise, we'll get him back." Jed never *promised* like that. He said it was the surest way to make shit hit all kinds of fans. But his voice was grim, serious, gaze unwavering from Anthony's. "So let's get moving." He turned back to the others. "Okay. Victor, Randall, you go back to the house," Jed said.

Randall immediately barked at him, setting his front paws and growling. Obviously not agreeing.

"Go back to the house, guys," Anthony echoed, looking down at Randall. "It'll be safer."

"We're coming with you," Victor insisted. "You're hardly going on some sort of *stealth* mission. Two extra bodies won't change anything. And Randall is an excellent wolf to have on your side at times like this."

"Yeah, but *you're* not," Jed said, exasperated. "You sound like a goddamn elephant running through the woods. I don't want to send you back alone. I need Redford, therefore Randall gets the short straw. Now stop fucking arguing."

Victor grumbled in exasperation, but he gave in. "Right, then. I'll hold down the fort." He sounded like he'd tried to inject some cheer and determination into his voice; it hadn't worked. "Randall?"

Obviously torn, Randall hesitated. But Jed just shook his head. "Don't, kid," he muttered. "We need blankets, hot water, and whatever first aid you have. Victor doesn't know where everything is. Edwin's going to be hurt when we bring him back, and I don't know how bad. So go, get ready. I need you both to do that so that we have someplace safe to take him to." Jed hesitated, looking over at Victor. "There are some spare guns in a hidden panel in the back of the Jeep. Get those. Lock the doors. Be ready. Okay?"

Victor still didn't look happy, but he nodded again and laid his hand on Randall's back in a comforting gesture. They left, and Redford turned his attention to Jed's bag. He pulled out his own gun and holster while Anthony shifted, and set about getting himself ready.

"Anthony, can you pick up their trail?" Redford asked, strapping the holster over his shoulder. He realized then that he was still in the clothes he'd worn last night, barefoot. Jed was sloppily dressed in what he'd tossed to the floor; Redford noticed that Jed's shirt was inside out. Neither of them had taken the time to hunt for new clothes.

Anthony circled the tree again and took off at a trot. To give Jed freer range of movement, Redford took the bag and slung it over his own back as they followed.

As they ran and as Redford thought, he felt a resignation settle into him. At the start of all of this, their only mission had been to help the Lewises find the Gray Lady's pack, but in doing so, they'd stumbled into a fight. And it still wasn't over—it would maybe not be over for a very long time, considering the visions Victor had had. And all

Redford wanted to do was take Jed to some remote little cabin in the mountains and fish from a stream.

This war they'd found themselves in might not end. This could just be the very start of it, and Redford didn't want it. He didn't want to get involved in something like this. But he couldn't back out now, could he? He didn't *want* to back out, not when the Lewises were in danger. Redford just wished this fight had never started at all.

When Anthony finally came to a halt, Jed and Redford stopped beside him. They crouched behind the low overhang of a hill to catch their breath. Redford tipped his chin up, testing the air with a deep inhale. "They're close," Redford told Jed. "Not even a mile away, and they've stopped." There was a certain scent that came with movement. Redford couldn't quite describe it, but it was something like a mix between the sweat of exertion and the pumping of blood. He couldn't smell that on the hunters anymore. Creeping through the scent of pain and sour fear was the crisp smell he associated with Edwin. Anthony seemed to sense it too, because his ears were darted forward, body in a line of tense anticipation. "Edwin is with them, and he's alive."

Jed pulled out a box from his bag and attached his second favorite sniper scope onto his rifle, easing himself up to rest along a fallen log. After a moment, Jed murmured, "I can't see any lights. No fires or torches that I can tell. We'll need to get closer."

Redford looked around for a twig. When he found one, he pushed the end into the dirt and started drawing a map. "From what I can smell, most of the hunters are gathered together," he said, keeping his voice low. "Edwin was telling me all about this area yesterday. There's a shallow stream that goes to the east of us, and an outcropping of rocks near where I think the hunters are. They've probably camped there for the night. Which means that we can't come at them from that direction." He drew a line approaching the west. "We'll need to go this way."

Jed nodded, looking over the map one last time before dashing it out with his foot. "Lead the way," he said, gun in his hands, dropping back behind Redford and Anthony.

"Wait," Redford hissed, throwing an arm out to stop Jed moving. Anthony had frozen as well, and together they looked behind them. "There's...." Redford sniffed the air, his eyes growing wide. "There's a few dozen wolves approaching."

"What the—" Jed cursed under his breath, fingers tightening on his gun. "Where?"

"Behind us," Redford replied. He inhaled again, trying to sort out the different scents the wind was carrying. "It's.... I think the Gray Lady is with them."

Jed darted a look at Anthony, as if for confirmation. Anthony shifted back, remaining crouched low to the ground. "It's her," Anthony agreed. "I have no idea *why*, but it's her. Mallory too."

"Not good," Jed growled, turning to face where they'd come from. "Not good, not good, *not good.*" His gun was out, leveled at the trees, and Jed was scanning the dark forest as if he'd suddenly be able to see more than a few feet in front of him.

Redford began to hear the quiet noise of paws moving over dirt, dozens of them running in unison. Then a bare minute later, he began to see shapes approaching through the trees. A sleek gray wolf emerged at the head of the pack, a wolf one moment and then human the next.

The Gray Lady, naked and as wild as the forest around them, regarded them calmly. "I see we caught up just in time."

Jed stood in front of them, between the pack and Redford and Anthony, gun in his hands. Unafraid. He faced down dozens of wolves without blinking. Which was probably idiotic. "We've got this under control," Jed told her lowly. "Though I'm sure if you need a place to stay for the night, you can take a detour through the Lewises'. But you don't need to be out this way at all."

"They've taken one of your own, am I right?" Her voice was nothing less than absolutely cool, but Redford still heard the growl of anger thrumming underneath. "They have been trying to take ours, still. We found notations on one of the hunters about where they intended to strike next. And we are ready to strike back."

"This is not a war." Redford saw Jed's hands tighten around his gun, his body shifting into a more defensive stance. "If you go over there, if you rip them apart, what next? They send more men. Better trained men. It's an arms race. You escalate, so they come back with bigger guns, with tanks. And then what do you do? You send more wolves in? So they start with planes. I've seen it before. It never ends well. Let me go in there. I can pull the kid out, send the hunters a message, without you throwing down the gauntlet."

"We are beyond *messages*, human," the Gray Lady said sternly. "There are consequences to what they have done, and they will know those consequences tonight. We are not weak. We will not lie down and let them continue."

"Anthony." Jed's voice was a quiet plea now. "This will start a war. Tell them."

"Jed's right, ma'am," Anthony said. He remained crouched, putting himself on a lower level than the Gray Lady, but his words were firm. "They can keep recruiting, but you can't. There's only so many wolves in the area."

It looked like the Gray Lady's patience was running out. Her wolves gathered around her, facing them down, with only Jed standing in the middle to stop them, and all of Jed's words and weapons couldn't stop the wolves from attacking if that was what they decided.

It felt like an eternity stretched past as the Gray Lady considered her answer, and Redford grew more tense with every second. Finally, she inclined her head, and for a moment it looked like she might agree.

She murmured, "Go. Kill them all."

The wolves flowed past them on silent paws, shoulders bumping against Jed and Redford's knees. Jed lifted his gun then, aiming it at the Gray Lady, finger on the trigger. But even he realized it would do no good. He closed his eyes, a defeated slump to his shoulders, and let the barrel of the gun fall, pointing harmlessly down at the forest floor.

Dismissing them, the Gray Lady shifted and ran off, leading the rest of the wolves toward the camp. Redford and Jed didn't move as the wolves streamed around them. Redford only glanced at Jed to see the resignation on Jed's expression that matched his own, and Anthony was staring after the pack, his jaw clenched tight. Moments later they heard the wolves attack in a flurry of noise: cut-off screams, barks and growls, and the dying moans of the hunters.

Everything fell to silence. Then a lone howl rose in the distance. "Edwin," Anthony gasped, sprinting toward the camp.

Redford reached out to take Jed's hand. "We should go catch up," he said quietly.

Jed looked like he'd aged about ten years. But he took Redford's hand without a word, and they made their way toward the wolves. The stench of death and blood was hard to miss. Even Jed grimaced as they got closer. And there was not much left of the hunters. There were eviscerated corpses strewn like fallen apples, the dark puddles of them against the ground. A few wolves looked to be limping, a few more were injured, but none had fallen. It looked like they'd caught the hunters mostly in the tents, a few of the bodies clearly cut down in an attempt to run away.

Jed made a quiet, choked sound. He abruptly turned and walked away, outside the tattered circle of the tents, back to the scene.

The Gray Lady was human again, standing in the middle of it like a queen surveying her land. A fine spray of blood marred her face, but she didn't seem to notice. Redford found his way to Edwin first, who looked banged up and bloody but alive. Anthony was already there, holding Edwin tightly.

"Never run off again, Edwin," Anthony was saying frantically.

In wolf form, Edwin looked strangely small, leaning heavily against Anthony's chest. He nosed into Anthony's throat as if reassuring himself of the scent, giving a pained yelp when he tried to take a step. Blood was matting his shoulder; clearly that was where the bullet had hit him. The hunters hadn't bothered to do anything to the wound.

Redford gently touched Edwin's uninjured shoulder. "I'm glad you're okay," he whispered.

"We're going back to the lake outside your cabin," the Gray Lady announced, seemingly having no time for reunions. "I assume you have your brother there, ready to give medical aid?"

Redford could only nod an affirmative before she was a wolf again, and the pack started leaving. Anthony scowled at their retreating forms and carefully stood, Edwin supported in his arms. "Where's Jed?" Anthony asked.

"Right here." Jed had found a shovel somewhere and was marching through the camp to the middle of the clearing. "Sick of burying these goddamn bodies." And he started to dig there, alone in the center of the camp and the corpses.

"You go back, Anthony," Redford directed. "We'll take care of this."

"No." Jed just kept his head down, digging. "You go too." A caustic smile touched Jed's lips, a weary slump to his shoulders. "It's a human thing."

Redford knew Jed didn't blame him for what had happened here. Jed wasn't an illogical person by nature, but Redford still winced at the tone in Jed's voice. He was a wolf too, or at least half of one, and right then the anger in Jed's body language toward wolves was clear.

Redford didn't blame him. He wasn't too happy with them himself.

Anthony left with Edwin, and Redford took a moment to stand by Jed's side, feeling useless. The smell of death was near-suffocating to his nose, and if he looked more than two feet in either direction, he'd see a severed limb or a puddle of blood. It had been a slaughter, a horrifically messy one.

Redford wanted to ask Jed not to take too long, but he also wanted to insist that he could take all the time he needed. The conflicting thoughts made him hesitate, and in the end he just wrapped his arms around Jed from behind, hugging him tight. "I'll see you soon," he murmured.

Jed's fingers tightened on top of Redford's and Jed nodded, eyes fixed on the ground. "I don't want to be in another war," he muttered, almost to himself. "This didn't have to happen. I'm not saying nobody had to die tonight. Just... not like this."

"I know." Redford laid his cheek against Jed's shoulder blade. "We'll talk to them, I promise."

It was different now. This wasn't just a pack of rowdy hunters that could be beaten off with a show of teeth and a trained force. This wasn't an office that Jed could stomp into and blackmail the ringleader into stopping. This attack had felt so much more *volatile* than the others.

Maybe it had been because of Victor's visions, and maybe they were just riled up from those. Or maybe there was just a feeling in the air, an intangible sense that this would lead to something so much worse, like the smell of burnt ozone after a flint had been struck.

Nobody *wanted* a war. But it looked like they might just get one.

Redford gave Jed a final squeeze and left for the Lewises' house. He looked over his shoulder as he did. Jed cut a very lonely figure, surrounded by blood and dismembered bodies. But Redford forced himself to keep walking, because Randall and Anthony would be more focused on Edwin right now, so somebody had to beg the Gray Lady to not escalate this into full-blown war.

The wolves were gathered around the edge of the lake when Redford arrived. Some of them were washing blood off themselves. Anthony was bundling Edwin into the cabin, though he kept darting glances back at the blood drifting into the water, a pained look flickering over his expression. Randall met them at the door, and they vanished inside. The Gray Lady was crouched by the shoreline, dipping her hands into the water to rub the flecks of blood off her face. Even now, with her white hair matted at the tips with red, she was the most graceful creature Redford had ever seen.

She was conversing lowly with Mallory, so Redford sat down on the front porch and decided to stay there. Waiting for Jed to return so they could speak to her together would probably be their best bet, because however much Redford could list off the exact same reasons that a war was bad, he knew they didn't sound quite as believable coming from him.

Jed had actually been *involved* in a war. People took his word on it much more seriously, and that was an advantage they were going to need.

There was the sound of voices from inside the cabin, soft noises of pain from Edwin, Randall's patient tone. When Randall finally emerged, his own hands stained red, he sank down on the steps next to Redford, looking decidedly unsettled. "Some days," he said, mostly to himself, "I wish I smoked. It's supposed to be relaxing."

"Jed used to smoke sometimes when I first knew him," Redford said contemplatively. "It doesn't smell nice."

"True." Randall stared down at his hands. "Maybe I'll take up heavy drinking, then."

Redford wrinkled his nose. "That doesn't smell nice either."

He was about to continue when he heard the sound of footsteps coming back through the forest. Redford could smell him long before he saw him. When Jed emerged, his forearms and clothing were streaked with blood and dirt. And he didn't wait for the

411

Gray Lady to be done talking, he just strode up to her and said, "Lady, you need to be real fucking careful about who you piss off."

The Gray Lady's eyes flashed in fury, though her expression barely changed. "Are you implying that I haven't thought about this? My pack is in danger, and I am within my rights to protect them."

"Sure," Jed agreed. "And that would be just fucking peachy if it was just your pack involved. But it's not. Take a look at this whole fucking mess we've been in for months now. It's not just wolves. It's humans too. There was a half blood playing middleman. There's a half blood sitting in that cabin right now, and you signed a goddamn deal with a half blood for freak solidarity. If you pull too hard at this string, it's not just wolves that are going to get hung by it. It's everybody. Those hunters aren't going to stop at wolves. Not now." Jed spread his arms, a rigid, too-wide smile creasing his face, making lines in the mud and dried flecks of blood. "Welcome to war, sister. It's open season on freaks, and you just fired the first fucking shot."

"They began this—" The Gray Lady started, but Jed was on a roll. He didn't even let her finish her thought.

"Oh, but you ended it, didn't you?" he bit out, jabbing his finger in her direction. "You let everyone know that you're big and bad and you've got fangs you're willing to use. And you forgot one thing in all your furry pride."

"And what is that?" the Gray Lady said coldly, her eyes glinting yellow in warning.

"Humans don't just retaliate. We go goddamn *nuclear*." Spinning on his heel, Jed stalked back toward the cabin, shoulders set in a furious line.

"Is that a *threat*, little human?" The Gray Lady sounded as though she was moments from ripping out Jed's throat herself.

But he just laughed. "Don't need to threaten when it's the truth, sister." He turned back to her, pointing toward her pack. "We know O'Malley hired those guys, but he says that chain of cash changing hands goes even further than him. He paid them. Gave them cash to leave their wives, their kids, their partners, and come out here to shoot at wolves. That was all. And I'm not saying they weren't going to die anyway. But you *brutalized* them. For no reason."

"And you haven't done the same," the Gray Lady snarled.

"Probably shouldn't use *me* as your moral goddamn *compass*," Jed shouted back. "Because I am *exactly* like those men. Hell, if Buck had called me first, I probably *would* have been. But me doing that shit? That's one thing. That's my life. You? You're in charge of the furry brigade. You didn't just retaliate. You started a *war*. If you thought they were coming after you before? Sister, you're tits deep in shit now."

"I did what I had to do." The Gray Lady drew herself up. "And I will do it again."

"Yeah," Jed muttered, turning his back to her and walking away. "You damn well will. Get used to the feel of blood in your fur, kids."

Redford noticed that most of the wolves had stopped whatever they were doing to listen. Half of them were still wolf, half were human, and none of them looked like they liked what they were hearing. But the Gray Lady didn't seem willing to back down when she was talking to Jed.

So Redford stepped up. As Jed walked away, the Gray Lady crouched back down by the lake, though she didn't resume washing the blood off herself. Instead she stared at the water, her gaze far away. Redford picked his way through the wolves and sat down next to her.

"Jed's been involved in a war before," he said, keeping his tone respectful.

"You think I haven't seen wars?" Far from the angry tone of before, now the Gray Lady just sounded weary. "I have seen all of them, child. I have seen what the humans do when they think they must kill something."

"So why do you want another one?" Redford didn't dip his own hands into the water. After what Anthony had told them yesterday, it would have felt wrong to mar the lake with blood. "This has to be avoidable."

She simply shook her head. "The only ways we would avoid this war are through extreme measures, ones that I do not wish to take. They found us in both of the places I had believed to be safe."

Redford refrained from pointing out that what she'd just done had been extreme enough. "What would the measures be?"

"Deep isolation." The Gray Lady rubbed her hands together, ridding them of excess water. She still didn't look up from the lake. "Much further than we went before. It would require a complete severance from the rest of the wolves. I would have to put out word for all the other packs to force them to choose, to come with us, or to be cut off from us and our help completely."

To Redford, that still sounded like a better option than war, even if it would be harsh to smaller wolf packs.

"There are many that would not come with us," she continued. There was an upset edge at the corner of her lips, a deep sadness in her eyes. "I don't think I could sleep at night, with the knowledge that many of my children would be so out of reach."

"It might not be my place to say so," Redford offered, "but I think that's the better choice. Jed's right about what the humans will do if this escalates. You might be able to take them now, but what happens when they bring in snipers? Helicopters? Remote explosives? They'll win through technology and numbers."

The Gray Lady almost smiled. "How strange it is to long for the days when man fought with their bare hands."

Redford didn't even try to imagine. He couldn't comprehend how long she had been alive, and the thought of truly understanding made him feel a little queasy—he didn't envy Victor, having seen all of that.

"And would it truly matter?" the Gray Lady asked with a sad smile. "There would be wolves beyond my reach. They would be slaughtered. And then what? Half bloods? The vampires, if they are not the ones behind this whole plot? And eventually, they would find me, little wolf. Eventually they always do. No, I am not afraid of war. It has happened before, it will happen again."

"It will," Redford agreed. "Victor's seen it, and this time it doesn't look like multiple choice. But we don't have to jump right into it." He found himself almost pleading with her. "We don't have to make it start right now."

He froze when she finally looked at him, all the weight of what she'd seen pinning him where he sat. "If we were to delay, to hide and hope for a few more years before this war, I would require every wolf to find a pack, if they did not come with me. Loners are a weak spot. They know too much, and information is too easily pulled out of them."

"Okay," Redford said, mostly for a lack of anything else to say. He'd admit he wasn't entirely sure what that meant for him—did he and Jed count as a pack? He didn't want to go find some larger group of a few dozen.

The Gray Lady looked over her shoulder toward the cabin. "Your group is particularly terrible at following orders," she said, and she sounded almost *fond*. "But I will speak to them anyway. Come with me."

Still unsure, Redford followed her into the cabin. The Lewises and Jed weren't in the main room, and Victor slapped a hand over his eyes when the Gray Lady entered. Redford had to take a moment to figure out why—he'd gotten so used to wolves going naked in one another's company that he'd barely noticed the Gray Lady wasn't wearing a stitch.

She sounded bemused when she asked Victor, "Will you go and get the rest of your company for me? I would speak to them."

Victor scurried out of the room to retrieve the others. He returned shortly with the Lewises, bandages standing out stark white against Edwin's sun-soaked skin, his arm in a sling. Jed trailed behind them, a flask in hand. He pressed it into Edwin's hands as Edwin sat and watched as he took a long, grateful pull before sagging back against the couch cushions. It spoke to Anthony's mood that he didn't even protest Edwin drinking mystery alcohol.

When Victor came back, he offered the Gray Lady a blanket. She arched an eyebrow at him, clearly bemused, but wrapped it around herself nonetheless. Even in a lumpy green afghan, she still looked regal.

Randall stood behind the couch, arms folded, head down. He looked as exhausted as Redford felt. "Is there something you needed?" he asked, voice little more than a low rumble. "I would like to get my brothers into bed before too much longer. They both need rest."

"We have two options before us," the Gray Lady said. She sat in a chair that Redford provided for her, the blanket bunching up around her legs. She looked at Jed, measuring him. "War is coming, whether I like it or not. I can either choose to fight it now, or gather what wolves I can and hope to delay it."

"I think you know which option we would choose," Anthony replied quietly.

"I do." The Gray Lady looked at each of them in turn, Jed and Victor included. "If I chose to hide again, I would cut my pack off from ties to the human world. Nobody would know where we are, not even other smaller packs if they chose to remain separate. My only order for the remaining wolf packs would be that they stay together. That includes all nonwolf ties."

"You mean me," Jed grunted, giving her a suspicious look.

"And the medusa," she confirmed.

"When you say 'stay together,' how closely do you mean?" Victor asked, squinting at her.

She seemed to smile. "Very closely. The six of you live in three separate residences, some distance apart. That would be a weakness."

"I think we've managed just fine on our own." Dread was dawning on Jed's face. "We're plenty good the way it is now."

"Then I will not go ahead with the plan to delay," the Gray Lady said simply. "Either every pack works with this plan, or we will be too fractured for it to succeed."

Redford, personally, didn't think it sounded *so* bad. For the past week and change they had already been at the cabin for a few nights, and seeing as Victor and the Lewises hadn't killed one another after living in the mansion for a week, they could obviously live together.

"There's no room for the Von Trapp Family Furries in our apartment," Jed pointed out.

Victor slowly raised his hand. "There's plenty of room in my house," he suggested. Randall gave him a sideways glance, and Edwin seemed torn between half falling asleep and watching Anthony for clues as to what he was thinking.

"Nope." Jed shook his head, arms folded. "You guys can do whatever you want, but me and Red, we're all the *pack* I can handle full time. We've got the cat. That makes three. That's got to qualify."

"Oh, come on, Jed," Victor said, starting to get exasperated. "You can live all the way at the other end if you like, and you'd never have to see anybody else. You heard the Gray Lady, it's this or fighting. Even you aren't that stubborn."

"You have no *idea* how stubborn I am, princess," Jed grumbled. But Redford knew that look, the way Jed would dig in his heels when he realized he had no choice but to go along. Same way he looked when Redford insisted they have vegetables on their pizza to try to stave off scurvy. In the end, Jed bitched and moaned about vegetables, but he always ate them.

Redford sidled over and put a comforting hand on Jed's hip. "Victor told me there's another kitchen at the other end of the mansion," he said encouragingly. "So it'd be like having half a mansion to yourself. Think of all the places Knievel could explore."

"Think of the yard," Edwin piped up, craning his neck to look back at them. "Redford could go with us every full moon."

Jed looked over at Redford, his eyes narrowed. "You want to do this?" he asked, clearly willing to keep fighting if Redford said no.

"I think we should," Redford replied. "It sounds like it might be the best thing to do." However much he loved their apartment, it was worth giving it up if it meant the Gray Lady would feel secure enough in picking the option that didn't involve going to war tomorrow. And Jed seemed to realize it. His eyes went to Edwin, half slouched on the couch, bandage bright white against his shoulder, and then lifted to the window. Outside, the wolves of the pack were spread out, some human, some still shifted, tending to wounds, resting, not more than three dozen of them. Redford could see Jed counting them, jaw tightening.

"You came all this way with barely more than a handful," Jed remarked, turning back to the Gray Lady. "What happened?"

She hesitated before shrugging, spreading her hands. "Hunters took some. We've had two new litters, so the pack isn't as mobile. I left the rest back with the main group, for protection. This is what I could spare."

Jed finally nodded. "Fine," he gritted, none too happy with the prospect. "We'll be a goddamn pack. You take yours and you go as far off the grid as you can. Keep the kids safe."

"We'll come too," Anthony sighed. "If that's okay with you, Victor?"

"Maybe we'll section the mansion off into thirds?" Victor tried to joke.

"I don't think that'll be necessary," Randall said. Removing his glasses, he bowed his head as he busily cleaned them. "Since we've decided, I really must insist that Anthony and Edwin get some rest. I assume you'll want us to do this as soon as possible?" His gaze flicked up to the Gray Lady, who nodded. "Right. Then we have a lot of work to do tomorrow."

"Very well, then." The Gray Lady seemed satisfied as she stood, looking over them again.

Redford couldn't help but remember first meeting her, and seeing her obvious disdain for nonwolf involvement with wolves. She hadn't liked that he and Jed had been together, and he imagined she'd felt the same way about Victor and Randall. Her attitude seemed to have softened toward that, as she appeared to be smiling at them all.

"You make for a very strange pack," she told them. "But perhaps a strong one because of that."

"Do you need anything?" Randall seemed to realize he'd been neglecting the visiting wolves. "We don't have much in the cupboards, I'm afraid, but I could go out and catch you something...."

"We are fine." The Gray Lady stood, inclining her head. "We have the water of the lake and the game of the forest. We will eat, rest, and be gone before dawn. Thank you."

Anthony stood to show her out, hovering at her shoulder as they left the cabin. They remained in silence until he came back a minute later. Anthony looked around the room and started laughing quietly.

"I guess we really are a pack, now."

THE WOLVES left as silent as ghosts near dawn, and the sudden lack of their scent woke Redford.

He blinked up at the ceiling, letting his eyes adjust to the darkness. He, Jed, and Victor had stayed the night at the Lewises to help them with packing, and at the end of the night, Jed and Redford had retreated to the guest cabin after picking their way through the Gray Lady's pack, that had parked themselves near the lake.

But now they were gone. Redford could only smell the faint hint of their trail. He wasn't surprised. The Gray Lady didn't seem like a person to indulge in drawn-out, formal good-byes. With the tension remaining between her and the Lewises, even though they'd come to a decision, Redford thought it was perhaps better that they had left without alerting anybody.

Unfortunately, now that he'd noticed, Redford was starting to feel too awake to get back to sleep. A quick glance at Jed revealed that he was still deeply dozing. Redford didn't want to wake him, because Jed looked like he needed the rest. Instead he carefully got out of bed, putting on clothes as silently as he could.

The outside air was crisp and dimly lit in the beginning of dawn. Redford wound up walking his way toward the edge of the lake, only to nearly trip over Edwin.

"Sorry," Redford blurted. "I didn't see you."

Bundled in a faded blue quilt, Edwin barely glanced up at Redford. "Smelled you coming," he said with a shrug, low and hoarse. "What are you doing up?"

"I couldn't smell the pack anymore, so I woke up." Redford awkwardly stuck his hands in his pockets. Edwin was seated on the same log that Redford, Anthony, and Jed had fished from. "Is it okay if I sit here?"

Edwin was oddly quiet, like he'd become a ghost himself, the mist around them softening his features, hiding him behind a gray thread of silk. "Go ahead." He nodded, knees drawn up to his chest, still staring out over the lake. "They left about an hour ago. It woke me up too."

Redford sat hesitantly. The way Edwin had spoken, Redford wasn't entirely sure if that was willing or grudging permission. He tried to study Edwin without being too obvious about it, wondering if his injuries were bothering him. "Are you okay?"

For a moment, Edwin didn't move. It was almost as if he'd been waiting for that question, gathering up his answers in advance, ready to say the same thing he'd been telling his brothers all evening. *I'm fine. It doesn't even hurt. I wasn't scared at all.*

Instead, he let out a slow breath, watching as the condensation curled up into the air, smoke signals lost again in the early morning fog. "Do you know what the worst part was?" Edwin turned then, to look at Redford, his brilliant-blue eyes clouded, the corner of his mouth tugged upward in a parody of a smile. "They knew. They knew I understood them. So they talked to me. They told me exactly what they were planning. And now I know what happened to the other missing wolves."

Most people listening to this, Redford was aware, would give Edwin a sympathetic *I can't imagine.* But Redford could. He'd been through it himself. Filtiarn and his wolves hadn't been kind.

"I've been kidnapped before," he offered. "It was the most scared I've ever been in my life. So I know how you feel."

Edwin seemed to absorb that, his gaze wandering again back out to the lake. Silently, he scooted a little closer to Redford, shoulder resting against his. "They're skinning them," he whispered, horror in his tone. "The wolves they catch. They liked my coat, so they didn't kill me. They were going to make a *rug* out of me."

What could Redford say to that? He shook his head, disbelieving at first, everything in him wanting to deny that that was what the hunters had been kidnapping the wolves for. It seemed preposterous, like something out of a bad horror movie.

But the hunters had spoken to Edwin, and they would have had no reason to lie.

"God," Redford whispered, stunned. He couldn't think of anything to say.

Perhaps luckily for him, he was saved, not by the bell, but by the sound of Victor groggily stumbling out of the guest cabin, his glasses held in his hand. "Does nobody sleep around here?" he grumped and parked himself on the end of the log on the other side of Edwin, still looking half asleep. "Why are you two not in bed?"

"Why aren't you?" Edwin returned, eyebrow raised.

417

"Because we can hear you two out here." Randall came next, following after Victor, winding up shoved up next to him, head resting on Victor's shoulder with a yawn. "Sound carries, little brother. And I could smell the wolves leaving, so I was awake already. What's going on?"

"Apparently nobody can sleep," Redford replied, bemused despite the horrible realization still circling around in his thoughts. Any second now he was expecting Anthony and Jed to join them. It seemed to be that kind of morning.

"What are you two talking about?" Randall asked, absently taking Victor's hand in his own, playing their fingers together.

Edwin hesitated, expression going a little blank as he ducked his head. Apparently he was more comfortable discussing it with Redford than with Randall. "I, uh—"

"What the fuck is going on?" As if summoned by Redford's thoughts, Jed was shuffling down toward them, hair all stuck out at ends, rubbing his eyes in sleepy confusion. "Redford? What's wrong?" He made it to the log, collapsing into Redford's lap and yawning hugely. "It's a fucking party and no one invited me?"

"God, can't a guy get any sleep?" Anthony came up behind them with a tray of mugs and a coffeepot. "What the hell. Are you all insomniacs?"

They passed around the coffee in companionable silence, the clink of mugs loud against the gentle lap of the lake's waves. When they all had their mugs, the steam rising from them to join the mist, Redford looked at Edwin again. He'd seemed hesitant to speak when Randall had arrived, so Redford decided to make the announcement for him.

"Edwin discovered what they were doing to the kidnapped wolves," he said.

Jed went absolutely still on Redford's lap. It only took a quick glance up for Redford to know that Jed had probably already known that particular answer. Shifting his weight, Jed cleared his throat, looking guilty. "Yeah, about that."

"They skinned them, okay?" Edwin was scowling now, hunched in on himself, practically disappearing into nothing but a pile of quilt and messy blond hair. "New topic, please."

Anthony was the only one not sitting on the log, Redford noticed. He was standing near the lake's edge, and where the mist was merely passing over the rest of them, it seemed to *embrace* Anthony, gathering and curling around his legs. Redford wasn't sure if it was a mystery of nature or a trick of the eyes, but he recalled the story Anthony had told them about his mate, and he thought it might be something much more than just randomly shifting fog.

"That's over now," Anthony said firmly. He looked nauseous at the revelation, but determined to help Edwin move past it. "They're not going to be kidnapping anybody else."

"You don't know that." Edwin's voice was quiet, something ragged in the edges. "We keep killing these guys or scaring them off, but more just keep coming. And they're all doing the same thing."

"Why didn't you say something before?" Randall's expression was one of pure horror. "While the Gray Lady was here? She should know—"

"You weren't there when they attacked." Edwin shuddered, gaze flicking up to Anthony and then away. "I could smell them. One more push and they'd be in full-on bloodlust and I just.... I didn't want to see that. I didn't want to know what they'd do."

"And you were right to do so," Anthony replied. He turned from the lake's edge. Randall slid off the log to rest against Victor's legs, giving Anthony his spot to sit. "They didn't need another reason to keep slaughtering." Anthony gripped his mug tighter, looking regretful. "I do wish we could have told them, though. Now we don't have the chance."

"What good would it do?" Jed had finished his coffee and had started in on Redford's. "Who cares what they're doing with them. I mean, no one thought these guys were taking the wolves to go live on a nice farm in the country. If they knew that the vamps are redecorating in furry style, there would have been no stopping a war. At least now we have time to check things out, make sure we're ready. Make sure we know who we're actually fighting."

"You don't think it's vampires?" Randall glanced at Victor, an unreadable expression on his face.

"I think we don't trust slippery guys in offices who pay people like me to go out and kill. The whole skinning thing is very Hannibal Lecter, liver and fava beans, yeah. It's sick. I'm not saying it's not. But it's also a detail that doesn't really matter, big picture." Jed reached out, gripping Edwin's shoulder. "You're alive. Let's count that as a win."

"I really wasn't scared," Edwin told Jed. "I mean, I wasn't doing a jig or anything. But I was more upset over what they were saying had already been done. I knew I would be okay." Edwin took a sip of his coffee, wrinkling his nose at the taste. "Anthony wouldn't let anything happen to me." He said it with such confidence, as if he were simply stating that the Earth was round, that the sun rose every morning. Not an ounce of anything but absolute faith.

Anthony looped an arm around Edwin's shoulders to pull him in close against his side. He seemed at a loss for a response, choosing to reply with actions instead of words. They all sat there, close and tightly packed together, a *family* in every way Redford understood it to be. Not all by blood, no, and not all the same, but just as important.

They watched the sun rise over the lake, burning away the last tendrils of mist, chasing the ghosts off in favor of a blaze of brilliant light. Today they would be moving into Victor's mansion, and Redford smiled at the thought of it.

He had a pack, now.

REDFORD HAD always known Jed was particularly picky about where he stored his weapons—he just hadn't thought Jed would actually search through each of the forty-six individual rooms in the mansion to find the perfect spot, before they'd even moved anything else in. Victor wasn't happy with the idea of guns and explosives being stored in his house, but after a fight with Jed in front of the furniture truck, Victor had eventually given in out of sheer exasperation.

There were three trucks crowded into Victor's driveway. Two were the Lewises', and one was Jed and Redford's. Though the mansion came complete with furniture, Anthony especially hadn't wanted to part with the chairs and the bed frames he'd made, and Jed had given Victor a twenty-minute lecture on how his couch was perfectly broken in to his ass specifications. He even demonstrated, pointing out the groove in the cushion. Victor didn't seem as interested in the subject as Jed.

Over the course of the day, Redford had figured out that he was best utilized helping with the heavy lifting.

"Jed?" Redford attempted to look over the chair he was carrying. He wasn't even sure where he *was*—the mansion's hallways looked very similar. He hoped he was going the right way. "Jed, if you're near me and if I'm not lost, can you tell me where you want this chair?"

There was a faint laugh and then Jed was behind him, wrapping arms around him, hands grasping the chair along with Redford's. "You are so hot when you're being all manly and strong," Jed murmured, kissing just under Redford's ear. "Come on. I've got the other chair. We're just down the hall."

At least Redford hadn't wound up totally lost. Relieved, he followed Jed and did his best to memorize what the hallway looked like and smelled like so he'd remember later. Earlier, Edwin had been telling him all about the best places of the mansion to sniff—Redford hadn't passed by any of them so far, but all of it smelled pretty interesting, like Victor's blood, only so much stronger.

Jed had bitched about leaving the apartment. It had been *his* for so long. But Victor had given them a whole suite of rooms to themselves, with huge windows and doors from the sitting room that opened out onto the grounds. They'd sat there, the two of them, talking about where they'd put their furniture, painting the walls, making it *theirs*. And it seemed better then. Jed had seemed more relaxed about leaving his home.

As he'd put it, the apartment had been for him. This was going to be for them. And Redford liked how that sounded.

They passed Anthony on the way down the hallway, his head in a blueprint, muttering to himself. Victor, Redford thought, might soon be regretting telling Anthony he could renovate rooms if he wished. Randall passed them, chasing after Edwin, who was carting a box of books away from the library.

"Bring those back, Edwin Lewis," Randall demanded.

"You don't need more books!" Edwin was laughing, grinning as he turned around to run backward, taunting Randall. "I'm setting them free. Free the books! No more stuffy libraries!"

From very far off, perhaps the next hallway, came a shout of, "Edwin, if you harm a book on my property, you'll suffer the consequences!"

That only served to make Edwin laugh harder, and Redford could see the start of a grin on Randall's face. "Oh, that's it," Randall mock growled, shrugging off his sweater, shifting as his pants hit the floor. And then, Edwin gleefully changing as well, there were two wolves wrestling in the hallway, Randall's usual reserve fading slightly, enough for him to just *play* for a bit.

Redford cringed as they wrestled a bit too close to a side table that held some kind of antique statue on it, but they were obviously conscious of it. Perhaps they'd received the same lecture Redford had a few hours ago.

When Redford finally got the chair to his and Jed's room, his arms were starting to ache a little with the strain. He set it down with a relieved puff of air and rolled his shoulders to ease the burn in the muscles. At least they had most of their furniture done already. Hand in hand, they walked back through the hallways to the truck, and Redford found he was unable to stop smiling.

It was early days, but it felt like the Gray Lady had been right. They did make an odd pack—three wolves, one not-quite-wolf, one human, and one half-blood medusa. And one very pleased cat, who was off exploring all the nooks and crannies she could find. But it was working, and it felt *good*. Redford couldn't feel the slightest hint of discomfort from his instincts. Edwin rolled past him on the floor, bumping against his legs, tail wagging eagerly, and Jed started to laugh.

"Go have fun," he murmured, kissing Redford's cheek. "I'm going to find Victor and make sure he's not having a panic attack from the hairballs."

"Have fun?" Redford questioned. "What do you mean? There's still furniture to get inside."

"I'll handle it." Jed squeezed his fingers lightly. "You go do wolfy things. Come on, Randall's got to have, like, a twenty-minute limit on acting like something other than a stick in the mud."

The idea of just spontaneously going to do "wolfy things" still didn't come entirely naturally to Redford, but he was getting there. The shifts were less painful now, and the instincts had calmed. Whether it was any one particular thing that had helped, or the combination of Dr. Alona, Jed's help, and the wolf pack, Redford still wasn't sure. The point was, he felt better.

Enough so that he just shook his head in bemusement and shrugged off his shirt. "I'll be back in half an hour," he promised.

Jed hauled him back for a kiss, grinning against his lips. "Love you," Jed said, pulling back, studying his eyes. "Happy?"

Redford nudged his forehead against Jed's, and he took a second to enjoy the moment. Jed was happy, and they stood alone in the hallway of a beautiful mansion that they now lived in with their own odd little pack. Anthony's treatment had started yesterday, and already he was showing signs of being able to move easier. Edwin had settled into the place like it was a second skin, and Randall and Victor were bossing them all around.

Two days ago, the Gray Lady and her pack had disappeared. There had been no good-byes, no closure. Redford was simply left with the vague feeling of unease, as if things had needed to be said, answers given, that had been left undone. He had hoped to find the reason behind Filtiarn, of what he had become. Instead there was only the bent grass where the pack had been, the silent reminders of something gone. They had left to hide, and Redford knew it was entirely possible that he would never see them again. There was still a threat of war. Victor's prophecy was still something they needed to figure out, though it was clear that Jed had banished all thought of it from his mind. But for now, they were safe. For now, they could live in peace.

"Yeah," Redford said. "I'm happy."

"Good." Another kiss brushed against his lips, and Jed gave him a playful smack on the ass. "Now get out of here. I'm going to drag Victor out of that library if it kills one of us."

Redford just laughed. "Good luck," he replied, and shifted just after he'd finished the second word. On four legs now, the mansion seemed to light up with scents, and after a fond nudge against Jed's legs, Redford took off down the hallway to find Edwin and Randall. They'd stopped wrestling and had instead started stalking each other through a strange room that was full of nothing but suits of armor. When Redford joined in, he did so by greeting Randall with a flying tackle.

Randall turned and snapped lightly at Redford's muzzle, and they rolled end over end across the room. Edwin galloped over, nipping at them both to send them charging after him, darting around the legs of the armor. They ran past Anthony in another room, who still had his nose buried in blueprints, and by the time they wound up outside at the back of the mansion, Redford was ready to have a sleep.

He flopped down on the sun-warmed grass. As Randall and Edwin did the same, Redford could have grinned with the contentment he felt. He had a *pack*. Jed found them then, one of the sofas from the back of the moving van on a wheeled trolley. Jed set it out on the grass and collapsed onto it, sprawled out lazily, head tipped back to the sun.

"Last thing," he huffed. "I need a cold beer."

Redford jumped up to sit on the couch beside him, contemplating something he wasn't even sure would work. He was going to try, though. Tipping his head back, he howled—quietly enough so that only those in the mansion would hear it. He heard a return from Anthony. A minute passed. Then Anthony came out with an entire six-pack straight from the fridge. There was no specific howl for "cold beer," so Redford had just tried to communicate the feeling of needing refreshment.

It had apparently worked. He gave Jed a wolfy grin and howled a second time, not for refreshment or anything in particular, just *peace* and family and feeling so at home that he almost didn't know what to do with the enormity of the feeling. Knievel curled up at his feet, finished prowling around the edge of the grounds. Jed had wrapped an arm around him, and Anthony was beside him. Victor was coming down from the house, Randall charging toward him, shifting halfway there, taking the robe Victor had brought him with a grin. Edwin was sprawled out in the sun, tail flicking absently.

And they were home.

EPILOGUE

Jed

"YOU KNOW what my apartment had?" Jed told Redford mournfully, shaking out his leather jacket, sighing at the cloud of fur that rolled off of it. "About a thousand percent less shedding. Also, no wolves running through my weapon room and scaring the shit out of me."

"Uh-huh." Redford was sprawled out on the couch in front of their fireplace, paging through a book. And clearly not as invested in this rant as Jed was.

Three weeks into moving into the commune, as Jed had decided to start calling it, and it was becoming *abundantly* clear that, however gigantic this mansion was, it was so not large enough. "I mean, don't get me wrong," Jed continued, slouching down to sit in the chair opposite, guns out on the table for cleaning. "They're not half bad." Which was pretty much the highest praise he'd be willing to give. "But does Edwin *need* to nap on my jacket?"

At least he wasn't using it as a chew toy. Jed should probably be thankful for small favors.

"Yeah." Redford nodded, turning a page. And Jed was now convinced he hadn't heard a word. Which was absolutely a tragedy, because this was a grade A rant!

"We need a job," Jed declared, pointing at him, waving his finger around. "I haven't stayed at my *old* place this long, much less in kiddie wolf camp."

Randall and Victor were positively *domestic*. Disgustingly so. Cooking dinner, working together, and they along with Anthony were eagerly working on turning the stuffy, dark mansion into something light and open. Hell, just yesterday Anthony had gotten Edwin's help in knocking out a wall and combining two small, dank rooms into what was apparently going to be a huge, open family area on the second floor.

It was a whole lotta family shit, was all Jed was saying. He desperately wanted to go out and blow something up.

No one was talking about the war. It seemed quiet, for now, and as far as Jed was concerned, they would take what they could get. He'd gone out the first night, checked the defensibility of the grounds. Appropriately enough, for a place that looked like a castle, pretty much all it was missing was a moat. It would be a fortress if they needed it to be, which made Jed sleep a lot better at night.

Didn't mean he didn't want a job.

"We need to *work*," he repeated, sullenly getting out his knives to sharpen them. Again.

"Absolutely," Redford hummed, eyes still on the book. "Sounds great."

Jed flicked a look up at him, eyes narrowing. "I think I'm going to start walking around naked," he informed Redford.

"Uh-huh."

"I might tattoo my entire body with a life-sized portrait of Margaret Thatcher. You know, in honor of my right ball."

"That's good, Jed," Redford murmured, turning another page.

Jed did the only thing he could. He stood up, undid his jeans, and shimmied them off his hips. His shirt was next, tossed off to land on top of Redford's head. Redford blinked, looking up at him, eyes widening.

"Take me to bed right now," Jed demanded. "You aren't listening to me. I think we need to rectify that."

He strode off toward the bedroom. Redford was right on his heels.

They had *much* better communication in bed. Jed made sure Redford worked on his listening skills. Namely listening as Jed begged for *more* and *harder* and *oh, God, just like that*. Redford was very attentive.

They lay in each other's arms quite a while later, content, Jed's eyes falling half shut as Redford ran absent fingers through his hair.

"You want a job?" Redford asked.

Jed raised his eyebrows as he looked up at him. Redford just smirked. "I listen to you," Redford assured him, dropping a kiss to Jed's nose. "You just had a nice steam worked up. I thought I'd let you go at it." A pause and he smiled, another kiss pressed to Jed's forehead. "Please don't get Margaret Thatcher tattooed on you. That would be... disturbing."

Jed snorted out a laugh and curled up farther into Redford's arms. "We need a job," he agreed. "I'm getting fat and lazy."

His phone chirped, and Jed sighed, looking over at it. "I didn't mean *now*," he muttered at it in a grump, considering ignoring it completely. Stupid thing had the worst timing. Reaching over, Jed grabbed it and squinted as he scrolled through the messages. One voice mail, unknown number.

Jed pressed play. And on the first word, the first smoky syllable, he was sitting up straight, eyes going wide.

"What is it?" Redford asked, concerned.

Son of a bitch.

"It's David."

ROBIN SAXON, born and bred in New Zealand, lives in the Midwest with partner Alex Kidwell. When not writing or daydreaming about ideas for more stories, Robin is usually found playing MMOs like *World of Warcraft*, reading, drawing, and fussing over their cats, Starsky and Hutch.

In the rare times when they are not being pestered by their cats, Robin also listens to heavy metal music and enjoys everything from classics like Chaucer to urban fiction, as well as cooking vegetarian meals and inflicting them on Alex.

Visit Robin's website, http://www.saxonandkidwell.com, find Robin on Facebook, https://www.facebook.com/robin.saxon.77, or e-mail Robin at robin_saxon@yahoo.com.

ALEX KIDWELL, confirmed geek and bibliophile, lives in the Midwest with partner Robin Saxon. Alex relaxes by slaying dragons in MMOs, listening to music that can be sung along with in the shower, and enjoying BBC programming.

Other than writing, Alex enjoys knitting and is currently attempting to learn how to knit in the round. There are plans for a future of cat hats, which Alex is certain will go over well with household-running felines, Starsky and Hutch. Alex also indulges in too many cooking shows, while owning only one pan.

Visit Alex's blog at http://saxonkidwell.blogspot.com/, Facebook at http://www.facebook.com/profile.php?id=100002270719608, and Twitter @kiddingalex, or e-mail Alex at alexkidwellwrites@gmail.com.

Sanguis Noctis Book 1 by

ROBIN SAXON & ALEX KIDWELL

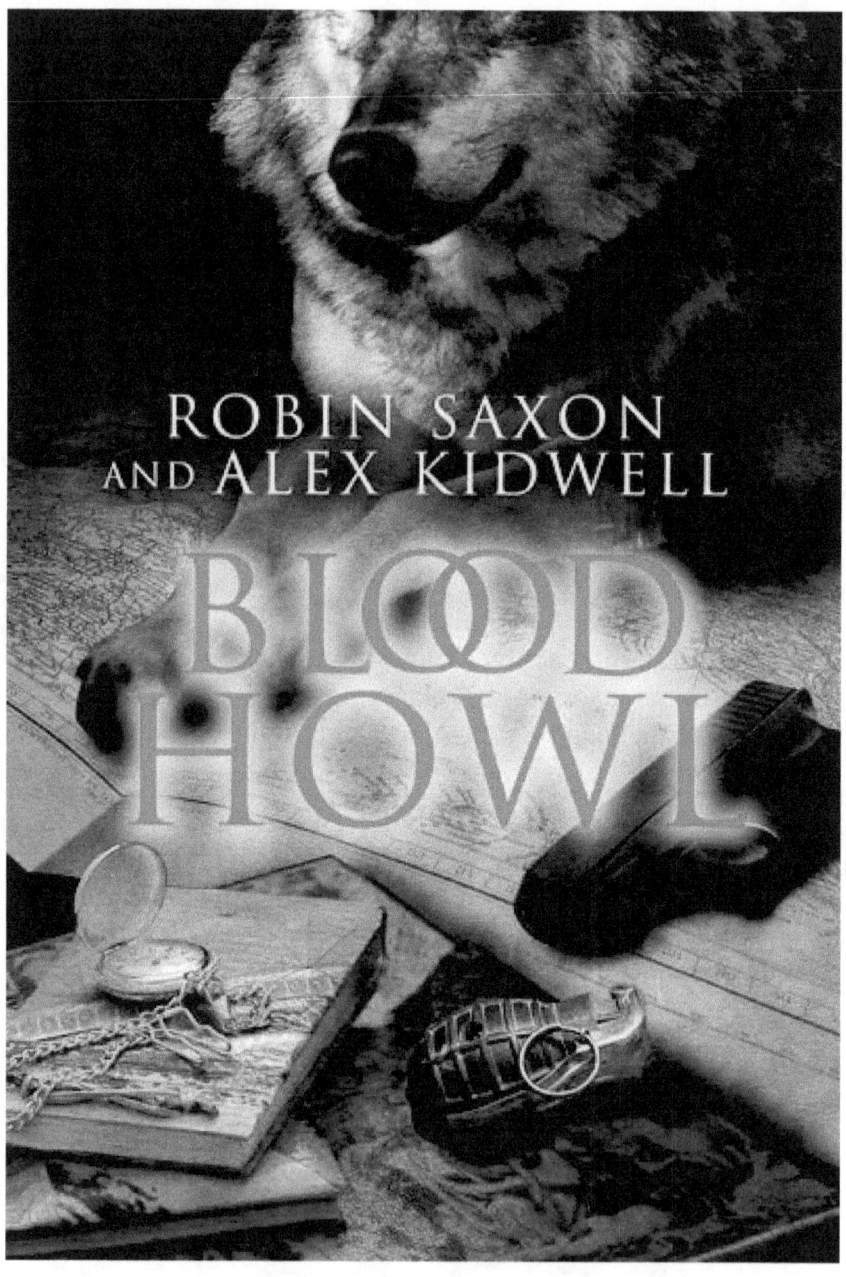

ROBIN SAXON
AND ALEX KIDWELL

BLOOD
HOWL

http://www.dreamspinnerpress.com

Sanguis Noctis Book 2 by
ROBIN SAXON & ALEX KIDWELL

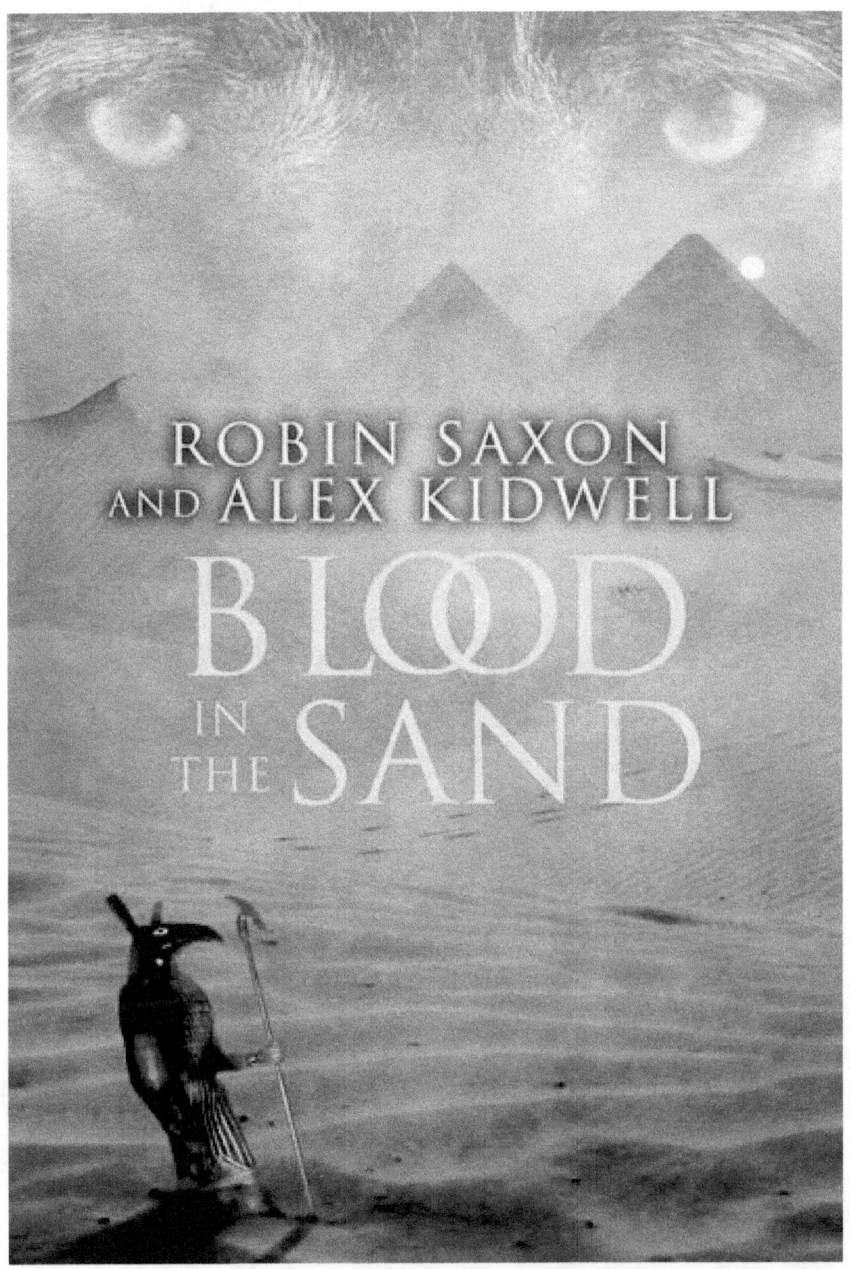

ROBIN SAXON
AND ALEX KIDWELL
BLOOD
IN
THE SAND

http://www.dreamspinnerpress.com

Also from ROBIN SAXON

Robin Saxon
The Royal Road

http://www.dreamspinnerpress.com

Also from ALEX KIDWELL

After the End

ALEX KIDWELL

Also from ALEX KIDWELL

http://www.dreamspinnerpress.com

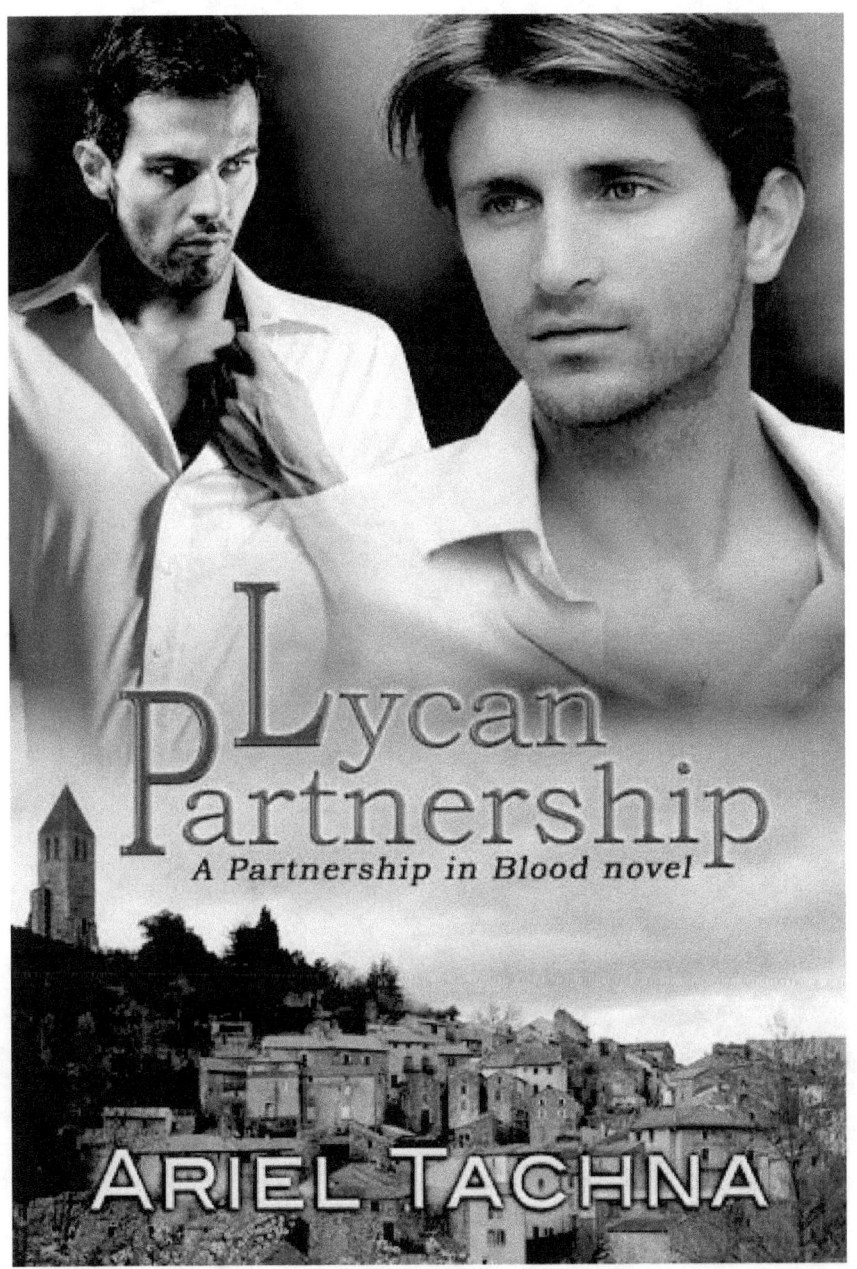

Lycan
Partnership
A Partnership in Blood novel

ARIEL TACHNA

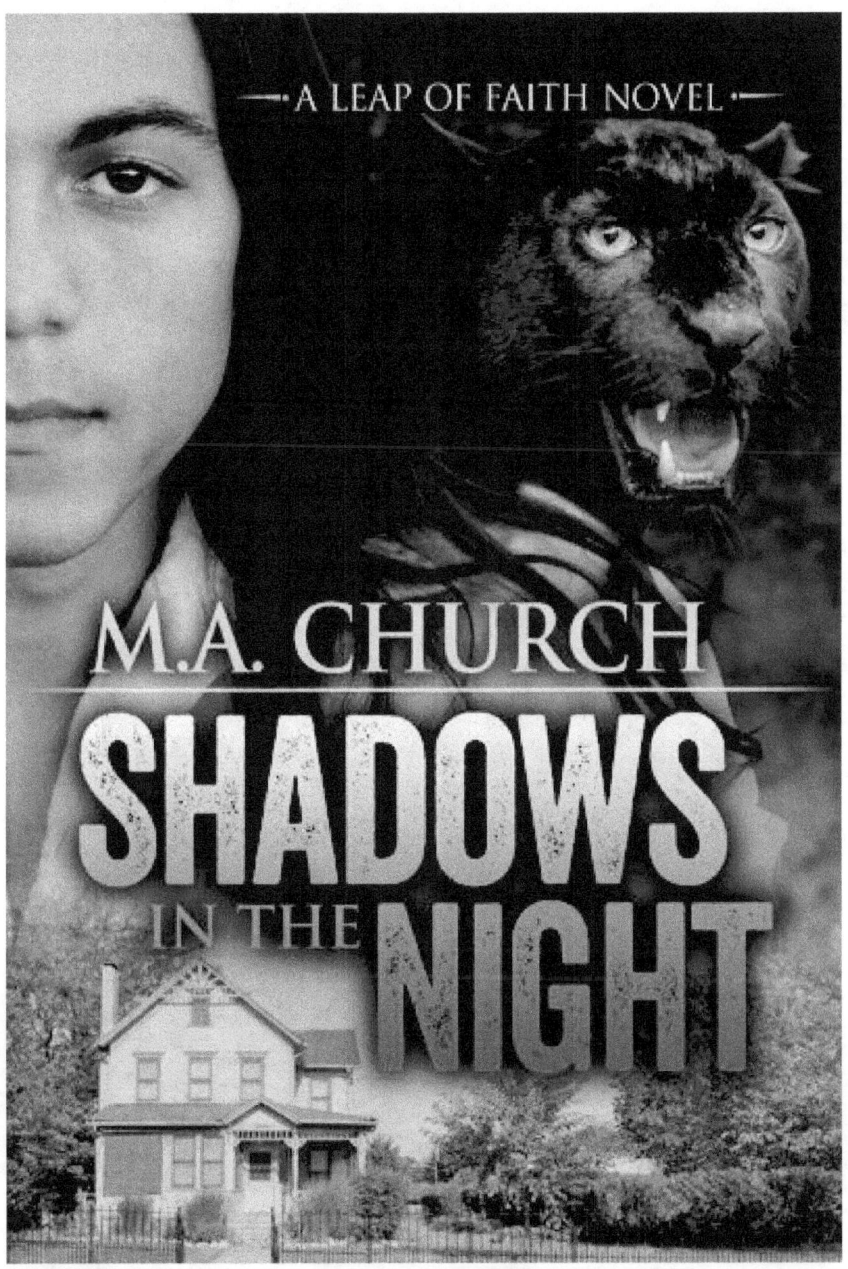